This book is a work of fiction, but some works of fiction contain perhaps more truth than first intended, and therein lies the magic.
– Anonymous

Copyright © Ben Galley 2020

The right of Ben Galley to be identified as the author of this work has been asserted in accordance with the Copyright, Designs and Patents Act 1988. All rights reserved.

No part of this book may be used, edited, transmitted in any form or by any means (electronic, mechanical, photocopying, recording or otherwise), or reproduced in any manner without permission except in the case of brief quotations embodied in reviews or articles. It may not be lent, resold, hired out or otherwise circulated without the Publisher's permission.

Permission can be obtained through www.bengalley.com.

All characters in this book are fictitious and any resemblance to real persons, living or dead, is purely coincidental. And weird.

FKHB1
First Edition 2020
ISBN: 978-1-8381625-2-8
Published by BenGalley.com
Cover Design by Pen Astridge
Original Illustration by Ben Galley
Map Illustration by Ben Galley

About The Author

Ben Galley is a British author of dark and epic fantasy books who currently hails from Victoria, Canada. Since publishing his debut Emaneska Series, Ben has released a range of epic and dark fantasy novels, including the award-winning weird western Bloodrush and standalone novel The Heart of Stone. He is also the author of the critically-acclaimed Chasing Graves Trilogy.

When he isn't conjuring up strange new stories or arguing the finer points of magic and dragons, Ben enjoys exploring the Canadian wilds and sipping Scotch single malts, and will forever and always play a dark elf in The Elder Scrolls. One day he hopes to live in an epic treehouse in the mountains.

Ben can be found on Twitter or vlogging on YouTube @BenGalley, or loitering on Facebook and Instagram @BenGalleyAuthor. You can also get a free Emaneska short story by signing up to The Guild at www.bengalley.com.

Other Books by Ben Galley

THE EMANESKA SERIES
The Written
Pale Kings
Dead Stars - Part One
Dead Stars - Part Two
The Written Graphic Novel

THE SCARLET STAR TRILOGY
Bloodrush
Bloodmoon
Bloodfeud

THE CHASING GRAVES TRILOGY
Chasing Graves
Grim Solace
Breaking Chaos

STANDALONES/SHORTS
The Heart of Stone
Shards
No Fairytale

For Dan

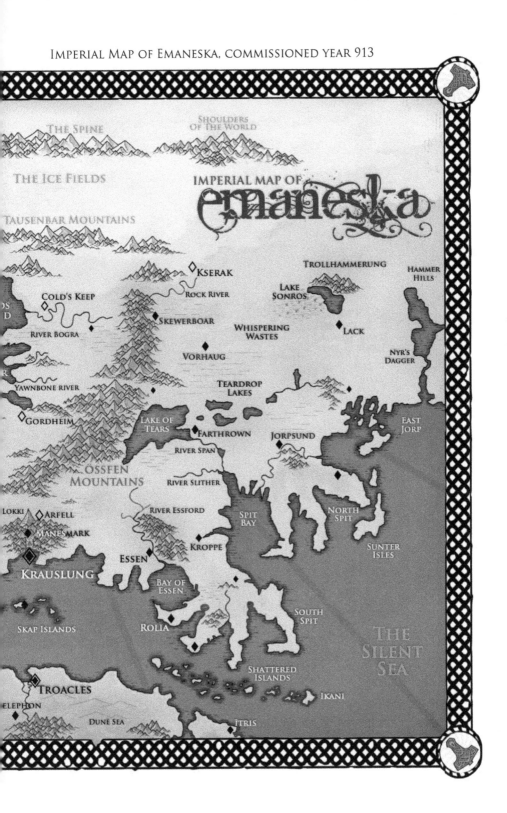

SCALUSSEN CHRONICLES BOOK ONE

Of What Has Come Before

While this account of The Forever King *is the start of the Scalussen Chronicles and a new tale entirely, its beginnings are rooted in the Emaneska Series.* The Forever King *is set after the events of the Emaneska Series, and thus, some outcomes of that epic tale may be hinted at or discussed in this book. Effort has been made to ensure readers who are entering the savage world of Emaneska for the first time can do so through* The Forever King. *If you, dear reader, have any concerns, begin with* The Written, *the first of four books in the Emaneska Series.*

For those returning to this winter-laden land, well met and good wishes to you. You will find a brief history lesson below. Be warned: the world is not as you left it.

A NOTE FROM DURNUS GLASSREN, ESTEEMED SCHOLAR, MAGE, AND GENERAL

YEAR 874

The world of Emaneska once enjoyed an age bereft of war. The Skölgard Empire kept to their borders. The Siren dragon-riders held a fragile peace with the south. The Arka and the dutiful arkmages saw to the governance of the use and trade of magick across the lands.

YEAR 889

Betrayal and murder changed everything. A simple theft of a spellbook set in motion a cascade of events that irreparably eroded the Arka's power. The Written mage known as Farden, previously hailed as the Hero of Efjar, was found to be the architect of the Arka's demise, a traitor of the highest calibre. With Farden at large, the Skölgard emperor took up the mantle of the Arka dominion, appointing the sole surviving arkmage, Vice, as his vassal king.

YEAR 890

In the years that followed, the Arka not only grew in power, but rotted from within. To restore the Arka's glory and stop its power consuming the rest of Emaneska, Farden led a bold invasion of the capital, Krauslung, with the help of the Sirens and Albion dukes. Though they were victorious, the cost was overwhelming. Farden consequently vanished into the Albion wilderness, beginning a hunt for the lost and fabled armour of the Nine, worn by the folkloric Knights of Scalussen.

YEAR 890-905

Once again governed by fair and just figureheads, a wise scholar and a mage, the Arka flourished in the vacuum of the Skölgard Empire. As did its enemies. An unknown force began to hunt down the remaining Written mages and long-dead daemons began to reappear in Emaneska, sowing discontent amongst the Arka. At the gods' behest, it once again fell to Farden to lead the defence against these most ancient of enemies.

YEAR 905

So began the Last War: a single battle of last hopes and brave effort. Its outcome reverberated through Emaneska, a bitter wind that changed the world forever. The heroes of the Arka returned to Krauslung to find themselves vilified, branded enemies of peace, and exiled by the new ruler: the opportunistic Malvus Barkhart. Unwanted, Farden and his remnant forces disappeared into the Bern Sea.

YEAR 906-9

As the Long Winter faded and the first summer in decades brought warmth to Emaneska, Malvus united the fragmented kingdoms. Proclaiming himself emperor, he decried magick and declared it the root of all of Emaneska's strife. The practice, use, and trade of magick was banned outright, and within years, the Arka dominion appeared to be a blessing of peace upon Emaneska.

The rebellion in the north, led by the traitorous Outlaw King, would disagree. Though the empire would have its citizens believe him a myth, his name is whispered in alleyways, painted on city walls. To most, it is a curse word, but there are those to whom that name is a beacon of hope. They know him by a different title:

The Forever King.

HOLLOW PEACE

CHAPTER 1
OF WOLVES & DAEMONS

The Spine of the World has Roots, and in those Roots burn the molten fires of the old giant. Burned forever, they have, and they will burn forever more.
FROM AN OLD SCALUSSEN SCROLL FOUND IN THE WRECKAGE OF THE HJAUSSFEN LIBRARY

YEAR 925

A whimper. A garbled moan of a half-prayer to an absent god. That was the sum total of the last words the woman was allowed before the noose slid tight against her pallid neck.

'The price of dallying with magick and disobeying the emperor's decree is death,' intoned the mage who stood alone upon that wretched stage with the condemned. His words lacked grandeur or ceremony. They wore the blunt edge of rehearsal. Bored, the mage sounded, and in that sense, callous, as were the shrieks of the rusted lever, the cruel clatter of the trapdoor, and the gap of silence before the woman met the scant limits of the noose with a jerk. The crowd cheered the snap of rope, applauding the limp convulsing of another heretic. Another traitor for Hel's clutches. The eyes of their children were not shielded; they were teased open so they could witness justice served before them. The price of magick. The parents sneered proudly as if the woman were a prize trout on a line. It did not seem to matter that her crime was as inconsequential as owning a faintly charmed heirloom.

The noose was knotted mercifully. The condemned did not suffer, as others had on those squat gallows. Rent the Hoary dangled choking for three hours straight before they had to pull on his legs.

With a last twitching gulp, the woman began her lonely walk to the goddess of death and her golden scales. Cheated of a grotesque performance, the crowd complained with handfuls of rocks and rotten vegetables thrown through the damp morning air. Their aim was poor: a curse of hangovers and those who had cursed the cockerel's crow. Only one struck the hanged, cutting the woman's grey cheek. The rest of the jilted missiles collided with the gallows or tumbled across the ground. With empty hands and the body hanging still in the breeze, the ennui set in rapidly.

Like autumn leaves, the people drifted and scattered back to their homes and empty tankards. A single figure was left standing before the dead. His hands were thrust in pockets, his hood draped low. Lips taut and shoulders drooped, he tore his gaze away from the corpse and trudged in the direction of distraction.

The gnarled coin slid across the marble with a banshee's screech. Heads turned. Eyes glowered. The quiet tavern went back to its murmuring conversation and idle slurping of ale.

'By the empire, you got a nerve, stranger,' said the barkeep, who rubbed furiously at an imaginary scratch on the white stone. 'You should have a care. Don't you know where this marble came from?'

'A quarry?' the hooded stranger took a guess.

'Yes. Well.' The barkeep harrumphed. 'At one point, I s'pose.' He spread his fingers across the marble as if he were the very craftsman who had hewn it from the earth. 'This marble,' he breathed, wafting a delightful mix of pipe smoke and garlic in his patron's face. 'This marble came from the shattered Arkathedral itself, from the broken floor of the Marble Copse when it was ruined by the Outlaw King's traitorous attack on Krauslung. This here stone is sacred ground, I tell you.'

As half-hearted booing came from the nearby drinkers, the barkeep thumped his fist into his palm in agreement. 'I bought it from a fat Manesmark stonemason and had it carried here on the backs of minotaur slaves.'

'That's some distance.'

The barkeep swelled proudly. His ruddy face creased to make way for a smile. 'That it is. It took two months and we left a share of marauders' corpses behind us, but here it lies in the *Patchwork Cat*: a testament to the everlasting power of the Blazing Throne. Perhaps even trodden upon by the emperor himself!'

'To Arka's glory!' cried a man lost in the crowd of drinkers. Appreciative echoes washed through the tavern. The drunker fellows clanged their tankards.

The stranger showed off his teeth. 'Incredible,' he replied, speaking loudly for all to hear. 'And here it lies, destined to have stew and ale slopped across it for decades to come. How fitting.'

Before rising from his stool, he watched the barkeep's proud smile fade like snow in a spring sun. A brooding silence fell. Ignoring the stares, the man sought out a table by a fireplace instead, eager to burn off the cloying cold of the road, to lose himself in the peaceful crackle of flames.

The stranger sighed wearily as he propped an ice-rimmed boot up on a stool. By the whispers turning to angry mutters, he could feel his comment gestating into an insult in the minds around him. He cared little. He simply waited and enjoyed what peace and quiet he was allowed.

It lasted exactly three sips of his murky kelp ale.

Tankards clanked on tabletops. Chair legs squeaked. Boots clomped upon the boards until three burly townsmen stood between the man and his fire.

'What was it you said?' one asked.

The man studied them over the rim of his tankard. Two looked to be brothers, one of whom had clearly received a larger serving of handsome and height than his sibling. Both had cauliflower ears and bushy blonde beards. The third, their self-appointed spokesman, was a weathered and wiry fellow. A bowl of black, greasy hair draped over his ears and cheeks. All of them typical Hâlorn brutes: too young in the head, never mind how many years stride past them, and with little else to do but brawling.

It was plain this had nothing to do with speaking ill of the empire. That was merely a convenient banner to fly. An excuse to scratch the itch of violence. The man could see it in the ripcords in their neck; the way they tensed beneath their leather and hide tunics. A fight had been predetermined no matter his response. He smiled politely.

'I don't recall saying anything to you.'

The wiry chap already had his words nocked and loaded. 'What did you say just then,' bout Leerol's marble? You said somethin' and we wants to know what it was.'

The man took his time. Another sip of ale, another sigh. 'I said, "And here it lies, destined to have stew and ale slopped across it for decades to come. How fitting." Now, what I meant by that was—'

One of the brutes kicked the stool from under the man's boot, causing ale to slop onto his sleeve.

'We know what you meant, old man.'

'Old? That stings.' The man slid back his sleeve to wipe the ale away, showing off scarlet and gold armour around his wrists. 'Then aside from exercising your general dislike of stools and spilling my drink, what is it that you want?'

'You insulted the emperor,' replied the wiry fellow, omitting more than one syllable. 'You don't just get to speak treachery and get away with it.'

Though conversation had but one outcome, the man had a casual interest in seeing how deep their rabbit-hole of stupidity went. 'Did I, though?' he retorted. 'If anything, I merely told... Leerol, was it? I told barkeep Leerol there that perhaps his reverence of the empire was misplaced in utilising such a fine piece of marble to serve such a functional – and let's be honest – *messy* purpose.'

The brothers looked between them as though the man had just spoken in Paraian. The one with the black hair fumed. His right eye twitched. 'You sound Krauslung but you don't look it. Don't act it. You act all foreign.'

Irritable growls of agreement sounded. More tankards clanked. The whole tavern watched on. All of them wore the same indignant yet leering scowl. The morning had cheated the townspeople of blood. They could taste it now in the tavern air.

The man swirled his hands. 'And therefore I am your enemy without question. I see.' He paused to drain his tankard, knowing it might be a while until his next. 'If I could offer one small piece of advice. One day, sometime soon, you should try thinking for yourselves instead of regurgitating the same old shit your beloved empire feeds you.'

The disloyalty was so barefaced it took a moment for it to make sense in the patrons' addled minds. The tavern erupted, incensed. Wild-eyed, the wiry thug let out an almost gleeful cry as he seized the man by his cloak's collar. His stupidity sealed his fate.

The stranger drove the empty pewter tankard into the thug's cheek. The weak metal crumpled under the force of the blow, driving sharp edges into vital places. Blood spurted. The fool howled but, to his credit, he did not let up his grip. A brisk kick to the groin from an armoured shin dislodged him for good and he fell writhing.

The brothers tried their best, throwing a few haymaking punches that were all too easy to avoid. As they tottered with momentum, the man broke a stool against the scrawnier brother's back. He was barged into the fireplace, striking his skull on the lintel with a fateful crunch before collapsing onto the flaming logs. He moved not a muscle.

In the panic, the larger brother managed to land a meaty blow to the man's stomach, but all that could be heard was wrist and knuckle bones snapping against steel. His roar of pain was strangled short as the man seized him by the throat and pinned him to a tabletop. To the horror of everybody present, blue lightning erupted from the stranger's armoured hand. The brute quivered like a pennant in a gale while smoke and sparks fired from his gawping mouth. The foul smell of pork seeped.

In the stunned silence that followed, as the stranger adjusted his collar and hood he wondered if the townsfolk had the smarts to stay put, or if they were the truly brainless kind and would challenge him further. His work was done, no more bloodshed was required. Judging by the fearful looks of the remainder of the tavern, they were in utter agreement.

Flashing the polish of red-gold armour, he pulled his cloak around him. Before departing, he slid another coin across the marble bar. The screech was protracted and piercing, but Leerol made no move except for wincing.

'For the damage those fools caused. The man drew the sword from between his shoulders and placed the blade gently on the veined stone. 'And this? This doesn't belong to the emperor, and it does not belong to you, let alone in some filthy tavern.'

Without moving, a violent crack of thunder split the uneasy air of the tavern. Bodies hit the stained floorboards like late apples, quivering to the ring of a sword blade.

When they finally peeled themselves from the floor, the stranger was striding out into the cold evening, cloak billowing in the wind. Patting themselves, everybody was proven whole and uninjured, if not a fraction deafer. Nothing was broken. That was until the door slammed.

Accompanied by a cloud of dust and a shrill scream from Leerol, the marble bar split in two directly down its centre and collapsed.

The barkeep blushed a shade of furious beetroot while he sucked in enough breath to bellow. 'F—fuckin' fetch the reever! And get that drunken twat out of the fireplace!'

By the time the outraged patrons of the *Patchwork Cat* had gathered at the reever's thatched cottage, they had roused the entire town to their cause. Keen for bloodshed and the sweet snap of neck bones, the crowd now stood in its scores and verged on a riot.

Guards stood awkwardly at the reever's door, trying to decide between their salary of pennies or a rock to the face. A handful promptly gave up their spears and iron helms and joined the gang of yelling townsfolk.

The commotion was impossible to ignore. The reever soon appeared in a high window, bleary-eyed and a mail shirt thrown awkwardly over his nightgown. 'What? What can be so bloody important at this hour! What is it? Another loose goat? A pickpocket? What?'

'More foul magick, yer honour!' yelled barkeep Leerol.

'Magick? Again? We already hanged—'

'It was a mage this time, yer 'onour! He killed Parsoks right in the middle of my tavern. Burned 'is brother up, too!'

A man with severe burns across his face was shepherded in front of the reever as proof. He attempted to speak through melted lips, but the pain seemed too great.

'Outlaw King's kind, no doubt!' yelled barkeep Leerol. 'Not just some travellin' crone.'

'He scarpered as soon as we challenged him,' bayed a man with a bloody face. Many amongst the mob knew fine well that wasn't the case, but eagerly adopted the more attractive lie with cheers and yells.

'Yeah, ran away! A pale man in a hood. Had red and gold armour on!' he cried louder, emboldened.

While the reever kneaded his tired eyes, the door to the reever's cottage burst open with a thud of oak meeting stone. Another sweating, shirtless man clad in moss-green and gold armour from the waist down emerged into the crowd's torchlight. They knew him as the emperor's man: the Krauslung mage fond of getting answers with the edges of his knives, and of tying nooses and pulling trapdoors. His face was expressionless, but the shine in his eyes brought the mob to a hush.

'Red and gold armour, you said?' he demanded, pointing at the speaker with a knife point.

'Aye! Finest scale plate I ever seen!' yelled the town's blacksmith.

'Which way did he go?'

A few dolts began to point in different directions, and the mage took matters into his own hands, seizing Leerol the barkeep by the fat of his throat and pulling him close. 'Which fucking way?'

'West from the *Cat*'s door. Barely half an hour ago!' he squeaked, before he was shoved unceremoniously into a half-frozen puddle.

'We'll handle this! You may go back to your feather bed,' the mage shouted up to the reever, as a dozen more soldiers in matching armour poured from the cottage. The emperor's mark of a white hammer adorned their breastplates.

Mobs were fickle beasts. All it took was a one loud-enough idiot to sway its mood. This mob had plenty of them, and they were soon drunkenly whooping as the emperor's soldiers went racing to serve the emperor's justice.

'Now clear off, or I'll have the lot of you in the stocks!' barked the reever.

The mob dispersed with grins and congratulatory pats on backs and took their cheering to the streets.

'This miserable fucking town,' the reever muttered while he latched his window. At least there would be another hanging on the morrow. A dead rebel mage should keep the townsfolk happy for a while. Long enough for the reever to get some godsdamned sleep.

🝮

Snowflakes traversed the broken shafts of moonlight, fat and lazy, unhurried to join their brethren on the forest floor. The air moved not a breath that night. The pine trees uttered no whispers.

A lone pair of boots broke the pristine surface of the snow at a slow but determined pace. The creaking, tutting sounds were loud against the silence. Plumes of hot breath spiralled behind the mage, now bundled up against the frigid night. A sword was slung across his back, poking between shoulders already heavy with snow.

He halted abruptly, head twitching as he caught a sound. He paused to roll up fur-lined sleeves, and the moonlight glimmered on polished metal: gauntlets and vambraces made of interwoven scales, crimson and gold.

Something threaded between the pines before him, silent as shadow. Not a breath escaped the mage's mouth. Even the snowflakes could be heard settling.

A timber wolf poked its snout from behind a black tree trunk, its eyes turned polished silver by the moon. It stared at the man with all the focus of a beast with an empty stomach Sharp ribs poked from beneath its worn pelt. The wolf's lips curled back to show its teeth. Its low growl rumbled across the snow.

Unperturbed, the mage took a step towards the wolf. The beast matched him, snarling, but the mage held out a hand to the wolf, flat-palmed, as if telling it to halt. The wolf bowed its head. Its arched, poised shoulders fell into a cower. The growl withered to a whine. Looking sorry for itself, it trotted through the snow towards the man's outstretched hand and began to lick the cold metal of the gauntlets. Clouds of breath billowed between its fangs.

'Hello, friend,' the mage whispered. While he ruffled the wolf's angular ears, he felt the animal tense beneath him. He looked up in time to see a crossbow bolt strike the wolf, sending it cartwheeling across the snow with a pained yelp.

'Bugger it!' came a muffled cry from the forest's shadow.

Any sensible soul would have scrambled for cover, but the mage stayed put. He clenched his fists, making the metal of his gauntlets sing.

A second bolt raced from the dark. This shot was on target, aimed directly for the mage's head. Before its barbed point could pierce his skull, it burst into splinters against an unseen wall.

'For the Arka's glory!'

A roaring ball of flame escaped the trees and painted the monochrome night a bright orange. The mage held his hand out, fingers crooked like eagle claws, and the fireball exploded in mid-air. The fiery remnants of the spell surged around his shield. Snow cascaded from the trembling trees. The resin in the pine-branches sparked in the heat.

As the fire died and the smell of smouldering wood wafted, he saw them in the faint glow: half a dozen figures, striding towards him with blades raised, fire and lightning spitting in their hands. No bandits, these. They wore full plate: gold and green marked with a smith's hammer. And marauders didn't use magick for fear of the noose.

Arka. And a full hunting party of mages, at that.

Even as their war cries rose, the mage stayed exactly where he was, content to watch his enemies approach. He even raised his arms as if welcoming them, a smile beneath the shadow of his hood.

The man waited until they were mere strides away before he pounced. With a bell-toll of metal crashing against metal, he slammed his vambraces together. Tendrils of crimson lightning surged from his straining fingers. The thick Arka armour counted for naught. The spell bored holes in Krauslung steel and reduced the meat beneath to cinders. Half of them crumpled to the snow at his feet, dead before they tasted the cold on their faces. The remainder that were still upright – but too stupid to stop – ploughed straight into the mage's sword and flaming fist. When only the injured were crawling through the snow, he went between them serving quick deaths with steel in their necks.

The mage paused amongst the corpses, watching the snow, listening to the crackle of the smouldering branches around him. Gradually, before his eyes, he saw the snowflakes begin to darken and fade to ash. The frigid air began to lose its knife's edge, growing warm. The flames shrank to embers before the shadow seeping between the trees.

The mage sighed. With a crack of his knuckles he threw out his spell. A curved wall of light appeared before him, and he hunkered down behind it in the nick of time.

A stream of crimson fire exploded from the pines. The mage's boots scraped through the snow even as the shield spell took the brunt of the force. Flames streaming inches from him, he grit his teeth and pushed back. Thunder split the air as the mage flexed his fingers, expanding his shield with concussive blasts until it was a spinning wheel as wide as a gateway. He took a step through the slush, and it was matched by a hulking daemon.

Its eyes were craters of forge fire. The flames poured from jaws lined with needle fangs. Each of its monstrous fists were wrapped around a pine to brace itself. Wings of smoke and darkness and ash towered over the lone mage, like the fingers of a fist curling inwards. Standing tall, shield held firmly, fire flowing in all directions. He endured while he waited for the daemon to run out of breath.

At last, the monster reached the limit of his foul lungs. The stream of flame sputtered out. The mage lowered his shield spell, sparing a moment to watch the daemon inhale through its furnace of a maw. Its fiery eyes narrowed. Sickle claws were raised. An unholy screech began to swell in the daemon's throat, now glowing white-hot. The mage simply crossed his arms and hoped his smile could be seen written on his face in the light of the blazing pines.

A dragon fell upon the daemon with all the speed and mercy of a plummeting anvil. The blur of sapphire crushed the foul beast into the loam in an explosion of snow and charcoal. The mage held up a single hand to shield himself.

When the dust and smoke cleared, the dragon was perched on the daemon's back. Her blue scales were smeared with its orange ichor, and yet they still glittered in the light of the flames. Curved talons, each as long as a farmer's sickle, had impaled the daemon's skull and neck. At least what was left of them. The daemon's wings of smoke had withered away, and the glowing cracks in its skin were fading fast.

'Kinsprite. Late, as usual,' chided the mage.

The dragon shook her head, rattling her long spines. 'I would call that perfect timing, Modren.' She bared her fangs in a fearsome smile, and he chuckled. He sat upon a tree trunk that had so far escaped the spreading flames. The dark, frozen forest had come alive with fire, and still the snow fell, uncaring.

'Our ruse worked well, then,' she said.

'That it did. Apparently I do a fine impression of our Outlaw King.' With a sigh, the mage removed his hood, revealing a shaved head interrupted by a stripe of silver hair, running forehead to nape. The scalp beneath was crisscrossed with white and pink scars. He clapped his red-gold gauntlets together, still in disbelief that the smiths had made such fine forgeries of the Outlaw King's fabled armour. 'The town's mage contingent must have run ragged to catch up with me. And to bring a war-daemon? When was the last time you saw an outpost put that much effort into chasing magick? Good to know the red and gold scales still carry the same reek of fear. If we keep this up, we might be able to draw half the emperor's hunting parties into a hunt, then slaughter them one by one. Maybe that will get the emperor's attention. The Outlaw King himself, roaming the wilds once more.'

Kinsprite dragged the dead daemon aside and retracted her claws. She sat in the half-melted snow, cat-like, her forked tail swishing through the steaming mud. A harness and saddle were strapped to her back. Her eyes were pools of molten silver, ever swirling. Even for a dragon, they held a heavy weariness.

'Hmph,' she sighed. 'You can hope. He will merely turn more towns into outposts, send more hunting parties, more mages, more daemons. We burn one Arka watchtower, two others sprout up. It has grown futile.'

'You know as well as I do that it can't be forever,' he replied, staring at the smoking corpse of the daemon. Modren's tired gaze matched the dragon's. 'We will have our war. No other option remains. In the meantime, we fight for who and what we can. That is our calling. It weighs as heavy on me as it does you, believe me.'

Kinsprite growled softly. 'Our king most of all, it seems.'

'He has plenty on his mind with running this rebellion.' Modren tapped his vambraces. 'With our little ruse, perhaps we help him. Finally antagonise that stubborn fuck of an emperor into coming north, where there's a spike waiting for his head.'

'I hope you're right, mage,' she tutted, but thankfully turned her mood with a wink of one great silver eye. 'Or should I say, Outlaw King?'

'That's the spirit.' Modren chuckled and hoisted his hood up with a flourish. 'The road calls us onwards.'

'*Road*, he says, as if we're walking,' Kinsprite grumbled as she crouched, wings flared and poised. 'I'm the one who has to do all the flying.'

Modren was seizing the opportunity for a much-needed piss when he saw it.

Where one of his spells had ripped through the armour of an empire mage, raw skin was left bare to the cold. Between the blackened threads of cloth and molten plate, Modren could see a black and disturbing shape.

'What do you see?' Kinsprite asked, sensing his caution.

Modren didn't answer. He moved slowly towards the corpse as if it were plagued and gingerly examined it with a dagger blade. Four lines branded the man's neck, burned by a salamander's tongue. Normally Arka mages wore three.

Etched into the man's pale skin in ink and needle was an elaborate rune. It looked scarred, the skin around it tortured, but it was plain and unmistakable. Modren could feel the faint magick still smouldering within it.

Kinsprite cleared her throat with a puff of smoke. 'When did—'

'I don't know,' Modren snapped. He couldn't bring himself to hear it aloud. 'What matters is they've already done it.' He slowly inched a dagger from his belt and pressed it against the skin. 'The king has to see this. No matter how dire the news, he needs to see it.'

The dagger blade slipped into the still warm skin and began to slice. It was an ugly cut and a grisly task, but Modren had no choice. Wrinkling his lips, he folded the scrap of bloody skin and wrapped it in cloth from his haversack.

'Charming,' muttered Kinsprite.

'Necessary.' With a heavy heart and numb fingers, Modren climbed the dragon's side and lashed himself to the saddle. 'West it is. We'll meet the *Revenge* on the coast.'

In a cascade of pine needles, the dragon leapt into the air and vanished into the snow-laden night, leaving only the moon and guttural flames to watch over the corpses.

CHAPTER 2
THE WRECK

I. From this day, the practice, manipulation, study, collection and wielding of magick or magickal items shall be forbidden throughout Emaneska.
II. Any soul found defying this decree or allowing it to be defied shall be hung by the neck until dead.
III. This decree shall last forever more, for the Arka shall never diminish. By order of his Imperial Majesty, Emperor Malvus Barkhart.
THE DECREE OF MAGICK, YEAR 907

Bare feet slapped the sand with a fervour and excitable abandon that only the youthful can muster. Grit flew from pale soles, ash black and tide wet. Sandworms were trampled mid-gasp as they reared from their holes for air. Great clouds of dappled waders took flight as hollering filled the unbroken, dawn air. Wordless cries of effort, challenges, and insults; they all rose to the granite-coloured sky. All save for laughter.

For this was a race.

It was said in the cliff-towns that the tides eventually return all that has been lost at sea. All one had to do was wait for the right tide. That morning, in the wake of the lashing winds and rain, the sea had regurgitated all kinds of lost treasures and delights.

The storm had broken the day before. It had besieged the Hâlorn cliffs for a week before its gales became a spent wheezing. Hurricane, the elders always called it: a storm god that roamed the seas, causing havoc on coasts and ships alike. He had brought ice rain and waves taller than the greatest pines, but the thunder, the lightning, they had not been Hurricane's doing.

Mithrid Fenn had glimpsed the ships through shutters and rain-soaked glass, refusing to blink should anything be missed. She and every other child in the cliff-village of Troughwake watched while the elders had cowered behind bedposts and cradled rusty weapons. Two vessels duelled between the roiling waves. At first, they seemed to exist only in the lightning flash. Then, as fires began to burn across rain-lashed decks and rigging, amber light sketched their shapes.

One ship she swore was as large as an island, square and fat. Likely some trick of the storm. The other had been smaller, an Arka warship. They were a familiar sight in Hâlorn, where the view was naught but a seascape. Always patrolling the waters, guarding the coasts from the rebels, as the elders told her.

For hours, the ships had battled. Lightning fell not from the sky but was traded between decks. Fire streaked the night. Unnatural colours painted the storm clouds.

As the storm died, so had the battle. The larger vessel limped away, listing to one side as it chased the winds north. Crippled, the Arka warship met its doom on the fanged reef beyond the narrow beach. Now its black carcass lay broken and awkward in the surf.

Mithrid bounded over a driftwood log. Sand scattered as she landed, causing the racer behind her to trip, blunder over the log, and get a face full of grit for her troubles. Mithrid was now a clear second. A boy with a tangled mop of black hair was out in front. Bogran Clifsson was nimble for somebody who closely resembled a toad.

With a quick shove to Bogran's back, she sent him reeling into the shallows, kicking icy water until he tumbled into the water and seaweed. Mithrid smirked as she sprinted past him, claiming the firmer ground. Father told her frequently how she had the legs of a marshdeer, and, more often than not, the flitting mind of one to match.

She fixed her eyes on the charred wreck. Pieces of its hull and innards had made their way ashore. The slate-grey beach was littered with wreckage, from splinters of wood and discarded boots to great chunks of hull and rigging. One section of mast had somehow righted itself in the sand, still doing its duty in vain. It looked like the surviving flagpole of a burnt-out fort.

Remina Hag was gaining on her. Mithrid could hear her desperate snuffling. She snatched a glance, and saw Bogran catching up, too. Mithrid lowered her head and forced her gangly legs to move faster. Copper hair streaming behind her, she hurtled for the finish line: a broad piece of ship's hull.

As Mithrid stretched out, ready to slap a hand onto the charcoal wood in victory, Remina threw herself forwards in a mad dive. Her arms flailed like an airborne squid. Bogran slid on his backside, toes pointed.

Thunk.

Slap.

'Shit!' Mithrid cried as she punched the wood in third place. It blackened her knuckles instantly.

Bogran arose, wiping sand from his wet trews. 'Ha! First!'

'Second!' cheered Remina Hag. Her face was a mask of grey sand and blood where she had squashed her nose into the beach. Her flaxen hair was all wrapped around her forehead. 'That's what you get for pushing me into a log.'

'Third,' muttered Mithrid. 'And you fell into that log yourself, you tit.'

A broom-handle of a boy sprinted up to them, slapping the hull as he zipped past.

'Fourth!'

Crisk was closely followed by Littlest. She had only seen nine winters, but as Remina's sister, she was determined to join in their games. She barely reached up to Mithrid's waist, and she giggled as she blackened her hands on the wreckage.

'Fifth,' she announced proudly.

Another boy was a large bull of a child, and the only child in Troughwake taller than Mithrid. Hence his nickname. Bogran and his father both held a strong suspicion the boy had minotaur blood in him, somewhere back in his line.

Bull lumbered up to the log and knocked charred splinters from it. 'Er…' he said, looking around with his sleepy eyes. 'What's next? Mith?'

'Sixth, you lump,' said Mithrid, pointing to where other groups of children were now racing down the steps of the cliffs. 'Come on. Quickly, before the old ones realise we're gone.'

Remina was everybody's senior by barely a winter and eager to constantly remind everybody of it. 'And remember! No hiding things, as per the rules!'

'Wipe your face, Remina. You look like a sand troll.' Mithrid flashed a smile.

There was foul muttering as the girl furiously scraped at her face with her sleeve. Mithrid shook her head and began her beachcombing. 'Hag by name, Hag by nature,' she whispered.

She chose to go further along the beach where a larger section of ship had survived the merciless battering of the sea. She spotted a box in the waterline, cracked but still whole, and dashed to it. There was no bolt, just a latch. Inside, the prize was waterlogged and smashed fruit. Mithrid wrinkled her lips and moved on.

Another box had fared worse, but inside there was a pair of fine shoes and some copper trinkets: bracelets and bangles and other such things. Mithrid slid a few onto her wrist, admiring them in the weak light. Holding the box under her arm, she kicked at a handful of charred planks that covered something deeper in the water.

A corpse without arms washed towards her in the flow of the waves. Mithrid retreated in a panic. Her yelp echoed against the stark cliff face that towered behind her, though it was not the first body she had seen amongst the jetsam. The Jörmunn Sea and the Coldcoal Bay were dangerous enough without ship battles and piratical rebels. Beachcombing was a game they played almost weekly. Mithrid took a breath to slow her heart, and after setting the box down, she moved back to the gruesome body. She knew what treasures pockets could hold.

Pulling a face, she delved aside the man's broken leather armour and felt for a pocket or purse. She found the latter attached to his belt, and inside, a handful of silvers and coppers. Mithrid's eyes widened. It may have been pittance in the empire, but it was half a year's wage in Troughwake. Without hesitating, she plucked the coins from the purse and tucked them into the folds of her seal-hide coat, behind a gap in the stitching. It was against the rules of the game, but she would be damned if Bogran and Remina got to fatten themselves up even more while she and father went hungry.

Mithrid calmly picked up the box and moved on. Crisk came racing past her, whooping, a stringless longbow clutched in his hand. Several other boys and girls were chasing him for some unknown reason. Youth didn't require one.

Beyond the body, there was a swathe of soaked and spoiled vittles. Apples bobbed on the waters or tumbled in the waves that washed over the shore. Mithrid picked at a few items. Most were badly burnt. She found clothing there, but no bodies. There were curiously few corpses, in fact. Perhaps the tides had dragged them out to sea, or perhaps foul magick had burnt them all to ash and charcoal.

Mithrid stumbled across wreckage that seemed at odds with the other jetsam: a section of hull complete with a broken shield still affixed. Its wood was barely charred, but deeply gouged as if it had been hacked at by a colossal axe. She moved closer, running her hands across the wet wood, where chisels had carved foreign runes into the hull. They felt cold to her touch, so much so they made Mithrid's hand ache.

Bending to the sand, she dug at a shattered shelf. A metal plate had been nailed to it, this time displaying writing she did recognise. Common-tongue.

'Re… covered from Arfell Lib—something. Year nine, one, three,' she read aloud in a whisper. She had never heard of such a place as Arfell.

Mithrid dug around the hull, finding more broken, empty shelves but no treasures. She was beginning to get frustrated; the warship was proving fruitless and already she could hear shouting from the buildings clinging to the cliff. The gang's time was running out.

Mithrid cast around, pulling slimy kelp and plank shards aside. A boot, complete with a severed foot, repulsed her but she kept digging. She yelped again as a wrackle jumped from the water, its tiny jaws gnashing. The slimy eel managed to seize the meat of her thumb, but Mithrid shook it off violently. Surprise overrode sense: wrackles had hooked teeth, and it was best to drown the bastards in air so they let go without leaving deep scratches. Mithrid clenched a fist, dripping blood in the water, and searched on.

Splashing water and detritus aside, her uninjured hand closed on something square and solid. And heavy. She hauled it with both hands, and with a grunt, she claimed it back from the sea.

Mithrid clutched it close to her belly. It was a rectangular block, the width of her outstretched fingers and twice as long. It was about three inches thick, and Mithrid would have thought it a jewellery box had it not been bound in waxy leather and had some spongy give when she squeezed it. It felt more like an old book. Mithrid clutched it tighter.

'Oi!' came a shrill shout.

With a groan, Mithrid turned. Remina and Bogran had appeared from behind some jetsam and were aiming for Mithrid. Bogran was carting a shield and a small cage. Remina was close at heel. Bull followed her. Littlest and Crisk were busy with their own merriment. What remained of the gang gathered in close council, in a tight circle turned away from the younger children of Troughwake.

'Show your treasures,' announced Bogran in a low voice, like a preacher holding sermon. He was taking his role as first immensely seriously, as always.

Bogran presented a dented wooden shield, circular and painted yellow with a boar in stark black. Something had blasted a bite-mark from one edge. Mithrid could have sworn the charred edges were still steaming, ever so softly. As well as the shield, Bogran had also found a birdcage with a dead sparrow swimming in it.

Remina held out her offering: a badly dented firkin of some sloshing liquid. It had a label scratched into it. 'Something called "slosk," ' she announced, shaking it to make it gurgle.

'Slosh,' Mithrid corrected. Remina had always been slower with letters.

The girl scowled deeply. 'Slosh, then.'

'Hmm. Next,' Bogran dictated. As first, he got the pick of any item the others had found. Unlike most of the old ones, he was far from interested in grog.

'And you, Mithrid?'

'Shoes, a ragged dress, some bangles.' Mithrid opened her smashed box to show them. 'And this leather thing. Maybe some book.' Though she didn't wish to draw too much attention to it, she saw the gang's eyes widen over the silver spiral on its leather wrapping. Books were rare in Hâlorn, items of suspicion, for books could sometimes be powerful and dangerous things. Their contents were a mystery until they were consumed. Even the humblest of stories could seed an idea in the mind, spark a fire in the heart. Such things were dangerous in the Arka Empire, or so Grey Barbo said.

'Nothing else?' Remina enquired, scowl still dominating her face. Her nose was crusted with blood, her cheek and back of her hands smeared with it.

'No,' said Mithrid, firm as cliff-rock, fighting to keep from clutching the lining of her coat.

'Cowshit.' Remina reached for her pockets but Mithrid slapped the girl's paw away.

'Back off. I ain't no liar.'

'Wouldn't be the first time you hid a find.'

'Says the girl who managed to stuff a whole loaf in her drawers.'

'You cretch!'

'Oi! Respect the rules!' Bogran snapped, clearly too interested in his own gains to care for their argument. 'Who's next?'

Crisk and Littlest appeared from behind a chunk of wreckage, as if they had been waiting for their cue. Crisk still had his longbow in hand.

'You first,' Bogran challenged the boy.

'Bow,' said Crisk before snapping his fingers. He fished something out of his pocket: a half-burnt candle. 'Or candle.'

'Littlest?'

With a proud thrust of her fist, Littlest produced a handful of chain. Loosening her fingers, a pendant dropped and dangled in mid-air. It was a shard of sun-coloured rock on a soggy twine, not gold but glittery enough to draw their gaze and cause a few moments of silence.

'Well. And you, Bull?' Bogran asked.

'Plant,' said the big lump, thrusting forwards a meaty fist that gripped a cracked porcelain pot with a withered plant. Its stems were a dark green and its leaves the colour of soured milk. Despite Bull's nonchalance, Mithrid was immediately intrigued.

A shout from along the beach stalled them momentarily. The elders – or "old ones" as they were commonly known – were wise to the games of their progeny and were now bustling down the beach in a tizzy. Voices floated on the morning breezes towards them. Harsh and damning.

'Right then,' said Bogran, eager to claim his prizes. His toad eyes flicked between the offerings of the group, measuring, calculating. He took his time deciding.

'Give me the book,' Bogran finally said.

With a heavy sigh, Mithrid handed it over.

'And I'll take the clothes and bracelets.' Remina snatched the waterlogged box from under Mithrid's arm. She would have slapped the wench if it wasn't her right as second, and if her hand was not wrackle-bit and bleeding.

As third, Mithrid ran fingers through her tangled mane of hair and eyed what was left to claim. The birdcage was disgusting. The shield and the plant had both caught her attention. Her gaze settled on Littlest's pendant for a moment. Tears immediately began to well in the little girl's eyes.

'You know the rules, little sister,' Remina warned.

'But I found it,' Littlest replied, voice wavering.

'Keep it,' said Mithrid, softly ruffling the girl's lemon hair with her hand. 'I'm going to take the shield, Bogran. Hand it over.'

Emitting a grunt, the boy relinquished it. Mithrid held it by its leather strap, down at her side as if she were playing a warrior.

'Bogran Clifsson!' came a holler from back along the beach, where a troop of old ones were making their way swiftly towards them. Mithrid could see her own father amongst them, and he was close enough that she could see both the tiredness and the anger in his eyes. The children were fleeing back to Troughwake, not brave enough yet.

'Quickly!' Remina hissed. The game played out rapidly, with Crisk choosing the birdcage for some unknown reason, Littlest taking the candle, and Bull, not understanding the rules even after all this time, trying to take the box from Remina. In a huff, he took the longbow instead.

'Hide the book, Bogran! Your mam won't let you keep something like that.'

Bogran nodded and got straight to digging a hole in the wet sand.

'*Above* the tideline, you nob,' Mithrid chided him, poking the boy with her foot.

He scurried away, though not without wagging a sandy finger at all of them. 'Not one of you touches it until I do. 'Specially you, Mith. In fact, look away!'

The rest of the gang stood their ground and waited for the scolding to rain upon them. Mithrid pasted her trademark smile. Remina raised her chin. Littlest was already tearing up again. Bull just scratched his head. Crisk was too busy poking at his dead sparrow to notice.

The old ones closed on them within moments, just as Bogran ran up, breathless and hands covered in sand.

Crisk's parents silently whisked their boy away, knocking the old birdcage and its dead resident to the sand. They were the silent type of angry, which Mithrid found far more disturbing than somebody like Mam Hag, who went about her scolding like a rainstorm dousing a town.

'Remina! Larina! Come here right now!' she snapped, swiftly seizing both Remina's and Littlest's ears. They were jerked forwards and held at their mother's sides. She was a large and muscular woman, was Mam Hag. Jurilda, as the elders called her. She was never seen out of her apron, whether it be mending trews, towing fishing lines, or sitting at table on Highfrost's Eve.

'What have we told you about this nonsense game? It's dangerous is what it is! Just look at the state of your face, Remina!' Mam barked. She grabbed Remina's nose and the girl managed to honk like a goose in pain.

'Maa!'

'You're lucky it's not broken, or I'd have broken it for you!'

Mithrid coughed to hide her chuckling.

'That's enough cheek out of you, Mithrid,' her father warned in a voice still hoarse from waking. He said nothing more, simply grabbing her arm and leading her away beyond the tideline. Even though he let the other elders do the admonishing, staying silent as they trudged, she knew better than to complain or speak another word. Mithrid saw him eyeing the char on the shield.

Old Man Clifsson, a man as toadish as his son, grabbed Bogran by the nape of his pudgy neck and marched him back up the beach. 'What did you bury?' he was saying.

'Nothing! I swear!'

'You think we didn't play this game when we were your age? What did you bury?'

'I didn't bury anything!' Bogran squealed.

'Really? How come I found a knife in your pocket after that fisher boat ran aground in summer, hmm? How did that mysteriously appear?'

Mam Hag was still blowing hard about the dangers of wreck-combing. 'Not to mention all the dangerous splinters, and the rain! You'll catch you cold, you two! Put that broken old thing down. Now! You want some dirty old shoes the sea spat out? Dear me.'

'But—' Remina wailed.

Mithrid's father let the other parents move past. They appeared far more eager to punish their children than he did. Bull's mother had not joined the search party. Not knowing what to do with himself, Bull had ambled after them, using his longbow as a walking staff. He still held his withered plant, too.

'Come along there, Bull,' said father, waving a meaty and calloused hand; what nature gave a man when he attacked trees with an axe all the live-long day.

'Ma's probably still asleep. She likes her sleep. That and staring at the sea.'

The poor woman had never been the same since a plague took Bull's father. Only his grandfather, Grey Barbo, remembered to feed and keep him.

'Then walk with us,' father told him.

They walked in silence for a while, letting the arguing of the others recede. Their feet swished through the wet, stranded seaweed, or kicked puffs of sand into the face of the cold wind. Mithrid's father still held her by the arm, not painfully tight, but firm enough to let her know she was in trouble. Mithrid's mouth dried up.

'Why is it you old—elders are so scared of shipwrecks?' Mithrid asked, breaking the silence so abruptly that she made Bull flinch.

Father liked to dwell on his words before speaking them aloud. 'Jurilda Hag speaks the truth, at least in part. It ain't that we're scared of shipwrecks, it's that you lot ain't scared enough. You rush in, alone and without thought.' He waggled Mithrid's captured hand for her, showing her its tooth-marks.

'Just a wrackle.'

'It ain't wrackles that worry me.'

Bull became curious. 'Then what, Master Fenn?'

'Look there.'

Father pointed them back towards the water's edge, where old ones had started a more organised, stately looting of the wreckage. Here and there, men and women dragged corpses onto the sand. Mithrid could already count a score of them. Many wore leather armour, marked with the emperor's crest of a white hammer. Others bore the crest on their cheeks or on their naked backs. Amongst them, here and there, were other bodies that did not belong to the warship's crew. Some were dressed in finer scale armour, or black chainmail. Another shield was rescued from the sea and tossed near the growing pile of bodies. If Mithrid looked closely, she saw the mark she and every other child in Hâlorn had been taught to fear since birth: a red skull, upside-down.

'The Outlaw King,' grunted Bull.

'Just a myth, Bull. Likely some warlord who thinks far too much of himself. They're no better than rebels. Enemies of the empire we find ourselves living in. Scum, just like any bandit stalking the clifftops.'

'But they're already dead.'

'Sometimes they ain't, daughter,' Father snapped, speaking while his eyes remained on the dead. 'Children have always played this game. I did. Old Clifsson did. And Mam Hag. Treasures from the sea, right?'

Bull nodded. Mithrid had been told this story before. She also knew what was good for her and pretended to listen avidly.

'We were lucky. Whenever a corpse came up gasping, it was always a fisherman, or sailor, or some pirate so glad to be alive that he ran straight off yelling his thanks. We got older and stopped playing, started treating it like work. Salvage, we called it, instead of a game. It's how the cliff-towns and villages survive, see? Other children grew on up, and like us, they also snuck out of their homes at the crack of dawn and raced to claim what they could before the elders got wind of it. Just as you did. You were too young to remember, but one morning a skiff got washed up. A boy of fifteen winters by the name of Fisle went out to the wreck before anyone else could even get their trews on.' Father took a moment. Mithrid felt his grip tighten on her arm. 'He found a body in the surf. Thought him dead so he started going through his pockets. He rolled the man over and before he knew it, he got a knife in the throat. Now he was strong, that Fisle, so he didn't die straight away. Instead, he tried to crawl back to Troughwake, but not before the man stabbed him a dozen more times. We found them both there, Fisle still warm and the man gasping and sobbing for air, staring at the bloody knife in his hand, and the boy its blade was still buried in. The boy who had only seen fifteen winters go by. One less than you, Mithrid. That is why we worry so.'

Mithrid spent the silence watching how the elders poked every body before touching it. She thought of the pale stump of the corpse she'd found and shuddered at what might have been.

'He was a rebel. A cursed traitor. I owe the empire peace and prosperity, but I owe the Outlaw King a piece of my mind,' added father. 'Now come. There's work to be done.'

'What work?'

'Not for you, daughter. You are going home,' he said, his tone growing stern. Mithrid tapped her teeth together.

'And what of me? What's my punishment, Master Fenn?'

The winds of Father's mood changed just as quickly, and he cracked a wide smile.

'You, Bull, will get no punishment from me. That's a job for your mother or grandfather, not me.'

Bull nodded, seeming pleased. Mithrid envied him.

'Run home, now.'

'Thank you, Master Fenn. Oh, and you can have this, Mithrid,' added Bull, catching himself as he turned to leave. 'Ma'll sneeze something' awful at it. And grandda might try to eat it. But I know you got your little garden. Maybe you can heal it.'

Mithrid couldn't help but smile as she took the limpid flower out of his saucer of a palm. She lifted one of its leaves as if shaking its hand. 'Thanks, Bull. I'll try.'

With a nod, Bull hurried towards the rope ladders that led up to the village, perched on the cliff face like wicker and hide barnacles on a hull. Her father marched her on slow yet steady.

Mithrid placed her foot on a ladder rung and paused.

'Go, up you get. And mind you don't drop that bloody shield on me,' he growled. 'Of all the things you'd want to pull from a wreck.'

Mithrid hopped up the ladder, looking for all the world like a soldier scaling a castle wall. Father was right: though she could out climb a crag goat, the shield was cumbersome at best.

'It's not all I found,' she admitted, once she'd climbed to the village. She was sweating, and not just from exertion. With her spare hand she plucked out several coppers and silvers and showed her father. 'Treasures from the sea. They're for us.'

He huffed. 'They better be. I'm not having my daughter get rich and leave me here chopping trees until I die. Now go.' He pointed to their cottage: a small, semicircle of thatch and wood affair that clung to the cliff at the end of the walkway. Its door was half-open. The night's candles still burned within.

The latch snapped shut behind Mithrid. The shadow of her father enveloped her. With shield held down by her knees, she swivelled to apologise.

Though her muscles were already tense, the blow caught her off guard. The back of that meaty, calloused hand struck her across the cheek. She spun from the force, falling heavy on the shield and her chin. The candles danced around her.

The strong fingers gripped the scruff of her neck and hauled her to her feet. Mithrid's feet dragged as she was marched to her bedding. She was still trying to count her teeth.

'You, of all the lost souls in this godsforsaken, grubby village, should know better, Mithrid. How *dare* you disgrace her by being so careless?'

There wasn't an answer in Emaneska that would have stopped his tirade. Mithrid owed it to the shipwreck, at least, to call him off. He dropped her on the floor with no more care than a sack of flour and thudded away.

Mithrid wiped her nose, leaving a long streak of blood from her finger to her wrist, and stared at the door as if her eyes were augers.

CHAPTER 3
BROKEN THINGS

The Outlaw King, the Outlaw King.
He'll steal your soul and boil your skin!
The Outlaw King, the Outlaw King.
Pluck your bones and make them sing!
POPULAR ARKA NURSERY RHYME

They say there is serenity to be found in watching a rainy day from the comfort of the warm and dry.

Mithrid could not have disagreed more.

Her day had been spent pressing her nose up against the glass of her cottage. The shutters had been slammed, reopened, and then slammed again in angst. Only planting the white flower had given her some distraction, at least for a half an hour. It looked at home between the clump of herbs and the red seagrass that was constantly attempting to crawl from the trough. Even her miniature garden could only hold her attention for so long. Before long, she was pressed to the window once more, her nose numb against the frigid glass.

From the vantage point of the cottage she was forced to watch the old ones pick apart the wreckage, building piles of various – and wholeheartedly interesting – things on the beach. With the spyglass she could pick out father hauling up plank after plank, gathering almost enough for two houses by the time the rain came in the afternoon. At least he would be worn out.

Sparking a candle against the gloom of the dying day, Mithrid caught her reflection in the smudged glass. She wanted to ignore it but that was easier said than done entrenched in boredom. The mark of her father's fist had begun to darken around her left cheek and eye. A fine match to the cobweb scar that reached from her temple to the corner of her lip. There was a cut on her chin, too, which bled profusely once she'd grown bored enough to pick it.

Once the wood piles were safe beyond the tideline, the elders retreated to sip stew and natter under the wall of the ochre cliff. Mithrid watched their mouths moving from afar, trying to guess words, grinding her teeth all the while.

When her father finally returned, the sun was fading behind the ceiling of slate clouds. He stood in the doorway, dripping with rain. There was a sack slung over his shoulder. Anything was a weapon in her father's hands, so Mithrid remained curled up by the window, spyglass threatening to break in her stiff grip.

Father regarded her with those eyes of his: always enshrouded in dark rings of tiredness yet refusing to burn out, like pearls at the bottom of a bucket. The mark of the weight of the world, he called it. His stare seemed stuck on her bruises.

'Have you eaten?' he asked gruffly.

'No.'

'Good.'

Mithrid huffed, ignoring him. She listened to the clomping rhythm of the sack meeting the floorboard, his boots being kicked away, and the door shutting out the night.

Something nudged her arm. Mithrid looked away and she was whacked instead.

'Ow.'

Mithrid saw a box at her side, a flat construction of green wood, engraved with strands of ivy. She traced the carving.

'Open it,' her father grunted.

It took some doing. The wood had swollen in the water, thankfully keeping the seawater out but making Mithrid struggle. She denied her father's help and with a growl of effort, pried it open.

Three small pale cakes sat inside, nestled in hollows carved in wood. Each was decorated with a beetle so lifelike that Mithrid almost threw the box aside. Emerald, sapphire, and ruby were their sugared carapaces. Spindly black legs, dusted in sugar, clutched each cake.

'Some officer has fancy tastes,' said Father. He tried an awkward smile. It didn't fit. 'Just like my daughter.'

'We'll share them,' Mithrid replied, meeting his eyes for the first time. 'What colour?'

'Green for me.'

Mithrid chose blue. The horned beetle was the hue of summer skies. It crumbled at the first touch of her tongue, fizzing away like a sandcastle falling to the waves. The sugar spread over her tongue as Mithrid bit down, halving the beetle. For all her stewing, she hadn't realised how ravenous she had become. It was like nothing she had ever tasted, full of flavours that set her mind afire.

It was no surprise the cake was demolished in moments. The only evidence of its existence were the pale crumbs spread across her knees and trews.

Father took his time. Once he had picked the morsels from his wiry beard, he gently closed the box and chose a place for it on the shelf beneath a shrine of shells and whetstones.

'For you,' he whispered, but not to his daughter.

Mithrid's stomach protested loudly.

'Almost time for the burn.'

'I guess I have to stay here,' she grumbled.

Father sighed as if he'd been holding his breath all day. 'As much as I despise it, you ain't a child no more despite what my eyes tell me, daughter. You don't know much of the world, but you've tasted its ugliness. As much as I tried to keep you from it, you learned young.' Father's eyes strayed to the small carved effigy sitting in the centre of the shrine. It was where most families kept their gods: Hurricane. Jötun. Njord. Not in this house. This was no god but a woman, as slender as the pine it was carved from. Her hair was stained red with sap, as wild as Mithrid's. The faintest smile lingered on the statue's face.

'Surely it's too wet?' asked Mithrid in an effort to distract both of them. She knew his hurt ran deeper than hers, a knife wound that refused to heal. Mithrid has been too young and the blade of sorrow had only raked her.

'Reesta donated some of his fishpickle grog. The stuff burns better than whale tallow or peat. It'll see to the bodies,' Father answered. 'Come now. We'll be late.'

Mithrid sought her boots quickly, before he changed his mind. The man had the moods of a winter gale. Even in this weather, he would have climbed the ladders to the clifftops and hacked down a tree to exercise his pain. Better than using his fists upon her, Mithrid knew, but she hated to see him hurting. He might not have been a shining example of a father, but she had none spare.

'Is the pit dug?' she asked.

'Pit's dug.'

'Then what are we waiting for?' she offered a smile.

His fingers trembled, but he reached out to rest a hand on her tangle of hair. He made it halfway before clearing his throat and seeking his pocket instead. 'You behave yourself.'

Even with their cloth-wrapped handles, the ladders were slippery that night. The sky was charcoal and the sea angry. The waves crashed first on the reef then second on the shore, deprived of their power but still seething with froth and foam. With the turning tide, more wreckage had appeared. Work for the morning.

The wet, charred wood took on a glasslike texture in the ragged light of the torches staked in the sand. They led a path along the beach, to where the denizens of Troughwake had formed a circle of seal hide and lemming fur around the pit.

Father found a gap for them and stood Mithrid at the edge. He timidly laid a hand on her shoulder as her morbid curiosity dragged her gaze down, to where the bodies lay in a puzzle of limbs and torsos. Driftwood planks crisscrossed half of them, green branches covered others, but Mithrid could still see gawping faces wedged into helmets, or hands still grasping for air.

It chilled her, more so than the biting wind or frigid winter's night, to see so many as young as her amongst the pile of dead. Useless and small, they seemed, and yet they had still been handed a spear and told to fight. It reminded Mithrid a wider world existed outside the hovels of Troughwake, one that asked children to fight, and that it was marching on without her. She was at peace with that. To Mithrid, Troughwake was a hollow in a world of sea-fog she hoped would never lift.

Between the packed fingers of the crowd, she caught the eyes of the others. Bogran stared at her across the pit. Nearby, Remina and Littlest stood wrapped in the protective embrace of Mam Hag, her hands clamped over their eyes.

Mithrid was allowed to watch, and watch she did. She drank in the warmth of the fire as it crept to and fro across the corpse pile until the pit roared with flame.

As the fuel began to dwindle, Mithrid found Bogran once more amongst the crowd. His head kept twitching to the left, encouraging a look past the crowds and further along the beach.

Mithrid couldn't make out his mouthings before the headman approached the pit to make the customary offering to Njord and his voracious sea. The old words.

'Always and forever, to the sea. Waves break and tides wane, ships break asunder, split in twain. What the sea claims she yearns to eat, all drowned sailors kneel at her feet. Take their souls down to the deep, oh Njord. Let no evil touch them. We'll hear their songs in crashing waves, laments of those in death's cold accord. Always and forever, to the sea.'

'To the sea,' spoke the crowd, in monotonous unison.

Mithrid mouthed the words. She had never quite understood the offering. If the sea wanted to eat what she claimed, she shouldn't have vomited it up on the beach.

'And to the empire,' somebody else called. That response was even more mechanical.

Her father tugged at her sleeve. Together they slipped into the departing crowd in silence. Mithrid looked for the gang in the press of people, many of which had the distinct reek of fish. At one point she saw Bogran, but he was whisked away as the queues for the ladders formed. Mithrid always imagined it as a siege, pretending they were an army of rogues assaulting the walls of a great fortress. If she'd had a wooden sword, she would have swung it.

Villagers peeled off onto their respective levels. Amidst the jostling, sharp nails grabbed Mithrid's forearm. It was Remina Hag.

'Midnight,' she breathed as she brushed past her, no friendlier than a stranger.

Immediately seized by the claws of both dread and excitement, Mithrid chose the former and shook her head. Remina's scowl faded amongst the crowd.

The click of the door shut out the bustle.

'Bed,' ordered her father, pointing to her cocoon of a room, its diminutive walls more cloth than wood.

Mithrid placed her hands on her hips. 'Don't you eat that beetle.'

He patted the box on the shelf. 'It's your mother's.'

She watched him, playing suspicious for a moment.

Her fingers stank of the pit-fire. Of driftwood char and corpses. Mithrid shuddered, as if a ghost had wafted by her. Chewing one of the sickly mint leaves her father insisted on gathering, she splashed cold water on her face and scrubbed with sand.

The girl wrapped herself in her woollen blanket and kneaded some of the knots from her pillow with her head. Father came to stand at her curtains, hands thrust deep in pockets.

'I...' he harrumphed. 'I am only stern with you because I care too much,' Father replied. 'You, you call us old ones, but another winter and you'll be one of us. Soon enough, you'll have to stop playing and start thinking like an elder. If you don't grow, don't learn, it might be you down in that pit. Just like Fisle.' He hesitated, rare emotion finding its way to his weathered surface. 'And I refuse to burn another soul I love. Your mother would say the same.'

Mithrid shut her eyes tightly, feeling the scar wrinkle. Saying no more, Father retreated, drawing the curtains shut and leaving her to sleep.

All Mithrid did was listen. She'd grown used to her father's evening ceremony. The scrape of the chair to the spot by the window. The salty winds blowing through where he unlatched it. The pulling of the floorboard he thought she didn't know about. And at last, the quiet, muffled squeaking of a cork being loosed from the mouth of a bottle.

An hour passed. Whenever Father shifted in his chair, or sipped too loudly on his firewine, Mithrid feigned snoring. Another hour, and it was he who slumbered, snoring with the indulgent, sonorous gurgling that only half a bottle of grog can yield. He sounded like a saw blade rattling back and forth across a rusty pipe.

Mithrid snuck from her bed to peek between the curtains. Her father's balding head rested against the chair back. The bottle lingered in his hand, teetering on the floorboards. Mithrid couldn't remember the last time he had actually fallen asleep in his bed. It was too big, he'd said of it one morning, when she had dared to press him about it.

She bit her lip once more, drawing blood from where she'd chewed it all evening, mulling over her father's words. Warnings, more like. *Threats.* Again, Mithrid felt the fragility of her world, felt the carelessness of childhood slipping away. Duties and work and responsibility were abhorrent compared to races and fights and odd books washed up by the sea. If it was to slip from her grasp, she would hold on for long as she could.

With a quiet tut, Mithrid fetched her blanket and trod softly towards Father, tiptoeing over the spots in the floor that creaked. Careful not to wake him, she draped the blanket over his broad chest before looking at the fingernail of moon breaking through the clouds. Somewhere high on the cliff, a watchmen sounded a low note on a ship's bell.

'Midnight,' Mithrid breathed, as she crept to the door. It required some patience to make sure the latch and bolt didn't squeak, but at least the hinges were freshly greased. Mithrid had made sure of that the previous evening. Picking up her shoes and coat, she slipped into the night.

The bitter air took her breath away, Mithrid hurriedly donned her coat and forced her feet into her shoes as she walked. The walkway of boards and tarred rope was dark, empty, and Mithrid dashed along it, keeping an eye on the torch glow above. The watchmen were tired old souls who had eyes only for the sea or the clifftops. Pirates and marauders were the only things that caught their attention, not a gang of children up to no good.

Mithrid saw other shapes in the shadows, swarming to join her. Only four of them tonight: Remina, Bogran, and Bull.

They descended silently, jumping from the rungs and onto the wet sand. Clinging to the cliff face, they jogged along the beach, heads low and silence reigning. Only the sea and moon were witness to their creeping.

Only when they were far enough from view of Troughwake and tucked into a crevice in the rock, did Bogran speak.

Mithrid shrugged off her hood. 'Where are the others?'

'Crisk and Littlest could not be trusted with this. They'd only let it slip.'

'Agreed,' Remina whispered.

'Think they found it?' asked Mithrid, uttering the question they had all spent the day wondering. She saw the unease in the others' wide eyes in the faint glow of the village. The pit was nearby, but its fires had long since died. It was now a black void in the beach.

Bull spoke up. 'What if they burned it?'

Remina shook her head. 'No. Can't have.'

'I buried it deep and high up the sands,' Bogran said, reassuring himself more than the others. He began to stride ahead. 'The old ones were working the tideline all day.'

Worry turned the gang's jogging into another race. Sand flew from their heels.

'Where is it, Bogran?' called Remina, having to shout over the crash of a wave. The tide was creeping in once more, hungry for what had escaped it.

The boy was dashing about between the thicker parts of wreckage that had yet to be hacked into pieces. 'There!'

Mithrid spotted the chunk of rebel ship at the same time. Bogran was already pounding back up the beach, counting steps out loud. Being far from the smartest in Troughwake, his numbers were in a jumbled order, but they made sense to him.

'Twenty-eleven! Here!' He hissed, kicking at a spar of wood sticking from the sand. He began to dig, down on all fours and using his hands as spades. It was a tense moment when he cursed and started to dig in another spot, then another, until finally he uttered a celebratory, 'Yes!'

The gang immediately crowded around him, but Bogran led them back to the rock, where an overhang cast them in deeper darkness.

'Remina.'

The girl had brought a candle. Bull produced a steel and with combined – if not lengthy – effort, they lit the candle. Every spark of the steel illuminated the cliff hollow in stuttering flashes. Mithrid imagined faces in the rocks, staring down at them, features disfigured by wind and wave.

Remina shielded the diminutive flame until it was strong enough to stand on its own. Its glow shone through her fingers. The gang leaned in, tightly knit, as Bogran reverently brushed the sand from the tome's face. He turned it over and over, prodding here and there at its singed or sodden corners.

'Open it already,' hissed Mithrid.

'It's my book,' Bogran tutted, placing it in the sand noticeably nearer to him. He saw to the latch on its cover. He might as well have been trying to thread a ship's rope through a sewing needle for all the fiddling he did. Mithrid fidgeted as the anticipation rose to infuriating heights.

'Bogran!' Remina squeaked.

'Got it,' he sighed satisfactorily. He peeled back the cover, showing a half-soaked page. The dull ochre watermarks around the edge made a dry island of white paper and flowing green text.

Bogran's rubbery lips quivered as he tried to read silently. His words were even less polished than his numbers.

'Mithrid?' he said. Eyes still locked on the page, he slid the book through the sand. The others leaned in like trees in a gale.

Mithrid angled her head to see better. The first line was written in some runic text, all harsh slashes and basic shapes. It was the kind of language designed to be carved in stone with a flat chisel. The next line was somewhat familiar in terms of lettering, but the words were all jumbled, foreign. The last line she recognised as the Commontongue, spoken throughout Hâlorn. It was old fashioned but readable.

'Book of the Myst–Mysticies of Con... Conjutar... Conjurating Trickery, by Master Kala... fan. Kalafan,' she said.

'That's not what it says,' insisted Remina, swivelling the book around to read for herself. It took some time, but finally she crossed her arms and pouted. 'Fine.'

Mithrid looked around the wide eyes and avid stares. 'What does it mean?'

'You're the smart one. You tell us.'

'Mysticies sounds suspiciously like magick,' Mithrid breathed, as if her father were eavesdropping. 'No?'

'Nonsense,' Remina scoffed, but she threw the book a sideways glance all the same. 'Magick has been banned. The emperor has said so. This doesn't look like an empire book. We should bury it.'

'Trickery sounds fun,' said Bull, in his usual innocent way.

'That it does,' Bogran began to turn the pages, unveiling diagrams and strange patterns marked in more unhelpful runes.

'Bogran, go carefully,' Remina cautioned him.

Mithrid blinked hard. Their intricate shapes blurred until Bogran came upon a page with a crude drawing of a skeleton key in blotched green ink. Below it were three more lines of text, each in its respective language. Below that, a block of scrawl that made her eyes ache, even upside down.

Bogran traced the boundaries of the key with a pudgy finger. 'I wonder what this means.'

'Don't read it,' Remina warned. All leaned closer save for her. She slid backwards on her arse like a hound with worms. 'Feels evil. Arka's glory, I don't like it.' She sounded just like Mam Hag. 'Bury the thing!'

'Crush, kill, bargain, slave,' Bogran read. As he spoke, his voice took on a depth beyond his years, as if somebody recited with him from the shadows. 'Stars, moons, blood, blame.'

A pain shot across Mithrid's forehead. 'Agh!'

Bogran was gripping the book with both hands. He wasn't holding it, but rather thrusting it away yet unable to let go. The words kept spilling from his mouth, now in a language none of them had ever heard.

'Bogran! Stop!'

'It's magick! He's reading a bloody spell!' Remina shrieked, hands framing her gawping expression.

Bogran went rigid, spine bent at an unholy angle. Jaw stretched to breaking, blue smoke arose from his mouth. The sapphire tendrils curled together, forming the roaring face of a sabrecat. Fear leaked from it, washing over them. Remina and Mithrid both scrabbled away but Bull stepped forwards, swinging a spar of driftwood. The stave cleaved right through the blue visage without harming it, but it did clip Bogran across the head.

The spell broke. The book burst from Bogran's hand and the boy was cast into the rock like a seagull striking a crab against a stone. A mushroom of blue smoke was left in his place. The spellbook crackled and fizzed, dancing about in the sand as if possessed. The night air grew hot.

'Do something!' Remina shrieked.

Mithrid acted fast, seizing the book to slam it shut. Scorching pain ran up her arm as soon as her fingers brushed it. Her vision failed her, but before she was enveloped by the darkness, she dragged the cover closed. The heat of the magick died. Green flames raced along the book's edges and scorched the cover and spine to ash. Mithrid's fingertips, lying barely an inch away, were seared pink but she did not flinch away. She could not. Mithrid lay prostrate in the sand, still reaching for the book, eyes rolled to the back of her head and limbs as rigid as fence posts.

Remina's screams, Bull's rough shaking, they mattered not. Mithrid was busy drowning in a black sea, with no star or moonlight to guide her. Echoes of a former life, now so distant it seemed a dream, escorted her into a void of silence.

North, where the cliffs thrust into the sea like a futile spear, pine forests dominated the precipices. They were known to sing when the winds blew strong and along the right line of the compass. It was a song no bard nor skald could do justice. It was an unearthly whining whose secret the pines kept to themselves. Some still believe it the song of spirits and phantom ship. On gusty nights, such as that particular evening, the wailing of the pines had been compared to that of a drowning crew crying out for salvation. If one listened closely, one could almost hear the individual screams.

Deep within the trees' shadow, the lance blade twisted and cut dead the man's screeching. The cliff peasant met the ground a corpse.

Masked figures with hoods drawn gathered around the body to watch it bleed. A dozen of them all counted. A spiral of corpses lay around them amidst the pine needles, some still twitching.

Unbidden, they methodically checked the bodies, moving as smoothly and coldly as machines. Knives ended misery before tearing tunics, revealing pale skin and emancipated spines. They poked, they prodded. Some of them carved stark symbols in the still warm flesh.

Before their macabre business was concluded, a change in the wind or some scent in the air made them all lift their heads. Still as paintings, they looked south, as if a lighthouse in the distance had swung its beam across the haunting forest.

No signal was given, yet they stood as one and immediately departed. No ceremony was given to the corpses. They were left to the devices of crows and rats.

CHAPTER 4
THE PRICE OF MAGICK

The wilds have become dangerous places in the Age of Magick. Evernia's gifts have become a curse, breeding all manner of chaos amongst beasts and men. Bandit mages prowl. Daemons snatch the lost into the night. Fenrir and icewights stalk the north. Trolls of all breeds roam the open moors. Wisps and fae are rumoured to have returned. Ghosts, even, drifting with the night. And still magick grows stronger every day. None can control its flow. Not the Outlaw King. Not the Emperor in his Arkathedral. Not even the goddess Evernia herself.
FROM 'THE NEW EMANESKA', BY THE EXILED SAGE OLE WRUM

Mithrid.

The voice boomed through the void. It was not hers; it was the voice of a god, grasping her empty world in its palm. She had no head to turn, no feet to kick out. She swam in a tide pool, drifting with an ocean's breath. Only her mind was imprisoned, adrift in that lightless place. Her body was gone. Taken. *Unmade.*

There was simply the voice and the void.

Mithrid.

Mithrid shouted for all her worth, but her voice was small and wordless in the vast emptiness. She strained the fragment that was left of her, and only felt the fainter for it. She was nothing but a dying star lost in the darkest corner of the sky. This was death, and no man had ever won against it.

༺

'Mithrid!' The strain in his voice was audible now, squeezed by panic.

Minding her burned fingers, Gammer Fenn held his daughter's cold, limp hand once more before rising from her bedside. Jurilda Hag stood behind, fiddling with an imaginary knot in her apron strings. Bartrum Clifsson cowered beside her. He was a broken man not worth berating. He wore the shattered, soulless gaze of a parent no longer a parent. It was not the natural order of life, for a father to bury his son. It was not right. His red eyes had yet to stray from the body upon the table.

On any given eve, the meagre driftwood table was normally set for three: two living, one passed and gone. That night, the chairs had been thrown aside. Instead of plates and forks, a boy lay atop it, covered with a grey blanket. Where a hole had frayed, bare, pallid skin showed.

They had found Bogran Clifsson slumped dead against the rocks.

Bull and the healer Reesta lingered in the doorway, along with a dozen other elders, still gawking at the contents of the Fenn cottage. Grey Barbo had a skeletal hand on Bull's shoulder. His sandy face was furrowed with tears. His hands still shook, no matter how much dunberry Reesta had fed the boy.

Useless man, Gammer cursed him privately. He was an old fool with seaweed between his ears, stubbornly clinging to remedies older than the cliffs.

'Is there nothing else you can do?' Gammer yelled. The healer and Jurilda flinched from their daze.

'I've done all I can, Fenn. Time and hope are her healers now, not I. Not you.' Reesta said, wringing his long beard between his hands. 'Your daughter breathes. She lives, at least. Take comfort in that.'

'Comfort? What good are you, man? Surely there are other medicines? Other healers?' Gammer did not care for the crowd's muttering. None of their daughters walked the precipice of death.

'In the larger cliff-towns. Wornspur, perhaps, or the skystreets of Hiren's Scarp,' the healer replied, stonier than before. 'But your daughter needs care and attention, not an absent father off on some quest to the city. She can be saved, unlike others.'

Gammer crossed gazes with Bartrum in passing, eyes red-raw from sorrow. His pudgy cheeks were drained pale as first snow.

Though the desire to hook Reesta on the jaw was mighty tempting, Gammer calmed himself. The anger fled from his shoulders. He felt empty without its fuel. He felt his old bones click as he sagged.

All his strength and care had counted for nought against a child's curiosity. Part of him wanted to shake Mithrid violently until she woke, if only so he could punish her. That was a darker man than he wished to be, and he hung there between the bed and the door, trying to trust in something he'd never believed in: luck.

'Where is that accursed book?' Jurilda broke the tension.

'Here,' said a faint voice. Fellow woodcutter Crallig came muscling through the onlookers. He had dwarf blood in him and was wide as he was tall. He didn't care who he barged out of the way to bring forwards a thick bundle of cloth and reed matting. The others formed a timid circle around Crallig as he laid it on the floor and began to gingerly peel it apart, like he was picking worms from a rotten cabbage.

Gammer watched the others cramming at the doorway to see past Bull's shoulder. The boy had shut his eyes, Njord bless him. He was taller than most of the elders and still petrified.

To an overly theatrical gasp that made Gammer scowl, the foul book was revealed. A blackened thing of crispy, charred pages, it filled the room with dread even though it looked destroyed. Crallig kicked it with a boot, drawing a nervous fart from somebody in the small crowd. Even Gammer recoiled.

'Is it... dead?' asked Jurilda.

Crallig itched his wire-brush eyebrows. 'Looks it. But I swear the thing whispered to me when I picked it up.'

'What did it say?'

'Nothing I wanted to understand,' growled the woodcutter.

Gammer approached the big lad by the door. 'What happened, Bull?'

'I told Master Clifsson already, Master Fenn. The book attacked us, throwing Bogran about and freezing Mithrid. I ran here as fast—'

'Tell us again, Bull. Clearer this time. Slower. Details, boy.'

Bull picked frantically at his fingernails, already too short to pick.

Gammer forced a smile. 'You won't be in any trouble for it. We just need to know the facts.'

Bull stared about the expectant circle of elders. His speech came slow and awkward. 'Bogran was first. First to the wreck, I mean, so he got first rights on the pickings. Mithrid found that book. Bogran wanted it, but the old ones—I mean... *you*, beggin' your pardon.' He pointed indiscriminately between the parents. 'When you came to catch us, Bogran buried the book up the sand, and after the fire was out, and you was all asleep, we four snuck onto the beach. Went back to the book.'

Gammer clenched his jaw. Emotions duelled within him. Mithrid had disobeyed him, and yet he had been too busy with his firewine to stop her. Its sour aftertaste in his mouth tasted suspiciously of guilt. 'Then?'

Bull's lip trembled. His eyes glistened with fresh tears. He stared at the grey blanket over the table. 'He... He tried to read the first page but couldn't. Not at first. Mithrid could though. And Remina, too, a little. Then Bogran finds another page, with a picture of a key on it.' Bull paused, remembering. 'He starts speaking all strange and this sabrecat comes right out of the book, smoking and shinin' blue and roaring. I swear on Hurricane and Njord and all the old gods. Bogran's shaking and crying, so I try to hit the cat. Bogran lets go of the book and something tosses him into the cliff. I see it – the book – shakin' in the sand, but afore I could stop it, Mithrid slams it shut.' Bull clapped his hands, making several of the elders jump. 'Her eyes were open, but she was shakin' and didn't wake up. So I ran with Remina. Ran all the way here, Master Fenn. Then we ran back, remember? To get them?'

Gammer held up a hand. 'That bit we know, Bull.' It had been the most breathless, savage sprint of his life. 'It's a fuckin' spellbook.'

'Nonsense!' cried Barbo. 'Nobody's seen a spellbook in Hâlorn for decades, even before the magick markets were burned. Trust me, I can remember. Arka torched most of 'em.'

'Then it must have come from that rebel ship,' insisted Gammer.

'And they bloody read it,' Jurilda breathed, one eye twitching. 'Magick words. Evil words. Cursed words. And they read them!'

Crallig took a hatchet from his belt and went to strike at the book.

'Don't,' snarled Bartrum, choking on his words. 'Don't you touch it. Don't you dare fuckin' open it. It took my boy. It'll take you, too.'

'Bartrum's right,' added Gammer. 'It's dangerous. Outlawed for sure.'

'Then we should burn it,' hissed Reesta. 'It's the only way to destroy it for sure. Before the emperor's men hear word of it.'

'Then we should do it now.' Gammer was already fetching whale tallow and tinder. 'Though it's not our empire I fear. Remember what our old ones used to say?'

Jurilda knew. Her hands had begun to follow her eye's example and were trembling noticeably. 'Magick brings magick, Outlaw King's summons.'

The whispers of worry were fierce now in the crowd.

'Reesta, fetch more of that fishpickle swill of yours! We make sure—'

Gammer was interrupted by the watchmen's bell sounding the lateness of the hour. Two bells had tolled last Gammer could remember. One lonely note pealed through Troughwake. Then the pregnant pause before another followed. The third toll was cut short, as if somebody had fumbled the bell's tongue.

Silence settled, only the sloshing waves below to disturb it. And in that silence, a whispering could be heard, faint as the scuttle of a mouse, sneaking in an open door as chill draught. It was in no tongue Gammer Fenn had ever heard, and from the stares around the circle, he was not the only one who heard it. All of them stared at the book.

Before a word could be spoken, a piercing shriek rang out from higher up the cliff. Moments later, a body wreathed in flame flashed past Gammer's salt-smeared windows and plummeted to the beach.

'What in Hel?' Jurilda yelled over the cries. The watchmen's bell began to ring furiously, singing a song of danger and death, reserved for marauders and pirates.

'To arms, Troughwake!' Crallig yelled. 'To arms!'

Gammer seized his broadest axe from beside the door and muscled his way into the panicking throng stuck in his doorway. 'Move, Bartrum! Can't you hear the bells, man?'

'Let them come,' said the man, stuck at his son's side. In that moment he was the calmest voice in the village. He reached towards the table to hold his son's grey hand. 'Our wives are gone. Your child still lives. All that can be taken from me has already been taken.'

'You keep watch on her!' Gammer glanced at Mithrid before he slammed the door and twisted its essentially decorative lock.

Gammer and Crallig marched along the walkway, axes in hand, necks craning to see the commotion through the masses of rigging and driftwood platforms of the village. Another dying wail cut the air. Gammer clapped a hand to his neck, feeling rain, but his hand came away smeared with blood.

'To arms!' Crallig kept bellowing. Those who could fight swarmed up the ladders or began to fortify levels. Those who could not scurried to their cottages to bar doors and pray.

There were few events more motivating than the need to fight for one's home and family. Gammer felt that surge of wild desperation in his chest as he put boot to rung. He looked up to see a watchman sail outwards from the cliff as if he'd been shot from a bow. Gammer didn't have time to watch him plummet, but he heard the impact in the shallows.

Two ladders up and Gammer finally caught a glimpse of the attackers. Clad in black to meld with the night, they smothered torches as they moved from walkway to walkway. Only flickers of sparks and fire lit their masked faces, curved blades, and the silver trim on their plate and mail. They were not the ragged, untrained bandits Gammer had seen before. These were soldiers in black cloaks. Cloaks that bore an upside-down skull. The sign of the dreaded Outlaw King.

Rebels.

Gammer held his ground beside a ladder, itching for a face to bury his axe in. Crallig was climbing below him, hatchet in his brown teeth. The screams began to overlap and multiply. A vicious heat filled the air as a fork of blue lightning lanced through two cottages. A window exploded as a man clutching his belly flew into the night. Fire bloomed on thatch rooftops. Gammer felt his mouth hang open. He had only seen magick like it once before.

A villager with a long knife climbed past him, heaving with effort. The fellow jumped to the walkway above, right into the path of a mage's spell. Gammer ducked as the man's scorched body tumbled down the ladder, taking Crallig with him.

'No!' Gammer cried, reaching uselessly for his friend as the woodcutter fell into the night with a stare of horror.

A bolt of green fire shot past Gammer's head, narrowly missing taking his ear off. Aiming for the level above, Gammer swung the axe at the very reach of its handle and lunged. The blade sank into something with a crunch. Gammer yanked hard, bringing a man and his severed leg toppling. The brief look in his eyes was one of forlorn surprise.

Arcs of flame streamed from the platform above. Villagers fell screaming by the dozen, lighting the night briefly before they struck the sand. It could have been the heat, or the smell of flesh in the smoke, but Gammer found his mouth parchment dry.

He did the only thing a father could do and scrambled down the ladder to fetch Mithrid. Silver ropes unravelled alongside him, whipping his arms. He looked up to see more mages sliding down the village's levels, hacking and slashing as they went with spears and swords. It was murder. Brutal, unstoppable murder with no purpose to be discerned except to the joy of wreaking havoc.

Snarling, Gammer swung onto a walkway, colliding with a mother and two young children fleeing for the beach.

'Wait!' He tried to haul them back, but in her panic, the mother ignored him. She had one hand on the ladder before a spear ran her through, shoulder to hip, and embedding itself in the walkway.

Gammer's axe was already swinging, and rudely introduced itself to the man's spine before he could even put boot to boards. Almost split in two, he plummeted with a burbling cry. Gammer threw his arms around the screeching children. They were pawing at their lifeless mother, still impaled on the spear. 'Go! To the beach! Run, children! Run!' he roared, scaring them into action.

The woodcutter followed them down the ladder, axe swinging in circles by his side. He struck at another dark figure, racing past with bare hands glowing scarlet. The mage was quick, dodging the blade and seizing the ladder instead. The weathered wood immediately crumbled into ash and splinters. Gammer flailed as the ladder collapsed. The earth pulled at him, inescapable. With a maddened cry, he reached out with the axe in blind hope. The jolt scorched his palms, but the blade had lodged in a walkway strut. With a swing of his legs, he was safe on the driftwood planks.

Though the screams of his kin and the roar of blazing cottages now filled his ears, Gammer was dead to any sound but his own slavering breath and the pounding of his heart. Boots falling like hammer blows, he raced for his cottage.

Gammer saw the blade too late. Scything out of the shadows, it made a mockery of his leather jerkin and sliced him to his guts. With a bellow, he came crashing to his knees, and curled around the wound. His hands were already slick with his blood.

A foot kicked his shoulder and splayed him on his back. A masked face, all eyes and brows, looked down upon him as if he were a fly with its wings plucked clean. Gammer swore it was the loss of blood, but darkness clung to the mage, eking from him like the black smoke of an oil fire.

'You're the sort we like to leave bleeding,' croaked the mage, in a voice that spoke of a lifetime sucking a pipe, and heavy with Krauslung accent. He bent down to grasp at Gammer's throat and whisper close. The shadows surrounded them. 'Teaches you a last lesson, see? For thinking you can beat us. You took two of my mages, and as penance, you will stay right here, dying one of the slowest ways a man can die. You look like a strong sort. Maybe you'll last an hour through the agony. Perhaps more. All the while, you'll be watching us go about our work, waiting for Hel to take you.'

Though the words were a blade in his heart, Gammer's only reply was a grunt of effort as he grabbed the axe with blood-slicked fingers and rammed it into the mage's neck. The cloak of darkness around them instantly unravelled, but the fingers at Gammer's throat squeezed harder. They felt like frozen steel, the kind of cold that burned. Spluttering, he grabbed the mage's head with his other hand and pushed. Blood spurted, slackening his grip further, but with a crack and a violent twitching of the mage's head, Gammer could tell he had reached spine.

The corpse fell limp across him, and it took a cry of breathtaking pain to shove it aside. Gammer retched as he dragged himself up. Clamping a hand to his split belly, using his axe as a crutch, and trying extraordinarily hard not to look at his insides or the amount of blood that was leaking from him, Gammer stumbled to the cottage.

He crashed through the doorway to find Bartrum kneeling beside the dead Bogran, his face awash with tears. He clung to his grey arm as if it were a fraying rope and he was dangling over a cliff's edge. Though the sight was pitiful, it relieved the woodcutter immensely. If Bartrum was alive, so was Mithrid.

'You'll die if you don't run, fool!' hissed Gammer as barred the door behind him. He wasted no time in kicking the burnt spellbook aside and heaving the bloodied axe blade into a gap in the floorboards.

'And what of you?' replied Bartrum, hoarse from his mourning.

Gammer pried up two boards, revealing a slim hollow set into the floor. He showed the man the crimson covering his belly and legs. 'I'm already dead.'

Putting his weight on the axe, he staggered to Mithrid. She had not moved, still as pale as a winter morning. Ignoring the ache in his chest, Gammer seized her arm. There was no time to be gentle and he had no strength to lift her, and so he dragged her to the hollow. Gammer knelt by his daughter's side. He spared but a brief moment to shift a strand of fiery hair from her face and tuck it behind her ear. A streak of blood painted her white cheek.

'When you wake up, I hope you can forgive me,' he whispered. 'I never wanted to let you down, but I made a life of it. This, at least, I will do right.'

Scowling back his tears, Gammer lowered the floorboards and jammed them back into place. A reed mat was dragged over it to complete the illusion.

Bartrum had been watching him, an odd mixture of jealousy and sympathy in his bulging eyes. 'I should have been more like you, Fenn,' he choked.

'No—'

'Stubborn. She'll live because of that. Because of you.'

Gammer bowed his head. He could feel his lip trembling. With a strangled growl of pain and effort, he forced himself to stand. Seizing his axe with his bloodied hands, he stood before the door, and waited.

'Run, Bartrum. At least save yourself,' he muttered.

'Too late for that now, judging by the look in your eyes.'

Bartrum got to his feet. He had a short knife in his hand It was the kind for filleting fish, not staving off rebel mages, but Gammer was glad for the company.

'That makes two dead men, at least,' he said. 'And two's better than —,'

Both of them flinched as the first fist pounded on the door, making it shake in its frame.

CHAPTER 5
THE COLDEST MORNING

Dim dawn breaks upon first snow fallen,
wind breathless, earth still, and colour stolen.
Stillness reigns, a king of silence forged,
by blades and bodies, food for ravens gorged.
In peace's name, through war and toil,
lives spent on blood-drenched soil.
Light breaks cross upon this promised calm,
mocking, lurking weight, devoid of balm,
Peace naught but lies to line rich purses,
peace, at the cost of the accursed.
POEM OF UNKNOWN ORIGIN, FOUND SCRAWLED IN BLOOD ON THE WALLS OF A RUINED COTTAGE

Nothing and nobody awoke her. Mithrid was not sure if it could be called waking. It was more akin to being dragged out a collapsing cavern backside first, through a mountain of biting rock and soil until she collided with her body. One moment, her soul had been adrift in a void. A moment later and she felt everything. Sensations, both jarring and painful, flooded her. Arms, fingers and toes she had almost forgotten seized up beneath clothes she had thought lost. Her eyes, though they took some forcing open, were still catching up. Mithrid saw nothing but familiar darkness.

Save for the void, the last thing she remembered was the accursed book, dancing about in the sand, and the lightning it sent racing through her veins.

The impulse to raise her hand travelled sluggishly from her skull, to her arm, and finally down to her fingers. With a loud clunk, the back of her hand met solid wood. Mithrid blinked hard. She saw nothing but felt the faint grain of wood at her fingertips. She recoiled, feeling pain in her left hand. Her fingers felt burned. Panic began to slide its hooks beneath her skin.

They had thought her dead and buried her alive.

She writhed against the confines of the space, finding it barely wider than her shoulders, and a hand's breadth of space between her nose and the wood. Naturally, Mithrid struggled harder, ramming her weak arms against the lid of this coffin. A faint smudge of light caught her eyes and she froze. Her weary vision was improving; she could see faint gaps between the boards, a charcoal grey beyond the blackness.

Mithrid steeled herself. This was no coffin. It was the narrow bunker father had made for his wine. The realisation made her feel ridiculous and yet filled her with dread. She felt around, feeling a clammy quality to the wood, as if something had been spilled while she slept. Either that, or she had soiled herself.

Soon enough, Mithrid found the catch, and pushed with her knees until the wooden hatch sprung free. Beyond was a dark cottage, eerily silent. She could smell wood smoke. Iron.

Mithrid scrabbled from her hollow, feeling a need to breath cleaner air, but before she could gasp, she found a dark puddle beneath her hands. It was blood, cold and half dried. Its pattern guided her eyes to a body lying not three feet away. Again, Mithrid blinked, taking in the torn ribbons of vaguely familiar trews, a shredded tunic. In the gloom, she saw more in shape than in detail, and she would have recognised that barrel-chested figure anywhere.

She crawled as fast as her numb limbs would allow, pawing at her father's arms and head to see if he still drew breath. He was not warm, but he was far from cold. An ugly wound crossed his belly. Another two punctured his chest. There were burns on his hand. Beyond him lay another figure, shrouded in black and just as limp.

Again and again she shook him, crying to Hurricane and Njord for a flicker of his glazed eyes, a catch of breath in his throat. The only life he showed was the macabre puppeteering of his body by her frantic shaking.

The girl fell backwards, almost pitching into the hollow. In an effort to catch herself, she looked behind her and saw yet another body lying face down in its own pool of blood. She realised now why her arms were soaked in it.

Despair, fear, and confusion combined forces to become a strong urge to vomit, but Mithrid held steady as she poked at the third body. It was Ole Man Clifsson. Where a dozen blades had run him through, the wounds glistened with frost.

Mithrid recoiled into a corner, trembling knees drawn up to her chin, arms wrapped around them. She rocked back and forth, hoping for this nightmare to fade away in sleep, and for her to wake upon the beach. Even the void was highly preferable to the murderous scene before her.

It refused to disappear. No matter how hard she clawed at herself, sobbed, or however many times she dug her thumbs in her eyes, the dead stayed dead. Even the occasional dripping of blood fell silent. Mithrid was undeniably, horrifyingly awake.

When the company of the corpses became abruptly too much to bear, Mithrid ached to escape. Her jellied legs were not so eager. The door was shut, but from the eerie stillness of Troughwake, Mithrid imagined that the nightmare continued on behind it. Even the rutlarks, usually so choral at the approach of dawn, were silent that dark morning. But Mithrid knew bad dreams. She'd had her fair share and more. If they had taught her anything, the worst ones were always waiting once a person falls back to sleep. Some needed to be seen through to be conquered.

Clenching her teeth until her jaw cramped, Mithrid pushed herself to standing. The effort made stars pop at the edge of her vision. She stumbled, she tripped, and a foot skidded in Clifsson's blood, but she made it to her father's side. She began to paw around in the dark, feeling for anything sharp. The black-clad figure that Mithrid didn't recognise had a curved dagger in its fist. It took some prying from the corpse's pale, rigid fingers. With a crack of knuckles, the dagger was hers. She hissed as her burned fingers protested. How they had been scorched, she had no idea.

Mithrid considered stabbing the body. It was a paltry kind of revenge; the tantrum of a child refused a toy. Instead she yanked its mask aside, revealing the porcelain face of a woman, perhaps thirty winters. She was so expressionless she almost looked peaceful, as if she merely slumbered. Her lips were black in the gloom.

Holding the knife low by her hip, feeling all colours of fear running through her, Mithrid tried the door. It was unlocked, propped against the latch. She noticed then how it was splintered and buckled; it barely swung right on its hinges.

The stench of smoke and blood and shit struck her, making her retch.

'Move, you idiot,' Mithrid chided herself beneath held breath. Another peek showed her the walkway was clear – of the living, at least. Two lumps occupied the wooden boards, curled in foetal positions. She had never seen black cloaks and silver trim like theirs on any passing traveller.

Cautious steps led Mithrid onto the boards, hating them for every creak they uttered. Troughwake was smouldering in a dozen places around her. The rusty glow showed her scene after scene of carnage. Where doors were broken or ajar, she didn't have to peek inside to know what she would find. She could tell by the footprints of blood leading to and fro.

Most of the ladders were gone. Only some charred rope and broken rungs remained. Below on the beach, a scattered trail of corpses led down the grey sands. Some were much smaller than others. She watched and she listened for signs of life, but none moved. Mithrid gulped, fighting back a sob or the urge to vomit; she wasn't quite sure which.

Mithrid tested a rope. It seemed stable, and so she climbed. With every level, her movements became less measured and more frantic, as though she were in the midst of drowning and the clifftop was the surface.

Propped beside the watchman's bell was Mam Hag. A ragged wound ran from her temple down to her collarbone. There was no sign of Remina or Littlest, and Mithrid didn't know whether to be glad or distraught. She just kept climbing. Her breath came in gasps by the time her hands grasped for a rung that was not there. Mithrid clawed at the brittle grass and dragged herself onto flat land. She lay face down, gasping the dewy scent of grass. The tears flowed no matter her fight to keep them back, pouring out all the fear and panic in uncontrollable measures.

It must have only been minutes she lay there for, but to Mithrid it was half a day. Gradually, forcing her limp arms into action, she propped herself up, slid her knees beneath her, and tried to breathe normally.

'Hello there,' said a voice.

Mithrid choked.

A man stood in front of her, wearing familiar black robes over charcoal mail, trimmed with silver. This one had no mask, no hood, just a pale, square face bearing white eyes and a shock of yellow hair. He would have been charming but for the scar across his nose, like a moustache placed too high. It took her a moment to make out the red skull, upside-down and emblazoned on his chest. The sign of the dreaded Outlaw King.

Drowning in fear. Mithrid tried to rise, tried to run, tried to do anything but stare, but strong hands gripped her shoulders and pinned her.

'No!' She looked up to find two more fellows standing on either side of her. These were more like the corpse in her cottage, with only a narrow strip of face showing. One of them stripped Mithrid of the dagger. He held the blade up to his mask and sniffed.

'I thought there might be one more hidden away amongst the mess,' said the blonde man.

'That was my home, you bastard,' Mithrid whispered.

He smiled and approached her with his bare hands held out and empty. 'Not any more,' he said.

Mithrid struggled in her captors' grip. They were firm as steel. 'Who are you, besides a bunch of fucking murderers? What did we ever do to you?'

The man reached out a hand as he muttered quietly beneath his breath. With a flick of his wrist, forks of blue lightning danced from one finger to another. Mithrid recoiled as far as she could. Her heart thudded against her ribs. *Magick*.

The closer his fingers came to her, the fiercer the lightning became: fizzling and crackling, almost blinding at moments. Mithrid turned her head, leaning away, blinking sweat from her eyes. She felt the heat on her cheek. He came closer still. The lightning stuttered, leaving a ringing in her ears. Beyond the bright glow, Mithrid saw the man gurning, as if magick took some concentration to wield.

'Please don't!'

With a clap of his hands, the lightning died, and Mithrid blinked at the white spots left in her eyes. The others were laughing. 'You're mages. Rebels. Outlaws.'

'That your first taste of magick?' asked the mage. He crossed his arms. 'Eh, girl? What do you know of it?'

Mithrid bit her lip. A worm of a thought had reared its ugly head. *The spellbook.* Reading it – even simply finding it – could have brought these rebels down upon Troughwake. The notion left her nauseated. *Her father. Ole Man Clifsson. Mam Hag. Littlest.* All dead because of some stubborn childish need to disobey. Mithrid wondered what she had missed, loitering on the edge of death. She had no idea how many days had passed.

'Nothing,' she said. It was too unbearable to admit it even to a stranger.

'We'll see about that. Bring her.'

'What do you want with me?' she cried out. Mithrid had no choice in the matter. She was carried aloft in the mages' tight grip. Her feet barely scraped the earth.

Along the clifftop path, a clump of pine trees grew a short distance away. Around the copse's seaward edge were the scars of woodcutters' work: piles of orange sawdust, stacks of logs, and tree stumps like severed necks.

Mithrid was marched into the underbrush. Her captors didn't care whether the branches raked her, they simply marched in a straight line, as if the world would bend and bow for them.

The mages brought her to a small clearing amongst the pines. There was light here: a ghostly glow that seemed to emanate from the hands of a dozen other mages. They glared at her as she was brought forwards. Mithrid wondered how many of them her father had killed before he fell. She hoped it was many.

Mithrid was surprised to see a ragged line of survivors there, bound like hogs and curled on their knees. There were seven all told. The eighth was a body bound in a grey woollen sheet. Its face was visible, and Mithrid felt a knot grow in her gut as she recognised it as Bogran. He looked gaunter than the other dead, but it made it no easier to see him lying there.

Mithrid could have yelped with relief when she saw Remina and Littlest there. Littlest was out cold, either gripped by terror or knocked senseless. Remina had a swollen eye and a missing tooth. Her lip trembled.

Bull was also one of the few. He wore a stoic face, staring straight into the loam.

The others were a mix of old ones with various, stomach-churning wounds. One she knew as Crallig, a friend of father's. He had seen better days: he was missing a leg and was the kind of pale that was one shade before death. His eyes were too glazed to recognise her.

The men deposited Mithrid before them. The blonde mage strode circles around her, giving her sidelong looks.

'What can you tell me of this girl? Hmm? Was she the one? Speak up, and you will be saved.'

Mithrid abruptly realised she might be more condemned than she realised. 'What one?'

Another mage cuffed her. The gauntlet he wore cut her cheek, and she felt the warm blood trickling down her neck.

The blonde man removed a charred, square lump from his cloak. 'Do you know what this is?'

It took Mithrid a moment. It looked like the spellbook, though half eaten by fire. 'A book.'

He huffed. 'What kind of book?'

'A burnt one?'

Another slap came, knocking Mithrid to her elbows. 'What do you want?' she gasped.

'I want to know where this spellbook came from! None of these fools seem to know. Perhaps you shall. Who touched this book? Who read it aloud?' he demanded.

No answer came. One of the old ones, a woman with grey in her hair, just whimpered.

'I am growing tired of this! I will start cutting throats if you don't tell me why you fish-smeared cliff scum have a spellbook! I know one of you read it. I know to my very core. Some of you reek of magick, and I will know why!'

Mithrid cowered at the volume of the mage's voice. He marched to Remina and grabbed her by her blonde and blood-stained hair. The girl screeched.

'Did you read it?' The man's milk-white eyes aglow. A blade appeared in his hand, and he held it against Littlest's throat. 'Tell me, or these two will be the first to die.'

Crallig, as pallid and weak as he was, struggled against his bonds, shouting hoarsely. 'Get away from her, you—'

'I know!' Mithrid yelled.

'We've got a squawker, Dromm,' chuckled the man that had struck her.

Mithrid levelled a finger at Bogran's body. 'He did. He read it aloud.'

'It killed him,' blabbed Remina.

Dromm wandered to the body, holding his hand over his chest. 'Where did the boy get this book? His father? A market? Speak?'

'I found it. In a shipwreck,' Mithrid explained. 'I gave it to him.'

'And who burned it? You peasants?'

Remina spoke up. She had a look of hope in her eyes, as if talking was the answer to living. She nodded towards Mithrid. 'She slammed it shut after… after Bogran was thrown to the rock. Then it burned itself.'

Bull talked for the first time. 'I saw it, sir. Blue flames running all across it.'

Mithrid ran her thumb across her burned fingertips. When she looked up, Dromm was standing over her, hand outstretched once more. 'I find that unusual,' he whispered. 'Unusual indeed.' His fingers twitched, his lip curled, and whatever he was searching for seemingly eluded him. He swept away. 'We'll take them to the helbeast. See what it says.'

'Says about what?' Crallig demanded. 'I asked you a question, you cretch!'

Dromm flatly ignored the woodcutter as he counted the line.

'All of 'em?' asked another mage, a musclebound fellow with a voice as deep as a cave. His hands were aglow with fire.

Dromm pointed to Remina, Bull, Littlest, and a lad several winters older than Mithrid. She only knew him in Troughwake as Hassamer. 'That lump of a boy, the girls, and that one there.'

'Let them go! Take us instead!' cried one of the elders.

Crallig had tumbled on his side and was yelling into the dust. 'They're just children, curse you! Heartless cowards!'

The big mage cared little for their protests. Hands sparking, bright as coals, he seized two of the old ones by the neck. Their howls were mercifully short-lived, the fire burned through their windpipes and spines fast. His work done, he moved on to the next unfortunate.

Mithrid shut her eyes but the screams scraped at her soul like glass on slate. She tried to plug her ears, but her captors batted her hands away. Littlest was awake now, and she screeched at the top of her lungs.

When the chosen few were left, the glowing hands turned to Mithrid. Once more, her cheeks prickled with the heat of magick.

'This one, too, Dromm?' he asked.

The mage regarded Mithrid with his bored gaze. She stared into those lonely black pupils, trying to keep her lip from quivering. 'Fuck it. Bring her. She'll be entertainment on the road if nothing else.'

Mithrid almost passed out with relief as they hauled her upright.

The rebel mages led them from the pines into a grey dawn. A mist hung in the air. Caring nothing for what they left behind, they put Troughwake and the sea behind them and headed east instead.

The captives had been bound with steel chains and arranged in a short train. None of them said a word. They simply trudged doggedly, too fearful to complain. The rebel mages – Mithrid counted eleven of them – walked alongside, eyes scanning the sky as much as the rolling grassy knolls and stark tors. Mithrid wondered whether they were expecting a storm.

Before long, the sun showed its face, casting pink light onto the sorry-looking collection of survivors. Mithrid walked at the rear of their linked chain. Their clothing was torn, scorched or missing entirely. Gashes and wounds still oozed. Bruises darkened as the sky grew brighter.

Gradually, the world took on colour again. The morning was a simple palette of ashen skies and the green of the rolling fields.

Mithrid busied her mind with counting the yards. The fear was constant, but it kept her awake and so she welcomed it. Vengeance had crossed her mind more than once, but as sweet as that thought was, staying alive always shouldered it aside. This helbeast sounded like a creature she wanted to avoid at all costs.

Remina walked in front of Mithrid. She whimpered constantly. Bull was a dejected lump, and his bulk blocked Littlest and the other chap, Hassamer, from view.

All of them were young, and for some reason that seemed to matter. And if it mattered, Mithrid deduced, then they were useful, and that might just keep them alive for a while longer. Long enough to make a run for it, perhaps. That notion kept her head up and her feet moving. It was oddly fortunate how the desire to survive could hold back terror. It was not her anger, nor her fear, nor the will for revenge that gave her strength, purely the need to live. All else could come after. *If there was an after.*

On the crest of every hill, Mithrid stared out over lands she had never seen before. Troughwake had been her birthplace, the provider of everything she had needed. All she wanted. Everything she had ever learned of the wider empire had come from elders' stories or a skalds' eddas, whenever they passed through the village. Now, gazing over the vastness of grasslands and rocky hills beyond, she was beginning to question just how wide the world might be.

Waves spread across the fields with every cold gust of wind. The rocky tors seemed plain at first, but on their landward side, colourful mosses grew. Each spur of rock seemed to be cradled in its own crater, reaching the length of the dawn's shadows. The grass grew sparse around them.

Mithrid saw distant watchtowers above the nearest cliff-towns, but the mages were not interested in them. They kept to wilder paths, where no soul lived nor apparently travelled. The only company they kept that morning was a pack of pinkish hogs with black spines protruding from their backs. They seemed unbothered by the mages and their prisoners.

The mages kept them walking until noon. The sun had slipped behind the sheet of grey clouds, but a dim orb could be seen overhead. Mithrid was deeply focused, deliberating whether the shadow in the distance was a cloud or a snow-capped mountain, when Dromm called a halt.

'Need to piss? Drink? Eat?' he called out to the prisoners.

Nobody answered. Unsurprising, given the mages had spent the morning treating the prisoners with hard shoves and smacks around the head at even the faintest complaint. Survival came in all forms and keeping silent was one its most preferred shapes. The survivors of Troughwake had resorted to keeping their dry, quivering mouths shut. Even now.

'Speak, curse you! Or you won't get another chance.'

As it turned out, the prisoners wanted all three. One by one, they were led into the grass, or fed sips from canteens and thrown hard tack biscuits like hounds.

Mithrid watched it all with a suspicious glare. The mood of the rebels had shifted too rapidly for her liking. They were prisoners still, but now treated with a shred of humanity. It felt fragile, like spring ice across rock pools, as if it would crack any moment. As such, she was remained as tense as a ljot string.

The respite was brief. Soon, they were marching onwards to where rocky hills rose from the grass and filled the horizon. The clouds proved themselves to be distant snowcapped mountains, and Mithrid had a hard time peeling her gaze from them, even when their path veered north, parallel to the range.

Mithrid had been attempting to squeeze her small hands through the black manacles for most of the journey. Every time she thought she was close the manacles somehow shrunk a fraction. All she'd accomplished was a bruised wrist covered in sores that burned at every touch of the metal.

The deeper they wound into the hills, the craggier the landscape became. Dustdevils spun and sputtered over the ridges, occasionally throwing stones at the travellers. The sun was teetering towards afternoon when Mithrid spotted the spikes of red tents peeking over the brim of their trail.

Slip-sliding down shale that sliced the survivors' hands and bare feet, they reached a flat pan of earth that looked like an old quarry. Claw marks streaked the ashen rock that walled one side of the clearing. The other edges sloped away beyond sight, presumably down into the vast moor and marshland that lay between them and the mountains.

Ignoring their bloody cuts, the mages pushed or dragged the survivors towards the small encampment. Nine red tents sat in a circle around a campfire near the sheer rock, with spears of pinewood set around it, similar to an ugly Highfrost wreath. Outside of the ring, four bulls drank from a trough beside half-empty wagons. A flag fluttered on a spear dug into the ground. A flag as red as blood emblazoned with an upside-down skull. A rebel's flag.

Other black-clad figures stood about or lurked in the shadows of their tents. They watched the survivors pass with leering grins and clouds of pipe smoke. It must have been the smell of the cook-fires or foreign incense wafting through the camp, but her head began to throb painfully.

A shirtless man swollen with muscle – almost comedically so – strode to block their path. His sunburnt skin was covered in tattooed swirls of black ink. His face held a stern expression. Mithrid saw the worry hidden beneath it. She had seen it on her father's face many times.

'What of the others? Where's Captain Svan?' the man demanded.

The blonde-haired mage, Dromm, met him head on. Mithrid had to strain to hear through the pounding in her head.

'Dead.'

'And Jaakan? Brista—?'

'Allow me to stop you there, Drisk. Anybody you don't see amongst us is bloody dead. I'm in charge now. Got it?'

This Drisk looked shocked for such a hardened, scarred man. 'Simple scouting, Svan said.'

'Well, something came up. A spellbook in a small gutter of a village. Svan ordered we take it, but the bastards put up a fight. During the brawl some bastard cut his leg off with an axe and he fell from halfway up a cliff.'

Drisk stared down the line at the survivors. 'All that for these scrawny cunts?'

Dromm barged past him, rather unsuccessfully. 'All the pickings we could find in their village, mangy cliff squatters. Don't worry. We killed the rest.'

That drew a sob from Remina, and a slap from the mage watching her.

'So now what, *Captain* Dromm?'

The blonde mage clapped his hands thrice as he called out over his shoulder. 'Bring out the helbeast, of course!'

Mithrid tensed as dozens of figures flooded from the tents, swarming to somewhere beyond the camp. Her hands took to trembling, no matter how hard she clenched. Further up the chains, she heard Littlest whimpering amongst the commotion.

The prisoners were dragged from the tents to where a crimson canopy stretched over a large box, masked in black cloth. Chains ran from its corners to heavy boulders. The rebels stood around it in a half moon, keeping a respectful distance.

As they were guided through the crowd, Mithrid noticed some of the bastards swapping bets behind their backs. Mithrid grew nervous. Perhaps she had drastically underestimated their worth after all. *What if they were sport for some monster? Mere entertainment for this troop of outlaws?* Her heart and head competed to see who could hammer the hardest.

Something resided within the box. That much became clear as soon as Mithrid saw the thing judder and noticed its chains. It was not a box, but a—

Cage.

Dromm swept the black sheet away, revealing a stout cage of dull iron and steel. Within it was a monster even the darkest recesses of her imagination recoiled from. Hassamer fainted almost immediately. Littlest wailed. Even stout, stoic Bull, whose only visible sign of discomfort was his profuse sweating, tried to back away. Mithrid stared, brimming with dread and unable to take her eyes from it. Around them, the rebels began to stamp their feet in unison.

The helbeast looked as though it had been ripped apart and then pieced back together, but it seemed its maker had grown confused halfway through and used other beasts to fill the gaps. Its head was that of a ram's, but it bared the jaws of a rabid wolf. Its six feet were clawed, cat-like, and yet its hindquarters were scaled and armoured, ending in a forked tail. The puckered scars that ran between its pieces were raw and pink, and between the balding fur, its skin glowed with firelight. As did its throat, and the eyes set between the curled horns burned like coals. It fit its name perfectly, and it filled Mithrid with dread.

At the sight of the prisoners, the beast screeched. Even though it did not pounce, maul the bars, or in fact do anything but merely tap its claws expectantly, every single one of Troughwake's survivors yanked against their manacles, only to cry out as the metal clamped down hard. Laughter was heard between the stamping of the crowd.

'Get the first one up,' ordered Dromm. Two mages seized Hassamer. No matter how many times he shouted, 'No! No!' at the top of his voice, he was unchained and forcibly dragged up by his throat.

All eyes were fixed on the lad as he was thrown down beside the helbeast's cage. The beast's calm vanished. It snarled and clawed for him through the bars, mercifully only snagging his shirt. The mages pinned Hassamer to the ground, just out of its reach. Still the beast groped for him, spittle flying with every snort.

Mithrid's heart stuttered as Dromm reached for the cage door.

'No!' screamed Hassamer.

But the door stayed shut. Dromm reached past the lock to slap at the bars. 'Hurry up!' he told the helbeast.

Through some foul intellect, the helbeast understood the mage. It hunkered down and pressed itself close to the cage bars, burning eyes fixed on the lad. Black smoke drifted from its jaws.

It hung there for a moment, staring at Hassamer while he convulsed with fear. All the while the rebels' stamping grew louder. Some began to chant. Then, with a disappointed whine, all tension crumbled like wet sand. The helbeast turned away to pad slowly around its cage. The crowd fell quiet, tutting or chuckling between themselves depending how their bets had gone.

Dromm threw up his hands. 'None in this one,' he announced. 'Put him with the other youngbloods in camp.'

Hassamer wailed for half the distance until a mage knocked him senseless.

'Next!'

Remina was dragged to the cage without moving a muscle, limp as a week-old fish. All colour had drained from her face. She looked dead but for her gawping, panicked eyes.

Once more, the girl was placed before the cage for the helbeast to stare and sniff at. Once more the stamping of feet grew. This time, the decision was quicker. The helbeast lunged for her. Horns crashed against the stout cage with a bell toll. Gnashing jaws spat hot sparks. Four sets of hooked claws reached out through the bars, thankfully only raking in the shale. She screamed all the same.

'A winner!' Dromm cackled.

A grumble of satisfaction came from the crowd as the girl was placed at Dromm's side.

'Winner of what?' Mithrid called out, much to the harsh booing of the crowd. This was a sport to the rebels – thankfully a bloodless one – but when in the clutches of torturers, surviving one trial only meant another waited to be endured.

'You'll see!' Dromm beckoned for another. 'Show him to the beast!'

Bull was brought up. He said nothing, but his face was half drowned in sweat. He walked slowly, making the mages work to push him.

Again, the helbeast tasted his scene, and again, it pounced for the boy, managing to rake Bull's forearm with a claw. Dromm didn't seem as pleased with this result as the last one, troubled, even, but he raised his hands and Bull was shoved to his knees beside Remina.

'The girl.'

Mithrid flinched, assuming he meant her, but a squeal told her it was Littlest next.

'Leave her alone!' Mithrid yelled, knowing how pointless the words were before they left her mouth.

The waif of girl was a fighter, though, a flurry of arms and legs, like a cat trapped in a box. The mages held her by the neck, choked the fight from her, and dumped her beside the cage. This time, the helbeast turned its back with an infuriated yowl, and Littlest was taken away just like Hassamer.

'A feisty one, perhaps, but not of magick.'

Mithrid was next. The trembling worsened, making the manacles and chains chime. Mages grabbed her arms and pulled her across the scree. Mithrid put up no struggle, she simply stared at the helbeast, and wondered what result she should be praying for. She was clueless, and that was far more terrifying than knowledge.

'Last one!' Dromm yelled. 'Tied at two a piece.'

The helbeast worked a slow sinuous path from the back of the cage to the bars. Its skin glowed fiercely. The wolf jaws snapped shut, over and over. A growl built in its throat as their eyes locked: Mithrid's pine green vying against two hot pits of ash and forge fire.

Mithrid clenched her teeth. A realisation dawned. Out of all the monsters around her, this one alone could not harm her, and so she silently dared it to try. What a faint and pointless challenge it was, but it was a small victory in a slew of defeats. It felt good to fight.

Mithrid narrowed her eyes. The helbeast scraped its claws on the cage floor. Its growl became an ululating whine. The helbeast lurched, half-heartedly pouncing then skittering back, claws dragging iron filings from the floor. It roared, wincingly loud. Hot, burning spittle landed on Mithrid's arm and she frantically wiped it away before it ate into her skin.

Mithrid faced it again and strained to push a singular thought into the helbeast's repugnant, horned skull. *Fuck. You.* Her head felt like a war drum but she fought through it.

Again, it pounced, withdrew, lashed at the air in frustration. In the end, it crouched down, legs bent at skeletal, arachnid angles, and swished its tail back and forth.

Only when Mithrid relented did she notice the silence. The pain behind her eyes was dizzying. Her head lolled as she turned to face Dromm. One side of his mouth arched upwards in a look of befuddlement. His eyes were peeled to the whites.

'I...' he said, hands waving about in the air as if summoning more useful words. 'Blast it.'

'Ain't never seen that before, Cap'n,' hissed one of the mages holding Mithrid. The girl tried to focus on the man, but he was a blur.

'What's the call?' yelled one from the crowd.

'Aye, we got coin on this one!'

'Shut your shit-smeared faces!' Dromm bellowed, before running dirty fingernails through his blonde mop. 'Bloody spellbook's doused you all with magick, I bet. Confused the beast.'

'Helbeast seems pretty certain to me, Cap. At least with the others,' said the other man. 'I can feel it in 'em.'

'You can't feel shit, Gurden. Put a stopper in that useless hole you call a mouth,' Dromm snapped irritably. 'Bring her here, curse it! We'll soon see, won't we? '

Mithrid was dragged to Bull's side as the crowd uttered a mix of groans and cheers.

Dromm stood over them, working spit around his mouth. 'Mark 'em and put them with the others.'

'What do you want from us?' Remina whined while a bucket was fetched, and red paint splashed across their chests.

Mithrid hissed at the cold touch of the paint. It was only when she started to shiver that she realised her trembling had stopped. Now it returned, fiercer than ever. 'You can mark us with your colours all you want. We won't be rebels like you,' she said, fighting to keep her teeth from chattering.

'Rebels,' whispered the captain, snorting. Dromm brought his pale eyes to within a few inches of hers and smiled. 'We'll see about that. A mind is a fickle thing, miss, and there is much in this world that can turn it. Especially for one as young as you.'

Mithrid headbutted him as hard as she could muster, driving her forehead into the bridge of his scarred nose. Suns and moons popped behind her eyes, but it was worth it to see Dromm yelp. Blood trickled from one nostril, the scarlet colour stark against his pale complexion. Behind them, the crowd lowed like cattle.

'You ungrateful bitch! I could have snapped your neck at any moment, and this is how you—'

Dromm stopped mid-tirade. The echoes of his words faded. His hand, raised and curled into a fist, quivered as he half-heartedly reached for something behind his back. Mithrid watched those white eyes roll up in their sockets before he toppled.

Whump.

The captain landed face-down in the dirt and rubble. Just like every other soul in that quarry, Mithrid stared open-mouthed at the shard of blue ice protruding from Dromm's spine. Frost still emanated from it.

'To arms!' somebody screamed.

A great whoosh of air made Mithrid cower, sparking some distant ancestral instinct. A dark, cold shadow washed over her, and then a searing blast of heat as fire rained from the heavens.

Half the rebel troop was consumed by the flames. The others scattered in all directions. Mithrid looked up in time to see the pale blue underbelly of a huge winged monster; a monster she knew only from fireside tales. She longed to speak to its name, but her tongue refused to move. Bull had no such trouble.

'Dragon!'

The mages standing over them snapped into action. Orbs of fire and lightning fled their crooked fingers. They missed the agile dragon, and rained scree on the rest of the camp instead.

Mithrid found her voice. 'We need to leave! No better chance than now!'

'But my sister! And Hassamer!' Remina squealed.

'We go get them, of course!' Mithrid was already beginning to crawl towards the tents. Her breathing came quick and sharp. A blue streak flashed between the hilltops as the dragon came for another pass. She couldn't steal her gaze away from it. She found Bull's arm under hers, keeping her up. Keeping her moving.

Before the dragon could return, flames exploded from within the camp. Mithrid saw the pine stakes tossed into the air like driftwood. One tent was gutted by a bolt of lightning.

Fell orders could be heard over the roaring fires and frenzied shouts. 'The prisoners! Kill them! Kill them all!'

Mithrid felt fresh dread clutch her as a bloodcurdling scream rose from the camp. She saw two young, skinny lads run from a tent only to be speared by two soldiers close on their heels. Freedom seemed so close, yet a glance over her shoulder told her that murder was closer still. She saw another two mages sprinting after them, fists wreathed in red flame.

'Run! Go, go!' she bellowed, causing Remina to scream. Mithrid cursed; the pain in her head had turned so vicious she felt close to passing out.

Bull threw her to the ground as the mages bore down on them. All he brandished was his manacles, but nevertheless he stood between them and Mithrid, ready to fight. She could only watch on in anguish as the mages raised their fists to smite the lad.

The shadow fell again, this time bearing claws as long as an arm. Two legs, thick columns of muscle and blue scale, descended on the mages and splattered them into the ground inches from Bull's feet.

There was no time to stare at the bloody, broken mess oozing from under the dragon's claws, or the giant, glittering creature now standing over them, wings arched like the roof of a great hall. Their only impulse was to keep running. Through blurry eyes, Mithrid felt Bull lift her up, and saw Remina sprinting onwards to the nearest tent, screaming Littlest's name at the top of her lungs. Bull's frantic shouts faded along with the clamour of fighting and dying.

Death was an escape, in a way, thought Mithrid, as she let darkness take her.

CHAPTER 6
OF BEASTS & REBELS

How better to whittle away at those who love your enemy than by making him a criminal in their eyes?
FROM 'GUTTER TACTICS' BY THE CRITIC ÁWACRAN, HANGED IN 909 FOR HERESY AGAINST THE EMPIRE

Of all the sights to wake up to, the immense sapphire snout of a dragon hovering inches from one's face is likely one of the most terrifying and trews-ruining.

Mithrid screamed at the top of her lungs. At least, that was the intention. It came out as more of a hoarse whine.

The dragon's scaled lips withdrew to reveal rows upon rows of sharp, ivory fangs, each as long as a quill. Mithrid could feel the heat wafting alongside the stench of old meat and charcoal. She covered her face, cursing herself for waking only to look her doom in the eyes.

'She lives,' spoke the dragon in the deepest voice Mithrid had ever heard. It shook her ribs and breathless lungs. She was shocked to hear such a creature speak.

Mithrid had been waiting for the searing heat to consume her, hoping it would be swift. She peeked between her hands instead to find the dragon attempting what could be called a smile, though that number of teeth would chill anybody to the bone.

Mithrid croaked, tongue sticking to the roof of her mouth. 'Will I stay… alive?'

'Yes, child. For another day, at least,' it replied.

The monster withdrew and with it, the shadow, casting the orange light of a sunset across Mithrid's face. As the dragon settled onto her haunches, the girl stared out across a familiar sea, and felt the stiff, icy breeze on her cheeks. A grassy knoll led down to a clifftop fringed with spiny grass and stakes holding rope ladders. Smoke drifted from smouldering embers far below.

For the briefest of moments, she clung to the notion that all the horror she had endured had been merely a dream, but then she saw the unmistakable shape of Bull huddled with Remina on the cliff's edge. Their slouched shoulders and vacant looks in her direction were full of pain. If she looked closely, she could see the fires of the encampment still burning in their eyes.

Mithrid looked around, finding the rest of the clifftop empty. 'Where's Littlest? And Hassamer?'

The dragon bowed its head. 'I don't know who they are, child. You three were the only ones found alive.'

Mithrid squeezed her eyes shut, fighting the flood of screams that echoed in her throbbing head. It struck her at last like a knife to the gut. This was no dream, and it surpassed a nightmare. Both fade away in the light of dawn, and this refused to dim. The blur of Troughwake's gutting was no hallucination but a memory now scorched into her mind. It was real, and heartbreakingly irreversible. Mithrid sank to the grass and hoped the clifftop would crumble away, sink into the sea at that very moment, and wash it all away.

When she had gathered herself enough to speak, Mithrid stared up at the dragon. She wanted to marvel at her serpentine neck, and the frills and spines framing her elongated, bony head. She wanted to stare at each plate-sized scale, and yet none of that mattered. She had to ask.

'Are you going to eat us?' Mithrid asked, meeting the dragon's orbicular eyes. They were flecked glass, the colour of a summer sea, and they held an entire night's sky within them. Mithrid almost forget her question.

The dragon huffed. A thin sliver of smoke escaped her nostrils. 'Why does your kind always ask that? Do I look some ragged, wild wyrm to you?'

Just as Mithrid was breathing a sigh of relief, the sound of a chuckle snapped her head to the right, where a man lay in the grass picking at a sliver of dried meat. He was wearing a burgundy tunic and muddy trews that looked as though they hadn't seen a washtub in a decade. His face was a day from clean shaven, with missed patches around the scars and pockmarks of his cheeks He was somewhat handsome, for an old one. A strip of white hair ran across his head, front to back. Its colour reminded Mithrid of Dromm, and she tried to haul herself away from him. Her arms flapped against the grass as if her bones had turned to kelp.

'You're too weak, girl. Calm yourself,' he said. 'We're not going to hurt you.'

'And why would I want to eat you, anyway?' grumbled the dragon, still sore over Mithrid's question. 'You peasants are too stringy for my tastes. Straw bones.' She rattled her spines as if in a shudder.

'I heard all the dragons had gone south or east,' Mithrid said, as if she were admitting a fault.

'You heard wrong,' rumbled the great creature. She had taken on a purple hue as the westward clouds blushed a deep scarlet.

'What do you want?' Mithrid asked, tentatively pushing herself upright.

The man chuckled some more as he tore off a morsel of meat. 'What do *we* want? Nothing. Fresh meal maybe. Hot spring bath. That would be nice. As for you, you're free to go whenever you please. As I said, we mean you no harm.'

Mithrid stared at him, trying to gauge the man. He was too calm for her liking. Too... *smug*. There was a pile of armour propping him up, and she had spied black cloth and fine, red-gold armour.

'You're a mage,' Mithrid accused him.

'That I am.'

Hope sprung within her. 'Then you must be Arka. An emperor's man.'

'Ah, no.' The man grinned.

The aforementioned hope was trampled immediately. 'But... you killed the rebels.'

He nodded eagerly. 'I quite like the term outlaw, too, you know. Has a certain ring to it.'

Mithrid curled her lip, edging away surreptitiously. He seemed far too proud of being a traitor amongst traitors. 'You would betray your own kind? Your friends? Why?'

The mage shoved what was left of his snack into a pocket. 'Because, girl,' he said, mid-chew, 'they were not our friends. In fact, they weren't rebels at all. They were Arka soldiers. And I'm surprised you're not thanking us, seeing as Kinsprite here and I saved you from their clutches.'

Mithrid pressed her forehead to her knees, staving off the dizziness, and realised then that her manacles were gone. The bruises and cuts remained. 'The emperor's own men?' she scoffed. 'I don't believe you.'

'Of course you don't,' he chuckled.

Mithrid tried desperately to make sense of the situation. Her mind weaved back and forth, unable to think in a straight line. No magick could be trusted. Once again, she found a trembling in her hands, and she rocked back and forth to hide it. Bull and Remina grew either curious or cold and wandered closer. They stood awkwardly, visibly wary of the dragon.

'Why don't you light a fire, Modren?' suggested Kinsprite. The mage – Modren – nodded. He reached into a bundle behind his back and brought out pine branches and logs. He didn't so much as arrange it on the ground as dump it in a pile. His hands hovered over the wood, and Mithrid saw light glow briefly within his tunic sleeve. Fire sprang up from the wood and crackled hungrily. She shielded her face from its foul glow. Modren left his bare hands in the flames, smiling at each of them in turn. He even wiggled his fingers.

'One of the benefits of magick,' he said, sitting cross-legged. 'Come, warm yourselves.'

'Not too close, Bull,' Mithrid warned, but the lad shivered his way close beside the fire. Modren passed him a stack of hard biscuits, and Remina a dry bread roll Mithrid had mistaken for a rock. For Mithrid, he had the remainder of a fillet of fish, so smoked and dried it could have been used as a doorstop.

Modren shrugged. 'All we have.'

Mithrid caught it awkwardly. The fish was greasy and stank of bonfire, but it lit a blaze of hunger in the void of her stomach. It tasted like saltash, but it was edible, and she wolfed it down in moments. Remina meanwhile poked at her bread roll, pondering how to break its shell.

A skin of water was passed around, and Mithrid's shaking fingers managed to direct at last half the water in her mouth. The rest went to washing away the blood and grime of the quarry.

Modren and the dragon watched them eat the meagre supplies in silence. The mage had a hard look in his eyes, as if he steeled himself against something. His jaw bunched.

'Now you are fed and watered, I imagine you want answers, don't you?' he asked.

Mithrid crossed her arms. Bull nodded. Pale Remina was the only one who spoke up.

'I want to find my sister,' she croaked. Her eyes were smoke-burnt and raw.

'I'm sorry for your sister, girl. I truly am.' Modren bowed his head.

'Lies,' Mithrid hissed, far from convinced by his act.

'Most gravely, you find yourselves amidst a war that has been raging since before you were born. A war fought for the oldest of reasons: who's right, and who's wrong. I can't find your sister for you, girl, but I can tell you who took her from you, and why they came to your doorstep. I can tell you the truth.'

'Again, why should we believe anything you say?' Mithrid challenged.

Modren fixed her with a stare as sharp as a spear. 'You don't have to, but you deserve to hear it at the very least and make up your own mind. Can an argument be an argument if one side is never heard? How better to sway hearts and minds than to only repeat the stories your emperor wishes you to hear.'

That silenced Mithrid, at least for as long as it took to hear this man's lies.

'Did the mages tell you why they attacked your village?' asked Kinsprite.

'We found a spellbook. Opened it,' Remina admitted with a shudder.

Modren nodded solemnly. 'They came because they can sniff out magick, as I can. As Kinsprite can. Magick emanates from people that have it in their blood. Bursts of it, such as spells, can attract unwanted attention.

Those mages came looking for that magick. And, more importantly, whoever used it.'

'Why?' Mithrid asked.

Modren, looked straight at her. 'The Arka Empire has outlawed magick and yet still wields it how it pleases. It is building an army, recruiting those who have seen rebels butcher their families in cold blood. That builds an army of vengeful soldiers, each one bloodthirsty and empire-mad. Which one of you wants revenge? You, girl? You look as though you want to kill me right now.'

Mithrid scowled. 'I want my life back.'

'Would you kill for it?'

She didn't trust herself to reply.

'That's the first step: to give you a reason to hate the rebels. Had we not attacked, they would've taken you east and south until they were closer to Krauslung. At that point, Arka soldiers would have miraculously rescued you, heroically defeating the Outlaw King's wretches and offered you safe sanctuary within the glowing capital. You're all tearful and grateful, and that's when you would be offered the chance to serve your glorious saviour of an emperor. To have your revenge. Sounds generous, no?'

Modren took a moment to let that sink in, scratching at his streak of hair. 'It is a ruse,' he said. 'A ruse to recruit those with magick ability while spreading the fearful lie of murderous outlaws roaming the wilds. Emperor Malvus sends his mages out into the wilds to wreak havoc and murder. The few they leave alive scream of cruel savages bearing the red skull. "Rebels! Rebels!" is all Emaneska hears, and it believes the lie all the more each time it's told. Clever, hmm? What do you think the routine with the helbeast was about? They were testing your magick, seeing if you were soldier or mage. As it turns out, it seems you have some trace of magick in you. An "old-blood" as they call it now.'

The words lingered between the three survivors. At any other time, not sat twenty yards from their ruined village, such a revelation might have been wondrous. For Mithrid, it only reaffirmed that they were the ones who had brought ruin upon it. There was no sweetness amongst that bitter knowledge.

The dragon spoke up, her voice like distant thunder. 'That is why the Arka ordered you killed when we attacked. Fewer soldiers for us true rebels.'

Mithrid's throat was tight. 'And what's to say this isn't the ruse itself? Lies upon lies. That your words aren't false?'

Modren smiled, holding up finger and thumb. 'Two reasons. As I said, you're free to leave at your leisure. No chains. No manacles. Secondly, there are fifty dead "rebels" a day's march east that would disagree with you if they still had tongue. You think we'd actually kill that many of our own for a mere trick?'

In the corner of her eye, Mithrid caught Bull nodding. She wondered what had been left of the encampment when they left.

'There is another choice. Come with us and we will give you safety,' said Modren.

Mithrid snapped her fingers. 'Aha! There it is,' she snarled. 'We're to serve the glorious Outlaw King instead?' she scoffed.

'Shut up, Mithrid,' Remina spat.

'Did I say anything about serving? Fighting? No. I said safety.' Modren pressed his fingertips together, forming a cage. 'I understand your pain, but open your ears, girl. Mithrid, is it? We're offering you sanctuary. A place where you can live free of empire and cruelty and explore the power in your blood if you so wish. Fight for vengeance, if you choose. At no time will you ever find a guard or a mage or a gate blocking your path. You may leave whenever you wish.' Modren got to standing, brushing the grass and dirt from his mail. 'Scalussen. Ever heard of it?'

The three survivors shook their heads.

Modren looked mildly disappointed but far from surprised. 'A city in the ice fields, as north as north goes. In a tongue this world has forgotten, it means "protection." Think it over. Our ship arrives soon.'

'Ship?' Bull whispered.

With that, Modren walked away, marching along the clifftop until he found a promontory from which he could watch the sun drown in the sea. The three survivors looked up to the dragon, who was regarding them all impassively with her cerulean eyes.

'He has given this speech too many times. Heard survivors like you spout back the emperor's lies, over and over. It pains him,' Kinsprite said, almost as if speaking to herself. 'It pains all of us.'

Bull nodded, as if his mind was already made up. Remina wore her hollow eyes, and they were full of pain and determination. Mithrid had no clue what she felt.

Doubt ran through her like a galloping herd of deer, and yet the logic of the mage's words stood stout. What Mithrid couldn't reconcile was that tampering with the spellbook was what brought the carnage upon Troughwake. Their disobedience cut down their fathers and mothers, slaughtered their friends. The guilt was too heavy a weight and she alone seemed to bear it. Blaming a dead Bogran felt too much like cowardice.

Kinsprite spoke again. 'If you need anything from your homes...' Her voice trailed off, but the meaning was clear. Mithrid stared at the bolts of the rope ladders, knowing well what waited beneath.

She was the first to push herself up, more in eagerness to get away from the dragon and her mage, if only to prove they weren't captors. Mithrid watched Kinsprite as she neared the cliff edge, silently challenging the dragon to stop her. Kinsprite merely flexed her wings, stretching as if she had just awoken.

As Mithrid hovered at the edge of the cliff, staring down upon bloody, corpse-strewn walkways, Bull and Remina joined her in slow, shuffling movements, full of trepidation and deep thought.

'You believe all that?' Mithrid challenged them as they came close.

'I don't know what to believe,' replied Remina. 'All I know is that they're not trying to kill us, and that's a nice change to the past few days. Maybe you should stop antagonising them before they change their minds.'

Reflex trumped sense and memory as Mithrid spoke. 'Your mam been teaching you big words again?'

Remina slapped her square across the face. Mithrid reeled, almost falling had it not been for Bull's grip.

'I'm sorry,' she muttered, but only after Remina had disappeared below the clifftop, descending into the dripping hell that waited beneath.

Mithrid watched Bull do the same. There was a strange mix of apology and sadness pasted on his broad, ruddy face. The girl bowed her head.

There was little to do but give up her protest and follow, even if it was the last thing she wanted. She could not stand to see her father again. Above the ladder, he and the cottage were still memories. Below, they were reality once more. The memories were brutal enough; they didn't need reinforcements.

Mithrid set her hands to the ladder and swung her foot over. The trembling made her unsteady, but she grit every muscle and forced herself down into Troughwake.

Some of the cottages were now burnt out, messes of charred thatch and driftwood. She tried her best to ignore the bodies. In the evening sunlight, their pallid skin took on a hue of the living, though the black pools of blood and gaping wounds were swift to remind her. Remina hadn't gone far. She was stuck at her mother's side, whispering something into her deaf ears.

Mithrid let her be and followed Bull down what was left of the ladders. The large lad was silent in his efforts. The closer they got to the centre of the village, the slower he became, as if a great gale blew against him, and him only.

'They killed grandda in our doorway,' he mumbled. 'Can't go in without seeing him.'

'Where's your mother?'

Bull shrugged. 'Don't know.'

'We can go together,' she said. 'If that helps.'

Bull immediately shut his eyes, as if Mithrid had offered to guide him. 'Alright.'

Together they stepped past fallen villagers and towards Bull's cottage. There lay Grey Barbo, just as described, half-in, half-out of his home. Bull had omitted that his head was missing. It was nowhere to be seen.

Mithrid guided Bull past the corpse until he was inside his home. There the boy began to gather clothing, doing all he could not to look at the doorway.

'You're going with them?' Mithrid asked.

The boy shrugged. 'Ain't anything else to do. Don't like being alone.'

'What if they're lying? Taking us to their ship to enslave us? Or worse?'

'No,' Bull said, with all the certainty in the world. 'They seem safe.'

Mithrid had always been happy being left alone and to her own devices. 'You'd call a dragon safe?'

'Don't know much about dragons,' said Bull, 'but if all the skalds said they're dead in the west, and there's one right above us, living, then that's proof the emperor lied, ain't it?'

The logic was simple yet flawless. Mithrid grumbled.

'Do you reckon there are more?' he asked.

'I don't know. I don't want to know.' Mithrid felt as though she rode a landslide, unable to change direction.

'I hope there are.'

Mithrid kept to her task of guarding the doorway, and when Bull was finished packing, he held out his hand. Once more, Mithrid guided him, and though his toe caught on his Barbo's jerkin, they escaped the cottage.

'You can go up, if you prefer.' Mithrid told him. Bull didn't need any further convincing and disappeared quickly up the rope ladder. She was left alone to stalk along the walkways to her cottage.

The dead mages were still there, untouched and uncared for. Mithrid moved on until she stood in her own doorway, staring down at her father, Ole Man Clifsson, and the mage they had killed. Her eyes shifted back and forth at first, but always they came back to the deceptively peaceful face of her father. Somehow, he managed to look asleep, as if she could wake him and still smell the firewine on his breath.

Mithrid stood there for a time she couldn't measure. It was only when the darkness claimed her father's features that she moved. First to check her tiny garden, tracing their leaves with her shaking fingers. Next came a few pieces of clothing, stuffed into a haversack. Lastly, she took the shield she had found in the wreck, and the axe from her father's hand. Mithrid stared at the blood on its blade. An axe was not like a sword or a spear. An axe was both a weapon and a tool. Its blade held both death and life. The choice belonged to whomever held the axe. Mithrid was not sure which she would use it for, but for the moment, she gripped the axe until her hands ached.

Before she left, she pulled over a stool and balanced atop it. She stretched up high to reach above the cupboard, grasping the box Father had found on the shoreline.

Prising it open, she revealed the last of the three beetle cakes. Mithrid looked down at her father. With great care and quivering fingers, placed the beetle upon his chest. 'You have it.' she whispered, before gently closing the door.

Modren lounged against a wooden strut, arms crossed. He wore a suit of armour now, and the girl saw the difference between him and the other rebels. The intricate grey steel plates were trimmed with fiery copper, and covered him from his wrists to his ankles. A black cloak hung from his shoulders.

'You're not like those others, are you?' Mithrid asked him, furtively wiping the tears from her face.

'I could say the same of you. But no, I am not, miss. I'm glad you're beginning to believe me, however.'

'Don't clap yourself on the back just yet,' she muttered.

The mage pointed to the axe and shield. 'Your father was a warrior, before?'

Mithrid ignored him. The pattern emblazoned on his breastplate was a pair of scales, perfectly balanced and trapped in a circle. She pointed also. 'Where's the skull the other rebels were flying?'

'The empire mages, you mean,' he corrected. 'That is a flag we true outlaws fly when we attack Arka watchtowers or encampments, to make them think that is our crest. When we see that skull, we know they're empire in disguise.' He dug a thumbnail into his chest. '*This* is the Outlaw King's crest: the scales of Evernia, goddess of magick.'

Mithrid slung the haversack over her shoulder.

'Why?' she asked, in a voice so quiet the question sounded like the mewing of a gull.

'Why what?'

'Why did this happen to us?' Mithrid thumped the haft of the axe on the walkway. 'Why do you fight each other, and what could be so important that my father and friends had to die for it?'

'That,' said the mage, 'is a long story indeed, spanning further than I dare to remember. The older the man gets the more his years dizzy him, like staring over one of your cliffs.' Modren beckoned towards the ladders and Mithrid followed in his shadow. 'I'll tell you on the ship.'

Where the breeze had blown gaps in the canopy of clouds, black pools of sky showed through, speckled with stars. It gave a faded, steel light to Troughwake, blurring the sharp angles of broken doors and limbs, wiping the colour from the spilt blood.

'Will you come with us?'

The girl shrugged, feeling anger stir in her gut, rising like a spring. 'I say I've got little choice in the matter, and yet I'm forced to make one. I didn't ask for this. Not one part of it. I never wanted the outside world, just for everything to stay the same.' The echoes wandered through the dead village.

'None of us wanted a life spent fleeing or fighting,' Modren replied, stepping closer. 'None of us asked for it. It was forced upon us by Malvus' betrayal of our freedom. We Scalussen survive, endure, and we stand up to fight back. That is all we are left with. That is our duty. The great war for magick is coming, and soon everybody in Emaneska will have to choose their side. If you want to spill Arka blood, then we can promise you that. Victory over the empire, possibly, if the gods are with us.'

Mithrid looked at one of the Arka corpses. Once again, she longed for petty violence. To bury her axe in its head, over and over. 'Will it bring my father back? Will it change anything?'

'Not for you, maybe,' Modren sighed. 'But for others who haven't yet woken to chaos and blood.'

Her voice was barely a whisper. 'I don't care about anyone else.'

The mage shrugged, surprising her. 'Then fight for yourself. Fight for something at the very least.'

They stood a while, with Mithrid staring at the dead mage and Modren patiently waiting.

'Your village. What did you call it?' he asked.

'Doesn't matter any more,' Mithrid tutted. Graves held no names. Her voice shuddered as if she were speaking heresy. But she knew the rules of death, and how souls were wont to wander if their ashes weren't sent to the ocean. 'We should burn it,' she said. 'Before we leave.'

Modren nodded solemnly. 'Kinsprite will take care of it.'

※

Atop the cliff, Remina, Bull, and the dragon were waiting for them. The dragon sat apart from them, preening the great, stretched canvas of her wings. Great clouds of breath emanated from her jaws. Mithrid found herself wondering whether a dragon was ever cold.

Bull looked down at the axe in her hand. 'What's that for?'

'We'll see,' Mithrid growled, her decision unspoken yet just as solid as iron. She looked at the packs hanging on their defeated shoulders. They were fuller than hers. 'You going with them?'

Remina sniffed. Her voice rasped like a nail against a file. Her lips were quivering in the cold. 'Nothing here for us no more. Nobody alive. Don't have relatives in the cliff-towns. No coin. In the north, I might be somebody. You saw the helbeast's reaction to me. What else is there?'

There was a question with few, if any answers, no matter how hard Mithrid wracked her brains. Father had taught her how to live above the cliffs. How to scavenge, how to hunt, how to make a fire, but nothing about how to survive a world of magick and murder, never mind seek her revenge against mages. Especially not alone.

'Nothing,' Mithrid whispered, gripping her axe tightly, thinking of how the helbeast had yowled at her also. Perhaps there was more to be found in the north than simple blood.

'And I never been on a ship.' Bull confessed.

Modren looked out west and north, where the sea was a black shelf reaching out to only gods knew where. 'And you won't ever step foot on a ship like it again, lad,' he said.

'What do you say?' Remina asked of Mithrid.

Mithrid propped the axe on her shoulder and looked to the mage instead. 'I say we'll see. Where is this ship of yours?'

Modren grinned. 'She's already here.'

All of the survivors looked around them. There was nothing to be seen on the black canvas of the sea but the occasional star reflected in a swell. They squinted, as if squeezing the sting of smoke from their eyes and could almost make out points of light in distant Albion. Far to the south, there shone a dim orange glow of another village, but there was no ship.

Modren raised and clenched his hand. A brilliant white light shone from between his fingers, illuminating the dark shapes of his bones. It faded as quickly as it appeared.

Mithrid caught the flash in the corner of her eye. Two matching bursts of light, coming from the middle of the sea.

Her head swivelled, catching the silhouettes of rigging and the inkblot of an immense sail. 'You expect us to swim?' Mithrid challenged the mage.

'No, girl, I expect you to fly.'

The dragon pressed her belly to the grass, like a cat lining up to pounce. Her wings spread flat, their bony ridges forming stairs to a saddle wide enough for two, or three at a squeeze.

'Climb on up,' Kinsprite rumbled.

The child stepped with mouths agape, jaws slacker than a windless flag.

'On that... ?' Remina whispered. 'I mean on *you*? On—'

'I don't see any wings on you, so unless you're hiding them somewhere, I suggest you climb on my back.'

Bull, fearless as a simpleton, climbed, placing himself in a leather saddle strapped to her back. Remina was more hesitant. Mithrid busied herself with strapping her axe to her haversack so she wouldn't be seen to look nervous. Once Remina had wobbled her way up to the saddle, Mithrid followed suit, taking her place at the pommel of the saddle. Modren checked to see if they were secure, pointing out stout straps that crossed their laps which did nothing to quell Mithrid's heart. She felt Remina's hands shake as they gripped the fabric of her sleeves.

'You better be right about this, Remina Hag,' she hissed at her.

Modren chuckled. 'Be gentle with them, Kinsprite.'

Before Mithrid could wonder why the mage found this amusing, her head was wrenched backwards as the dragon launched herself into the air. It was a highly unnatural feeling to see the ground recoil so swiftly beneath her. Great lunges of Kinsprite's wings tested Mithrid's grip. Her eyes went wide with terror as the clifftop fell away. The dragon fell with it. The wind sought to tear her from the saddle, rushing past her ears like the roaring of a mocking crowd. The black depths of the beach flew up to meet them.

A hair's breadth before Kinsprite's snout ate sand, she flared her wings with a loud snap. Mithrid felt her body compress like an accordion. A huge weight enveloped her. Even the skin of her face seemed intent on falling. Mithrid grit her teeth, but it was a brief sensation. She was soon marvelling at the dragon's clawed wingtips clipping the foamy peaks of waves. The wind still buffeted her awfully, but the awe had set in. She was flying, Njord damn it, and clinging to the back of a dragon, no less. Mithrid found a peace in it, an elixir for her heart's wounds. She half-closed her eyes and listened to the skin of Kinsprite's wings crackling as they bent the air.

Mithrid knew better than most that memories were hard things to kill, the painful ones most of all. But, for a blessed moment, all could be forgotten, last to the sea-salt air and moonless dark.

Against the smatter of grey stars on the horizon, Mithrid made out the faint outline of several ships huddled together. At first she was confused, assuming she had heard the mage incorrectly. Yet as they raced towards them, curving a path to their seaward side, the shapes knit together. It was not three ships, but one gigantic vessel dominating the waters. Remina had seen it, too, if the tightening of her grip was anything to go by.

Kinsprite's wings beat harder, rising up once more. Soft red lights bloomed along the ship's side as they approached. Portholes and arrow slits glowed like myriad eyes. Mithrid picked out loose sails that hung from masts that rivalled the cliffs for height. Their cloth was blacker than the night. Her eyes ran from the rearing armoured bow that looked like it could spear an island, to the monstrous castle at the stern that bristled with fortifications. Between them, diamond spears ran the length of the deck, and three towers rose up around the masts, amongst a forest of rigging and lines. Two more dragons poked their heads from hollows in the ship's stern. Crimson light shone from behind them, making their silhouettes look haunting. They made a curious chattering sound as Kinsprite hovered over the deck.

Mithrid was having trouble keeping her jaw from hanging open, but the stomach-churning drop did it for her. Kinsprite thudded onto a platform jutting from the aftcastle.

'Welcome aboard the *Winter's Revenge*,' she growled, bending a wing for them to climb down. They did so with shaking hands and trembling limbs. Remina almost ploughed into the deck.

Mithrid stood by the dragon's side, wary of the small crowd that hovered on the edge of the platform. Their shapes were etched by the ruby light, but their faces were draped in shadow. The fear crept into Mithrid again, and she cast a questioning look to Kinsprite.

'Worry not,' said the dragon, before throwing herself from the ship with a piercing whistle. Her dark shape sped across the waves.

'Welcome aboard, indeed!' announced a deep voice. Bull stepped in front of Remina and Mithrid, guarding them.

'Come now, you arse-scratchers!' it barked. 'Give them some bloody light.'

As the red glow strengthened, heavy bootsteps came pacing across the deck towards them. A tall, thickset fellow in a stark uniform of black and red emerged from the crowd. A potbelly clung to his midriff. He was bald, and his ears were like two miniature cauliflowers stuck on either side of his head. Though the man's craggy, weathered face had its rifts and potholes, it also held a gap-toothed smile. He walked with a scarred hand extended. His fingers were covered in rings of all colours.

'Call me Roiks, captain of the bookship *Winter's Revenge* and admiral to the Rogue's Armada.' said the man.

Bull shook the hand warily, somewhat confused at how it seemed to dwarf his own sizeable paw.

'Welcome, lad. You're safe here. Safe as a coin in a taxer's fist. Welcome, missy.'

Remina was too stunned to do anything but have her hand shaken vigorously.

'And you as well.'

Mithrid kept her hands around the straps of her haversack, still wary and busy wondering exactly what a bookship was.

'We won't bite, girl,' Roiks said, widening his smile. 'We're an ugly bunch, I know, but that don't mean we act ugly, see?'

Unable to deny the grin and waiting hand, Mithrid shook it firmly, as Father had shown her. Roiks yelped immediately, making the other sailors spring forwards. He hopped backwards, holding his hand and furiously blowing on his rings.

'What is it, Cap?'

'Hot!' Roiks gasped. 'Bloody hot.' He looked to Mithrid, who had recoiled to the edge of the ship. There was no accusation in his eyes. If anything, there was amusement. Mithrid flinched when the admiral began to laugh heartily.

'You got some fire in *you*, miss, that's fer feckin' sure,' he brayed.

Mithrid felt the stares of Bull and Remina upon her.

'And serves me right for buying shit-cheap charmrings, don't it!' Roiks clapped his hand on the nearest sailor's shoulder, almost batting him into the sea. 'Come now, you must be starving.'

Before they could protest, the survivors of Troughwake were ushered into the vast innards of the ship.

CHAPTER 7
KINDLING

Power is a river: some may dip their toes into it, others may wade or bathe, and some will let power's strong currents sweep them away to be drowned.
SPOKEN BY THE SCHOLAR ARFALSSA, FOR WHOM ARFELL WAS ORIGINALLY NAMED IN YEAR 307

When a timid dawn broke over Hâlorn's coasts, the dustdevils were still playing at covering and uncovering the dead.

One spiral of wind would cast gravel over the mess of battle. Another would wander along shortly after to blow the dust and corpse flies away. It was an elegant, lazy argument between impish spirits. It would have no doubt carried on for days until the rot set in, had it not been for the arrival of greater predators. There was hierarchy even in the worlds of the dead and ancient.

Before a single rock had been disturbed, the dustdevils seemed to sense it. They slowly whirled away from the burnt and broken camp, fleeing at the speed of cumbersome crabs. Few had made any real escape when the air above the bodies began to warp, then fracture. A crack of thunder sounded as two clouds of ash and onyx dust exploded into being. As the winds dragged the smoke away, two fell figures were left standing amongst the rocks and blackened bodies.

One wore wings of shadow draped behind his hunchback shoulders. Decorating his reptilian face was a lion's mane of barbels that leaked black smoke. The other stood taller and was crested in bony spines, like some grotesque thistle. Each daemon's skin was a mix of leather hide and volcanic crust. Both their veins and eyes glowed with inner fire, as if furnaces raged beneath their vile rinds.

Fearless, they strode across the scree, breaking stones as easily as skulls. They picked through the dead, examining any crests and banners that had survived the fire. The winged daemon tasted several of the corpses, partly in investigation, partly in hunger.

'You choose to consume such foul meat?' cursed the other daemon in a hoarse voice, like iron grinding against slate. 'Better when alive and full of magick, Baltharad.'

With a snort and a smile that held far too many teeth, Baltharad tore an arm from a fallen, and half-rotten, soldier. 'Ravenous, I am, brother Malphet. I will take what meat I can. You continue to starve away. More for me.' He munched away on the hand with careless abandon.

Malphet looked on, unable to ignore the roaring in his belly. With a snarl, he swiped the remainder of the arm out of Baltharad's grasp and tore a slough of grey flesh from it.

'Foul,' he mumbled around the meat. 'Maggot-eaten.'

Baltharad was insatiable. 'A garnish,' he cackled. 'What do you see, brother? You have better eyes than I do.'

Malphet grunted, solitarily bearing the burden of their task once again. 'A massacre, brother, by the look and smell of it. All the empire's meat. Not one rebel amongst them. A dead helbeast, too. Marks of dragonfire. Magick.'

'And of the emperor's runed mages?'

It took some scraping and bothersome digging, but the daemon managed to find a glint of mage armour amidst the dust. He soon unearthed a corpse lying in what used to be the doorway of a tent. 'Here, brother.'

Baltharad moved with all the alacrity of a spooked cat. He pawed at the corpse, ripping the remaining armour and cloth from it. He sniffed deeply at the black marks tattooed into its back. 'The magick, brother. Can you smell it?'

'Indeed, Baltharad,' Malphet spat, feeling the hunger in his own gut yet refusing the dead meat. He yearned for a fresh soul.

While Baltharad sank his teeth into the corpse's ribcage with a crunch, Malphet stalked up a nearby hill. Shale and rock clattered and cracked beneath his heavy claws. The dustdevils, who had crowded like crows to wait for the daemons to leave, scattered in clouds of dust. The daemon clambered between colossal boulders to escape the battleground. He took a stand upon the tallest one and let the wind through his spines. His skin seethed and smoked, giving him a black cloak of smog. He stared west, across the rolling, pockmarked hills to where pine forests decorated the land. He snarled. Wasted space. Far too alive for his liking.

The voice was so surprising, Malphet almost tumbled from his rock.

'If would be almost peaceful if you removed the infestation, wouldn't you say?'

A short man in a long and pristine brown coat lounged against the neighbouring boulder. Shorn gold hair escaped his hood to flow in the wind. His young face stared idly into the distance.

Flame bloomed between the cracks in the daemon's skin. Malphet didn't wait for an explanation. He swiped for the human, intent on popping his eyes out of his skull before crushing him for his sneaking.

'Wait one moment,' spoke the man. His words failed to slow the grasping claws, but what the man swept from his coat worked wonders. It was a glass cube, and within it a pure and blinding light burned. Malphet blurted ancient curses as he recoiled. The skin of his arm was more charred than usual.

'I think you'll want to hear me out,' said the man. His face didn't move, but his eyes smiled for him: a deep brown flecked with fiery orange. They were not the eyes of a human. They burned with sparks of world long turned to ash. Lost to millennia.

Malphet sniffed, still shielding himself from the light. 'You reek of god-kind.'

'Strange, that.'

Malphet sneered. 'Little god. I know you: the god who fell from the sky with the wrong kind. You wield scant power, for a god. Why should I listen to you?'

The man waggled the cube. 'Besides the obvious?'

A deep and impatient growl emanated from the daemon.

'Because I know what your kind longs for. It is not so different from what I want.'

'You know nothing, little god.'

'You long for a time when you mattered: when you ruled Hel and the souls within it. When you feasted on souls and meat by the mountain. Ruled the virgin lands with elves at your bidding. Every one of you kings. Now look at you. A lackey to an empire of men. You long for different.'

Malphet's claw lingered in mid-air. 'I...'

The god winked. 'Come.'

Despite the daemon's guttural complaints, the god was swift, bounding between the boulders and down the hill. He even managed to surprise Baltharad, still hunched over the dead mage's body.

'I have spent a decade or more walking the paths of the world,' said the god. 'Emaneska has changed much in my absence. Looks to me like you've grown fat and lax in your idleness.'

Mouth full of a leg and half-eaten boot, Baltharad screeched in indignation. 'Brother! Who in Orion's fire?'

'A little god with a proposition for us.'

Baltharad recoiled, hissing as the god's light touched his wings. 'Godblood!' Fear lingered only briefly on the daemon's face. Hunger immediately replaced it. Godblood was poison, but the stench of the magick in the air was enchanting.

The god looked about the corpses. 'I want you to escort me to Krauslung. I need safe passage.'

'We do not take orders from you,' replied Baltharad.

'No, you take them from the emperor instead, don't you? A daemon taking human orders. My, much has changed indeed,' he replied. The god's smile was infuriatingly mocking. He looked around at the corpses. 'What happened here?'

Malphet began to pace around the broken campground. 'Emperor's hunting party. Slain.'

'All of them? Then why are you here?'

'We hunt the ones who slew them.'

'And who are they?'

Baltharad began to circle now. The little god held the glowing cube tightly.

'You have been gone a long time,' the daemon purred, forked tongue wetting his leather lips. 'The rebels. Outlaws.'

'No,' the god tutted. 'Who are *they*?' His finger pointed to the half-eaten corpse and another body Baltharad had unearthed for sharing. 'These poor creatures with runes on their backs.'

The daemons looked down at the grey skin, and the simple runes and symbols tattooed into it in stark black.

The god was insistent. 'Who are they?'

'The emperor's men. New mages.'

The god smiled as if he had been waiting to hear those words for weeks. He tossed his cube into the air and caught it with a curiously heavy thud. 'I see,' he replied. 'A shame that you are wasted on mere hunting missions, cousins. Even if you do get to fill your stomachs along the way. Where is the great war Malvus foretold? Two decades and still these rebels rebel?'

'The Outlaw King is... persistent.'

'The Outlaw King,' echoed the god. He laughed unabashedly. 'I like that.' With a flourish, he palmed the cube and the light was quashed. The daemons visibly tensed to spring, but his words held them back.

'Are you not bored by your measly existence? Angry at what you have become?'

'We are scattered,' growled Malphet.

'We are few.'

'More of the ancient world exists than you think,' said the god, 'I am not your enemy. Traitor you called me, and traitor I am. That is why I have a proposal for you. You will take me to the city of Krauslung, and I will find out from the emperor himself. I will find out why the once proud kings of this land are now servants to a mere man, beasts to order here and there. I will set you free. You will have the great war I know your kind thirst for. Orion's vision will be realised.'

The daemons threw back their heads and roared at the name of their dead king. When the echoes had faded into the hills, they advanced. Baltharad spread his wings wide, hovering over the little god. Still, he did not move. He did not uncover the light. He stayed stock still, waiting for his answer.

They did not admit it aloud, but the god's words had driven a splinter beneath the daemon's skins. Baltharad and Malphet locked eyes. The former slathered profusely, as if already imagining skinning the god for his insults. The latter bared his teeth.

'Calm, brother.'

'What?'

'We will see what our prince makes of the little god. If he disappoints...' Malphet stared down into the god's glowing eyes.

'Then Gremorin will tear his soul from his bones and eat him anyway,' finished Baltharad, baring a ravenous smile crammed with fangs.

It was the god that smiled. 'Precisely.'

When the black smoke settled on nothing but the footprints of gods and daemons, only then did the dustdevils pluck up the courage. The game was continued. Grain by grain, the gloomy skies the only witness, the dead were buried.

CHAPTER 8
THE *WINTER'S REVENGE*

With no library or spellbook safe from Malvus' decree, the bookships were a necessity rather than a show of might to throw in Arka faces. Though, as fortune would have it, the bookships had that effect, too. Word has it that when news of the Summer's Revenge reached Emperor Malvus, he immediately had half the Krasulung shipsmiths burned alive, just out of – I suspect – pure jealousy.
FROM THE WRITINGS OF GENERAL DURNUS GLASSREN, YEAR 915

Living a life beside the sea counted for nothing when forced to venture out on the open ocean. No other terrain forged by the gods could turn a stomach as deftly, nor as swiftly. Especially when there were storm giants battling for the skies.

An entire day had passed and Mithrid was still vomiting. She had filled three buckets and was close on setting a record with a fourth. They lay in various corners of the room like shamed children. It was all Mithrid could do to stay upright, propped up in her cabin's corner and moaning to herself.

The only blessing was that it was all that occupied her mind. Not her destination, not her dead father, not her village lying in ashes, not her life stripped away. Not even the fucking Outlaw King could occupy her as avidly as the need to vomit.

Mithrid heaved once more, wiped mess from her lips, and set her head against the wall with a thump. She wished she had stayed on the cliff.

A bright morn had poked its head through the cabin's porthole at first light. Mithrid had almost forgotten the whole world, staring at those gossamer clouds. She had watched them swallowed by a dark squall, and that squall turn into a tempest. The ocean's fields had turned to deep valleys and crumbling mountains. Even for a ship of this immense size, it bucked and lurched.

Mithrid didn't know whether it was she had nothing left to give to the buckets or her sea legs were coming in, but the urge to vomit finally, thankfully faded.

'No...' Mithrid groaned, chiding her stomach. 'More...'

Standing was a feat of sheer willpower, but she managed it. She sat against her bed, the only furniture in the cabin, and stared at the door. Going beyond it meant questions, both the asking and the answering. Mithrid pinched the brow of her nose and sighed. She looked instead at the axe she had propped up against the wall. It had fallen over repeatedly with the swaying of the ship. Instead of fighting the inevitable, she picked up the weapon and thumbed its steel blade. The only parts of it remotely sharp were the notches and burrs under her thumb. That would not do.

Relinquishing the sanctuary of her cabin, Mithrid exhaled slowly, navigating a dangerous belch. After clasping her hands to her stomach, she reached for the door handle.

The expansive corridor awaited her. Glow-worm lanterns lit the steps both down, deep into the ship's bowels and up to the deck. Everything groaned or creaked. Seawater sloshed down the nearby stairwell and gurgled into gutters and grates. The *Revenge* bucked again, turning Mithrid's heavy steps into a dizzying lightness.

Fresh air had always calmed her. Many times, her father had found her standing on the beach and daring the lightning to strike near her. Seeking that familiar respite, Mithrid set foot to the stairwell.

The storm winds hit her in the face like a fist. It was part exhilarating, part terrifying. Mithrid gradually found her feet. The deck was coated with a sand that helped her boots stick. Hands clasped around the railing, she looked up into a world gripped by a storm. Beyond the taut half-sails and screeching lines, the clouds were a charcoal black. Only lightning showed their crags, and when it flashed, Mithrid swore she could make out the shapes of great forms fighting. Every time they clashed thunder shook her bones.

The girl wasn't sure if it was raining or if the sea was whipped to a spray. Perhaps both, but in either case, she was drenched to the bone and shivering by the time she reached the rampart-like gunnel to look at the waves.

There was no land that Mithrid could see. Just a confined world of leaden cloud and deafening noise. Her stomach churned again, but she managed to swallow it back. The wild sea air was helping. At last, Mithrid took a moment to study the vessel she'd come aboard.

In the faintest daylight, she realised how truly massive the *Winter's Revenge* was. The ship rivalled some cliff-towns for size. Mithrid could barely see the far end of the ship amongst the spray. Across the decks, men and women in both red soldier and sailor's garb toiled away, fighting the storm to keep the *Winter's Revenge* afloat. Half of them stretched their arms to the skies or waters, concentrating on something deep and meaningful. Their hands glowed, sparking occasionally. The other half hauled lines or saw to stray cargo. Several were clinging to the three giant masts, perched above the stout towers that fastened them to the deck.

The almighty afterdecks stretched several levels into the sky like a castle of wood and iron. They held more sailors, each frantically working on something. Mithrid could only wonder at what it took to keep this colossus from sinking. *And why?* she wondered. *Why build something this huge?*

Lightning struck one of the masts, blasting a pennant to cinders. The *Revenge* soldiered on unfazed. Amongst the gale, Mithrid could hear the deep booming shouts of the admiral.

Step by step, she climbed the slick steps to the height of the aftcastle. The sea was so far below it felt as though she stood upon the cliffs once again. There, Mithrid saw three giant wheels embedded in the architecture. Admiral Roiks manned the largest, central one. Two other beasts of men saw to the others left and right.

'Five degrees starboard, lads!' yelled Roiks. The sailors heaved in unison with their admiral, and Mithrid felt the giant ship slide to the right, right into the face of a smoky precipice of water. Mithrid was shaken to her knees. The impact ran through the ship like an earthquake, and yet the *Winter's Revenge* won the battle. The wave broke before the vessel, and the *Revenge* soldiered on into the darkening day.

There were others clinging to the deck nearby. One human, one far from it. Modren and his dragon were braving the storm, watching the admiral go about his work from a safe distance. Modren, wearing a coat of sabrecat fur and leather instead of armour, was fixed in place by some unknown means. All Mithrid saw were his hands outstretched to the deck. Kinsprite had her eyes closed as if she was enjoying this. With her scimitar claws deeply embedded in the expansive deck, the wind and waves were powerless to bother her. The dragon's scales steamed with every splash of seawater. Droplets skittered across her armour as if racing each other.

'A fine afternoon, no?' rumbled the beast, sensing the girl's presence without opening her eyes.

Mithrid had no chance to respond.

'Hold!'

The booming shout from Admiral Roiks froze her. Somehow despite the cacophony of the weather, it sounded as though he were yelling uncomfortably close to her ear. She had little time to ponder it.

A dark green cliff face of water had arisen in the ship's path. A rogue of a wave, towering above its brethren, sweeping towards the ship like a mountain with a grudge. With an arse-clenching rush of speed, *Winter's Revenge* descended into its trough: an anvil of seething water for a god-sized hammer. Thunder cackled overhead in mockery.

Mithrid craned her neck, watching the water rear up, surely twice the height of Hâlorn's coasts. With a horrifying roar, the wave began to topple. Though she was drenched by the storm, her throat was desert dry with fear.

No order had come. Roiks' eyes were narrowed and fixed straight ahead. 'Mage!' she cried in hopelessness to Modren and Kinsprite. Her fingernails plucked splinters from the deck as she tried to find something to hold onto. The dragon shifted a wing and pinned her flat. Firmly, but not painfully.

'Stow sails!' bellowed the admiral.

With a screech of ropes and canvas, the wall of sails that powered the ship shrank back into the masts and spars. All the ferocity of the wave was revealed in wrenching detail. What scant light the day still offered died as the wave curled over the *Revenge*.

'Shields!'

Hatches burst open across the ship's fortifications. Modren threw his hands to the air. An unnatural heat spread across the deck. Mithrid squirmed at the prickling sensation on her skin. It took her a moment to realise the rain had died. Not one drip of sea spray met the deck.

'Dig a hole!'

A blast of air whipped her drowned hair into a blindfold. Fighting to control her locks, Mithrid glimpsed the wave being torn and blasted asunder by unseen forces. There was no fire, no lightning, but only pulsating waves of green light. Above, the wave's breaking tip collided with the ocean, and the world began to collapse.

The noise reached a painful crescendo as the *Revenge* broke the wave's back. While any normal ship would have been crushed by such unimaginable force, the bookship skewered the wall of water like a spear through flesh. After a choking flood of water washed the decks, Mithrid found herself blinking in disbelief at the sight of clouds and a world beyond the crushing fate that had seemed so certain moments ago. The storm raged on, uncaring. High above, the dark silhouettes of the storm giants paused their battles momentarily to consider the *Revenge*. The rain and spray returned almost gleefully as the ship's invisible barriers faded. Mithrid was glad of their cold touch.

'Half sail and onwards leisurely! No more running for us tonight!' Roiks ordered, and a great cheer came from the crew. The admiral gave up his wheel to his officers and clapped Modren on the back with a resounding clang. 'That felt almost bloody personal. Haven't seen a wave that big in all my life,' he huffed.

The mage was stretching his hands. 'Farden said he wanted a ship that could make the gods jealous.'

Roiks stamped the deck with a boot. 'And the shipsmiths fuckin' did it as well.'

Kinsprite had forgotten the girl and seemingly fallen asleep. Sliding from beneath her wing was like crawling from beneath a scaled mattress. Mithrid stood adrift, brushing seawater from her face as she tried to connect what her eyes witnessed compared to what her mind knew and trusted.

'What in Hel is this ship?' she asked, catching the two men off guard. 'And who's Farden?'

Modren laughed heartily. 'Your foul tongue is catching on, Admiral.'

Roiks beamed as he scratched his nose with one of his gold rings. 'Farden is the name of our king, miss. The Outlaw King himself. The ruler without a throne. Hero of bloody Efjar. Finest fighter Emaneska's ever seen and ever will see. Even the years can't cut him. Don't worry. You'll see him soon, if the Arka don't sink us.'

While Mithrid pursed her lips, Roiks stamped his soggy boot with a resounding squelch.

'As for this old girl. You stand upon a bookship. Largest vessels ever built. Was supposed to be a simple mage-powered ship, but we got... *ideas*.'

'You said that the night I came aboard, but that doesn't mean much to me.'

Modren simplified the matter while he wrung out the ends of his cloak. 'A bookship is a floating library, Mithrid.'

The offence was written across Roiks' furrowed forehead. He even went as far as to shove the mage. Modren just grinned. 'The *Winter's Revenge* is the highest class of warship in Scalussen possession. The first of three so far constructed. The biggest, too,' said the Admiral.

'Now, now.' Modren wagged a finger.

'*Second* biggest. Fine. You understand numbers and measures, girl?'

Mithrid nodded. 'My father... I've been taught.'

Roiks looked pleased. 'Seven decks to the top deck, four more in aft-castle. Two more up front. She's iron-hulled, runecrafted, and got clockwork throughout her. Five hundred feet long, she is, I tell you. The masts are pure Scarala rimewood. Place your hands against one between the armour. You'll still feel the cold of the ice the trees were dug out of. No taller masts have ever been raised.'

Mithrid crossed her arms, bored of the bluster. This chap Roiks seemed overly concerned with measurements and lengths, and Mam Hag had always said those sorts of men compensate for lacking in other, sensitive regions. Besides, she was still busy trying to privately figure out what a library was without sounding a complete dolt. 'And why does a library need to float?'

'Because the books we carry are banned, and the empire wants them for themselves. And we can't allow that to happen.'

'Spellbooks,' Modren muttered, as if the storm would whisk his words all the way to the emperor.

He was watching her face closely. Mithrid was glad the seawater had numbed her cheeks. The memories of that night where like a shattered mirror. She glimpsed herself, poring over the book, reading its words, but if she dwelled too long on one reflection, it began to cut her. Mithrid shuddered.

'And where better place to hide than in the open ocean. Only fair battlefield in this world, I say,' Roiks was saying. 'They hunt us and the other bookships for all their worth, but this beast has teeth.'

'Plenty of them,' growled the dragon, now awake and letting her fangs protrude from her lips.

'Three more dragons are aboard. Three thousand sailors, soldiers, and mages.'

And three strays of Hâlorn, thought Mithrid. 'Where are my friends?'

Modren tapped his foot. 'Belowdecks, sick as pigs on rotten acorns. You're the first one to make it upright. Last time I saw that Bull fellow, he'd redecorated half his room in spew.'

Roiks looked concerned. 'He's done what?'

Mithrid braced herself as the *Revenge* ploughed into another wave and sent spray scattering. Both the cold seawater and the news were refreshing, and vaguely cheering. The shake seeped out of her limbs, and Mithrid forget her sorrow and sickness for a hallowed time. A grumble of hunger from her sore gut chose that moment announced itself.

Either the dragon had ears that would make owls cry in shame or the blasted beast could read minds, but in any case, it spoke for Mithrid.

'Vittles, Modren. I think the girl might need some,' she rumbled.

'No,' Mithrid corrected her. Petulant, maybe, but if the dragon dared to read her thoughts, she would make her look a fool. 'I just came to find a whetstone for my axe.'

The mage chuckled. 'This is a warship, girl. We can do one better and show you to the blacksmiths,' he said.

'Admiral?' came a gruff call. At first, Mithrid mistook the sailor for a scarecrow severely out of place. His drenched clothes hung loose on his skeletal frame.

'What is it?'

'Sprung a leak again,' called the skeleton man.

If there were four measly words that could fill any novice sea-goer with dread, they were it. Mithrid immediately sought a handrail.

Roiks waved his glittering fingers. 'No cause to worry! An old wound from almost a week ago. She's seen deeper cuts and lived.'

'Come with me. We'll find you that blacksmith.' Modren extended a hand towards her, but Mithrid snubbed it. She was no frail maid. Instead, she waited for a level moment in the waves and walked herself back to the deck.

'Fire, like I told you,' she heard Modren mutter to Roiks, shortly before she was heartily slapped in the face with spray. Spitting salt, Mithrid found the stairwell from which she'd emerged. She turned to find Modren not six feet behind her. Even with the roar of the storm, he should have thudded down the stairs like a shod donkey.

'Lurker,' she accused him.

'Fetch your axe, Mithrid,' he ordered. No smile this time. Mithrid followed behind his blustering cloak until they were in the shelter of belowdecks. The mage waited in the corridor, picking at caulk in the bulkheads while Mithrid retrieved her axe. She was well aware that compared to the mage's armour and weapons, to the marvel of this ship that encased her, her axe must have looked no fancier than a stone club, but it was hers and hers alone. Value was not always based on how many coins a trader would pay.

The mage reached for the axe, and, after an uncomfortable moment, Mithrid handed it over for him to examine. He left wet fingerprints across its rusted head, grunting at its notches as she had.

'Might be some fine steel under all this dirt.'

Mithrid snatched back the axe and clutched it to her. The mage shook his head but did not chide her.

'We all have keepsakes, Mithrid.'

Mithrid had no idea what a ship's insides were supposed to look like, but she was surprised this much iron and tarred wood could float, never mind sail through entire waves. Alternating between huge chambers and shrunken corridors that weaved dizzyingly, the innards of the *Winter's Re-*

venge were vast and complicated. Mithrid felt as though she had woken up within some colossal, living beast.

Modren guided her past cabin after cabin, map rooms, storage closets, armouries, workshops, and steaming galleys where copper vats bubbled and hissed with every lurch of the ship. The inside of the ship seemed even busier than the frantic top deck. Those that weren't crammed into hammock-lined barracks, toiled at frayed ropes or rushed about from one issue to the next. Shouts volleyed back and forth. How anyone slept amongst this maelstrom, Mithrid didn't know. Merely navigating the throngs of crew and avoiding being barged into a cabin door was hard enough.

Here and there along their journey, she glimpsed script chiselled into walls and bulkheads. At first, she thought it was graffiti, but it was too consistent, too deliberate to be the idle scrawl of sailors and soldiers. It had the purpose of design. What bemused her thoroughly is that aside from the smell of sweat, cooking, and the occasional latrine they passed, the *Revenge* was a machine of organisation and cleanliness. Every section of brass and metal shone. Every piece of cargo and clutter had its place. Even plates and cups stacked into pillars. Each time the corridor swung close to the outer layers of the ship, Mithrid saw giant ballistae poised to shoot at battened hatches.

Once they broke free of the bustle of the upper decks, a different world awaited in the levels below. Beyond the capstans and rope stores and the business of keeping the vessel moving, the *Revenge* became a sedate and dignified affair.

At last, the narrow corridors ran beside great, dark halls that spanned two or three decks at a time. Though the halls were decorated with the steel trimmings of a fortress, Mithrid saw men in mustard robes walking their levels, bearing lanterns of glowing moths. Figures in copper-coloured armour and full visors stood guard at every doorway and junction. In the faint light, shelves covered every available wall, bulkhead or column. Mithrid had to peer hard to make out their contents.

Books.

Thousands of them, from tomes to scrolls to sheaves of paper. All of them were behind bars that kept them in place. Some were even locked in cages. Whenever a lantern passed by, their colours blossomed. Though plenty were leather or cloth bound, the rest shone with colours even the rainbow had forgotten. Mithrid was staring so hard another headache grew behind her eyes.

Modren had noticed she had paused at a railing to stare. He hovered at another stairwell and watched her, waiting for her to speak. Mithrid let him wait, but in the end, it was she who proved uncomfortable.

'This, Mithrid, is a library. A haven for books. I saw it in your eyes earlier. The word has grown foreign since the Last War.'

'I didn't know this many existed,' she breathed.

'Thousands. And yet still a poor shadow of the knowledge this world used to hold. There used to be thousands more before the empire burned Arfell.'

Though the mage's sigh was wistful, Mithrid stared at the shelves like she would a vicious razorcrab trapped under a glass bowl: curious, but immensely thankful for the glass. These books held a dormant danger she could almost taste over the dust and thick air.

'Are they all spellbooks? Magick?' she asked.

'Not all. Some hold histories or accounts the empire would rather Emaneska forget. Others were saved from the northern land of Nelska before it was overrun by fire and ash. Old songs and memories of dragons stored in what they call tearbooks. The majority, however, are concerned with magick, whether they teach it or hold it.' Modren paused. His lips were pursed, white as his hair. 'Just like the spellbook that washed up on your shores.'

Mithrid's first instinct was to take the axe to the nearest shelf. Modren could clearly sense her anger and beckoned her on. The next stairwell led to the very bowels of the ship, where the libraries ended and the cargo holds took over. The sound of water rushing over the hull became louder. Between the roots of the colossal masts, sailors worked away on clattering pumps. The air felt wet. Hammering could be heard up ahead.

'Roiks fought off three ships last week. The last was wrecked on the beach.' Modren stared straight ahead as he walked. Mithrid hunted for any expression. 'The other two were pushed south by the storm. During the battle, the *Revenge* was damaged and a hole blown in the armoured hull.

The crew patched it, apparently, but not before the starboard library was damaged. A score of books were lost. One, seemingly, was discovered. That part you already know.'

Mithrid saw the source of the hammering. A gang of sailors were battling to keep water from spurting from a mass of fresh planks and hasty caulking. Tar was being slopped onto any gap. A woman stood nearby, hands outstretched to the hull and her face contorted with strain. The water ran in odd directions, spreading up the wall or bubbling up in strange shapes.

Mithrid looked back to find Modren staring at her.

'I'm sorry, Mithrid,' he was saying, 'that this war spilled into your lives. If that spellbook had never washed ashore...' The mage was clearly terrible at this, but Mithrid saw he was trying. She became aware of her teeth squeaking she was clenching her jaw so hard.

'Looking back over your shoulder all the time means a life spent walking into walls,' she replied quietly.

Modren's eyebrow made its way up his creased forehead. 'Did your father say that?'

'No,' said Mithrid. 'Mam Hag. Remina's mother.'

'A wise woman, then, for she's right. Regret is a slow poison. Don't let it wither you away. We can look at the angles of the past and wonder if we could have shaped them differently, but that brings only pain. We can only walk forwards through life. The future is what we have a chance to mould. That,' he gestured broadly around them, 'is what this ship and Scalussen is all about.'

Mithrid was in little mood to let this stranger teach her lessons of life, but he made an irritating amount of sense. Imagining a different outcome to the last few days was indeed painful. They were set in stone. Mithrid could spend a life scratching her fingernails to the bone trying to etch it out, and nothing would change.

She shrugged. 'If your words are to be believed, the war would have reached Troughwake eventually.'

Although she still looked for a sign of lies, she saw none. Modren bowed his head and spoke through clenched teeth. 'That it would have.' He did not dwell, but instead called to the woman standing over the frantic sailors. 'Under control?'

'Aye, Undermage,' she hissed. 'Storm ain't helping.'

'I'll fetch you help.' Modren swept away, leaving Mithrid to catch up.

'Undermage?' she asked.

'An old title for the right hand of Krauslung's arkmages. Doesn't mean much these days,' he replied. He grabbed the first guard he found and muttered an order. The man scurried off.

'You seem pretty important around here.'

Modren smirked. 'That's because I am. The Outlaw King and I go back almost thirty years. Forty? Evernia's tits, I can't remember now,' he cursed with the name of the banned goddess, the creator of magick.

'You've been fighting the empire all this time? You might want to look for a new career, *Undermage*.'

'I'll take your cheek as a sign of healing, girl. But no,' he replied. 'Once, *we* were the empire. The Arka kept magick under control and the world had fewer problems. Or so we thought. Greed and ancient grudges changed all of that. Now they call magick the problem.'

Mithrid weaselled out of the conversation by holding up her axe.

'Ah, yes.' Modren knocked on the breastplate of a passing man and pointed him along the corridor. 'Lend a spell or two, would you?'

After winding back up through the ship's innards, Modren led Mithrid to the bow of the ship. She felt the heat and smelled the tang of metal long before they found the blacksmith. Between the crowded ballistae and hammocks, a workshop had been staked out and roped off. A forge burned quietly. Tools and contraptions lay about. Mithrid sensed it was the kind of mess that looked chaotic to all except the person who created it. She was highly familiar with the method.

A stocky woman sat slumped in a chair draped with sheepskin. Her arms were crossed tighter than a belt and her eyes squeezed shut. She was trying immensely hard to ignore the presence of her visitors. Mithrid spent the wait marvelling at the woman's... *scales*. There was no politer way to say it. Small diamond-shaped scales, dragon-like, encrusted the ridges of her face, from brow and cheekbones to jaw and collar. They were a yellow so dusty it encroached on grey. The scales gave her an aged look, but the snow-pale skin between them made her look barely thirty winters old.

'Thron's balls. What now?' asked the woman brusquely.

Modren waved his hand dismissively. 'Nothing you need get out of your chair for.' The woman still didn't open her eyes.

'Don't be touching anything. You know how shit you are at the forge.'

Modren twitched as if the insult had physically poked him. 'It's not a skill Written ever needed to learn. Shame, really,' He raised a clenched fist and let flame simmer between his knuckles. Mithrid was wary, but guiltily enraptured, even though the bright flames hurt her eyes and brought a sharp pain to her head.

'What's a Written?'

'This twat,' Akitha pointed at Modren, eyes still very much closed. 'He's a Written. Mages that think they're so special they can swagger about my forge as if I am their personal smith. You all do it. Inwick. The bloody king himself.'

Modren sighed. 'And this ray of summer sun is Akitha. Don't touch her tools.'

'All I need is a grindstone.'

That cracked one of Akitha's lids. A yellow cat's eye fixed upon Mithrid. 'You're new.'

'I am.'

The eye shifted to the small wheel of sandstone sitting upright and attached to a bench. 'Know what you're doing?'

'I do.'

'I like this one. She don't flap her mouth like the rest of you human bastards. Go ahead.'

Mithrid had only just sat on the grindstone's bench when the words settled in her ears. *Humans*.

'Akitha is dragonkind. Siren. A survivor of Nelska.'

'Before the fire-springs filled its mountain halls with molten rock and flame. Before a thousand years of building and tending out land count for fuck all.'

Mithrid took a deep breath and set to work. Her fill of strange names, people, and places had been reached. The most exotic person in Troughwake was Halinan, who had once travelled to every duchy in Albion. On rare, fair days, Mithrid could see the Albion coasts from the clifftop.

Modren extended a half-hearted hand to help. 'Do you need—'

With a confident kick, Mithrid set the grindstone spinning. When its surface was an ochre blur, she hefted the axe into the right position, and with utmost care, touched the blade to the wheel. The sparks were always a joy, and with eyes upon her, she let them pepper her hands and feet, ignoring their burn.

'I shall leave you to it then, before this ship sprouts any more leaks.'

'What?' Akitha blurted.

The mage ignored the smith. 'Your cabin is all the way aft and one deck up, Mithrid. Sleep. Rest. We have another six days of sailing.'

Mithrid watched him leave before continuing. With gentle, fine touches, she carved the rust and imperfections from the steel until it shone. Only once did she look away, and that was to meet the Siren woman's gaze. Both eyes were shut again. She appeared asleep.

The metal screeched as the axe juddered.

'Eyes on the wheel!' called Akitha.

When the axe head's fresh metal shone, Mithrid tested its edge. The blade could have spliced a leaf. Mithrid found herself pressing her thumb against it. It was too sharp to feel her skin part at first. Only when the pain came, and blood ran down her palm did she stop.

'No point spilling your own blood over it, child.' Akitha had sat up, disconcertingly awake and wide-eyed.

'I am not a child.'

'I'm two hundred and fucking three years old. Everyone is a child to me. If you got to cut something, cut them.' Akitha pointed sternward. 'The bastards that did… whatever they did to you.'

'Modren already saw to them.'

Akitha cackled mockingly. 'Oh, my dear child. Bless your heart.' The Siren's eyes burned. 'Does that satisfy you? Doesn't look it. Why sharpen the axe? Let me tell you, there ain't many trees in Scalussen, but there are many, *many* more Arka to kill. That's the way you win a war, right? Kill more of them than they do of us? Save that blood, girl. Nurture that anger and put it into every swing of that axe. If you got magick in you, then use that, too. Wind's have changed. The war's coming.'

Mithrid was bold, perhaps too much so. 'What happened to you to make you fight for the Outlaw King?'

The smith's face fell serious. 'I fight for my people and for freedom. The Outlaw King fights for the same thing. He is not my king, I follow the Old Dragon, leader of the Siren Remnant, and he follows Scalussen.'

Mithrid stood. For a quick a tongue as hers, to stay wordless was upsetting. Instead, she let her father's axe hang by her side and left.

Akitha called after her. She was already reclined in her sheepskin rugs again, eyes closed, and hands clasped behind her head. 'Time. Give it to them. Trust is a gift. Don't give it easily, but don't keep it to yourself all your life. Take it from me.'

After getting lost several times trying to locate her minuscule cabin, Mithrid closed her door, propped the axe up, and sat on the cot. The vomit buckets had slopped in a number of places. One had tipped over completely and drawn some artistic yet grotesque pattern on the floor as it had presumably sloshed back and forth. Mithrid fought back another retch as she stared at it.

Instead, she chose the porthole. She pressed herself against it and cursed when the ship rocked, knocking her forehead on the glass.

Mithrid searched the ramparts of the clouds for lingering storm giants. The darkest clouds seemed behind the ship. A lighter remainder of the day awaited them in the north. Not fair weather, by any means, but by the intermittent shafts of sunlight, and the copper-green patina of the ocean, it looked as if they had escaped the storm.

She looked as far south as possible, thankful for her cabin being on the backwards-facing curve of the ship's gigantic buttocks. Threads of lightning could still be seen jumping through the clouds to finally hurl itself into the sea.

One fork led her eyes to a smudge amongst the violent horizon. Wrapped in rain and sea spray though they were, two dark notches sat upon the gloomy horizon. Mithrid couldn't ignore them. She had watched enough cargo cogs and Arka vessels pass the cliffs of Hâlorn to recognise a ship when she saw it.

While she watched, two smaller, darker shapes emerged from them, but vanished into the curtains of rain. Mithrid rubbed at the glass and cursed the specks of tar and salt rime.

It was a fine distraction, watching those unknown ships fight to remain on the horizon. But with a headache growing and her eyes aching from the strain, she retired from vigil and sought the cot.

The floor had other ideas and decided to shift rudely from beneath her. Mithrid hit the boards hard, and, to her disgust, sprawled amongst the largest section of vomit art.

'Ugh.'

As she slipped and slid in an effort to get up, Mithrid heard the frantic voices bellow the word as one, heard it echo through the ship, deck by deck.

Dragons!

CHAPTER 9
THE HUNTED

Oh, how I long to view the gleaming gem of Krauslung! Tales abound of its glory and the emperor's dispensations. Streets of glistening steel and glass. Ports bursting with ships. Is it true, cousin, that the cathouses of Krauslung cater to any desire imaginable? Yurina glares at me even as I scribe this letter to you. I swear she is wise to our plans. Find me some Paraian silks to shore up my lies, cousin. I shall see you soon.
FROM A LETTER FOUND IN THE POCKET OF A CORPSE FOUND FLOATING IN THE PORT OF RÓS

As another shockwave struck the bookship, Mithrid staggered through the doorway. Axe firmly in one hand, the other frantically searching for handholds, she charged to the stairs.

Remina was hanging onto her door for dear life, green-faced and looking about twice as thin as when she came on board. 'What now?!' she yelled.

'Stay in your cabin. Away from the window!' Mithrid yelled right back.

Remina had a sour face. 'Who put you in charge, cretch?'

Mithrid emerged into a scene of chaos. Two great serpentine heads reared above the deck, clad in misshapen plates of bronze armour. Their claws were embedded in the bulwarks, their wings flapping frantically behind them. When they weren't snapping their jaws at sailors and soldiers, they were roaring at a deafening pitch. The noise weakened Mithrid's knees and she tumbled to the deck. Blood trickled from a cut above her eye as she cowered behind a crate to watch.

Flame poured from one of the dragon's mouths, kindling a blaze on the foredeck.

'Water!' came an order from the tower around the mainmast. Modren was there, directing the defence of the *Revenge*.

Two giant shapes fell from the heavens like burning stars. The Siren dragons collided with the attacking beasts like pickaxes meeting rock walls. It was Kinsprite and another. Landing claws first, they broke the dragons from the side of the *Revenge* and drove them into the sea. The ocean was churned into a frothing mess of water and wings, turning the surrounding water a sickly violet colour.

With a roar, Kinsprite burst from the waves. Blood streamed from her wounds, but she bore the tail of the other Arka dragon in her jaws and was refusing to let go. Her prey came up spraying water a moment later. The stocky dragon thrashed and wailed, roaring his complaints.

'Ballistae, first volley!' cried the mage.

Mithrid felt the wrenching power of the machines through her body. The *Revenge* rocked slightly as the ballistae fired spears with tips wider than spades from beneath the decks. She rushed to the splintered bulwark to watch.

Five fired. Four hit their mark. The Arka dragon was skewered like a hog in a pit. Kinsprite somersaulted as she slammed the dying beast into the waves, his wings flapping uselessly.

The other enemy was mightier and managed to wrestle itself clear of the Siren dragon. It exploded out of the water and grappled with the deck again. Mithrid was thrown a dozen feet across the boards and left to stare up in horror. In the moment before the dragon launched itself into the air, she locked eyes with it and glimpsed its burning, rabid desire to kill. Not a hatred, but a hunger. It looked starved.

The blast of air drove her up against the mast. She was pinned, unable to do anything but watch the dragon unhinge its jaws.

'Mithrid!'

Boots skidded on the deck beside her head. A mere moment later, fire engulfed them. Mithrid had buried her head in the crook of her arm. She cowered at the deafening roar, but to her surprise, there was no searing heat, no crackling of skin and grisly death. She opened her eyes to find the fire spreading outwards from where Modren held his hands, as if he held a shield of glass.

The relief was momentary. The deck smouldered, and Modren's armoured grip was sharp and painfully hot as he seized her by the neck and dragged her into the mast's tower.

'I told you to stay in your cabin!'

Mithrid bared her teeth. 'No, you told me where my cabin was.'

'I—' Modren halted. 'Fuck it. Go!' he ordered, shooing her up the spiral stairs curling around the mainmast. Roiks was right about the rimewood: Mithrid ran her hands across the ship's iron bindings and she could still feel the cold emanating from it. 'Do you somehow *attract* danger? By the ice, you do remind me of somebody.'

'Who?'

Mithrid didn't get an answer. The mage stood above the wooden and steel ramparts and scanned the skies. The Arka dragon was being chased by Kinsprite and two more allies. It was trying its best to lay more fire upon the *Revenge*'s decks, but every time it came close, a volley of arrows, spears, and firebolts would fend it off. After three attempts, the bronze dragon swung south to join the specks on the horizon.

'Foul bastards,' Modren cursed, before taking a relieved breath. 'Admiral Roiks! I'll take all the sail and speed you have. Mages! Get that wind blowing in the right direction. I want a constant watch on that fucker in the south.'

'Aye, Undermage!' chorused the crew.

Mithrid craned over the rampart to watch them scurry into action. Her heart had not yet calmed. Modren's judging finger did little to help.

'Stay below while we are still in the open ocean.'

'How was I to know there were dragons waiting to fall out of the sky?'

'There's a lot you don't know, Mithrid!' he snapped.

Mithrid lifted her chin. 'Perhaps one day I'll be as wise as you.' She dropped that comment like a vase. It shattered between them, and she trod upon its pieces as she departed the tower. She did not care for the stares of the other soldiers and mages atop the tower. She took her axe and left, heading for her cabin.

Modren was left kicking at the deck. He, too, felt the weight of the eyes upon him. He looked around at the crowd and clapped his palms together. 'Don't you dare give me that look. Work!'

The gaggle of men and women quickly dispersed. A few got awkwardly trapped by their own indecision and pretended to examine the ramparts for damage.

The mage tutted as he laid hands to the iron ladder that ran up the giant mast. Refusing to take a break on any of the three levels that interspersed the mast's height, he kept climbing until his thighs and shoulders ached.

The *Winter's Revenge* had three distinct crow's nests, and each was a turret stocked with longbows and glass vials that, when thrown, exploded with ice or fire.

Atop the main turret was a contraption that looked simple from a fair distance: just a bulb of iron with a long snout, angled at the northern sky. Iron wires ran in complicated patterns. Half a dozen plates with hand imprints pointed in all directions. Glass chambers filled with green liquid ran along its base.

The bulk of its design had come from Paraia, where sorcerers dabbled with the finer magicks of time, distance, and light. The rest had been cobbled together by Scalussen's General Durnus and the rare spellsmiths that came from all corners of Emaneska to escape the empire.

After Modren had huffed and sweated atop the ladder, he gestured to the mages stationed in the nest. There were seven, each staring south to the Arka ships, fingers pressed to temples and their pupils swollen to black pits.

'It's time to use this blasted thing,' Modren ordered.

Five of them peeled away from their watch. 'Aye, Undermage.'

Climbing atop the contraption's platform, each mage put a hand against the plates and pressed into the grooves for fingers and thumb.

'Concentrate, as you were trained. Light and fire.'

'Yes, sir.'

Together, the mages wound up their spells and fed their magick to their machine. The glass vials of liquid glowed brightly. The contraption whined like a whipped mule, and when it reached a piercing note, it bucked in its cradle and unleashed a searing firebolt near vertically into the sky. Its flames burnt so hot it shone a faint blue colour. For a short time, it was the only sun the vast, roiling ocean had seen all day.

Modren and the mages craned their necks to watch the fireball punch through the clouds. Even behind that staunch grey ceiling, they could still trace the flickering light until it fell again, plummeting into the sea many miles north of the bookship.

'And now, below,' Modren sighed as he set foot to the ladder again.

The sweat dripped from him by the time he reached the deck. 'Evernia, do I need some more exercise,' he muttered as he swaggered to the forecastle and his cabin.

Modren kept a stark room consisting of two mannequins struggling under the weight of suits of armour: one his own grey and copper, etched with script, the other made of scales of red and gold. He snorted at the latter and sought his bare desk that faced a window high on the bow. From there, he could admire the swell rolling to greet the ship and breaking beneath her.

A wave slammed into the figurehead below, sending up curtains of spray in the shape of butterfly wings. If there hadn't been dragon's blood splattered across the windowpanes that day, Modren would have found himself entranced.

Instead, he knuckled the coarse tabletop. *No rest 'til justice served.* The Outlaw King's standing order. The words had been an electrifying fanfare when Modren had first heard them echoing around Frostsoar's courtyard. A decade later, the words had begun to feel like an iron mantle hanging around Modren's neck, constantly seeking to pitch him on his face and bloody his nose. Duty was a cumbersome burden in the face of times as dark as Emaneska faced.

Modren pressed a hand to the foul trinket he was keeping within a hidden breast pocket in his cloak; the skin he had cut from the mage in Hâlorn. He didn't dare dig it out. Not since it had developed an interesting aroma.

As he bent to open a nearby trunk, the mischievous sea decided it was a fine moment to serve the bookship a deep gutter of water. The *Revenge* pitched, and Modren thumped his head on the edge of the desk.

'Oh, that's just fucking perfect…' Modren shook with vexation as he gripped the edge of the table. Smoke curled from between his fingers. He pressed a finger to the spot on his forehead and pressed until the pain died.

Cursing the shipsmiths' lack of love for smooth edges, Modren opened the trunk and dug out a book that weighed far more than its size suggested. He hefted it onto the desk with a loud thud. The desk creaked.

Its cover was made of thick copper bound in stripes of brown leather. Heaving it open, Modren revealed pale green pages. Durnus had compared their hue to sunlight across ocean waves. To Modren, it was the colour of a recruit taking too much magick in his first day. The fringes of the thick pages were a bloodshot red, and strangely, there was not a scribble to be found on any of them. It was utterly blank from cover to cover.

Modren left it open, the pages splayed upright. He felt no breeze, but the pages stirred nonetheless, flitting back and forth until the book flattened as if smoothed by an unseen hand. Modren took an inkwell and clipped quill from a nook in the desk and poised over the book, waiting.

A ghostly splotch of ink appeared on the green paper. It smeared across the page in a crude zigzag. Modren snorted in amusement. Script appeared below the smudge. Words formed themselves, stroke by inked stroke. The mage read the phantom's message.

Stupid bloody book…
We saw the signal.
Danger?
F

Modren rolled his eyes and bent his quill to the page.

Of course there's danger. What? Thought I fancied some fireworks, did you?
We have company tagging along.
M

Every drop of ink he laid on the page vanished an instant after he'd finished writing. If Modren didn't know better, it would be an infuriating joke. According to a boring conversation with a Siren scholar he'd once endured, that was how inkwelds were first invented.

The reply came momentarily, the phantom hand and quill scrawling letters once more. And so the disjointed conversation proceeded:

How many guests?
F

Two ships. One dragon. seem determined to chase us north.
M

We'll lay out the welcome mat.
F

Warm up the mÖrd
M

Modren snorted but smelled a waft of the dead skin and pulled a face. He would tell Farden in person. Anything else was too dangerous, even via an inkweld.

There came a knock at the door. Modren bid them enter once he had closed both the book and the wooden trunk.

It was Roiks, and by the look of him, he'd been stung by a quillhog. 'What in Njord's balls was that?'

'Dragons, if I recall—'

'Not the blasted dragons, Modren. The signal you decided to flash to everyone with eyes from here to Gordheim. There are more ships on the seas than just those two.'

'Which I am fully aware of, Admiral! If you must know, I was calling reinforcements from the north. We haven't a dragon to spare.'

Whether it was the iron weight he carried, the constant running battle they were fighting, or simply that sting across his forehead, Modren didn't know; but nevertheless his anger spilled like wine from a drunkard's cup.

Roiks worked his jaw for a moment. By the clenching of his fists, Modren half expected him to swing a punch. Such was the blade of anxiety and stress that the crew of the *Revenge* balanced on. The mage caught himself, realising he was not alone in any of this struggle.

'I'm sorry, I—'

Roiks swallowed, his neck bobbing. 'Onwards it is, Undermage. At your order.'

Before he left the cabin, Roiks' gaze lingered on the four scorch marks on the edge of the desk, the perfect shape of a man's grip. The slam of the door was his punctuation.

Modren growled to himself. He knew himself to be a better man than to let his emotions rule him.

Shuttered by the persistent swathe of clouds, the sun's death went by largely unnoticed. A faint stain of orange marked its western grave, refusing to fade even when the ship's bells rang evening counts. The northern nights never gave in completely to darkness in the summer months. Deep in the north, past the Tausenbar Mountains, upon Scalussen's ice fields, it was said the sun never truly set in summer, skulking about the foothills of the horizon for weeks. Faced with the endless sunlight of the north, many a scout or soldier had returned from those far reaches foaming with madness. A mind needed the cadence of night and day to sense time passing, to know that existence had not halted.

Its path lit by red lanterns, the *Winter's Revenge* continued to plough through the iron-coloured waters of the Jörmunn Sea. Aiming north and a fraction east to pass Nelska, the winds took on an icy bite. Frost grew across the decks like a chalky lichen. Ice wrapped the intricate tangle of lines. Fur and seal-skin coats were broken out, and sailors worked with hammers to keep the lines from freezing.

Through the night, the wind mages plied the sails with their power. When one would faint or falter under the strain, they were immediately replaced with a fresher mage. It kept the *Revenge* shifting, even when the winds turned westerly and threatened to sweep the bookship closer to the black, jagged coasts of volcanic Nelska.

The dawn was weak, but with the clouds blown east, its powdered yellow light gave most of the souls aboard a reason to come above decks to stare at where their travels had taken them and to feel the *Revenge* flying across the waves.

Mithrid, woken by the light bleeding through the half-frozen porthole, was one of them. She had mustered Remina and Bull and forced them onto deck. They had complained in muted voices hoarse from sea-sickness, eyes were rimmed with red from grieving, but faced with the icy, crisp morning and the smack of salt-laden air, their faces were pinched rosy.

'Not going to vomit, are you?' Mithrid watched the two of them warily.

'I'd be vomiting up my own guts if anything else came out of me.'

Mithrid couldn't help but smirk at Remina. The girl usually pretended to be so superior. She looked offended, but then sighed. 'The fresh air helps.'

'How are you feelin', Mith?' croaked Bull.

Mithrid just nodded and pretended to smile. The nausea had gone, but her insides were still taut with the task of keeping the ever-present anger, trepidation, and sorrow all cooped up inside her. When Remina narrowed one eye, she shrugged the question off.

'Fine as can be expected,' Mithrid said.

'Where are we?' Bull's head switched back and forth. The deck was so full of activity his poor mind couldn't concentrate on one thing alone.

'Off the coast of Nelska, young'uns,' croaked a one-eyed sailor. He stood nearby, arms loaded with fur coats. 'Here, afore you freeze. They say the Long Winter's finally given way to summer, but that don't matter in the far north. We ain't far now.'

Tightly wrapped in their coats, the three Troughwake survivors went to the bulwarks and stood upon crates to see the places they had only heard of in stories, and in the ballads and eddas of travelling bards.

Gone were the heaving, storm-driven waves. Gone were the howling winds and vicious rain. The Jörmunn Sea could have almost been called placid. A gentle swell still kept the bookship rocking. A sea-mist cloaked the coastlines, but even through the haze, it was easy to see the imposing cliffs of the country they called Nelska, a dead country where the dragons were supposed to have lived and perished in fire.

It was as though some god had carelessly painted a thick line of black paint across the horizon. Jagged islands stretched all the way into the *Revenge*'s course. Beyond the sheer charcoal cliffs, the shadow of great mountains dominated. One broken and frosted peak soared above the rest, haloed in a cloud of its own making, built of the smoke and steam emanating from its black crags.

Before Mithrid could ponder anymore, a trumpeting roar deafened her. Mithrid saw Kinsprite's long neck arched to the sky, jaws wide. Two other dragons spoke out from the *Revenge's* bow. They sounded pained.

Bull clamped his hands over his ears. 'What is that?'

'Dragon song, boy, and a doleful ballad at that,' said a woman's voice. It was the blacksmith, Akitha. Her searing yellow eyes gazed far past them, fixed on Nelska. Bull and Remina couldn't take their eyes off the woman's scales and colouring.

It took Akitha a moment to realise why they were so quiet. 'Never seen a Siren before either, have you? Thron's arsehole. I'd blame your parents for your lack of education...' Akitha stopped herself as she remembered how the three had arrived on the ship. 'But... I know the only history the empire wants to tell is its own. Look.'

As the dragons' roars died to a sorrowful echo, Akitha pointed to the mountaintop. 'That is Hjaussfen. Once my home. A grand mountain fortress that was never breached by any army.'

Bull barely paused to think. 'What happened to it?'

Akitha was lost in the distance again. 'War and fire happened, boy. The Arka Siren war, the battles of Carn Breagh and Krasulung... they hacked at our numbers until there was almost nothing left. We joined with the Lost Clans – northern dragons and riders wilder than Sirens. You met two of them earlier, Mithrid. They betrayed us for Emperor Malvus, murdered us, and forced us into exile. Then our very home forsook us, consumed by the ice in the north, and the south destroyed by the fire springs that once kept the mountains warm.'

'Just like us,' said Bull with a wistful sigh. 'War and fire.'

Mithrid stared at the big lump. One village did not equate to an entire population, but to Bull, it did. Mithrid understood. That was all the world they had known.

Akitha saw the simple lad for what he was: genuine. 'Just like many homes,' she said, and paused to look along the *Revenge*'s side to the dark weather in the south. Mithrid saw them, too. They seemed far closer than before.

'You'd think they would be happy with the empire they have. No. They want it all. Power demands more power. Fucking hopeless,' Akitha cursed, making her leave without so much as a farewell.

Remina cleared her throat. 'A charming folk,' she replied, unconsciously performing her finest impression of her mother.

If Mithrid had learned anything from the voyage so far, it was that her concept of distance was deeply, shockingly flawed. A whole day they spent watching the world pass by, and there seemed no end to the landscapes of both ocean and land. The world beyond Troughwake was wide indeed.

The *Winter's Revenge* skirted the fang-like islands of Nelska, momentarily losing sight of the pursuers as it weaved between dangerous rocks. Dirty ice frosted their points, a stark contrast to their black volcanic rock. The island crags were also white in colour, but that was thanks to an overwhelming predominance of bird shit.

Every nook, ledge, and hollow were stuffed with every kind of seabird Mithrid recognised and twice as many she didn't. Their combined squawking was thunderous. Gromorants, skewers, gannets, rimelings, and petrels fell from the sky into the waters around the *Revenge* in a near-constant barrage. Mithrid and the others watched, fascinated, as they folded their wings and speared the surface of the water at breakneck speeds.

Fat, cumbersome birds dressed in what appeared to be black and white suits waddled over the crags. Here and there, they toppled from the ledges as if they were committing suicide, but as soon as they were underwater, they swam with shocking yet graceful speed, chasing scarlet fish between the rocks.

Minuscule birds with sword-like beaks dashed about in tight flocks until they, too, would plummet into the water, taking on entire schools of fish and white squid that churned in the bookship's wake. Great numbers of them stole a rest on the *Revenge's* lines and masts.

Beyond the raucous cawing of the islands, as the hours slipped by with splash and spray, the granite of the rocky horizons was bleached by cold. Snow began to decorate the coastlines. Far ahead of them, snow-capped mountains rose up above a vast and frozen country.

It did not take long for the first enormous lump of ice to come floating past. It was smaller than the bookship, at least on the surface. Admiral Roiks gave the thing a wide berth, and Mithrid could see why: its pale blue roots spread out far and wide, twice as large beneath the water than above.

By the evening, the ice chunks had become larger and more numerous. The *Revenge* plotted an undulating course between the biggest ones, slowing the ship down and giving the smaller Arka warships time to carve up the leagues between them. Over the past few hours, they had inched ever closer. A keen eye could now pick out the shape of a white hammer on their sails of moss-green.

Mithrid and the others were perched at the bow, placing idle bets on which chunk would escape the bookship or be crushed. An hour had passed since the sun dipped into the sea, and yet it was already rising once more in the same place. One half of the sky was velvet black, but the west still shone. It was highly unsettling.

When red lanterns blossomed across the side of the ship, Modren joined their small huddle at the bowsprit. He was watching the skies closely as he leaned against the iron ramparts of the ship. The next batch of clouds had rolled in from the east, streaking the sky with thick ribbons.

'Not far now,' he told them.

'How long?' asked Remina.

Modren took his forefinger and pressed it to his temples. His eyes transformed from their usual moss-green to a burnished gold. His pupils swelled deep and black as he looked north to the mountaintops and gathering clouds. 'We'll be there by morning.'

'Will we last that long?' Bull enquired. There was a tremble in his big paws that Mithrid suspected wasn't just the icy air.

Modren seemed to guess it, too. He laughed and clapped Bull on his slab of a shoulder before fetching the three of them more fur blankets. They caught them awkwardly.

'Those ships?' said the mage. 'This will be the last sunset they see. You'll get your first taste of retribution come dawn. Now, let's see if I can't help some more…'

Modren reached to an iron box nailed to the prow of the forecastle that loomed over them. With a flick, he unshackled its bars, and it collapsed to reveal a smoky glass sphere. It was not smooth but had faces like a tortoise shell. Modren stretched his fingers and ignited a flame in his hand. He gripped the sphere for a moment, and when he withdrew and extinguished his magick, the flame remained. Within the dark glass, a miniature firestorm whirled. The heat was immediately noticeable. Both Remina and Bull stretched their hands towards it. Mithrid was fascinated, but her eyes didn't seem too keen on the flame. Despite its subtle glow, it stung her eyes. Her palms prickled.

'Magick wins again. Fasten the box back around it and it will go out,' Modren instructed before he moved to leave.

'Wait,' Remina piped up. 'Who are they?'

She was pointing aft, where two skinny, almost identical figures stood alone at the bulwarks, breathing hard into their hands and squinting in the wind.

'Them? They're like you. A brother and sister from further down the coast towards Midgrir. Roiks found them half-drowned and half-dead on the shoreline. Apparently, they jumped into the sea from the cliffs to avoid getting captured by an Arka hunting party,' the mage explained. 'Incredible, what fear will make you do. Must have fallen a hundred feet before they hit the waters. The lad will have a limp for the rest of his life.'

Whether the wind had carried his words or the pair had the hearing of cliff bats, they were looking to the bow.

'I'll leave you to count the bergs and swap your tales. Speaking your story airs your soul, so they say,' advised Modren.

Mithrid looked around, confused. 'Count the what now?'

Modren pointed to a pale peak of ice drifting along the port side. 'The bergs. Icebergs.'

'Berg,' Bull repeated it, as if enjoying the shape of the word on his lips.

The mage made his departure, leaving the two siblings of Midgrir to amble up. They were scrawny waifs. If it hadn't been for their heavy fur coats, Mithrid was sure the wind would have blown them away like kites with cut strings.

Though the sister had half a foot in height on her brother, they were otherwise identical. Freckles ruled their faces, covering their cheeks and foreheads in abundance. Each had tails of dark hair that brushed their necks. They were an odd pair, to tell the truth, but their smiles were wide enough to see they were harmless.

Mithrid wasn't fond of the idea of strangers, even ones her own age, but Bull and Remina had already decided for her. Remina took her opportunity to play host, as if she had just welcomed the twins to her front door. Mithrid couldn't help but stare and watch the ghost of Mam Hag live in her lips and gestures.

'Njord's balls!' the brother greeted them in the squeaky voice of youth.

There was a moment of sidelong looks.

'Ha,' cackled the sister. 'He's been in his cabin for weeks, what with his broken ankle and all. He heard all the sailors saying it this morning and thinks it's a greeting.'

The younger boy looked immediately horrified. 'Ain't it? You told me—'

'I know.' The sister grinned at the others.

Mithrid wasn't sour enough not to enjoy a fine prank when she saw one. She went as far as to offer the girl a smile.

'We're Trenika and Lurn, of Hogswash. Well, used to be. Arka burned us out of our cottage weeks ago. Hung everything on two and four legs from the willow trees. Father included. Been running ever since.'

'Remina Hag. They slaughtered us, dragged us in front of a helbeast before we got rescued.'

The big lump extended his hand. 'They call me Bull.'

Mithrid pointed to the boy's leg with the head of her axe. She still hadn't let it out of her sight. 'Modren said you fell off a cliff.'

Trenika looked confused. 'Who? Oh, that chap! Yes. Powerful one, he is, by all rights.'

'What do you mean?' asked Mithrid.

'A powerful mage. The sailors have been telling us all about him. A Written, they call it. A mage with a whole spellbook inked into his back. One of the last of his kind he is, just like the Outlaw King in his ice palace. I hear there's no shortage of strays like us in this place we're going.'

Mithrid wondered why they were so contrastingly enthusiastic, having just fled a burning town and likely the corpses of those they cared about. 'You seem somewhat excited.'

Trenika nodded. 'Happy to be safe and free, is all.'

Lurn piped up. 'Ready to cut Arka throats.'

'Or so they keep promising,' muttered Mithrid.

The twins regarded her with smug looks. 'We know what you're feeling. Feels like your guts have fallen out of you, learning you've been lied to since you crawled out your mother. To find out the rebels were true and just all along, when all you've ever heard is horrors and skald's whispers of fire-eyed evils in the north.'

Mithrid shrugged. 'I'm still waiting to see.'

'Why?' Remina looked as though Mithrid had just pissed in the twins' laps.

'To see what?' Trenika pushed the matter.

'Proof, with my own godsdamned eyes. After what happened to us, I trust nobody. Especially fairytales of kings sitting in ice palaces.'

Lurn chuckled. 'You'll see. Our Da told us all the banned stories. Knew we had oldblood from the start, he did. Knew there was a war coming.'

Trenika rubbed her fingers together as if twiddling coins. A few meagre sparks popped and jumped. Bull and Remina were immediately fascinated. 'We learned to hide it, but one slip and it's the noose. That's what took Da. We've travelled north ever since, like we promised. Slowly, mind. Warily, but to where we belong. Where magick is as free as it should be.'

Mithrid turned so she could stare out at the fields of floating ice. Stars had appeared. She idly traced their shapes while the others prattled on behind her. About the Outlaw King, about magick, about whatever a Written was. She cared little except for sunrise and the answers it might bring.

Mithrid clutched her axe and her coat around her, and let the judder of the racing bookship rock her to a fitful sleep.

CHAPTER 10
CHAOS SOUND

Lies will always run faster than the truth.
OLD SKÖLGARD PROVERB

'Up, Mith,' Bull whispered to her.

He narrowly avoided an axe head to the snout. Tangled in her own fiery hair, the girl came awake with a start. The boy managed to dodge the weapon and clasp her hands in his.

Mithrid was breathing heavily. Her darkened dreams of screaming and murder faded before her eyes. She found a pale day awaiting her instead. A thin patina of cloud hovered above, featureless and ethereal. Fog lingered around the base of the bergs, which had only grown in size and number. The coastline had become pinched, and the bookship was heading for a channel that led deep into a field of white, endless ice. Mountains black as Hâlorn soil towered ahead. Their jagged crags were ominous at best. Somewhere to the east, a dawn was rising.

'Morning,' Remina bade her sternly. She had a face on her as if she'd swallowed a cup of warm piss.

'What's wrong with you?'

'Nothing.'

Mithrid was too tired and too bemused to coax the girl into talking. The two Midgrir twins, Lurn and… Whats-her-face, were standing nearby watching a colossal shard of blue ice pass by. As it caught the lights of the *Revenge*, a massive silhouette could be perceived. Something was buried deep within that ice, and it was far from human.

'Welcome to Chaos Sound,' spoke Modren gruffly. The mage hovered close. He looked as though he hadn't slept a wink.

Mithrid felt as though she were too young for things in her spine and ankles to click, but click they did as she hoisted herself up and tottered to the bulwark. The Arka warships had gained on the *Winter's Revenge* during the night and were gaining still. Once she rubbed the blur of sleep from her eyes, Mithrid could see the ice on their rigging, and the movement on their decks every time the ships crested the back of a wave. The pallid hammers emblazoned on their sails undulated with each freezing gust. She could see fire, too, burning in barrels and ready for archers, Mithrid presumed. The single Lost Clan dragon hovered high in the sky, far to the south.

'Who called it Chaos Sound?' she asked, moving to Modren's side.

He snorted. 'We did. The Last War ended on these ice fields. Further north still, but in the battle the ice broke up under the force of daemons falling from the sky or the heat of dragonfire. The Long Winter fading melted the rest. This path we marched still remains, be it water or ice. Now it leads through a maze in the moving ice to Scalussen. Only the bookship admirals and captains know it. But before we enter it...' Modren cast a glance over his shoulder. 'We've got to shed these barnacles.'

'I want to watch it,' demanded Mithrid.

The mage smiled as he pressed his gauntlets and vambraces together, almost a strange gesture of prayer. 'I want you to stay here, with me. No arguments and no deciding orders don't apply to you.'

Mithrid raised an eyebrow. 'Is that an order?' She didn't remember bowing a knee yet.

'Why, yes, it is. All of you stay put.'

'Yes, Undermage,' replied Trenika, Lurn, and Bull as if they had been inducted into the cult of the Outlaw King in the night. Mithrid rolled her eyes but agreed.

The *Winter's Revenge* swung around an iceberg and entered a clear bay of stunning emerald water. Here, the west and east coasts met. Sweeping cliffs of ice stood before them. Deep, thunderous cracking echoed across the sea as sections of ice tumbled and fell at random intervals. Foam and slush-tipped waves surged outwards to greet the bookship. The ice was broken in one place only: a great notch that interrupted the walls of white ice as if some godly chisel had been driven between them.

'Slow your spells!' came the booming cry of Admiral Roiks, far back on the aftcastle.

Mithrid pitched against the railing as the *Revenge* slowed. Her black sails crackled and flapped as their manufactured wind died. Mithrid could hear the faint sounds of clanking machinery and screaming orders coming from the ships behind. They had split apart to assail the *Revenge* on both flanks.

'Look ahead,' Modren ordered, pointing north. There was a quiver of pride in his voice and a shine in his eyes that Mithrid found hard to look away from.

When she did, the girl saw unnerving waves racing towards the bookship. The waves moved unbidden, not caused by any swell or falling ice, but by dark, fell shapes beneath their rippling waters. Tall, obsidian fins breached the surface, along with gusts of steam that lingered in the air as the creatures sprinted on.

'Blackfish,' Modren breathed. 'Seawolves.'

Down, they dove, under the sharp bow of the *Revenge* and deep into the emerald abyss. Mithrid glimpsed white patches on the monsters' sides as they passed.

'Water mages! Spiral!' came the next order, this time echoing from officer to officer until Modren bellowed it.

Above them, in the ramparts of the forecastle, mages went to work. As Mithrid watched them weaving their hands in spirals, she felt a strange wash of heat that dizzied her. A sharp pain flared at the base of her skull.

Mithrid had no time to complain. The water immediately ahead of the *Revenge* was starting to churn. A whorl grew bigger by each precious moment, drilling deep beneath the waves. The bookship's momentum carried it straight into the churn, and Mithrid had to hold on as the vessel lurched violently sideways on the spot. Mithrid was bemused until half the top deck roared as one.

'FIRE!'

With startling bangs, hatches across the bookship flew open. The noise of half the *Revenge*'s ballistae firing at once felt as though the vessel had run aground.

The crew of the bookship were fine shots. The ballistae bolts ripped into the Arka warships, blasting apart bulkheads and puncturing sails. Mithrid watched, rapt, as one bolt skewered three sailors before digging into the forecastle. Screams echoed across the arena of ice and water.

The Arka ships tried frantically to turn sideways as fast as the *Revenge*. Their mages did their best, but the surprise end to the chase had rattled them. As each warship began to bare their broadsides to the *Revenge*, Mithrid instinctively took cover, but Modren hauled her back up by the scruff of her shirt.

'You wanted to watch. Watch,' he hissed.

Before the words had escaped his mouth, an inky mass of water began to build between the opposing ships. The roiling wave careened towards the left warship. Mithrid saw its name: *The Heel of The Emperor*. She pulled a face.

Despite harrowed shouts from the Arka sailors, they could not escape it. The wave surged inexorably onwards. At the final moment, the blackfish dove, pitching the ship into a deep gutter to raise the hammer of the wave even higher.

The dismayed howls of the sailors were snuffed by the booming crash of water. They had opened their hatches at just the right moment, and with the *Heel* rocked to one side, the wave pummelled the main deck. The ship was awash in moments. Sailors who chose to abandon the ship immediately regretted the cold, or the sharp jaws that churned the water a foul scarlet.

Mithrid was having trouble tearing her eyes away, but the *Revenge* was not done. She was spinning still, bringing her starboard side to face the other warship. Once again, the ballistae fired, striking havoc amongst the Arka. They returned a volley, during which Modren forced Mithrid and the others into cover, but their bolts went wide in their panic.

With a screech, the Arka dragon entered the battle, rocketing down from the clouds with fire streaming from its jaws.

Mithrid was about to ask Modren why he was chuckling when a colossal streak of gold intercepted the beast. The crack of the dragon's spine was like boulders colliding. Cartwheeling in a blur of scales and limp wings, the Arka dragon collided with the sea. Another feast for the blackfish.

From the seasoned veterans to the survivors of Troughwake, there wasn't a head that didn't turn to watch the dragons. Their colours were bedazzling: emerald, ruby, sapphire, regal amethyst, and even one humongous dragon dressed in glimmering gold. Their trumpeting roars shook Mithrid's very bones.

As they swooped to pass the ship, Mithrid noticed figures perched on the dragons' backs, between the spines and beating wings. They hefted spears or sniped with bows, bellowing their own war cries with their dragons.

Together, they unleashed an onslaught of flame that consumed the warship. The Arka shield spells spared them for moments only. The masts and sails were engulfed like pines in a forest fire and screams joined the roar of beasts. With the *Revenge*'s mages now adding to the fray, Arka's doom came swiftly. Fire from above. Teeth from below. Death reigned supreme.

And Mithrid drank it all in. The details were marred by smoke and flame, but she could still hear the screams and imagine every last one of them as a murderer, a kidnapper, and a lying wretch. As she watched, she spotted a young man swimming towards the Revenge with the desperate, flailing strokes of a madman. Somehow, he had so far escaped the blackfish.

'Help! I surrender! Take me prisoner!' he cried out.

Modren made no move. His lips were drawn tight and his eyes narrow. Mithrid's stare switched between the two men.

The man's screams didn't last. With a last fearful yelp, he was dragged beneath the water and to the crushing depths.

'Would you have saved him, if you could?' she asked.

Modren turned the same impassive gaze upon her. 'Question is, Mithrid: would you, now that you know who the Arka are?' As if he already knew the answer, he didn't wait for a reply. He raised a fist as the dragons whirled overhead, a halo for the *Revenge*'s spire-like mast.

'To Scalussen!' came his order, once the last of the Arka had sunk beneath the waves.

Once more, the mighty sails of the bookship billowed, and the frigid waters of the north began to slide by once again. With its entourage of monsters in tow, the *Winter's Revenge* nosed into the great canyon of blue ice.

Mithrid was left to watch the bloody waters churn, to think upon the sailor, and admit one quiet word to herself without the mage hearing. 'No.'

☙

Mithrid spent the next several hours feeling painfully assured the ship was doomed to be crushed.

Barely for a moment did her eyes return to the deck. They were affixed to the sheer, towering edifices of ice that dwarfed even the bookship. The ice walls made a mockery of the masts, so much so that the daylight was lacking. What little found its way into the channel was dyed blue by the ice.

High above, near to surface, more dark shapes could be seen, frozen in their state of rigor mortis. Inhuman shapes, their limbs sharp and splayed. Others were clearly dragons, wings still aloft as if in flight. The small, hopeless shapes of humans lost within a frozen sea. The ice claimed all.

White, crow-like birds chattered on the edges of the ice cliffs. Small barges bearing mages used fire and bright light to turn wayward spurs of ice flat and glassy.

The sheer canyon twisted this way and that throughout the journey. Admiral Roiks called every turn before they reached it, a testament to his skill.

Before long, the canyons gave up their narrow squeeze for a wide, open bay ringed by walls of ice. A small town of wooden buildings half-swallowed by snow protruded into the blue waters. A narrow strip of bare land separated the harbour and the black mountains. The colossal teeth marched east and west into a featureless, white desert of snow. Here, at the further end of their reach, the mountains were fewer, smaller, but no less breath taking. Mithrid wondered how they were going to pass their fearsome wall.

Another giant ship was berthed at the harbour, rivalling the *Revenge* for size. Two smaller ships, sleek and built for war, lingered beside it, dwarfed by its bulk.

Mithrid stared at that giant vessel, measuring its lines against the *Revenge*. It looked incredibly similar to their ship. It, too, was swollen with fortifications and clad in armour.

'The *Autumn's Vanguard*,' said Modren, who had barely left the bow. 'Roiks will forever be vexed that she's four feet longer than the *Revenge*. He will argue for days that the *Revenge* is still faster and taller. Admiral Lerel has none of it.'

'And don't forget she can put out more sailcloth, too,' came a gruff shout from above. The admiral had come to stare at the small harbour.

Mithrid managed to smirk at that. She looked back to the mage and found his smile outlasting the moment, teeth bared to the cold wind. He was peering through the mountains' peaks and troughs, as if trying to glimpse something.

'What is that infernal smile?' she asked.

Modren turned to look at her. 'Me? I miss my wife.'

Mithrid was a little taken aback. She hadn't taken this war-scarred battler for a man to settle down with the wife and fireplace.

'Where is she?'

'Through there,' he gestured to the wall of black rock and ice. Mithrid swore the white mountaintops scratched at the sky, drawing white scars of cloud. 'Past the Tausenbar Mountains. Half a day's journey using the tunnels.'

'Tunnels?' Bull asked, visibly swallowing. There was something about the nature of being underground that terrified the big lad. Bogran had tried to bury Bull with a bucket of sand once. It had taken weeks for Bogran's broken nose to heal. Bull hadn't stopped apologising for a year.

'He's deathly scared of being buried,' Remina explained.

'There's plenty to be scared of in this world. These tunnels aren't one of them.'

'She a Written mage, too? Your wife?' asked Mithrid.

Modren just chuckled at that. 'No, she's not, but Elessi is as fierce as one.' His levity faded momentarily. 'There are only three of us left now, including myself. The rest have died or turned to madness, as is the fate of our magick.'

The *Revenge* took its sweet time idling up to the broad jetty. The blackfish also came to berth here, gathering in great groups around the edge of the ice. The monsters had voices. They whistled and played ululating notes from their pink, fang-ringed maws. Mithrid was so fascinated the others had to tap her on the shoulder to remind her it was time to depart.

Even after such a short time at sea, the fact the land did not rise and fall jellied her legs for the first dozen paces. Remina wiggled about like a newborn goat. Bull went as far as to clasp one of the jetty struts and thank Hurricane and Njord loudly for their blessings.

Only Modren, Akitha, and a score of mages and crew disembarked the ship with the refugees, who stood blowing steam on the jetty, wondering to which unholy frozen land the bookship had brought them. A man with a face that was more beard than face stood holding two young women, presumably his daughters.

A willowy woman of sun-drenched and desert climes stood nearby, looking especially bitten by the cold. Furs swaddled her. A headdress of amber cloth tried in vain to hide the stubby deer horns that poked from her temple. She was Paraian, if Mithrid remembered Halinan's stories, and she was the only refugee who didn't flinch as Kinsprite swooped low over the jetty and landed with a shower of snow on the shore.

Modren clapped his gauntlets together. 'Time's wasting. Rebellion waits for no man.'

Mithrid set her jaw, half to stop her teeth chattering and half in silent disgruntlement. Kind and welcoming these rebels had been, but there was still much to be proven. She thumbed the frosted blade of her axe. *Much to be claimed.*

Guided like sheep from the jetty, their throng ambled through the town. Here and there, residents would emerge from their huts and houses to applaud. It made Mithrid want to shut the hood of her coat around her face.

'Why are they doing that?' she hissed to Akitha.

'They're applauding your choice to join us here at the edge of the map.'

'Choice?' Mithrid snapped, catching Remina's glare. 'There is nothing to applaud about how I came here.'

Beyond the black houses, the yellow grass and frozen earth led them to the roots of the Tausenbar Mountains. Their foothills, if they could be called that, were a jumbled mess of boulders and ice blocks so big a village could live inside one.

A well-trodden path led between the crags until they came to a sharp gulley. A wall of dirty ice blocked the way, looking like a clenched fist trapped in the rock. Others in fur coats and patchwork clothing waited there, but for what, Mithrid didn't know.

Their small crowd opened up with the arrival of Modren. Whispers skittered about as the undermage spread his hands across the ice wall. Cracks followed his touch. Meltwater dribbled down in steaming rivers. White ice turned translucent, unveiling a blue glow, and with one push, the wall shattered like weak glass. Beyond the hole, a half-circle of a tunnel stretched deep into the mountains. Its walls were solid ice and hewn rock. Lanterns had been drilled into them at intervals and stuffed with glowing worms. Their pallid, cobalt light gave the tunnel an eerie aura.

'Nope,' Bull said to himself, loud enough for half the crowd to hear.

Modren reassured them. 'Straight through this tunnel is Scalussen and the Frostsoar tower. Not long, now.'

One prim elderly woman was in the middle of asking whether they must walk the entire way when a strange yowl sounded. Everybody present peered into the tunnel as a stream of musty air began to waft. It smelled like wet hound, with a touch of stale cheese thrown in for good measure. A rasping, scraping noise grew louder. One by one, the lanterns winked out, smothered by some invisible blanket.

It took several uneasy moments for the daylight to illuminate whatever beast or contraption was making that horrendous noise. It turned out to be both. First, claws like sword blades and piggish, twitching snouts heavy with thick whiskers emerged from the gloom.

Moles.

Three giant moles, each the size of a cow. They were pearl-white with tony black eyes embedded in their thick, northern fur. They were tied in tandem by stout leather and wood harnesses. Ice chips flew from their claws.

The vehicle they were hard at work dragging soon followed. It was a sleek, barge-like affair, but instead of a keel, it had runners of steel, like long knives biting into the tunnel's floor. A man in a fur hood and leather tunic waved and smiled cheerily. He made no noise, just a rapid clicking that the moles seemed to understand. After turning in a tight arc, the sled poked its backside from the tunnel and a set of steps clanked onto the ice.

Modren ordered the refugees onwards. Benches had been bolted to the sled. Handles, too, as if the moles were capable of lurching rapidly. By the way their bellies hugged the ice, and their limbs splayed while they panted, Mithrid didn't imagine there would be much lurching at all.

She imagined wrong.

No sooner had Mithrid taken a stand next to a standing Bull and sitting Remina, did Modren give the warning to hold on. With one flick of the driver's cane, the moles sprang into action. The barge leapt on as if this was no tunnel, but a pit they plummeted down.

The moles' claws, both front and back, were the secret. Mithrid, once she had managed to escape tumbling from the sled and wrangled her rusty hair out of her eyes, stared at the creatures in disbelief. She felt cheated. Lied to by their flabby white coats and squinting, half-blind eyes.

'Pride of the ice field snowmads, these moles, and only the moles of the Driftracer snowmad tribe go this fast,' Modren was explaining to some nearby refugees. Mithrid tried to make sense of the names, but the rest of his words were lost over the rush of cold wind.

The moles laughed in the face of distance. The frozen detail of the tunnel walls flashed past in a blur. The lanterns came, adding another beat to her staccato heart.

Bull shut his eyes for the entire journey, most likely pretending the same thing. Every twist made him groan, and whenever there was a large bump in the ice, he clasped for Remina's and Mithrid's hand until they grew tired of his crushing grip.

'Brace yourselves!' Modren shouted, when the pinprick of light appeared over the moles' shaggy backs. The beasts hurtled towards it, as if, oddly, they longed for the sun as much as the passengers. Mithrid felt the tunnel sweep upwards.

With a spray of ice, the vehicle bounded from its dark vein and out into a blinding field of white snow. The moles slowed to an idle canter. The harsh scrape of the tunnel had reduced to a muted grumble. Mithrid stood tall to look around. She had to blink every other moment to keep from tearing at the sheer brightness of the landscape.

A vast swathe of pure snow stretched endless leagues to both horizons. No trees, no bushes. Nothing grew here to interrupt the cold wasteland. Behind them, the Tausenbar Mountains stood quietly frozen, a formidable wall between this land and the south. Another range crowned the north, and even leagues ahead, Mithrid could tell they dwarfed the Tausenbar. Dark clouds swaddled their black, snowless peaks. She swore she could see fire in the far distance.

In a slight notch in the mountains, perched atop the only slight mound for miles, Mithrid saw the place they called Scalussen. It was as featureless as the terrain, decorated by a smear of smoke and steam. To Mithrid's half-blind eyes, all it consisted of was a dark wall stretching around the most boring tower she could have imagined. It was a granite cylinder, nothing more. A splinter of stone poked from one side of its flat top. If it hadn't been dizzyingly tall, Mithrid might not have been impressed.

Modren was standing tall beside the driver, arms crossed proudly. Perhaps it was the days of travel irritating her, but she decided to poke at the man.

Stepping through the refugees – and treading on several cold toes to do so – Mithrid barged into the one-sided conversation he had been having with the snowmad driver.

'Is that it?'

'Yes, that's it.'

'I thought it was supposed to be an ice palace. Some great centre of civilisation, not a skinny tower and some bare walls around a town.'

Modren wasn't letting her ruin his good mood. 'Tell me, Mithrid, do you always judge things so quickly? You're still half-blind from the sun. Patience.'

Though Mithrid grumbled, under the snow moles' power, Scalussen quickly began to loom. And loom. And loom some more. Refusing to admit her eyes had lied to her, Mithrid blamed the featureless ice and the northern sun.

It was no town, but a citadel built on a rise of ice, its back to a hollow in the colossal black mountains. As the sled – not "barge" as Remina had corrected Mithrid several times – got ever closer, the city and its spear of a tower grew ever taller. Before long, her neck took on an ache from staring upwards so much.

Scalussen's walls were colossal. So much frost clung to their roots they looked to be made of ice, but the stark, bleak granite blocks that emerged from the frozen armour proved otherwise. A smattering of scarlet pennants snapped in the breeze. The grey soldiers watching the sled approach were numerous, yet pea-sized, even once the sled had reached the foot of the gates. Dragons glittered between the battlements.

Featureless was a word that described Scalussen well from the outside. Barely an arrow slit or gate dared to break the monotony of cold, mountain stone. One road led to its main gatehouse, an H of stone that bristled with steel spikes. The gate beneath it was clad in stone so as to appear seamless. Its only markings were lines and lines of script chiselled around its edges.

Mithrid had never heard such clatter as the gate cracked open. Somewhere inside the gatehouse, chains rattled. Something clanked like anvils colliding. Dust and snow cascaded as the stone separated. Mithrid swore she glimpsed the script shining with golden light.

Within Scalussen, "featureless" would have been a dire insult. Mithrid bit her lip, like a latch to keep her jaw from hanging slack.

It was as if the builders of the citadel had spent years harvesting every scrap of colour from the north and hoarding it within the walls. That was the only explanation Mithrid had for the ice fields' bleakness. Flags flapped proudly from every building's weathervane, gutter, or iron spike. Streamers spanned the gap between the walls and the city that huddled around the Frostsoar, forming a threadbare roof over the bustle. The crowds of people milling about the vast, ring-like inner courtyard were equally colorful in dress, in decoration, and in all the shades the gods forged their children in, as Mithrid's father once put it. Her pale Hâlorn skin was just one colour in the broad palette of the crowds: from the scales of the Sirens and dragons, to the tanned skin of the Paraians, to the strange beastpeoples covered in hair and hide, stalking on hooves, wearing more twisted horns of goats, deer, or even the tusks of a hog. A smattering of dragons poked their bejewelled heads from eyries bored into the Frostsoar's towering heights.

Wafts of food from nearby markets reminded Mithrid she hadn't eaten since the previous day. Bull was already sniffing at the air. Remina pointed to where fragrant clouds of steam and coloured smoke arose from a section of crowded buildings.

She was ready to follow the growl of her stomach, but Modren had other ideas. It was then that Mithrid noticed they were not the only new arrivals. A crowd of queues and waiting people stood either side of them. They were waiting to pass through a bottleneck of a wooden fence. Its gap was guarded by men in armour, a turquoise dragon, and a woman who Mithrid would have betted coin on being a witch.

'What now, sir?' came the question from a fellow confused refugee.

'A fine question, madam,' announced Modren, raising his hoarse voice in an effort to be heard over the commotion of voices and city echoes. 'You will be weighed and measured.'

The mage could see the collective shudder that ran through the crowd. Mithrid wondered if they had all been shown to the helbeast like she had.

'Fear not, we keep no daemons here,' said an ancient-looking man accompanied by a white-haired woman in armour. His black robe was caked in dust, and he wandered through the crowds, repeating his reassurances. 'The dragon will know your heart, whether it true or false, and the lady Wyved will sense your magick.'

The dusty elder beamed warmly at Modren as he ambled forwards, his walking stick tapping on the flagstones. What concerned Mithrid the most was the fangs that protruded from his smile.

'Back so soon, I see, Undermage?' the woman challenged.

Modren shrugged. 'Didn't plan to be, but such is war.'

'Tiresome, painful, and inconvenient at best. That is war,' advised the old man, speaking to the crowd as he turned to examine them. His eyes were the colour of the palest winter sky. 'But necessary in times like these when conversation and diplomacy have been exhausted. Many of you have come simply to survive, and we welcome you. If you have magick, or the strength, then we invite you to fight this war. To topple this cruel empire. But we will only ask, not force, and we will only ask once.'

His worrying smile was as pervasive as Mithrid's staring. *Fangs. What kind of man had fangs?* The simple answer was no man at all, but a vampyre.

Somehow, Mithrid missed the reassurance that seemed to envelop everyone else like a warm blanket. The bearded man began to clap, accidentally and momentarily throttling his daughters with his big arms in the process.

The old man led their group towards the lines. Mithrid hung back, waving Remina and Bull on and waiting to drift past Modren, who was staring intently up at the tower.

'More doubts, Mithrid?' he asked without looking.

'Who is that old man?'

Modren chuckled to some private joke. It was a habit that was beginning to irritate Mithrid.

'Old, you say? Ask him how old he is sometimes. He won't mind. But that, girl, is General Durnus. The greatest mind left in the lands. A scholar of centuries, a healer, and a devastating mage of magicks I've never seen the like of. He ruled as arkmage before Emperor Malvus usurped him.'

Mithrid blinked, trying to digest that. 'And the... fangs?'

'He was once blind, you see. To cure himself, he willingly fell under the vampyre's venom. It's a powerful curse but he tinkered with it as he likes to do. The blindness went away. Fangs came back. He calls them a side effect, just like his frail bones, but I suspect he likes how they look. He never admits it, but I have a bet he enjoys being a vampyre. Again.'

'Again?'

'He was, then he wasn't. Now he is. Sort of.' The undermage laughed. 'Long story.'

'One of many you've yet to tell me.'

Modren began to stride towards the lines. She chased him.

'Where did all these other people come from?' Mithrid asked.

Modren snorted. 'You know, Mithrid. Some things will naturally be answered, if you give yourself a chance to breathe and look about.' He whirled around, making her stumble. 'Or are you still hunting out some great lie? Hmm?'

Mithrid crossed her arms. Her doubts had been trampled but she didn't let Modren know. 'I'm naturally curious.'

'They came from the *Vanguard*. The *Summer's Fury*. They come across the ice on ramshackle sleds and bleeding feet. Look there. Those are called quickdoors. Portals that can take you a thousand miles in a blink. They used to stand all over Emaneska. Now, they're rarer and more dangerous than ever. These we have kept open for as long as we can, keeping us tied to outposts hidden throughout the lands.'

Mithrid looked to the door set upon a pedestal in the centre of the main courtyard. A man circled it, chanting from a book held in his hands. The door itself was a simple arch of black rock. The air within shimmered as though one of Morden's water mages had convinced a pool to lie on its side. As she stared, a man in lord's dress came hurtling through it. Somebody had thoughtfully laid out some pillows around the pedestal to stop the man from breaking his face.

'Happy?' asked Modren.

'Recently? Rarely.'

'Time, Mithrid,' said Modren as he gestured to the line. 'It heals.'

Mithrid shuffled in time with the queue. The process of approaching the woman and dragon seemed simple. Brief. There was a moment of eye contact and then Scalussen was open. Workers stood by to guide people hither and fro.

The dragon's eyes were like orbs filled with swirling, tropical seawater. Mithrid met its narrowed gaze several times, and felt the hairs rising on her nape each time. It was something different from awe. It was the knowledge of being prey. She felt like a mouse examined by an owl. Worse, she felt the dragon searching her very soul, not just meeting her gaze. She tried to look away to no avail. The dragon's gaze was a searchlight that found her each time.

'What is it doing?' she hissed to Remina.

'I don't know.'

Bull swallowed, his wonder for dragons squashed. 'It looks hungry.'

'Next!'

Bull staggered forwards, unsure of what to do. The dragon bent its long serpentine neck to regard the boy. The woman, old, leathery, white as a snowdrift and with her hair matted in thick strands, craned her neck to take all of Bull in. She was a witch; Mithrid was sure of it.

With a flick of her head, his sentence was passed. Bull was guided towards the left, where others spoke of swords, spears, and shields.

Remina stepped up, standing proudly and with her eyes gazing off into some imagined distance. It seemed Remina had some magick in her, for the woman raised a hand, and Remina was sent right. She flicked her hair as she walked.

Mithrid's turn. She approached slowly, more fascinated by the turquoise dragon scales than the woman. Before she could stand before them, a commotion broke out in the line behind her. A fell shout cut the quiet, contented bustle.

'For the Arka's glory!'

It was the bearded man with the daughters. All three of them produced knives from their cloaks and surged into the crowds, stabbing at anything and anyone that got in their way. A half dozen refugees fell before their blades before the soldiers could intervene. The Paraian woman was amongst them, sweeping the legs from beneath one daughter and bringing a heel down onto her neck with an audible crunch.

Modren was deep in the panicked fray, wielding not magick but a long sword. He sliced the other daughter down before the man retreated, spinning shapes with his hands. He threw up a shield spell before Modren's fork of green lightning could gut him.

The two circled, the undermage and the assassin. Their arena was a border of tense bodies, eager for righteous blood yet terrified to edge closer. Shouts echoed across the walls, bringing more from Scalussen's streets to watch the outcome. Struggling to part a space between elbows and fat bellies, Mithrid pushed to see, more entranced than horrified.

Modren was holding his hands low and clawed, causing the flagstones to quiver and crack around the assassin. Arrows bounced from the man's shield all the while.

Before the thought of stalemate had dared to creep from the shelves of her mind, stormless thunder rocked the courtyard. Between Modren and the assassin, the air itself shook. A rushing void of air and light held for the briefest of moments before a figure burst through it.

He was wearing Modren's armour of red and gold scales, but something about this metal seemed different. It was not restrained to his arms and shoulders but rather encased him in a full suit of scale plate that shone so brightly Mithrid initially thought it was aflame.

Before the assassin could react, the newcomer threw a fist against his shield that forced him to his knees. Another blow, a flash of green light, and with a heavy wave of hot air, the shield exploded into vanishing shards.

The two parried blows, the knife blade screeching weakly against the russet armour. In four moves, the newcomer had outfoxed the assassin, sweeping a free hand under his guard. He gripped the bastard's neck, lifted him from the ground, and unleashed his magick.

The man's head was enveloped in flame so hot it flared white. The man's screams were painfully short-lived as his flesh and then skull were burnt to nothing but ash. The headless corpse slumped to the cold earth when there was nothing left.

The silence was condemning.

The armoured man swivelled to take in the crowd before removing his helmet. He must have seen barely forty summers; the shaggy mop of black hair bore only a tinge of grey. His eyes, however, looked as if he'd stolen them from an older, wiser man: the colour of sage moss on grey granite.

'That is what happens to assassins and spies in Scalussen,' was all he said, before tugging a circular gold disk from his belt. He cast one look at Modren, and with a crack that made everybody flinch, vanished into thin air.

'And that, ladies and gentlemen, boys and girls,' Modren said, with a roll of his eyes that said he had seen these theatrics before, 'was the Outlaw King. Or, as some of us have taken to calling him, the Forever King.'

Mithrid stared at where the air still wobbled where the king had vanished and narrowed her eyes in a scowl.

'Next!'

Somebody jostled her forwards, and the king, whatever they called him, was forgotten as Mithrid was swept back to the old witch and dragon.

'Meet her eyes, child,' rasped a woman standing by the witch's side. Mithrid swore she saw a tiny bird hiding in her matted hair.

Mithrid did as she was bid.

The witch leaned out of her chair, eyes pinched between skin as crinkled as walnuts. She hummed, louder and louder until she reached for Mithrid's hand. She looked down at her soot-stained skin, at the tattoos of feathers and serpent skins that hid beneath the muck.

'I...' said Mithrid, but she was already reaching.

Touching those ashen fingers was like putting a hand between a hammer and its anvil. She made no sound. Deaf were her ears. Black shadow clouded her eyes. Mithrid felt herself falling into a familiar void. As the crowd faded, her own voice held the last echo.

Not again.

CHAPTER 11
SKIN IN THE GAME

/ A Written will serve the Arka and the Arka only.
// A Written will never reveal their Book to another, nor allow it to be revealed.
/// A Written is forbidden to breed with Written, mage, or otherwise.
//// A Written shall not seek to use their powers against their fellow Arka.
/\ A Written will serve the Arkmages, the Undermage, the Magick Council, and the Arka with their life.
//\ A Written, like any Arka mage, is forbidden to consume the poison known as Nevermar.
///\ A Written, if their Book has taken their mind, shall face permanent exile or death.
////\ The penalty for breaking these rules is death by hanging, unless pardoned by the Magick Council.
THE RULES OF THE WRITTEN – UPDATED CHARTER, YEAR 815

The blades of wind clawed harmlessly at his armour and whined in frustration. Farden defied them recklessly, as he always did, standing alone with the point of his boots poking over the sheer, unguarded edge of the Frostsoar. Arms crossed against his fiery breastplate, without helmet and bare face to the elements, he stared out across his frozen world with narrowed eyes. Frost had already begun to gather in his eyebrows.

The huge gryphon lying at his side trilled musically. Farden shook his head and gently ruffled the wind-harried feathers of the beast's mane.

'Not now, Ilios,' he said softly.

The gryphon clacked his hooked beak before swiftly falling back into sleep. How jealous it made the mage.

Like Ilios, the mage visited the Frostsoar's peak to find peace. The others said there was peace to be found in solitude and silence, but Farden found the featureless swathe of ice, frozen earth, and mountain rock was a poor distraction for a busy mind. It was a vacant stage which he had no choice but to fill with his thoughts. Some days he managed to direct them into order and made sense of the riotous voices in his head. Other days, like that day, the stage might as well have been on fire for all the clarity it offered.

Distant thunder brought him welcome diversion, and Farden faced north, where the great Spine made a mockery of all the mountains to the south. The stark edifices blackened half the sky with ashen clouds and smoke. It was not thunder, just the mountains of the Spine of the World arguing with each other. Moments later, Farden felt the feeble tremor making its way up the tower. He eyed the faint splash of scarlet staining the clouds. Amongst the cold mountains of the Spine were the Roots: volcanoes that had burned since the dawn of Emaneska. Volcanoes the snowmads called the Emberteeth. One alone sat higher than its brethren: *Irminsul*, in Siren tongue.

The clang of a steel door spun him around. Modren emerged from the spike that towered above the Frostsoar's flat roof. He sounded like a forge bellows, breathing in great gasps of air. His shaved head was slick with sweat.

'You...' the undermage panted. He put his hands on his knees and spat on the frozen stone. '...bastard.'

'Good to see you, too, old friend.'

'Didn't want to take me with you? No. Lifts and stairs for Modren, is it? Fine,' he grumbled. The undermage collapsed to the stone and exhaled with an exasperated growl. 'Fuck me, we're getting too old for this work.'

Farden chuckled as he looked back to the Emberteeth.

Modren threw up his hands. 'Oh, excuse me. The *rest of us* are getting too old. The Forever King stays the same age.'

'You know I don't like that name. Call me Arkmage or nothing.'

'And you have yet to tell me why.'

Farden thumbed the scales of his Scalussen armour. 'Too much pressure in both those words. Pressure, I have enough of.'

'Don't we all.'

'Anybody hurt?'

'Ten dead, two almost so. Siren healers are tending to them. One of the assassins is still alive. She's being taken to the dungeons as we speak.'

Farden raised an eyebrow. 'It's been a while since we caught a live one. It might make up for the lack of news coming out of Krauslung.'

'Still no word from your blind spy?'

'Not for a year.' Farden paused to face the mage. The question had to be asked. Though recently questions produced more problems than they did answers. 'Why are you back so soon, Modren? Did pretending to be me not lure the Arka like we'd hoped?'

'Better than we'd hoped. An Arka contingent came chasing the moment I showed the fake armour in a tavern. A dozen mages and a daemon permanently removed.'

'Then what?' Farden could see by the wrinkle in Modren's lip that the news was the kind that stuck in one's craw. 'Don't torture me.'

Rummaging in his cloak, Modren threw a package on the stone between them: the cloth wrapping covered in dubious stains. Farden opened it with the toe of his boot and the help of the wind. A square, grisly patch of flesh lingered in the package.

Farden scowled at Modren.

'Turn it over.'

Farden had given up being squeamish at some point during childhood, in the vicious Written School of Manesmark. Spill enough guts, and a man tended to grow used to it. Farden did not dare to count the bodies of his past.

Farden flipped the flesh over, revealing grey skin on the brink of rotting. It was the rune tattooed into the skin that caught his eye. 'Is this real?'

'As you or I.'

'No trick?'

'Took it off an Arka mage. Officer of some kind.'

Farden crossed his arms once more and searched the sky for calm. A thin stream of steam escaped his nostrils as he growled deep within his chest. 'As if I didn't already have enough battles to fight.'

'This could tip the balance of the war if—'

Farden cut him off. 'I don't want to hear it. Where is that cutthroat?'

'In the dunge—'

Farden threw his cloak aside and seized the golden Weight hanging from his belt.

Modren 'Wait…'

The air crackled deafeningly as Farden folded into nothing and disappeared.

'…for me.'

With much dramatic heaving, Modren got to his feet. Warily, he eyed the flecks of people and smudges of houses far, far below. He wasn't as fearless as Farden when it came to heights.

'For fuck's sake,' he cursed, before heading back to the stairs.

'Where is the would-be assassin?' Farden demanded, before the healers had recovered from their fright. Half of them were still cowering on the stone, hands clasped to their ears and whispering to Thron for mercy.

'What in Emaneska do you think you are doing, using that Weight so frivolously?' came a rasping, chiding voice. 'You could have lopped some unfortunate's arm off with the shockwave. Or worse!'

Durnus came tapping his way down the corridor, slowly but surely. The years and his experiments with magick might have ravaged the man, but his ferocity refused to dim. His spring-ice eyes were wild, fangs bared. He had a retinue of generals with him: Written mage Inwick wore a stormy face, hands poised on her shortswords. Eyrum, the bear-sized, one-eyed Siren dominated the rest of the corridor.

'This is urgent, Durnus.'

'We are at war, Farden. Everything is urgent!'

Farden was not in the mood for wisdom, but for answers.

'Farden!' boomed the Siren, but the quivering healers had already pointed the way. Farden strode down the dark, damp corridor and followed the echoes of screams and cursing. In one of the larger cells they had dug into the bedrock of Scalussen he found her.

The Arka spy couldn't have been older than fifteen winters, yet she had the rage of two grown men. She spat and gnashed so vehemently her lips were covered with foam. She bit at anything that came close to her face. There came a clang as one of the guards was kicked in the groin. Armour wasn't just useful on the battlefield.

'Be still!' Farden commanded.

For a fleeting moment, the woman stopped thrashing and stopped to take in the armoured man standing before her. Realising who Farden was, she cackled and struggled all the harder.

'Be still, you bitch, or we'll put you out of your misery.'

Durnus' voice floated past his shoulder. 'She came here to kill or be killed, Farden, same as all the others who have snuck into this fortress. Death would be welcomed. What makes you think she is different from the others?'

'I don't,' Farden snapped. 'But as usual, I have little choice in the matter.' He thumped the grisly wad of cloth and flesh on her chest. 'When did your emperor start tattooing mages with spell runes? Speak!'

'Gods save us,' Durnus breathed in shock.

The woman just grinned through bloody teeth. 'Doomed! You're all doomed!'

Farden barely resisted the urge to forcibly remove them from her mouth. Even so, his fist hovered above the scrap of dead skin, poised far too close than was comfortable for his generals. The seething woman locked eyes with the mage and dared him to strike.

'Farden,' Durnus spoke, softly. 'She won't tell you even if she knows.'

The mage snatched up the skin. 'Lock her up on her own. No light. Give her a month and then toss her with the others in the Cold Dark. She does not deserve death. Let her wither away in a dank hole beneath the ice.'

Her sentence delivered, the woman went wild with panic. Poor justice, perhaps, but any justice in this world was a welcome thing.

'Kill me, you craven traitors!' she cried, before she was muzzled and gagged.

In the silence of the corridor, Farden stared between the Siren, the mage, and Durnus. 'What?'

'Should have killed her,' Inwick growled.

Farden waggled the rancid flesh in front of her. 'As briefly satisfying as that would be, if this is an omen of what Malvus is planning, we have greater problems. Summon the Old Dragon.'

Once again, Farden departed at the speed of an arrow, forcing the others to chase after him through crowded corridors. The city was becoming so crammed since the Frostsoar had begun to take on refugees.

Stair by stair, corridor by corridor hewn from black rock, he wound up into the Frostsoar, listening to the shrill bell ringing somewhere beyond the walls. He climbed until he reached a great hall that the others affectionately called the Wolf's Hall. Farden refused to have an actual throne – he never sat down long enough to make any bloody use of one – but he had settled for the necessity of a meeting hall.

It was a stark affair with no trimmings of a king in sight. A black granite table, carved into an intricate map of Emaneska, occupied the floor. A set of golden scales perched upon it. Around the hall, where stalactites and stalagmites met, intricate statues had been carved into their pillars. Their stone glowed with an unusual yellow light: a magick of the original and ancient Scalussen smiths that had yet to be explained. It was one of Durnus' great irritations as a scholar.

One entire wall of the Wolf's Hall was missing, forming a dragon door. Steel shutters stood like accordions on either side. A small balcony with no railings extended past the sheer sides of the Frostsoar. Scrapes and gouges decorated the flagstones.

When the others found Farden, he was standing with his shoulders arched and his head low, poring over the markings of the tabletop. Modren had caught up, and one by one, the mages, vampyre, and Siren took their places around the table.

'Well?' asked the undermage, when the hush became unwieldy.

Farden held up a finger as a gust of frozen air swept into the hall. The featureless blue of the sky beyond was broken as a giant golden dragon rose into view. He shimmered as though his scales were liquid metal. Once his claws had seized the balcony, the dragon tucked his wings back and strode inwards.

If there were any true king in the room, it was the Old Dragon: Towerdawn, heir to the Siren Remnant. Not only did his gold scales scream opulence and royalty, the memories of centuries resided beneath his skull and spines. With every clack of his scimitar claws on the stone, every ripple of muscle or crunch of his armour, every moment the unblinking ferocity in his eyes roamed the hall, Farden felt like a jester in a king's costume.

'Old Dragon,' he announced with a bow.

Towerdawn lowered his spiny head to the stone. 'Farden, my friend. It has been many weeks since you called a council.'

'It has indeed, but that was until our good undermage found *this* in his travels.' Farden cast the scrap of skin on the table. 'Carved it off the back of a mage in Hâlorn. And I'll be the first to say this is one fucked up gift you've brought us, Modren.'

He shrugged. 'They say it's the thought that counts.'

While Farden ground his gauntlets into the stone, Towerdawn settled onto his haunches. 'Spell runes. How long has Emperor Malvus been meddling with such magick?'

Durnus was peering at the skin, and by his slatted eyes, he was not convinced. 'Does it matter? If this is all Malvus can achieve—' Durnus rapped the table with his cane '—poorly-replicated runes without context, then we have no need to worry.'

'And what if it *isn't* all he can achieve?' growled Farden.

Eyrum thumped the handle of his great axe on the floor, bringing them all to silence. 'You all speak too quickly and without explanation. Why does this flesh have you all so concerned? Explain.'

Durnus held up a hand, claiming the air. 'You are, of course, aware that Farden, Modren, and Inwick have Books upon their backs? Tattooed spellbooks?'

Eyrum grunted. 'Of course.'

'Then you will know these Books are highly dangerous, due to both the power they give to their bearer as well as to anyone foolish enough to look at them.'

'Mhmm,' the Siren growled, sharing a glance with Farden. He knew very well. The first time he and the mage had met in Nelska, decades before, a Siren healer had proven stupid enough to read Farden's Book and turned his own mind to mush.

'Up until now, Malvus has not marched for fear of Farden's power. This crude attempt before us shows our good emperor is trying to recreate the power of the Written and to level the battlefield,' Durnus explained.

'Albeit poorly. Still no match for us,' Modren muttered, that old pride of the Written kindled for the first time in what felt like a decade. Farden forced a smile.

'With no Book in his grasp, Malvus has nothing to work from. He is clutching at reeds with this! These rough runes add *some* magick skill, perhaps, but nothing like a true Book,' Durnus explained.

Towerdawn settled onto his haunches, stretching his foreclaws. 'What would it take for Malvus to recreate a full Book? His own Written.'

'Another Written. And none exist outside the fortress walls,' answered Farden. Only ten of the Written kind were left in Emaneska after the Last War's carnage. 'That is the reason Inwick and I have stayed behind the walls, and why Modren alone acted as my decoy.'

The dragon fixed the mage with a mesmerising stare of swirling gold. 'Are you sure of that?'

A contemplative silence fell. For Farden, the years stretched far into a dark distance he didn't want to explore. Unsure, but unwilling to cause concern, he bit his tongue and stayed silent, guarding his mind against the Old Dragon.

Durnus was not convinced. 'Even if Malvus had access to a Book, the skill required to recreate it is considerable. The only individual capable of creating Written was the Scribe, and he died before all of this began. Not to mention that half of all those who underwent his Ritual died from the strain or went mad. That was forty years ago, when the magick of this world did not seethe and bubble as it does now.'

'Even without a Book, Malvus will kill dozens of mages trying,' the Old Dragon added.

Eyrum flexed his wisdom. 'And if enough of these mages survive, they could turn the tide against us when Malvus at last arrives at our gates.'

Farden growled deep in his throat. 'I think it's time we speak to our old spy in Krauslung. Lady Jeasin.'

'Jeasin?' Modren looked appalled. 'Why in Hel would you do that, after what she did? She turned her back on Scalussen years ago when she failed to warn of us the Kserak Massacre.'

The mage flinched at the name. It had been two years, but his failure was still raw, no matter how effortless it was to blame Jeasin. 'I remember well enough what she did, Modren. That is why I will go speak to her myself. With Malvus meddling with tattooed runes, I need to have a pair of eyes in the Arkathedral now more than ever.' Farden replied. 'Even blind ones.'

'You cannot go!' Durnus looked horrified. 'Your Book is the most dangerous of all.'

'It'll be the last place he'll suspect me to go. He thinks I'm skulking in the wilds. It's time for the so-called king to leave his castle.' Farden shuddered at using the moniker of "king". That was their moniker for him, not his.

'Want company?' Modren asked.

'Now that you mention—'

Modren clapped his hands together. 'Good, because you can take Inwick. I have other matters to attend to. Namely a wife.'

Inwick snorted. 'Be sure you reach Elessi before the rumours of your return do. You know she won't tolerate dallying.'

'Not even war is a good enough excuse any more.' Modren sighed.

Farden clasped the undermage's hand, and the black, key-shaped tattoo on Modren's lower forearm and wrist sparked briefly with white light. Farden felt the burn beneath his own vambraces, where his own keys resided.

'Don't die,' Modren bade him as he quickly exited the room. 'Not again.'

Farden rolled his eyes. Inwick did not look too enthused about journeying south, but she had never once turned down an order. Not since the Last War. If there was anyone that Farden trusted besides Modren to not curl up and die, it was Inwick. The second to last Written the Scribe had ever forged. A woman so vicious with her swords, he swore she had sabrecat blood.

'Travelling by Weight?' she asked.

'The helbeasts will sense its echo,' Farden unhooked the heavy disk from his belt and tossed it to Durnus. The years might have ravaged him recently, but the old man still caught the thing in one hand without a blink.

'We'll need somebody fast,' Farden said. He turned to Towerdawn. The Old Dragon was perched on the balcony and poised to soar.

'Surely not,' he rumbled. 'She is too unpredictable. She would likely leave you in Krauslung if only to follow a feather on the wind.'

The situation might have been dire, but sure enough, a grin snuck across Farden's face. Any excuse to ride a dragon was a good excuse, even when it's the Mad Dragon.

'We'll meet you in the Dragonfields,' replied the mage.

Beyond the rebuilt city of Scalussen, closer to the Spine where the heat of the Emberteeth thawed the glaciers, lay the Dragonfields. The earth there was black soil and pumice. Meltwater poured in colossal waterfalls that steamed with volcano heat. Above the pockmarked crags, dragons of all colours soared on the hot thermals, and roared in unison with the thunder of the distant volcanoes.

Thin air snapped as the four bodies emerged from the Weight's spell. Durnus remained its master, stowing it deep within his robes. Together, they trudged across the scorched earth and deeper into the Dragonfields.

A number of roosting dragons poked their heads from their nests and caves at the sounds of passers-by. In honour, they roared to Eyrum in their own language, and called to the others in the Commontongue. With so few survivors of their kind, surviving another day was always a cause for cheer. Farden greeted those he recognised. Ever since he had washed up on the shores of Nelska as a young, shipwrecked mage, his fascination with dragonkind had never waned. Only deepened.

Though many dragons spent their time guarding or mingling in Frostsoar, it was in this valley of ash the surviving dragons of Nelska had made their new breeding grounds. Unlike everything south of them, the dragons had prospered. Far from interference, dragons had laid eggs for the first time in decades. Such eggs were kept in deep and roasting hot caves, and no two-legged creature was ever allowed near them. Not Farden. Not any Siren. Not even the dragon-riders themselves. Dragons tended their eggs constantly and in private. They guarded them even more fiercely now that fewer than a hundred of Nelska's kind remained in Emaneska.

Amongst the spindle crags and huge, scaly bodies, Farden looked for the Old Dragon or his Siren Queen Nerilan. Eyrum trailed behind, speaking with riders and other Sirens that lived in stubby towers amongst the rocks. Durnus tottered about amongst the shale and dark sand with Inwick.

Once they had arrived at the Old Dragon's usual perching spot: a great platform of stone, steel, and rimewood, they found Queen Nerilan sprawled there alone in a sea of cushions. Though his favour with Siren Queens had historically been severely lacking, Farden bowed to Nerilan all the same.

'Beat him again, did we?' It was somewhat of a silent game, for Towerdawn to race Farden's Weight.

'Once again, magick is cheating,' grumbled Nerilan, as she pointed a single finger upwards.

The golden shape descended from the clouds. Towerdawn flared his wings barely a dozen feet before the ground. The rush of air threatened to topple them all. The dragon dropped to his platform with a thud that rattled Farden's armour.

The Old Dragon lowered his head and Nerilan arose to run a hand along his snout. The queen bore a glaive with a curved and hooked blade, and rider's armour of steel scales shaped like feathers. An obsidian circlet sat upon her brow. Her scales, too, were golden, the only Siren to bear such colours. Her slate hair, slicked back by wind and some Siren concoction, only served to make their colour more obvious.

'Malvus is creating Written, I hear.'

Farden was well aware of the mind connection between rider and dragon. It made it no less infuriating. Farden had also found that Sirens, given some of their dragons' ability to read hearts if not minds, appreciated their information served simply and honestly. 'Possibly, Queen. That is why I need to go to Krauslung to find out more. Stop him, if I can.'

'Dire news indeed,' spoke the Old Dragon.

'And you want the Mad Dragon?' Nerilan asked, mouth halfway to a bemused grin. 'Why bother? She is sullen. Distracted. Barely listens to her kin, never mind humans.'

Farden shrugged. 'She listens to me.'

Nerilan looked personally offended by that claim.

'We share a certain… outlook.'

Durnus waggled a finger. 'And there is none faster without a Weight or quickdoor.'

'I would not repeat that around Ilios,' said Towerdawn.

Nerilan threw up her hands in exasperation. 'Thron save us.'

'Thron save us indeed,' growled Towerdawn, as he raised his spiny head to the sky and canopied his wings. His voice split the quiet of the fields. Dragonspeak always sounded like a guttural roar to Farden, but somehow, they constituted words to the big beasts.

It took barely a moment for something iridescent to dart between the Siren towers. Farden shook his head, knowing better than to give the damnable creature the satisfaction of applause.

Only when he heard the clomp of heavy claws in the dust did he turn, finding a dragon whose scales couldn't decide whether they were blue or green. The dragon was big for a creature so comparatively young. Farden knew she had fifty years out of her egg at least, but that still made her a juvenile.

Fleetstar had the iridescent patterns of her mother, Brightshow. Farden missed that dragon dearly. Often, he saw shades of her in Fleetstar's rows of needle teeth and her diamond scales. Her eyes held the fire of youth, but behind the freneticism, there was wisdom. Dragons suffuse their knowledge into their eggs before they hatch, and Brightshow had given her daughter all she knew. That meant the memories of meeting Farden almost thirty years ago.

'What do you bloody want now?' she muttered, one eye twitching. She was highly fond of the foulness of the Commontongue, a habit that Nerilan held Admiral Roiks personally responsible for.

Farden smirked. Mad, they called her, but there was a streak of something in Fleetstar that was like looking into a mirror of old. 'A good sleep and peace and quiet, as always,' the mage replied, stepping close to the dragon until he could taste the sulphur in his own breath.

'Sounds as boring as staring at shit,' said the dragon.

'Doesn't it just? But tonight, we need answers to difficult questions. And we need them quickly.'

'Quicker than these old goldscales?' boasted Fleetstar, making Towerdawn and several other dragons grumble or put claws over eyes.

'A moment, Farden?' asked the Old Dragon.

Farden walked aside to take council with the golden king. 'I do not have to remind you of our circumstances, do I, mage?' he whispered. 'Our kind are few, and if you have your war, we are likely to be fewer still. I will not have my dragons idly wasted simply for speed and convenience.'

'You should know by now I'm only careless with my own life.' The mage bowed low, wiping his smirk away. 'Fear not. I'll look after her, Old Dragon.'

Towerdawn's sinuous neck stretched over Farden as he brought his giant snout close to Fleetstar's.

'Keep him safe, young wyrm. That is all that is required. We have not come this far to lose our precious young to carelessness. You will obey Farden as if he were I. Understood?'

Fleetstar blinked solemnly, even though she watched a snow hawk far above.

Once a saddle was fetched and strapped between her crest of blue spines, the dragon extended her wing as if casting a giant blanket wide. Farden's boots found the ridges in her skeleton as he scaled her thick hide.

Inwick joined him somewhat hesitantly. No matter how many years and missions passed, the Written had never grown used to dragons. Whatever magick kept such beasts and birds in thin air, she had no desire to learn. She had barely finished muttering an old argument about humans and why the gods hadn't blessed them with wings when Fleetstar exploded from the earth.

Three stomach-lurching beats of her wings, and the dragon was darting through the towers of vertical rock.

Farden drank in the cold northern air rushing though his visor. Though his mission was of war, soiled in peril, he had learned the value of enjoying these moments of simplicity, when all the toil and concern of fighting an empire, of saving the world once more, could melt away. The mage blew a deep and meaningful breath, focusing solely on holding tight to the saddle's pommel, and watching the frosted ground shrink beneath him. The war could wait.

CHAPTER 12
A WAR TO END ALL

The Dromfangar Fealty was a dire day for Emaneska, taking place amongst the ashes of the Last War, before the very tears had dried on our faces. Malvus Barkhart, as the self-proclaimed leader of the Arka, demanded court with Grand Duke Wodehallow, who had consolidated power in Albion, and Saker, Lord of the Wind and Lost Clans. There, desecrating a burial ground with their mere presence, they made their pact. Malvus would rule, but for the promise of greater power. Something even fifteen years later he has yet to do. Only the Arka have flourished. All else dwindles in Malvus' shadow.
FROM 'THE NEW EMANESKA', BY THE EXILED SAGE OLE WRUM, YEAR 920

It was not the pathetic mewling of the wounded and weakened soldiers shivering on their knees before him.

It was not the rude intrusion of the daemons, nor their unannounced swagger.

It was not the fact that he had already spent an entire day swatting such problems like pestering saltflies.

It was the filth smearing across the perfect, milk-white floors of the Marble Copse that vexed Malvus Barkhart. Blood, bog mud, and sweat glistened in dirty streaks. The daemons leaked ash and cinders and came with a sulphurous stench that Malvus had spent twenty years failing to grow accustomed to. Of course, it was not the purity of the expensive marble that truly concerned him. He was not some boarding house madam asking every visitor to wipe their boots. It was the respect. Or the distinct lack thereof.

Emperor Malvus, politic as always, let his anger burn privately beneath his vaguely curious exterior while he studied the three bodies the daemons had brought him.

Pitiful, was his first impression. Their armour was either broken or missing entirely. Each was caked in mud, both wet and dry, and bore some wound or another. Accidentally or on purpose, the men had been dumped before the glow of the Blazing Throne in order of consciousness. The man on the left was slowly forming a puddle of black blood beneath him. The woman in the middle was either in a state of blinking or wincing at the vicious burn across her neck and collar. The man on the far right was awake enough to be mightily afraid.

Malvus stared at the marks of rank on his neck. Three red tallies, branded by a salamander's tongue. A mage. One of his runed mages, at that.

'Speak,' the emperor ordered.

'The Forev—' began the man, before being elbowed in the ribs by the woman.

'The *what*?' Malvus glared. The nickname was a thorn in his palm.

'The *Outlaw* King, Imperial Majesty. Have mercy on him, please. His mind is addled. We have not slept, only run. We came here as fast as the wind would carry us to deliver the news to you.'

'The traitor destroyed our entire company,' the woman croaked. 'Malvus looked to the daemons. Though each daemon in their pack towered over the Imperial Guard, one beast alone dominated the room. Prince Gremorin. *Orion's Shadow*. His ashen skin, veined with red, bristled with spines. They quivered as he heaved with breath, leaking smoke from his serpent's mouth. Above his head, a circlet of fire hovered, slowly rotating. By the shade of red in Gremorin's four eyes, Malvus could tell the daemon prince was deeply vexed. However, Malvus had no idea how three soldiers could cause him so much insult.

Gremorin did not speak, but his lieutenant, Hokus, confirmed their story instead. 'They did not flee from us when we caught them on the border,' he snarled.

'What news?'

'The entire Company of Fenris is… er, gone, Your Majesty,' spoke the man, shivering relentlessly. 'We were waiting on another company, east of the cliff-town of Coalscry. Captain Larsness and his daemon envoy. They were supposed to meet us but never did.'

What sounded like distant marching proved to be Gremorin growling.

'Captain Svan took his rebel-dressed mages to raid Hâlorn's coast. Died there, we was told. Mage Dromm was in charge when he came back. Had some recruits with him. We was in the middle of testin' them when the Outlaw King 'imself ambushed our camp in broad daylight. Came with a dragon, too. We're all that survived!'

'Lies!' Malvus spat. 'My spies tell me the Outlaw King has not left the north in years.'

'Truth,' Gremorin spoke, the sound like oaks being ripped asunder. He pointed to a pair of daemons lurking behind him, Baltharad and Malphet, if Malvus wasn't mistaken.

'My kin went to the camp in search of our dead brother. We found none alive.'

It was General Toskig, a troll of a man encased in emerald armour, who spoke up. 'We continue to underestimate Farden, Your Imper—'

The emperor's fist collided with the marble of the throne so hard he thought he had broken a bone. He hid the pain well. 'Do not speak his name!' Malvus barked. He could feel the heat in his cheeks and forehead. 'Not in this chamber. Not in this city. Not in this empire. Only *I* may utter it. You, Toskig, should know better.'

The general's eyes slipped back to their vacant, military stare. 'A lapse in concentration, Majesty.'

Malvus watched him for a while before seeking Lady Jeasin's silent counsel from halfway across the Marble Copse. As always, the blind woman was somehow staring straight at him. Her face was dour, one shade from boredom, but Malvus knew her too well. Where Toskig leaned toward mercy and caution, she could be counted on to be as unflinching and remorseless as he. For all her failures, he could count on her to keep his fist iron and his mind true. Her face was a shade from expressionless, but even so, Malvus caught the slightest shake of her head.

'Failure,' the emperor uttered, making the survivors flinch, 'cannot be tolerated. It must be bred out. Stamped out. You call yourselves brave survivors, eager to deliver me warning? I see you for what you are: Deserters. Liars. Traitors.'

Malvus got to his feet, ignoring the crunch in his hip, the ever-present reminder of age. In the constant light of the flaming throne behind him, he cast a long shadow over the survivors. 'Prince Gremorin,' he said, making the daemon look up. 'A gift. Consider these three meagre compensation for your dead kin.'

Gremorin and his daemons didn't allow the survivors to emit barely more than a squeal before they descended upon them, ripping souls from bodies before fighting over the bones and torn limbs.

Malvus stayed standing. He fumed; his eyes locked on the spatters of blood. He raised a finger for quiet, and then pressed hard on his lips as if trying to hold back the flood of anger.

With much restraint, he managed to grind out some words. 'Do you not have lairs of your own for such grotesque behaviour? Instead of soiling my throne room with your FILTH!'

The flood had broken the barrier. The echoes of Malvus' yell brought the daemons to a standstill. Their eyes flashed dangerously.

Gremorin, caring little for blood, approached the Blazing Throne in three great strides. The golden imperial guard lowered their lances, skittish at the size of the beast looming over them. Toskig rested a hand on the hilt of his great sword.

'Lairs, we have. What little and few you have awarded us. You forget our pact, Malvus. We built you this empire.'

Malvus snarled, showing the daemon prince the whorl of a scar that decorated his palm. Burns tended to be the most common side effect of shaking hands with a daemon. Besides being betrayed by one.

'Do I, Gremorin? Two decades might have passed but I remember it well. I remember your kind being defeated in the Last War, forced to crawl into the wilds like whipped dogs. I remember you coming to me. Offering partnership, power. I remember giving you a space in this world instead of letting Farden and his virtuous kind hunt you down. I think it is you, who forgets. How many does that make of your kind now? Fifty? Not enough to take this empire from me, I think, let alone control it. No human would follow you, Prince.'

The average person, had they not already quailed in the sulphurous presence of the prince of daemons, might have quailed then: a pole's reach from Gremorin's fangs and fire-lit eyes, enshrouded in the smoke of his wings. Even the lances levelled between the daemon and emperor trembled.

Gremorin withdrew, much to the muttering of his brothers. Dragging their bloody morsels with them, they stalked from the Marble Copse and left a foul trail behind them. Before the great golden doors were shut, Gremorin trained a scythe of a claw at the emperor. 'You promised us war.'

War. The daemon's echoes ricocheted about the vacuous hall, taunting Malvus. *A war to end all.* The very words he had spoken when their pact had been forged upon Dromfangar's wastes. A war that had taken twenty years to start. There were few in Emaneska, in the firmament of stars or Hel beneath, who were more frustrated than Malvus.

In a whirl of rage, Malvus descended from the throne and screamed at the closest pair of guards. 'Clean this foul stench up before I return!'

Malvus stamped his way through a pool of crimson, leaving a grisly print in his wake. Where Lady Jeasin swept across the marble gracefully with no more than a whisper from her silk and peridot dress, Toskig clomped after his emperor like a doting hound, despite his age. Malvus might have loathed the man for delivering him nothing but problems and ill news every day, but at least he bore respect. Even if it was pretence, at least the man was loyal enough to pretend.

The boar of a man wore his usual face of unimpressed thunder. Acting bodyguard, he marched ahead of the emperor, opening doors and checking every corridor even despite the constant presence of imperial guardsmen. The gold and green-clad guards lined the opulent marble corridors of the Arkathedral like doors along a street. They came to attention as they passed; a constant breaking wave of rattling armour. White hammers, set in pearl, shone upon their breastplates

Malvus would have called it excessive had it not been for the spies and would-be assassins that once dared to infiltrate his imperial court. It had been marginally inconvenient hanging the entire of his court, but at least it had made for quite the display. Malvus had them strung like festival lanterns throughout the city for weeks.

At a stout doorway, Malvus snapped his fingers at Jeasin, making her startle. 'Leave us, Jeasin. I've told you; this is not for your ears. Ready my chambers. Have Master Findling send his Paraian whores. Fresh this time!'

Lady Jeasin grumbled but knew well enough not to argue. She slipped away, leaving Malvus and Toskig to wind deeper into the myriad levels of the Arkathedral. Leaving daylight behind, they took a corridor deep into the mountain rock the fortress laid its foundations on.

The screams came before the smell. Howls of madness and pain filled the stuffy air, garnished with the stink of shit-buckets and fear. There was no other smell like it. The guards standing sentry at the next few doors all wore masks. Several had wool stuffed into their ears.

When Malvus and Toskig came to the limits of the burrowing tunnel, they stood before a long wall and a selection of doors, each guarding a cell of stone and each built with barred windows and a steel door marked with runes. A variety of screams, cries for mercy, and moans emanated from the cells. Nervous huddles of attendants hovered in coffin-shaped alcoves. They held towels of linen, some fresh and pale like virgin snow, others soiled with blood and shit.

As Malvus was taking breath to address them, one of the middle doors flew open, unleashing a hail of pained screeches. Hands slick with black ink and crimson, a man tottered out of the dim candlelight of the cell, shivering violently.

'I can't... I can't,' the scribe was whispering, staring hard at the long whalebone needle in his hands. He tore the thick plugs of candle wax from his ears as if they did nothing for him. The scribe was reaching for a towel when a pale, human hand reached from the dark of the cell and seized him by the throat. Panic ensued, but not before a succinct crunch could be heard as windpipe was mashed into bone.

'Guards!' barked Toskig. Armoured figures streamed from the shadows. Spears were thrust into the cell as if the man inside were a caged boar. His manic, desperate screaming outlived him, echoing down the corridor, seeking witnesses but finding nothing but plugged ears.

The scribe was dead. He lay on the floor with a surprised look stuck on his dead face. His hands were gnarled like oak branches.

'Take them both away. Clean up that cell,' Toskig ordered.

Malvus took his hands from the pair of knives hidden within his grand emperor's robes. With the guards paying close attention, he began a tour of the barred windows. The first three held shivering, seething specimens, their shoulders or arms swathed in bandages and poultices. Two women and a man. Their eyes glinted like feral cats between their cries for freedom.

In the next cell, Malvus saw little fruit of his labours. One man was scraping at the walls even though his fingertips were already worn past the nail. The next, another young fellow yelled streams of unconscious madness between racing around his cell. The rest lay splayed or huddled in their cots, dead or dying. Only one soul was currently undergoing the tattooing process.

The bars were cold against Malvus' nose and cheeks, but he needed to watch. A shirtless woman sat upon a wooden stool with her back to the emperor. Three runes, puckered and scarred red, already decorated her spine and left shoulder. A scribe, sweating like a waterfall, bent double over her skin. His eyes flashed from the scroll laying propped open upon his lap and the needle in his hand. He had to hold himself by the wrist to keep from trembling. An inch of runic script had already been etched into her back. The woman was taut with pain; it was obvious from the cords in her neck, and the clenching of her fists every time the needle stabbed her skin.

'Promising,' Toskig breathed over Malvus' shoulder.

The emperor flapped a hand heavy with rings at the general, shooing him back. 'Personal space, Toskig! By the Copse, you have a nerve,' he tutted. 'Promising indeed, but hardly enough to face *him*.'

A scribe had edged close to their conversation. He sucked his teeth to announce himself, thinking it his place to speak up. 'Almost two hundred have undergone the needle, Majesty. Almost half survive. More, if these survive the night. Your runed are growing in number.'

Malvus nodded appreciatively.

Through the searing pain, the woman had heard their discussion. She turned to face the emperor, showing him not just the tears of effort rolling down her face and torso, but the ferocity in her eyes. The determination. Malvus had little doubt the mage would survive.

A scribe hovered annoyingly close. 'This one veritably bleeds magick. Three runes and no adverse effects. No madness. No ruptures. No clawing out of the eyes. Always nice.' His timid chuckle died away with his spineless smile.

'Her name?'

The woman spoke for herself. 'Corcoran, Majesty.'

Despite wincing every time there came a lunatic's howl from the neighbouring cell, Toskig seemed impressed. 'We need more mages like her.'

Malvus matched the mage's glare until the pain stole her attention. 'We don't just need more, General. We need more power. These runes are not even half-measures.'

The scribe moved closer to poke eagerly at the door, but Malvus batted his hand away. One of his gold rings drew blood.

'T—This is the first full spell we've attempted, Your Majesty,' the scribe stammered.

'It is not enough!'

Malvus bellowed so loudly, even the experiments fell silent for a moment. The scribe was leaning back as if a gale threatened to topple him. The emperor could have sworn tears were welling up in those wide eyes.

'I need a *Written*, not some botched attempt!'

'B—But, Sire, as we've said for years, we can't hope to create a Written without a Book. That secret died with the original Scribe, decades ago in the Manesmark fire—'

Malvus shoved the man into the grip of two guards. 'I know my history!' he snarled.

A moment was spared for the attendees to drag the body of a dead mage out of another cell. His veins were black as ink, swollen, and his eyes so bloodshot they looked burst.

'A convenient vacancy,' Malvus chuckled. 'Lock him in there. Have him tattooed like the rest.'

'What? I... Your Majesty!' the scribe babbled, before realising the order was for the guards. He was summarily thrown into the cell with a garbled wail. The door was already locked by the time he threw himself against it in panic. 'I have no magick in my blood! It would be poison! Please!' he begged.

'Precisely.'

Malvus dusted his hands in front of the bars before sweeping away. The echo of his boots was rapid. Remorseless. He spared not a glance as the man howled his name.

'I cannot abide complacency. Can you, General?'

'Not in the slightest, Majesty.'

'And yet the daemons continue to accuse me of it.' Malvus threw open the door, finding bright sunlight again. He whirled on Toskig before the general had a chance to blink. 'Do you agree, General? Do you think I fear marching north?'

Toskig visibly quailed, which was an amusing sight for a man so large and with a history as barbaric as his. He snapped heels together and stared out over the valley of Krauslung beyond the windowpane. 'No, Majesty. The army is not ready. The runed mages are only a beginning. You have told me many times that you will know when it is time to put an end to the Outlaw King. Gremorin is merely impatient.'

Malvus let his glare soften. He even went so far as to reward the general with a smile. 'You have learned to be diplomatic in your old age, Toskig. Such balanced words.'

The emperor joined him in regarding the city. The ever-present smoke obscured much of Krauslung, but a number of spires and rooftops reached for the sun. Their emerald pennants and weathervanes hung slack and still. Where the sea met the city's edges, bright blue waters sparkled.

'It is not I that is afraid. Farden refuses to march against Krauslung. *He* has forced *my* hand. Forced me to harvest the wilds of magick and soldiery. But I am tired of skirmishing on the borders, chasing that mage and his dragons. Tired of an empire that still refuses to obey me. Tired of growing old with waiting,' Malvus growled his words. 'This was not the future I saw,' he breathed, thinking back to his youth, and the painted pebbles a seer with one arm had read for him. A fortune full of power and promise. No road as long and as treacherous as this. His darkest doubts told him he had strayed from the path of fate. Ruined it in some way, and yet beneath that foolish uncertainty, he knew it was Farden's doing.

Malvus pressed his fist against the glass, ignoring the ache of his arthritic joints, the constant rasp of phlegm in his chest. 'I would have my war tomorrow, Toskig. Understand that. I will have us obliterate Scalussen and put an end to Farden's fable once and for all, as I am supposed to. An empire with no enemies is a contented empire. Then, they will not bicker.

Then they will see me as their true emperor. That day will come, but only when we are prepared.'

Toskig grunted in agreement. That was about the height of the enthusiasm Malvus ever managed to squeeze from him. 'I hold no doubts, Majesty. You need not explain your mind to me.'

And yet, Malvus felt as though he must. Without a voice to speak its thoughts, the mind knotted into a festering tangle. The knot in Malvus' mind had been growing for far too long.

'Imperial Majesty!'

Malvus felt a fist in his gut as he heard the messenger's shouts come clattering down the hallway. As he waited for the lad to sprint the distance, Malvus wondered how much of the Arkathedral servants he could execute in one day without making the rest flee.

'Imperial Maje—'

'What?' Malvus bellowed.

The lad deflated like a torn wineskin. 'I... there, er... another riot, Imperial Majesty. In the Gutters!' panted the messenger. 'Message from Watch Captain Thornss... something.'

Toskig answered on the emperor's behalf. 'Have the Street Legions haul them away and thrown in the stocks!'

'That won't work this time, General, sir.'

'You presume to know tactics, boy?'

'There are many of them, Imperial Majesty. There are barricades...'

The rest of the lad's calamitous words faded behind him as Malvus began marching alone. Toskig and the messenger darted after him, but the emperor ignored them. He thought solely of the fire he'd seen in the young mage's eyes. The unquestionable determination.

Malvus knuckles popped he squeezed his hands so tightly.

Krauslung had pushed and pushed him. From the moment he had taken the Arka throne, they had opposed him. At first, they called for the end of war and mayhem. They wanted peace, and Malvus had given it to them – he'd banned the root of all chaos. *Magick.*

The ungrateful peasants were outraged. They called magick a right. They were furious the magick markets had been ripped apart. Outraged by the fines and punishments imposed by the new city watch. Magick for all, they had protested. When their threats had fallen on deaf ears, they had rioted for days, turning street after street to ash and rubble until Malvus had every ringleader publicly drowned in the port. The outrage and protest had died with every last bubble.

Yet somehow, though the masses now cheered the emperor's name, the unrest had continued, suppurating in the city's darkest corners. It did not matter that under Malvus' reign, the Arka had become history's most powerful empire. It did not matter how the city glowed or how the foreign ships queued to dock or how many leagues the Arka armies conquered, there were those that still resented him. Pamphlets with tales of the Outlaw King would mysteriously spread through the streets. Guard captains vanished mysteriously, turning up flayed or hanged. Unlawful shrines or god-cults were found beneath sewer grates. And, when the outrage had built to fever pitch once more, some idiot plucked the courage to start a resistance. Each time, Malvus had them put down by fire, blade, or arrow.

This particular uprising seemed different.

In the centre of the city, past the gleaming rows of merchant and noble houses, where the main concerns were poetry and wine, where the valley and streets met their deepest point, lay the Gutters. Krauslung had always been known as a hive of debauchery and sin, even before Malvus ruled, and the Gutters were its sordid core. There, tall buildings of wood and stone leant conspiratorially close to each other. Their architecture gave the narrow streets their name, for they ran with effluence of all kinds, but mostly the kind that walked on two legs.

In the absence of the magick trade, businessmen had turned to brothels, smoke-houses, gambling dens, and lewd theatres. It was where morals came to die and where coin flowed faster than the salted winds that flowed through the narrow streets. It was where people came to forget or to be forgotten.

An entire neighbourhood had been barricaded off with tables, doors, and sharpened stakes. At the centre of the makeshift fort stood a tall and crooked tavern of old black beams and white plaster. Like the other buildings, it had been boarded up and fortified. Their balconies bristled with people holding window shutter shields and rusty blades, mostly the kitchen kind.

Standing upon an armoured pedestal behind a wall of shields, the emperor's gaze roamed across the crowds squeezed behind the barricade. For a brief moment, recognition flooded him as he spotted a youthful face and sand-blonde hair. The face was lost immediately. Malvus bent an ear to their chanting.

'No rest 'til justice!
'Down with the Blazing Throne!'
'We want peace!'

Malvus ground his teeth together, forcing a smile. 'Forwards,' he ordered.

The pedestal was drawn by a throng of persnippen: great two-legged birds covered in pink, leaflike scales instead of feathers. They stood taller than a human, with a dark leather head strapped around their heads and sinewy necks. They looked like serfs tending a field. As their minders tugged their reins, they rasped like clogged drains.

Malvus adjusted his bejewelled crown as the pedestal jolted forward on iron wheels. On either side of it marched a fresh complement of a dozen runed mages. Like the imperial guards, they wore full battle armour: gold and emerald, outshining the grubby Street Legion soldiers and the fat, leather-bound city watch who lined the barricades and streets for half a mile around.

The sun had fallen behind the western peak, Hardja, casting shadow and lighting fires amongst the fort of uprising.

General Toskig stood amidst the shield-wall. He levelled his greatsword at the dissenters. 'Who speaks for you?' he challenged.

'Nobody!' screeched an eager woman, whose face and hair were painted the most lurid shade of red.

A man with overgrown hair as crimson as blood stood tall amongst the crowd, presumably on some kind of crate. 'We are a collective, Your Imperial Majesty! We bow to no leader. We stand for justice, peace, and freedom of magick! We stand here in protestation of your laws, Emperor. The laws that are bleeding the life from our cities, our people! Crime runs rife! The mages and Street Legions rule the streets with an iron fist, unchecked. Those who aren't forced into your armies or mage schools are beaten or taken hostage every day. We are told of victories in the north when strangers bring us tales of defeat and lies. We have had enough, Emperor! We demand fair rule! We demand peace and justice! We demand the chance to be heard!'

The more the man talked, the more animated he became. The crowds growled and shook their fists to his words, but once he had run out of those, an awful pause hung over the streets.

All eyes turned to the emperor. The crowds of traitors fidgeted nervously. Malvus felt the air grow hot as his mages let their magick swell.

'No,' Malvus replied.

'No?' The ringleader crowed and the crowds began to seethe anew.

Malvus loathed repeating himself. 'No,' he replied, smirking in a way that roused angry shouts. 'You have no power over me. You are dissenters. Traitors by any other name. No better than the rebels who cower in caves to the north!'

'You cannot lock us all up in your dungeons!'

The barricades bristled as more of the traitors took up arms and readied their defences.

Malvus tilted his head. The man was painfully correct, and unwittingly, he had sealed his own fate. Until that point, Malvus hadn't considered more than severe whipping and perhaps a handful of executions. In that angry man, in the frantic waving of a banner bearing Evernia's scales, Malvus saw embodied every dissenter. Every snarling daemon. He saw Farden. There was no violent outburst, no crescendo of emotion, merely the knowledge that Malvus' very last thread of patience had, at last, withered and died.

'Correct! I cannot,' he announced. 'Mages! Bring me their heads.'

Screams rose up first, then bolstering shouts cut through the panic. Proud words of noble sentiments. Justice. Peace. *All that shit.* Clods of mud, glass tankards, and rocks began to rain. They bounced harmlessly from the shield spells his mages cast.

Toskig threw the first blow, driving a foul wind in from the surrounding streets, ruffling torches and casting muck and detritus into the barricade.

Once the runed mages had formed a line before Malvus's pedestal, they wove fire in their hands. Fireballs struck the barricades in a flurry of bright flame and screams. Toskig's wind spell whipped up the flames. The wooden defences began to catch, and Malvus began to smile.

Vexingly, there were magick users amongst the dissenters. Fountains of water sprayed across the barricade. Forks of lightning split the air, swiping several of the city watch from a wall. One man broke both legs and went to his grave howling. The rest ran away with their tabards aflame. For now, the traitors seemed to be fending off the attack surprisingly well.

It took a flaming arrow to turn the tide.

The missile dug into the foot of one of his imperial guards, who had been holding his shield spell too high. As he tumbled from the pedestal, his spell tumbled with him, leaving the emperor dangerously exposed, just long enough for a shard of glass to slice Malvus' cheek.

With shouts of, 'Death to the emperor!' ringing in his ears, Malvus put a hand to his face. It came away bloody and shaking with indignation.

'Toskig!' Malvus called to the general, as more makeshift missiles began to rain.

'Majesty!'

'Fetch Prince Gremorin. Tell him a feast has been kindly laid out.'

Toskig spun around so quickly, Malvus was surprised he didn't snap his neck.

'Majesty,' he breathed, troubling to find the words. 'Never have the daemons been allowed that deep into the city. We cannot use them against our own people!'

Malvus stared at the ringleader and his disgusting flag. 'They are not our own, General! Do not be so blind. They are usurpers. Anarchists no better than the Outlaw King!' he bellowed. 'Now. Fetch me Gremorin!'

There came a crash as the mages drove their fire spells into the centre of the barricade. The traitors were ready. Sharpened staves and swirling water filled any gap. Street Legion soldiers tried to swarm a weak point but staggered away with injuries. One soldier took a spell straight to the face. Shards of skull rained down on the Arka ranks.

The chanting was now a roar, shaking the very air. The whole city must have heard their cries.

Death to the emperor.

Death to the emperor.

The roll of thunder made Malvus turn. There, filling the narrow streets with shadow and smoke stood three daemons. Gremorin stood wreathed in his own flame. Two giants, war daemons, stood tall behind him. They each bore iron cutlasses as long as a ship's oar.

'You sent for us?' Gremorin stared at the barricaded compound and the tavern shining with torchlight. His expression was one of confusion at first, but the fires of hunger and chaos soon glowed in his eyes.

Malvus dismounted from his chariot, making the guards scramble to protect him. He stood before the sulphurous stench of the daemon, barely reaching Gremorin's hip, and drew one of his prized knives.

'You wanted your war? This is the beginning of it. You may do as you wish with these traitors.' Modren pointed his blade at the barricade, where the mages were just beginning to make a hole. 'I will break their spirits once and for all.'

'And we shall break their spines!' snarled Gremorin. He knocked soldiers and mages alike aside as he and his dark brothers entered the chaos.

The chants died instantly, replaced by screams as traitors quailed beneath the shadows of the daemons. The broken barricade was torn to splinters by the daemon prince alone. His long claws were the harbingers of death, sweeping through the crowds where they pleased, making two of everything they touched. The fires and torches were extinguished with blood.

It took mere minutes for the rebellion to be crushed.

Malvus followed in the path of the daemons. With both knives unsheathed, he stalked behind the destruction, boots splashing on the bloody, burnt cobble. The dying still groaned or pleaded. Some cursed with their last breaths. All their work had been turned to splinters. All their hopes dead alongside them. All their lives, pointless. The pitiful few who had escaped the daemons' wrath and the soldiers' swords were being hauled away to dungeons or workhouses or factory forges. They bawled or ranted with what voices they had left.

'Gods curse you, Malvus Barkhart!' came a cry from above, shortly before a man plummeted from a rooftop, a great chunk of rock in his arms.

He might have crashed down upon Malvus had it not been for the daemon's claws that swatted the man against a broken window and smeared him across a wall.

Malvus moved to the tavern. The sign had been crudely repainted in scarlet before being dislodged and stamped into the mud. It read *The Emperor's Head*. A grinning skull accompanied the letters. Inside, mages were still scorching traitors out of cupboards and cellars.

The emperor trawled the walls, decorated with a depressing display of wanted scrolls torn from street corners, and in their absence, names burnt into the plaster. Malvus grew bored after the first dozen. Scrolls bearing rewards of fortunes for the Outlaw King or a Written mage's head were stuck in high places like trophies. The phrase "Magick or Death" had been written across the ceiling in many different hands and languages, from High Paraian to old Skölgard and Siren dragonscript. Malvus wanted to spit on the words, but the risk of wetting his own face was high.

Curious, half searching for an answer to these rebels' foolishness, Malvus followed the trail of rebellious propaganda up the stairs, much to the delight of the ache in his hip and back. He ran a knife blade across the wall as if slicing a throat. Plaster pattered behind him. Guards apologised for the inconvenience as they dragged a senseless woman down the stairs legs first, so her head bounced like a ball.

Smoke masked the upper rooms, drawn in from the fires sprouting outside. Malvus found another barricade, where soldiers jousted with spears at stubborn individuals refusing to submit. A dozen of them had holed up in the top floor. No daemons could reach them here. Some half-trained sorcerer kept up a stuttering shield spell, and, like stubborn whelks, the traitors refused to be winkled out.

Malvus half admired, half coveted them. He wished his soldiers fought with such conviction. With more roars of freedom, peace, and death to the empire, he retraced his steps to a large, shadowy bedchamber bare of furniture, presumably to hold meetings. At the far end, between the trickles of blood dripping through the floorboards, he found a colony of molten and flickering candles gathered like a shrine. They illuminated a particularly huge sign affixed to the wall. The kind that used to hang on the city walls.

Malvus stood before the massive depiction of Farden, twice life-size and crudely drawn in charcoal, but still unmistakeable. Untamed hair escaping a persistent hood. Scars and square jaw. The words "FOREVER KING" were emblazoned above him. Beneath, a promise that his time was nigh. Malvus could still feel the ridge of scar beneath his beard where the cursed mage had struck him once.

The emperor slowly pressed his knife into the mage's forehead, hoping that somewhere, hundreds of leagues to the north, Farden would wince in unknown pain. A cough took him then, phlegm catching in his chest and causing him to retch. He could taste the copper blood in his mouth. He forced himself to swallow, refusing to acknowledge it.

A scrape of a boot on a floorboard betrayed his watcher. Subtle, faint, but Malvus felt the prickle crawl over his skin as he became aware of a presence. He did not take the knife from the wall. In the corner of his vision, he saw the shadows stretch over the spattered plaster, reaching for him. A cold air drew sharp. The emperor's breath steamed before him. He held it, but something else breathed behind him.

'Yah!' Malvus howled as he spun around. His knife cut the air so quickly it uttered a whine. Air was all it cut. No figure loomed over him. No rebel with a cause. Instead, there stood a pale-faced figure so enshrouded in shadow Malvus had to squint to be sure he wasn't imagining it.

Malvus startled when it spoke. Quiet, almost a whisper, yet audible over the ruckus of battle.

'If only he could feel that,' said the man.

'Who are you? Guar—!'

'You shan't be needing them.' The face bore a smile now. Malvus heard no footsteps, but the man approached. The shadows moved with him.

The man chuckled, and that sound tickled a memory in Malvus' mind. 'Do you not remember me, Malvus?'

'You will address me as Emperor…' his words trailed off as he caught a glimpse of straw hair, a fair face, and eyes that shone with no human colours. The tall collars of his coat rested against boyish cheeks.

'I will take that as a no. But I remember you, Council Malvus Barkhart. Full of heart and vigour. Full of ambition. I see that hasn't changed, despite the wrinkles on your brow, the faint limp. Bad hip, is it? Time is a cruel companion, is it not?'

Malvus swiped a knife at the man. 'You will tell me who you are!'

The man's stature grew. The shadows pawed at the walls. 'I am the Morningstar. I lead the dawn. I alone fell to earth from Haven and I alone have what you need, Malvus Barkhart.' His hand swept in a mock bow. 'I am Loki.'

Malvus felt a dribble of sweat on his temple. 'Only the daemons fell from the sky during the Last War.'

'You are not the only one to make a pact for your survival.' The man held up a pale hand, unscarred. 'I was wise enough not to shake hands.'

'How do you know…?' The realisation struck before the question had left his mouth. A chill shook him. 'You are but a shadow of a god. A mirage.'

The apparition sneered. 'Shadow, you say? Perhaps when we first met, but no longer. Not just the daemons fell from the sky that day so long ago.'

Malvus was torn. The presence of a true god rattled him. Even with a daemon prince under his boot, meeting a god was not something that occurred often in Emaneska. If at all. Then again, these creatures who called themselves gods had never answered a single prayer of his. They had only doted on the Outlaw King.

'And what do you believe I need, god?'

Loki gestured broadly to the state of the bedchamber. 'Besides a good night's rest, to do a finer job, by the looks of it.'

Such words would have earned any mortal man a slit throat.

'I have travelled a long road a long time. I followed roads that have no names to coasts that have seen no ships. I have walked lands where the moon alone rules. Where waterfalls run in reverse. You can imagine my surprise, when in the furthest east, sitting beneath the shade of a tree so large dragons make their nests in its branches, I heard talk of a glowing empire in old Emaneska. An empire stretching from wild Albion to Kroppe, from the Troacles to the old borders of the Crumbled Empire. I heard talk of a place called Krauslung, a jewel of trade and power. Of its glorious emperor that at last keeps the wild nature of magick in check. An Emaneska in peace at last? This, I had to see for myself.' Loki paused, gazing off at some memory in his eyes. 'And when I looked, I saw a battlefield of dead mages. A port so crammed ships sink hourly. Starving daemons picking for scraps. And this. Rebellion in your own jewel of a city. You are a rotten oak, Malvus Barkhart. Sturdy to all who look at you, but hollow and full of mould.'

'I will kill you where you stand.'

Loki looked him up and down and grinned like a jester. 'You need a better hand in this game of fate, I think.'

God or not, Malvus poised to strike as Loki reached into the fold of his coat. Instead of a weapon, he withdrew a large and heavy tome. How in Hel's name he managed to hide it in a mere pocket confused Malvus deeply.

It was an ugly thing, with a sandy leather cover all beaten and scarred, repaired many times. A heavy iron lock kept it closed. The pages did not look to be made of paper or even parchment. Their curled edges were yellow, dusty pink, or grey. It came with a reek of dried meat and damp. Malvus scowled as the god dropped the thing on the floorboard between them. It was inordinately heavy.

'The Hides of Hysteria, I call it,' said Loki.

'And?'

'Let us test your rusty memory, shall we? Before the end of the Last War, before you stole the throne of the Arka and carved up Emaneska between the Lost Clans and the daemons, the Written were hunted down one by one by a wild force. Do you recall that?'

It was a vague memory amongst the mist of two decades, but Malvus nodded. 'I do.'

'Then you'll no doubt wonder what happened to those Written.'

The emperor scowled. 'Lost to time and rot.'

'Incorrect. It was no force, but the same girl who dragged the daemons from the sky. Her history is veiled by lies and death, but what I have pieced together is that she did not work alone. She had a mentor. A guide. An old, one-armed seer by the name of Lilith.'

A one-armed seer. Loki's eyes roamed Malvus' face, searching for recognition. Malvus had never heard her name but he kept his expression blank all the same. The god deserved no satisfaction.

Loki continued. 'While the girl killed, the seer harvested, cutting the skin and tattooed Books from the backs of the dead Written.'

His eyes strayed to the ugly tome. 'You're telling me—'

'I am telling you that this tome,' Loki rested a boot on it as he spoke, 'contains the hides of more than a score of Written.'

Malvus' throat was dry. Still, he tried to act nonchalant. 'And why would I be so concerned with such vile items, god?'

Loki's fiendish smile was becoming infuriating. 'Because I am far from a fool. I've seen the runes and spells you've been carving into your mages and soldiers. Even had I not, it is the next logical step. Farden and his remaining Written are too powerful even for your horde. You need similar power to guarantee victory, and I can provide you that power. With this tome, you can create all the Written you desire, Malvus. Replicas of mages long dead.'

The emperor sheathed his knives, taking great care and ceremony. 'I take it the gods are not used to bartering, hmm?'

Loki looked incredibly far from worried. His face was an oil painting for all it moved.

'What's to stop me from feeding you to the daemons and taking this tome for myself? I'm sure they would gorge themselves on such a grand soul as a god's. Or stop me from killing you right here myself?'

Loki chuckled. 'Nothing stopping you from trying. Then again, for a man chasing a future he has long envisioned yet cannot grasp, it is always useful to have a guide. An ally,' he replied. 'I can give you Farden.'

Malvus hated how much this god knew. The seer had not predicted this interference, and, not for the first time, he doubted that prophecy of fire and gold she had shown him. 'I don't need a god's help,' he snapped.

They let the lie linger and crumble between them.

At last, Malvus spat on the floor beside the tome. He knew well that desperate men were simple to manipulate. Malvus had never known desperation until that moment. To make a pact with a god was a price he had never expected to pay for victory, and yet here he was, biting his tongue to stop from blurting yes.

'Why would you assist me? What grudge does a god hold against a mage?'

A crack appeared in Loki's smile. 'No grudge. Farden is simply an imbalance that needs to be corrected.'

Imbalance. It was the kindest word for traitor and scum Malvus had ever heard. He bared his teeth. 'You lie, you cheat, you steal, you so much as fart in the wrong direction, and I will flay the pale skin from your back myself. God or not.'

'A fine and eloquent deal,' replied Loki. He removed his boot from the tome and kicked it towards the emperor.

The Hides of Hysteria was awkwardly heavy. It reeked of decay and oil. Malvus unhinged the cold lock and hooked a finger under one of the stout, gnarled pages of skin. Loki held up a hand.

'You remember the rules of the Written, do you not, Malvus? Tell me it hasn't been that long?'

'A Written will never reveal his Book to another, nor allow it to be revealed,' muttered the emperor. *Hides of Hysteria, indeed.* And yet, dangerous things hold a terrible allure. Malvus glimpsed the faint trace of faded script beyond his finger and felt the urge to read it all. A commotion beyond the smoking tavern drew him back from the brink. 'Does Farden know this exists?'

Loki replied instantly. 'No.'

The way his tone bent, Malvus knew the god was holding back some jewel of immense interest. The candles sputtered distractingly. His pervasive cough pounced once more, and he thumped his chest, eyes squeezing shut.

At that moment, imperial guards – seemingly breathless over having lost their emperor – crowded into the doorway of the room. Blood soaked their armour. One had lost his helmet and taken an injury, leaving a black hole where there should have been an eye.

'Stow your arms, you halfwits. This man is with me!' barked the emperor.

'Majesty' stammered their captain. 'What man?'

Malvus turned around to find nothing but vacant shadow. The tome still rested in the emperor's arms, weighing as much as a pig. It took a while for him to speak.

'To the Arkathedral.'

Beyond the immense walls of Krauslung, bristling with lances and crenellations like a quillhog, beyond the shanty towns and makeshift streets that clung to the city, the valley swept up to Manesmark.

A black stone tower lay in ruin upon the crest of the hill. The years had decorated it with moss and vines. The iron-coloured skeleton of a dragon lay nearby, undisturbed yet spoiled by crude graffiti. At the tower's foot, a town spread outwards like a mould. Manesmark's proud years of military glory had been utterly trampled. Armourers and soldiers, mages and trainers had once toiled day after day here for the Arka's might; a shining example of training and order. Now, taverns outnumbered barracks. Law was held in each person's fist. The streets were clogged with tents, lean-tos, and ramshackle billets. Manesmark heaved with bodies. Two hundred and fifty thousand of them to be correct.

When the air wasn't filled with clanging armour, it was filled with the roar of yelling voices or erupting laughter. Where fights milled, the occasional fireball would streak into the sky, bringing sergeants and captains bearing switches and sticks in swarms. It was revelry based in boredom, and that can be the most dangerous kind.

Beyond the human quarters of Manesmark, where the mountains met the valley floor, a choking smoke hung in the air. Fires burnt like eyes staring out from veils. Here, Gremorin's daemons had been given their paltry cut of Emaneska. It consisted largely of a crater of bare dirt where nothing grew and stone houses where the oldest of daemon kind held their courts. Save for the spoils of war, deliveries from the dungeons, or the occasional drunken idiot, no human dared wander this scorched earth.

Loki was no human.

He trod the dust, listening to black grass crumble to ash beneath his boots. Dark shapes sputtering with flame tracked him through the smog. Where he couldn't see them, he could feel the heat and magick around him. He knew they sensed him.

Loki needed no blade. No insurance. His safety had already been bought days ago. A promise is all it had taken. Even so, his hand still strayed to his endless pockets, feeling for the shining cube of glass – Jurindir's Candle. A pretty trinket, useless to most humans, but it was a weapon to a god. It was not like him to doubt himself, but it was also not like a god to enter a daemon prince's enclave.

Gremorin sat hunched upon a throne of boulders, two helbeasts chained by iron at his feet. Like all daemon architecture, the concept of comfort was a slur, synonymous with kindness and mercy. Such creatures had no need for gilded trappings nor marble floors. The prince's wings arched over him, blacker than the night. His entourage crowded behind him. They were an undefined mass of black hide and ash, only distinguishable by counting the pairs of eyes.

'Little god,' Gremorin rumbled. He idly picked a chunk of meat from his teeth and flicked it at Loki's feet. The apple-sized chunk nudged his boot and the god forced a smile.

'Speak,' ordered the daemon.

Loki did not bow. He did not blink. 'It is done,' he said. 'Malvus has the weapon he needs to march north against Farden.'

'Then war is at last upon us,' Gremorin growled. His daemons raised their foul voices to the sky. It brought a momentarily lull to the swollen Manesmark.

When the noise had died, Gremorin levelled a sword as long as a pike at Loki. 'You have kept your bargain, and so shall we. No talon nor fang will be laid upon you as long as you serve us. But tread carefully. We know your ways, godling. We know what you are the patron of, besides the morning's light and what charge they gave you.'

Loki crossed his arms, clenching his fists unseen. Oh, how he tired of "little" being used to describe his stature. 'Oh? And what is that, pray?'

Gremorin leaned forwards to stab the earth with his sword. 'Lies.'

Loki let the smog envelop him as he retreated, a white smile lingering on his lips.

'Be ready, Prince,' he said.

part two
REVENGE LOVES COMPANY

CHAPTER 13
TRUE MAGICK

The Kserak Massacre was possibly the darkest day in Emaneska's memory since Malvus first took the Arkathedral. Kserak once stood on the empire's eastern fringes, far enough for the empire's lies to whither, and for Farden to hope to save the entire city from Malvus' clutches. Along with Inwick and Modren, he took a risk and showed his face. After saving three would-be mages from the noose, the Arka governors and soldiers were hanged instead. But empire loyalists betrayed his presence there, and Malvus responded with force. As ten thousand soldiers arrived by quickdoor, his dragons turned Kserak's walls to ash before the city could barely fortify itself. In the chaos, no more than two hundred souls escaped alongside the Written. Malvus retook Kserak, yet instead of reinstating the loyal to the Arka, he slaughtered every last inhabitant.

Six thousand perished that day. Kserak was reduced to a scorched crater in the earth. A sole "survivor" was left to tell just the tale the emperor wanted. How curious that Krauslung was on the verge of rioting in days prior.

From that day, Farden's soul has been scarred indelibly. He spiralled into seclusion for several months and has not left the north since. The blame he places upon himself is an ugly, heavy shackle.
FROM THE WRITINGS OF GENERAL DURNUS GLASSREN, YEAR 924

Mithrid was beginning to despise this habit of unconsciousness she had developed. So much so, in fact, she awoke from the cloying, echoing darkness with a scream of rage.

The sound of whimpering and pounding feet opened her eyes just in time to see a small, scuttling figure slam a door.

Mithrid blinked, taking in a stone room filled with beds: some stacked upon each other like crates, others dizzyingly high, swinging from platforms where walkways riddled the walls. Far above, in the vaulted roof, scarlet plants dangled from the rafters and dark thatch. Moths fluttered about their diamond leaves, glowing different colours as they collided with things. Mithrid wondered at first whether she was dreaming.

Back on the solid and patterned floor, ornate iron braziers burnt with white fire in the corners. Not a soul occupied the room besides her.

That changed with the creak of the door. hairy fingers curled into view, followed by a sharp snout. Before Mithrid could get a look between the forest of bedposts and mattresses, somebody pushed past the creature and entered. Mithrid swore the braziers brightened at her entrance.

It was a girl near to Mithrid's age, perhaps two winters older. She had the paleness of a northerner, but the flaxen hair of eastern blood. She wore it in an intricate braid that confused Mithrid's eyes. Her clothing looked to be some kind of basic uniform: a padded tunic and a cloak of scarlet. Her ocean-coloured eyes were mirthful.

'Knew it,' said the girl in a coarse Dromfangar accent.

'Knew what?' wheezed Mithrid, trying to find some saliva in her mouth to speak with.

'Knew you'd be alive. You seemed like the tough type.'

Without invitation, the girl sat on the edge of her bed, squashing a toe in the process. Mithrid drew the blanket around her.

'I passed out again,' she growled.

'That you did. Right on the witch's feet, too. Your overgrown friend said it's happened before. Even so, you passed through the test, and so we brought you here to rest up.'

'Why does this keep happening to me?'

'It occurs more than you'd expect. Magick has never been more powerful in Emaneska than it is now. It has strange effects on people. Me? Passed out first time I was in a fight. Woke up with the Forever King himself staring down at me.'

Mithrid found some solace in the girl's words but no answers. 'I heard Modren calling him that. Why?'

'The Outlaw King suits Emaneska fine, but there are others in Scalussen that see him as more. Because of his armour. It's the last of the Nine, armour made for the Knights of Scalussen when it was its own kingdom. That was more than a thousand years ago. Rumour has it that that metal's got the blood of the Allfather himself forged into it. Farden never takes all of it off. Not in decades. Roiks says even time itself can't cut him.'

'Well, can this immortal king of yours wind time back, so I can go back to my old life? Not freezing my tits off in this infested place?' she uttered and pointed at the moths. Why the girl found that so funny, Mithrid didn't know, but it jilted her.

'This place, Mithrid, is your new home. If you want it to be. The Underspire, as we call it. A fancy name for a burrow full of barracks and forges, but as high as the Frostsoar reaches, its roots go almost as deep into the ground. Deep and safe. Warmer, too.'

That explained the quiet. And yet, the days spent on the *Winter's Revenge* had left echoes of the sea in her ears. She swore she could still hear the waves in silent moments.

'What do you want?' asked the girl. 'Drink? Vittles?'

Seeing movement, Mithrid broke her burning stare. She abruptly noticed the dark and hairy shapes lingering behind the nearest beds and froze. Mithrid might not have heard of Nelska or the Last War or libraries, but every child has heard tales of the voracious lycan.

There were four, surrounding them completely. Their hooked claws gripped at mattresses. Amber and summer-yellow, their hungry, leering eyes were fixed solely on Mithrid. Breath rattled in their throats.

'What in Hel?' she whispered, too panicked to move.

'It's fine,' spoke the girl. She simply waved them away, as if four lycans prowling the chamber was as perfectly normal as sunrise. 'They can be quite a shock if you missed the introduction. First night I was here, some dimwit who hadn't listened goes for a stroll. He opens the door and finds Kurulach over there right behind it. Poor lad was so scared he shat across three separate beds as he fled. Works in the kitchens now.'

The lycan called Kurulach could be heard quietly and gruffly snickering.

'These lycans are perfectly civilised. They patrol the Underspire once the evening meal is over and the braziers are low. They normally keep to the hallways, but General Inwick was suspicious of you. There's not a sounder sleep you can have under such watchful eyes.'

'That's mad.'

'We're all mad here, in the eyes of the empire.'

A shout interrupted. 'Hereni!'

'That's me,' said the girl, before coming to attention. The door gave way to a newcomer once more, and in strode a Siren who rivalled the lycans for size. Had it not been for the lack of fur and the grey scales hanging like a beard from his angular bones, Mithrid would have assumed he was one of them. A large scar carved a path from his forehead to his cheek, proof he had gotten in the way of a blade at some point. A patch of slate-coloured hair had been braided down the back of his neck. Plates of carmine armour covered his torso.

'How is the Hâlorn girl?' His voice was so gruff Mithrid could barely make out the consonants.

'You can ask her yourself, General.'

The big Siren looked Mithrid up and down with his good eye. 'How do you feel?'

Apart from a few aches from either the collapsing or the carrying underground, and a gentle but constant headache, Mithrid felt fine. Ravenous, but fine. She said as much.

'Fine is good enough for me, child. Come this way. You're late.'

'Already, sir? The undermage said it might not be the best idea.'

The general gave the girl a haughty look that immediately quailed her. 'You, of all people, Hereni, know how short time is,' he said, before retracing his steps.

The girl's face hardened. 'Yes, sir. Right away.'

Before Mithrid knew what was going on, the blanket had been torn away. She was clothed beneath, but Hereni pressed a fresh tunic and burgundy cloak into her hands.

'Put these on. Boots as well.'

Hereni was right: the lycans were civilised. As Mithrid changed, they turned away to face the door, left ajar by the general. Mithrid saw a winding staircase and honeycomb chambers.

Her minder was drumming on the nearest mattress with impatience by the time Mithrid was ready. Panic swooped like a vulture. 'My axe. Where is my axe?' Mithrid was already half breathless as she cast around.

'In the armoury with your name on it.'

'That axe shouldn't leave my side.' The fact somebody had merely touched it vexed her sufficiently.

'It's safe. Farden doesn't allow recruits weapons in the Underspire for the safety of everyone here. Not any more, anyway. Not since... well. Malvus likes to send spies and assassins, as you saw the other day. Come on. General Eyrum's increasingly irate these days. Modren says he's missing Nelska, but I think he just needs a good woman.'

Infuriatingly, Hereni didn't explain further, but took Mithrid by the sleeve instead and guided her towards the doorway.

A woman with salt and pepper hair was at that moment descending the stairwell. She made it to the threshold without jumping at the sight of a lycan. 'By the gods! Every damnable time I come here,' the woman scolded the lycan. 'Must you lurk like that? Jötun save me. Ah, Mithrid Fenn, is it? You're awake and well.'

'And wanted in the yards an hour ago,' sighed the girl.

Mithrid didn't get a chance to speak before a vial of brown liquid was pressed into her hands and unstoppered.

'If Eyrum insists on such pressure, then take this, girl. It's *syngur*. It ain't the nicest tastin', despite my recommendations to the Sirens, but it'll keep you on your feet. First day is the 'ardest, they say.'

Mithrid was already being marched up the stairs. 'Erm. Thank you... ?'

'Elessi.'

'You're Modren's—'

'Better not keep Eyrum waitin'!' her holler chased them up the coiling stairwell.

Perhaps she was still dizzy from fainting, but Mithrid swore the steps climbed with her. They pushed against her feet, making the ascent up the wide tower beneath the ice faster than it should have been. She stared and she stared, but she could only catch the stairs moving in the corners of her eye.

Magick might have assisted her, but Mithrid's heart still pounded with the effort by the time they reached the top and a wide tunnel. Hereni moved on, not dragging Mithrid this time but still moving at a rapid pace.

Other people walked this passageway, and the girl didn't care who Mithrid had to collide with to keep up.

She managed to catch her before she reached a thick, iron wrapped door. 'Enough! Not another step.'

'What do you want? We—'

Mithrid's voice was a dangerous whisper of strain to keep from shouting. 'What I want, Hereni, is to drag the sun back across the sky so I never found that fucking spellbook, nor had to stare into my father's dead eyes, nor saw my friends slaughtered. Seeing as I can't very well do that, and neither can your Forever King, I want to gut the men who took my life from me. To carve piece after piece from them. I want to sit and watch them bleed buckets before they die. That's what I fucking want. I have said I'm not here to join a cause, yet since the moment I accepted Modren's offer of safety, I've been dragged against my will to this frozen arsehole of nowhere, tested again, and now I'm wearing colours.

'I was told I had a choice, but I don't see it. Even when I collapse, nobody seems to give a multicoloured shit about me! Everybody just nods along, saying war is coming, adoring a king despite him doing nothing but hiding in the snow. That is why I am not taking another fucking step, not until somebody explains to me why I should fight for anything within these walls, and not go slit throats myself.' Mithrid threw the vial of liquid down to punctuate her anger, smashing it against the wall in an ugly brown smear.

She knew bystanders were staring. She could hear them depart with an awkward shuffling. A piebald lycan hovered nearby, watchful. Mithrid did not care.

The girl was paused with her hand on the door. She looked at Mithrid with narrowed eyes that were a varnished pine. She sucked her teeth as she thought. 'Woke up one night a year back with a tingling in my fingers. Clenched them up so hard, I did. Gripped my sheets to get the feeling back. Accidentally singed them and left charred finger marks all over. Managed to bury the sheets in the orchard behind the cottage before father or mother or my brother found out. I knew it was outlawed. I knew it was wrong, but I couldn't refuse it. I spent nights practising magick in the cow barn.' The girl spared a moment to pinch her tongue between her sharp teeth. 'It drew them. Emperor's men. Father had his throat cut to the bone and was left to die the snow. Mother was locked in the cottage to burn as they torched it. My little brother was thrown into the blaze as callously as a log. I listened to them die as they dragged me into the snow.

'You say you want to spill blood, Mithrid? Good. So do I. So do *they*.' She slammed her boot against the door and kicked it open.

A rush of glacial wind chilled Mithrid's skin. Blinking, she saw a vast courtyard filled with two things: snow and people.

Nearest to the door, four-score stood in the same burgundy cloaks, trying awkwardly to tighten up their lines and formation. Beyond them, hundreds more parried with weapons of both wood and iron or took aim at targets with lance and bow. Further still, where mages trained, fire and lightning raged against the frozen, ice-gripped walls of the fortress.

'Take a dozen of these people and ten will tell you a similar story of dead fathers, raped mothers, and friends disembowelled with hearts still beating, right before their eyes. All because of what they were born with, or for listening to the wrong story. If you think you are the only one struggling with sorrow and fear, lashing at the world around you to give you some semblance of control, you are sorely mistaken. We all pine for revenge. Five years, I've waited and mourned. Some here have waited twenty and more. Understand this when I tell you: as the king once told me, you're not unusual, Mithrid, you are not special. You are not prophesied or chosen by the gods. You are one of us: the downtrodden and lied to, and that is fine, because together, we are something. A force that can wipe clean this hate-filled, blood-drenched world we find ourselves trapped in.

'We are taking revenge on all of the empire, not merely a handful of murderers and rapists. The empire who banned a world drenched by magick and hangs us when we can't deny our power or ask for freedom. That is why we fight, and why we hope you'll fight with us, but if that doesn't suit you – if you can't wear colours – then leave. You're welcome to take your axe and claim your revenge by yourself, just know you will be on your own.' Hereni half grinned, half snarled. 'You'd better believe war is on its way. Our protests were not heard. Our rebellion is not enough. War is inevitable. If you'll battle alongside us, we will train you, make you strong, give you every weapon you need to spill as much Arka blood as you want. You don't have to bow to some king if you don't want. Fight for yourself if you want, but all we ask is loyalty and trust. Now get the fuck out there and never speak to me like that again.'

Mithrid wasn't pushed, she wasn't dragged, but she burst into that training yard all the same with the girl's words still ringing in her head. She didn't know whether to be insulted or inspired.

'Captain! Nice of you to join us at last,' boomed the huge Siren standing at the front of the red-cloaked ranks. 'You! Get in line.'

Captain. Mithrid inwardly groaned, watching her saunter to Eyrum's side. *Of course.*

Unable to see Remina or Bull, and pretending to ignore the irritating Midgrir twins she spotted, Mithrid shunned the multitudes of eyes upon her and just stood in a gap at the end of the ranks. An older, fatter man tutted at her for blocking his view with her wild locks.

After dwarfing a stone plinth, the general addressed the crowd. Though he was not the most eloquent or effusive speaker, his booming voice carried effortlessly over the multitudes. Mithrid felt as though he shouted directly in her ear.

'You are here because you have nowhere else. You are here because somebody took something from you. You are here because you chose to come. You are here because the world doesn't look right to you any more. You are here because you are terrified, outraged, or mourning.'

Eyrum's eye scanned over the crowds as each person tried to figure which category they belonged to. Mithrid could see it in their pursed lips and nervous eyes.

'You are here because you will take a stand against injustice and tyranny, and whatever circumstance brought you to this place, know that you are united in the goal of freedom and peace from a cruel empire. And whether we die in its pursuit, we stand together. Mages. Soldiers. Emaneska.'

Mithrid hadn't expected the cheer. She felt the wind of the roaring voices buffet her.

'*You,*' Eyrum said, now stabbing a finger at the crowds, 'are here because you have either shown some skill with magick already, or you've been deemed worthy by the witch. We want to show you how to use it, both for the emperor's sake and ours. Some of you will be able to withstand this power flowing through your veins. Some of you might be able to wield fire and light like Scalussen mages do. Others will struggle. Others will fail.'

Mithrid groaned. She had known little failure in her life, and that meant any hint of a challenge devoured her. Once, Remina had dared her to climb the cliff face. By Hurricane, Mithrid had made it halfway before she fell. The leg had healed but her pride had not.

'Magick is dangerous. Always has been and it keeps getting stronger. It has killed and will kill again. I have seen recruits consumed by flame for not concentrating hard enough. I've seen limbs severed by wayward spells. I have seen eyes melted straight out of faces.'

Amidst the muttering, everybody around Mithrid surreptitiously searched the stone, re-examining every scratch, char mark or dubious brown stain with fresh understanding. Mithrid kicked curiously at a few shattered pieces of what looked like bleached ceramic. Her headache swelled in that moment like a skald's crescendo. She clenched her jaw and fought through it.

'If you are concerned, scared, or in doubt, there is no shame in fighting with blades and might. Magick is for all, but not all are for magick. Now is the time to step forwards.'

Not a boot stirred. There were a number of awkward, panicked faces, but that was all. The general seemed satisfied enough. He looked the sort of man that didn't know the meaning of smiling, but his curt nod to Hereni said it all.

'Spread out!' yelled the captain.

There was no military precision in response to that order, just an awkward shuffling until there was an arm's breadth between everyone. Mithrid still found herself on the fringes again, not knowing where to put her hands.

'Magick,' Hereni began, 'as a greater mage once told me, is a song. An endless song, ever flowing. It has no beginning and no end. It was written before Emaneska was born, and it will echo long after you and I are gone.'

Hereni waited for that to sink in.

'Those of you who can stand it may let that song flow through you. When you become attuned to the feel of magick, you will feel its waver, its crescendo, its power. Know that this power is greater than you and I. It does not originate within you. We can only borrow it. Summon it. We can write it down in spellbooks or speak it aloud, but as such, most of us will never know the full breadth of magick's song. Some of you will be able to learn more of it than others. Some of you will learn a different song. One of fire, perhaps. A common one.'

Hereni held out a hand. A red flame sparked into life, hovering above her palm.

'There are many schools of magick. Fire. Quake. Will. Lightning. Water. Vortex. Light. Thunder. Zeal. Illusion. Shield, and they are but a few. Some schools we do not dare invoke, as they verge on sorcery.' The flame was quenched between her fingers. 'You are all here because you have some form of magick resonating in your blood and in your bones. Many of you might have already wielded magick before, with or without training, accidentally or on purpose. Many of you will have found yourselves speaking aloud, unbidden. This is the most basic form of wielding magick: the recitation of spells that mages traditionally memorise. Siren wizards read aloud from scrolls. But magick has changed. The song has grown louder, stronger. Some amongst you may only need to hear the voice in their head. Others might not hear a voice at all but will be able to wield magick like flexing a muscle. That is intrinsic magick, and unless you are like our illustrious leader and have a spellbook carved into your skin, that is unreachable for most of you. But we can still aim.'

Hushed whispers spread about the crowd as rumours were either confirmed or questions sprouted.

'Silence!' Eyrum roared.

Hereni continued, casting a side eye at Eyrum. 'Know this! There is no failure here. There are many weapons to wield in the fight against oppression, and magick is merely one of them. We are not rivals but allies.'

Mithrid had to admit, she had balls for a girl so young. Why Hereni's gaze found Mithrid amongst the crowd at that moment, she didn't know, but it nettled her nonetheless.

'Row by row, you will come forwards and you will taste true magick.'

Those words set off a bell in Mithrid's mind. One that old habits tugged frantically on. *True magick.* She wondered what her father and mother would think watching her now, taking that collective step with the crowd of strangers. Her heart thrummed so hard she could see its beat in the twitching of her robe hem. Her gut felt twisted.

Between the mass of bodies, it was hard to see many details. Hereni and Eyrum moved down the ranks, recruit by recruit, speaking to them directly. It seemed tasting true magick was largely uneventful. Something would abruptly glow, or smoke would puff into the air. A loud pop echoed through the courtyard at one point, causing a smattering of applause.

Mithrid tried her best to see without breaking rank. As she leaned back and forth like a sapling in a storm, the lines moved forwards again. This time, she managed to glimpse an older gentleman with a bald head as shiny and hairless as a shore pebble. He was instructed to hold his hands out, flat and ready. There was silence while the man went from trembling to violent shaking. Hereni yelled at him to focus. Focus. *Focus!*

A timid blue spark flashed between his palms. The man was white as a sail from the effort and yelped with surprise or pain, but otherwise he beamed at the applauding ranks behind him. Eyrum directed him towards one of two groups standing nearby: one of mages on the left, one of soldiers on the right. His fellow mages pummelled his back in congratulations.

By the time Mithrid was standing one rank from next, a large number of recruits had joined the mages' group. Their members stood there, swollen with pride, and watching eagerly to see who was worthy to join their tribe. Hereni's cautions had already fallen from their ears.

A portly man of Albion looks was next to try this song of magick. His tonsure of mud-brown hair was greying at the edges. Two crystal spectacles trapped in wire balanced over his flat nose. He had the look of a pig dressed in a coat, who had suddenly found its ruse turned far too serious.

Mithrid watched intently. Her fingers twitched as she mentally mimicked Hereni's instructions. The man had a pair of glistening palms out, flat this time. The captain had whispered a series of instructions to him already with no luck. Now she had given him a tiny scroll of paper to read, and he chewed on the words slowly and to himself. All of a sudden, he began to jiggle violently.

'Hold it now,' ordered Hereni. 'Draw that power in and push it out through your hands. Use your mind instead of your body. Feel it at the base of your skull. Concentrate.'

The man was oblivious, staring with wild eyes at his hands as they became a blur of trembling effort. Several of his neighbours edged away. He looked to them for help, breaking his adsorption.

'Focus, man!' barked Eyrum. He was already beckoning for a troop of black-clad workers, standing by with all manner of objects, from buckets of water to racks of medicinal vials.

With a sound like that of old fishpickle grog bursting its cork, a deep red fire exploded upon his palms, consuming his arms in a brief shroud of fire. Pitch-coloured smoke enveloped his face. His screech was doused with a mouthful of ice water. Another bucketful put out the fire and the spell sputtered out. The portly man was left quivering and dripping wet, his entire front blackened and crisp. A large gap had been burnt out of his ring of hair. Fresh, pink, and greasy burns adorned his palms and wrists. Another bucket of water hit him before Eyrum guided him away to the right-hand group. None of them as burnt or as jaded as the Albion man but each looked forlorn. *No failure here, Hurricane's balls*, Mithrid thought.

Watching the man seethe with pain, she put a hand to her own scar. That fire was dead and gone, but its grave remained emblazoned on her cheek.

Two more went left and one right before it was Mithrid's rank. They began at the far end. Some fat louse of a child showed off by making the water slide across the cobbles. He threw up a fist to the applause he got. The next was Remina Hag, of all people. None were as shocked as Mithrid when the girl managed to summon the faintest waft of steam from her hands. Hereni was nodding appreciatively, saying, 'It will come to you in time and with concentration.'

Bull was there, hidden by the length of the line. He stepped forwards and tried his best, staring at his hands as intently as a half-blind scholar reading a note. It looked hopeless, but he perked up when Eyrum took him by the elbow and showed him to a seat in the group of failures. They grinned at him. They didn't look so secondary with him amongst them. There was no winning or losing for Bull, and Mithrid was jealous.

There was nothing to do but wait and watch almost every other recruit in the line succeed at some form of magick; be it the common shaking like a leaf or as mesmerising as an orb of light dancing over knuckles. Or even the woman next to her, who bent her shadow into strange shapes.

At last, Hereni and Eyrum stood before Mithrid.

'Hello again,' greeted the captain cheerily. Mithrid didn't know what to do but stick her hands out as she'd seen others do.

'First things first. Close your eyes. Feel your breath mix with the air. Feel the ground pressing against your boots. Feel their power. That is magick. When you think you can, grasp it with your mind. Pull that power towards you.'

Mithrid reached out, clawing at nothing. She heard every shuffle of soles and whisper. She felt the ache in her body, and the dizziness of darkness.

'Feel anything?' came the gruff bluntness of Eyrum.

'Give her a moment, General,' Hereni whispered. 'It will feel like heat, sometimes cold, or a rush of blood.'

Mithrid stretched her arms and ground her teeth. Every muscle strained, teeth breaking through taught lips, she tried to feel this flow of magick. All she felt was lightheaded. The murmurs of the others grew louder.

Then, a twinge in her mind, as if one of her thoughts had been caught on a fishing hook. Mithrid, desperate, seized it. She felt a growing prickle of heat in the soles of her feet and in her fingertips. Once more, a sharp pain struck at the back of her skull. Her face felt numb, yet on she pulled.

'She's found it,' Hereni muttered in encouragement. 'Draw it in and then focus it into your hands.

The more the sensation flooded her, the harder she tensed, the more vicious the pain became. Her head throbbed. Mithrid opened her eyes to look at her rigid fingers, expecting fire, or light, or green tendrils. There was nothing but her grimy hands.

In that one blip of confusion, the magick petered out. If it had even been magick at all. Though the tingling still remained in her fingertips, all she had to show for it was a cramp in one arm.

A quite sigh of disappointment emanated from the crowded group. Mithrid looked to Hereni. The captain kept her cheery face up, but her eyes were fidgety. Eyrum guided the way with his axe, and no matter how pleased Bull looked, Mithrid found herself discouraged that the magick had failed her. She hadn't endured everything since the shipwreck just to accept that she had failed it.

Hardly any time passed before another recruit was successful. Mithrid watched the scrawny lad take his place. Watching his grinning, doltish face, she met Remina's gaze. It was far too haughty for Mithrid's liking, and she hated the girl in that moment. She turned around to find the portly Albion man staring at her through soot-covered spectacles and groaned.

An hour passed before the ranks were divided into their halves. Halves was a kick in the face. The witch and dragon had been mostly correct. The recruits who had shown promise as mages now occupied the other side of the training yards. If Mithrid's keen ears were correct, Hereni and another mage were currently yelling all the wonders of magick at them.

Eyrum stood guard over the soldiers. 'You stand there, thinking yourself lesser than those. But let me tell you, recruits, every mage has to swing a sword at some point. There are times when even magick fails, and all that is left in the gnashing, fearsome dark are these,' Eyrum held up two hands, one clenched into a fist the size of Mithrid's head, and another holding an axe. 'And what strength the good gods have gifted you.'

With no further chatter, the towering Siren swung his axe for a nearby climbing pole. Though the pole was almost as thick as a tree, it came apart as easy as a dandelion. With a loud crunch and a shower of splinters, the pole was severed. Eyrum shoved it from its shattered roots, and let it fall to the stone.

'Magick may not be your weapon, so we will have to make you a weapon instead,' he spoke.

The workers swooped in once again, carting barrels of quarterstaffs, spears, and blunted swords and axes. The recruits moved forwards to try a few of them out. Bull hung beside Mithrid. Aside from punching Bogran once, she knew the big lad had never swung a weapon in his life.

Under the watchful eye of Eyrum, Mithrid reached for an axe. A worker lifted up a wooden broadsword instead. 'Perhaps a practice sword instead, miss? These are hea—'

Mithrid's swing snapped the wooden weapon in half. The worker dropped the other half in shock, eyes trying to trace the path Mithrid's axe had taken so quickly.

'Now, see here!'

'Disappear,' growled Eyrum and the worker scurried away. The Siren looked her up and down as he hefted his own weapon. 'Nothing wrong with an axe.'

He swung it in a wide, reckless arc, forcing everybody present to scatter. The bespectacled man threw himself needlessly into a clumsy dive. Mithrid tottered backwards, almost falling. Eyrum's blade came perilously close to her shoulder before biting into the stone. She swung her axe madly as if she swiped at an encroaching bat.

'What you need,' Eyrum grunted, somehow finding the time to lecture between the flowing arcs of steel he directed towards her, 'is control.'

Mithrid ducked, pausing just long enough to see three fiery hairs float past her face.

'Speed.'

Either she was being made an example of, or she was being tested. Mithrid despised the idea of both. She swung her axe in a wild attempt to fend him off. She caught the faintest glimpse of surprise in his face before he pirouetted away. Mithrid's axe whistled past his beard of scales, and as the momentum sent her reeling, Eyrum kicked her legs out from under her.

Mithrid heard the whoosh of the blade and the nearby screams of panic, but no more. When she opened her eyes, its honed edge rested an inch from her nose.

The Siren stood beyond it; one eye fixed on Mithrid. 'And accuracy,' he said.

Embarrassment. Uselessness. Outrage. She felt them all, breathing hard, emotions ruling her, Mithrid pushed the axe head aside, glowering at the bully towering over her. She was about to give him a piece of her mind and tell him how she hadn't been dragged a thousand miles to be tormented, when the Siren thrust out a huge hand.

'Again?' he offered her.

However small that smile was – more a wince with some teeth thrown in – it completely punctured all of Mithrid's anger. It was still a smile, and that mattered. She let that hand seize hers and firmly, but gently, drag her upright.

Eyrum spoke to the gathered others. 'You cannot get a job done without the necessary tools. Ask any Scalussen architect. Our job is war. Our tools are weapons.' He took a breath to bellow. 'Now, FORM UP!'

The hour was late when Mithrid wound down the empty steps into the bowels of the Underspire. She was so tired, so wrapped up in her aches, bruises, and scratches, she almost forgot all about the lycan guards patrolling the Underspire.

Frightened half to death by one of the leering wolfmen standing in her path, Mithrid staggered towards the barracks she had woken up in.

Despite her hopes, the silence of the morning was gone. In its stead rang raucous conversation from every bunk and hammock. The barracks were split by age only. It seemed any refugee or citizen under the age of sixteen winters had been lumped together. Where the older recruits were, and the quieter, emptier barracks, Mithrid wished to know.

Shepherded in by the lycan guards, Mithrid carried her tired limbs into the room. She arrived mostly unnoticed. It seemed swiping at the blowing moths and red plants, or hurling things back and forth at great speed between beds, or simple nattering was far more interesting than a late arrival. Here and there, a few exhausted bodies slept on through the noise.

The very young seemed gathered nearer the door and lower to the floor. Above and beyond them, the bunks were occupied by older survivors. Amongst them, smaller hierarchies had been drawn between top hammocks and bottom hammocks. Mithrid wondered why, left to its own devices, society always seemed to draw its own lines.

As somebody who had spent the first night unconscious, she accepted her lot of a lower bed and the theft of one of her pillows. At least a tray of food had gone mostly untouched. All except for a square void where cake crumbs lingered. It was only when she started to crawl into bed that somebody hollered her name.

'Mithrid. Why are you so late?'

Remina Hag was still awake and perched on a high hammock. Trenika and Lurn were with her, and two others, an older boy and girl that Mithrid had seen chosen as mages.

'Wanted to keep training,' she lied. She had been avoiding her hunger and tiredness for the last hour, waiting for the barracks to fall to slumber so she could sneak in unbothered. *So much for that plan.* She avoided any further questions by stuffing some loaf into her face.

'Still trying?' Trenika baited her. 'A shame.'

Mithrid rolled her eyes in the shadow of her bunk, refusing to answer, but the pause grew too lengthy for Bull. The big lump was on the opposite bed from her. He piped up on her behalf, the lummox.

'What?'

Nudged by the others, Remina spoke up. 'To not have you with the rest of us. The rest of us mages, that is. You, too, Bull.'

It sounded too pleasant for Mithrid's liking. Normally when Remina was nice, it meant she either needed something or was poised to ladle on the mockery. Mithrid checked to see if she was able to contain the sneer that was so plain in her words. So far Remina had yet to break.

'I don't care. Like they said, we're all in this together now,' Bull replied. A few others murmured in agreement, both soldier and mage recruits, Mithrid was satisfied to see. She had to smile at Bull's purity. It should have shamed Remina into silence, but she had clearly been waiting to lord it over Mithrid.

Remina hummed. 'How strange that both the witch and the helbeast made a mistake. Almost like you tricked them by fainting both times, and now you've been caught out.'

'I'll take brawn over magick any day, you cretch.'

Remina raised an eyebrow. 'Sounds like something a soldier with no magick would say.' Sparks scattered at a snap of her fingers.

Mithrid's entire day had been spent getting beaten and battered about. She refused to spend the evening the same way. She stepped from her bunk. 'Magick's gone to your head that fast, has it? You seem to have forgotten all too quickly what brought us here. Your sister? Your dead mother? Classic Remina. You've been given an inch more than the rest of us and you treat it like a mile. One day here, and you're already pretending to be queen of the Underspire. Being better is so important you'd trample on anyone, wouldn't you? Even Bull and me. I never got to tell you with Bogran and Crisk all wrapped around your finger, but you've always been truly pathetic.'

The low groan of intrigue from around them was painfully predictable. Conversations died. Bodies scrambled for a better view.

Remina swung down from her bunk. There was an assuredness about her that Mithrid hadn't seen in Troughwake. Her cheeks were flushed crimson.

'I haven't forgotten. I mourn by getting on with it. What's pathetic is *you*. We've been given a better life here, and all Mithrid Fenn can do is mope about, questioning everything and everyone. You're the one acting important, as if your sorrow's somehow greater. As if spilling blood for your worthless, dead drunk of a father is so—'

Mithrid's arm was swinging at the word "drunk". She socked Remina square in the jaw. It was a clumsy blow, hurting her wrist as much as Remina's face.

'You always were a cunt,' Mithrid spat.

The barracks were filled with hollering as Remina Hag came up swinging. She loosened one of Mithrid's teeth before she was put on her backside once again with a swift kick to the shin. Mithrid thanked Eyrum for that move.

'Stay down,' Mithrid spat, unsettled by her own lust for violence. Her fists ached to pummel the girl into mush.

Remina was beyond listening. She got to her feet. Before anybody could intervene, she was muttering into her hands, eyes wild and arms shaking.

'Stop her!' somebody cried.

With sparks sputtering around her hands, Remina reached for Mithrid. She yelled out as one caught her wrist. Mithrid shrank away, kicking at the girl to keep her at bay. 'You're mad!' she cried, unable to ignore the fiendish look in Remina's eyes.

Bodies scattered as the lycans came racing through the bunks. Two of them skidded between Remina and Mithrid. They snarled in each girl's face, baring hideous fangs that dripped with far too much saliva. The piebald lycan from before fixed her with a stare Mithrid would take to her grave.

Remina, meanwhile, was incensed to see what was happening. It took the lycan roaring in her face to send her white as a sheet. She fell on her plump arse, much to the sniggering and whispering of the onlookers.

'So eager to fight you must battle amongst yourselves? Ridiculous. Asleep! All of you!' came a bellow from the doorway. Eyrum cast a long and monstrous shadow into the room. As the barracks calmed into quiet muttering, and the lycans began to patrol the bunks, Mithrid finally managed to eat her vittles in peace. It was plain fare, but to her tired, starved palate, they tasted like scraps from a king's table.

The piebald lycan remained nearby, as if expecting another fight. Mithrid was silently grateful on the matter. She could hear him sniffing as she chewed, and in thanks, slowly slid a piece of loaf and salted meat towards him on a board. The speed with which he snatched the meat away was frightening, and highly comical.

For the first time since setting foot beyond Troughwake, Mithrid relaxed.

CHAPTER 14
SOME WOUNDS NEVER HEAL

Burned to charcoal and dust. That is what the Outlaw King made of my city. He came in the night to burn us in our homes. He slit half the throats of my family before I awoke and escaped to safety. I alone made it free. I alone, out of six thousand.
A SPEECH MADE BY A SURVIVOR OF THE KSERAK MASSACRE TO THE PEOPLE OF KRAUSLUNG. INCIDENTALLY, THE SURVIVOR IN QUESTION WAS NEVER HEARD FROM NOR SEEN AGAIN

From the jagged teeth of the Össfen Mountains, in the lack of moonlight, Krauslung looked to be aflame. Columns of smoke arose like the buttress roots of eastern trees, coalescing into one great tower of smog and char. The winds bent it north, and like a scar it sat across the lands. A constant storm with no lightning nor thunder to offer, just ash flakes for rain.

A hot eye of flame glowed in the Arka capital's central district. Several buildings had been recently razed by the looks of it. The rest of the pollution was the fault of the smelters, tanneries, and forges that spread from the Port of Rós to the northern backside of Manesmark, at the neck of Krauslung's valley. Where the city wasn't choked by the business of making arms and armour for war, trade commanded. Factories belched all manner of coloured ethers from their brick chimneys. Some spewed sparks. The industrial districts looked like no city at all, but a breathing blight trying to consume a once great monument. The only magnificence to be witnessed in Krauslung besides its heaving sprawl was the Arkathedral. A colossal, tiered cake of marble hugging the opposite mountain. It glowed in the combined torch and firelight of the city. Mansions and rich abodes clung to its sheer walls. They clambered over each other like citizens fleeing for city gates when the enemy hordes arrived.

At least that's how Farden saw it.

Fleetstar's claws crunched in the permanent ice that refused to vacate the peaks of the mountains, even since the Long Winter had thawed. 'You used to call this home?' the dragon hissed. A smoke ring puffed from her nostril before being snatched away by the winds. A shade of teal washed across her black, camouflaged scales for a moment. A tiny lapse of concentration.

'It wasn't always like this,' answered Farden. He didn't want to admit how much it had changed since he had last left the Frostsoar.

Inwick quietly scoffed.

'Fine. It was dirty and depraved, but at least it had an order to it. Unity. The arkmages protected Emaneska and we all pretended to be civilised. At least until the sun went down.' Farden clenched his fist to send another wave of heat rolling through his body. 'Malvus has ruined all that.'

Fleetstar's eye's shone fiercely. 'I say we find his bedchamber and fill it with flame. What's to stop us?'

Inwick was busy picking her nails with one of her swords. 'Helbeasts, Lost Clan dragons, daemons, and about half a mile of marble, soldiers, and mages. The emperor might be worth less than the shit scraped off the wall of a privy, but he's not stupid. He never was.'

'Modren told me you hit him once, Farden,' Fleetstar cackled. It was an odd sound, a hoarse burbling. Farden could feel his ribs shuddering under the saddle. 'Right in that excuse for a face you humans have.'

'That I did.' Though his memories of those years were occasionally hazy, more so as the years slid past, Farden would often think of that punch and smirk.

'I often wonder where we'd be now if you had thrown him from the roof of the Arkathedral,' sighed Inwick.

'Me, too. But some other bastard from Malvus' cult of the Marble Copse would have taken his place. Saker of the Lost Clans, perhaps. The most disturbing about all of this is that people agree with Malvus. Believe in him. It boggles my mind.' Farden felt the frustration bubbling like a stew left too long on the fire. He took a breath and clapped his gauntlets together. 'Inwick? Our messenger.'

She produced a tiny wooden cage from her haversack and passed it to him with a wrinkle of distaste on her lip. Inwick had never grown a fondness for small, wriggling creatures.

Since the Arka had started using Paraian vuleguls to patrol Krauslung's marred skies, no hawk lived long enough to deliver a message. A Bethmuir bat, on the other hand…

At the taste of fresh air instead of the musty bag, the diminutive, indigo creature jiggled inside its cage, chirping a note so lofty it sounded like something scraping the inside of Farden's skull. A cloth bag dangled from the cage. Its patterned weave writhed gently. Inside were a collection of dozy worms, and Farden dangled one for the bat to gulp down.

When the little thing was fed, it stared at Farden from between the bars with its bulging brown eyes. *One clear thought.* That was all the bat needed, he knew. *One clear thought.*

Farden thumbed open the cage, and the bat tore into the night as if the goddess Hel herself chased it. Not one chirrup broke the silence of the mountaintop.

'How do you know where Jeasin is?' Inwick asked.

'I don't,' replied Farden. 'but I know where Malvus likes to keep her.'

Right by his side.

Five scribes it had taken for the Book to be forged on Mage Corcoran's back and shoulders. Barely an hour had each lasted before the magick claimed then, until their mouths foamed, and they were dragged quivering from the cell. In went the next scribe, forced to pick up the ink and needles and continue the grisly task.

Loki grinned when the mage finally moved. Watching through the bars, he had thought Corcoran dead for some time. The stench of rot, the blood dripping in quiet patter from her bare hips and elbows. A twitch of the finger was all it was, but enough. Next came her eyes, red raw, all white forgotten. Her teeth were a snarl of effort. Up, she staggered, and as she turned, Loki saw what the scribes had written upon her. *Carved*, would be more accurate. The script of her stolen Book was no more than jagged, black wounds oozing blood. Black veins spread across her arms and face. Ashen was her skin. But between the mess of flesh and ink, amongst those borrowed, maddening words, white light flashed as the magick settled.

'You are not Written,' Loki breathed. 'We will call you the Scarred.'

Of all the sounds that Lady Jeasin loathed above all else, it was snoring.

It was an annoyance of two parts. First, the guttural hawk rattling through the back of a nose. That was bad enough. Then the silence, the gentle breath that lasts just long enough to make one hope that snore was the last… But no. There it was again.

Malvus was a torturous snorer with wine in him. How unfortunate, then, that he never went to bed without wine to dull him.

His drunken whores, their limbs sticking all directions from the bed, compounded the abuse. The four of them made a disjointed melody like that of a choir of frogs.

Jeasin pushed herself from the bed, letting the tangled sheets fall from her. The steps from the vast bed didn't even need to be counted any more. When she felt the cold wall, she traced it to the various items of furniture she knew her clothes lay upon. The servants would not come until the morning to dress her. They knew it best to leave the emperor alone when he was in a dark mood and lusting for wine and women.

After shimmying into her gem-studded dress and a scarf of fur, she paused at the door, listening once more to the clatter of snoring. Jeasin had sipped her wine slowly, as she had learned to do long ago in an Albion cathouse. She had no need to feel dizzy nor drunk. Her world was dark enough without muffling it further, and she knew how most worries were impervious to drowning, no matter how much wine they were doused in. They always waited to greet you in the morning light. There was only one thing that ever soothed the steady crunch of her mind: knowledge, and, in its refined form, secrets. They had kept her alive and at the emperor's side so far.

Thirty paces to the door, and Jeasin was weaving through the corridors. Lanterns crackled softly at intervals. The gentle clearing of a throat and creak of armour told her where the guards stood.

'Lady,' they bid her quietly.

She said nothing in return. Women of her stature did not need to. Jeasin stared emptily ahead, and retraced steps she had taken countless times in the last two decades. It had taken her a year at most to learn its myriad stairs, rooms, and levels. Another to learn the streets. It helped having the escort of the emperor's guards and favour instead of pawing around in the dark, mocked by strangers.

From Malvus' self-imposed prison at the core of the Arkathedral, Jeasin worked her way outwards to where the edges of the citadel were forged in glass instead of stone. She liked to trace her fingers across the vast, cold panes, and feel the vibrations of the city beneath her. She also liked to cause the guards to scatter to make way for her. Simple pleasures, more for the ego of the filthy peasant girl residing deep with her, than the lady of Krauslung.

Five flights down.

Malvus' mood, which had been darkening like brewing tempest for the past year, had abruptly brightened two days ago. Though usually he spent his days hunched in the Blazing Throne, screeching at ingrates and fools, or staring north and brooding, he had been a bundle of activity.

Fourteenth corridor.

Not levity, mind. The years of fighting to rule had utterly soured him, but he worked with a renewed purpose that Jeasin needed to understand. Even despite her decades of cleverly-constructed loyalty, it was vexing that the emperor still did not completely trust her. It rattled the foundations of all she had built.

Two lefts, straight.

A visitor with a gift. That was all Malvus had told her. Something for his experiments in the dungeons. She had heard the screams every night for the past six months, emanating through the stone. Since this visitor had arrived, those screams had only grown louder and more numerous. Jeasin followed that haunting clamour now. She knew what they were: Malvus was making mages.

Seventh corridor.

A stamp of a foot caught her in her tracks.

'Emperor's orders, Lady Jeasin,' said a guard. 'Can't let you in.'

She scoffed haughtily. 'Don't you now know who I am?'

'Course, Lady. But the emperor said no admittance but himself, General Toskig, or—'

'Who?' Jeasin demanded, hands on her hips. 'Who else is there?'

A door opened, briefly releasing a cacophony of screams before they were muffled by a slam. Jeasin felt wintry air blow across her naked feet. It took her a moment to dig up the memory of where she knew that feeling from: of a shadow cast by no sun. A shadow with breath. A scent of fields and primordial forests she would never set foot in.

She had never forgotten meeting the shade of a god.

'You,' she spoke. *The visitor.* 'Loki.'

'Me, indeed,' came the reply, in an accent foreign and familiar all at once. 'And you, the whore from Albion. You have aged, Jeasin of Tayn.'

'We humans tend to do that. Why are you here?'

Loki chuckled. 'I could ask you the same thing. My, what fine work you've done. From a cathouse in Kiltyrin Duchy to the Arkathedral and emperor's side. And twenty years with the same client is rather impressive by itself. Especially when that client's known for burning people on pyres for so much as saying the Outlaw King's name. Though, that's the dream, right? Even changed your accent. My, my, I dare say there's not a more successful whore in the lands.'

Jeasin reached out to slap the bastard. She had no clue why, seeing as the creature was just shadow and dreams, but it was the gesture that counted.

Nobody was more surprised when the slap connected with skin. Rough like sand and cold like metal, but skin all the same. *No mere shadow.* Jeasin would have tripped backwards over her own superstitions had it not been for the vice-like grip that seized her elbow and escorted her from the guards.

Once striding up stairwells, she shrugged Loki away. 'Release me! How did…'

'Not like you to be speechless, from what I remember of our previous meeting in Albion.'

Jeasin was confused. 'Why are you helpin' Malvus? Your kind favours the Outlaw King, not the daemons.'

'My kind? I alone stand outside the realm of the gods. Though I hear they call it Haven now. I would have gone for Prison.'

'Then why aren't you lapping up praise, like any god would, instead of being a lackey to the emperor? Without magick there is plenty of religion to occupy people in this city. Plenty of cults.'

'All in good time, Lady Jeasin,' he replied. Jeasin could hear the curl in his lips. 'We have shared interests, let's say.'

'Farden,' the name was said through a clenched jaw, half spat. The habit had started out as rehearsed, something to throw Malvus off the scent of her spying for the Outlaw King in the dawn of the empire. As the years had passed, and her position as the emperor's woman had grown ever more entrenched, and Farden's summons became ever more precarious, the loathing had become more a part of her than she realised. Jeasin recited the story she had clung to for decades. 'Farden kidnapped me from Albion and abandoned me here. I detest that mage and all his kind.'

'How the years poison the soul!' Loki remarked, hearing her emotion. 'I remember a time when you were on his side, even helped Durnus and Modren escape the Arkathedral's dungeons.'

Jeasin thought she knew where the god stood, but her sharp fingernail met stone instead. 'You keep your forked tongue behind your lips. That's a filthy lie!' she hissed, straining to hear the presence of others. They sounded alone.

Loki sounded impressed. 'A lie long hidden, I must say. Well done. You and I could work well together.'

'What do you want?' she asked.

The god spoke from behind her, making her whirl.

'I want you to tell Farden everything.'

Jeasin's snorted with laughter. 'I don't know what you mean. That would be treachery.'

'Naturally.'

Wind toyed with her hair. She caught the scent of chimney smoke on it, telling her they were near the roof of the Arkathedral. Loki chatted idly like an old friend come back to visit. Jeasin hoped he wasn't here to stay permanently. He was a rogue nail in the floorboards. A jester in her deck of cards and game of power. He had upset her balance.

'I hear Malvus calls this the Eyrie now. Shame nothing nests up here besides these ugly birds.'

Jeasin heard a movement of cloth and a wretched squawk from one of the vuleguls. They had always sounded ugly. Carcasses must have been strewn around her given the stink in her nose. She ran her hand across the marble trees. They were more weathered than their cousins below the stone at her feet in the Marble Copse. For almost a decade now, they were the only forest she had been allowed to experience. *Still beat scraping a whore's living in an Albion duchy.*

'Why are you helpin' Malvus?' Jeasin asked. 'Tell me.'

'I suppose you could call it helping,' mused the god. 'Because Farden will never come south, and without me, Malvus will not march north. He languishes here, growing older and angrier by the day. Simply put? He needed poking.'

'How?'

'By giving him the weapon he needs.'

'I thought those runed mages were the weapon Malvus needed.' Jeasin had felt their presence in the Arkathedral. They smelled of dead meat and sweat.

'Amateurs and lucky accidents. He needs real magick, and seeing as all the spellbooks are either stolen, lost, locked away, burned, or floating on Farden's great ships in the ocean, I brought him a better one.' Loki's steps punctuated the rhythm of his words. 'Thirty Books carved from the backs of Written mages, all wrapped up in leather, ready to carve into unwilling backs. You remember Farden's Book, don't you?'

Once upon a time, Jeasin had run her hands across all of Farden's scars, even the ones in writing. He had never let her trace the script, in case she read it. *That way lies madness,* he had said.

'Now, Malvus' new mages – the Scarred – can be exactly what he wants: rivals to the power of Farden's remaining Written. Rivals to Farden himself, perhaps.'

Despite the sour feeling the man's name gave her, Jeasin still spluttered with laughter. 'Sure. You and I know better than that cowshit. The only mage who could defeat Farden would be 'imself.'

'Imagine that,' Loki chuckled. 'Two Fardens in the world. Evernia save us. There would be no hope for anything between Haven or Hel.'

Jeasin pulled a grim smile. One mage was troublesome enough. She heard the god's footsteps depart, making the vuleguls scatter. 'I 'aven't spoken to Farden in two years, and nor do I want to. It's too dangerous. I need to protect what I've made for myself,' she called after him, hands to her fur scarf. It was always gratifying to speak a truth when one lived a life of lying. Like finding a gold piece in a pile of dragon shit.

'Maybe you should speak to him, for old time's sake. Oh, and when you do, ask him how Farden Four-Hand killed Duke Kiltyrin, all those years past. He never did tell me.'

Nor her. Jeasin thought.

'It's pointless. Farden won't come. He blames me for not warnin' him of Malvus' plans to attack some city called Kserak, even though it would have seen me hanged.' Jeasin was a stranger to guilt. It took her a moment to realise what the sensation was. 'I made my choice long ago. This ain't my war.'

But the god chuckled his way below. 'We'll see.'

Jeasin stayed atop the Arkathedral, glad for the music of the rushing winds, and the rumble of the city beneath her. Screams, once again, not from within the fortress, but down in the streets. In the darkness behind her eyes, she saw the lights, the streets knitted in stone. She imagined it all, and yet every time she heard a scream or a cry, her imagination crumbled.

Vexed, she gave up. Jeasin was stamping after the god to give him a piece of her mind when she heard it: a piercing chirping, quiet and yet growing louder. It came zipping past her, painfully loud before disappearing. One or two of the vuleguls who had heard the noise took chase, but Jeasin knew the bat would already be long gone. She hung her head and took a slow breath.

'Fuck these gods and mages,' she grunted, wondering how they plotted such perfect timing.

Farden had returned to Krauslung.

※

Besides sliding down the precipitous sides of the mountains, the safest way to sneak into Krauslung's city valley was via its port. And when lacking a boat, a dragon will have to do.

The Port of Rós was a yawning mouth choked with all manner of vessels. From a league south, the port shone like a bonfire on a black coast. Myriad ship lights and boardwalk lanterns shone golden. Ships drew sketched silhouettes against the glow.

Fat cogs, sloops, and overloaded skiffs occupied the eastern side of the port. The western half was swollen like a tumour of rigging and sailcloth. Warships crowded together, and plenty of them.

Fleetstar thundered through the air, barely a foot from the waves. Farden tried to count shapes amongst the mess. The distance was shrinking fast, but the wind was bitter to the eyes. He looked aside, watching the blur of back waters, tantalisingly and terrifyingly close. How Fleetstar flew so fast just by gliding, he had no idea, but it thrilled him. Perching on the Mad Dragon's back felt like riding a crossbow bolt.

Cold knuckles crunched as Fleetstar swerved. Farden had been expecting her to avoid the glittering patrol ships sitting a mile out from Krauslung. Instead, she aimed for them. Her wing-claw cast up an arc of sea spray.

Fleetstar! Farden yelled in his mind, as Towerdawn had taught him.

The dragon's cackle boomed in his skull.

As the ship approached faster than the swing of an axe, Farden felt Fleetstar tense. Her scales shed every last glint of shine to them, darker than pitch. The mage winced.

Fleetstar missed the ship by yards only. Farden almost snapped his neck trying to chase the ship as it passed by. He managed to catch a glimpse of a confused sailor steadying himself against the strange wind.

The dragon's laughter echoed through his mind.

The ships began to grow in number. Those that couldn't squeeze into the huge port anchored in the Bay of Rós. Fleetstar slalomed between the bigger ones. A thrust of her tail almost capsized a small faering. The drunken, alarmed cries of the drunken fisherman chased them into the dark.

Fleetstar.

Oh, fine.

With a raised fist, Farden signalled Inwick, and felt the mage hunker close to him. Fleetstar opened her jaws wide, not to roar, but in a great inhale. Farden did the same. This time, it was he who tensed, watching with wide eyes as the black sea inched closer. A lurch elicited an involuntary groan from him as the dragon folded her wings back and dove into the frigid waters.

Farden's curses were a stream of bubbles. The cold tried to force his precious air from his lungs and seeped through every crevice of his armour. He had a hatred of cold water. Surviving several shipwrecks will instil that in a person. He would have cast a heat spell, but it was too dangerous to use his magick so close to Krauslung.

Great sweeps of Fleetstar's wings thrust them through the void-like water. The dragon swam deep, making the mages' heads pound with the pressure. There was no light besides the rippling glow of Krauslung. Farden couldn't help but stare below into the formless deep. However he tried, he couldn't avoid recalling the leviathan he had once seen in the Bay of Rós, bludgeoning a ship to splinters. A dragon could make an easy morsel to a creature like that.

Farden shuddered as a dark, oval shape passed over them. It was the fat bottom of a ship. Another followed, and another, until Fleetstar was weaving around keels. He was grateful for the tight straps on a dragon-rider's saddle as she spiralled through the sea. One slip and he would have sank like… well, a man encased in armour.

Their lungs were burning by the time Fleetstar had entered the port's boundaries. She arched her back, raising the mages out of the water briefly to gulp down their air. Once more, she submerged, and led them on through the maze of crowded vessels. Bilge waste turned the water foul. All manner of junk floated in that muffled underworld, from glass bottles to lost crates. Even a smattering of corpses rotted in the port's water.

In the shadows between two spice-reeking schooners, a dragon's black snout and two pale faces emerged from the water without so much as a drip. A leaky rowboat was cut from its line, and after the dragon had slipped back into the water, the mages rowed their way into the light.

Sitting hunched with hoods up, they passed for any number of shady characters plying the waters or boardwalks. Ports bustled, and bustle is a fine distraction for those roaming the night. Combine that with souls who had been stuck at sea pining for the pleasures of a city, and iniquity flourished. It had been this way since before Malvus, and in that way, Farden felt almost at home in the Port of Rós. At least for a moment.

With the boat tied off on a quieter jetty, the two mages began to filter through the crowds of sailors, traders, craftspeople, pleasure seekers, and drunkards. Street Legion guards and the grubbier city watch clumped together on every corner, watching for any excuse to harass a citizen. It was pathetic. All that elevated them was a tabard and some chainmail, and yet they acted like they alone bore the emperor's will. Authority was their poison.

Farden stared at the Arka warships, trying to count their shapes amongst the mess of wood and rope. They already outnumbered the Scalussen fleet by double. At least none of the Arka vessels could rival his bookships in size.

'Farden,' Inwick whispered to him, motioning ahead. At a junction between two main thoroughfares, the Street Legion had company. Two Arka mages in steel plate and dirty white capes. One struggled to manhandle something, and as the crowds shifted, Farden saw the helbeasts.

Lipless faces dripping with teeth and black saliva, the creatures were small, barely cubs, but they still strained against their iron leashes. When they weren't sniffing the night air, choked with the strange blend of gutters, bilge waste, and a variety of cooking smells, they snapped at the public trying their best to avoid their reach. The beasts must have been starving.

'Suppress,' Farden replied. He did the same, drawing his magick in from his extremities and pushing it deep into his bones. His armour was completely covered by his disguise of drab and patchwork cloth, which was enough to keep it hidden. Daemons and their helbeasts only reacted to the sight of it, as if it shone with a light that human eyes couldn't see.

Even so, they wound through the busy boardwalk and took another street. Farden's stomach rumbled as they passed long queues of skinny doorway vendors. They sat elbow to elbow, each manning a charcoal stove that spat steam and smoke. Coloured streamers crisscrossed the street, reminding Farden of the Paraian markets. He eyed the sizzling meats and ignored his stomach's rumble.

'Where will she be?'

'Hopefully,' Farden answered her, 'in the old bakery.'

'Hmph,' Inwick grunted. Like many in Scalussen, the Written mage had become increasingly irascible of late. Inwick was a particularly fine example. As the years of strife grew heavier each passing day this stifled war went on, she had withdrawn into herself. Serious, she had always been, but that sombre exterior had darkened, weathered. Cracks had started to creep through her skin. Farden couldn't help but hold himself accountable.

Leaving the port behind them, they weaved an unpredictable pattern between the buildings to avoid helbeast and mage patrols. Farden's gaze roved over every busy tavern and boarded shopfront, marking each change he didn't recognise. The further they moved from the boardwalks, the more he felt like a stranger.

Farden faltered upon seeing a body hanging from a pole between two buildings. The corpse was too rotten to make out who or what it was, but the scales and the word "Treason" were painted in white paint across its naked chest. Below it, on any stretch of wall not occupied by door, window, or sign, graffiti reigned.

Seeing his own face, or a poor copy of it, at least, never failed to bemuse Farden. He had always lurked on the fringes of these people. Half of them hadn't been born when he saved Emaneska the first time. Now, he was a symbol. A hooded, square-jawed figure pointing out from the wall, accompanied by words like *solidarity*. *Patience*. *Justice is coming*.

Some lump of a man decided to shoulder the mage as he barged past.

'Watch it, shitfuck,' the man growled, pausing momentarily to see if he'd successfully sparked a fight.

Farden's knuckles popped as he clenched his fist.

Inwick shook her head. 'Ungrateful bastard.'

'Fear. When the world changes around you, you clutch at what you can control. If that man needs to pummel others to assuage his fear, good luck to him,' he muttered.

The meeting place was a crooked house lashed like a mast to three other buildings to keep it upright. Rotten scaffolding hung from it like lank hair. Its roof had been pilfered for its tiles. The signs that hadn't been defaced spoke of danger and collapse.

After lingering by its boarded door for a moment to watch the crowds for spies, the two mages splintered a panel and slipped inside.

Farden had no idea what purpose the building used to serve, but in its dying days he would have guessed a place for storing shit. Piles of... something lingered in every corner. The smell was enough to fell a minotaur.

Clamping hands over noses, Inwick and Farden proceeded up the rotten stairs to the tallest point, where the only roof was a smoky night sky. Nests of twigs and bones and hair balanced on surviving rafters. A lone seagull eyed them suspiciously. White dung had replaced the old colours of the walls.

'Took you fuckin' long enough,' said a voice from the corner. Jeasin leaned against a rafter, pretending to watch the streets below through the cracks in a black windowpane. 'I've been waitin' for an hour.'

While Inwick waited by the stairs, hands on her hilts and watching Jeasin as if she were a condemned thief, Farden stepped into the faint city glow.

'If it isn't Lady Jeasin,' he grunted.

Jeasin's hair had grown past her shoulders, tinged with silver. Her face had not softened, still that arrangement of sharply beautiful features, always puckered in a scowl. Beneath her silk, gold, and furs, she reeked of perfumes, to a degree almost as eye-watering as the rest of the smells in this city. *How far she had risen since Albion*, Farden thought. *How alike Malvus she had become.*

Farden cocked his head towards the window, trying to remain civil. 'The helbeast patrols have doubled since last I saw them. More mages, too. Seems every other building is a blacksmith.'

'You should see Manesmark. I 'ear it's not even a town any more. Just one giant war camp,' she muttered. 'Shall we speak of the weather next? The rise in port taxes?'

Inwick spoke up. 'What about how you betrayed us, leaving thousands to die?'

Jeasin snarled. 'I got nothin' to apologise for.' I risked my fuckin' neck for years payin' my life-debt back to you, Farden. I told you I was done, yet you kept thinkin' of me as your spy. Kept sendin' your bats and clickin' your fingers to summon me. I was finished bein' your traitor before Malvus told me of his attack on Kserak. Me, and only me. I wanted to tell you, I did, but Malvus would have gutted me. Even now, do you know what I risk to be here?'

'Perfume and jewels, by the looks of it.'

'You're damn right.' Jeasin turned then. Despite her clouded eyes, she always knew exactly where Inwick stood. 'I don't give a fuck if you're a Written, there'll be two blind bitches in this room when I'm finished with you.'

Inwick drew her shortswords. Farden took a step, teeth bared.

'Enough! The past is set in stone. Jeasin's chosen her side.'

A crash of glass and raised voices drew the mages' attention to an alleyway, where some street legion guards were breaking their way into a house.

'We don't have long, Jeasin. Help me one last time, for Kserak, and you will never see me again. Keep your jewels and your palace,' Farden bargained. 'We know Malvus is trying to make his own Written mages. I need to know his plans.'

Jeasin chewed her lip for a moment. 'He calls them runed mages. I hear more and more of them every day. You should hear the screamin'. Somethin' awful, it is,' said Jeasin. 'Every day and night for six months now. Almost every recruit Malvus drags into his dungeons for tattooin' either dies or goes insane. I wager he has almost fifty of them runed mages, now more every week. How many are left of you now?'

'Not your concern,' Inwick snapped.

Here, Jeasin chewed her words. 'Well, they ain't much match for you Written, it pains me to say, but the new ones might be.'

'What in Hel do you mean?'

Outside the decrepit building, a man and woman had been arrested for some infraction or other and were being hauled screaming across the broken glass and cobblestones by soldiers. Farden's jaw tightened. He ached to intervene. 'Tell me quickly.'

'Loki is back.'

All of the city noise fell away as Farden turned back to Jeasin. 'W— what did you say?'

'Loki, he's back. And he's real, Farden. He ain't no shadow. He ain't no ghost. He's got flesh and power and all. He's helpin' Malvus. Brought 'im a gift. Something that'll make the runed more powerful.'

While she spoke, Farden searched his memories. The realisation hit him like falling into a snowdrift. Chilling. The Written before the Last War had been hunted down, one by one, until only a score of Emaneska's finest mages remained. Since then, only three had survived the fight for freedom since, a fact that made Farden's heart ache if he dwelled upon it.

'Books, Farden. A book of... Books. He calls it the Hides of Hysteria. He gave it to Malvus to turn his best mages into *you*. Loki calls them the Scarred.'

The Scarred. Farden's stomach knotted. He remembered a seer. A woman with one arm. The wretch that guided the world to calamity. 'I have to stop him,' he snarled. 'He can't do this.'

'He can, and he is. With Loki's help.'

'I'll...' Farden seethed. He glared at the glowing Arkathedral between the rafters.

'Go on, then, Outlaw King, blast your way through the fortress. Take on Malvus and all his daemons by yourself. Worked out well for you last time. Probably exactly what Loki wants,' Jeasin snorted. For all tonight's disappointment, at least Jeasin could be counted on to be right.

'Farden,' warned Inwick.

Farden felt the magick churn temptingly in his veins. She hissed in his ear.

'King!'

Farden caught himself. He trembled with anger, but he held on by a thread.

'He had a message for you, mage,' said Jeasin, smirking as if she enjoyed this. 'Loki, that is. He knew you'd come. I don't know how the fuck he knew, but he is one smart god. He asked me to meet you, to tell you everythin'.' Jeasin smirked as if she enjoyed this. 'And to ask you how Duke Kiltyrin died, that night in Tayn twenty years ago. How Farden Four-Hand killed him. You never told me, but Loki said you would know exactly what that means.'

Farden had not heard that name in years and had forgotten how much he loathed it. The lack of the smallest finger on his left hand was enough of a reminder of a man he had once been. Four-Hand had been his name.

'Search that building!' came a shout. Its proximity was alarming.

Inwick was wide-eyed, strangely jittery. 'We have to leave.'

Farden levelled a finger in Jeasin's face, wishing she could see the scorn in his face, the fire he felt scratching his eyes. 'Enjoy your time in the Arkathedral, Jeasin. It won't last much longer.'

Jeasin just smiled and waggled her fingers farewell.

Casting their hoods over their heads, Inwick and Farden threw themselves from the building. They collided with the sloping roof tiles, sliding through moss and rotten feathers. The tiles bore the mages' weight for the most blessed of moments before collapsing into the front room of the building; right on top of a legion captain.

'Oof!' wheezed the obese man, accompanied by a foul splattering noise. The man had somehow simultaneously shat himself in either surprise or from the impact.

'Thron's balls,' Farden remarked to Inwick, while the guards stood shocked and frozen before them. 'I've never literally scared the shit out of somebody before.'

One of the guards mastered his flapping jaw. 'Halt! In the name of the emp—!'

Farden's sword stole the man's words away, spraying his blood across his comrades. As one died, the others came to life, clumsily waving their clubs and shortswords. Farden's sword danced between them, taking a limb or two while Inwick wound up her force spell.

All the air vacated the room as the spell crescendoed. The entire front of the building detonated, thrown outwards in a blast of masonry and green lightning. Guards cartwheeled like circus toppers before colliding with neighbouring buildings. One chap sailed straight through a window of a cathouse, interrupting a couple in the most tender of moments.

'Don't spend yourself so quickly, mage,' Farden reminded her.

Inwick's twin swords glittered almost as dangerously as her eyes. 'To the port, then?'

Casting one last look to Jeasin, standing over them, face hidden in shadow, Farden began to sprint. 'Where else?' he yelled.

The warning bells had yet to sound. Only the baying of nearby helbeasts could be heard. Their escape looked fruitful until they came face to face with a contingent of legion guards, presumably investigating the ruckus. Farden's armour was bared for all to see, and to his dry amusement, they had skidded to a halt exactly opposite a crude, graffiti sketch with the words, 'Repent' splayed across it.

Inwick rolled her eyes.

With a clang of metal, Farden slammed his vambraces together. The power he knew so well surged through his arms and rattled through every muscle.

'Ears,' he said to Inwick, seconds before clapping his hands together.

The shockwave raced along the street, shattering windows before it struck the guards. The mages raced ahead in its wake. Guards toppled left and right as the spell worked, bones breaking, noses bleeding. Farden and Inwick spared them no mercy. Their blades fell, darted, and hacked at anything that moved as they galloped towards the port.

Now the bells were ringing. Now the beasts were baying. One came charging from an alley mouth, its chain trailing like a whip behind it. As it sailed through the air, gruesome jaws opened wide, Farden pivoted, braced his sword arm, and held.

The helbeast skewered itself like a street vendor's meat. It took precious moments to wrench his sword free. He roared as he managed it, raising the weapon aloft and letting flames climb its bloody blade.

'Farden!' Inwick yelled, yards ahead and holding a shield spell in each hand. Great crowds of citizens were scarpering in every direction, eager to escape the commotion. It kept the guards and mages at bay for now, but their crossbows and feeble spells could still reach.

Farden swiped a firebolt aside, crushed the magick between his gauntlets and sent it straight back at its caster. The man sailed to the next rooftop, landing as a charred husk.

He could see the boardwalk now: a slice of crowd between the jumbled buildings. Inwick and Farden dashed for it, caring not who chased them or who was ahead.

Another spout of fire from Farden's hands was enough to scatter most people who had yet to notice mayhem barrelling towards them. The mages' boots clomped on the wooden boardwalk. One, two, three, and then silence as they sailed through the air and into the water.

Guards spewed from alley and street in chase of the wayward mages, and as they crowded against the railings, each pushed the other forwards as they fought over who was swimming.

Fleetstar solved their argument for them, rearing from the murky waters and drenching their crowd in dragonfire. The screams were muffled by the rushing waters as the dragon sped away beneath the waves and hulls.

A lung-crushing journey later, and the Fleetstar hauled herself from the sea, claws crunching on barnacles and mussels. She poked them with her snout as the mages caught their breath and strapped themselves into the saddle.

'Did you get what you wanted?' asked the dragon.

'No,' replied Farden, flatly. 'But I know where we have to go next.'

Inwick's face took a downwards turn. 'And where is that?'

'Albion. Kiltyrin Duchy to be exact. Before Malvus beats us there.'

'Beat us to what? Why?'

Farden did not answer.

CHAPTER 15
A CITY CALLED SCALUSSEN

If you tell a lie large enough and tell it often enough, it will be believed.
FROM THE MOUTH OF COUNCIL MALVUS BARKHART, YEAR 876

'Again!'

Early mornings were the bane of any existence, but Mithrid felt this torture especially. It was made worse by the fact that sun still refused to dip even halfway below the horizon. On clear evenings, it would sit like an eye amongst the mountains, beadily watching Scalussen as if it did not like this mar upon its land. This cursed, frozen land.

If it didn't hurt so much to look at the glowing ball of disgust, Mithrid would have been levelling an almighty scowl at it. Not that she had the time.

'AGAIN, I said!'

General Eyrum's order boomed across the training yard, so loud it seemed to come from right next to her.

Mithrid wrenched her axe from the log that vaguely resembled a human enemy. A mightily short and disfigured human, the victim of countless assaults, but it was more satisfying than swinging at thin air.

Splinters scattered in the path of the axe blade. Mithrid held it fast again in both hands, ignoring the cry of the raw blisters on her palms.

A step forwards.
A feint.
Block.
Sweep the leg.
Hack.

The log's crudely-shaped face was halved by the blade. The reverberations ran through Mithrid's shaking arms and pained bones. Days, she had spent training. She was improving, she could feel it, but she had yet to make up her mind whether it was worth the pain.

The porcine Albion man by her side, Savask, yelped in pain as he overshot the mark. His fingers hit the tree instead of his axe blade. Strangely, he hopped on one foot while sucking his fingertips.

'Savask!' came the cry, the echo of a hundred times Eyrum had already shouted the man's name. 'In Thron's name, are you blind, man?'

Eyrum was between Savask and Mithrid in moments. His own axe was strapped across his back. It would have dwarfed Mithrid. 'Step, feint, *then* block! Your balance is off by the time you strike, meaning you are ill-prepared. And what does ill-preparedness bring in battle?'

The crowd of hundreds had heard this question many times in the last few days. They – Mithrid included – uttered in reply.

'Death.'

'Correct! Even the most inexperienced of Malvus' men have been training for years longer than you have. Where magick can't save you, brawn, speed, and accuracy can.'

Mithrid nodded, but within, a sour taste spread throughout her. She looked to the other side of the vast courtyard at the Frostsoar's foundations. Even without looking, Mithrid could feel the concussion of the trainee mages' spells drifting across the flagstones. As a cheer rose up from their crowd, she gripped the axe so tight she burst one of her blisters.

'I... I...' Savask stuttered. He held his axe as if it were diseased: arms out full and his face one of nausea. 'I can't do this. This axe is too light.' His excuse sounded like a question.

'That is where you are wrong.'

Eyrum wrested the man's axe from him. In a blur of flesh and steel, the Siren carved the log a new face.

'A useless workman always blames his tools,' the Siren growled, before shoving the axe back into Savask's chest. The man almost fell to his ample arse.

The horned Paraian woman that had been with Mithrid her first day stood nearby, swaddled in furs so that only her face and hands showed. She was the kind that barely spoke and left her face to tell her story. Currently, that story was one of disgust. She seemed the sort that had been born with a blade in her hand. Why she even trained alongside the others was a mystery: she treated the wooden targets as if they were the emperor himself. With her curved, golden sword, the woman had carved the log to a shiv. She stood in a graveyard of chunks of wood.

'Aspala,' Eyrum called her, though Mithrid had never heard her name offered before.

'Well done,' he said. 'Fine work. You'll make this rebellion proud.'

Mithrid wouldn't have called it a smile, barely a slight upwards curve to Aspala's face rather than the severe downturn she had worn since arriving in this frozen wasteland.

Mithrid waited for Eyrum's praise to reach her, but she was ignored. The big Siren marched down the lines, slapping limbs wherever they showed poor form.

'Again!'

Over and over, Eyrum had them repeat the form. Mithrid was sweating profusely by the time the yards fell silent. Unlike the others, she did not stop. She hacked again and again, like her father used to vent his rage upon a stubborn tree stump. Between her strikes, Mithrid saw ugly faces staring out from the splintering log. The Arka mage who had stolen her from Troughwake. Modren, who had dragged her here. Malvus, or what she imagined from the likeness of his coins, and her father, for all the things he never told her of the world. Mithrid hacked at them all.

She felt a presence beside her, and though some semblance of control within her screamed to stop, she swung for it anyway.

Savask's mask of terror could do nothing to stop the axe's blade. Fortunately for his continued existence, Eyrum was closeby. The axe met the Siren's gauntlets with a bell-toll of metal vying against metal. The interruption of the force staggered her. The axe was wrenched from her grip, and quite abruptly, Mithrid found herself sat on the cold flagstone, blinking.

Eyrum held onto the axe, sapphire first clasped around its blade. Barely inches from his knuckles, Savask's face was whiter than the mountains' skirts. His jowls flapped as the man shivered uncontrollably.

'Emotion,' Eyrum said, in a tone that suggested he'd never felt a thing, 'can be the death of you.'

Mithrid's shock had momentarily kicked the anger out of her. Standing there, with every eye locked on her, wide in surprise or narrowed in disappointment, she felt the fool. The girl stared accusingly at the Siren and Savask, as if they had gotten in the way.

'Give my axe back.'

Eyrum held onto her weapon as if it were his own. Mithrid pushed to her feet.

'That was my father's!'

'Then he should have taught you to wield it better,' muttered Aspala, in her thick accent.

Mithrid longed to punch her. After seeing how swiftly it shut Remina up, the solution seemed all-encompassing. Her fists clenched, but her feet at least had some sense.

'Walk away, recruit. Take your anger with you. You can return when you are calm enough to learn.'

'Learn what?' Mithrid. 'To take on an army of logs?' She regretted the words before they had even escaped her mouth, but there was nothing to do but let the air carry them. A low murmur of disgust ran through the makeshift, fur-wrapped army. Mithrid glowered at Eyrum, secretly hoping he would bark at them all to keep training. He did not. He simply stared and waited.

Walk away. The words reverberated in her head all the way to the edge of the training yard. There, three mage recruits had been taken aside. Remina was there, eyes already glinting at the sight of Mithrid sweaty and flushed pink. Trenika and Lurn sat nearby. Hereni stood over them, in the middle of schooling them on something ridiculous like posture when she noticed Mithrid stalking past.

'Mithrid? Where are you—?'

'Anywhere. Wherever that is.'

Remina and the twins sneered, laughing between themselves before Hereni snapped at them.

'Idiots,' Mithrid hissed to herself as she strode south for the gates.

'What is wrong?' Hereni demanded of Eyrum. 'What did you do?'

'Nothing, except try her patience. She will learn to manage her anger.'

Hereni snorted. 'Some don't.'

The Siren scratched his beard of scales. 'You may be skilled beyond your years, little mage, but you still have much to comprehend.'

'And you two have got nothin' but dough for brains,' a voice chided them.

Elessi stood behind them, face stormy and arms crossed high on her chest, looking for all the world like a mother who had just discovered two fractious offspring in the midst of strangling each other. With a tut, she swiped the woodcutter's axe from Eyrum's big paw and started after Mithrid at a determined, yet arthritic pace.

'What did we say?' Eyrum grunted. He was staring at a mark in his gauntlets: a notch crossing the metal palm. A gouge, more than a scratch, but still shallow. Hereni had followed his gaze. She tested it with her hand.

'That's not supposed to happen to Scalussen armour,' she whispered. 'Not with an axe.'

There came a cough.

'Perhaps you could be gentler with us?' Nearby Savask spoke up, holding up a pudgy white finger like a child with an answer.

The man squealed as Eyrum grabbed him by the collar and carried him forcibly back to his log.

'AGAIN, YOU INGRATES!' the Siren yelled.

Where the stone gave away to the natural ice of the north, Mithrid's march became less a clomping and more a crunching. Snow had fallen in the night, crystallising over every rut and dent, forming a miniature landscape. A landscape the girl busied herself with obliterating in her borrowed boots.

Mithrid's path was southbound, but as much as she tried to follow the curvature of the walls and stay removed from anyone or anything, beyond the training yards, Scalussen's city occupied every possible scrap of frozen space. Treading its streets was inevitable.

With paving beneath her feet once more, Mithrid shoved her fists into her pockets and kept a scowl on her face. She wished she had a hood to hoist and hide under. Hoods were perfect for that sort of ominous treading, where people scattered to avoid a person. These crowds of people didn't seem to care. Several cheery idiots had the gall to wish her a fine afternoon.

Try as she might, Mithrid couldn't avoid soaking up the sights and sounds around her. They were garish and loud enough.

The Forever King had built himself a busy city, far taller, broader, and squeezed tighter than she had ever seen in the cliff-towns and villages of Hâlorn. When she wasn't craning a neck to take in a squat, stone tower, or a wooden edifice of floors and windows, Mithrid's eyes skipped like a fish out of water between the bizarre shopfronts and front doors. Every building had a dual purpose. A trader or smith toiled away on street level while some other business sat upon them. All manner of abodes perched atop those, and so on. The shortest structure she saw was a bathhouse draped in steam.

The shops and taverns weren't content keeping to their frosted, crystal windows and open doors. Half of them spilled into the streets. Minor traders and merchants filled the gaps. They didn't hawk and bray like many she had seen in the towns, trying their best to shove wares into the flinching hands of the passers-by. They chatted at leisure between themselves and customers, swapping hazy mugs of liquid as if the war were a myth for Highfrost's telling. Even a skald, who played a harp-like thing with one string, sang meaningless songs of summer fighting winter. Every skald that had screeched in Mithrid's ear growing up had warned of magick or praised the empire. Or damned the Outlaw King and all his kind. This skald performed a jig for a woman walking a white boar on a leash. The plump beast squeaked. They laughed. Mithrid almost forgot her mood, her lips half-heartedly mimicking the smiles from across the street.

Mithrid looked around at the Scalussen folk. She wondered if they called themselves subjects of a king. The details were hypnotic in their strangeness. Even amongst the snowmads or beast people of distant deserts, Mithrid was shocked by their individuality. Two goatish men stood together on their strange, backwards legs, gabbling on about bolts of cloth. Even they were wildly different from one another, one gaudy in amber sashes and silks while the other was covered almost entirely in grey paint. A loincloth and tabard were all he called clothes.

Her eyes had grown weary of flitting about, but Mithrid was powerless against drinking it in. No matter how much she stared, however, not a single overflowing gutter could be seen. Taverns and brothels existed, but they did not seethe with music and leak questionable characters into the streets. They were orderly, well-kept affairs. When she spied words and runes sprawled across the side of a building, Mithrid thought she had spied a crack in the sheen of Scalussen. The graffiti turned out to be a fresco so intricately drawn in ash and dye that she stumbled into a cart trying to take it all in.

'Sorry,' she mumbled to the cart's owner. The woman, who looked as though she had eaten nonstop since birth, had an expressionless face. Her eyes smiled, though, as Mithrid irritably rubbed at her knee. The girl found a cup thrust into her face. Shredded, greasy meat sat within, soiled by some violently red liquid.

'Try,' said the merchant, speaking the Commontongue. She gestured to her cart of various roasted things, even vegetables and fruits. Seeing Mithrid's hesitation, she tried another word. 'Free.'

Such a word needed no further encouragement, and Mithrid slurped it down.

As if the meat was on a string, yanked upon by the merchant, Mithrid spat it straight back out. She had been poisoned. There was fire in her mouth. Some trick of magick, no doubt. To add insult to poisoning, the merchant was chuckling, her eyes so shrouded by creased jowls they were tiny raisins.

'It spice. Spice!' She said the word slowly. A cup filled with what looked like curdled milk was offered. 'Drink.'

Mithrid warily slurped the drink. It was ice-cold, and it quenched the fire rapidly. Clicking her tongue against the roof of her mouth, she nodded politely to the woman and made a swift exit before she tried to give her anything else.

Within a street, Mithrid found herself in the expansive courtyard between the front gate. There she found a hole in Scalussen's commitment to peace. Where the buildings bordered the plaza, great gates and portcullises were tucked away. Hidden, but ready enough for battle. Out of the narrow streets, Mithrid saw archers and mages standing on rooftops and the stubby watchtowers, watching all. This peace was an illusion. War waited beyond the mighty gates like a wolf.

Ignoring the muted thump of the quickdoors spewing out individuals, Mithrid glowered at those gates. She rehearsed Modren's words as she strode towards them. *At no time will you ever find a guard or a mage or a gate blocking your path. You may leave whenever you wish.*

It was time to test that promise.

A hundred guards must have stood on either side of that gate, never mind the thousands who stood atop it. Most watched outwards, or patrolled, but a score watched the girl approach, hands stuffed in pockets and simmering like a cauldron.

The gates were locked, and neck-achingly tall. Mithrid almost faltered at asking them to open the whole city up, but she saw a smaller door embedded in the stone: two halves of stone-clad iron, slightly ajar but seamless when closed. Mithrid marched towards it.

One Scalussen soldier held up a hand while she was still a score of paces away. 'Where you going, miss?' he challenged.

'Out,' she replied, like spitting a cherry seed.

Mithrid readied herself for the shake of the head, or the laugh, or the clang of spears as the guards barred her from passing. None of them came. The soldier stepped aside, even opening the gate wider for her.

'Mind how you go,' he said.

Mithrid had one foot across the threshold when a shout caught her. She almost cheered.

'One moment!'

'What? Am I not allowed to leave?' Mithrid demanded.

A second guard, even with half his face obscured by intricate armour, looked positively confused. 'No, just your name for the ledger. Forgive him,' he said, nodding to his comrade. 'Somebody's head is still soaked in last night's wine. Name, then?'

Mithrid saw no ink or parchment or ledger in anybody's hands. 'Mithrid Fenn.'

'Be safe,' said the guard. Mithrid backed away onto the snow and shadow of the thick walls, but they did not follow.

She traced a rough path to where the sunlight lit the ice like a field of diamonds buried in the floor. There, she stood in the weak sunlight for all the guards and mages to see. The sun itself was lingering in the west, barely an inch above the snow.

No shout came. No warning, and Mithrid teetered between jaded and impressed. Whatever flaws she hunted for had resoundingly eluded her.

The footsteps betrayed the old woman's approach. Mithrid saw her winding from the gate, tracing the girl's path. It was Elessi, Modren's wife. She had no doubt followed her from the training yards, where she tended to lurk, seeing to cuts and burns. Mithrid frowned, and busied herself with carving a perch in a frozen wave of ice. She sat there, eyeing the sun and ignoring the woman. She wanted this moment to herself. It had calmed her to stare at the sea in Troughwake and she was determined it would work now scowling at this featureless sprawl of white.

'Mithrid, isn't it?'

Mithrid couldn't remember telling the woman her name. She did not turn, forcing the woman to find her own perch nearby. Elessi hovered in her peripheries.

'A knack I have. Rememberin' names, that is,' Elessi told her, wagging a finger.

Mithrid glanced at the ugly purple scar on the woman's neck, hiding between her curled and silver hair. It reached below her fur collar. Morbid curiosity hijacked her. 'How'd that happen? Rude to ask, I know.'

Elessi touched her neck gingerly. 'Not rude, girl. It's 'ard to miss, I know. You know, there are people in that fortress from towns and lands I can't even pronounce, let alone point to on a bloody map. You know what everyone has in common, though, whether they're from Paraia or Albion? One thing we all share? Scars.' She winced momentarily as if the wound was still raw. 'I was almost gutted by a daemon, I was, when this war of magick truly started. It was my wedding day and all, wouldn't you have it?'

'Why would you have a daemon at your wedding?'

Elessi laughed easily. Though the grey of locks and the wrinkles in her features told of one age, the way she spoke and carried herself told of a woman far younger. 'Daemons have a habit of appearin' here and there when they want to. Quite the frustration, as my undermage husband puts it. That's why they carved runes into the walls to interfere with the daemons' magick.'

Mithrid nodded, her curiosity spent. Elessi waited a while to speak. She stared at the peaks of the Tausenbar as if watching something Mithrid couldn't glimpse.

'What brought you here?' she ventured.

'Revenge, or so I thought. Would be a lot easier with magick, but it seems that isn't my destiny.' Ice chips flew as she hacked at the ice.

'No, girl. What are your scars?'

Mithrid hacked once more, saying nothing. Though her emotions were still an echo of that dark morning in Troughwake, she had taken the details, buried them deep in her mind, and boarded them up.

'I can see the memories festering' in you like an infection. Nothing better for damp and rot than fresh air and sunlight, the healers say. You can speak to me, girl.'

It took some time to unclench her jaw enough to speak. 'They turned my home into a butcher's floor. Killed my father, slaughtered my friends and everyone I knew. Even the children who ran along the beach. The Arka slew them hunting for us. Me.'

'Why you, if you aren't a mage? Beggin' your pardon.'

Mithrid growled as that familiar guilt stuck its dagger in her gut once more. 'We—I found a book. A spellbook. I read it, the Arka felt it, and they came for us. Now I'm here. I thought I might have magick in me after that. And with the helbeast's test. But no. Magick chose others instead. Others like Remina Hag.'

'Modren told me about you. He tells me about all of you. Look at me, though. I don't have magick in me. I've known Farden and those Written mages a long time. From what I've seen, all that magick brings you is trouble. Look at Emaneska.' Elessi sighed. 'But it doesn't 'elp hearin' you're just one of many, does it?'

Mithrid found herself pressing the axe blade into her thumb again, not cutting, but threatening to. 'Not much.'

Elessi sniffed at the breeze. 'Revenge is no friend of patience, Mithrid.'

'Which wise mage told you that, hmm?'

'None of them. Learned that one myself. I was consumed by it at one point. We all have been. Farden with Malvus. Modren with the daemons when I danced on Hel's doorstep. It 'asn't been easy but we've learned to wait. Revenge demands blood straight away 'cause you can't stand the pain or guilt of it all. And there is nothin' like anger to bury a feelin'. But that's when you verge on the reckless. In that sort of mind, everybody looks like an enemy. Even those friends trying to help. Anger rules you.'

Mithrid realised she was scowling even then, and quickly hid it.

'Trust me. You think I'm sayin' *don't* seek revenge. I say feel free. But the best revenge is the kind you wait for, plan for, train for. You're a fiery sort, but you think you can take an Arka mage, right now? No, girl. To get revenge you have to be able to take it. Make whoever killed your da truly pay. That's why we're all bidin' our time in this freezin' corner of nowhere. That's why we all pretend life goes on, making as much of our time in any way we can, because we know what's coming. Mark my words, girl. You won't 'ave to wait long. I can feel it.' Elessi looked to the mountains. 'The wind's blowin' strange today.'

Mithrid stared at the ice instead. The old woman was right. Mithrid had carved her grief into a new and jagged shape, painted it a furious red, and called it her destiny. *Revenge*. It almost sounded ludicrous. It had burned raw in her heart, but now she could feel it turning sour, poisoning her as it spread.

She nodded. 'It doesn't help I've had a splitting headache since I arrived here.'

'Force of the magick and so many mages in one place. Worry not. Otherwise you bloody should be content!' she chided, playfully, and with the cheek of a young girl. 'You've come to the freest place in all of Emaneska. Why do you think we're so cheery? Because each of us is free to do as we please, so long as it doesn't 'urt another. Farden's first rule. The empire has to go without such a thing, from Krauslung to Lord Saker's domain in the east, to my home and to Albion where King Wodehallow the bloody Second sits in fealty.

'As for Eyrum, that's a sour suck for you, miss. No excuses there. Nothin' worth havin' comes easy or fast. You want to make a difference, then learn. Just bargain with yourself that it'll be worth the wait.' From her furs, she withdrew an axe. Mithrid's axe. Elessi handed it to her without hesitation and with a beaming grin. Mithrid now understood where she had earned those creases and wrinkles.

'Now let's get our arses off this ice, otherwise we won't be able to shit for a week.'

Mithrid had to grin at that.

※

'Here she is, General, do your worst,' Elessi spoke for her. Unexpectedly so, but Mithrid put on a determined face of scorn just in case. So be it, if this man was destined to torture her, she would bend all the knees and carve all the logs she needed to get past him. He was but an obstacle. A big one, but all trees fall, as her father once said.

'Ready to learn?' the general asked. Hereni stood nearby with a contingent of mage recruits. Older specimens, not the beginner's ranks that Remina belonged to. Mithrid had still spotted her nearby, astride the benches lining the yards, arms crossed and bruised face pouting not to be involved.

'More than you know,' Mithrid replied.

'We're practicing against magick. Something you should be keen to do,' advised Hereni. Her eyes held a glint of caution in them, a silent message for Mithrid.

The girl swung her axe. 'Teach, General.'

The big lump of a Siren growled at being told what to do. He snatched her axe from her, tossed it into a pile, and passed her a wooden facsimile instead. Mithrid shrugged, and while he arranged the lines, one mage to one army recruit, she watched Remina whispering into Lurn's ear, who – after cackling heartily – turned to another friend to whisper. And so on, until the chain of whispers had reached the nearest mage in their pathetic coterie.

'Get 'er Krommish,' mumbled the last chap in the chain, loud enough for Mithrid and her partner, Krommish, to hear.

Mithrid looked at her aggressor, not liking the fact she had to look up to meet his beady and eager eyes. Whether he had heard of the cause of Remina's bloody nose and didn't care, or was none the wiser, he squared up to her. Mithrid was reminded of the Arka mage upon the Troughwake walkway, and felt the shiver run across her shoulders. She gripped the axe with tired, cold hands. Elessi stood nearby, eyes half-closed and trusting.

'Mages, a simple force spell will suffice. Army, you are to follow the instructions from before. Time them right, and it will be a mage in the dust and not you. Otherwise…' Hereni let the threat hang.

Mithrid steeled every muscle in her body.

'And attack!'

Ten feet must have separated them, but the mage came in quick, taking a step nobody else did, and putting Mithrid off her stride. He knocked the axe away and struck Mithrid in the ribs with his spell. She was thrown into the ground as if swung by a troll like a bat.

Laughter rose up before General Eyrum cut it dead with a bark. 'Stay put, you fool. Too close and you'll crack a bone.'

Krommish played the buffoon, backing up to his mark and tutting at himself.

Mithrid shook uncontrollably as she came up, her head pounded with her heart. She caught the eye of Elessi, and the gentle shrug she gave. Not urging calm. But permission.

Krommish readied his hands again as the ranks reset. His lips moved as if in silent prayer, and Mithrid wondered what spells he uttered. She glanced to Remina just as the orders split the silence.

'Commence!'

The mage unleashed his spell right on the heels of the Siren's words, catching Mithrid on the leg as she dodged. Spinning like a top, she tumbled, half-blind from the pain splitting her skull. Mithrid came up seething. Nothing obscured her vision. Not Elessi. Not Remina. Just this piece of shit before her. Mithrid twirled the axe in a figure of eight, making even a wooden blade whine.

Krommish's grin didn't falter as he readied another force spell.

'Recruit!' yelled Hereni, hands outstretched and plucking the air like unseen harp strings.

'Get fucked!' Mithrid roared, throwing a hand towards him while raising the axe in another. Too focused on the lad's overbearing forehead, she did not notice the ripple of force that spread outwards from her, nor the fact her headache melted with her cry, nor the fact that Krommish's hands curled up like a crone's claws. She only cared for bringing the axe pole down on the recruit's head.

The sound was almost musical. Mithrid didn't know whether it was the wood or his skull, but a resounding *thunk* sent him sprawling. Hereni still reached towards her, clawing at the air but scowling at her fingers as if they refused to move. Another one of Remina's sidekicks, stupidly aiming for the status of hero, tried to throw a spell of his own at Mithrid, despite Eyrum's outraged order of, 'Hold!'

A mere spark popped between his palms before he doubled up in abject confusion and strain.

It took barely a moment for a small circle to appear around Mithrid. As she looked around her, the seconds dragging past like hooks pulling at her skin, her headache returned like a distant drummer racing towards her. Dark nausea clawed at her gut, but she fought to stay within the light. As she felt the ghostly claws of Hereni's spell clutching her at last, somehow it brought her back to the moment. Hereni's spell stuttered, but it bound Mithrid tightly until Eyrum could relieve her of her toy axe. Even that was apparently too much. Words failed her. Mithrid was as bemused as the faces that stared at her. Every single soul in the yards watched her and waited.

'To the Underspire with her, Hereni. You know where.'

Mithrid's feet scratched unbidden against the cold flagstones as Hereni pushed her towards the Frostsoar's foundations.

'I can walk,' Mithrid growled. She was surprised when Hereni let her go. Perhaps the spell had broken, but Mithrid didn't question it, and let herself be led to the Underspire.

It was strange, how something so weightless as a stare can drag a person to the mud.

CHAPTER 16
MISTAKES MOST DIRE

People talk of the Last War as a mortal history, and yet it changed the very fabric of power. I have seen beyond the veil of death, friends, and it no longer leads to the great void, where souls belong, the other side, but in the domain of the gods. Haven. Hel. These places are one and the same, one above and one below. They are grain houses of souls, to feed the gods through their winter. Reject your praises! Give them no prayer! They need no more power than what they have.
SERMON BY THE HERETIC FALSO, WHO DIED MYSTERIOUSLY NINE DAYS LATER OF DEVIL'S SPOOL POISON

The dungeons of the Arkathedral were feared throughout the empire. Those dank cells had housed the greatest warlords, the most nefarious of sorcerers, and rumour had it even an arkmage or two in their long history.

Loki was not interested in such esteemed visitors. That night, he sought a most inconsequential man. So inconsequential, that Malvus had even forgotten the man existed when the god asked. He had not forgotten.

The corridors were a honeycomb of shadow lit at punishing intervals by oily torches, but Loki trod the grimy flagstones and chose junctions as if a map resided in his head. Mould coated every wall to knee-height and sprouted from corners. Only the doors remained pristine. Dusty, yet free of rust and rot. Their oak and runed steel held too much magick for decay.

Keys jangled in Loki's fist. Though stiff with lack of use, the lock surrendered to them. Runes glowed across the door as the spells relaxed their hold.

Within, the cell was as cold as mountain roots. The stench of piss was overwhelming. Days of wooden plates, licked clean, were stacked by the door, clattering as Loki swung it wide. In his other hand was the Jurindir's Candle, useful for more than just fending off slavering daemons. It lit filth-smeared stone, a cot of folded blankets dirtier than the floor, and a bald wretch of a man cowering in the far corner.

'Mercy, Lord. Mercy or death, I beg of you,' he said, words malformed as if he had not spoken in some time.

'Loffrey of Albion,' Loki said, curbing his candle's light. 'Often they are one and the same.'

The man looked around as if that name belonged to somebody else in that empty cell. 'You are not Malvus.'

'Thank the gods.'

'Who are you?' his shit-stained hands wiped a nose broken sometime in the past.

'I am not important. But you are, Loffrey of Albion. A man who's wandered almost as many miles as I have, a scholar by any rights, a hunter of trinkets and treasures.' Loki examined the mould on the ceiling. 'Or should I say Loffrey of Krauslung now? You've been in this cell long enough, I hear. Eleven years. All alone. What a waste.'

Again, he looked around, seeing ghosts Loki was blind to. 'Malvus was displeased with me.'

Loki crouched down by the man, tapping him lightly on the cheek. He was too petrified to shrink away. 'That's what you get for promising the emperor that you'd find him ancient Scalussen armour. Pieces of the Nine, no less. How long did it take you to realise that Farden has the only full suit left in existence?'

Loffrey picked at scabs around his lips, chewing at the pieces of skin he peeled. He didn't answer.

Loki continued to tell the man's story for him, opening up drawers of memory that this cell had shut. 'And before that, you promised the same to the late Duke Kiltyrin. Again, bold. Especially trying to sell Farden to him. You were wise to run once the duke turned to madness.'

'They said Farden did it. Made the duke mad,' Loffrey whispered.

'No doubt. He was seen running from the castle. But I heard there was never proof. And, what's more, his wife and son vanished not an hour afterwards.'

Loffrey's eyes slithered up to meet the god's gaze. 'Who are you?'

'Just a man who remembers your worth. A time when you served dukes, when you knew half the secrets of Albion and exactly where to find the other half. What happened to the duchess and the boy? Do you remember their names?' Loki held the man by the chin.

'M... Moirin. And Timeon.'

'Good. Where did they escape to?'

Loffrey began to melt into an ugly sob. 'Mercy, lord. Mercy. Release me.'

'I shall, worry not.' Loki assured him. 'Where are they?'

'Last I saw, north Albion, through Maudlow Duchy to Clannor. Caught them south of Clannor, but with the dukes in an uproar, nobody cared for Kiltyrin's widow. I let her go.'

'What was in Clannor?'

The sobs were becoming pitiful. 'Nothing. Just the furthest east as Albion reaches. Old daemon scorched lands. A black mountain called Old Man Grey,' he stammered. 'Who are you, my lord?'

Loki released him and put a hand on his cheek in comfort. 'I will never forget how useful you've been, Loffrey of Albion. Just the rest of Emaneska.'

With a violent shove, Loki rammed Loffrey's temple into the wall. Blood splotched the stone. His skull cracked on the third strike, collapsed inwards on the fifth. Loki stood over the faceless wretch. Though Loffrey was naught but a corpse, a whine emerged from him, accompanying the glowing soul that was peeled from his still-warm bones. Loki pulled it to him, inhaling it until the glass cube lingering in his fingers glowed so hot the swathes of mould puckered and smouldered. The soul's scream faded into a mere ringing in his ears.

Loki trembled, and the shadow returned with his shuddering breath. What fools his kin were, to subsist solely on prayer. The daemons knew the true meaning of these two-legged cattle. Loki chuckled to the silence as he put the dungeons behind him.

Within the upper layers of the vast Arkathedral, where marble and gold ran side by side, and where guards lined the halls more frequently than windows and sconces combined, Malvus had made his opulent den.

The imperial guards regarded Loki with suspicion and a smattering of fear. He flashed them winning smiles as they moved aside to admit him. Inside the murky room of marble and silk, Toskig was slumped in a chair reading a scroll. He hid it immediately at the sound of Loki entering, like a child with a stolen apple.

'What do you want? His Majesty is busy. Go away, little god. Come back tomorrow.'

Loki could already tell by the choir of screams and yelps coming from deeper within the emperor's chambers.

'And you don't get to partake? Why aren't you darkening the doorway of a brothel this evening?'

With one mangling of the general's lip, Loki saw to the core of the man. Duty and honour were his spouses. Devoted, he was, but Loki saw the shame lingering under his skin. Like a spouse who had spent twenty years in a marriage they had never planned. Loki didn't break a step.

'Stop, I say!' Toskig began to follow with a clatter of plate armour.

Loki led him through another room, and another, and yet another until he found the emperor's bedchamber. Loki did not knock, instead pushing his shoulder against the door.

Three naked women wrestled on the expansive bed, laughing and cavorting. The good emperor himself stood naked over them, watching, leering, occasionally spitting his wine. The Lady Jeasin was seated in the corner of the room, a diaphanous robe running across her chalk skin, a bored look on her face, and goblet of wine in her hand. She alone noticed the god first.

Much to the shrieks of the whores, Loki stood in the doorway, ignoring Toskig's apologies and attempts to remove him. The general seemed afraid to touch the god.

'Get out, you wretch! How dare you barge into my chambers unin—'

'Farden is in Albion,' Loki said, arms crossed and admiring every part of naked flesh in the room with a smile. The women dragged sheets around them. Lady Jeasin just continued to drink. The emperor was not so shy approaching Loki with his manhood still at half-mast. His eyes swirled with wine. Crumbs punctuated the grey of his stubble. Loki matched his gaze and waited for the words to burrow into his sweat-smeared skin.

'How do you know for sure?'

Loki tilted his head. These mortals and their doubts. The gods had failed their creations deeply. A curse of imperfect makers forging imperfect beings, forever succumbing to lust, and fear, and fight. So predictable.

Malvus' fierce eyes switched between Jeasin and Toskig. 'And yet where was this information two days ago? When that red-gold cunt dared to walk my streets in broad daylight! Unimpeded!'

Loki shrugged.

Malvus took a moment to scrape a smear of wine from his cheek. He spoke in a measured tone, but Loki could see the fervour shaking through his arms. 'Are they ready? My Scarred?'

'We have three, Majesty.'

'Fetch them!' he shouted. 'We are going to Albion!'

For one to have admitted they adored Albion precipitation was normally a quick way to get knifed by most of the populace. Even by tourists. Even by allies.

The way Inwick kept blowing the raindrops from her nose and cursing the earth god of Jötun for crafting this accursed country, Farden decided staying silent on the matter was best.

What it was about the rain that bewitched him, he could not tell. Whether it was its erratic patter, or its callous indifference to what it soaked, or even the gloom that tagged along like a sibling, something gave the mage a respite he found in few places. If any. Perhaps it was merely the fact he had grown up in this sodden land; spent years here enduring much worse than rain.

Inwick blasted the wet wood with another spell, determined to make it burn. The pines swaying above gave little shelter. 'Where is that blasted mad dragon when you need some proper fire? Something in this foul earth dampens my magick.'

'Nonsense, you're just not focusing.'

'I'm beyond you teaching me spells.'

Farden's one-eyed scowl reigned her insolence back. 'I'm as miserable as you are, Inwick.'

'At least you know why you're here.'

It was veiled, but Farden counted that as the tenth time Inwick had asked. He feared judgement from her. From all of them in Scalussen if he should tell her. But the problematic nature of carrying out this mission *without* telling her was much more persuading.

Farden opened his mouth, but it was unexpectedly filled with silt as the confounded dragon landed far too close and far too rapidly.

'Evernia's tits!' Farden spat grit.

'I found a cave.'

Inwick was immediately curious. 'Far?'

'Not at all,' replied the dragon. 'You idiots should be using your light spells or something, instead of settling for the first hollow you find.'

Farden acted as if he were none the wiser even though his fondness for the wet and the storm had kept them in the forest. Trailing behind Fleetstar's irritably swishing tail, he and Inwick raised their hands and let light burn between their fingers. The darkness was thrust back, but the storm was relentless. Inwick was right: he could feel the wind dragging at more than just his cloak; it pulled at his magick as it reached through his armour and grasped at his insides. It did not dampen the magick: it collided with it.

Fleetstar led them to a dark maw between two tors meeting. Their dark towers were lost to the gloom and weather. Yellow paint had been daubed across the bare rock, the marks of some long-lost gang of marauders, no doubt.

A timid wind howled from the back of the cave – suggesting an exit – but it was dry enough. A skeleton wrapped in mouldy rags still slept peacefully in the corner. The knife that had stolen his life still protruded from his ribcage. Farden was curious about what else had been stolen, and why.

'Durnus and the others will be able to find us in here.'

'I don't see why they had to be summoned at all.'

'Because this might take more than just the two of us if it goes wrong.'

Inwick raised an eyebrow. It stuck halfway between insulted and confused.

'Not questioning your power, Inwick. We need tact. Knowledge. Legs that haven't been stuck on a dragon for days.'

'Grow some scales on your arses like true riders then, and stop whining.' Fleetstar let the threat linger as she took up guard at the mouth of the cave, back turned, yet tail curled in a protective wall around the mages. The rain steamed on her hide. Farden knew how the dragons preferred the cold. It was to be expected for a furnace with wings.

Inwick sat propped up by the dragon's tail. Farden stood arms crossed, staring out at the night like Fleetstar.

'What?' Farden knew without looking. 'You've got more in you. Spit it out.'

'After the Kserak Massacre you vowed not to leave Scalussen until war comes, and yet here you are, barely two years later, promise forgotten and skipping across the lands. It seems peculiar to be taking such great risks, Farden. What's so important you'd dare Krauslung's very bowels, and now come here, to Albion?'

'The very arsehole of Emaneska,' scoffed Farden.

'It is a serious question.'

'And one that will go unanswered until the others get here, mage. If there's one right I'll claim as arkmage, it's—'

Inwick tutted mockingly. 'You still can't say "king" after all these years?'

'—it is not to repeat myself. I'll call myself king when Emaneska is free.'

'They've already chosen you, *Arkmage*. Whose face did you think they were painting on the walls of Krauslung? Malvus'? No, the Forever King's. I'll be damned if that doesn't have a ring to it.'

Farden touched his red-gold armour in silent thanks for its constant power. Seventy winters had passed him by, and thanks to the last suit of the Nine, he hadn't aged a day since the daemons had fallen. 'Leave the jealousy to Modren. I like you as the quiet, murderous one.'

Shutting her eyes was a clear signal their conversation was over, and Farden was glad for it. The three left the talking to the wind's shrieking voice and the incessant grumble of the rain.

※

Farden awoke not remembering drifting off. A small patch of cinders smouldered between him and Inwick. Fleetstar's tail was still curled around them. Farden's hands groped for his sword and armour, checking both. He could have sworn he had been deep in conversation. With whom and what words had passed him by, he could not recall. Farden never trusted dreams, not when forces in the world could weave their own.

'They're here,' rumbled the dragon. Farden blinked owlishly as he rubbed the confusion from his eyes.

The storm held the sky jealously, keeping the dawn from Albion's view. Light and colour had been sapped from across the forest and tors. The wind's teeth gnashed no more, wheezing to a breath sometime in the night. The rain now fell as a faint, yet all-drenching mist. An Albion staple. Drizzle of the highest and most bothersome quality.

Two dragons descended from the sky like dropped anvils. Their wings and tails shoved aside pines and saplings like a man might stride through long grass. Kinsprite and Shivertread, two dragons that almost rivalled Fleetstar for youth and speed. Orphans of Nelska's destruction.

Kinsprite gleamed in the wet. Shivertread was the first of what the Sirens had come to call a scaleshifter; his colours changed between green and earth-beige as he stretched his wings. Flying so far so fast must have been exhausting, never mind carrying three bodies apiece.

Farden stepped between the great beasts, bowing his head as they lowered theirs, and smiled to their bedraggled, windswept passengers. 'You made good time.'

'We had the teeth of the ice fields chasing us,' Durnus replied, as he began the arduous task of climbing down from Kinsprite's flanks.

Farden hid a smile. Despite Durnus' experiments with the vampyre curse to cure his eyes and his oldest injuries, the magick had worked dark trickery on the old man. He could see, and sunlight was no longer his enemy, but much of the strength had been sapped from his body. Not the magick, mind. And yet, Farden knew how the old scoundrel liked to exaggerate his weakness. The fangs betrayed it: a beast still dwelt within him, just a greyer and older one.

'What by Evernia's wisdom have you dragged us back to this miserable land for, Farden?' Durnus grumbled. With his wizened stick, he poked the mage in the chest with a musical chime.

'Old mistakes,' answered Farden. He used the excuse of greeting the others to say no more. 'Wyved, Peryn.'

Wyved said nothing. It was far from unusual; he had yet to meet a witch clan elder that did speak. She was perhaps the eldest of them all, a figure they called the High Crone. The rain had washed streaks in the paint and soot decorating her face. Her dreadlocked hair, sewn with vines and braids of coloured twine, reached to the back of her knees. Beneath her bulky cloak, something – or somethings – chirruped frantically.

Peryn, meanwhile, seemed too intrigued by her surroundings to be miserable like the others. She had no hair to be matted, just a pale scalp with tattooed swirls that reached beneath her eyes. She forwent a cloak, leaving her painted arms bare. 'I've heard much of Albion, King, but never thought I would see it. Such trees. Such life.'

'It grows old surprisingly quickly,' muttered Durnus.

The last figure to disembark the dragons did so with a jump and a stout thud. A man of bulk and muscle, Ko-Tergo was covered in matted grey hair, snow white in places. Had the man not been wearing a jerkin of leather, he could easily have passed for a lost bear. Ko-Tergo grinned with fangs like that of a floeshark, so jagged they raised the question of how the man closed his mouth without carving his lips off each time. The rest of him was covered in matted grey hair. Had the man not been wearing a jerkin of leather, he could have passed for a lost bear.

'I was promised a feast, but I see it not!' he greeted them warmly.

'It's coming,' Farden said, trying to ignore the squeak of his gauntlets as Ko-Tergo gripped his hand. Yetins were smarter than their lycan cousins, but still hadn't grasped the concept of tact. Like their snowmad brethren, any sentence successfully spoken in Commontongue was a cause for celebration.

'Thank you for coming. No journey should be taken lightly. Not in this time, and especially not in this country,' Farden announced. Under Grand Duke Wodehallow II's rule, this country was a lackey of a vassal, a slavering hound to its Arka master. 'We'll need to move quickly before we bring the duchies and the Arka down upon us. Rest for a moment, break your fast, and we'll move on. No fires and keep watch.'

The old vampyre shuffled after Farden, into the cave and out of earshot. 'Is this about the runed mages? Explain, and explain quickly, Farden.'

'I agree,' Inwick muttered.

'You're here because I made a mistake twenty years ago, and because I need help rectifying it.' Farden wished his words could remain as memories, trapped in his skull. He gave them no frills, no gilding of any kind, and instead let them land in the mud at their feet. 'A copy of my Book exists here in Albion.'

Durnus groaned. Inwick stared accusingly.

'How is that possible?'

'It's not a pretty story. One I haven't told any of you apart from Durnus, but the fact of the matter is I once slit throats for Duke Kiltyrin.'

'Why does that not surprise me?' she huffed.

'Perhaps because it was foul work that suited the foul man I used to be. I didn't think of the numbers, but I know it was years. That was, until Durnus sent Loki to bring me back to Krauslung to fight the Last War. He found me half dead after Duke Kiltyrin tried to betray me. I got my revenge the only way I could think of; not to take his life, but his mind, his rule. In a moment of what I can only recall as violent stupidity, I made a copy of my Book, strapped him to a chair, and with a knife, I, well... *forced* him to look at it for a prolonged period.'

It was a despicable punishment, even for an Albion duke. Any more than a glance at a Written's tattooed back can lead to madness. A mortal mind simply cannot handle the force of the magick the Scribe imparted in the Written mages.

'I left a raving Kiltyrin there with my Book and was too foolish to retrieve it. My stupidity didn't end there. I made another copy, with Loki's help, I'm ashamed to say. And that, as you both know, I burned to ashes a decade ago for this exact reason: to keep it out of Malvus' hands.'

'A wise decision,' Durnus said, 'sadly built on the backs of many poor decisions.'

Farden frowned. 'You don't need to remind me. Why do you think I fight over each decision, even now? As you told me not long ago, Durnus, what is old age, but reaping the past? My past just so happens to be full of mistakes.'

The vampyre's ice-blue gaze could still pierce Farden even after all these years. 'Where is it? The copy?'

'I don't know. I had assumed it destroyed. Burned along with Kiltyrin himself. Lost in Albion's upheaval. The Last War was somewhat distracting on that matter. I had not thought of it until Jeasin reminded me.'

'And how does she know?'

'Loki told her to ask me "how did Kiltyrin die?" when she saw me next. The perfect words to remind me.'

'*Loki*?' Durnus spluttered. 'The gods told us he was dead! Killed in the last war. How can that be?'

Inwick snapped the pine branch she clutched in her hands. 'Does it matter? Somehow the traitorous cunt has returned, and is now somehow in Krauslung, aiding Malvus and asking Jeasin to deliver messages to Farden.'

'He is goading you. Luring you at the very least,' said Durnus. 'This is Loki's deception, surely. That god – that *creature* – tricked us before. Threatened the very existence of sky and earth. What is to say he is not lying now?'

'Of course he is, but we can't afford to ignore him,' Farden exhaled. 'Not if that copy still exists.'

Durnus must have seen the anxiety in the arch of Farden's weary back. 'What else did Jeasin tell you?'

'That Malvus has a book of Books, cut from the backs of Written during the Last War by Samara's seer. He has the cheek to call it the Hides of Hysteria.'

The vampyre was so horrified he forgot to speak.

'You said it yourself: unless Malvus has a Written's Book, his runed mages were little threat. Now he has what he needs to try making his own

Written. His Scarred, as he calls them. It's too late to stop that, and we'll deal with that when we must—'

Durnus beat Farden to the crux of the problem. 'But if Malvus gets his hands on your Book, and manages to recreate it, this war of ours will take a dire turn. All hope we have fought and built for will be a bloody and ashen steak across the north.'

Durnus stared at the ragged tips of the pines, at the roiling clouds beyond. A contemplative tongue wound around his fangs. 'You made the right decision to summon us,' he said. 'This stinks of a trap.'

Farden tried to hide his sigh of relief. No matter how many years flew past him, no matter how many times they called him king, Durnus would always be his superior. The mage owed him too much. Forgiveness, for one, despite all of Farden's missteps and all the foul gullies he had fallen into. His life, on several occasions, too.

Though he could see the news weighing heavy on his comrades, like snow weighing down a bough, they looked determined. 'Where is the copy? Are we close?'

Farden smiled awkwardly. 'Somewhere in Albion.'

'Thron's balls, Farden...' Inwick's words were ground to a meal between her clenched teeth.

'I left Kiltyrin's wife and son Timeon alive and sane that night. Moirin was always kind to me, for all my failures and spilling guts for her husband. As far as I can know, Timeon was never made his heir. Kiltyrin's land was claimed by dukes Wodehallow and Maudlow after I left Albion. They must have fled, but if we find Moirin, or her son Timeon, we'll know what happened to the Book I left behind.'

'I see now why you asked for the witches.' Durnus said. 'As sound a plan as I've come to expect from you, Farden. But we will have to execute it quickly. We saw Lost Clan patrols to the north. Arka mages reside to the south. Their helbeasts will taste dragon and mage scent soon.'

'We've wasted enough time.' Inwick strode from the cave checked the straps of her armour and small buckler shield before striding from the cave.

Durnus was chuckling at something private. Farden nudged the old bag of bones as they gathered with the others once more, their council of the cave concluded.

'What's tickled you?'

'Odd, is all: how our whole saga began with a theft of a book. Now, it hinges on another. Time is a wheel, Farden. We mustn't let it crush us.' The old vampyre whistled sharply. 'It is time, ladies, gentlemen, and dragons. We move on.'

'Where to?' Ko-Tergo's voice had the quality of a boulder being dragged along the ice.

Farden gestured to the witches. 'That is for our good witches to tell us.'

Peryn managed to drag herself away from the apparent fascination of the damp undergrowth. She was holding a crest of mushrooms and quickly stowed them in a pocket. 'Right you are. What is it we are hunting?'

'Me,' Farden replied. 'A part of me, at least. A copy of my Book, to be precise.'

Though the others traded concerned glances, the High Crone had no cause for hesitation. Standing at the centre of the circle of dragon-scale and armour, Wyved stooped low to the ground before arching her back violently. Farden had seen this ceremony many times during his hunts for recruits and refugees, but the pop of the witch's old spine never failed to make him shudder.

'Never tracked a Written before. Never mind a king,' Peryn was muttering as she hoisted Farden's left hand up. She patted his red-gold palm. 'If you please.'

'Must I?'

'Like a wolf tracking a scent, we need yours.'

Farden set to removing his gauntlet. The magick of the Nine adhered to its owner in more ways than one: the armour only responded to his touch.

The mage flexed his fingers. With a pinch and a pull, the metal scales at his wrist whispered as they parted, flowing like hot wax. It was the work of moments, and Farden bared a pale and scarred hand, missing its smallest finger. So long had it been since he had last removed all of his armour that the hand looked almost foreign to him. It took the cold slap of a witch's palm to remind him it was his.

Wyved was in a trance, eyes rolled back to their whites and hands shaking intensely as if she rattled a pair of tambourines. From soot-marred cloak to her matted hair, her body began to… *squirm.*

A lone bird abruptly popped its head from the folds of Wyved's rags. A finch, no taller than a thumb, twitched its tar-dipped head back and forth as if looking upon the miserable, wet world it had found itself in and thinking, 'what the fuck'. A shuffle of its wings bared sky-blue feathers beneath. Its black eyes centred on Farden, and with a chirrup, it landed on the mage's palm.

Farden held the bird up close, trying to see a mind in those black beads of eyes, eyeing the hooked beak that should have belonged to a hawk.

'Bah!' Farden bit his tongue as the finch dug its beak into his palm, drawing a smear of blood.

'Necessary,' Peryn replied, almost chiding him. Farden saw Durnus hiding a smile. Ko-Tergo stared at the whole business with abject boredom until he saw the blood. His eyes clouded black, but he restrained himself with a grunt.

The finch burrowed back into Wyved's clothing. The witch did not break her pose, arched back, drizzle washing her face, soot streaming from her peeled-grape eyes like black tears. Farden had just enough time to replace his gauntlet before Wyved unleashed her flock.

A cloud of turquoise and pitch birds erupted from the witch's rags. They moved like a shoal of fish trapped in shallows, moving as one animal in tight, fluttering formations around the witch.

Between the boiling fray of tiny wings and cheeping, Farden could see the High Crone. She strode from her horde with several birds still tangled in her hair, too lazy to fly. The rest swarmed above her in a hypnotising figure eight.

'We move west,' said the witch.

'Where?'

'West.'

And so they did. With their passengers mounted, the dragons soared high into the slate skies where the winds still raged. The flock of witch-finches stayed unseen below the clouds. Farden kept his eyes open despite the sting of the wind, letting his tresses whip his neck. He snuck looks at Wyved, perched behind Peryn. She looked dead, frankly. Her eyes were solid white. Her body barely moved with the flow of Shivertread's body.

Farden reached out with his own magick, feeling the wind once again snag at his power. He could feel magick's threads, running unseen through the air, vibrating like ljot strings as the god Heimdall had once explained it. The knack was tricky, surrounded by other mages and the dragons, but once he had closed his eyes, he could almost see lights sparking like ship's lanterns on dark horizons. The rest was as intangible as feeling the presence of somebody standing behind him.

'King!' yelled Peryn.

Farden had lost himself to darkness and effort. Time had slipped by as if he had accidentally fallen asleep once again. Farden's eyes snapped open. A carpet of clouds stretched out before them, and at its ragged border, a rusted land sprawled. The sun now showed its face, and they appeared to be chasing it before it could sink into the endless Lonely Sea.

Following Peryn's finger, he saw it: a mighty snow-capped mountain. It had no lofty brethren, no foothills to call servants. It sat alone, perched on the edge of the ocean, surrounded by leagues of black beaches and scorched, wasted earth.

'Old Man Grey,' Farden whispered. Albion's only peak worth mentioning, and yet a fabled and haunted place, long avoided. Even the Duke of Clannor, the excuse for a ruler who owned the lands beneath them, had rejected it, refusing to lay claim to the cursed mountain and its shadow.

It looked like the last fang in the jaw of a long-dead and titanic creature: a lithe, granite shard that dominated all else on this godsforsaken land. The permanent ice that decorated its top quarter was stained the colour of cow piss. A half-hearted trail of smoke leaked from its jagged top.

'There?' Farden shouted.

Peryn shrugged. Divining magick was not a pure science. It wasn't even an art. It was as simple as better odds.

After the dragons had swung beneath the cloud cover, Farden spotted the flock of finches, their form spread like a hand towards the mountain. No sooner had they landed upon the crusty wasteland did the finches seek out their witch. Wyved soon bristled with birds.

The dragons left them there, to soar in the breathless reaches of the sky where they were mere specks.

Spread in a line, the makeshift hunting party trod the broken earth: two mages, two witches, a yetin, and a vampyre.

CHAPTER 17
OLD MAN GREY

The snowmads tell of the yetine that stalk the Tausenbar Mountains. The saying goes, "if you see a yetin, it is already too late for you". Fierce and strong as storms, they are men beneath their mounds of muscle and white fur. Some say they are cousins of the lycan curse. Others believe their ancestors laid with the snow bears that used to roam the north in droves. I, thankfully, have been fortunate to never see hide nor hair of one, though I have heard their songs when the moon is full.

FROM 'NORTH AS NORTH GOES', BY WANDERING WALLIUM

The walk took two hours at most, but it was a slog by every right. Where the ground blistered, foul yellow mosses crept over the earth. They cast up a vehement cloud of spores, capable of stinging eyes and throats. Once Farden's and Inwick's faint vortex spells had solved that problem, the earth itself proved itself a trickster. What seemed to be a flat landscape was a field strewn with sharp rocks hidden amongst sand, inexplicable boggy patches, and crumbly dust plateaus that stank of salt and crumbled beneath every footstep. The air was still, thick, and cloying.

All of them were of a bitter and vexed complexion when they entered the shadow of Old Man Grey. The chill wind that sprung up was far colder than it had any right to be. The sand shifted in the breezes, spinning whorls and spirals around their boots. Farden swore he heard voices in the wind. Magick, too. Plain as sunlight. It ran across the deserts like a storm blowing in from the ocean.

'You feel that now?' Inwick muttered beside him. A strand of silver hair divided her narrowed eyes.

Farden nodded, raising a fist to let fire burn around his fingers. The flame ran raggedly like a torch harassed by a gale. That was not usual. Magick barely responded to the natural elements.

Durnus' cerulean eyes came into view. He lifted a skeletal, clawed hand. The light that burned on his palm left a smoky trail. 'How peculiar.'

'Onwards,' Farden ordered. Still in their line, though with the Written gathered around their leader, they began to jog towards the mountain. The wind whispered to Farden, calling his name, or so it sounded between the crunch of boots. *Nonsense*, he thought, until he saw the hunting party exchanged wary glances.

'You hear that?' Peryn shouted to them.

'Voices,' barked Ko-Tergo, bending his pointed ears to the winds. 'A name.'

'Whose?'

Durnus was still cradling light in his hands. 'Your name, Farden. Over and over.'

Four-Hand.

Farden flinched, throwing a fist at thin air, as if the speaker had hissed in his ear. The wasteland was empty. 'What the fuck is going on here? Who called me that?'

'Nobody said a word, Farden.'

Farden felt the pressure and heat around him as he pressed his vambraces together. He kept his magick back, not wishing to give the others a splitting headache. With Emaneska's magick burning brighter than ever, two Written flexing their power in one spot was enough to give a bystander a nosebleed.

On, they pressed, until the sheer granite broke through the waste at an abrupt angle. Farden pressed his hands against the stone. It thrummed ever so faintly, as if one of Scalussen's forges ground away beneath it.

'Shit,' he cursed as the stone seemed to bite him. 'Whatever this place is, I already hate it.' Farden shut one eye and concentrated. *Can you hear me?* he asked of Fleetstar.

Her reply was faint, but audible, accompanied by a cackle. *Unfortunately*, she replied.

The mage tutted. *Keep watch.*

'An opening,' Durnus pointed without looking. His vampyre senses be damned; Durnus' years spent as a blind man had given him a sense of awareness that rivalled a god like Heimdall's. Whether it was the wind, something in its whine, or just a guess, he was right.

The party stood in the gap of a great fissure, a cavity in the sky-scratching fang. That was where they found the first of them. A carving hewn into the rock. It curved across one flat plane of granite in a diagonal line. Three other gouges crossed its centre. Red paint – or possibly blood – coloured their gutters. It took a moment and a slight tilt of the head, but Durnus and Farden realised simultaneously.

'A rune,' hissed the vampyre.

'Beat me to it.' Farden threw up his hands. 'What's an Arka rune doing here, old friend?'

'What's more important, Farden, is the language of the rune. Not Arka. It is Akatarsen, the direct descended dialect of Servaean and elvish.' Durnus had noticed the confused stares from around him. 'The language of the spellbooks the Scribe once tattooed into the backs of Written.'

'I refer you to my previous question.'

Durnus thrust his stick ahead of him. 'I suggest we find out. I imagine there is only one place somebody could have learned that language, seeing as it died with the Scribe more than thirty years ago.'

The interior seemed night-like in the orange sun, but once inside, with eyes adjusting, it was easy to see a trail winding into the crevasse.

Rusty streaks of quartz in the granite glowed softly, lighting their way. There was a singular path. All offshoots had long been blocked by rockfalls. It worried Farden to have one escape, but there was little choice. Every dozen yards, another crude rune was carved and painted. They were getting more intricate the deeper they tunnelled.

The Forever King. Is that what they call you now?

Farden recoiled again and stared vehemently at Inwick.

'What?' Her face could have soured milk at a glance.

'Did you... ?' Farden shook his head. 'Never mind.'

As the rock squeezed them into single file, Farden raised a shield spell in one hand and a light spell in the other. Both stuttered. Crimson light flashed through the quartz.

Under the mountain, the air was stifled and growing hotter with every step. The smell of rotten eggs was disturbingly prevalent. Farden had tasted the same odour in the Dragonfields.

Farden. The voice came again. The mage steeled himself, growling beneath his breath for it to shut up.

'What is that noise?' Ko-Tergo's ears trumped all of theirs, even Durnus'. It soon grew louder, a feverish hammering of some kind. It set the party on edge. No mountain made that noise, just like no mountain carved its own runes. Farden pushed his shield spell out, grating against the granite on either side of the tunnel. Here and there, where script had been chiselled into the walls, sparks flew as his magick clashed with it.

When a wind railed at them, he knew an opening was coming. 'Get ready,' he hissed to Inwick. She put her hand on Farden's shoulder and dust poured around them as their magick shook the rocks.

Pushing around a protrusion of granite, the mages burst into a tremendous cavern filled with a crimson light. Huge, and empty. The hammering had stopped abruptly. Inwick pushed a candle spell high into the air. It hovered above their party like a flaming arrow caught mid-flight.

Come at last.

All of them heard those words. They were deep and booming, as if the bowels of the mountain itself were speaking to them, a voice made of boulders and stone. A circle was formed, claws, spells and pointy things facing outwards.

'Why do I want to say "trap"?' asked Inwick.

'Because it is,' Farden growled, stepping around a needle-sharp stalagmite that towered over them. He reached out to Fleetstar. *Can you hear me?*

Whispers. That was all he could hear, a whole crowd of them clamouring to be heard. At first it was a low susurrus, but the deeper they went into the cavern, the louder it became. Farden did not see it in the others' faces. They were too busy staring up at the runes decorating the hollow chamber.

'Show yourself!' he roared. He clapped his hands, sending a shockwave of an echo spreading through the cavern.

Something, or somebody, yelped, then cackled madly. The mages moved swiftly, racing through the ranks of stalagmites until they found the centre of the grotto. A broad space had been cleared and fashioned into some kind of beggar's workshop. Stone chips and iron chisels blunted to nubs lay about the place. Detritus filed the gaps between an ornate wardrobe that looked uncomfortably out of place and a bed made of what could only be described as filth. A disquieting number of human skulls lay about the place. Zero to one tended to be the customary number. One skull still wore the rotten strips of a face.

Where a skinny stalactite speared the workshop from above, ropes had been tied like a spider's web. Pulleys and spindly ladders ruled the mess.

And there, in the middle of it all, shirtless and breathing hard, a blunt hammer in one fist, was a grinning man with hair the colour of flame. He could not be more than thirty winters, but the subterranean hue of his skin, the gaunt ribs poking through his skin, and the mess of a rusty beard around his face made him look older. Wilder. He wore nothing but trews cinched at the calves. His skin was covered in smeared diagrams and more runes.

Despite the man's pleasure to see visitors, Farden's heart fell. There wasn't glee in this man's eyes, but a fiendish spark that the mage had the displeasure of seeing only twice before. Once, in a Siren healer's eyes. *The madness of magick.*

The man spoke then, revealing an array of missing teeth and others filed into points. His voice was quiet amongst the clamour of the whispering voices.

'You don't recognise me, I see?' The man's grin did not return. He stared at the ceiling and his carving work as if trying to remember his lines. 'I... hmm. You were supposed to.'

He paced for a time until Inwick took a step. The man raised the hammer in threat.

'Back! You are in *my* house! My workshop. My stone temple.' He leered wide-eyed at Farden and instantly bowed. 'To the Forever King. Come at last.'

Farden felt the others surreptitiously spreading outwards around the edges of the grotto. 'How do you know how to write these runes, sir?' he asked.

'Sir,' he whispered. The noise that spilled from his mouth was a slide from polite tittering to hysterical baying. 'SIR!' he screeched, his legs rigid while he pulled himself up by his own hair as if he dangled from it. 'You astound me, Farden. How little you care! How lightly you tread on others' necks! You don't remember me? Perhaps my mother?'

The man scooped a skull from the bare stone, one with a fracture across the forehead and eye socket. 'Funny! And we both thought my father would kill her first. Wrong again! It was you.'

Farden saw it now. In the scowl. The boy had always been one giant scowl. The name came unbidden from Farden's mouth.

'Timeon… By Evernia, look at you.'

'Timeon.' Spittle flew through bared teeth. 'Son of a duke. A bright future, lad. Chin up. Straight back! Here comes Farden Four-Hand.'

That name was an old wound opening. Another name for another mage. Farden held his hands out, approaching the man slowly. 'I saved you from your father. Saved all of his duchy from him.'

Timeon cackled again. 'You saved yourself. Straight back!' He thrust out his chest. 'Cut father's eyes open. Showed my father the dark words and saved yourself. You left us. Killed us. No boy can be the duke, they said. No boy! Showed my father the words. We ran. They chased. Mountain called us. Mountain saved us. Not you. Not Farden Four-Hand.'

Farden could feel the others staring at him. 'And what happened to the dark words? The page I showed Kiltyrin?'

The man snorted as if Farden had asked a highly stupid question. 'Mother read it first. She tried her very hardest not to, but it called to her. Chin up! You killed her, Four-Hand. Told her to carve her face with a rock.' Timeon dropped the skull, snapping its jawbone. Farden clenched his jaw, throat rising. Moirin did not deserve that, not even in death.

For the first time, Timeon turned and showed them his spine-ridged back. No paint or ink lay there, but scars, poorly done in fury and haste. It seemed no threat, but Durnus took no chances.

The clatter of his stick on the ground caused Timeon to sprint to the far edge of the workshop and sprawl against a wall of rock, trapped. The vampyre's spell dragged him to the earth. Tentacles of green light seized his limbs and held him still. The skulls jittered on the rock.

'Aaagh!' Timeon shrieked.

'Where is the page? Where is the Book?' Durnus demanded, now standing over the man. The tentacles obeyed every twitch of his claws.

'Durnus! Stop!' Farden yelled. The runes around the chamber flickered as Farden's magick flared. Shafts of light fell across a shape standing in the shadow of the cavern's wall. 'Look.'

In the crimson light, they peered at the jumble of boulders. They were unavoidably... *human*. There were limbs. A torso, and a head. Remarkably for the madman, he had actually managed to carve a hood across the face, showing only some ghastly, daemonic jaws. Two jewels had been hammered unevenly above.

'By the gods, Farden. He built a... *you*,' said Peryn, sounding somehow impressed.

'My shrine!' gasped Timeon, breathless with a spell strangling him.

'What about that, Farden?' Inwick asked. Farden shot her a dark look.

Every inch of the statue's skin bore the marks of a chisel. Most of it resembled Written runes, but the rest was a language Farden had never seen before.

'Don't you touch it! Don't you dare! He will save us. Not kill us like you, Farden!' Timeon shrieked. It was then that Farden caught the betraying direction of his gaze. *The wardrobe.*

Armour chiming in his hurry, Farden tore open its doors open to unleash a stench of rot. A whole deer leg lay rotting on one shelf. On the other, several more skulls all enraptured by a scrap of paper nailed to the wardrobe's back wall: his Book. The paper was ripped and repaired many times over, yet the black script had refused to fade.

'Found you,' uttered Farden. The Scalussen metal rang like a bell as he slammed his vambraces together. The cavern glowed as if Old Man Grey burned like the Emberteeth. The ground shuddered, the incessant whispering grew to a scream, but Farden pressed on, dragging up the full weight of his magick.

'Don't you dare!'

To the music of Timeon's screams, white flames flowed from Farden's fingertips. The wardrobe burst into cinders and flaming rubble, but the page refused to wither. The mad mountain screeched, as if feeling the sudden pain that wracked Farden's body. It felt as though fire surged beneath his armour. With a cry, he wrenched his spell clear and stood seething. Farden glowered at the accursed relic of his darkest years, refusing to catch light even lying in quivering cinders. Durnus was steadying himself upon the shaking ground, but he was staring intently.

'Gods only know how, but it's connected to you.' Inwick stepped up, flames surging her wrists. Her eyes roamed everywhere besides the Book itself. 'Want me to do it?'

'No! Leave it.' Farden snatched up the page and swiftly crammed it beneath his breastplate as a stalactite crashed into a workbench. 'I'll deal with this later when we haven't got a mountain trying to crush us.'

Inwick stared for a moment, one brow raised in silent question.

Farden pushed past her. 'It'll be safe with me. Safer than here!'

The screeching stopped abruptly, replaced by the laughter of a lunatic. Still in the grip of Durnus' spells, Timeon seemed to be cackling into the crook of his arm until they noticed the blood streaming down his elbow and spreading across the floor. All eyes had been on Farden.

'Stop him!' The mage raced to his side, but Timeon's filed teeth had already lacerated his arm to shreds. Blood could not leave his body fast enough. He pawed at the statue, and where he left bloody marks, the cuts in the stone seemed to shine.

'You think it a shrine, Farden Four-Hand?' Timeon asked through incarnadined teeth. 'I have spent years building. Learning. Chin up, straight back! Building and learning your magick. I knew you'd want to see it. My Farden. My *golem*, I call him,' Timeon babbled while he stared at the blood gushing from his wounds. 'Before you die, Farden Four-Hand!'

Farden's patience broke like a damn. He backhanded the man away from the statue, knocking him senseless. Judging by the ragged crunch of stone, the squeaking of pulleys, and the glowing red script shining across the statue's stone, Farden was too late. For what, Farden imagined he would find out forthwith.

'What is it?!'

'Some kind of automaton! A machine of stone and magick!' Durnus cried, already winding up his spells.

'Keep him in place!'

Vortex spells obliged, but the golem thrashed to be free of its ropes and shackles. Timeon laughed as the stone beast took its first step.

'Spark!' Farden barked.

Lightning crackled in the mages' hands. Blue bolts crackled over the creature's skin to no effect. Quite the opposite: it seemed to fuel him, especially whenever Farden's magick struck it. It would shiver and groan with its carved mouth.

'Quake!' Farden yelled another school of magick.

The ground beneath the golem sunk, sending it off balance. It speared itself on one of the stalagmites, and, for a blessed moment, Farden thought they had victory. That was until the golem extricated itself from the spears of limestone in one slow, yet inexorable push. Before they could retaliate, it swiped through the spears of stone, sending shrapnel flying.

Shield spells dealt with most of the shards. One cry rang out from Peryn, who had a dagger of rock embedded in her upper arm. She wrenched it free with a cry while pulling two vials from her belt. One, two: they flew from her fingers, the first staining the grey golem orange, and the second exploding in a deep red flame that appeared to gnaw into its stone.

Farden fell back, looking to Durnus. The vampyre was building to his moment, waiting until the golem was in the right place. In one violent movement, he clawed for the ceiling of the cavern. Old Man Grey gave up one of his teeth, and it fell like a thunderbolt, skewering the golem through its torso and breaking it in half.

For a blessed moment, the clamour of voices died in Farden's ears. 'I think we—'

The screech of stone was torturous, made worse by the rush of voices flooding Farden's head. He staggered, but Inwick grabbed him.

'It's your own magick, you can't fight it,' she grumbled.

'Then burn him. Melt him!' Farden looked up to the glowing script carved in chisel and paint. 'We burn it all. Timeon has cursed this mountain.' *And it's all my fault*, was what he wanted to add, but he couldn't voice it.

With much heaving and scraping of its giant claws, the golem reared up once again, its jaw now loose and emitting a chilling howl. The blood upon its stone flaked away as its magick burned brighter.

Bright and furious flame poured from Inwick's fingers. The golem was doused in fire. It roared, sending more shards of stone flying in their direction. Farden and Durnus kept them at bay, letting the stone shatter against their spells.

Relentlessly, the fire raged around the golem. It did not take long for its rocks to begin to glow. It threw a punch towards the witches and yetin, but they were too swift of foot.

'How long will this take?' Inwick yelled over the rumble of flame.

Farden bared his teeth, working patterns with his red and gold fingers.

'That's not wise, Farden,' Durnus warned him. 'Let me.'

'Do what you will, old friend. I'm going to wipe this slate clean once and for all.'

With that, Farden drew his sword. Lightning claimed the blade. He ran towards the golem, one hand holding the sword poised and ready, the other hand clenched, wreathing his body in a tight shield. The river of Inwick's fire engulfed him, but he sprinted on. The golem saw Farden coming. It raised its swollen lumps of hands and aimed to smear him across the stone. The mage slid through rubble, ducking the fists by an inch. He rode the shockwave of the golem's missed blow and swung his glittering sword at its knee. With a piercing grate of metal and a shower of sparks, the leg was severed.

The golem came crashing down to one side, landing hard on its stump. Farden vaulted its flailing limbs and came down hard on the other knee. The cursed granite, already weak under the heat, withered before the blade. Within two strikes, the golem had been immobilised.

Sweating and breathing hard beneath his shield, Farden rapidly withdrew beyond the flames. The golem uttered another unholy roar as it tried to reach for the mage. Its jaw sagged, molten. The runes and carvings around the cavern glowed furiously. Stalactites began to crack and tumble. The workshop was an inferno, and now smoke was beginning to fill the chamber.

'Durnus, we can't leave this here,' Farden pointed to the walls. 'Not a trace of the golem or Timeon's carvings can survive. We cannot risk Malvus finding it.'

Before Durnus could offer any advice, the golem made one last feeble grasp. It was far out of reach of Farden, but there was still power in its malformed hand. The earth cracked beneath the mage, pitching him and Durnus to the ground.

'Is it me, or are the walls trying to move?' Peryn shouted.

'We need to leave!' ordered Farden, while muscling the old vampyre along with him. 'Now!'

Falling rubble sought to squash them as they dashed for the narrowing tunnel. Old Man Grey seemed to be exhaling, collapsing into the crevasses that riddled it. Maybe it, too, wanted to be rid of the cursed magick within it. All Farden cared about was running. With Ko-Tergo carrying Durnus like a sack of flour, and Inwick and Peryn both supporting Wyved, they fled the death grip of the mountain's innards.

Racing from the crimson light to the pale day turned everything a strange shade of blue in their eyes. Farden came last, a cloud of dust and cinders gnashing at his heels. They choked on it until they managed to escape around the lee of the mountain. Rocks tumbled after them as the mouth of the crevasse collapsed. Old Man Grey rumbled angrily. At its peak, black smoke belched.

Sprawled against a boulder. Farden rubbed at his eyes. Though his lungs had turned to acid and his heart galloped, the voices had not died with Timeon nor his stone creation as he had hoped.

Farden!

'Go away, I say!' he snarled at them.

Farden! Can you hear me, you bastard?

Farden's eyes snapped open. That was not Timeon.

'Fleetstar!' the mage yelled, both out loud and his own head like a novice rider. He cast around, neck craned to the sky. The dust obscured all.

Where the fuck have you been?

A long story. What's wrong?

Malvus is here.

Farden staggered to a halt.

You hear me? Malvus is here. He's come for you!

Durnus must have seen the twitch in Farden's face. He tottered forwards, stick held like a longsword. 'What is it?'

'Malvus. He's here.'

Farden wove a shape with his fingers. Wind whipped his hair, and he pushed it outwards to clear the dust from the mountainside.

There, at the very peak of the mountain's shadow, stood a line of a hundred Arka soldiers and mages. A Lost Clan dragon lurked on one side of their ranks with a handful of daemons for good measure. Three shapes stood front and centre, standing upon a chariot and guarded by hooded warriors in black. One stood shorter than the others, and even with the haze and the fierce, biting gale still blowing across the wastes, the mage knew him.

Salt and cinder crunched beneath his boots as Farden strode out towards the enemy's lines.

'Farden, no!' the vampyre bellowed.

'Did you bring the Weight, Durnus?' asked Farden.

'No.'

'Then I guess we're flying out of here.'

Farden walked in the shadow of the mountain. The sun burned low over the Lonely Ocean, bathing the wastes in orange. He soon heard footsteps behind him, and without turning, he knew the others had joined him. They walked in an arrowhead, Farden at their point. With the curse of the mountain broken, their magick ran ferocious and free. Dust scurried from them. Something peculiar in the wind still pulled at their brewing spells, but it was a faint flicker compared to its previous hunger. Farden paid it no heed. He was wholeheartedly focused on the three figures standing loathsomely proud at the head of this small army.

Coming to a halt an arrow's reach away, lingering deep in Old Man Grey's gloom, Farden took his moment to examine every inch of his enemy, from the lines in Malvus Barkhart's jowls to the streak of grey beneath his lavish and overly bejewelled gold crown. Farden could see the dark hollows around his eyes, poorly hidden by the powder and gem-dust.

Dour Toskig, once a welcome yet stern shadow in the magick schools of Manesmark, stood beside him. The strip of face windowed by his gold and green visor looked weary, as if a feather bed could fell him as much as a sword. Farden swore he heard a constant growl emanating from him.

And beside him, Loki. Farden saved him for last, making him wait. His gaze narrowed at the flaxen-haired fucker. Farden had been betrayed many times in his life, throughout this sordid journey of his, but never by a god. He was vexed to see that Loki's infuriating smirk had not withered with time. He had not aged, as such, but Farden could see the years upon him. And yet, despite the smattering of golden mail he wore, he still insisted on that interminable brown coat.

Farden felt Malvus' furious gaze searching his face for wrinkles and creases. The mage had gathered only scars, and even they were few in number.

The emperor's voice was hoarser than Farden remembered. 'How many years has it been since we last crossed paths? Five?'

Farden's reply was spoken like a curse. 'Two. Kserak, if I remember rightly.'

Malvus made a show of summoning a faded memory. 'Kserak. Ah yes, that charming town. Wherever did it go?'

'You're not looking too healthy, Malvus, I must say,' Farden called out. 'The weight of rule must be getting to you,' Farden said. Antagonising anyone that displeased him had always given him great pleasure. The voice was a weapon as much as fists and feet. As a wise, yet psychotic man had once told him, words can't hammer in a nail, but they can start a war. And that was exactly what Farden wanted.

'I told you he would try to goad you, Emperor. He has no class,' Loki said loud enough for Farden to hear.

'And you, Loki!' Farden sighed. 'What a shame you are not dead, as we thought. Another in a long line of disappointments from you.'

'Life is full of disappointment, Farden, when you expect everything on a gilded platter.'

'I expect freedom and nothing less. Malvus will tell you all about that. We've argued about it for quite some time, haven't we?'

'Indeed we have, Farden. But no more. Our stalemate must end. I have grown very tired of waiting for your ragged band of rebels to march against me. Your rebellion has come to an end.'

Farden's eyes shifted back to the traitorous god, wondering if he could see the puppet strings tied to Malvus' back. 'Now who's being goaded?'

Loki grinned a perfectly pearly smile.

A clang echoed across the wastes, as Farden pressed his vambraces together. Dust motes spun around his boots. 'Why don't I save us all the trouble and kill you both right now?'

Malvus bared his teeth, too, even as flames began to trickle along the mage's arms.

The fire began to spin in great arcs between Farden's hands. The ground turned black beneath his feet. The air was heavy with magick and fierce heat. He grinned like a madman, jaw aching through stretch and strain. This moment had taken far too long to come, dangers be damned. A war cry tore from his throat as he unleashed the inferno that he had longed to level at Malvus for twenty years.

The firestorm fled across the wastes. Farden pushed it with all his might, hands outstretched and clenched to talons. Between the streaks of blinding flame, he saw the hooded mages scurrying. His grin became triumphant as the spell exploded against Malvus' ranks.

Or so he thought.

The shockwave of returning magick pushed his boots through the grit. It railed against him like a gale. There was no smell or taste to magick despite what one imagined, but this had a… *colour* to it, one of a tempestuous darkness and flame. It felt like being amongst Written, but wilder, skin-crawling.

The Scarred. As the flame dissipated into the sky in a great black cloud shaped like a mushroom, Farden saw them: three black-clad mages formed in a line before their emperor. Two men and one lofty woman. The air shivered before their shields spells. Through them, Farden saw Malvus smiling, clapping mockingly slowly.

'A dying breed no more!' he crowed. 'Your reign of power is over, Farden! Meet your match!'

'Inwick! Durnus!' Farden called for his own reinforcements. To his surprise, they were already behind him, a testament to how ubiquitous the hatred for Malvus was. Inwick juggled spheres of light around her. The witches held vials and wicked daggers that dripped something blue onto the dirt. The finches swarmed around Wyved like a personal storm cloud. Ko-Tergo was blowing breath after breath as he removed his jerkin and bared his white fur to the world. His muscles bulged. He put his paws together in an effigy of prayer and rumbled like a landslide

Durnus stood beside Farden. He spoke in his whisper of paper ripping. If possible, his face had turned paper, almost translucent. 'You were right about the Scarred, Farden.'

'Gods, do I hate being right.'

Durnus put his claws on Farden's shoulder. 'We cannot defeat him here. Not today. We are stronger together behind our walls.'

'But he is here, alone and without his horde.'

'As are we,' Durnus snapped. 'And more Arka will come. We are far from home.'

Farden turned to his old friend, face a deep glower, but Durnus was adamant.

'You will not make a corpse of Malvus here. Wiping all traces of your Book from that mountain is the mission we came for.'

Farden spat grit from his mouth. 'You know what? I hate it more when you're right,' he replied. 'Time, I can give you. Tell the dragons. Let's test the mettle of these Scarred and see who's better. Shields!'

The concussive blast of the Written's spells igniting was enough to entice Malvus' forces forwards. The emperor was also in a rush for vengeance. Though it pained him to defend instead of attack, if there was anything Emaneska and rule had taught him in the past two decades, it was a thread of patience.

Though the Scarred irritatingly held back to protect the emperor and his pet god – or rather the god and his pet emperor – fireballs surged in from all directions as Arka mages advanced. Forks of lightning skipped between Scalussen shields, probing for a weakness. Farden, Durnus, and Inwick held firm, resisting all punishment. A cloud of grit and smoke billowed around them.

A faint shout floated across the dirt. 'Vilespar!'

'Inwick! Ko-Tergo!' Farden yelled as he switched one hand to his sword. 'Like we practised!'

No sooner had the words left his mouth than the cloud scattered like a herd of deer before a wolf. A Lost Clan dragon, to be precise, swooping over their shield-wall and aiming to out manoeuvre them. It dropped fangs and claws first, but the witches and yetin were too fast for it. Dust was all the dragon murdered. Before its wings and tail could begin to thrash, Inwick cast her spell: a shining green orb that exploded above the dragon's head and forced its face into the dirt. Vilespar's eyes rolled with the blow. Green vines of light burst from the earth, wrapped around the dragon's extremities, and lashed it to the ground.

The yetin had grown a head in height and maybe two sideways. His eyes were washed black, and his fangs bursting from his gums. Ko-Tergo came in like a boxer, punching the dragon thrice in the jaw and eye, caring not for the iron-like hide of the beast. Farden's sword pierced the armour just behind the great crest on its neck. Vilespar lurched with pain, casting the mage back, but they were death throes, and short at that.

'Well that went surprisingly well,' muttered Farden.

'They advance!' Durnus yelled.

Seeing the ranks now charging towards them, Farden turned on his heel, forcing the vampyre's shield outwards while Inwick delved deep into the ground. The wasteland rippled as her quake spells bent the earth to their will. Ko-Tergo, who had now practically doubled in size, chased it with a bloodcurdling roar.

The Arka charge was utterly ruined. There were few spells, if any, for sure footing. Arka mages and soldiers alike tumbled into each other, and before they could right themselves, Farden and his hunters were amongst them.

Whether it was a finch pecking at eyes, a mage's spell ripping a hole through armour and entrails, a witch's dagger darting too fast to see, or a godsdamned yetin tearing the legs and arms from anything in his path, it was safe to say chaos descended. The Arka's taste for blood was quickly spoiled as they alone stained the wastelands scarlet.

Farden tore through the lines as if Malvus hid beneath every helmet. His sword carved a pattern of silver. Arcs of blood and sparks chased the blade. Lost fingers, legs, and other important things rained. Those that managed to block his furious attack found themselves engulfed in flame, or the mage's fist between their ribs, splitting them in half with lightning. Farden felt the brutality of it but refused to stop. This was vintage rage, bottled up and fortified until it had become something pure yet scorching. There was no stopping it. Farden even glimpsed the same pent-up fury pouring from Durnus. The vampyre was unleashing magick Farden hadn't seen in years, from darting a dozen places in a blink, to using force spells to collapse armour and ribcages.

Farden spared a glance for the great cloud of smoke that rose from Old Man Grey's sides, and for the three serpents that spewed flame upon it. *They had to be almost finished.*

The mage caught a fireball, crushing its fire to ash in his palm. Before he could spy its caster, what felt like a warhammer collided with his ribs. The force sent him spinning along with his sword, rewarding him with a mouthful of dust. It was then the pain struck; the heat searing through his armour. Whipping raven hair from his face, Farden sprang upright to see one of the Scarred mages standing on the edge of the fray. Whatever Malvus had done to them, they looked half-rotten. The pallid man wore an impudent grin though not a tooth resided his mouth. His eyes were red sores, but they still sparkled with mirth.

'Let's see what you're made of, Scarred!' the mage barked. He marched out to meet the abominations, lightning burning in one gauntlet, fire in the other.

Farden felt the rumble in his boots before the spell came. He dodged as the spear of rock thrust from the earth and retorted by pouring magick on the Scarred. The man was swift, throwing up his shield spell at the last instant. While he reeled, Farden sprinted for him, swinging a fist trailing green light. Curving around the shield, he hammered the Scarred in the armoured gut.

Wreathed in a cloud of dust, the pale man came up spitting blood. Farden cracked his neck from side to side and heaved at the ground. The dirt beneath the Scarred burst upwards, striking him in the chin and sending him right back on his arse. He failed to see Farden's glowing hand, held flat and blade-like, until it had cleaved into his throat.

The Scarred toppled to the earth, his head rolling once before it came to a rest, staring back at Malvus. Another Scarred mage walked out to meet him: the tall woman, with thunder crackling around her.

'Farden!' came Durnus' shout. 'It's time!'

With much reluctance and a dash of infuriation, Farden tore his dust-sore eyes from Malvus and Loki and began to retreat. The dragons were racing across the wasteland towards them, throwing dust clouds in their wake.

Malvus' order was an avid howl. 'After them!'

Closing the distance between them and their scaled escape, Farden heard the crackle of more daemons appearing on the plain, wreathed in rags and clouds of smoke. Their screeches were chilling.

'I will hold them off!' Durnus yelled, almost causing Farden to stumble. He ran like a chased hound, eyes glued behind him and spittle streaming.

'You'll *what*?'

Durnus held his hands high as if leading a sermon. Farden could not make out what spell he was attempting, but he felt a chill wind chase them. Trails of sapphire smoke poured from Durnus' claws, each wisp seeking a nearby corpse.

Farden saw no more. The dragons swooped towards their hunting party, with claws splayed like eagles hunting fish. With a shared groan, they all quickly reversed course as they realised what the dragons intended. Even though it was perfectly safe – and quite necessary when speed was of the essence – Farden always found it mildly terrifying. Some ancestral memory, perhaps.

With a gut-wrenching lurch, his scarpering boots left the dirt and rose up. Farden saw Durnus' magick now, and his insides performed another twist. Between the charging Arka and the hammering tread of the daemons, the corpses were rising. *Reaching*, more than anything, but they grasped at any passing leg and sowed panic in the ranks. It was an odious magick he had never seen before.

It was momentary: Shivertread scooped up Durnus in his claws seconds later, and the horizon spun like a baton as the dragons dodged errant spells and arrows. Dark shapes of reinforcements were approaching both by land and sky, rushing to the emperor's aid. More mages, by the feel of it, and half a fleet of Lost Clan dragons.

Farden snarled at their odds. The day had slipped inexorably from his grasp. 'I'll see you in Scalussen, Malvus!' Farden baited him with a roar.

Dousing the Arka ranks one last time with dragonfire, they made their escape north and sped low over Old Man Grey's wasteland, away from Emaneska's madness.

Safe in Fleetstar's grip, Farden let his ache-wracked body hang limp while his mind worked to torture him with second guesses. And third guesses, and so on. Doubt was a foul road that led to regret, and if one followed it far enough, madness. Farden knew that, but as Albion disappeared beneath him, he closed his eyes, and walked that road, exploring all the worries of Scarred mages, and gods playing puppeteers.

For the first time in half a decade, Farden felt adrift.

Amongst the mire of the Arka's chaos, a sole figure stood motionless. While the mages chased the dragons with spells, the archers strained to bend bows double, and others fought desperately to drag themselves clear of the dragonfire, Loki surveyed Farden's escape with a satisfied smile.

Nearby, the emperor was stolen from his constant stream of orders by a ragged cough. Eyes watering from the effort of dragging breath, Malvus wheezed into a kerchief. General Toskig tried to shepherd him towards the chariot but the emperor shoved him away.

'Search that mountain. I want to know what Farden was doing.'

No matter how fast Malvus pocketed it, Loki spied the blood in the silken kerchief. The emperor caught the god's stare with narrowed eyes.

'I wouldn't bother your men or waste the time, my good Malvus,' Loki called to him. The smoke and dust was still rising from the mess

Farden had made of Old Man Grey. The magick that had flowed from the rusted spearhead of a mountain before was now dead and cold. 'Whatever Farden came to this bare scar of Albion to accomplish is finished, I would wager.'

'Then what are you so pleased about, bastard?' Malvus rasped. A fleck of blood decorated his lower lip.

'Because,' Loki said, 'I imagine you will not let such a trespass go unpunished, Emperor. And with your Scarred proven, what else remains but your war?'

Malvus regarded the god with a haughty stare. Loki knew there was no better leash for a man like Malvus Barkhart than his own pride, and he waited patiently while the emperor found the alternatives lacking. Toskig stared on, gaze flicking to and fro.

'Hawks, General,' the emperor spoke at last. 'I want one dispatched to every outpost, regiment, and hunting party. Summon my vassals to Arfell.'

'What message, Majesty?'

Malvus stabbed at the marred sky with his knife, in the direction Farden had disappeared.

'What else, Toskig?' he cried. 'To prepare for the greatest war Emaneska has ever seen!'

CHAPTER 18
A DIFFERENT KIND

Never before has neighbour stood so vehemently against neighbour. Borders of belief divide towns, cities. Never before have arms been taken up by so many innocents. Never before has east been so far from west, north from south.
PAINTED IN MANURE ON THE WALLS OF THE ARKATHEDRAL

The metallic crunch of the locks made Mithrid sit up like a sprung trap. Through the conservative gap, a tray poked into the room, was placed on the chair, and the trembling hand quickly withdrew.

Mithrid rolled her eyes. 'I told you, I am not a spy!' she yelled after them, whoever the coward was.

The cogs jiggled back into their locked position. Mithrid's spine bent as she slumped. A day and a half, or so the shaft of light told her, she had been in this room. Mithrid didn't care how plush the chairs and bed were, or how sweet the scent of the candles, or even for the washed-out frescoes showing some ancient history, this room was a prison cell by any other name. Her crime was unuttered and unknown. The events of the training yard were a blur to her. A blur that had resulted in her being dragged promptly into the Frostsoar and a door locked in her face.

Mithrid seized the tray so viciously a bread roll tumbled across the varnished floors. Wrinkling her lip, Mithrid left it be. The stew, dried meat, and hard cheese did her just fine. She had grown use to this "spice" Scalussen insisted on using, and after stirring the meal all together in one bowl, she wolfed it down.

Belly full and gurgling, Mithrid made laps of her room, resorting to poking at the frescoes and wondering who all these old and important people were. Her roaming took her past a stone cube propped up on a table. It contained a miniature glass sculpture of a tree. She'd stared at it for hours, but never this close. It was far too intricate to be made by human hands.

To her abject surprise, with a gentle brush of a finger, Mithrid realised it was not glass, but an actual plant. The little tree swayed under her touch, its arrowhead leaves jingling softly like chimes.

'What in the—'

Before Mithrid could investigate further, the door locks spun again. If they thought they could placate her with dessert they were sorely mistaken.

She found Hereni standing in the doorway instead. The mage had a furrow in her brow that Mithrid didn't know whether to call concern or unease.

'At last,' Mithrid spoke before she could. 'Somebody has come to explain why I'm suddenly a prisoner.'

'You are not a pris—ah, fuck it.' Hereni gave up on lying. She closed the door behind her – not completely – and stood arms crossed. 'I'm sorry, Mithrid. In this age of traitors and spies, we can never be too careful.'

'Modren himself insisted I come here.'

'You'd be surprised at the lengths some of the Arka spies go to.'

'I'm not a spy!'

'I know.'

Hereni answered her so quietly, Mithrid wondered if she had misheard an errant scrape of a boot. The mage was staring at her intently.

'How do you feel?'

'Bored. Irritated. But otherwise fine.' Mithrid took a moment. The answer was illuminating. Ever since being stuffed into this room, her constant headache had vanished. But that was inconsequential. 'Why am I locked up in here? What happened in the yards that made you all piss in fright?'

'Time,' Hereni replied. Her steps were slow and cautious, and she kept flexing her fist as if testing her fingers still worked. 'We needed it. We've never seen magick like yours, Mithrid. We sought out Durnus, but he was summoned south in haste to Farden. We had to delve into his libraries ourselves.' Hereni puffed out her cheeks. 'How the old coot isn't ever buried in an avalanche of scrolls and parchment, I don't know.'

Mithrid held her breath. *Magick like yours.* The words were so fragile, she worried they might shatter if she repeated them alone.

'At first we thought it was leech magick, perhaps voiding. Or maybe presence magick you didn't know you could wield.'

'What are you saying, Hereni?' She had to hear it.

'That you've got power in you, Mithrid. But without Durnus, we don't know what kind. That's why we kept you here, to stop you hurting yourself or others. Well, *another.* You gave that recruit quite a lump. He's had a shake in his hands ever since.'

Mithrid swallowed, nervous. A crack had appeared in her hope, spreading slowly the more Hereni spoke.

'Too much discovery of magick is accidental and explosive. Ever notice that new patch of flagstones in the western yard? Paraian man came to us years back. Had never seen thunder spells like he could wield. One morning, he burned too hot. Magick ripped from him, part vortex spell, part fire. As well as burning the skin from his entire right side and setting light to four other mages in the process, he threw himself a hundred feet in the air. Ilios just about managed to catch him.'

'What's an Ilios?'

A boot kicked the door inward and Modren finished off Hereni's sentence for her. 'Long story short, we don't fuck around and take chances on what we don't understand.'

Behind him, Elessi stood warily in the corridor, wringing her hands and staring at Mithrid as if she were a plague victim awaiting Hel's welcoming touch. Eyrum was there, too, a makeshift door blocking the dead-end hallway. His face was parchment blank as always.

'So... what?' Mithrid shrugged, vexed that her heart fell without her permission. She hated the false hope Hereni had given her. 'What will you do with me? Are you sending me away? Banishing me?'

Hereni's laugh was either painfully cruel or a blessed thing.

'Gods, no, girl,' Modren clarified. 'We made a promise to train you. Make you dangerous in one direction only.' He pointed a thumb in what Mithrid assumed was south. The undermage's words were final, and with boots squeaking on the floor, they about-faced and escorted her from the room.

Mithrid's heart had changed its tune, now drumming a lively beat. She whispered to Hereni, who walked behind her, keeping a strange and constant distance. 'Does this mean I'm a mage after all?'

Hereni tutted. 'I don't know. But we'll find out.'

Mithrid walked a little straighter, a little surer than the hunch she had adopted in her plush cell. When the cold sunlight struck her, she blinked at a full plaza of trainees, spending the afternoon hours batting each other with spells and sticks.

The sergeants and captains kept them hard at work while Mithrid's guardians trod the fringes, near the walls of sky-blue ice that hemmed in the training yards. The small procession still gathered attention no matter how hastily they walked. Mithrid searched for Remina in the crowds, wanting to challenge her judging eyes, and the gossip that had no doubt flown about the Underspire in the last day.

'Fuck you, freak!' came a muted cry, half-hearted and shouted behind a hand. Lurn, by the voice.

Hereni shot a dark look into the crowds and signalled to the captain overseeing them with a wheel-like motion of her finger.

'About turn, you miserable weaklings!' Mithrid heard the captain bark. 'Twenty jumps! Quickly now!'

'Don't get cocky, Mithrid,' Hereni chided her. 'I would have done that no matter what they shouted. Your friends need to learn discipline. There were recruits like that when I trained. Even on a level field, people will always build mounds to stand above others. It's juvenile, but it's in our nature. Only cure for it is time and hard lessons.'

'You would have thought seeing your family murdered was a lesson hard enough.'

'We all deal with grief in our own way.'

'Pipe down, you two. We're here,' Modren snapped, motioning to a hollow of ice half hidden from the rest of the yards. It looked like a range for archers, spears, or far-reaching spells. Instead of targets, a table had been set up. A variety of objects perched upon it, from ornate torches and a conical lockbox, to a jiggling hawk made of cogs and springs. Mithrid raised an eyebrow.

'What are these trinkets for?'

'So you don't have to practice on us. Not yet, at least,' answered the undermage. He and the others had arranged themselves behind her, eyes wide and curious. 'All of these trinkets are charmed so that they use magick to work. The torches, for example, will stay lit for years unless extinguished by a word. Try them first.'

Mithrid stared at the torches. 'Try what?'

'Using whatever magick you used on that young recruit. Aim it at the torches.'

No matter how hard she tried to untangle the blur in her mind, no details came forth. She remembered pain, anger, and the overwhelming need for the smug bastard to kindly fuck off. She had reached out, or so she recalled. Mithrid mimicked what she had seen the mages do, aiming a splayed hand at one of the shining torches. She had no idea what she was doing, but she exerted herself all the same, wishing the flame to sputter out.

'Get closer,' suggested Hereni.

That was no help.

'Closer.'

Still nothing. Mithrid's hand was now an inch from being burned by the flame. Enduring the warmth, she clenched her jaw so hard her teeth squeaked, wishing, hoping, and demanding the flame die. When screaming in her head didn't work, she resorted to verbal abuse.

'Go out,' she hissed. 'Go out, go out. Go out, you bastard!'

She most likely imagined it, but Mithrid swore the flame glowed only brighter. She threw up her hands in sour defeat. Her hope had been shattered. 'It doesn't work.'

Hereni shook her head, as if she knew something Mithrid didn't. 'Try the hawk. Put your hand on it.'

The intricate creature was made of metal plates and screws. Under its shell, springs, levers, cogs and all kinds of details clattered away, making a metallic racket. The hawk's eyes glowed green even in the daylight. Mithrid blew a cloud of steam over it and muttered a prayer to Hurricane before clapping a dejected hand on the witless creature.

'See?' was what Mithrid had been poised to say. It came out more like, 'Sssss… ' as she stared in shock at the hawk. The contraption had fallen deathly still, its glowing eyes dead as stone.

The others traded glances.

As soon as Mithrid lifted a hand from the warm metal, the hawk once more began to flap its wings. The glimmer sputtered back to life momentarily before Mithrid quashed it again.

'Leech magick. It has to be,' she overheard Hereni whisper.

Modren scowled. 'Only if she is absorbing it. And we know the dangers of that.'

'Cessation, then, or dispelling. Even shield magick can act like this.'

'Why don't you talk to me, instead of between yourselves?' the girl challenged them.

It took a moment to realise what the deep grunting sound was. Mithrid looked around as if the hollow was set to cave in on them. But it was Eyrum, chuckling to himself. The Siren swept his axe from his back and used it as a leaning post.

'I am starting to like this one. Tell us, Hâlorn, what does it feel to you? Do you feel like you are drawing power into yourself?'

It did not.

'Does it feel like you're pushing against the magick?'

'No.'

'Burning? Tingling?'

'Warm under my hand. That's all.'

Hereni pointed. 'Try the box. It's locked by magick and magick alone with Siren spells.'

Mithrid obliged, eager to test the ugly lump of iron. At first, she tried it with her hand apart, but nothing happened. When her fingertips graced its pitted surface, there was no solidity there, but what felt like the surface of water. Mithrid stared but saw no such ripples in the iron. She pushed down, driving her will past her flesh and bone and down against the perplexing water. The iron box shuddered violently until a crack shot through its lid. Its front fell open, revealing runes that steamed gently.

'Well, Mithrid, you've broken the spell completely.'

'Is that bad?'

'It's interesting. Some spells are flexible. Others are not.'

Hereni took a step out of line. 'Try me.'

Modren stamped a foot, casting ice chips. 'Hereni, that is not wise. We don't know if Mithrid's power is lasting. Don't make me order you back.'

With a click of her fingers, Hereni lit a flame in her palm. 'With all due respect, Undermage, it needs to be tested. And I trust Mithrid.'

Nobody was more surprised by that statement than Mithrid. She momentarily lost her gaze in Hereni's amber eyes.

The undermage may have growled his displeasure but he stayed silent. Mithrid caught the glimpse of the faint green glow around his gauntlets. *Ready*.

Mithrid's heart hammered as Hereni approached, one hand aloft and one outstretched. Mithrid slowly clasped her armoured fingers, and the more metal she touched, the more Hereni's flame began to spit and sputter. The mage pushed harder; Mithrid could feel the power rushing against her like a river. She had no explanation for it, but she could feel it as clear as if somebody had tossed a bucket of water over her. Mithrid tensed, trying to match Hereni's strength.

The flame went out with a snap of hot air.

'Hereni!' Modren yelled.

She didn't answer, but she withdrew from Mithrid swiftly, having to rip the girl's fingers from her gauntlets. She cupped her hands together and whispered a stream of panicked words to herself. Flame sparked immediately, and she visibly deflated in relief.

'It's not permanent.'

'Fortunately for you, mage.' Modren cocked his head as a loud trumpet blast sounded.

Once, twice, and while Mithrid waited for a third, the undermage already pacing across the flagstones. 'What is it?'

Hereni shook her hand as though she had slept on it for an hour. She pointed to the streaks of colour racing past the Frostsoar.

'The king has returned,' Eyrum rumbled, before following Modren.

'And after this display, he'll no doubt want to meet you,' added Hereni.

Mithrid felt for the axe at her empty belt, seeking something solid and familiar, but was dismayed to find it wasn't there. Instead she clenched her fists and wondered what in Emaneska her father would say.

Magick like yours. Magick like hers.

It was a guilt-ridden thrill that ran through Mithrid.

The dragons were exhausted. Their claws sparked against the Frostsoar's stone as they scraped for purchase against the winds. Fleetstar gave up completely and slumped into a heap. Shivertread had turned a pale, weak grey.

The passengers fared little better, even after they had prised themselves from the saddles. The witches picked ice from their braids with jittering hands. Ko-Tergo's fur had been frozen in great spikes behind him, as if he were still in mid-flight. Inwick and Farden were in the best shape, having stuck to their heat spells, but Durnus had turned a soft shade of blue. His teeth were bared to keep from chattering, and his legs bent so much he looked moments from collapse. Whatever magick Durnus had summoned in the shadow of Old Man Grey had drained him. And rightly so, thought Farden. That breed of power was never to be trifled with.

Inwick's hands were clamped to Durnus' forehead. Between her fingers, Durnus stared into vacant space, his eyes glassy.

'Get him syngur, or firewine, and quickly,' ordered Farden.

'What are you—?'

The slam of the heavy door sliced Inwick's question in half.

Farden descended the stairs as fast as his aching legs would carry him. Mages and healers scrabbled to greet the arrivals, bobbing quick bows as they passed him on the stairs. Farden kept his eyes flat but nodded to each. If they were going to call him king, then he refused to be known as a cruel king.

His door could not come quick enough. Red scales covered a central circular portion, with a hollow shaped perfectly to fit Farden's right gauntlet. He rammed metal against metal, listening to the ring as the magick fused with the door. A deep clicking sounded, and with a twist and push of his hand, the door to his chambers split down its centre. The stone rumbled as pulleys and mechanics beyond Farden's need to understand went to work.

The stark stone room was cold. Windows had been left ajar. Ice had gathered on sills. A nearby couch was white with frost's chalk. Farden did not care. Dallying not in the lounge, he sought his inner chambers, where a matching door waited. *Click, twist, push.*

To the unwary visitor, Farden's hideaway would have looked like a shrine. The stone altar was the focus of the cylindrical room. Shelves wrapped the walls, holding not only weapons and trinkets, but a smattering of ivory candles, each carved to resemble a face. A plain wooden chair guarded a dead fireplace jealously.

The altar was bare but for a stack of books, a lectern bearing a colossal tome, and an iron frame for holding armour. Currently, all it held was a shining helmet, the same autumnal metal as the rest of his Scalussen pieces. Its etched face and hollow eyes stared at him expectantly, one twitch from mocking.

As the door thudded back into place, Farden seized the helmet from the stand and thrust it over his head. He felt the metal scales sliding across each other to match his shape, and to intermingle with the plates of the cuirass, forming its ridged spine. Farden felt the armour's power run through him: glacier melt cascading through his veins. It caused him a shiver, one that ran down to his injured ribs.

The chair creaked threateningly as he slumped into it. Though Farden hunched before it as if it blazed, he kept the fireplace cold. Instead, he stared at the coals with his head cradled in his hands.

There was no singular concern disquieting his mind. Merely a hive of hundreds, buzzing away in a constant drone – a wall of noise and perturbation. No sooner would he swat one did another sting him.

Such was the mantle of being a so-called king, Farden thought. There were too many strings attached to him, pulling him hither and thither. Oh, how he had longed to cut them free at first. Then came the learning; the adjustment to a crown he hadn't ever wanted. Two decades since, and those strings had only grown tauter. Each one of them now a soul who depended on the Forever King to keep their skin on their backs. To keep their heads attached to their shoulders.

Here, in this sanctum, that mantle could be put aside at least momentarily. Farden could once again be himself; be like that lone wolf of old, hunched in a cottage by the sea, free as the gulls and forgotten by all. Farden bent the fingers of his left hand, curling all but his missing finger.

The murderous old Farden Four-Hand. The mage snorted. Responsibility might have been an anchor dragging in the dust, but the toil had carved him into a better man. It was simply a high and heavy price to pay. Farden picked up a half-finished candle and used a sharp edge of his gauntlet to turn a smile into a sour pucker.

He blew a long sigh before casting the chair aside. From the folds of his cloak, he withdrew the rolled parchment, squashed and battered after the fight and flight but still as dangerous as ever. His Book felt hot in his hand, even through the Scalussen steel. Unrolling it, he stared at the flowing script one more time. Fortunately for Farden, Written were able to regard their own Books without adverse effects.

Four complex runes for fire, light, quake, and spark were surrounded by script so intricate it quickly hurt his wind-bitten eyes. These were Farden's chosen schools of magick. He could still remember the searing point of the whalebone needle as the Scribe inked them into his shivering body of barely nineteen winters.

He held a veritable mistake in his palm: a dire poison in parchment form. It should have been reduced to ash immediately, he knew that. Farden tried once again, half-hearted, but the spark still jolted through him instead of the Book. He grimaced and wiggled his arm. It was a piece of himself, irrevocably intertwined. Farden traced the runes with his finger. *For posterity,* he thought, whatever that might look like.

Farden placed his Book between the pages of a leather notebook so weathered and ragged-edged it looked as though it had been in a fight and crawled away with its life. Within were sketches, diagrams, and notes on his old hunt for the armour of the Nine. A charcoal portrayal of a rat, too, beady-eyed and long of tooth. Whiskers. A companion long gone and still missed.

The tome on the pedestal called his attention. Replacing his helmet and gauntlets on the stand, Farden placed his hand upon the gigantic book. The thing was the length of his elbow to his fist and just as wide. It had grown thicker than his hand span in the last decade, like a plant fertilised by death and chaos.

'Grimsayer,' Farden breathed, and as always, he swore he caught the whisper of the book repeating its own name in foreign tongue. In all the years since stumbling across the tome in the Hjaussfen libraries, he had learnt nothing of the book's strange and ancient magick beyond its purpose.

With a grunt, Farden heaved the book open, filling the empty half of the lectern. The Grimsayer sighed, breathing dust. He spread his hands over the blank and silken pages for a brief moment before recoiling.

'Tyrfing,' Farden spoke clear and loud to the tome.

It took a moment before the pages began to flutter. They turned with quick snaps, first dozens at a time, then hundreds, until the tome neared its end. With a shiver, it fell still. Gleaming points of amber light emerged from the gutter of the spine. They darted across the page like insects with tails of fire. They were mere pinpricks, but combined, their frantic dance wove a sculpture of light that hovered above the Grimsayer. A man, no bigger than Farden's palm. He flickered as the sculpture changed ever so slightly, as if the man walked under the sea.

Farden smiled without humour. It was to keep from suffering any other emotion. Decades had passed since his uncle Tyrfing, the greatest Written ever inked, had passed into Hel. Every soul referred to him as dead, but Farden knew. He had made the journey beneath the world with his uncle, to the dead ship and its mistress. He had been there, when his uncle had given Hel his soul as payment for Farden's return from the nethers. In his long lifetime, Farden had paid many a dark toll for his actions, but never one as leaden and sharp as that. It still cut into him.

'How I could use your guidance now, old man. Now more than ever.'

When Farden managed to tear himself away from the Grimsayer and close the pages upon his uncle, he steeled himself before parting the door. What waited beyond was inescapable. He donned a cloak, levelled the hood across his eyes and pressed his vambraces against the door.

CHAPTER 19
KING'S PROBLEMS

Pale Kings three and Pale Kings free,
daemon's blood, burnt ashen tree.
Orion's lust and mankind's trust,
fell seeds fallen, smiths of dust.
Pale Kings stalk and Pale Kings wait,
to sow chaos oathed to father late.
'BALLAD OF THE PALE ONES', AN OLD SKALD'S TALE

Undermage Modren waited in Farden's grand lounge, arms crossed and picking ice from the couch, the fault of a window left open. Beyond the frosted panes, the north spread into vast leagues, devoid of horizon and blending into one blinding sky. A black cloud hung over the Spine, washed red by the glow of Irminsul and its fiery brethren.

The undermage offered his hand and Farden clasped it to feel the heat burning across his wrist. Modren's forearms were bare and the black tattoo of a skeleton key across his forearm glowed white in kind.

'I see Scalussen hasn't burned to the ground while I was gone.'

Modren smirked. 'And what about the rest of Emaneska?'

Farden followed the curve of the windows south, imagining a fleet of black and steel dragons ascending above the Tausenbar Mountains. 'Malvus found us in Albion. He knew exactly where I would be, likely before I knew where I was going.' Farden waited for his friend struggle to swallow that information. 'Walk with me.'

'Spies, then?' Modren asked. 'Strange, as you spoke only to the council about it.'

'It's Loki's doing.'

'Excuse me? You seem to have said "Loki" but that's impossible.'

Farden's heavy footfalls punctuated every loathsome word. 'That bastard is back. He had Jeasin remind me of a copy of my Book I foolishly left in Albion. He knew all too well I'd chase it down and put Malvus on my scent. That traitor god has his hand so far up Malvus' arse he could waggle the emperor's tongue for him. What's worse, he's given Malvus the power of the Written, stolen from our dead sisters and brothers cut down before the Last War.'

Modren blushed with anger. 'By your…'

'Yes, by my daughter,' Farden grumbled. He led Modren down level by level to the stout, winch-powered lifts that removed half the stress from climbing or descending the Frostsoar. Farden slammed the doors and kicked the lever that balanced the weight of the lift against iron slabs dangling below.

'He's made Written, Modren. Malvus has his own Written mages. Scarred, he calls them,' he said.

'Evernia's tits, didn't you bring back any good news?' Modren spat. 'They any good?'

Farden patted his side, where the Scalussen metal was charred and blistered.

The undermage looked unimpressed. 'Gods. You getting sloppy in your old age, Farden?'

'Too close, is all,' Farden replied, brushing off his concern.

Modren clapped him on the shoulder. 'Too close is all it needs to be.'

'There is some good news. The copy of the Book has been destroyed. Malvus would have found it and put it to his own use. At last, a splinter of my past is finally gouged out and in safe keeping.'

Modren leant against the lift's struts. 'We're all paying for past mistakes, Farden.'

'I seem to be paying double. Jeasin has turned from us. Malvus has his Scarred. Now he has a god on his side…' Modren was grinning at him. 'What?'

'Anything else you want to pile upon that cart of responsibility you're dragging around?'

'You don't understand—'

'Don't I? Being undermage isn't exactly a glass of mörd and boots up by the fire, Farden. A king can't rule without his advisors and captains. How many times has Durnus told us all that? Let us help carry the weight of all of this.'

'How many times have I said I'm no king?' Farden growled, feigning annoyance. It was the mention of the vampyre that had turned his face to stone.

'There's more, isn't there?'

'Nothing else,' lied the mage. Durnus was wrong. Modren didn't need to be burdened like Farden was. None of them did.

The air had changed from cold to a humid warmth by the time they descended into the depths of the Frostsoar. As the foundations spread into the rock, a cavern unfurled beneath them. The lift descended like a fishing hook into the depths of a smoky sea. The memory of tracking the ancient kingdom down always pounced upon him here.

Scalussen had died a fiery death more than a thousand years ago. The bones the hordes had left behind had outlasted countless empires. For nine weeks, Farden and the survivors of the Last War had traced the oldest maps and songs of the snowmads, forging a path to where Emaneska's first great civilisation had been left to become legend.

Farden had almost killed himself burning the ice away with his magick. Malvus' claim upon Emaneska had driven the newly-appointed arkmage almost to desperation. Farden almost drove the survivors to mutiny before Farden found it: a broken foundation of the old Scalussen spire, where the Knights of the Nine had turned the world to jealousy and chaos.

'Thinking of old days?' Modren waded into his thoughts.

'Constantly, at the moment. I'm sure time erases the darker details, but it all seemed simpler before all of this.'

He and Modren stared out across the array of factories and forges that fed Scalussen. From above, the city might have seemed an idyllic refuge amongst the ice, but beneath, it was a machine of war, a crunching, grinding, never-ending effort to prepare for the battle to end all battles.

Volcanic vents steamed night and day, keeping the tower and refugees above a fraction warmer than they should. Gigantic pans and glass spheres boiled above their chimneys, feeding all kinds of contraptions.

Glowing streams of metal cascaded down blackened conduits into fields of furrowed moulds. Trees had been dragged from the south, and rimewood delivered from eastern Scarala. Teams of workers desiccated them like ants, trimming planks for bows, axe handles, spears, or to build the complicated siege engines that waited for their day in the sunlight: the ballistae, catapults, trebuchets, and other dastardly apparatuses that waited to spill Arka blood.

Magick lingered here, carved into forges and cauldrons of boiling metal to add strength and power to whatever shape it found itself poured into. Runecrafting was an old art, passed down from Scalussen to Emaneska when the gods were still new stars and revived by Tyrfing before the Last War.

Where walls of glossy blue ice or black rock formed the edges of the caverns, tunnels had been bored, from a slim hollow for a bunk to a whole house burrowed into the walls. Few workers ever left the forges to keep spies from coming and going, yet Farden gave them every treatment those above received. It was voluntary, paid well in food and warmth, and between the anvils and foundries, inns and betting arenas thrived. The occasional roar from those off their shifts always gave Farden a smile. Doubt will always wither in the light of accomplishment, and, beneath the ice, he could bury his frets for a time in the rebirth of Emaneska's most fabled forges.

As Farden strode to the nearest blacksmith's workshop, he shot Modren a question. 'Without wanting to sound rude—'

'You? Never.'

'—why did you come to see me?'

'We have an interesting development.'

'Did you not hear the long list of problems I already have? You thought you would bring me another?' Farden groaned, tossing his cloak aside.

Modren pressed him. 'This may be a solution. One that needs your attention, Farden.'

With a slithering of metal, Farden unfastened the cuirass and let it peel away at the shoulders so he could remove it. The lightness of Scalussen metal always escaped his understanding. He took a wire brush to scrape the char from it. It was unbroken yet scorched deeply.

'What is it?'

'There's a girl. The one I saved from a cliff-village in Hâlorn along with several others. She has a magick I don't think I've ever seen before.'

'Sure she's not a spy? Wouldn't be the first time they went to such extremes.'

'I don't know yet, especially if Loki's back and giving Malvus ideas. But I don't believe so. If so, then she's the finest actor that Emaneska has ever seen, and she let her father die to play the part.'

Cuirass cleaned, though wearing a few more scratches than he would have admitted, Farden slammed his sword on the table and fetched a whetstone. 'What kind of magick?' he asked.

'I don't know. Leech, possibly. Some shield and cessation combination. Yet this shadow drifts from her hands. She choked the magick right out of Hereni with just a touch. Eyrum saw her rip the spells from two recruits during a duel.' Modren shook his head. 'She reminds me of somebody I used to know.'

The mage looked up. 'Is that so?'

'Full of fire and hatred. Brimming with emotion.'

'Weren't we all?'

Farden threw his sword on the blacksmith's table. The notches were deeper than a quick fix, and if there was anything Scalussen wasn't short on, it was blades. He chose a new sword and a matching knife from a shelf brimming with fine swords, and after fastening his cuirass around himself, he motioned back to the lift.

'I'll see her. Tonight. First, let me speak to Durnus,' he replied. 'He and I have business to attend to.'

Back turned and face to the fire, the mage got no welcome on entering the vampyre's haunt. It was a chamber similar to Farden's, but with a distinct lack of windows and an overabundance of literature. Farden was constantly surprised the Frostsoar didn't lean to one side with the weight of buckling shelves and tables trembling with mountains of books atop them. They could have built another bookship just for Durnus alone.

The logs sparked, turning Durnus' head ever so slightly. With a clatter of wood on stone, Farden dragged an armchair close and sat opposite the old vampyre. The pipe in Durnus' hand was not lit. His eyes were closed in meditation. Farden glowered.

The vampyre had left some of his wrinkles in Albion's wasteland, it seemed. His face had shed ten years like a travel-dusted cloak after a good shake. Ten years wasn't a lot to somebody who verged on thousands of years old, but to Farden, who knew every peak and valley and crag of that old vampyre's face, it was noticeable.

'Explain yourself,' Farden ordered.

Durnus kept his eyes shut while he spoke. 'You know of the research I conducted when the Frostsoar was still wrapped in scaffolding. When I began to investigate whether the vampyre curse could take the blindness from me, and clean my blood of its daemon poison, I realised it is one rooted in the darkest of magicks. It might grant immortality, healing, but it is death magick through and through. That is where the bloodthirst comes from. My research took me to places I never thought I would wander to search for answers. I discovered many solutions to my blindness that would have granted more than sight yet cost more than fangs and a cripple's limp. As any scholar worth his salt would do, I studied such things, Farden. Do not blame me when I use that knowledge for good. For your war.'

All of Farden's argument sank like a ship stricken by a reef. The risks still remained, and so did his anger. 'Toying with such magicks is dangerous, even for you. You've shed years, old friend. Something in those spells of yours fed upon those dead souls, and fed you like a warm neck. Now if that isn't how daemons conduct themselves, then please correct me.'

Durnus ignored the accusation. 'I believe such spells were necessary, and they will be again.'

'I will not have you raising the fucking dead, Durnus!'

The vampyre dashed his pipe to pieces on the floor. 'It's not—Gah! Of all people, I thought you would understand. It's not *raising*, it is *animating* the dead. It is not soul-tearing, nor necromancy, nor any of the darker schools you fear.'

'It is one inch from it. I swore never to hinder any practice of magick, but I will if it threatens Emaneska in any way. I'd rather fight Malvus for another century than have a world glowing with ghosts and ghouls. You didn't see the number of the dead below the earth that I did.'

Farden needed twice as many hands and feet to count the number of mages, wizards, and spellsmiths he once knew who had tumbled over the line of control into the abyss of the darker magicks. The power of such schools was far too alluring, too easy to grasp, and as addictive as nevermar. Farden had felt such attraction before; felt the grip of reckless abandon around his neck. Felt his mind swirl with power. Even with the simplest, purest spells, mages walked a thin precipice of control.

'For years you have had me search for weapons to help us defeat Malvus. Now that I have found one, you wish to ignore it?'

'Not this. Never this. Any other weapon than death magick.'

'Then what do you want of me?' Durnus asked.

'To help me,' Farden sighed, throwing his head back into a cushion. 'It's another worry in a long queue that I'm starting to think doesn't have an end, and I don't need you becoming one more. Find something else.'

'Modren's right, you know.' The vampyre attempted a smile. The tension withered like a cinder beneath a boot. 'Ever since Malvus destroyed Kserak, a raindrop falls and you expect the whole sky to follow. Looking for problems that do not exist will only find you problems. You have one task to focus on: winning this war as you said you would. That is all. The minutia we can handle. You do not need to handle latrine schedules for the south walls. Yes, I saw you there, last week. You have an undermage, generals, and captains for a reason.'

That name again. That scar of bones and ash that was once a city. *Dead because of him.* Farden shook his head as if shaking the memory free. 'The decisions are still mine. I knew responsibility in years past, but now I feel every decision I make or don't make has the fate of thousands attached to it. One wrong move and Kserak happens all over again. Here.' Farden prodded the chair's arm. 'How did you do it? You and Tyrfing, when you were arkmages. How did you not go mad from the weight of it all?'

'With much cursing on Tyrfing's part. And mine,' Durnus admitted, baring fangs.

'I wish he were still alive.'

The vampyre sighed. 'As do I. We were trying to fix a broken idea, thinking we could save it. You are protecting an idea that needs to be saved. Both are arduous tasks, never simple, and both will result in war. At least this time, it was us who chose war rather than having it thrust upon us. We wrought this storm.'

'And what if we have wrought a maelstrom?'

'Then you'll fight that, too. Trust in the fortress you've built. You are the weapon it wields, Farden. The Outlaw King and his Written. Or should I say Forever King? I see it scrawled on Frostsoar stone more and more these days.'

There came a loud pop as Farden ground his knuckles together. He said nothing.

Durnus shifted in his chair. 'Where is that Book of yours?'

'Safe in my chambers.' Farden patted his vambrace. 'Under lock and key.'

The vampyre shuddered. 'By the way, there are... *other*... benefits of the magick I've been attempting.'

One of Farden's eyebrows scaled his forehead.

'Magick that could erode the barrier between the living and the dead —'

'Durnus!'

'Hear me out, mage. I speak of communication only. A way to speak to the dead. One in particular. Your uncle.'

Farden's other eyebrow joined the first.

'It is a theory many years in the making and nothing else, but important enough to share. I have known many hardships in my centuries. Daemonblood in one's veins will have that effect. The vampyre's curse. Decades in darkness. What hurts the most is being stranded on your own island of understanding. We are all islands, in a way, marooned with our own thoughts and none others'. Help and solace only come from those whose island is similar. But to truly understand, one must have experience. That is why I still cannot imagine the task of carrying magick like you do, Farden. I will never understand, but Tyrfing might. More than anyone. It might just be possible to speak to him. Perhaps he can help bear that burden.'

Farden swirled those words around in his head like the dregs of wine at the bottom of a cup. 'What would it take?'

'The Grimsayer. Time. Patience. Some help and sources from Scholar Skertrict when he arrives back from wherever he's roamed.'

'And it will be safe?'

'Trust me, Farden,' said the vampyre, wearing that grin again. 'Like you used to.'

'Still do, old friend.' Farden arose. 'Weapons, Durnus. Find me weapons. Preferably before Malvus knocks on our gates.'

'But you—'

'The Written aren't alone in the world any more, Durnus. I fear even we're not enough. Not I, nor the remaining Written.'

Farden didn't allow the vampyre a chance to reply. He pulled the door shut, sealing Durnus in silence. How so many had so much faith in him, when all Farden felt was doubt, was utterly perplexing. He wished he could pull their trust off like a mask and show them all the wretch inside. For now, he had other work, and it waited for him in the corridor.

Modren stared at the lantern-fire of the city and its walls. Night had fallen at last, for the first time in a month. It wasn't the pitch black of a winter's night, more of a russet shadow and hours brief, but a sign Emaneska's summer was fading. Frostfall and winter awaited.

'Where is she? This recruit of yours?' Farden asked.

'In the yards, still waiting.'

Farden felt tiredness assailing him. 'Magick like you've never seen, you said?'

'I wasn't eavesdropping, but I heard you well enough at the end. You doubt yourself, I understand that. You want a weapon. Mithrid could be exactly that.'

Farden tugged at his dark locks. 'Mithrid. A Hâlorn name if I've ever heard one.'

Modren waited, arms crossed and patience fraying before Farden's eyes.

He sighed. 'Send her up.'

The crunch of ice betrayed the undermage. Modren emerged into the torchlight, where Hereni, Eyrum and Mithrid stood staring at the rare stars. Mithrid was still panting, exhausted and aching from the long hours of training.

No. Training suggested honing a skill. Mithrid's power was a party trick. An inconvenient knack. Unless she was able to touch her prey, her abilities seemed nonexistent. What more Hereni and the lump of a Siren could rouse from her, Mithrid didn't know. All she'd earned was a headache. The torches still burned. The magick clockwork still rattled on.

'Any luck?' Modren asked, the hope in his voice annoyingly shining a light on Mithrid's failure.

Nobody spoke. Eyrum shook his head.

'Doesn't matter,' the undermage pressed on. 'He's ready.'

'Fucking finally,' Mithrid muttered.

Hereni poked Mithrid in the shoulder before rapidly withdrawing her touch. Mithrid felt a shudder in her heart and wondered why she was so nervous.

Why the king of Scalussen insisted on meeting at the very top of his tower was a question that burned hotter than Mithrid's work-sore legs. The mechanical platform only lifted them so far into the sky. Stairs led the rest of the way.

Modren and Hereni climbed without words. It was as if the night's dark demanded a respectful silence. Every glass pane drew Mithrid's attention, dizzying her with the height and miniature world spread out below. Perhaps this was why Farden chose such lofty views: to gaze upon rooftops and streets as a bird would, all neat and sensical. Easy to watch over.

Guards upon guards watched over them. Every break in the stairwell, every corner or important-looking door bristled with them. She had grown bored of seeing the Scalussen crest when Hereni spoke up, making her jump.

'There is one thing to know about the roof,' she said. It's not just the king's haunt. It's home to another old friend of ours. Don't be afraid of him, but to be on the safe side, avoid standing in his shadow or meeting his eyes for prolonged periods.'

Mithrid's gut churned. 'What? Why?'

'Don't worry,' Hereni hissed.

She and the undermage had stopped at another ornate stairwell. This one disappeared in a coil into the Frostsoar's impassive stone. Mithrid could hear a wind keening through the gaps in a door above.

'After you.'

With her thighs screeching at every last step, Mithrid climbed to the door. She elbowed it open, battling the wind that immediately made a tempest of her fiery hair.

An empty stone circle was spread before her, one that ended in a violently bare edge. No railings or parapets offered safety. A large, crooked shape stood shrouded in darkness. The light of the two torches burning behind her failed to illuminate it.

Something whistled. The shape sprouted dark wings and a swishing tail. Beside it, she could make out the shadow of man. They approached together, slowly. An enormous beak and a pair of golden eyes were the first to emerge into the circle of light. Mithrid's pounding heart told her to look away, but she couldn't help but stare into those pools of liquid gold.

A weathered hand rested on the beak. Its owner stayed hidden, and Mithrid squinted to discern out the figure's obscured features.

She became painfully aware that Modren and Hereni had not followed her all the way up the stairs. Though they remained in the doorway, it felt like it was just her alone with the Outlaw King, and the icy wind seeking to sweep her from the stone.

Trying to hide her fear of the beast, Mithrid crossed her arms, waiting while her hair whipped her face. Her heart thudded against her hand. The Outlaw King was clearly taking the measure of her, and Mithrid didn't like it.

'Am I supposed to bow? Or curtsey, or something?' she asked, the wind snatching away the volume of her words.

A faint Arka accent, eroded by years of exile, replied. The voice was deep and ragged at the edges. It sounded neither old nor young. 'I'd rather you didn't,' he said, surprising her.

'Thank the gods,' Mithrid muttered. She waited nervously for the beast to settle down, his fearsome front end in the light, sharp claws tapping the stone and those golden eyes half-closed in a bored slumber.

'What is that thing?'

'A gryphon. From Paraia. His name is Ilios.'

'So that's what an Ilios is. And what do I call you? Sir? Majesty?' The word felt awkward on her tongue.

'Farden is my name. Use that. Never have liked the idea of being a king. Arkmage, fine, but that role has long withered away.'

'Farden,' echoed Mithrid, trying to surreptitiously stretch an aching leg.

'Looks like Modren and Hereni put you through your paces.'

'It was one way to pass the time while we waited.'

The chuckle was curious, too. There was no regality in this man. No arrogance of entitlement. Mithrid didn't know whether she found it disarming or disturbing.

'Modren was right. You are full of fire,' muttered Farden.

'Father said it was why I had this colour hair. From my mother.'

'And where are they?'

Mithrid looked past him to the mountains. 'Dead and gone. Mother when I was very young. Father a week ago now,' she replied, loudly and confidently. 'I assumed I was coming here for answers, not to be questioned again and have wounds reopened.'

The gryphon growled deeply. There came a clank of metal meeting as Farden also crossed his arms. 'Do you always speak your mind so frankly?' he asked.

Mithrid shrugged. 'Why else have a mind?'

Boots scraped as the shadow drew back across intricate scales of metal. Scarlet and crimson, so finely made Mithrid thought at first it was dragon skin. The Outlaw King emerged into the torchlight, his head without helmet and his hands bare. The rest of him gleamed even in the fluttering fire. His dark, almost black, hair trailed in the air, half hiding a face of stubble and scars. Mithrid would have guessed him to be barely forty winters old, or a harsh-lived thirty. The marks of old wounds and fresh exhaustion were the only creases she could see. Farden's eyes, however, held the burden of years in them. Stuck somewhere between grey and green, they had seen more than his face gave on.

Oddly, the wind felt warmer near to him, as if Farden defied the north's icy bite and burned with an inner flame. A pressure, too, as if his very presence weighed Mithrid down. A pain needled the base of her skull. But above all else, the mage smiled at her cheek.

'You and I are going to get along just fine,' he said gruffly. He swept away in an arc, more touring the city views than circling her. 'I don't relish in asking you your story. My mother and father are also dead. My uncle, too. My daughter. Countless others. Those stories are like chewing wasps to tell.'

Mithrid's head was immediately crowded with questions.

'I ask to see if you have any roots of magick in your family. Whether you are an oldblood, with magick passed down directly, or a newblood, when magick springs into being along dead lines. Hereni was once such a mage. She was one of the last I saved. Feels like yesterday.'

'No magick,' Mithrid sighed. He seemed genuine enough to deserve her story. 'My mother was struck down by a mage for having a magick ring when I was three winters old. My father was a woodcutter.'

'Then what?'

The guilt was still raw there. Too fresh a wound. 'Didn't Modren—?'

'I want to hear for myself.' Farden still faced away, watching and listening to his city.

'We found a spellbook in a shipwreck. A summoning book. We opened it. Read it aloud. A creature came from the book and killed my friend, and I woke up to a village dripping with blood and my dead father next to me,' Mithrid replied, finally remembering to take a breath. 'Modren and Kinsprite plucked us from the hoax of a rebel camp.'

Farden was silent for some time.

'And what happened the other day in the yards?'

'I don't remember. All I know is they were taunting me. I wanted them to stop. I reached out, and Krommish... *stopped*.' The moments were all blurred together.

The Outlaw King did not reply. He stared back at the city. By the movement of his jaws, he could tell he was chewing or mouthing something.

'Do you have questions for me?' he finally asked.

Mithrid had plenty. They all clamoured to be asked first. A child's wonder won over anything practical. 'Are you really immortal?'

'Time will tell.' At Mithrid's pause, he turned to face her at last, grey-green eyes shuttered. 'That normally gets a chuckle, at least.'

'Then how old are you?'

Farden snorted as he shook his head. 'Elessi tells me this will be my seventieth winter.'

And now, the practical. *The important.* 'When will this war of yours begin?'

'Soon, I feel. Is that why you are here, Mithrid? For Malvus?'

'Not for him. My own revenge.'

'A fine reason. I've travelled half the world and back again for revenge.' Farden waved a hand across the stone. A flame appeared between them, a spear's reach apart. As it crackled and sparked, Farden kept his hand towards it, and looked to Mithrid.

'Show me. I want to see this magick that's got everybody foxed.'

Mithrid inwardly groaned. She had already scorched one finger getting too close to those confounded torches.

With an experimental flexing of her fingers, Mithrid took the stance Hereni had showed her, reached out with her mind – or whatever Eyrum had babbled about – and tried desperately to make the flame do anything, never mind extinguish itself. She strained and she pulled at nothing but air.

'I can't,' Mithrid snapped. 'Not without touching something. All day trying, and that's all I can do.'

'Then explain what happened in the yards.'

'I don't know.'

Farden whistled sharply. The gryphon sprang to a crouch, eyes popped open and a sabrecat's growl reverberating through the stone. Its white feathers shone orange in the fire.

'What is it doing?'

Farden whistled a fine impression of an owl.

Mithrid began to back away as Ilios began to stalk her. 'What are *you* doing?'

'Why are you here, Mithrid? Are you a spy?' Farden yelled.

'No!'

'You're saying it was an accident?'

'No! I—'

The mage came striding, beating the gryphon to her. Fire burned in his hands.

Mithrid stumbled over her own feet in fear. She flailed with panic, and in amongst her wild movements, Farden stopped dead. Threads of shadow drifted past his armour like obsidian sand. The fire in his hands had sputtered out, and he stared at those cold palms, his apparent anger vanished. Mithrid was still breathing heavily, fists up and shaking.

Modren and Hereni came charging through the door. Hereni placed a hand on Mithrid's shoulder, but the girl shrugged her away.

'Leave her!' Farden yelled, still unable to tear his eyes from his hands.

In the light of the stairwell, Mithrid saw what bewitched him. A single spark tried its hardest to cling to life before dying. Farden was clearly disturbed. His stare crept painfully and slowly from his hands to Mithrid and bored into her. There, behind those weathered eyes, she saw an unexpected fear burning.

It was all she saw, even after Farden had turned and the spiral stairs flew by beneath her feet. Though the levels of the Frostsoar and cold city passed before her, Mithrid paid them no heed. The image of Farden's pale face was affixed in her mind, like a bare room with a single, immense painting hanging on the wall. All the while, she clasped her hands as if opening them would unleash something she did not understand.

The piebald lycan barring their path was what shook her out of her stupor. He stood guarding the stout door that led to Mithrid's solitary room, drooling slightly from one side of his mouth. Modren waved him aside. He acquiesced but followed in curiosity, likely hoping for more scraps.

To her surprise, more figures hovered nearby, not looming as enemies but gathering as friends. Bull, Savask, and Aspala looked on, concerned for their comrade.

Hereni playfully elbowed Mithrid in the ribs. 'Not all is as it seems. Once you can control it, you'll be back in the barracks.'

Mithrid gave a faint wave before disappearing within, left alone with nothing but the ice tree. She thought of Remina and Trenika, and what gossip they might be sowing in the Underspire, but it was a brief pondering. There were more important thoughts afoot, namely how she had put fear on the face of the Outlaw King; the same look Hereni had worn at Mithrid's touch. That power did not thrill her, as she might have assumed, but was deeply unsettling, like a cliff's edge crumbling beneath her feet. *Freak*. The word echoed in her mind and pursed her lips.

Only once did she try the door, and found it unlocked. She took an apple from a nearby basket somebody had left and put it in the gap of the door.

It took a moment, but a thick hand of black and white fur snatched it away. With a faint smile, Mithrid closed the door on loud crunching.

CHAPTER 20
DARK COUNCIL

Knowledge is power, so it is said, and a power that not all should wield. As such, I decree the foundation of the Grand Libraries of Arfell, a sanctuary to store the vast knowledge of Emaneska. To provide a safe harbour for power unsafe in hands beyond the Arka's. To build a shrine of learning, so that we might glean the lessons of the past. Such is the monument we will build amongst the Össfen Mountains.
FROM A SPEECH BY ARKMAGE AND MASTER BUILDER SVADILFAN, YEAR 305

Broken, cracked earth and spurs of ruins long hollowed to claws by wind and sand. That was all that remained of the library of Arfell. Once the fires had gutted its ancient halls, the stones had toppled down the mountain like a common landslide. Their rubble lay in a scorched arc where the flames had reduced the forest to ashes. It was a most depressing of meeting spots, to be certain, but far from prying eyes and far too curious ears.

Malvus stood alone upon the tip of a great thrust of stone foundation, smoothed by wind so the builders' mortar looked like veins of mica. He waited with his hands on his hips and gaze affixed on the sky, as he had for several hours now. An emperor easily forgot the pain of waiting, when servants wait on them hand and foot. Even minutes now proved torturous to him. Hours verged on insulting.

Lord Saker was now a fleck in the northeastern sky, growing larger slowly and at his leisure. Grand Duke Wodehallow was late without apology, and Prince Gremorin was nowhere to be seen.

Malvus stirred his aching hip and surveyed the ashen clearing. The two Scarred standing nearby were restless. Corcoran insisted on pacing. Her new subordinate twitched sporadically. Toskig, Loki, and Lady Jeasin waited by the dormant quickdoor at the foot of the spur. He glared at the latter. Ever since Jeasin had been found in the bowels of Krauslung the same night of Farden's incursion, lying amongst wreckage, he had imagined a noose around her neck. He had yet to decide whether to pull it.

As Malvus stalked across the rock, a rancorous squawking grew to disturb the deathly silence of Arfell's grave. He looked west and saw a cloud of crows tethered by ropes emerge above the pines. There must have been a thousand of them lashed together, and as they ascended with a deafening fuss, their peculiar cargo was revealed.

To the chorus of yells and whistle blasts, a fat longship rose into view in time for its flat bottom to brush the treetops. Rows of shields in Albion colours of yellow and orange gleamed even in the overcast day. A dragon figurehead curled in on its own neck. Large jewelled eyes stared blankly at the world below.

The sky-ship's decks were swollen with Albion men, frenetically working levers and plucking strings to control the birds. Malvus watched impatiently as the craft wallowed in the air for some time before descending in jerking increments to the burned soil. Once the swarm of crows had roosted in the V-shaped masts, a gangplank was lowered, and the Grand Duke of Albion, Wodehallow II, finally arrived.

Plump and many-chinned like his late father before him, Wodehallow was swaddled in a thick cloak of ermine fur and green trim. What he lacked in stature he made up for in swagger, the sort of swagger that wasn't earned, but inherited without reason or substance.

Wodehallow bowed curtly to the emperor. His entourage of roundshields and dishevelled mages bowed also.

Malvus extended a hand to let the man kiss his ring, swift to prove the hierarchy in front of these unwashed Albion men. Wodehallow obliged somewhat begrudgingly.

'My Imperial Majesty,' he said. 'Where is Lord Saker?'

Malvus pointed upwards, where the Lord of the Winds was now circling the clearing and waiting to make his entrance. What an unnecessary display of an entrance it was. His dragon Fellgrin plummeted from the sky, casting up a cloud of dust and dead pine needles as it crashed to the earth. Fellgrin belched smoke as she took the measure of the surroundings. The dragon had scales like rusted iron, sharp and ragged plates covering a stout and strong body. The Lost Clan dragons were smaller than their Siren cousins, but just as unapologetically vicious.

Saker dismounted with a grunt. His attire of leather, fur, and bone bracelets gave him the look of a barbarian, but Malvus knew the sharpness that hid behind that disarming, jagged smile of filed teeth and impassive, yellow eyes. A curved sword hung at his belt. His hand lingered upon it as if expecting betrayal.

Last, but not least by any means, came Gremorin. The daemon prince split the air, emerging in a blast of heat and ash. The stench of sulphur rolled through the clearing, making some of the weaker-stomached soldiers gag. Half the Albion lot were already too busy gawking at a daemon up close. Never mind a daemon prince.

Gremorin's greeting was no more effusive than a loud grunt. He folded his arms and waited.

Malvus took a breath. The cold mountain air caught in his throat. 'So kind of you to come,' he greeted his vassals hoarsely.

Saker and Fellgrin shared similar expressions of distaste and suspicion. 'Why have you summoned us?'

'Because I have every right to.' Malvus glanced to Loki. 'And because the time has come. At last we march north.' Though his words sounded like fanfare in his head, the gravitas escaped his guests.

'Truly?' asked Wodehallow, his chins wobbling. 'Almost two decades have gone by since you promised us war, Malvus. And yet... I had assumed you were happy with your borders.'

The omission of his title stung the emperor deeply, but he didn't let on.

'Well, now I fulfil that promise. Our armies are built. The Outlaw King has shown himself. War has come,' Malvus said, his voice rising as he spoke.

'What guarantee do you have of victory?' Wodehallow had the cheek to ask. Even Gremorin growled at that, as if he took the insult personally. The fat lump had clearly grown used to settling squabbles of lesser dukes and landowners and had forgotten his place in Malvus' empire.

Malvus levelled a finger at him. 'You, Wodehallow, will dispatch every able body and ship you have to Dromfangar, Hâlorn, and Midgrir, where you will join with my forces and the Lost Clans. Together, we will march north to face Scalussen. Farden thinks he is prepared. He has even built himself quite the fortress in the snow, but our forces will overwhelm him in numbers. Not to mention with the Scarred at our side.'

Saker and Wodehallow followed Malvus' gaze to his homemade warriors. 'Scarred?'

'The Written are no longer a dying breed. Our new mages will outmatch theirs. Perhaps even the Outlaw King himself.'

Nobody, even Malvus himself, seemed convinced of the truth of those words, but they sounded too important to dismantle.

Apathy. That was the parasite that had apparently sunk its mandibles into Saker and Wodehallow. Not fear. They had instead let slip from their minds Farden's capacity to be an enemy. Malvus sought to remind them.

'That reminds me. My condolences, Lord Saker, for the recent death of your kin.'

Saker cocked his head as if suggesting this was news to him.

'One of your dragons loaned to Krauslung, Vilespar, was killed by Farden's very hands.' Malvus played dumb. 'I had assumed you knew…'

Fellgrin roared as she scraped furrows in the earth. The dragon-rider bristled, the furs at his neck trembling slightly. 'When? Where?'

'Not two days ago.' Here Malvus turned to Wodehallow, knowing he was the sort to be jealous with his power, overprotective of his precious and rather meaningless borders. 'In Albion. Clannor duchy, to be precise. The Outlaw King trespassed upon your lands, murdered several of your countrymen and mine, and then vanished north, as if our rule means nothing to him.'

Wodehallow worked his jaw. Malvus couldn't figure out whether he was annoyed or digging remnants of food from between his teeth, but his silence was telling.

'Farden has grown confident, fat, and rich from our patience. We have given the rebels their chances. They have sent our messengers back beheaded and blood-slick. We have tolerated their harassment and treachery. Too long has that fool in the north mocked us with his opposition. No more. Now is the time we make Emaneska ours forever more. It is time to lose the idea of rebellion to history.'

The clenched fist and grim nod of Saker and Wodehallow was all Malvus needed to see. He looked to the hulking daemon casting shadow across them all.

'When?' Gremorin rasped.

'We gather in a week's time,' Malvus announced. 'Speak nothing to your advisors or courts. Make no speeches nor announcements. Simply march, and we will crush every Scalussen outpost and camp between here and the north. We will cut them off and paint the north red with rebel blood. Farden's skull will rot on a stick on the gates of Krauslung upon my return, and we will build an empire to last a thousand years.'

Malvus' audience was small, but he had won them just the same. A few cheers broke out from the gathered Albion mages, while appreciative grunts rumbled from his own guards. Loki grinned like a fool, drawing an uneasy stare from Wodehallow.

'We are in agreement.' As much as Malvus spoke those words as a statement, the others seemed to take it as something to consider. With no parting words and barely a shallow bow sketched poorly, the Lord of the Winds vaulted upon Fellgrin. The dragon left as she arrived, blinding all those nearby with dust and needles.

Gremorin wrapped himself in his dark wings and vanished from the clearing with a sound that popped the emperor's ears.

Left abruptly alone, Wodehallow looked around at the settling dust, as if wondering how to make his long journey more worthwhile than a mere short discussion of war.

'Will there be anything else, Grand Duke?' Malvus stared down at the rotund man.

'Erm. I thought I might sample the streets of Krauslung after making such a journey.'

Malvus crossed his arms and kept them there until Wodehallow smacked his lips. 'Well, look at the sun.' He waved a pudgy finger. 'A week it is.'

Muttering something about messenger hawks and tried and tested methods being the best, he boarded his flying longship and disappeared within its small tent of a cabin. The crew poked the birds into action with long, skinny poles, and soon enough the ship was ascending above the pines once more.

Malvus found Loki standing uncomfortably close. 'Think they will join us?' asked the god.

'I do not care if they do. My hordes are unrivalled. I have the daemons. I have the Scarred.' Malvus stared at the fat-bottomed ship as it snapped the tip from a spruce. 'Besides, little god. They will either stand with me, or I will wipe them from the map on our journey back to Krauslung.'

'A fair deal.'

Malvus looked down at him. 'A coin bearing a crown and face does much to remind citizens who rules an empire, but it takes blood and blades for them to believe it. It is the same with allies and vassals.'

Loki nodded. 'What a shame you have no heir to pass this wisdom down to,' he said nonchalantly.

Lady Jeasin snorted from ten paces away. The blind woman's ears had only been honed with age, not dulled. The emperor's virility was a subject Malvus had killed others for broaching. The blame had lain with Jeasin for years. The barren Albion whore, he had branded her. Time had only proven him right, but no better. No matter how many he took into his bed, whether he fucked Krauslung's whores or Paraian slaves, his seed refused to sow.

Malvus glared, fingers touching his knives, but a cough interrupted him, hoarser than usual. He wheezed to keep from descending into a coughing fit. He had fought against its itch since their council had begun.

Loki tutted. 'I would take a healer with you to Scalussen, Emperor. Or several, to make sure you can last the northern cold. How unfortunate it would be, were you to perish of the flux before seeing Farden's head on that spike.'

Malvus sought to shove Loki in the chest but thought better of it. A thin strand of superstition held his arm back. 'I am no weaker than I was when I broke the Twin Thrones and built my own upon their rubble!' he snarled.

'For a man so close to completing his empire, you don't have much time to enjoy it, do you? Your health is declining. No heir sired to continue your good work. What a shame it would be to see the Arka fall so soon after their great rise. Leaderless.'

Malvus slid a knife from his sheath. The god seemed undeterred, even guiding him up the incline of the stone spur. Lichen crackled underfoot.

'After all, that is why you hired Loffrey of Albion, was it not? The man who you hired to find the Nine. You feared death so much you wanted to cheat life.'

'I remember him failing miserably.'

Loki shook a finger. 'The man might have failed in finding you Scalussen armour, but there are other ways to extend a life. I can see the longing in your eyes even at such a tiny whiff of hope. Ways you have come across before without knowing.'

'I have had scholars scour every surviving book, dispatched riders past Kroppe and the Hammer Hills—'

'And none of their tinctures or rituals seemed to work, did they? There are many promises in the world, and far too little proof.' Loki picked at something under his nails. 'The seer, Lilith. When she cast her stones for you, she looked not a day older than when she cast her stones for old Arkmage Vice, more than a decade before you even sat on the Magick Council.

'How?' Malvus hated the speed at which his heart drummed and cursed the god for stoking it. 'Speak plain!'

Loki began to circle him, still whispering. 'Daemonblood, Malvus. Just as godblood lends Farden's armour power, the blood of our friendly daemon kin can stave off the ravaging of human years.'

Malvus felt something pressed into his palm. A hefty vial shaped like a teardrop. Its glass stopper was waxed shut. 'This could be poison, for all I trust you.'

Loki tittered. 'Then you'll die now, rather than on the ice fields, coughing blood on white snow. Same difference.'

Malvus flinched as if the god's words had stabbed him. *Coughing blood on white snow.* A perfect echo of the old seer's words. He caught Jeasin staring at him with her blind eyes. Her face was sour pucker, more so than usual. Malvus gently slid the vial into a pocket on his cuff. 'Where did you find this?'

Loki patted his coat. 'I can find all manner of things that are truly lost. Not buried. Not hidden. But lost. And there is plenty in the world that is lost.'

'Riddles! Always riddles with you!'

The god had begun to walk up the mountainside between the ruins. Malvus yelled after him.

'Where do you think you are going? I did not give you permission to leave.'

Loki flashed a smile and sighed dramatically. 'What is a dog to a king, Malvus Barkhart?'

Malvus narrowed his eyes. 'Nothing.'

'Then what is a king to a god?' Loki answered.

Nothing.

Malvus swore he heard Jeasin mutter it. 'Fetch him!' he ordered.

As the Scarred sprang to obey, Loki reached into his coat and drew forth a cupped handful. He blew hard, spraying cinders and black smoke in a rapidly-expanding cloud that obscured him completely. When the Scarred managed to disperse it, the god was gone.

Malvus was not the kind of man to wallow in rage. He was already making for the quickdoor, standing alone on a mound of earth, yelling at the top of his voice. 'Get that spell working!'

Jeasin sighed as he passed her. 'He is the trickster god for a reason, Malvus. Loki exists to either betray you, or very least annoy the shit out of you. And you let him play you like a bard plays a ljot.'

Malvus backhanded her. Hard. The blind woman sprawled upon the stone before Toskig could help right her. Ash smeared her silken robes.

'I thought you appreciated my honesty,' she muttered, glassy eyes blinking in surprise. The last time he had struck her was lost to memory. 'You said nobody else speaks it to you. Not even this big coward of a general.'

Toskig let her go, and she tottered, wiping blood from her cheek.

'Lying whispers and false encouragements, for all I know. You have still yet to explain how you were found in Krauslung, directly where Farden attacked.

Jeasin blinked. 'I have told you. I was at a cathouse findin' whores for you. He attacked m—'

Malvus inhaled deeply. The earth here still smelled of ash, despite fires decades old. 'From now on, Lady Jeasin, your mouth will either be shut or at work on the emperor's cock. I have a new councillor now.'

Jeasin covered the tremble of her lip well with derisive scorn. 'What, the councillor who just disappeared. He wants whatever suits him most, just you watch.'

'That may be.' Malvus wrapped a ringlet of her dark hair around his gauntlet and pulled her close. Her perfume might have stirred his britches, but he felt no fondness. Where along the path that had died, he did not remember. The truth was simple. 'But he has given me more in ten days than you have in twenty years.'

He left her there cowed and hunched, striding for the quickdoor. In his palm, hidden within a velvet pocket, the emperor gripped the vial as tightly as he dared to without crushing it, and cursed the god in all the shades he knew for knowing the depths of Malvus' heart.

CHAPTER 21
ANTITHESIS

Even the most ordinary of minds can birth the most extraordinary of ideas.
ARKA PROVERB

They say it is a curse for kings and similar kin to be plagued with unrest. Farden was inclined to agree.

Sleep made a mockery of him, as it did on many nights, dancing away from his grasp no matter how empty Farden made his mind, how close he coaxed it.

So it was the mage found himself treading the dark stairs of the Frostsoar. Ilios was awake and standing guard over the city, watching a fresh dawn emerge over the slumbering Scalussen. It had the colour of warmth, but the sun's rays were feeble, a faint touch. The ice glistened like countless diamonds strewn across a blood-washed canvas.

'Can't sleep?' Farden asked, as he ran his hand across the gryphon's feathers. 'Me, neither.'

As soon as the mage had a firm grip, he felt the iron muscles beneath fur and feather tense, and Ilios plummeted from the edge of the Frostsoar's summit. Farden closed his eyes to the rushing gale, letting it chill his face. Shudders ran through the gryphon as he fought the fall to a level flight, and with heaves of his eagle's wings, they left Scalussen behind them.

They skimmed the ice fields, so low that Ilios drew patterns in the undisturbed snow. Farden stared back at the fortress, somehow already small amongst the expanse of featureless landscape between the impassable walls of the Spine of the World.

A deep and distant rumble sounded. The northern sky blushed a brighter shade of red. It was no dawn's glow. The sunlight held no sway over the choking clouds that never left the Emberteeth.

Ilios seemed to follow Farden's gaze, soaring high enough to rival the highest of the Emberteeth's black crowns. Dragons patrolled the morning skies, trumpeting to the gryphon and performing corkscrewing dives.

Past their sacred fields and over the barren lands of obsidian crags of vents that spewed yellow steam, the gryphon swung through the jagged peaks, testing Farden's grip as well as his empty stomach. Ilios trilled, making the crevasses and cliffs sing back to him.

Soon enough, as they neared the Spine's volcanoes and the great peak of Irminsul, the air grew warm and acrid. Rank sulphur and char filled their noses. The heavy skies were more ash than storm cloud. Lightning flickered occasionally, devoid of thunder. That was the mountain's duty. The Emberteeth were never silent; they grumbled and roared. Landslides flowed constantly like waterfalls, molten rock churned in craters, and crags whistled and gargled with steam.

Irminsul made Old Man Grey look like a crooked watchtower. It towered over all. The snowmads told a preposterous tale that if the peak ever toppled south, it would reach all the way to Dromfangar. False, of course, but the eyes longed to believe it.

Its sawtooth and hollow summit vomited a constant plume of oily grey smoke. Its sides were pitted with streaming craters. The only foliage that decorated its slopes were swathes of red ash, scars of tumbling boulders the size of taverns.

It was not just fire and heat that ruled this charred landscape. The Emberteeth were awash with power. If Farden concentrated, he could feel heavy waves of magick in the air, emanating from Irminsul. They were dizzying in their concentration. A dull ache took up residence in his skull.

As Ilios circled higher and higher, Irminsul spoke. A deep snap of something enormous broke within the earth. It shook the air, followed by a huge belch of ash. Orange fountains of glowing, molten rock arced from its crater. As the gryphon pirouetted over its peak, Farden glimpsed a crimson eye at its very centre, leagues within its rock. There, rock churned like broth.

If history were to be believed, the fires that had created Emaneska still burned deep within the Spine of the World: where the lonely giant, baring the burdens of ice and fire through the empty skies, had met his doom and curled up to form the world. This was the giant's fatal wound, and it would never be healed.

Farden stared at the volcano long after Ilios had grown tired and turned back to Scalussen. Even when the gryphon's claws rasped against the Frostsoar's stone, Farden stayed standing, captivated by the black crown of smoke dominating the northernmost reaches. Their clouds reached south with ashen claws on winds higher than Ilios dared to soar. What appeared to be rain had begun to fall upon the Dragonfields. Farden knew better. It would not be the first time ash had fallen from the sky. For a moment longer, he let the dust flakes land upon his vambraces and gauntlets, while still wrapped in his thoughts. Ilios was not so impressed, sneezing several times before seeking shelter in a dragon nest below.

Alone and wrapped as tightly as a hostage in his thoughts, the arrival of the goddess went by unnoticed. She had always trodden softer than a falling feather, but in the quiet whisper of falling ash, she was silent as shadow.

'You seem troubled, Farden.'

Hiding his jolt of surprise with a muttered, 'Fuck's sake', he turned around to face her.

Evernia's gossamer hair floated in the opposite direction of the breeze. The ash did not linger on her shoulders or head, instead tumbling through her wraithlike form. Her robes of silver reflected nothing of the dawn's light, now bolder, and had turned Farden's armour to molten fire. The more he stared, the more she seemed to shiver as if spring water ran a river between them.

The goddess of wisdom and magick waited patiently for a response.

'War is finally coming,' he replied at last. 'I can feel it.'

'Heimdall has seen it. Malvus can avoid mortal ears and eyes but not Heimdall. He held a council of war.'

'You came here to warn us, did you?'

'I did.'

'Good to see you so invested in our survival. What has it been? Ten years since a shadow of a god fell upon this fortress?' Farden accused. If Durnus had stood there, he would be sweating and cringing at the mage's tone. Farden's respect for the gods had died some time ago. After what they had put him through, Evernia was fortunate for an audience. 'What a pity you could not warn us of Loki, who now stands at the emperor's side.'

Evernia's form shifted, stuttering closer without her taking a step. 'Loki?' she asked, her voice shrill. 'He fell into the void.'

Farden crossed his arms. 'Did he? Because I saw him several days ago.'

'We...' It was peculiar to hear a deity of wisdom stutter, but Farden relished in it.

'You knew. You just didn't tell us. Old gods up to their old tricks.'

Evernia hissed. 'You forget your place as always, Farden. We glimpsed him once and for the briefest of moments when his body fell as fire, in the Last War. We knew he lived, nothing more. Since then, Heimdall has been blind to him. He has walked this earth beneath a shadow that only daemons seem to wear, into realms beyond our pantheon's borders. We are as surprised and concerned as you are to find him returned.'

Farden was always chafed to find the gods discussing such human emotions. All they knew was cold calculation. 'Well, I appreciate the warning.'

'We wish...' Evernia caught herself, eyes heavy and lowered to the floor. 'Our kinds will be reunited again, Farden. In time. Like magick's force, we have grown in power. Belief still feeds us and now the souls we give safe harbour in Haven and Hel give us strength even after death. Hope is still strong. Even in Krauslung, in dark corridors and lost alleyways, they still build their shrines. Gods will one day walk upon Emaneska's soil once more. No longer will you fight against darkness alone.'

'Until then,' grumbled Farden. 'Death and glory, it is.' *Useless beings.*

She paced around him. 'We have seen other shrines, Farden, though they are few. In Krauslung and in hovels across the south. No offerings are made as they are to us, but candles lit all the same, and the same words scrawled on brick. In ink, paint, and blood they write them. Not to a god, but to a myth. A man of hushed song.'

'What in gods' – *your* name – are you trying to spit out, Evernia? I'm not in the mood for riddles. Cold, iron facts are what I crave.'

'The Forever King,' she spoke.

'I don't like that name in the mouths of my friends, never mind you, goddess. King is abhorrent enough.'

'Yet that is the name they write and whisper in hope that you will return the world to order and not tyranny. It is our hope, also.'

The mage moved to walk away but found a precipice before him. He tutted. 'No pressure, as always.'

Evernia's hand rested on his shoulder. Somehow, he felt the weight of flesh and bone, inordinately heavy. 'A warning, if you wish for one, Farden. If Loki has returned, the game he plays is greater than Malvus'. You fight not against the emperor, but a god. Kill him at all costs. It is he who brings hordes against you.'

Was that fear Farden heard in the goddess' voice? 'You'd have me kill one of your own? How?'

Evernia's shadow faded in a flurry of ash. Gone, to the plain of stars the gods clung to. Haven, where the souls of the dead found peace.

Spending a few more moments in solitude to shake the echo of the god's voice from his head, Farden took one final look at Irminsul, scowled, and began the task of war.

Killing gods could wait.

'Next one falls,' said Bull, thumping his new longbow into the slush. 'Two nuts.'

'Raise you one.' Savask dug into his meaty palm and tossed three nuts into his threadbare hat.

Mithrid took the bet, following with three of her own. She sacrificed one of her coins, cracking the nut's shell to nibble it. They were addictive little things to a ravenous appetite.

Aspala held off, shaking her head. Her hands were held protectively around the pile of winnings in her lap.

With captive breath, they watched the quickdoor. Several minutes passed and no joy. Then they saw the flicker in the veil of the arch's surface. The guards tensed, lowering their spears once more. A fur-bundled form came cartwheeling from the quickdoor as if he'd been hurled through by catapult.

While the man stumbled upright, dazed and eyes still spinning in their sockets, their small group cackled with hearty laughter. Even though they sat a good stone's throw away, the arrival heard their derision and flashed a foul gesture before being led to the queues for the dragon and white witch.

'Aspala wins again,' Bull announced with a hint of sadness. He was down to his last handful.

The Paraian woman grinned as she accepted her winnings, caring enough for Bull's plight to leave him two nuts.

Mithrid chuckled. She had longed for the simplicity of games. Games were a chisel to the boulder of boredom and brooding. For a blessed moment, she had forgotten the aches laying siege to her body. She put the rankle of the king's meeting aside.

The morning had broken on the cusp of brittle dreams filled with unease over what she had or hadn't done to the Outlaw King. Modren and Elessi had made no mention of the meeting when they had fetched her and let her out into the yards. No mention of fault or punishment. They had even returned her axe, left in leaning against the wall. Mithrid was free to wander, just so long as she, 'didn't fucking touch a soul', and stayed away from the mage recruits. Mithrid had smirked at that, suspecting – hoping – it was for her safety over theirs. Being dangerous had never been a quality she'd had, and it had injected a slight swagger in her walk.

Bull and the others had been waiting for her in the yards, kicking stones, and Savask babbling about the vast variety of pies one could find in Albion. Theirs was an odd group from whichever way she looked at it, but as Aspala had informed them during one of her sparse vocal moments. 'When a world is divided in war, every kind fights side by side.'

A rare day of rest had been granted the burgundy cloaks, the freshest recruits, and while they made the most of their hallowed freedom, the remainder of the city seemed gripped by a frenzy of preparation. Scalussen's quickdoors were abuzz with comers and goers. Mostly the former, it seemed. Earlier that morning, messenger hawks had fled the Frostsoar in shrieking flocks, calling all reinforcements, recruits, patrols and anyone that harboured the faintest grudge with the Arka Empire back to the Outlaw King's fortress, or so Aspala said. The Paraian called it a guess, but in a world where spies lurked behind every smiling face, Mithrid couldn't help wonder *how* she had guessed.

War. The word was on everybody's lips. It seemed Scalussen's wait was to be over soon.

Getting out of the way of the bustle proved difficult in such a hive of commotion, until they found a small knoll overlooking the quickdoors. Barrels of something had been stacked in a row, and to Bull's mind, they made the perfect seats. Thumbs twiddling, yet eyes busy with the bustle, like the best games, their game had sprouted from the simple roots of gambling. They bet on which new arrival would walk even remotely upright from the quickdoor, and who would fall on their faces in the slush. The former was infinitely rarer than the latter, and therein lied the wager.

'Next one walks,' Mithrid said, tossing her bet into Savask's cloth hat.

'Falls.'

'Falls.'

Aspala took a moment to adjust the silk tied about her head like a pirate's cap. 'Walks.'

If there was god of luck, he smiled broadly. Two fur-clad strangers strolled out of the quickdoor side by side, with no more fuss than entering a room.

Mithrid put half her winnings back into the hat. 'Walks.'

All but Savask agreed.

They did not have to wait long. From the nearest quickdoor, a shrewish man emerged, bearing an armful of cylindrical cases that looked suspiciously the same size as scrolls. A book was strapped to his side instead of a sword. His clothes were patchwork and road-weary. Bespectacled and wearing a mop of greasy, flaxen hair, the man skidded once, teetered, but otherwise stayed upright. He beamed at the guards, who looked otherwise unimpressed. Before the bets could be collected, he spotted the gang and wandered to them.

'Greetings! Have you seen General Durnus this fine day?'

Mithrid shook her head, staring at the shiny scar of a burn across the man's lip and cheek. 'Try the Frostsoar, sir.'

'Scholar Skertrict. Good to be home.' The man gave no other conversation and promptly flounced towards the Frostsoar.

'Jötun fuck it!' Savask cursed when he was out of earshot. He picked up his hat and strangled it. Nuts flew everywhere, much to the others' laughter.

'Keep that anger for the battlefield,' Bull remarked with a grin. The lad had stolen some of General Eyrum's quotes for his own use. It gave him immense pleasure whenever he remembered one correctly.

Savask muttered darkly. The man wasn't a complex chap. He was full of bluster around anyone he could out-think or out-talk. On the training yard, that accounted for nobody. Even here in the group, that proved to be Bull and Bull alone, and even that hierarchy was looking shaky. He changed the subject back to Mithrid.

'Did you meet him, then? Word 'as it Modren took you up the Frostsoar.'

Mithrid nodded, detesting gossip for its rapid legs, yet hoping it had made Trenika and Remina stew in jealousy for the evening. 'I did.'

'And?' Savask pressed her. He, like most others in the Underspire, held Farden in some mythical regard. 'What did he look like up close? Did you see his armour? What'd you talk about?'

Mithrid flicked a nut at him to cork his babbling. 'Just a man, dark hair, three dozen winters at a guess. A tired man by the hollows in his eyes. And yes, he wore his armour. You know he never takes it off. He asked me questions. Who I was. Where I came from.'

'Troughwake,' Bull answered as if it were a question for him.

'Yes, Bull.'

'What else?' Savask asked.

'There was nothing else.' Mithrid didn't mean for the words to sound so clipped. In the pause, they watched a man land face first in the mud and chuckled between themselves.

'So, are you a mage now?'

'No. Nothing of the sort.' That much was painfully true, at least. *Not yet*, Mithrid kept telling herself. Aware that Aspala was staring at her avidly, she shrugged off the interrogation. 'Was just an accident. Some quirk of that recruit's magick.'

Voices made themselves clear over the noise of the bustling city. They had company, and it came in the form of Remina, Trenika, and a handful of mage recruits. Mithrid recognised one of them as the mage she had duelled. *Krommish.* No wonder he looked sheepish when the others scowled or grinned.

Lurn had a quarterstaff. He pointed it as if he were poking a poisonous wrackle. 'There's the freak.'

'Thought earlier in the Underspire you called her an Arka spy?' Bull yelled back, much to Mithrid's smirking delight.

'She's both,' Remina decreed, standing with hands on hips and face a pucker of discontent. 'Bewitched you all, she has.'

'You've known me all your life, Remina, you fucking dunce. Or has magick melted your mind already?' Mithrid growled. 'I am no spy.'

'Don't you dare talk to me like that, cretch. You're a traitor for sure after what you did to Krommish.'

Trenika had her arms folded. 'She didn't even get punished for it, either. Rewarded, even. Got to meet the Outlaw King. What makes a new blood like you so fucking special?'

A shadow washed over across the ice and gravel between them. Remina's cronies quickly retreated, and for a wrenching moment, Mithrid thought it was her shadow, her power. She whirled to see Bull and Savask standing with eyes wide and full of wonder. Not for her, but for whatever shook the ground as it landed behind her.

Encased in full armour save for a helmet, Farden sat astride his mighty gryphon. Ilios emitted a shrieking warble and everybody present took a step back. The creature's golden orbs seemed fixed on the girl, and remembering Hereni's warning, she fought desperately to avoid its gaze.

Motes of red and gold light scurried across the ice as the mage dismounted. Bull bowed deeply, but Farden gestured for the boy to stand upright. 'That won't be necessary,' said the mage, taking Bull by the sleeve and guiding him to his feet. 'Gods, you're a big lad, aren't you? If I didn't know better, I'd say you were the spawn of a certain Siren general.'

Bull looked mighty pleased.

Farden greeted Aspala in a language that sounded as though he had lost the use of his tongue. Aspala bared her teeth and bowed deeply. Savask, whose jaw hung slacker than a hammock as he tried to take in the intricacies of Farden's armour, babbled nonsense.

'Sir... Majesty. Mister... er King.'

'A pleasure, I'm sure,' replied Farden, politely ignoring him and stepping close to Mithrid instead. 'Trouble?' His eyes switched to Remina and the mage recruits, who were now standing at attention.

'Nothing I can't handle,' Mithrid said, and she meant it. Her face stayed grim, but inside she laughed at Remina's dour and confused face.

'Good. Come with me,' ordered Farden. He was momentarily distracted by Aspala, who was bowing to Ilios. The gryphon whistled like a songbird and bowed his head.

'Where? Why?' asked Mithrid.

By the look Farden levelled over his shoulder at her, the questions could have been curses. Before she could protest further, another shadow passed over them, larger than Ilios'. Stirred by some long-lost instinct of eons past, Mithrid looked up so quickly her neck audibly cracked. A black dragon circled above them, carrying what looked to be Elessi and Modren.

Once the mage was astride the saddle, Mithrid used the gryphon's wing to climb behind him. Ilios seemed to quiver momentarily at her touch. He screeched one last time, directing it at Remina's gang. The girl scuttled behind Trenika far too quickly and fell promptly on her arse in the slippery slush. Mithrid grinned but her satisfaction was short-lived. Ilios leaped into the sky, and she was squashed into the saddle with a force that tested the fortitude of her bowels.

Being only her second flight, and her first aboard a gryphon, Mithrid's knuckles turned immediately white with concern as the spear-lined walls began to grow small beneath them. She had no understanding of how the wings of birds and beasts worked. Mithrid tread the line of blind trust and despairing terror.

As if Ilios sensed her unease, he flew straight and true, gliding more than flapping, and by the time they were soaring low over the ice fields, Mithrid's fear had dwindled – not vanished, but quieted enough for her to be engrossed in watching the furrows and frozen ripples flash past.

'River or forest?' Farden's words were muffled by the rushing air.

'What?' Mithrid yelled back.

'River or forest?'

It was an easy choice, though how such a thing existed in this frozen waste, she had not a clue. 'Forest!' she challenged him.

A roar half deafened her, painfully close by. The black dragon soared a wing's length behind and on their flank. Something in its tone sounded joyous. She heard Elessi repeating a rising cascade of the word, 'No!' over and over. Mithrid's heart rose with it as she soon understood why.

The black dragon tucked its wings and rolled. Elessi's scream was cut short by the jolt of the dragon catching the air again. With two huge beats, he was level with Ilios once more. Elessi was a faint green. Modren was busy trying to contain his howls. Mithrid caught Farden's laughter on the wind, and found her scowl easing slightly.

The flight was short: the gryphon led the way, skimming a glacial pool the colour of flawless turquoise. She was transfixed. It looked too perfect to be natural, as if painstakingly painted by an artist not of these lands. Its river curved south to worlds unknown to her: a blue vein that tunnelled and spilled over the marble ice for miles.

Two spurs of black rock reached from the Spine of the World like a mother's arms, forging a small crater of a valley at the edge of the ice fields. Dark veins of fauna spoiled the whitewash. Mithrid was already craning her neck before they landed, then swiftly slid from the gryphon's wing.

Trees. They were larger versions of the sapling in her chamber. Their brittle leaves and branches were so fine and glasslike they gave the appearance of loitering mist. Their trunks were blackened by some mould or moss, and when Mithrid kicked the snow from the ice, similar dark roots tunnelled into the ice, far below into either soil or sea.

'What do you call these?' Mithrid breathed, running her hand along the nearest branch. The cold of it stung her bare hands. While the translucent bark was smooth like an icicle, the leaves were as fragile as frost and crumbled beneath her hands.

Elessi lingered nearby. 'The snowmads call them *theranthagar* and also something else that's highly unpronounceable. The Sirens have taken to calling them verglass trees.'

Farden clapped his hands with a metallic clang. 'Enough with the trees. As fascinating as I'm sure they are, I didn't bring you here to stare at flora, Mithrid. I brought you here so you could train without worrying about prying eyes or unfortunate accidents.' He shooed Elessi and Modren away across the ice. 'You two carry on and enjoy your... *picnic.*'

Elessi snapped her fingers in the Outlaw King's face as if she had known him since a babe. 'Excuse the husband and wife for wantin' to have one last meal out in the peace and quiet before all Hel comes down on us.'

Farden shook his head. 'It's a picnic,' he mouthed at Modren, and the undermage threw up a finger.

Elessi and Modren were digging into haversacks, drawing out breads and cheeses and a small table, as if they were making camp for the night. Had Modren not been in full armour, and a war brooding on the horizon, Mithrid imagined it would have been what the skalds called romantic. It seemed at odds with this frozen landscape, bent so singularly to war; a humanity she hadn't expected, a glimmer of a normalcy she had forgotten.

Farden gave the pair a respectful distance, standing near the gryphon and dragon, who was now white instead of black. Mithrid blinked as if she were going mad.

The mage saw her confusion. 'Shivertread tends to change colour. He's the first dragon to do so, the Old Dragon tells me.'

'And the only,' grumbled Shivertread with a toothy smile.

Mithrid stood a spear's length from Farden, arms crossed. She could count the number of apologies she had uttered in her life on two hands. Once they had failed, again and again, to stop her father's knuckles from falling on her, she had given up on their use.

Mithrid worked her gums. 'For whatever I did, I'm sor—'

'No,' Farden sighed. 'For last evening, it's me that owes you an apology. The mages at the old Manesmark Written School knew it best: the simple fact of the matter is that nothing unearths magickal ability like rage or fear. All other emotions pale in comparison.'

'So, you provoked me?'

The mage nodded; his stare fixed on her. 'I did. And for that, I'm sorry. It's never enjoyable.'

Mithrid fidgeted in relief. 'Luckily for you, it worked.'

A smile emerged on Farden's face. 'Yes. That it did. A little too well, if you ask me.' With a flick of his fingers, a fireball burst into life. 'Fortunately, it's not permanent. You certainly have a power in you, Mithrid. What it is, we'll see.'

'But I have to be angry, or scared, to use this power, this… *thing* that you don't know anything about.'

'You can say magick. The word won't hurt, despite what the empire would have you think.'

She was not convinced. 'Magick.'

'And no, we don't know anythin' about it, but we want to find out,' called Elessi. 'Carefully, mind.'

'You concentrate on your pig pies and marmalades over there. Let me do the training.' Farden told the couple. Elessi shook her head, even throwing a chunk of bread across the ice. Ilios sniffed it with no interest.

The mage shrugged. 'She's right. Understanding is the key to control. We need to know what you can and can't do.'

Mithrid looked around, catching Modren's sidelong stare. She measured the distance between her and Farden and realised it had grown. She didn't feel dangerous. She felt diseased. 'Why do you care? Because you're worried I might steal your magick?'

Farden drew his sword, flourished it to the whip of metal against cold air, and dug it into the ice. He chuckled coldly. 'Yes, frankly. But we care because we don't have hearts of pitch and tar, despite what Malvus would have you think. You have a right to know what's within your blood. And, because you have a power that could be useful in this war. An edge.'

'So you see me as a tool?'

The mage tapped his sword hilt. 'In war, tools are called weapons, Mithrid.'

With a sharp clang, the Outlaw King knocked his armoured wrists together. The air popped and shivered. A circular pane of glass hovered before Farden's hands, fizzling ever so slightly, distorting him. Its facets flowed as water. *Shield magick.*

'First test,' he said, making Mithrid jitter. 'Break through my shield.'

'Break through it, you say…'

'You heard me.'

Mithrid pursed her lips, stretching her fingers and having no idea if that helped. 'Will it hurt?'

Farden shrugged. 'Feel free to stop if it does.'

Mithrid reached out her hands, walking forwards until she felt a faint breath at her fingertips, colder than the winter air. With each crunching footfall, that sensation grew until it felt as though she had dipped her hands into the snow.

The memory of home had a sting in its tail: a genuine stab of pain beneath her skull that made her wince. The shield sparked. Farden saw her pain but did not relent. She met his blurred, expectant gaze. *Anger. Fear.* They were two friends she had carried since the last day in Troughwake. They had yet to leave her side, lingering never far away.

Holding her hand a fraction from Farden's shield spell, she thought of her father's dead gaze, still forlorn in never knowing whether he had done enough to save his daughter. She thought of the panic, scratching at blood-soaked boards to be free of darkness.

She winced as the pain in her head grew. The shield hissed once more, and again the mage held fast.

'Focus,' Modren instructed.

Mithrid wanted to curse him aloud. *What else was she doing but bloody focusing?*

The shield now hissed and crackled beneath her hand. She flinched as a spark stung her.

'Come on, you're not focusing.' Farden said, voice distorted, but clear enough to stoke her. He had touched a nerve and noticed.

Fear withdrew. She was not scared of these people. She was not scared of Malvus or his war-making. She was not scared of this power within her. Memories of Troughwake, burned, charred, dripping with blood, came to her stark and cold. Her footprints on the sand, yet to be washed away by the sea's forgiveness. Her world cracked open like a villager's skull. That is what they stole from her. *Life.* Every step taken for sixteen winters. No choice given, no question asked. The whims of the powerful and the inexorable unknown had changed her life without her consent. Now she was here, forced to be questioned and suspected and made to perform—

Snap.

A glaring crack appeared in the shield. Its ragged edges were torn away and vanished in the breeze. Mithrid pushed forwards, her hand a blade to force the gap wider. The shield recoiled like the broken tension of spiderwebs.

As Farden let the spell falter, Mithrid was pushing so hard she almost toppled. She jiggled her numb hand. The Outlaw King was impassive, giving nothing in the way of congratulation or disappointment. He backed away, leaving a hand trailing behind him and two score paces between them. Threads of apple-green light flitted through the air towards her.

'Second test,' he ordered. 'Defend yourself.'

Mithrid held an arm across her face and wished the foul magick away from her, as she had the false rebels. The green tendrils sought to grip her, but at their ends they frayed as if burned away. Farden pushed her. She felt the surge in power, a cold pressure in her veins. Mithrid sought to rid herself of the horrid, mauling spell.

It was her turn to push. Shadow leaked from her skin. The shout came from her unbidden. 'Yah!'

Farden's spell unravelled, consumed like rope catching fire. Her shadow chased the magick until the mage was forced to recoil. He exhaled slowly. 'Well done, Mithrid. Distance does not hold you back after all, it seems.'

Mithrid caught Modren and Elessi staring, their food now forgotten and hovering between plate and mouth. Mithrid's breath was short as if she had sprinted here. A bead of sweat raced down her cheek.

'Any more?' she asked.

It sounded, faintly, like Modren was laughing. Farden's face was framed in scowl, but in the way that Mithrid suspected it hid a grin.

'She has fire indeed, Modren!' called Farden. 'He was right about you. You learn quick, but take it from me, that fire inside you can be dangerous.' He put a finger to his nose.

Mithrid wiped her face. The back of her hand came away bloody.

'Just as blades and fire can cut and sear, magick can do the same within us.'

Elessi was now on her feet, edging closer with her hands clasped like a manservant with bad news for his lord. 'You're pushin' her too hard, too fast, Farden.'

Mithrid surprised them all. 'Next test,' she demanded.

Farden obliged her, but not in the way she expected. 'Why are you here?' he asked.

'I told you last night. Modren saved me—'

'You never answered me.' Farden wrenched his sword from the ice and pointed it at her. 'Why are you here?'

Distracted momentarily by the frozen blade, Mithrid tried to swallow her emotion, even though she knew he was goading her. 'To have my revenge. For my father.'

The sword cut the air. 'I don't believe it.'

'And for all the others in Troughwake—'

'Why are you here?'

'For me!' Mithrid yelled, shocked at her own selfish truth. 'For the life they took from me!'

She saw the ice scurry from around her feet, saw Farden wince as if her very voice had battered him. He flexed his fingers, sparking a meagre flame. It grew quickly, and he held it out before her. The flame leaned away from Mithrid. Somehow, she could feel its presence, not in heat nor light but in magick.

Farden shook his head. 'That is your third test, controlling whatever is in you. If you can't control it, I can't help you, and you can't help me.'

'I don't need your help.'

'The motto of a reckless fool, girl. Trust me, I know that motto well.' Farden smirked. 'Going to kill Malvus all by yourself, are you? Please do. That would save me a lot of trouble.'

'Why haven't you done that, then, and saved us all the trouble? I thought you were all powerful, or so everybody likes to say about you.'

The laugh was like two rocks knocked together. 'Not even the gods are all powerful.' Farden sheathed his sword behind his back. He kept the flame burning, staring deep into it. 'And I have tried. We have tried. Many, many times. I took every dragon the Old Dragon Towerdawn offered and fell from the sky at night like a flaming hammer. We almost broke the

Arkathedral in two, but Malvus repelled us. A lot of us wear the scars from that last attempt. Since then we've built our forces, built our walls, and waited to fight Malvus on our own terms.'

Modren thumbed a pink ridge across his white scalp. 'Attacked him at sea once. Thought that one might work, but he surrounds himself with too many mages. Too many soldiers. Walls too thick.'

Farden ran his hand across Ilios' forehead and beak, making the monster purr. 'This is why we search for weapons that can help us kill him. And everyone that stands with him.'

The notion of war that lurked in Mithrid's mind darkened. It had not worn a friendly visage before, but thanks to the glare of her burning desire for revenge, Mithrid had yet to question whether she would survive it. Once again, she had created a bubble for herself, and imagined its film to be steel.

'Here I was thinking *you* were the weapon,' she said, hating the way her voice quavered.

Farden stared north, into the crystalline copse, saying nothing.

'We'll take every weapon we can get,' Modren answered for him. 'Concentrate. Draw your power in like holding your breath.'

Mithrid, still clueless to the mechanics of her power, did just that while Farden approached with a handful of flame. Once again, the spell leaned away from Mithrid as if threatened by her. She clenched every muscle she knew, becoming a statue of herself.

'Calm,' he whispered, watching both the flame and her half-closed eyes.

She tried. Her emotions were a fierce conflagration to quell. Farden came to a rest mere paces from her. The flame in his hand spat and withered for a moment. Mithrid held herself tightly, trying to imagine her body shrinking in on itself. Farden's spell remained a glorified candle, but it held.

Silent, Farden swept away. He was shaking his head over and over.

Mithrid was breathless. 'Is that it? Did I do it?'

Farden avoided her question. She looked to Modren and Elessi instead, noticing a dark curiosity in their eyes. The clearing was deathly silent. 'Did I do something wrong?' Mithrid asked.

'You've done nothing,' Farden said, voice rasping. 'You've proven yourself better than I expected. It's what you could do that concerns me,

Mithrid.' Farden crossed his arms with a crunch of metal. 'You have a gift, Mithrid. I've never seen anything like it in a mage before. I have, however, felt this magick elsewhere.'

'Where, Farden?' Modren was on his feet now.

Mithrid slowly began to retreat. She was abruptly aware of how alone she was, how distant from the Scalussen tower.

'Nevermar,' Farden growled.

The word meant little to Mithrid besides it being a rare red moss that grew on trees. Her father had dubbed it a poison. Farden fortunately explained.

'It is a drug once banned to Written. Even a small dose can render a mage powerless. A poison, for all intents and purposes.'

'What are you sayin', Farden?' asked Elessi.

'I harboured this suspicion since last night.' Farden at last locked eyes with Mithrid as he spoke. 'This is no leech magick. It's not magick at all. I'm saying – and I can hardly believe these words – that you appear able to unravel magick, Mithrid. You can erase it. You are the inverse.' He turned his next words over in his mouth. 'You are its poison.'

All Mithrid took from Farden's words was slight offence at being called "poison". But judging from the paleness of Modren's face, the mage's words were grave. Silence fell once more. The trees whispered like distant chimes.

'I don't understand. This has never happened before?' she asked, but found her voice ignored.

Modren was quickly at Farden's side. 'That isn't possible, surely?'

'I don't know. Durnus might. Though, if I've learnt anything about the nature of magick, and of this world, nothing is ever set in stone. Everything is possible.'

Freak. She heard Remina's voice as if she hid nearby behind a snow drift. 'A poison,' Mithrid whispered.

'I...' Farden bared his teeth as if in pain. He did not seem well-versed in reassurances. 'You—'

'You are not a poison, Mithrid,' Elessi chimed in, glowering sideways at the mages. 'You are unique. Unusual, yes. But remarkable. No freak, but a gift.'

Mithrid was struggling to agree. Farden was still staring at her as though she had just trodden gull-shit across a marble floor.

Elessi held Mithrid by the shoulders. It had been so long since Troughwake, another's touch felt foreign to Mithrid.

'A weapon you wanted, Farden,' she said. 'A weapon you've got. Who are the Scarred without their magick?'

'And who am I, without mine?' Farden said as he walked away. Modren strode after him, leaving Elessi standing besides Mithrid. The Albion woman sucked her teeth and sighed.

'Pig pie?' she offered, attempting – and failing rather miserably – to assuage Mithrid's roiling mind.

From stomach-churning heights above, Scalussen had the look an ant's nest. Multitudes scurried in clumps and rivers. Smoke and steam spewed from blackened vents, wreathing the fortress in its own cloud.

On the tabletop of ice, more figures could be seen making the desperate pilgrimage to the north. Their trains spread from Scalussen to the faraway harbour hidden in Chaos Sound, where, if Mithrid's wind-swept eyes could be trusted, three giant bookships now berthed. *The Rogue's Armada.*

Their descent was a tight spiral around the Frostsoar. Every window was being boarded. Spears bristled from every balcony. Platforms were thrust from any opening. Gigantic crossbows and catapults inched into position to the song of, 'Heave! Heave!'

The dragon and gryphon's claws skidded in the snow. The frozen earth had been churned like a tilled field. Where the buildings encroached on the gap between the walls, more activity was afoot. Cranes had appeared on rooftops, currently busy hauling stone slabs upright. Each one could have been the side of a house. Gates, previously tucked into walls and out of sight, now swung forwards and locked off streets, one by one.

Ingenious was one word for it. Splashing slush across her legs with an ill-placed jump, Mithrid stared at the bustle, confused as to why she hadn't seen it before: whatever city Scalussen might have boasted was a ruse. Every street formed an inner wall. Its bricks were the buildings, carefully placed in rings around the Frostsoar, interrupted only by the training yards. She had wondered why very few of the buildings faced outwards towards the gate; why their walls were so deceptively thick.

Preparation was never evident until it was needed, and Farden had seemingly spent every waking minute of the last twenty years preparing. Mithrid, despite her head being a tangle of woollen, frayed thoughts, was impressed.

The quickdoors were still expelling refugee after refugee. The grand courtyard between the gates and city was full to the brim. Scores of mages in red or black Scalussen garb gathered in ranks. Queues snaked from the dragon and witch's gate and curled around the walls like unruly hair stuffed beneath a cap.

'Where are they all coming from?' Mithrid asked Farden, as the mage landed beside her.

Whatever had perturbed the mage in the verglass copse seemed forgotten. They had spoken no more of Mithrid's power, and simply eaten Modren and Elessi's vittles in silence.

'From the edges and shadows of Emaneska. We have outposts and camps throughout the lands, protecting the last quickdoors that Malvus doesn't control and acting as a haven for those who can't reach the north.'

While they stared, two men holding a stretcher came flying from one of the quickdoors. A claw of flame chased them into the mud.

'Arka!' came their cries. Farden and Modren were already racing across the mud.

Mithrid, despite Elessi's complaints, ran after them, barely an arm's reach behind them. Young legs held the edge, and hers had been honed on Hâlorn sand.

'Help us!' the man yelled, even while being dragged upright and wrapped in a fur cloak. The stretcher held another man, an elderly chap with three arrows protruding from his belly.

When the refugee saw the red-gold armour bounding in his direction, he fell straight back to his feet with a squelch. Farden seized him by the collar and dragged him up.

'What is it?' the mage barked.

'Arka, m—my king!' the chap gabbled. 'They're attacking the outpost!'

'Which one?'

'Rolia!'

With barely a look swapped between Farden and his undermage, they drew their swords with an inharmonious screech. Mithrid felt the air shift as their magick bloomed.

'With me!' Farden ordered.

Mages and soldiers streamed towards the arch of stone. The thin veil of magick stretched across its mouth swallowed body after body. Ripples of light burst with each passing. Soldiers barged Mithrid aside to close in their fence of spears and swords around the quickdoor. She fought to stay amidst their throng, drawing out her axe to look like one of them. Her feet jerked as if to race after Farden, but the spitting surface of the door held her back.

Behind its blur, she could see a warmer light than this northern sun. Sand, instead of ice. Scents of fruit and spices breezed through the portal. She could vaguely make out an odd tree, with all of its leaves stripped back to a green crown. Beyond that, fire bloomed, and the dark paint-strokes of smoke could be seen. The sound of steel biting steel was muffled but loud.

'Mithrid!' yelled Elessi, already trying to chase her down through the crowds.

The quickdoor rumbled, as if straining. Its window darkened like ink dropped in water, until three refugees, blood-soaked and caked in amber sand, came through. Mithrid was desperate to know where in Emaneska that door led.

Modren emerged from the quickdoor with two survivors, one trailing in each fist. 'Stay put!' he yelled at two soldiers that raced to join the fray. Instead, with a shockwave of hot air, two orbs of flame ignited in his palms.

'Hold!' he roared through the effort.

A handful of Scalussen soldiers appeared and tumbled into the mud. Red and gold light filled the quickdoor now. Flame curled around the edges of the portal.

'Hold!'

Farden burst into view. He came flying from the quickdoor, arse first, and dug a furrow in the mud as he skidded. Flame still circled his wrists.

'Kill it!' he bellowed.

Before he or Modren could level their magick or a single blade could tough the quickdoor's spell, one last arrival broke through. A ragged Arka appeared, wearing the black and red skull of false rebels and a lunatic's grin. What looked like a pickaxe was poised in one hand, moments from crashing down on the Outlaw King. Shards of memories sliced through Mithrid's mind; of familiar armour and a leering face bearing down on her.

Farden had already raised his sword, but Mithrid acted nonetheless. She needed no magick, none of the so-called poison in her veins; she whipped her axe over her head and threw as her father had taught her, as if his corpse was still at her feet, and this Arka bastard stood above him with a dripping sword.

The axe bit deep between the plates protecting the Arka's ribs. He landed spread-eagled at Farden's side. Modren's boot raced to beat Farden's blade to murder the man. With a crunch of steel and a sickening squelch of skull, the Arka lay dead. Not a twitch.

Farden roared again. 'Shut the door!'

Modren's fire was unleashed, making the quickdoor shudder on its foundations. A faint scream could be heard over the roar as something else tried to arrive. Soldiers took up hammers and attacked the stone arch furiously. The portal began to whine.

General Eyrum came wading through the masses, a gigantic axe raised over his shoulders. People scattered as he stretched for the swing.

Mithrid wasn't sure if the light was from sparks or from a spell collapsing. In any case, the courtyard shone as if lightning had consumed the sky. The whine was silenced with a resounding boom. The force knocked half the crowd flat, Mithrid included.

As the dust cleared, the charred stones of the quickdoor lay in pieces no bigger than an apple. Mithrid found herself surrounded by heavy breathing; the only sound left after the explosion. She looked around to find a multitude of soldiers staring at her. A few nodded in grim appreciation.

Mithrid met Farden's gaze. The mage tugged her axe from the dead body and weighed it in his hands.

'Fine work,' he growled when closer, which was about as much praise as Mithrid received. 'Fine work to you all.' Farden counted the faces around him. His jaw bunched as he looked to the remaining two quick-doors. 'Modren, I want two phalanxes around these doors night and day. Mages and archers at a distance.'

'What of me?' Mithrid piped up, catching him by the arm.

Farden turned to stare at her hand. She backed away, but he shook his head, and placed the bloody axe in Mithrid's hands. There was no trace of concern or fear in his face, just the fading traces of battle-fury.

'I don't care why you fight, or how, just as long as you put this power of yours to work for me,' he growled. 'For Emaneska.'

Mithrid gripped the axe, hands slipping in the blood of another person. She didn't want to betray how much they were shaking. 'Fine,' she said.

Farden clapped her on the back, knocking the wind from her. 'Then for now, you train.'

CHAPTER 22
DEATH & GLORY

Outlaw King? That traitor is no king. He is but a murderous fool! He preaches freedom yet marauds the north, killing, razing, and raping where he pleases. He would sooner gut you than look at you. He is more beast than man. A wild savage who must be destroyed. Fight for your emperor's quest for peace! Fight for your lives!
A RATHER SENSATIONALIST PAMPHLET FOUND LITTERING KRAUSLUNG'S PORT OF RÓS

It took three days for Scalussen to cease being a city and to become a tool of war.

As the furtive sun set upon the ice, and the world was coloured a cinder's glow, Scalussen shone like a beacon. The work to prepare for war was barely started, never mind finished, but the city had changed irreversibly. Gone was the veneer of peacetime pretence. No more traders brayed their prices. No more ladies and gentlemen walked their pet pigs and geese on leashes. No window was left unshuttered. No door left unbarred.

War consumed all. All, that was, except for the taverns. Ale would have flowed even if the whole world burned.

Farden watched every firefly-like torch and shadow that moved below. Hammers kept a constant drone with boots tramping back and forth. Shouts of captains floated above the noise. Farden could have drowned in the ruckus.

'It's time,' Modren muttered.

Farden did not move.

'Farden?'

'I heard you.'

Modren joined him at his giant window. A small gap had been left between the metal shutters, melted into place by smith-mages. They both stared at this strip of dark world.

'Decades waiting,' Farden breathed. 'Decades of fighting, of preparation, and now that this day is here it all seems too sudden. As if I've forgotten to lock some vital door. Or left a fire burning.'

'War is never easy. We've fought enough of them to know that.'

'Elessi said the same thing.'

'Aye, she's a wise woman. That's why I married her.'

Farden's mood broke with a slight grin. 'Don't pretend you had any say in the matter.' He sighed. 'You're both right. And yet I can listen to all the wisdom in the world, and somehow, I still don't believe it. I forget it too quickly. I feel too... *full*. As if my head is boiling. One thought will be hijacked by another. And just as I have them detangled again, something else appears to tangle it up again. There is no peace from it. There have been times I've wished to just disappear.'

'Mithrid's got you doubting yourself again, hasn't she?'

'And you aren't?'

'Of course! To have all our training and knowledge ripped away that easily? Chills me. And I thank the gods we found her first.'

'That girl is...' Again, Farden's words trailed off as he searched for better ones. 'A force we never expected, yet one I'm immensely glad we have on our side. But she scares me. She is dangerous, Modren. She is nevermar incarnate. The antithesis of magick. If she grows stronger, loses herself, she could render us all powerless in the middle of battle.'

'Or, render the Arka powerless. She could be the winning hand.'

'Or she'll be the death of us.' Farden shook his head. 'In any case, far too much responsibility on one so young. You and I know that feeling, and how responsibility can crush a person like an apple in a vice. Worse still, kill them. I will not force that upon Mithrid.'

'The way she acted today, you may not have a choice.'

Farden snorted, breaking his eyes away from the world beyond the glass. 'Come. Let's go decide how not to die.'

The Wolf's Hall gleamed unusually bright. Shutters and dead candles kept this place Farden's preferred brand of dim, but today, the dragon door was wide open, angled directly towards the setting sun. Deep windows omitted more of the evening sky's fire. The statued columns glowed with it. Lanterns perched on scores of poles arranged in rows, each smoking away. Even the candelabra, made of iron and verglass wood, shone with every candle lit.

The table at the hall's centre matched the shape of the walls: round, and made of smooth, black rock. Its centre had been shaped by smiths into the topography of Emaneska, as far as the most recent maps told it.

Seats and platforms knelt before the table. Most of them were already occupied by bodies, large and small. One empty chair sat alone and avoided, one that Farden approached with the haste of being late.

'My apologies to all for keeping you waiting.'

Nobody arose. Nobody bowed. *Just how Farden liked it.*

Modren and Elessi sat together, arms on the table and fingers intertwined. Curving around the table from them sat generals Eyrum and Inwick. The latter looked hollow-eyed, as if she had chased sleep for the last few days. She twiddled green light around her fingers in fidgety boredom. Rumour had it she'd spent plenty of time on the walls, staring out across the ice, unblinking for hours. The matter of her control over the magick in her Book – well known for its poison of madness – was a problem he could not begin to broach, not even with himself.

Across from Inwick perched Siren Queen Nerilan, whose eyes were closed in either meditation or silent conversation with Towerdawn, it was hard to tell. The Old Dragon sat on his haunches like an over-sized golden cat, tail swishing back and forth to mark the passing moments of the silence.

Nearby sat High Crone, Wyved, always a diminutive figure yet somehow as imposing as the dragon. Today, the witch-queen's braided hair covered her face and much of her torso, a sign of contemplation. Stone beads and bones hung from the strands in greater numbers than before. A lone finch perched upon her crooked hand. Three other witches stood by her, two in blue hoods and masks, and Peryn, who stood with her hands on the Crone's shoulders.

Ko-Tergo and a fur-clad snowmad clansman shouldered Durnus, whose favourite scholar Skertrict stood by him, clutching a pile of scrolls. The man had just returned from some pilgrimage of knowledge, hunting out books in the south and east for Durnus. From the dark bags behind his spectacles and the creases in his face, it looked as though the long road had ravaged him.

Lastly, but by no means least, were the admirals of the affectionately named Rogue's Armada, from half-shaven Roiks and burly Sturmsson, to Admiral Lerel, whose feet hadn't touched land for almost two years, yet still spoke for the Paraian tribes and beastpeoples that now called Scalussen home. She had, after all, grown up in the deserts and sandstone alleys of Paraia. Lerel stared at Farden, wearing her trademark expression that teetered between scowl and smile.

Farden's gaze lingered in her for a moment before he remembered to finally breathe. 'The day we've waited twenty years for has come. Malvus marches against us at last. He has begun to cut off our quickdoors and outposts.' His mouth was dry. 'You've put your trust and your peoples' lives in my hands in a time of rebellion. I ask you to do that again now in a time of war.'

Farden bowed his head, gauntlets gripping the back of his chair. 'In truth, I can't promise you anything. I've made so many promises of safety, so many of freedom and revenge, but the price of such things is danger and bloodshed. Bitter battle, and one I cannot promise we can win. But I can forge one pact with you, and that is to try. To try, with all my might and magick and knowledge and rage, to win you that revenge. That freedom. That new Emaneska we dream of so often and fought so hard to build here, in the ice.'

He took a moment to breathe, skipping between the expectant eyes watching him. Farden stood on the same floor as they did but he felt upon a stage.

'When I'm done explaining, if any of you wish to leave Scalussen, travel east or south with your people, then I wish you well and won't stand in your way.'

Towerdawn's voice made the furniture tremble. 'Tell us your plan, Forever King,' he spoke with bared fangs. A dragon's grin.

Despite himself, and despite the loath he had for that name, Farden smiled as he took his seat. The weight not only lifted from his legs, but his shoulders.

'First, we evacuate those who can't or won't fight. Put them on one of the bookships. Two, if necessary. We do this at first light, and we do it swiftly. Malvus may still have spies amongst us.' Farden knocked his fist on the stone twice. 'Next, fortifications, supplies, shoring up. I want constant patrols over the Tausenbar and Chaos Sound.'

'After that?' Inwick spoke up, clearly eager to get to the matter of bloodshed.

'We wait.'

'What?'

'Wait.' Farden leaned forward, spilling a mind he had held onto for many months, years even.

'We let Malvus drag his horde over mountains and cold like they've never known. We let them form up on the slippery ice and attack our walls in their droves, and we'll repel them. We will bleed them for all they've taken from us. They'll come at us time and time again until their food runs out and their hearts tire of fighting for Malvus' greed. Then, once they are desperate, we strike.'

'A siege,' spoke Durnus. 'You are suggesting a siege instead of open battle.'

'Aye.' Farden watched the vampyre for any flicker of doubt, but the old creases did not budge.

Ko-Tergo was tracing coastline with his claw. 'How long do we have to last?'

'Perhaps a month. Two, if we prove Scalussen as impregnable as we think it is.'

Each of his council members muttered to neighbours or to themselves.

Farden pressed on. 'We have the supplies to last six. We have the weapons. We have every trick cocked and loaded. Let Malvus dash his forces on our walls until he seals his own fate. In open battle, with his numbers, he could outmanoeuvre us, trap us. With Scalussen as our home, we'll defend it until their last man.'

'If history is to be consulted, it is a plan that has worked many times before. The Siege of Essen, for example,' Skertrict added in his cracked voice.

Farden watched the changing faces around the table.

'What of the home we have built here? Of the Dragonfields and our eggs?'

'To be evacuated, just like ours,' Farden replied, playing to the Sirens' love for frank speech.

The Siren Queen's scales were turning a russet gold. 'You wish us to uproot at a click of your fingers—'

'Nerilan,' growled Towerdawn.' We built a fortress for a reason. In all truthfulness, we all knew this was to be the plan. Our king has only stuck to it, whereas we have forgotten.'

Nerilan slammed the handle of her glaive on the stone. The blade sang a haunted chime.

'Thank you, Old Dragon,' Farden drummed his fingers upon the table. 'That's the plan. Leave now if you want out of it.'

Once again, not a soul stirred. Farden could have acted king-like, as Durnus was always urging, but he was never going to exude royalty. Never going to wear a jewelled crown nor sit his arse upon a throne. Farden let out his relief in a sigh and saw the smiles curl around the council. 'Thank you. All of you.'

'What of the armada?' Lerel asked.

'Where do you think we're evacuating to. You'll take everybody who can't fight and sail out west, hiding in the Nelska islands out of the reach and mind of the Arka ships. We can't fight a battle on two fronts.'

'Reinforcements, perhaps?' ventured Roiks.

'If the day comes, perhaps. For now, keep those who can't fight safe. Old Dragon, I would ask you to send the bulk of your dragons to protect the ships. Leave a score here to keep any Arka spies guessing. When Malvus comes against us in force, you can attack his hordes from the flanks and the rear.'

Again, the echo of Nerilan's glaive meeting stone. 'The Lost Clans have fewer numbers than we do. It will be an easy fight.'

Eyrum's fingers scraped against his slate-coloured scales. 'Speaking of reinforcements, do we have any allies we have yet to summon?'

A wry chuckle spread around the room.

'We have exhausted all avenues. Either our friends and allies are within these walls, already on their way, or they are no allies at all,' advised Durnus.

Farden sucked his teeth. 'There are still the minotaurs. Each of them are worth twenty soldiers, or half a dozen mages, easily.'

Silence lengthened.

The vampyre remained unconvinced. 'Yet they still refuse to fight. Our hawks never return from Efjar. Eaten, most likely.'

'I reckon I could convince them, now that Malvus is finally coming to war,' said Farden.

Modren's laughter was harsh against the stone. 'You? The Hero of Efjar, who slaughtered minotaur clans for the Arka? Out of all humans, they hate you the most.'

Farden shrugged. 'Worth a shot.'

'And what of the threat of these new Scarred mages?' Durnus asked.

Farden thought of the black hoods, faces caught in a laugh. Too bold. 'They will fall like the rest of them.' He listened to the lonely echo of his words and hoped to the gods that they would ring true.

'Scarred mages?'

Durnus templed his skeletal hands. 'Malvus' poor facsimile of a Written mage, forged from stolen Books of mages twenty years dead. He toys with powers he doesn't understand. That none of us truly understand.'

'Anything else, King?' growled Ko-Tergo.

Farden took a moment to answer, as he picked at a section of coastline in the table. 'Yes, indeed. Tonight, we feast.'

The vacant looks silently begged explanation.

'I don't need to have a dragon's senses to feel the uncertain mood of this fortress. It's a palpable breeze. A stench of fear and angst. Suspicion over spies runs rife. Every neck cranes south waiting to see Arka banners.

They deserve to forget war and death for one night. We will remind them why they're fighting and what we struggle for.'

Durnus raised a finger. 'But—'

'No buts. No arguments. Tonight, we forget war and remember who we are.' Farden stood, pressing knuckles to the stone. 'You insist on calling me king? Then consider this a decree.'

Feet, claws, fists, and a glaive thudded upon the ground in cold, grim accord. The path ahead was set. It was a bloody-soaked country it led to, but there was no other route to take. Farden watched Towerdawn closely. The dragon's giant golden eyes studied the mage in turn. Farden buried his thoughts, hoping Towerdawn wouldn't know the truth in his heart: the truth Farden had failed to mention to the council.

One by one, they filtered from the Wolf's Hall in a slow trickle. Conversation was quiet yet buzzing. Ko-Tergo and the snowmad clansman babbled in their guttural language. Admiral Roiks and Sturmsson disputed currents and tides.

The mage felt a presence by his side. 'Lerel,' he greeted her without looking. He could smell the sea's perfume on her.

'Farden,' she said. Even her tone was a puzzling mix between disappointment and amusement. 'How exactly does one kill a god?'

'My question exactly,' Durnus piped up. The man had a fantastic knack of injecting himself into conversations where he wasn't needed. Farden cursed his vampyre's ears.

Farden shrugged. 'I'll guess we'll have to find out.'

Skertrict made a show of adjusting his spectacles and flicking through one of his tomes. 'I will begin to research—'

'Save your eyes, scholar,' Farden said. 'I'll slice his head off with my sword and go from there.'

Skertrict smiled politely, edging away with Durnus to leave Lerel and Farden to bring up the rear of the council.

'It goes without saying, but you haven't changed a bit. Longer hair perhaps. And what is this? Some salt in that pepper.'

Farden irritably plucked at the hair she had pointed out. 'It's stress, is what it is. This fucking war.'

Lerel's smirk gave way to a clenched jaw and pursed lips. 'Between you and me, do you think we can pull this off?'

'Like we have a choice. Loki has seen to that.'

She looked confused. 'Loki?'

Farden took her aside, away from Durnus and his scholar. 'He's somehow returned and is now tugging firmly on Malvus' puppet strings. He helped him create the Scarred and drove us against each other in Albion.'

'Nothing is ever simple with you, is it? You can't even hold a good old-fashioned siege without attracting complications,' Lerel tutted.

'I would argue, but after six decades spent battling such complications, I'm inclined to agree.' The years sped past his eyes in the form of fractured memories. Of Manesmark. Of Albion. Of the Arka's fall. The older memories had grown blurrier with time. He usually blamed the years spent in a nevermar induced stupor. It was such complications that had lost him the kinship – possibly the love – of Lerel. The mantle of king and protector had kept him too busy, and her love for the Lonely Ocean now ruled her heart.

Farden realised he was staring at her. After all these years since Tyrfing had transformed her into a cat and back again, there was still something feline about her. He looked away, clearing his throat.

Lerel snorted. 'Come along, Outlaw King. You promised me a feast.'

As it turned out, trying to win a staring contest with a lycan bordered on the impossible. The confounded hairy lump barely rose and fell with his breath, never mind blinked.

Mithrid raised a piece of hardtack biscuit halfway to her mouth. The lycan licked its lips, tongue darting fast around his fangs. She lifted it a fraction more, and there it was: a blink. Victory at last.

'Ha!' she cackled. Twice in one hour, she had won, yet had been defeated dozens of times. She nibbled the biscuit and gave him the rest: two more lingering in a wasteland of crumbs on her bed.

The piebald lycan lurked by the door, nibbling with two paws instead of wolfing them down in a single gulp. She busied herself by listening to some sort of commotion going on outside the Frostsoar, some clanging of more fortifications being built.

Somehow, she had slept through the clamour. Her training had drained her, made her muscles shake and her bones weary. It was why she yawned now, eyes watering it was so forceful.

Until this point, every lycan she had seen in and about the Underspire had been deathly silent.

They were considered mute by the recruits. So it was that Mithrid nearly jumped from the bed when the lycan spoke.

'You are a mage now?' The wolfman's lips barely moved. The voice was deep in his throat. Guttural and thick with an accent she had never heard.

'I... what? Since when could you speak?'

'We always have. Just not to you.'

'Hmph.' Mithrid studied him. 'Where I'm from, we have tales of wolfmen and boarmen who are half human and transform with the face of the moon. Does that mean you were a human once?'

'I was.' The lycan bared his fangs. Mithrid didn't know if he was smiling or offended. 'Those are too young. Have not learned control. I am of three hundred winters.'

'Why does everybody around here insist on refusing to die at a normal age?' Mithrid muttered.

'I forget the man I was before. Now better. Stronger,' the lycan beat his barrel-chest with his fist. 'Smarter.'

'Do you have a name?'

He growled something that sounded like, 'Roglurg.'

'And you like this work?'

'Blood is coming. Tonight's feast is not ours. Ours will come later.'

Mithrid couldn't argue with that. And here she was, feeding biscuits to a wolfman.

'Wait... what do you mean "feast".'

No sooner had the words left her lips did a hand pound at the door. Savask opened the door, saw the lycan, and jumped impressively high for a man of his belt size.

'Sorry,' he wheezed. 'Old habits.'

Roglurg resumed his silence as Bull barged past them both.

'The king's called a celebration. A feast, Mithrid.'

She wondered whether this was customary before war. 'Why?'

'Because we may not get another chance, girl,' Aspala shouted from the corridor. Her honesty was irrefutable.

Dragged from her bed by her rumbling stomach, Mithrid was amongst them before they could say another word.

A feast, Farden had promised, and a feast he had delivered.

As quickly as Scalussen's streets and buildings had been wrapped in armour and made ready for war, within hours, they played another character: one of frivolity and celebration of survival. The pikes, lances, impassive gates, and walls of spikes were an ominous backdrop, but the eyes were distracted by bright streamers, variegated pennants hanging from ropes, to the flags billowing from windows. Every crest, every clan, every sigil, every sonnet, saying, and proverb were evident in a multitude of languages, all crackling in the cold wind beside proud faces and cheering hearts.

Bonfires raged between the rings of the city. They blazed bright and fierce, keeping the cold of night at bay. The greatest of them sat before the gate, where the crowds were at their fiercest and the music played loudest. A hundred ljots and flutes battled to be heard above the horde of voices. Circles of dancing had grown. The air was busy with whoops and hollers. Even the dragons performed their rarely seen dances, swirling around each other, entwining necks and tails in a hypnotic pattern in mid-air.

There were no partitions, no borders. All mingled together, newcomers and veterans, old friends and even enemies, or so Aspala said, after meeting a fellow Paraian with a cold nod of mutual respect. All had come to be united in hatred of Malvus, and tonight, they celebrated that common ground.

Tables lined the streets, bowed under the weight of bowls, platters, trays, buckets, and any other receptacle serviceable for bearing vittles. Steam and char-smoke from cook-fires and kitchens gave the streets a dreamy haze. Lanterns sparkled on zig-zagging lines, blotting the stars with their own myriad lights. There was food there that Mithrid had never seen the like of; dishes and recipes she could not name, let alone describe. Swollen boars roasted on spits. Cakes with five levels or more teetered while forks mined at them from all angles.

Where food didn't command the tabletops, barrels and kegs held court. Their most loyal subjects swayed and cackled close by, waving tankards to snatches of songs. Two were in the midst of their own edda, arms crooked around each other's necks and deep in concentration.

From purple wine and ale to the foul-smelling spirits that the Sirens and their dragons seemed fond of, alcohol seemed to always be the lubricant of festivity.

The world and war had been forgotten, lost beyond the walls. They might as well have floated through the black ocean of stars for all the care Scalussen seem to give their time and place. Tomorrow was an eternity away. History was merely a tale for the bonfires, or a cause to clank tankards. Though she looked, and looked hard, Mithrid saw not a single wet eye of sorrow or shaking fist, or heard a raised voice that wasn't in jest or song.

'Look at that!' Bull, who had regressed a few more years and scampered around the feast like a hound, pointed upwards, beyond the lanterns and pennants.

Dragons. Dozens of them, wheeling around the Frostsoar in ever-tightening circles. In the fire and glow from the fortress, their colours shone.

'That Outlaw King knows how to throw a party,' Savask said, sparing a moment to doff his threadbare hat to the dragons. The man was busy attempting a self-set record of sampling as many dishes as possible. Some even twice. 'What did he want with you today? That was quite an exit.'

Mithrid smiled, thinking of Remina's face. 'Nothing, really.'

Even Bull was confused by her evasion. 'He summons you for nothing?'

'To talk about what I'd seen in the south, before coming here. Information, was all.' It was a nimble lie, but it seemed to do the trick.

Savask threw a piece of fruit high in the air and caught it in his mouth. 'You've got magick, 'aven't you? You can't hide it. What kind?'

Bull grimaced. 'Does that mean you won't be a soldier any more?'

'No,' Mithrid answered flatly. 'I... Well, look who it is.'

Mithrid may have pretended to be crestfallen, but it was an act. Secretly she had hoped to see Remina. Farden was right: there were greater enemies than their jealousy. As difficult a crop to swallow as it was, it needed to be spoken aloud. Remina could make her own mind up.

Waiting until a free space opened amongst the eddying crowds, Mithrid slowed and waited for Remina's gang to catch up.

'If it isn't the king's pet?' Remina began. She had a bottle in her hands of smoked glass. It sloshed as she pointed, perhaps half full.

Trenika stood beside her. 'You think you can be a mage like us, I hear?'

'No,' said Mithrid, and that was the truth. Her emotions were already rising, her power with it. She sought calm, scrabbling for it like a frayed and fleeing rope. 'But this, whatever problem you have, needs to stop. The enemy is out there,' she mimicked Farden. 'Not here. Look around. You see anyone else itching for a fight between themselves?'

Mithrid stared at the recruit she had first unleashed her spell on. Krommish was standing as if somebody had pumped him up. His fists shook.

'Let it rest,' Bull summarised, helpful advice always.

'You're a coward,' said the lad, stepping up to him with the help of a shove from Lurn. 'And the king isn't here to watch over you.' Bull stretched to his full height, beating Krommish by a head.

'I don't need protecting,' Mithrid matched his advance. 'Fancy another go?'

He postured for a moment before Remina put her hand on Krommish's arm.

'She's right,' she said, with an air that was either deadly serious or painfully sarcastic. 'We don't need to fight. If Mithrid thinks she can be a mage, then let her try. She'll have to prove it to us soon, won't she?'

It was the latter. A challenge thinly veiled in niceties.

Mithrid saw that this ran deeper than her tripping Remina in a few races, than the off-centre bridge of her nose. 'How bloated and selfish you've become, Remina, obsessed with little things. I don't have to prove anything to you. You're late in realising what I have: that games and gangs are long gone. We are not vying for first, second, and third place any more, but to live.'

Bull might not have understood all of it, but he got the gist. 'Yeah. Get your narrow head out of your arse.'

Remina turned the colour of beetroot. Mithrid extended a hand.

'Allies?'

Mithrid's hand hovered in mid-air, alone. Remina looked at it as if Mithrid were plagued. She ached for the bitch to take her hand, for her to take some of the magick from her.

Bull loomed, growling, until Remina capitulated. She seized the proffered hand, and as gently as she could, Mithrid let her power go to work. Disguising it with perhaps a few too many shakes, Remina staggered backwards, eyes blinking.

A figure barged into their little circle. It was Hereni, dressed in a black and gold cloak that crackled behind her with sparks. 'Problem?' asked the captain.

'No problem here. A resolution, in fact,' Mithrid spoke for them all.

Hereni was not convinced. 'What the fuck is this, Hag?'

'What?' said Remina. Dazed, she hid the bottle too late. Hereni grabbed her arm and smacked the bottle from her grip. The drink smashed against the nearby wall. An orange liquid oozed across the cobbles.

'Really? You're given one night of freedom and you think you can drunkenly brawl your way through it. You forget your place. To the Underspire with you.' Hereni shooed them away. 'All of you.'

One by one, Remina's gang filtered off. Trenika was the last, giving Mithrid a curious, lingering look.

Mithrid found Hereni standing before her. Her voice was a chiding whisper. 'What are you doing? You are not supposed to be socialising with anyone, especially people who make it painfully clear they don't like you. Never mind touching them!'

Savask's head popped into view. 'We weren't doing anything. Mithrid was telling them the feud was pointless.'

'Stupid,' grunted Bull.

Mithrid crossed her arms while Hereni studied her face. It took some time, verging on awkward, before the captain's stormy scowl broke, and a wry smile dawned. 'Gods, you're irritating, you know that?' she said. 'Come, to the big fire and first courtyard with you all. Enjoy yourselves.'

Mithrid obliged eagerly, but found Hereni's hand hooked around her arm, holding her back. 'What did you do to her, Mithrid?'

'Nothing.'

'Farden told me your power. I want to call it a magick, but…'

Mithrid cursed the girl's perceptiveness. 'I shook her hand. Held back as much as I could.'

Hereni tutted, releasing her. 'For your sake, that better be true,' she said, unable to avoid laughing. 'Or at very least, not doing anything permanent to her.'

Mithrid's grin betrayed her.

'I knew it!'

The music drowned out any more conversation. Between the shadow of the crowds and the glare of the blazing bonfire, Mithrid walked through a jostling world of whirling dancers, and revellers. The heads and arching wings of dragons stretched like canopies here and there. Thicker crowds gathered around mounds of barrels.

All were welcome here. Cups were pressed into their hands, even Bull's and Mithrid's. The liquor tasted sweet, of cardamom and herbs, and had a heat that traced a path from her tongue to her belly.

'Jenever. Paraian wine, of sorts. Don't drink it too fast, you two. I meant what I said to Remina.'

Aspala seized the nearby flagon in a flash, pouring herself a liberal dose. She knocked back the jenever, spilling it down her furred chin. 'A taste of home I have long wished for. Where did this come from, Captain Hereni?'

'From the Paraian outposts, evacuated after the Rolia mess.'

'Thank Bezarish,' Aspala gasped, shuddering as if somebody had crossed her grave, as Old Man Clifsson used to say. She poured herself another cup with a cackle.

As swiftly as the spirit crept into her head, Mithrid found herself relaxing. It was not so foreign a feeling; she had tasted firewine and fishpickle brew before, on another night spent hidden in a cove with forbidden items. Much less harmful ones than spellbooks.

And so the night wound on, full of music, and dancing, and blind ignorance of everything beyond the guard-crowded walls and their lantern light. Nothing existed beyond the next lively tune and the next cup or plate. Even Mithrid forgot herself and all the horrors of Troughwake and the war to come, spinning in the frenzied circles of the Siren dancers, cavorting with the other recruits. As Scalussen became a wheeling blur of colour and sound, she found Hereni's hand grasping hers, leading her on into the night from marvel to wonder and back again.

The First Dragon's Wake, as they called it, shone above them all, dancing its own dance throughout the feast: ribbons of blue and red entwining for the watchers below. Upon the ice, all the way to the Tausenbar and Chaos Sound, the snow-foxes and icewights and the blackfish yowled in harmony. And the gods, in a distant fortress of their own, watched on, no doubt, and listened to the echoes of mortals' songs.

'Fuck the Underspire,' muttered Remina. She turned to see if Trenika agreed, but the girl had disappeared. Her brother Lurn was gone also. They had stood behind her only moments ago, wandering lazily with her through the now dwindling tables of food.

Remina rubbed her forehead, trying to knead the dizziness out of her skull. Whatever diluted cindergin was, it had not agreed with her. The drink of true dragons, the man had called it. Then again, she had not felt like this until touching that cretch Mithrid.

'Trenika!' yelled Remina. The noise of the street drowned her out effortlessly.

There. A glimpse of her blonde hair between stalls. Remina tracked her to an alley between a tavern and cobbler.

'Where are you going?' she called after her, hoping the echo would carry her voice. No luck. Instead she was forced to chase the figure. Running was tricky, so she adopted a meandering jog. Trenika was moving quickly, sticking to every shadow the festivities cast.

Remina felt as though an hour passed before she broke out into the open. The details of her vision blurred, but she could make out the tip of the training yards. Several dragons and some kind of raucous game appeared to be happening at the far end. Remina ignored them, watching three dark figures racing across the pale flagstones instead.

Three did not make sense. Holding her tongue this time, she pursued the curious silhouettes. She had to blink hard to keep the world from tipping on its side. *Curse that cindergin poison.*

Now in the shadows of the grand walls, Remina was half-blind while her eyes adjusted from torchlight. Her feet fell softly on the earth. She could hear whispering. Either that, or that bitch Mithrid had cursed her good and proper.

She was right not to trust her. It was she, after all, who had read the spellbook, and now she thought herself too good for the Underspire. Mithrid might have conned the Outlaw King, but she had yet to con Remina Hag. Her mother had been right: that girl was the daughter of a witch and a drunkard.

Remina swallowed the sorrow that pounced, catching her off guard. She refused to think of Troughwake; she did anything she could to bury it. She had assumed the cindergin would be a fine way to accomplish that. Regrets were brewing.

'Trenika?' she called again, growing impatient with doubt that she had seen anything but dragon shadows. The whispering had stopped.

She was about to turn when a hiss caught her. 'Remina.' *Trenika's voice.*

Three figures crouched by an elbow of rock that nestled under the walls' shadow. Lurn had something in his hands that rustled. The other was hunched over, not tall but wide, and his face obscured by a scarf.

'She followed you,' he grumbled, in an Albion accent. There was an age to his voice.

Trenika's eyes were fixed on Remina, but she didn't speak to her. 'She's drunk.'

'Remember what the emperor told us,' said the wide man. It was hard to define in such thick dark and through blurred eyes, but he appeared to be coming closer to Remina. 'No loose ends and plenty of sacrifice.'

The snap of beating wings swept past her head. Against the sky's glow, Remina saw a black hawk flapping high.

'Emperor?' Remina began.

As dragonfire bloomed in the sky, Remina saw his face beneath a hood. One she had sneered at only recently.

'Savask? What are *you* doing he—'

A sharp pain in her ribs stole her breath. She looked down to see a knife-blade piercing her tunic. The blood was faint until the man calmly and coldly twisted the blade free. Gore began to pour from the wound. Then came the pain, outshining the numbing alcohol. She raised a hand, trying to summon her magick.

No matter how easily the spells came to her in the yards, they abandoned her now. Savask regarded her feeble attempt with a curled lip. The knife came again, punching four more brutal holes in her stomach and chest. Remina buckled under the pain. She coughed, finding warm liquid in her mouth. She coughed, spattering the flagstones black.

'Savask!' Lurn snarled. 'You'll expose us all.'

Remina was on her knees now, trying desperately to understand what was happening. The wet knife touched her neck. Strong hands grabbed a fistful of her hair and showed her the stars.

'Let them wonder and worry. Let them fight amongst themselves,' he hissed, before beginning to cut. Remina drowned in blood before she could begin to scream.

part three
SHADOW'S RAGE

CHAPTER 23
WARBRINGER

After becoming a war hero of the Efjar Skirmishes, Farden was set to become a powerful name amongst the Arka echelons. His uncle's madness, and Tyrfing's rampage through the city, skewered that fate like a hunter's spear through a hog. A pariah by association, Farden resigned himself to the fringes of Albion. Serving his own introspection as much as the Arka's orders, he sank himself into his duty, and to quell his sorrow, the drug nevermar, for his faults. I knew, but never stopped him. Like his uncle, Farden was cursed with power, and that is a difficult weight to bear.
FROM THE WRITINGS OF ARKMAGE DURNUS, YEAR 901

Krauslung had been emptied.

High upon the mountain of Ursufel, on a perch of frosted rock and purple moss, Emperor Malvus watched his hordes march like a master cardsman watching a pile of coins slide towards him.

Rivers of steel and leather flowed between the dawn-red crags of the Össfen Mountains. Thousands upon thousands of bodies, the sound of their boots and hooves and wheels a constant, rolling thunder. They left behind a blanket of dust that choked Manesmark and Krauslung, as if a bank of mist had tumbled in from the Bay of Rós. The crowds of spectators squeezed against the valley walls or crowded atop buildings looked like threads beside a tapestry. Despite their few, their applause was raucous. Flags and banners flapped violently.

The combined magick of daemons and a hundred thousand mages moved like a storm front, drawing dark clouds to their power. Birds, too: great swarms of them summoned by some magnetic force, or the expectation of corpses to dine upon. Malvus vowed they would not be disappointed.

He stretched out to feel the wind rush through his fingers. The constant trumpet blasts were his fanfare. The beat of the war-drums an echo of the gratified, smug pounding in his chest.

Higher, the emperor raised his hands, as Krauslung's contingent of dragons skimmed Ursufel's peak. The wind from their wings rocked Malvus onto his heels, and they filled the mountains with their voices.

To the far south, a multitude of horns blew. Amidst the haze, Malvus watched his fleets disappearing beyond the headland, each ship and vessel heavy in the water with more souls and arms heading for war.

Malvus heard her complaining before she was manhandled up the steps to the mountain peak.

Lady Jeasin. Ever the pleasure.

One of the Scarred had a scratch across his nose, likely from her sharp nails. The other looked beyond bored of her complaints.

'I demand you let me go! Who the fuck do you think you are, touching the empress like this?'

Malvus gestured with a hand heavy with rings. 'Unhand her.'

'About bloody time!'

The Scarred let her go, letting her follow Malvus' voice up the steps.

'They stink of magick and rot. I could have come here by myself.'

'Witness it, Jeasin. What power! What force. What carnage we will wreak in the north,' Malvus crowed.

Jeasin crossed her arms. 'Twenty years, and you still forget I can't fuckin' see.'

Somehow, she anticipated his movements and tried to bat his hand away. Malvus seized her by the throat. He did not squeeze to choke the air from her, but to let her know he could.

' "Empress", the chambermaids tell me you fancy yourself, though I have never given you even the faintest suggestion of such a title. You seem far too sure of yourself,' he whispered in her ear, 'for a traitor of the highest order.'

Malvus felt her swallow against his hand. Her blind eyes flicked back and forth.

'Whatever Loki's been whisperin' in your ear, it's a lie,' she gasped. 'All that god speaks is lies.'

Malvus laughed. He hadn't needed the god to feed the wildfire of his suspicion. The more he had stared at her, the more he remembered nights long past, and other excursions of hers to cathouses. Patterns had emerged. *Who had brought her to Krauslung in the very first place but Farden?* 'Tell me once more, what it was you were doing in Krauslung's streets, the night Farden showed his face?'

The lie was too slow. Too damning. Her last test had been failed. 'I was servin' you, as I always do—'

'I know you have been helping the Outlaw King.'

'You're wrong, Malvus. I've no love for Farden,' she rasped. 'The bastard abandoned me here. Cheated me. I've devoted myself only to you.'

Malvus squeezed.

Jeasin's eyes bulged, racing back and forth. The truth came spilling now. 'I stopped, I swear it! I never told him of Kserak. Never told him anything since then.' She choked.

'Until the other night.'

Malvus gripped tightly, feeling the stiffness of the tendons under his fingers. She was a traitor, but if Jeasin was anything, she was a witch of his heart. Domination, victory, absolute power: these were what Malvus longed for, and yet even now, though the fondness and appetite for her had long since evaporated, there was value to her that, like a trader clutching his last coin, he did not want to give up.

But what was war, but a time of sacrifice?

The emperor released her. Jeasin staggered back, her Albion skin more pale than usual.

'Your days of basking in my glow are over, Jeasin,' he decreed. 'I would have Farden wonder why you are absent from my side. You are worth no ransom. I doubt he would surrender anything for you.

'Go on then, kill me,' she said, a sneer creeping across her face. 'I know how you treat your scorned. I've had a finer life than any Albion whore.'

'Such a swift ending is not to be yours, Jeasin. Do you take me for a monster? No. Instead, you will remain in the Arkathedral until I return victorious. Then, we shall discuss your punishment.'

Jeasin bunched her jaw, surprise plain on her face. 'Well, I—'

Malvus clicked his fingers. 'To the dungeons with her.'

'No!' Jeasin shrieked. 'Don't put me in those cells! You can't do that!'

'I am the emperor of Emaneska, Jeasin,' he said with a flashing smile. 'I believe I can do what I please. Take her away! Let the cold stone and silence teach her the lesson of loyalty.'

'No! I beg you!'

Black hoods and masked faces seized her. What noise she had made climbing Ursufel's peak was exceeded on the way down to the Arkathedral. Her curses and threats filled the air until they drowned out the sound of the Arka hordes. Rumour had it the cramped dungeons could sieve the mind from a man as easily as a rock from grain. All it took was time.

With a sigh, Malvus turned back to survey the flood of humanity escaping his city. Alone again, he allowed himself a well-deserved grin. It grew into a chuckle, which graduated quickly into a laugh. He raised his hands as the familiar pain shot across his chest. Something ragged caught in his throat. The laugh was cut short by a hawking cough, one that doubled him up.

Malvus spat on the bare rock and froze. Blood decorated the stone. Briskly, he wiped his lips, his hand coming away a bright scarlet.

How long he stared at that unwanted sketch of blood, Malvus didn't know. By the time he looked up, Manesmark was a barren ghost town. The hordes had consumed the mountains.

With a hand that quivered in a way that he cursed, he felt for the vial Loki had pressed into his palm. He stared at the dark liquid, a red bordering on black.

Poison. Malvus could not shake the word from his skull. He had debated asking Gremorin, but he had never been one to reveal his hand at the first opportunity. A good gambler never showed his cards, even once the game is over.

A cough pounced again, and Malvus thumped his chest. With a flick of his thumb, he broke the seal and stopper, and brought the vial to his lips. The smell was of char and vinegar, foul even from the faintest of inhales.

Malvus stared north, past the dirty silver clouds gathering above his armies, past the black wall of Lokki, Össfen's proudest peak, to the faint blur of the north, and as he stared, he threw that vial back and let the liquid pour onto his tongue.

Just a sip. That was all Malvus took. He was glad for it: the daemonblood stung his throat as if he had swallowed shards of glass. The pain came swiftly, folding him onto to his knees. Clutching at his stomach, he tried to curse that bastard god, but the words came out as a strangled cry.

Loki had ruined him.

Poisoned him.

Killed him.

Alone, he lay on the rock, convulsing, eyes full of pained tears, feeling daemon's magick course through his veins.

Malvus was frankly surprised to awake. He gasped, finding granite beneath his face. Spittle dangled from his lips. He spread a quivering hand across the rock and found a black and chainmail boot beneath his palm. His bones were afire yet filled with an energy he hadn't felt in years. Malvus craned his neck. Corcoran and her Scarred were gathered around him, staring silently and morbidly. Vuleguls waiting for a plague victim to die.

Malvus pushed them aside, shifting his legs beneath him to stand. He did so unsteadily. He turned, taking steps at the mages, testing his aching joints. The song of pain in his hip he had endured for a year had fallen silent. He took a gulping lungful of mountain air, testing his ribs, he breathed so deeply.

Corcoran removed her mask, revealing purple lips and scabs around her mouth. 'Your orders, Emperor?'

Malvus flexed his fists. 'North, mage. Glory awaits.'

'Malvus marches!'

Elessi's cry ricocheted across the training yards. Skirts hitched up and curls flowing in her haste, she cupped a hand around her mouth and shouted again.

Farden, Modren, and Hereni were gathered around something by the walls, hunched and heads conspiratorially close. They did not turn, even when she shouted again.

'What on earth has got you all—I, oh.'

Elessi saw the pool of blood before the body. Dark and crystallised, it formed an ugly cartography across the snow and flagstones. It seemed too much for one person, and yet as she squeezed into the tight circle, only one body lay on the churned snow.

It was a girl, her head masked in golden hair, stained with blood. While her body lay slumped facing the sky, her head was at another angle. Elessi felt the bile rising. The girl's throat had been sawed to the spine with a blade. Stab marks decorated her chest and stomach.

'Who is she?'

Modren's voice was hoarse from the night of revelry. He clutched a steaming cup of Siren syngur in one hand, utterly forgotten. It would have been a fine cure for a hangover had murder not become involved. 'Remina. Remina Hag. I saved her from Hâlorn along with Mithrid.'

Hereni piped up. 'One of the mage recruits. The one that was antagonising Mithrid. A guard spotted her this morning, when the light rose.'

'You don't think…' Elessi stopped herself before she said it aloud.

'No,' Farden growled deeply. He stood slightly apart from the rest. 'I don't.'

'I did find them together last night. Mithrid had offered her a truce,' offered Hereni, barely audible.

Elessi spoke the word that was a needle in everybody's ears. 'Arka spies.'

'Perhaps she stumbled across them.' Farden stepped respectfully around Remina's body. 'Bird shit here, maybe from a messenger hawk. More footprints. They didn't bother to cover their tracks. It's like they wanted this to be seen.'

'Wars are fought in the mind and heart just as much as on battlefields. Suspicion is already rife in this fortress, and now they're trying to push us to fear. Tear us apart,' said Modren.

'It's not goin' to work,' Farden snapped.

Hereni throttled the hilt of her sword. 'What will you have us do?'

Farden looked up to the walls. Guards and soldiers were staring down over the crenellations. 'We give Remina Hag the pyre she deserves, but we speak nothing of how she came to her end. Wrap her body. No announcements. No warnings. Go about finding the killers quietly. We cannot afford doubt, not now.' Farden muttered, half distracted by the walls. 'We're all too busy looking outwards. I want every shadow burned away, a candle in every corner. Guards facing in as well as out. Have the lycans patrol beyond the Underspire and station dragons at intervals around the walls. No hawk leaves this fortress without our permission. Shoot any others down. If one of Malvus' moles even so much as fucking farts, I want a blade in his throat.'

Hereni caught the mage by the arm before he could turn away. 'And what of Mithrid, Farden? She could be in danger.'

'Or, did you ever consider she could be behind it?' Farden retorted.

Both Modren and Elessi scoffed in unison. 'You can't be serious,' she said.

Farden said nothing, turned on his heel, and tramped across the cold flagstone.

'But...' Elessi called, waving the scroll the hawk had delivered. 'Where are you goin'?'

'To find Mithrid!' he yelled, causing Hereni to scamper after him.

'Malvus marches.' She offered the scroll to Modren. Her husband clutched her spare hand instead and pressed the warmth of the syngur into her palm, clutching it with her.

'About time,' he sighed. 'Farden was right.'

Elessi studied the bruises of weariness under his eyes, deeper than usual. 'What a mornin' to have a hangover,' she said.

Modren shook his head. 'I blame Eyrum's drinking games. And how Durnus has never found a spell for a hangover will be a constant source of annoyance for me.'

Elessi pushed the cup to his lips, and brushed snow from his scarred forehead. 'Come along, Undermage. Let's tend to this poor'un. The sooner this war begins, the sooner you can end it, and at last we'll have that peace you've always promised me.'

'Retirement, I think the vampyre called it once.' Modren looked wistful.

'Good,' she said, patting his breastplate before heading to find a blanket. 'Because you and I are getting too old for this shit.'

By the sounds of the footsteps, the girl came stumbling to the door, still stumbling on the choices of the previous night.

A squinting Mithrid answered the knock, bleary and confused. The hour was still early, but Farden saw the hollow eyes and crusty face of a soul still sodden in last night's drink and poor choices. It was infinitely preferred to finding her lying in a pool of her own blood.

'How do you feel?' he asked. It would have been amusing had he not just left a bloody body in the snow. Hereni joined them, hovering in the corridor and looking a dozen kinds of concerned.

Mithrid scrunched her face. 'How do you old ones cope with this?'

'You're not far from an adult yourself. But don't worry, it gets worse with age.'

That elicited a groan. 'Then how in Hel do you feel this morning, immortal king?'

Farden squinted. 'Fresh as Frostfall snow.'

'Urgh,' Mithrid turned to Hereni, trying to smile. 'And you?'

'Terrible,' came the mage's quiet voice.

'I'd like you to come with me. Put on your armour,' Farden instructed.

'Where are we going?'

'Efjar.'

It didn't look like Mithrid was the most familiar with the war-torn, festering swamp populated almost exclusively by minotaurs. Farden waited a polite moment behind the door. He nodded to Hereni, releasing her.

'If I truly thought she was the culprit, I'd have her in chains already. This is about her safety instead of suspicion.'

Hereni blew a braid out of her vision. 'Safety. In Efjar?'

Farden wanted to smile but he tutted instead. 'Don't let how impressed I've been with your aptitude for magick over these years make you forget I'm still in charge. You should know how important it is she learn to protect herself. Especially now. Go. Leave her with me.'

Hereni squinted but followed his orders.

Mithrid poked her head from the door, wearing the simple yet formidable scale-mail the forges churned out for recruits. She was attempting to tame her wild scarlet locks with little luck. 'Efjar. Is that nearby? Wait, not... *Efjar*, the marshlands, with the minotaurs?'

'You've heard the rumours, I see.'

'A travelling skald came by the village once. He didn't make it sound like a place where anyone should go.'

'Consider it your next test. Diplomacy,' said Farden, performing a sharp about-turn and leading Mithrid from her room. The girl trailed at his side, clearly brimming with questions. He could see she chewed over them, deciding which one was more important.

'Ask away,' he invited her.

'Why me?'

'Because I think you need to see the wilder world. See what fighting for Emaneska's freedom looks like.'

The girl was smart, he had to give her that. 'That sounds like an excuse.'

Farden stopped dead before the door. 'You're quick, Hâlorn, but you're too suspicious for your own good.' The mage held his tongue, lest he say anything else. He would tell her of Remina, of course, but not yet. There was still a depth to this girl he wanted to dig out, to see who she really was beneath the blind vengeance of her exterior.

Farden said no more during their walk, weaving along the edge of the Frostsoar until they were striding across a courtyard littered with discarded pennants, tankards, even a shoe or garment here and there.

Two of the three quickdoors still burned away. Soldiers and mages surrounded each one like a spiked shackle. Spearpoints and swords menaced the portals constantly, wary of Arka tricks. A Siren wizard stood nearby wielding a spellbook, manhandling the magick to point to an Efjar quickdoor, a vestige of old skirmishes.'

Farden knew the quickdoors would not last. Keeping them open gave refugees vital escape, but as Malvus marched across Emaneska and more of their counterparts fell, they would soon become a weakness. In order to keep Scalussen safe, they had to shut their doors eventually.

'I take it we're using these, instead of a dragon. Isn't that a bad idea, given my intolerance for magick?' Mithrid whispered, out of earshot of the quickdoor guards.

'Hold that power of yours deep within, hold your breath and close your eyes,' Farden answered her. 'Quickdoors look fierce, but their magick is simple. Stable, for the most part. They do not interfere with their travellers, just throw them halfway across the world.'

'Comforting.'

'Convenient,' Farden countered. 'Keep to what I said and you should be fine.'

Mithrid frowned at him. 'These are not the most comforting of words.'

The soldiers parted before them. Several bowed low, whispering, 'King', and 'Majesty.' Farden made sure to nod his thanks.

The quickdoor hissed quietly, waiting patiently. The surface of the portal sizzled in places where foreign raindrops sought to sneak through. The world beyond its door was a depressing palette of grey and brown, as if somebody had smeared shit across a slate. Instead of cold and wet, Emaneska's recent summers seemed to have just made Efjar more of the latter.

'I'll go first. Remember what I said,' Farden said. With a nod to his soldiers, he stepped up to the quickdoors, and with a gasp of breath, drowned himself in the portal.

A guard waved Mithrid forwards with his spear. 'Step up, miss. First time's the worst.'

Another chap decided to wade in. 'It's just like diving into an ice pool.'

And another. 'Sooner you get it done…'

'Yes, thank you,' Mithrid put a stop to this impromptu advice circle.

The quickdoor fizzed unexpectedly, but the gloom on the other side did not change.

Mithrid drove every ounce of air from her lungs, took a gulping breath, and charged for the spell's surface.

The guard had been right: it was an ice pool. The innards of the quickdoor were shockingly cold, the kind that seized her arms and legs in rictus. Her lungs screamed for breath, but Mithrid fought the instinct, more concerned with the sensation of hurtling through thin air at a terrifying speed.

The world screamed at her. There was no gloom beyond the portal but a scape of burning light behind her eyelids. The rule demanded to be broken, and for a brief moment, she opened her eyes. Before her eyes, and beyond the strange fibres of tunnel she raced through, colours ran like rivers. Where they crossed paths, the purest of light burned, so bright Mithrid was sure she would emerge from the quickdoors blind. There, in the aftershock of the light, the shadow lived. A face carved of raw bone. Hollow sockets of a skull. Mouth agape for her.

With a thunderclap, the quickdoor released her. Rain pelted her face as she burst into another world. Half-blind, she swung her arms like cartwheels in a failing effort to control her momentum. She would have simply let herself fall, if it hadn't been for the rusty halberds and spears lined up to greet her.

Something made of stone hooked her, almost jerking her arm from her socket.

Mithrid, still blinking the light from her vision, stared at the point of an iron spike, resting barely an inch from her eye. Black blood decorated it, and further along its jagged edge, a scrap of mouldy skin, complete with a sprout of hair.

She turned to find Farden's hand had seized her by the elbow. 'Welcome to the Efjar Marshes,' he whispered.

The mage released her. Mithrid let out the breath she had been fighting to keep. Her ribs shuddered. Her stomach clenched uncontrollably as a wave of nausea mingled with the relief. The vomit spewed from her mouth.

'It'll pass soon. Always happens the first time.'

'Conveniently left that out,' Mithrid spat between wiping her mouth. 'Why would you leave this sort of dangerous junk here?'

Farden remained unblinking, busy watching their surroundings. The fat, heavy raindrops ran freely down his face. 'We didn't,' he replied in a hushed voice.

'Then who did?'

Farden's laugh was hardly a cursory sniff. 'You'll see.'

Minotaurs. The question was answered by his silence.

Mithrid only knew what the skald's song had told her. 'The Minotaur and the Raven,' it had been called, in which a bird had conned the minotaur into essentially bludgeoning a whole village so the raven could get to their grain. What Farden wanted with these fearsome, idiotic beasts, she had no idea. All she knew was that they were an army of two, and she barely counted as one.

A screech came from nearby as it lost its life. Mithrid's eyes had adjusted, and she had not missed much. A flat marshland stretched out to distances hidden by a curtain of mist. It reminded her of the days the sea-fog hugged Hâlorn, shrinking the world to a tiny patch of beach and water and making all else a veiled memory. Glowing insects buzzed lazily from reed to reed, pool to pool. Bile-coloured flowers nodded under the hammer of the rain. The reek of bitter almonds and what smelled to be latrines vied to dominate Mithrid's nostrils. Another scent lingered, faint, but unmistakeable. *Death.*

She stood, finding her boots squelching. 'Should I be worried you haven't brought mages or dragons?'

Farden stalked west, away from the pale saucer of sun that tried in vain to poke through the veil of mist. 'No. Force offends them. It's taken us decades to learn that.'

'Not even one mage?' Mithrid shivered as a raven cawed.

'No need to soil your britches. You'll be safe. If not, then it's a good time to learn how to fight, isn't it?'

Mithrid seized her axe. Farden's chuckling was almost lost in the drumming of rain. Even so, he placed his helmet over his head. Mithrid marvelled at how the metal latched itself together, until she became remarkably aware of how thin and basic her armour seemed. She pulled her hood up and cursed as she almost lost her boot in a bog.

'How far?'

Farden looked around. His eyes were black slits. 'Not much further. We're already being tracked.' He pointed with a nod. 'The quickdoor will have got their attention.'

'Oh, good.' Mithrid peered into the mists, but the only sign she caught of them was a stink of beast. Her heart rattled.

'Your axe, Mithrid. It might have worked fine against that Arka, but you know it's not the kind for battle.'

'It was my father's.'

'Tell me about them.'

Mithrid's jaw clenched. 'Mother, I only remember parts of her. Memories. A smile. A scar on her hands. The way she would swim alone for hours in the sea. I can't remember her voice, but she used to sing to her plants.'

'Plants?'

'She liked to grow things. Something else I inherited. She would find the tiniest sprig of some withered plant and nurse it to life.'

'And what of your father?'

Perhaps it was the dregs of wine swishing around her uneasy stomach that loosened her tongue, or the need to ignore the ghoulish sounds of the marshes. 'A drunkard, once she died. Spoke with his fists and his axe instead of his words. When there were no trees to punish, I bore the brunt of his pain and regret.'

Farden regarded her with his helmet's vacant eyes. 'That is never easy. I'm sorry.'

She shrugged off his condolences like an ill-fitting cape. 'Don't be. He was a good man beneath the skin of regret and anger he grew for himself. He loved me in his own way, I know, when he didn't have the drink in him. He would have hated you, being a mage.'

'You speak with more years than you have bending you, Mithrid. You sound like you've thought about this long and hard.'

'I took me many black eyes and broken lips to understand it, but I do now. And I don't blame him. I reminded him of mother, and at least it made sense. Simple, in some upturned way. Makes more sense than being in this war. Or in this place, for that matter,' she said, momentarily distracted by a corpse. The first she had seen but far from the last. This particular specimen was half drowned in a bog, with his legs still poking up in the air. The child in her found it darkly comical. The new adult growing within her shivered.

Farden's voice sounded metallic. 'Northern air will never smell sweeter. I spent my early years as a mage here, fighting for the Arka against the minotaur clans.'

'For the Arka?'

'I *was* Arka, before Malvus turned them into the empire we know and hate. So was Modren. Durnus was even arkmage. That is why they call us rebels. I fought with a contingent called the Iron Keys. I was greener than spring grass, eager to prove myself. Somehow I survived and they even called me "hero" afterwards. The world made perfect sense to me then, too. Allies and enemies. Kill or be killed. Until my uncle Tyrfing succumbed to the Written's madness, and all changed.'

'Why become a Written, if that's what happens to you all?'

Farden chuckled wryly. 'I never questioned it until the day they found him clawing at the city walls without any fingertips left. A story for another day, perhaps. We Written either die in battle or live long enough to find out if we're one of the lucky ones. Lucky is dying in your bed an old man. The rest – half of us, maybe – have their minds slowly gnawed upon by the magick in our Books. Three of my Written have already succumbed since the last war. That is why there are only five of us left.'

'And why do you wear that armour?' Mithrid asked.

The mage tapped his helmet. 'You've got a knack, girl. After Tyrfing, nothing felt the same. I clung to the idea of duty like you cling to your vengeance. Served on the fringes as far from Krauslung as the Arka would permit me. And yet despite my efforts, I was dragged back in. Shown the true pain of betrayal until I found myself adrift in this dark age of Emaneska.' Farden's voice had become a growl. 'Simplicity fades with the years, I think, as if every action we take tangles the threads of who we are. Every day, another knot. So it is with this land, ageing with us. Nothing is simple any more. Not for me and not for you. It will sweep every soul into this war for Emaneska's soul.' The mage seemed to catch his tirade and smother it like a cork in a bottle. 'We all must choose a side. Even our most trusted can turn into our enemies when it suits them. That is what I've come to tell the clans.'

Mithrid stopped, letting him trail off until he noticed the lack of squelching boots.

'No time to linger, girl.'

Mithrid had an itch in her mind, and Farden had put it there. 'There's something you're not telling me.'

The mage kicked at a knoll. 'I always found bad news was best washed away with rain—' He trailed off, staring into the marshes around them, nothing there but mounds of mud and swords buried in the backs of rotting corpses.

'What?'

'Down!'

Mithrid hit the muck as a rock wrapped in leather came hurtling from the mist. Scalussen metal rang loudly as Farden met the missile with his fist. It fell in shards at his feet.

The air shook with heat and pressure as bright orbs of light kindled in each of Farden's palms. The colour that hid within the gloom came to life. Even the mist shrank slightly. He kept his hand from his sword.

Roars arose from the marshes around them. Threats in a harsh tongue that sent her spine crawling. Brutish, horned shadows appeared amongst the murk. A spear bannered with black cloth skewered the ground, piercing a gigantic mushroom and sending foul spores aloft. Mithrid's fingers dug at the loam. The mage's light stuttered as if bothered by a moth.

'Hold back your fear, Mithrid. I need my magick,' Farden hissed.

Mithrid swallowed against a dry throat. She nodded, saving her words for the effort.

A deep voice filled with gravel boomed across the marshland. 'This clan land, Arka! Not and never yours!'

'Turn or die!' ordered another.

'Shall we do what they say?' Mithrid breathed.

'No,' Farden scoffed. 'We're not Arka. Doesn't apply.' He cupped his hands around his mouth. 'We are Scalussen! We come in peace!'

She wondered if they knew the meaning of the word. Mithrid's head snapped back and forth as the shadows emerged from the mist, growing flesh and muscle. She wished the minotaurs had stayed shadows, still myth and folktale. Her eyes stretched so wide they stung. The real thing was terrifying.

From their bulging horns to their hooves stamping divots in the mud, everything about a minotaur was the very definition of monstrous, both in girth and having the wrappings of a nightmare. Their height alone made her cower; even the smallest minotaur Mithrid could see would have made General Eyrum look stunted and underfed.

Beneath their enormous, curling horns, cow-eyes bulged with fury and vacuous nostrils billowed. Their bovine heads sat in valleys of swollen shoulders, bunching as they growled and wound themselves up for battle. Arms that rivalled pine trunks led to fists that could have enveloped Mithrid's head. Beneath their matted, painted hair, or patchwork armour, the beasts were so exaggerated and inflated with muscle she was unsure how they didn't sink into the soft earth every time they tried to move. Despite the muck that clung to them and the waft of manure-stink, Mithrid was surprised to see gold hoops in their twitching ears and gemstones hiding in braided beards.

'You fought these things?' she stammered.

The mage was barely audible over the cacophony of snuffling and grunting. 'Many times. It's the bloodmongers you have to watch for. The captains. Like this one.'

One minotaur in particular came closer. Bright blue paint crisscrossed its charcoal hair. Three copper rings punctured the ridge of its snout. His left shoulder was encased in a dented pauldron, bearing two black spikes decorated with skulls that looked unmistakably human.

The beast jabbed at the trespassers with a mace that was the length of Mithrid. 'Care not if you not Arka, magicker,' it boomed, in a voice that sounded jarringly female. Mithrid had not expected that. 'We allow no power of yours here.'

The light crept inward as if reconquered by the gloom. For a moment, Mithrid thought it was her, but it was Farden dimming his spells. Once the colour had been sapped from the Efjar bogs, Farden raised his hands open and wide, free of magick. 'I have come for a moot,' he called out. 'To speak to your warbringer.'

While Mithrid pondered what that meant, the minotaurs found this cause for great amusement. The bloodmonger thumped the earth with her mace. Insects escaped in a cloud as mud rained.

'Why speak with your kind? Always you bring death, never words.'

'Not me. I speak for a different kind entirely. We want to parlay. To help you survive the Arka.'

This was apparently even more hilarious. The minotaurs brayed like drunken donkeys. All except the bloodmonger, who just stared.

Farden crossed his arms, acting casual, but Mithrid caught the shift of his foot, his hands tensing. Somehow, she felt his magick against her skin. His shout cut their laughter cruelly short.

'Then ask your warbringer if they wish to speak to the one you call Scourge of Efjar.'

A moment of barking and shouting in minotaur tongue ensued. It sounded like an argument to Mithrid, but whatever its outcome was, it resulted in several minotaurs charging at her and Farden. The bloodmonger roared, but it seemed a rebuke rather than an order.

'Hold yourself, Mithrid,' Farden growled.

She tried desperately. 'What's a warbringer?' she strained.

'A chieftain of sorts. The finest killer of every clan.'

One beast, coat as rusty red as Mithrid's hair, came at Farden. Back hunched and horns down, he sought to stampede the mage. While Mithrid looked around for a marsh pool to fling herself into, Farden stepped in front of her to meet the minotaur's charge. He raised no sword, no flaming orb, just a forearm, as if fending off nothing but a closed door.

With the minotaur's black horns barely inches from them, Farden unleashed a force spell with all the flexibility of a fortress wall. The huge beast was compressed into a disjointed heap and collapsed into the mud with his eyes crossed and snout pouring blood.

The next minotaur used its weapon instead. Farden ducked the axe's arc, severed its handle with a blade of green light, and whipped the marsh from beneath the beast's hooves with magick that rippled the earth.

The third thought better of it, snuffling to his leader instead.

'I told you, I didn't come for blood, but for a moot. I would rather be taken to your warbringer peacefully, then have to fight my way through you all.'

The bloodmonger heaved with angry breaths. She watched her kin crawl away before speaking. 'You risk much. Speak you shall.'

Mithrid decided it was actually more disconcerting to see the minotaurs fade back into the fog. Now she knew what it hid. The only beast that remained was the bloodmonger, who turned her back on them and beckoned them to follow. Splashing and squelching followed them.

'See? Easy,' Farden whispered.

Mithrid threw him a sidelong look. 'They really seem to hate you, Scourge.'

Farden pulled a face. 'I was the newest face of old grudges. Older than me. But, in fairness, I did kill a great many of them.'

The marsh's corpses grew in number, as if they waded through a recent battlefield. Most had been piled naked and left to rot, some stretched on poles like grotesque flags, perhaps as a warning. Other piles solely consisting of bloodied gold and green armour, weapons, and other useless trinkets. Bloodied tree stumps, still with axes buried in their faces, lingered near those piles. Death hung heavy in those places, the kind that ran Mithrid through with horror.

'Do they...' Mithrid began, but struggled to say the words. 'Do they *eat* us?'

'That they do,' Farden whispered, 'when we're stupid enough to run into clan territory. I've seen them boil a whole scouting party alive.'

'How many of them are there?'

'Clans? Perhaps four or five left, but word has it they have banded together under one warbringer. As for how many individuals, we fought the minotaurs almost to extinction once or twice. The Arka never knew how many have survived. I'm hoping hundreds. Maybe even thousands.'

They walked for what Mithrid counted as an hour, trudging through ever more churned mud. The fog stole all concept of time from the day. Mithrid spent most of the journey swatting at bloated flies with spindly legs that took a shine to any bead of sweat on her bare skin.

When at last they came to two fangs of white rock that had no business being in the middle of a swamp, the bloodmonger blocked their way with her mace.

'Wait here.' She vanished into the murk as the noises around them began to die away to a slow, drudging rhythm of hooves or fists on barrel chests. Mithrid's head swivelled back and forth like an owl's until she noticed a small wisp of light drifting towards them. Mithrid dreaded some kind of marsh-sprite, but it was soon revealed to be trapped inside an orb. That orb was attached to a stick, and that stick attached to a hobbling grey minotaur.

Its stature might have been halved by its hunch, but it was easy to see this creature was once a giant even among its own kind. One of its horns was broken halfway. A swathe of beard ran from its chin into a kilt of blue silks and chainmail. In its other hand hung a warhammer of terrifying proportions. It looked as though some foul blacksmith had stuck an anvil on an oar. Its spiked end dragged in the mud.

Bloodmongers, wearing suits of patchwork armour and bearing axes over their shoulders sauntered alongside their chieftain. Mithrid could feel the weight of their hooves reverberating through her boots.

With a hoarse bark from the old minotaur, the beastly entourage halted. Metal whispered as Farden removed his helmet to slowly and respectfully approach. Mithrid mimicked him, even when he bowed deeply, and then knelt in the mud. She fought not to scowl at the cold water seeping through her mail and trews.

'Warbringer,' Farden spoke. 'I've come to—'

'Scourge of Efjar,' spoke the minotaur. Despite the beard, her voice was familiar, the same timbre as the bloodmonger that now stood behind the warbringer. Now, in proximity, Mithrid saw the family resemblance between them. 'Lies, I thought they bring me. The Scourge, returned. Now I know. I see armour I see before in years lost. Though you wear more today than when we fought. You remember me not?' The warbringer paused for an angry snuffle. Mithrid saw a mad look in those dark, glassy eyes.

'Many years have passed since I last—'

'We forget not! You have nerve to cross our borders again, Scourge. To dare call for moot. Many here long to spill your blood, cook your meat, gnaw your bones. As do I.' The warbringer's staff flared brightly. 'Tell us why we should not claim revenge long awaited.'

One of the bloodmongers licked its lips. Mithrid felt that nausea again.

'Because I no longer fight for the Arka. Instead I fight against their empire, to keep Emaneska from being overrun as you almost were.'

The warbringer bared her teeth. They were no cow-teeth for chewing the cud, but fangs, for ripping flesh. She hissed. 'You are still magicker. Our blood still on your hands. No difference.'

'Emperor Malvus is different. He has more soldiers and mages now than the Arka ever dreamed of, and now that horde has left Krauslung. It will sweep west through Efjar on their way north. He has delivered an ultimatum to Emaneska. Fight with him or die as a traitor to his empire.'

'These marshes ours before you named them Efjar, not Arka's.' The warbringer's ears flapped, scattering flies. 'We have no place in your war.'

Farden sneered. 'Malvus doesn't care what you want. Only whether you bend the knee.'

The warbringer roared. Her kin and other bloodmongers bristled. 'None shall rule us! Into marshes we were born, and in marshes we will live on! The world burn around us if it must. We clans live on. Your warning useless.'

'The fire will consume you, too. It's coming here as we speak. There's no standing against it alone. Join us. Join the thousands of others that have come together to overthrow this empire. I can give you refuge and safety, repay you with glorious battle and a chance to be left alone for ever more. No more enemies. Only freedom.'

'Join pink-flesh?' Warbringer snarled again. 'We had freedom before magickers came. You take from us and ask us to fight for it back? We defeat him as we defeated you!' She shook her head violently over and over, until the bloodmonger rested a hand upon her shoulder.

'No,' Farden said, raising his voice. 'You won't. I wish you could defeat him, but not without Scalussen. All of free Emaneska has gathered there, waiting to meet his hordes.'

'You dare—!'

'I dare to speak the truth! To put old grudges aside for a common enemy. Malvus' daemons will turn this marsh to ash. He has dragons. Machines of war. A dozen times the force the Arka idly threw against you forty years ago.'

'Take them!' the warbringer began to say, but a distant blast of a horn stole her attention. The bloodmongers were marching to seize them when a deep shudder shook the earth. The mist to the east shone orange and faded red. A long and pitiful roar hung in the air, like a breathless wind still moaning in a dark night. Mithrid shuddered. It was no human and no minotaur.

'The Arka have come.' Farden clasped his hands together in one last plea. 'We can use the quickdoor to escape, Warbringer, if we're swift.'

His words fell flat in the mud and were trampled. 'Leave now, or at last we find out what Scourge tastes like!'

'See sense, damn you!' Farden bellowed before he could catch himself. 'Save your clan.'

Axes were raised. Farden even drew his sword for the first time.

It was the charcoal bloodmonger that kept blood from spilling. She snarled at her chieftain in their foreign tongue. For a moment, the warbringer tried to straighten her crooked back, tried to raise her warhammer higher than her shoulders. She failed at both. Mithrid felt the scene tug at her heart as she watched. For a moment, with the bloodmonger's mace raised, she feared that a cruel death would be dealt to the mother, but though they were barbarous beasts who butchered their enemies, no blow fell. Instead, to the rhythmic thumping of the bloodmongers' hooves, the warbringer held her warhammer in two hands and dropped it to the earth with a thud and a bowed head. Her daughter seized it in one hand and twirled it experimentally as if it were as light as a broom handle. Mithrid swore she heard screams and moans emanating from the hammer as it cleaved through the air.

'We will join you,' she announced, to the grunting of her bloodmongers.

'I...' Farden hesitated. 'Is that it?'

'Forty years, you say, and still you think us animals,' growled the bloodmonger. 'I am chieftain now, I decide. We have no roads. No castles like you. But we are Emaneska as much as you. I not let the last clans die for pride,' she added. Mithrid saw those bulging shoulders droop ever so slightly, and the sidelong glance to her mother, who had retreated into the care of the other bloodmongers.

'Thank you,' Farden sighed in relief, 'for listening. What should I call you?'

'You call me Warbringer,' the minotaur said, barging him aside. A horn was lashed to her belt, and with it, she trumpeted three short blasts. The mists thundered in response, and in a slow stampede, the minotaurs came together in their droves, bound west for Farden's quickdoor.

Mithrid spent the journey staring up at the growing, lumbering crowd that spread around and behind them, and wondering if she would ever be powerful enough to wade confidently amongst them as Farden did at her side. If he had known fear, he had hidden it well.

'That was close,' he whispered to Mithrid, with a spark in his eyes.

'I thought they were going to eat us. What if the other minotaur hadn't agreed with you?'

Farden pulled back his cloak to reveal a golden disc hanging at its side. It was marked with swirling, complicated inscriptions. 'A Weight. An old relic of the Arka before the empire. A miniature quickdoor, if you will. We were never far from escape.'

The commotion chasing them was growing louder and closer by the moment. Mithrid heard the cracks of whips. 'What's that noise, Farden?'

'Daemons.'

Mithrid felt her face grow cold as the blood drained from it.

'We faced their kind before,' Warbringer said beside them, hefting her hammer. The weapon sighed and moaned whenever it moved; Mithrid had not imagined it.

'They bleed like any other. Just fire and smoke instead of blood.' Farden pointed at the warhammer. 'I sense magick in that thing. And, if my memory serves, I heard stories of such a weapon in the skirmishes. What is it?'

'This?' the minotaur snuffled. 'This Voidaran. The Soulcatcher. Each life it claims is trapped, never to see the Bright Fields.'

Mithrid guessed Haven and Hel were not ideas reserved for "pink-fleshes".

Fire bloomed high overhead. A shadow passed between the sun and marsh.

'We need to move faster,' Farden yelled. He drew his sword with a crackle of sparks. At Warbringer's orders, the minotaurs began to run. Mithrid was bespattered with mud flying from hooves. Farden's arms fended off the jostling beasts for her.

A knife blade of shadow and fire split the air to their left. If Mithrid had been shaken by the minotaurs' appearance, she was quite literally floored by what emerged from that burning rift. Farden swept her up by the scruff of her cloak. She stared, chin glued to her shoulder, as they ran at the head of the minotaur crowd.

The daemon was wreathed in flame as if it wore it as a cloak. Its tar-black body seethed with an inner heat. Its skin was covered in arching spikes like that of a quillhog. Threads of lightning ran between them. It swept claws like broadswords at the minotaur herd. Sparks flew as ancient blood clashed.

Another daemon emerged from nothing. And another. Wherever they appeared, the noxious gasses eking from the marshland caught light, sparking into gushing clouds of flame. With the mist banished by the heat and smoke, Mithrid could see other figures racing behind the daemons. They were not minotaurs, but soldiers in pale armour, black masks and hoods.

Mithrid felt the sting of sweat in her eyes as Troughwake rushed back to her. Memories and reality tangled far too effortlessly, and she stumbled again. Gripping her axe, she used it for balance as she scrambled over corpses and through sodden grass.

'Scarred!' Farden bayed. 'I feared as much.'

'You? Fear? What are they to worry you?'

'Malvus' attempts to copy Written,' Farden's eyes remained fixed on the pursuers.

With as much alacrity as their enemies allowed them, the minotaurs sprinted for the quickdoor. Barging aside the barricade with their brute strength, the big beasts began to charge through the portal, their size limiting them to single file, so close they could have been holding onto each other's kilts. Mithrid's neck ached she had turned it so much, switching between the beasts continuing to emerge from the mists and the battle bearing down on them.

The bloodmongers, to their credit, were keeping the daemons at bay in marvellous fashion. One daemon was already shrinking away, a minotaur horn and two spears embedded in its chest.

'Move! Move!' Farden yelled, pushing on the coarse, iron-skinned hides surrounding them.

Mithrid watched one minotaur hustle forwards, a small, hairy babe in her arms. Others allowed her through, giving up their space for her. Other mothers and minotaurs that stood no taller than Mithrid appeared. The blood-stained axes and chopping blocks were all but forgotten in an instant.

The Arka soldiers were closing the distance. Mithrid stared, both nauseated and fascinated, as a man was cleaved in half from scalp to sole by one of the bloodmongers. She had never seen so much blood, nor the insides of a human neatly cross-sectioned for her study. The marsh pools were washed red.

'Stay put, Mithrid!' Farden ran to join the fray, leaving her awkwardly trapped between battle and a crowd of minotaurs dwindling painfully slowly.

Mithrid stood there in the mud, axe in one hand, waiting. The bloodmongers and mage slowly gave up ground. The quickdoor was shrieking. There must have been fifty of them left to escape. She could hear the bellows of the beasts who had trailed behind.

A rising shout caught her attention. A mage was running at her, fire trailing around his raised fist. Mithrid became suddenly and terrifyingly aware that she was alone in this fight. Farden was sprinting for her, sliding across the earth at an unnatural pace, but he was still too far. The bloodmongers raced with him.

Mithrid could do nothing but throw her hand out, as Farden had taught her, letting all her fear boil down to one shining point of power. She screamed as she unleashed it.

All murder was driven from the mage. He shot a look at his empty and extinguished hand in confusion while his feet tangled beneath him. With a squelch and a gurgle, he came down on his face.

Later, she would thank Eyrum for drilling his tactics into her ceaselessly. His will, manifested as training, moved her body unbidden. Even as the axe was carving through her peripheries, she did not stop it. She watched it fall upon his skull.

Blood sprayed her. She tasted it in her mouth, felt it sting one eye. She stared down at the bloody gutter she had made of the man. What surprised and chilled her, even as memories of broken, butchered villagers flooded back, was the urge to keep swinging.

Farden yelled in her ear. 'Mithrid! Behind me!'

She didn't complain. A tide of Arka armour was sweeping towards them. Charging feet threw up fountains of marsh-water. Spells simmered in fists. Weapons held poised to slice. Only Warbringer stood against them while the last dregs of the minotaurs were finally limping to safety.

The mage grabbed her, speaking rapidly. 'A confession, Mithrid. You were right: bringing you here was an excuse keep you out of Scalussen for a time. To give you news that I take no pleasure in.'

'What?'

'Remina Hag was killed last night. I know now you didn't do it. Arka spies murdered her during the feast. Call it blind hope, but I need whatever rage or sorrow that news stokes in you, and I need it fast.'

Remina. Dead.

Whatever she had become, Remina had been kin. Chest tight, guilt and confusion raging, Mithrid stared at the snarling, roaring faces bearing down on them. She stretched out her arms, feeling the ice-water in her veins. She could feel their magick breaking like a wave, and, with a clawing of her fingers, she snatched it away from them.

Spells failed one by one, only fuelling Mithrid's rage. Farden and Warbringer met the frontrunners with a complete absence of mercy. The soldiers were brutalised, reduced to nothing but meat in metal wrapping. Fear was piled atop the bewilderment of the mages.

Half a dozen Scarred broke out of the ranks, fire and lightning already screeching in their hands. Before they could level them at Farden and the minotaur, they met Mithrid's wall. Immediately, their spells faded. The mages dragged. They heaved. They made the very ground tremble with their efforts, but Mithrid drained them with everything she had.

One withdrew his mask, staring through the curtains of blood and smoke at her. Mithrid sneered back, cursing them and their kind. *The murderous, conniving bastards.*

Farden abruptly stood beside her, barking something about the quickdoor.

'They're through! We need to go!' His words were muffled through the wind that roared past her ears. Her crimson hair billowed.

Farden seized her arm. It seemed to pain him, but he clung on, shaking her free of her ravenous trance. 'Mithrid! Pull back!'

The mage held the Weight in one hand. His sword raised to the sky with another. Without their spells, the Scarred came at them with blades instead. The quickdoor exploded in a shower of stone behind them as another daemon appeared. The dying spell flashed with white fire.

Mithrid shook with the power running through her. She felt like a dam against a storm surge.

The mage shook her. 'Control it, curse you!'

Mithrid clenched herself so hard it felt her teeth might break. Behind her scrunched eyes, light burned, and a shadow grinned through a mask of rushing colours.

'Hold on!' Farden yelled.

She let the roaring world back in for a moment, long enough to see a pillar of lightning collide with Farden's sword. Magick swept from him, uprooting marshland and corpses. The tidal wave of energy was short-lived. The world split in two, and Mithrid was dragged into the screaming light once more.

Cold slapped her with a ring-covered hand. It felt strangely comforting against her blazing skin. Mithrid let herself lie there, face down in the ice, trying to keep her head and stomach from spinning.

'Mithrid!' came a distant and hollow cry.

Strong, searing hands seized her. She tried to shrug them off, panicked. She felt the power leak from her.

'Fuck's sake,' Farden cursed, shaking his hands. 'That stings. I thought you were dead for a moment.'

'I thought we were going to be,' Mithrid breathed. Her heart hammered so hard her cloak shook. 'That was close.' Then, for a reason she knew not, except to show the foreign sense of excitement that ran through her, she found herself smiling. She had leapt a rift and seized the other side with but a finger. She had stared at death and survived. Even better, Mithrid had *won*.

Farden grinned right back at her. 'You've got the streak of a maniac in you. Good. Though just remember, a rush, it might be, but don't go hunting it. That's the path of a fool. Let it find you.'

It was fleeting as sensibility and conscience struck. *Remina*. The crushed skull of a mage. The bloody axe still in her hands. The fever of battle faded, leaving a cold draught in its wake. Mithrid shivered.

A snarling became apparent to her deafened ears. Several hundred minotaurs prowled around a smoking, charred quickdoor. The Scalussen guards looked somewhat confused and slightly shaken. Modren was there, keeping the peace. Eyrum and Ko-Tergo, too, squaring off against Warbringer and her surviving pack of bloodmongers. They bled with Arka blood and from their own wounds. Three dragons perched nearby on rooftops and inner walls. Fire washed around their fangs.

Mithrid saw Bull, Aspala, and Savask, their faces frozen in concern.

'What welcome!' Warbringer roared. Voidaran waved back and forth with pitiful moans. 'You promised peace, Scourge. A trick, was it?'

Helmet clutched by his side, the Outlaw King climbed the nearest crate to stand above the courtyard. 'Back off, all of you! These are our new allies.' His voice was unnaturally loud. The shadow he cast in the frozen muck grew.

Spears angled to the sky. Swords slid into sheaths. Spells sputtered out.

'Undermage! Give Warbringer and her people, room, food, and care. No question. Warbringer!'

The giant minotaur lumbered to the mage. On his crate, Farden was just above the minotaur's eye level. 'I can't just keep calling you Warbringer.'

The minotaur growled something unpronouceable. 'I am the Broken Promise. Katiheridrade.'

'Warbringer it is. Can I trust you to respect our rules?' he challenged. She snorted, clearly loathing being spoken to like this by a pink-flesh, but she nodded all the same. Mithrid guessed the underlying question. *Will you promise not to eat any of us?*

She ground her fangs. 'I am... grateful,' she said. 'The Scourge is no more. Consider your skin safe, Farden of Scalussen.'

As Farden bowed, and the tension in Scalussen's courtyard disintegrated, Mithrid forced herself to her feet. 'Who killed Remina?' she demanded of Farden. 'Why?'

He jumped to the mud with a crunch of armour. 'I told you: I don't know, but we'll find out. Hereni seems to think they were after you.'

'Then let them try. She was a fool, but I never wished her dead.'

Mithrid caught the eyes of the gathered crowd. Some of the mage recruits were there. Trenika stared daggers at her. Others whispered. Mithrid suddenly became aware of the blood soaking her. She tried to sheath her axe, only to realise the handle was cracked and missing a hand-span of wood. She closed her eyes to see a caved-in skull and clenched her teeth. What worried her was not that she had killed, but that she had enjoyed it. It shocked her, and in her confusion, it came out as anger.

'You shouldn't have taken me to those fucking marshes,' she hissed at the mage, before storming across the ice towards the Underspire.

CHAPTER 24
THE BEGINNING OF THE END

Nine smiths together.
Nine suits of life.
Nine pieces beaten.
Nine years of strife.
Nine kingdoms covet.
Nine thrones of spite.
Nine armies marching.
Nine fires ignite.
Nine smiths are murdered.
Nine suits are stolen.
Nine pieces scattered,
and lost for evermore.

FROM THE 'EDDA OF SCALUSSEN', AN OLD FABLE FROM BEFORE THE SCATTERED KINGDOMS

As the week slid by at the pace of spilled treacle, it soon became apparent that waiting for a war was as torturous as fighting it. The entire fortress busied itself as much as it could. There were plenty of distractions to be found, but every soul, in moments of quiet or stillness, found their heads turning south, watching the skies. Watching the endless ice.

Behind the walls that bristled constantly with full contingents of warriors, all trace of a city had been wiped away. The vast main courtyard was now a stretch of earth designed specifically to hinder and kill. Pits yawned and spikes dripped with witches' poisons. Where the forges, Frostsoar, and Underspire had run out of space to house every fighter comfortably, tents and pavilions had sprung up.

Half the training yards had been taken up with camps for minotaurs. The handful of dragons that had stayed behind roosted in the Frostsoar's nests, giving the tower a look of an old pine infested with colourful birds. They roared and trumpeted night and day, much to the displeasure of all those who had decided to stay and fight.

The refugees who would be nothing but casualties and corpses once the battle was joined had streamed from the fortress for four days straight. In the daylight, their trains undulated across the ice like jewelled snakes, shining all colours in the pale northern sun. At night, when torches and lanterns blazed, a constant procession of fireflies headed to the bookships and other vessels of the Rogue's Armada beyond the Tausenbar.

It was far from empty or silent in the fortress, even with a third of Scalussen now at sea. The thousands that weren't keeping guard spent their days in an endless rotation of drills and practise. Sleep and stuffing food down throats were the only escapes. Though it seemed a fine idea to erode the hours, such activities only seemed to restrain time's cogs. Where camaraderie should have blossomed – and in many places it did – tempers became frayed. Irritation ran rife. Arguments flared and were quickly quashed.

Such was the wait for war, and such was the poison of gossip.

Despite vowing to keep the murder as silent as possible, word had snuck out before the door of secrecy could be closed. Guards talk on long watches. It was natural, and before long, like a humble spark igniting dry bracken, a conflagration of suspicion had spread. Boredom fanned the flames. Reports came in their dozens to the captains and generals. Undermage Modren's days had become endless witch-hunts, putting a halt to this rumour and that.

Even under such watchful eyes, no spy had been caught, never mind confirmed. No Arka worms had reared their heads. That was a thistle in Scalussen's paw for certain.

The higher amongst the hierarchy of the fortress, the more torturous the week became. Hawks had flocked to Scalussen with message after message from the south. The scrolls came hastily written, many stained with blood or filth. Most called for help, or warned of what was already known. Malvus was sweeping all of Emaneska before him, friend or foe.

A handful came from those who had saved their last moments to curse the Forever King for not doing more. For his treason. Those messages

Farden had hurled from the peak of the Frostsoar and let the Mad Dragon turn them to ash. Between delivering orders in ever more frantic bursts, he sequestered himself within his rooms, carving candles into stubs and listening to the whispers of the Grimsayer. Mithrid's scorn had cut him. At dawn and sunset, he would leave upon Fleetstar's back, winging north to the Emberteeth alone. Ilios tried to follow the first time but was turned back.

Farden's life had always been plagued by secrets, and yet his own he kept for himself, holding it close to his chest like a beggar might clutch a jewel found in the gutter.

It was upon the ninth day the smoke appeared on the southern horizon.

At first the guards called it fog, swaddling the Tausenbar Mountains. As the day wore on, it had only grown instead of withered under the sun. Before long, the southern parapets were dangerously crowded. The yellow and grey smear was tell-tale of Malvus' warpath. Little existed south of the mountains besides stubborn farmers and hamlets of trappers. They burned all the same.

By the time the sun hovered near the skyline, black columns arose from the mountain peaks. Specks materialised on the ice, racing as fast as they could to Scalussen.

This was no charge, but fellows fleeing the Arka hordes. Dragons were dispatched to help, and, one by one, the survivors were dropped at the gates of the fortress squealing or frozen stiff in shock.

It was Elessi who first said the words, long before the keenest eyes confirmed them. She knew from the vestigial ache in her daemontouched wounds, all those years ago.

'Daemons,' came her hushed warning, passed along in mutters and whispers. It would be muttered later between the guards that every jaw or arsehole along those walls clenched. Mithrid, standing with Bull, Aspala, and Savask lingering nearby, was wracked with a deep shiver. She still had not rid the snarling, glowing face she had seen in Efjar from her dreams.

The fortress watched on as larger, winged shapes appeared from nowhere amongst the fleeing escapees. They were still nought but grains at that distance, but the frozen winds brought them the faintest of howls and screams. Forty, they managed to save from the daemons' clutches. The vile shapes disappeared, lingering in the mountains no doubt.

It was a sombre mood that set with the dying sun upon Scalussen. The crowded walls filtered away as the ice took on a scarlet hue, as if Emaneska itself was trying its hand at foreshadowing.

The first blood of the true Last War had at last been spilled.

※

The lift creaked ominously, and Mithrid's hand flew straight to the rough oak railing. She felt her cheek twitching while she watched the stone walls of the borehole slide past. Mithrid trusted these Scalussen contraptions less than she trusted magick. The pulleys shrieked again, and she dug a splinter from the railing with her finger. She could smell ash and tar wafting from somewhere. A heat prickled her legs.

'I shouldn't have dragged you into that situation,' Farden was apologising – or trying to. 'I expected to have more time in Efjar. Malvus must have sent an advance force.'

Mithrid nodded absently. The slow days and hours had been a twisted mirror, and in it she had glimpsed a different girl of Troughwake. Revenge had been taken. Her father's axe wrought death. What bunched her fists was her simmering need for more. Every teaching of Grey Barbo's, every fable, every travelling skald, they all painted her as the villain for such a desire.

Farden cleared his throat. 'If it's any consolation, you did well. Defended yourself proudly. Even managed control. Exactly as I'd hoped.'

It was not.

Mithrid's tone was low and careful. 'Do you... enjoy killing, Farden?'

Farden blew out his cheeks. 'Thron's balls, girl. That's a tough question, even for your inquisitive mind,' It took some time for him to come to an answer. 'I saw the blaze in your eyes the other day, axe broken and wanting more. Understandable, in such times. There is a faded line between vengeance and murder, or grim satisfaction and enjoyment. What side of the line I stand on depends on whom I'm killing. I have only known the latter once or twice.'

The mage let that remain his answer, and before Mithrid could press him further, the walls of inky stone fell away, leaving their contraption to dangle hundreds of feet above a swarming mess of activity, smoke and flame. It was a shameful thing for a cliff-dweller of Hâlorn to admit, but if there was one fear Mithrid had adopted in recent times – other than minotaurs – it was a fear of heights. She cursed Farden as she clung to the railing with both hands and stared.

Below her lay a veritable cavern, speared by the thick, central foundation of the Underspire: a featureless island of black rock that ran close by the lift. No wonder Mithrid had heard distant clatter all through the nights.

Fields of workbenches and grindstones and anvils gathered before giant forges, the like of which Mithrid had never seen. The one blacksmith of Troughwake had used a small pit hollowed from the cliff face, a peat fire, and had made Bull work makeshift bellows. These forges were thick towers, gushing smoke from their fierce glowing vents, where it found its way to cavities in the ceiling. Many of the towers did not look manmade, but protrusions of volcanic black stone, merely shaped and tamed, and surrounded by rings of walkways so that smiths could work in great numbers simultaneously.

'Welcome to Scalussen's forges, Mithrid. The fire of the Emberteeth also burns here, deep below us. The Smiths of Scalussen harnessed it more than thousand years ago, and over centuries, they culminated in this.' He tapped his cuirass. 'Once we found the ruins, and dug deep enough, we rebuilt and reignited them.'

Mithrid was too entranced by the glowing aqueducts of molten metal that poured from blackened crucibles the size of fishing boats. They ran in all directions, feeding racks upon racks of moulds. Virgin swords and axe heads glowed like candles in the hazy half-light of this underground world.

At the frozen and stark rock edges of the cavern, Mithrid saw houses perched on stilts, or burrowed into the smoke-stained ice. A tumult of hammering came from a crowd of workers there. Doing what, Mithrid didn't know.

Once the lift had thankfully wobbled to a rest atop a platform, Farden led a weaving path between rows of clattering smiths. Each of them tipped their hat. A few went as far as to bow. Farden welcomed each one but did not stop. Mithrid had realised that king was a mantle he wore awkwardly. A man cooped up by responsibility yet yearning for lost years. *Or new ones.*

She avoided the curious eyes of the smiths and workers. The rumours of Mithrid Fenn had spread far in recent days. The attention was bittersweet; she was glad to be of consequence but haloed in suspicion. Although those beyond its chambers knew only of a girl favoured by king and generals, Remina's disappearance had not gone unnoticed by the Underspire's recruits. Whispers abounded in any case. Nobody shouted. Nobody harassed her. They simply kept their distance to stare and spoke amongst themselves.

Instead, Mithrid took notice of the strange loam and moss that softened her step. Wherever a mound of black rock protruded from the ground and breathed steam, umber and emerald vegetation grew. Mithrid ran her hands through its tiny fronds.

To say that they entered a quieter section of the forges was untrue. It was simply a fraction less deafening. General Eyrum was there, bent over a stone anvil and bare from the waist up. He was busy filing and scraping at some poor piece of metal. Mithrid eyed the grey scales that ran across his shoulder and down his spine, only barely outnumbering his battle scars. She wondered how many decades Eyrum had lived to wear so many.

Modren, too, was present, along with Inwick. Each of them was working on their own weapons or armour. Another familiar face toiled away amongst them: the Siren blacksmith from the *Winter's Revenge.*

Akitha spotted Farden coming and muttered something about his presence. She hurled down her hammer, pounding a dent in the stone floor.

'Oh no. Not now, King. Every one of you Written wants me to oversee something. Tonight, of all nights. You had a whole bloody week, but *no.* Does it matter to any of you I have two suits of dragon armour to finish before—'

'Akitha!' Farden cut her off. 'You done?'

'Hmph.'

'It's for Mithrid. She needs a new axe.'

The Siren tongued one of her sharp teeth, measuring Mithrid up and down as if she'd never seen her before. 'There's plenty in the storerooms.'

Farden was adamant. 'No, this one needs re-forging. Means something.'

'Means more than something.' Mithrid raised her father's axe. It didn't even have a shine to it any more. The edge could have been used as a comb it was so notched. Never mind the cracks running through the metal and its broken handle.

Akitha reached for it, peculiarly calm in that movement. Mithrid gave it up willingly, but not comfortably.

'This old thing? This was made for tree stumps, not for bone and Arka steel.'

'Worked fine so far,' Mithrid interjected. Akitha raised her scaly eyebrow.

'Fine! By the storm god's arse crack, you've got a nerve, King.'

Farden and Modren shared a look that involved much pursing of lips and holding back of laughter. What they didn't see was the surreptitious beckon Akitha offered Mithrid.

'What are you going to do with it?' asked Mithrid, trailing her to a workbench.

Akitha's ears were apparently attuned to the constant drumroll of the forges. 'The axe is the head, not the handle. I'm going to put a handle on this excuse for a blade that won't break, then I'll mix some Scalussen steel around the existing piece, inscribe a spell or two on the blade for strength, and then hopefully you'll all leave me the fuck alone.' Akitha stared back at the mages with her vivid yellow eyes, challenging them to ask her something else.

Turning back to the axe, Akitha knocked the head from the handle with a hammer blow. 'You gave it time, I see,' she whispered, winking. 'Told you it was worth it. Now look at you.'

Mithrid nodded.

'Taken a few lives, has it?' Akitha thumbed the notches. 'How'd that make you feel?'

Mithrid swallowed, keeping her eyes on the axe head. 'Better.'

'But not better enough, right?' Akitha chuckled. 'War's not won by righteous deeds and honourable nights, child. It's won by killers.' With a pat on the back that almost drove Mithrid into the workbench, Akitha disappeared to the nearest forge, yelling, 'Give it 'til the morning!'

'She's the best smith in the forges, and gods, does she know it,' Farden chuckled.

Modren nudged the mage. 'So are you making a speech, or not?'

'What do you mean, speech?'

'There's always got to be a rousing speech before a war, hasn't there?' Modren asked, half-scoffing as if Farden had never heard the word. 'Before the blood and shit starts flying.'

'I'm not making a speech,' Farden crossed his arms. 'We'll fight just as fiercely.'

Mithrid found herself smirking. 'An inspiring statement, then,' she said. 'Always happens in tales and eddas.'

Farden looked shocked. Modren chuckled. 'See? Even Mithrid knows and she's seen fuck-all of the world. Speech it is.'

'I've done plenty already for this fortress, thank you, they don't need a speech.' Farden replied curtly.

Modren kicked the ground for a moment, watching Farden beneath his white brows. Inwick's vision darted between them. Eyrum just kept filing away, until at last, his deep voice could be heard muttering, mocking.

'The Old Dragon would make a speech.'

Farden threw up his hands. 'Oh fuck off, all of you. I'll make the godsdamned speech.'

'Bet it'll be short,' Modren said. He quickly found Farden's finger in his face.

'You're bloody right it'll be short,' the mage grinned. 'Just like Malvus' stay in the north.'

Mithrid looked on, watching them laugh, squinting at humour she enjoyed but didn't fully understand. It seemed forgetful, out of place. The notion of long-promised blood on the morrow kept her throat dry.

It was Akitha, once again, who educated her. 'It's how they deal with it, child,' she said, waggling some sort of pronged chisel. 'Laughing in the face of danger or sorrow files its fangs just a little. You ain't wrong for doing it.'

A musclebound man covered in white matted hair came wading through the benches and steam vents. He looked as though he had tried transforming into a bear had got stuck halfway. 'Brethren!' he called, baring jagged teeth in a chilling smile and beckoning with black claws. 'You will want to see this!'

Dropping tools and armour with a clatter, they strode briskly for the lift in the wake of the bear-man. Akitha's voice chased them from the forges.

'And stay out!'

The Tausenbar Mountains had been lit ablaze with torch and campfire light. A myriad of lights, stretched from east to west even beyond the mountain passes. Even with the hordes lost in darkness and glare, those pinpricks of orange and ochre alone seemed to outnumber Scalussen's forces.

Once more, the walls were packed with onlookers. Guards, soldiers, mages, and everyone else thirsting for the morning gathered to stare and lose count of the lights. No sound besides the occasional cough or shuffle of frozen feet came from the masses. Those who could not fit on the walls clambered the Frostsoar and crowded every window.

Atop the Frostsoar's peak, all of Farden's council had gathered, from the Old Dragon and the Siren queen to Ko-Tergo and Wyved.

'Gods aid us,' breathed Durnus, vapour streaming from his lips in the frigid cold.

'You know as well as I do that there's nothing they can do for us except watch,' replied Farden. In the glare of the Arka fires, even the stars had faded away. They cowered on the horizon instead. The mage put his hand on Ilios' head and felt the gryphon shiver beneath him. Modren, wrapping Elessi in his fur coat, grumbled beside him. Inwick breathed deeply, blowing great clouds of steam. Even Mithrid watched, standing on the edge of the group. They all looked to him for hope. Even in the gloom, Farden could see the flicker in the glass of their eyes.

'No, old friends. It's down to us,' he said. 'And that will do just fine.'

On a parapet of wind-shaped stone high in the southern peaks, attainable by no path except wings or magick, Emperor Malvus stood watch.

There was no mistaking the howling. The jeering. It was no mockery of the freezing wind, but of Scalussen's. The sounds of the fortress and its moronic inhabitants washed across the dark ice. Though frost clung to his brows and lashes, he studied Scalussen endlessly. Diminutive, it seemed from that distance, barely the size of his thumb. A simple circle of grey walls and a spike Farden called the Frostsoar, or so his spies had informed him. It glimmered with specks of flame, pitiful compared to the blazes that lit half the ice fields orange. Behind it, a wall of black rock was illuminated by orange skies at the crest of the world. He had perused maps of the Spine of the World and its fiery Roots. They would make a fine backdrop to the slaughter.

Fire in the west distracted him. Lost Clan dragons danced around the Arka ships crammed into the ice-locked bay. Below him, spread across a glacier, he could see his vast numbers, and he saw them take pause to listen. Malvus sneered at those that braved the winds nearby. Toskig was bundled in two cloaks. Gremorin glowed like a fanned forge, a thick banner of smoke streaming behind him. Lord Saker stood with one leg on a rock, a half-empty bottle of repugnant wine in his hand, pissing off a precipice. No spherical Wodehallow in sight.

Malvus was on the cusp of ordering the bastard to light half the mountains aflame when he caught the shriek of a hawk on the wind. Sable plumage shone in the fires below.

'At last,' Malvus muttered to himself. The emperor held his arm out, letting the bird circle to it. Claws clinked on Malvus' armour, and he untied the message from its shivering leg. The last message sent by his eyes and ears hidden amongst Farden's fools had reached him a day beyond Krauslung. All numbers and scribbled maps, and the mention of a mage of some interest to Farden.

Malvus glared over the scrap of paper as Toskig's scraping boots ruined his concentration, Malvus snapped his fingers to beckon him closer.

The general looked highly confused by the emperor's minimal attire of a robe and armour.

'Are you not cold, Emperor? Your health—'

'Is none of your concern.' Malvus refrained from patting the half-empty vial tucked close to his heart.

The general pointed to the hawk. 'Spies? I thought they were dead.'

'It appears a handful have survived.' Malvus let the general read the message. He did so with it barely an inch from his eyes.

'Fifty thousand, no more. Inner walls... Supplies for months. A siege it is then.'

'As I suspected.'

Toskig cleared his throat. 'And who is this Hâlorn mage that's mentioned. A girl? New ally, it says.'

'A fine question, General Toskig.' With a heave, Malvus let the hawk take flight, and watched it soar south into the darkness of the Tausenbar crags. *Coward*, he thought. 'One we will have to ask Farden on the morrow, won't we?'

'Yes, Imperial Majesty. Please, however, you'll catch your death before the battle begins.'

Malvus looked over the edge of the frozen rock to find the daemon prince looking up at him with suspicion in his amber eyes.

The emperor grinned. 'Find Duke Wodehallow. His Albion forces will be the vanguard tomorrow. Might as well trim some of the fat from Emaneska while we are here, General!' he ordered, fixing his sights firmly on Scalussen once more. 'This will be a short war, I feel.'

CHAPTER 25
A BATTLE JOINED

It is reported Skölgard Emperor Kuhrnan raised the greatest army that ever stood upon an Emaneska battlefield. Six hundred times six hundred souls fought at dawn in the narrow Skewerboar Pass. Half of them lay dead and picked at by vultures by noon, all for Kuhrnan's impatience.
EXCERPT FROM THE MILITARY MANUAL 'SKULLS OF VORHAUG'

The sun arose upon a new north. The white flesh of the ice fields had been tarred with shades of brown and pitch. The stain had crept north from the Tausenbar at first light: a sea of moving bodies, steel armour and leather plate. Green, black, gold, and blue splashed here and there where banners streamed in the morning's sharp winds. Northern winds howled to the thunder of their advance, as if bemoaning their presence.

The cold and the rugged terrain tried their best to slow the tide of humanity, but by the time the sun was at its peak, the Arka horde had spread in a monstrous crescent across the frozen fields, cornering Scalussen against the black foothills. They seemed without end. Beyond count, were Malvus' hordes.

To the continued dread of the watchers, they replaced every mile of ice between the mountains and Scalussen. When veritable orchestras of trumpets called them to halt, snow trembled from the fortifications of Scalussen.

The emperor had arrived, and it appeared as though he had brought all of Emaneska with him.

Far out of range of anything but dragons or Weights, Malvus made his camp. Even without spells or spyglasses, the faint outline of tents and war-machines could be made out. Trenches were being dug, ranks of stakes outlined. Flags raised on poles to stand crackling in the wind.

Farden and Inwick stood with fingers pressed to their temples, pupils swollen twice the size and faded golden. They spoke in turn.

'Catapults and mangonels of Skölgard design.'

'Kroppe crossbowmen.'

'Helbeasts, but no daemons.'

'Dromfangar beastmen.'

'Fenrir, too,' Farden eyed the giant wolves, cooped in iron cages or held on chains as thick as his arm.

'And plenty of those Scarred. Maybe a score of them now.'

'How many?' Durnus hailed them, still tottering up the stairs to the gatehouse. For a man that was so pale as to be almost translucent and walked with a cane, his ears were still mind-bogglingly sharp.

Farden shook his head. 'Too many to count,' he whispered, conscious of eavesdropping soldiers. Scalussen teetered on a knife-edge between disembowelling fear and the righteous anger that had brought them to the top of the world. Farden could almost taste the sweat in the air, and he could certainly smell the piss on the stone.

'Six... eight hundred thousand. Maybe more,' mumbled Inwick, one of her hands shaking. She bundled it into a fist and said nothing of it.

Farden leaned closer to Durnus. 'What's the word for when you run out of thousands?'

'A million, or so the Rolian numeralists teach. But surely not...' The old vampyre's words were thieved by the wind, and by the sheer expanse of the army that had gathered on their doorstep.

'Twenty years,' he said. 'We've spent it building a fortress. He's spent it building *this*.' Durnus' took in every part of the horde, his head swivelling from his right shoulder to his left.

'Can you feel it, Farden?' asked Inwick.

The mage nodded. He had felt the pressure building like a storm for days. Now the hordes stood before him, and the feeling of the combined magick was a constant weight against his skin, as if the air had thickened. He was surprised the weight of the magick and that of the hordes hadn't cracked the ice.

For another hour, they watched, darkly fascinated as the horde took root. There was pleasure to be taken in the fact that a great many hundreds of them looked ill-prepared, shivering as they sat or camped upon bare ice. The wind was teaching them a cruel lesson, whipping up snow-devils to tear lines from hooks, canvas from shelter. If Farden looked as far south as he could, past the smoke of their fires and the horde's ragged tails, he could see limp forms left behind upon the ice. The north had already claimed its first blood.

Just as Farden was about to turn his back, a gold and green bannered procession emerged from their front lines, like an impudent tongue poking from a mouth. Barricaded by soldiers, mages, and three dozen Scarred, two armoured chariots crept half the distance to Scalussen, and then stopped. They were joined by an iron-coloured dragon, who roamed back and forth like an impatient hound.

Farden didn't need his magick to see who each figure was. He had fought all of them personally but one. 'Gods. Malvus wants to talk, does he?'

Inwick was scraping her armoured fingers across the crenellations. 'His kind always do. Otherwise how else would we know how mighty and clever they are?'

'Keep it calm, Inwick. As much as I also want to separate his head from his neck, that won't win this war. They've come too far. So have we. The very ideas of the empire and Arka need to be eradicated, as much as it pains me to say.'

'Who's going, then?' she rasped.

'It'll do Malvus good to see you again, Durnus. Modren. All of us. He wants to talk. Let us talk.'

Farden slammed down the visor of his helmet and descended from the gatehouse. Hearing the horn, Towerdawn swooped from the Frostsoar, wings flared and beating like a landslide. His head, belly and tail were encased in burnished armour that flowed with the movement of his scales.

'He seeks to parlay with us?' the dragon boomed, armour rattling as he spoke. His eyes burned beneath his visor. Nerilan, perched atop his back, clad in matching armour and wielding her long glaive, looked far from impressed.

'An ultimatum, I'm sure,' she said. 'One last offer of servitude to make himself look the benevolent emperor.'

Durnus shooed them to the gate. 'Of course. Let us hear his lies. It has been a while since I heard a good joke.'

Farden cackled behind his visor.

With the golden dragon walking like a beast of burden, the gates were cracked open and their entourage emerged. The journey across the ice was tense and full of silence. It was eerie to have the hordes and fortress so quiet. Untold thousands of eyes watched on.

Even before they drew close, Farden could feel the magick of the Scarred pulsating, washing across the ice. He let his magick unfurl. He felt Inwick and Modren do the same. Their power clashed like two flames competing.

What drew all of Farden's attention was the fact that Malvus looked younger. Not the fat son of Wodehallow, his father's effigy. Not the grinning and tooth-filed grin of Saker, so-called Lord of the Winds, nor Toskig, as barrel-like as ever. Nor even that Jeasin was missing. It was Malvus, and how the creases had faded from his face, taking years with them. There was no denying it and much to suspect. Youth did not come easily to those but the gods.

Each stared at their equal: Towerdawn and Nerilan stared at Fellgrin and Saker. Modren and Inwick at the Scarred. Farden at Malvus.

Farden cleared his throat. 'You've come a long way for disappointment, Malvus!' he hollered. He saw Modren nodding appreciatively.

'You are right about that, Farden. I expected more than… *this*. Is this what you've spent your time on? Just a tower and some walls?' Malvus shook his head. 'I will show you mercy if you capitulate now,' came his offer.

The Written mages found themselves laughing. Even Nerilan found a smirk in her.

'You don't know the meaning of the word.' Farden countered. 'I will not grant you the same. I won't even give you a chance to leave. You've come for a fight and you will get it. Take your mercy and blow it out your arse.'

This Modren very much appreciated, snorting before he caught himself. *And why not invite a little humour into death's court?* thought Farden.

Malvus took a moment to chew his gums. Wodehallow and Saker looked on, like a toad and cat waiting to pounce on the same meal.

The emperor made a show of shaking his head. 'Do you really think you can win this battle? Your... *castle* is already surrounded. We will crush you within days. It is inevitable.'

'Try us, and see what happens.' Farden stared at the Scarred, silently wishing they try him. 'We're ready for you, Malvus. We have been for years. Upon our walls is where you realise the error of your ways, and that your ideals mean nothing but lies and death. That you are a poison to Emaneska, a plague, a blight that I will take significant pleasure in eradicating. We will restore freedom and peace to this land, even if it means cutting through every last one of you.' Farden let his voice spread with a subtle spell, soaring across the ice to the ears of the front ranks.

The emperor raised his hand, and a thunderclap of arms on shields rolled across the ice. The Arka formed into lines in one swift movement. 'Proud words. You almost suit the name of Outlaw King.'

The mage chuckled. 'Up here? They call me the Forever King,' he said, watching Malvus' eye twitch. *Worth it, despite how sour the name tasted.*

Farden began to step backwards, the others with him, but he froze at the emperor's parting words.

'Give my regards to that Hâlorn girl of yours,' he said. The wink he added was detestable, and had Modren not held him back, Farden would have taken on his entire entourage just to scrape it from Malvus' face. Flames spiralled around his arms and fists.

Instead, they retreated as the Arka advanced, running for the walls. The colossal gates slammed behind them with a sonorous boom that shook the earth. The cogs within spun and cranked cantankerously as the steel bolts, each the size of tree trunks, barred the gates.

'Farden,' Modren hissed in his ear. 'He knows about Mithrid. His spies must have told him.'

'Told them nothing of use, I bet. Even so I want her off the walls and in the Underspire, guarded.'

'She won't like that one bit.'

'Mithrid will like a knife in the back a lot less. It's for her safety,' growled Farden.

'I can guard her.'

'Not today.' Farden had already spotted her in amongst the ranks, standing with the large man-boy who insisted on trying to kneel. He was not the only one. Several mages bent the knee.

The mage swept her along as he continued his march. 'I want you in the Underspire for this battle.'

Mithrid's boots scraped to a halt. 'What? But I've been training for days. I'm ready!'

Even lowered to a whisper, Farden's voice felt too loud. He bent close to her ear. 'Malvus himself wished you his best.'

The girl had the look of a deer finding an arrow in its side. '*What?*'

Farden huffed. 'Use more vocabulary in the future. He knows you are important and that makes you are a target. Now go! No arguments, or I'll have you dragged to the Underspire.'

Modren muttered his apologies to her as she stormed off. The lump of a child called after her, but she didn't turn. Two of the soldiers nearby watched her long after the horde had stolen back the attention of the wall.

Farden took the gatehouse steps two at a time, to the rising clang of spears to stone, of swords upon shields, and of fists on breastplates. He pinched his fingers in his lips and whistled loudly until a shadow fell over him. Farden climbed upon the crenellations and to a few confused gasps, he jumped.

Ilios caught him almost perfectly, and as soon as Farden had a grip, they rose above the walls to the beat of the gryphon's wings. Drawing his sword, he cast his voice far and wide.

'Once before, this fortress fell in the face of greed. To hordes like this one. Not a second time! Remember the blood spilled that brought you here! Remember every lie you swallowed before finding the truth. Remember every soul fallen for the empire's profit! Remember it all today and days to come, when we will be warm at our own hearths, free people! Everything that future requires is here, before you, ready to bleed in payment! Take it! Forge a new Emaneska at my side!'

Sending snow and ice scattering across the fortress, Towerdawn's remaining dragons took flight, hovering or swooping in tight circles, flexing claws and spitting flame. Ilios darted amongst them, shrieking his war song. Even the minotaurs joined them with zealous bellows. It sparked a cascade of voices, from war cries to wordless yells. Every mouth turned to the sky. Scalussen roared.

Ilios reared before the gatehouse, wings spread and beak agape. His claws had barely scraped the stone before Farden had jumped to the parapet. Modren sidled up to him, both staring across the chanting hordes.

'Nice speech, Forever King,' he whispered.

Farden rolled his eyes.

'Be honest. Did you rehearse it?'

Farden had; sat staring at his faded Book, with carved candles glowing about at him, but he admitted it not. 'Prepare for battle!' he roared.

Within moments, a forest of lances sprouted across the walls. Shield spells shook the air. Bows creaked as they stretched. Braziers flared as spears, arrows, and missiles dipped in tar were lit. In the courtyard, the war-machines rumbled as they were pushed into position and cranked. Scalussen seethed at the challenge. Fear had transformed into gut rivalry: a burning need to survive.

Whatever challenge the Arka offered was staunched by the sound of multitudes upon stubborn ice. Malvus and his captains stayed where they were, letting the hordes flood around them. The charge was meant to be swift, but with boots sinking and ankles twisting, and with long ladders to carry, the first ranks seemed to take an age to begin their sprint to the gates. They did so with a rising shout, far feebler than Scalussen's.

'Archers! Mages! Loose!' Modren yelled at Farden's signal.

The charging roar was punctuated with cries as the archers and mages let fly their volleys. Fireballs, bolts of lightning, and arrows slaughtered hundreds.

With a clash of steel colliding, the Arka met the gate and staunch walls. The soldiers hammered uselessly on Scalussen steel. While mages set their fire and force spells to work, the runes carved into the fortress beat back their magick. Farden watched with grim satisfaction as weaker mages were catapulted into their comrades.

The ladders that dared to touch the walls were immediately repelled, either by burning them to cinders, pouring hot tar down their rungs, or by knocking them sideways. Those low enough jumped, some impaling themselves on friendly spears and lances. Those too high hung grimly on as they tumbled, hoping to land on something soft. Their hopes were dashed as savagely as their brains and innards.

As the cries of bloodthirst turned to pain and panic, Farden knew the battle was well and truly joined. It had happened too quickly, too rashly on Malvus' part; it did not seem real. The battle seethed before him as Farden stood upon the crenellations, shield spell in hand, hair whipping his face, staring down at the so-called emperor. *This* was what he had built. He would show Malvus before the sun set on this first day.

'Mages!' Farden bellowed to the winds.

All along the walls, mages stood on their platforms, gleaming in their full suits of Scalussen armour. The air grew hot as fire spells ignited by the score. Lightning crackled. Quake and vortex spells turned the battlefield into a quivering maelstrom.

Farden gave his signal, unleashing the flames that burned around his right gauntlet. The metal glowed, the magick burned so hot. His spell sent dozens screaming, straight into Modren's swirling dervish of fire. Inwick hurled bolt after bolt, not satisfied by the blood she had already shed. Her face was a mask of ferocity. *Pure murder*. Years of pent up frustration were dealt out in savage doses. Durnus kept his word. He sent whirlwinds battering through the makeshift shield-walls. More fruit for the archers to pick off.

Pandemonium had been well and truly sown amongst the fields of Arka. Their charge stalled as those closest to the carnage tried to retreat. With more pressing in, not an arrow nor spell nor slingstone missed. Farden defected a volley of Arka firebolts and took stock of the walls.

He watched the war-painted snowmads hurling iron pellets the size of melons over the fortifications. One flattened an Arka soldier into a gory heap. Beside them, lycans hurled javelin after fire-hardened javelin. Throughout the crowded walls, ten-bodies deep, his mages wielded their vital shields, fending off stones and arrows and spells. Only ricochets and misfires made their way into the courtyards.

Tremendous clouds of purple flame exploded across the Arka ranks. Even when soldiers threw themselves to the ice, the fire refused to die. This was no magick, but simple Paraian science. Behind him, on the lower ramparts, beastpeople and minotaurs spun in circles with ropes lashed to smoking clay pots. At the apex of their twirl, they let loose the pots, and shaded their eyes to watch them soar high over the walls and shield spells to whooping cries.

Dragons turned the handful of armoured battering rams to bonfires. Soldiers fell screaming and aflame from their heights. Throughout the frenzy, finches and sparrows darted. Eyes were pecked. Faces savaged. More screams joined the din of death.

Farden drowned in such clamour. Firebolts streamed from his hands, sending soldiers flying. Wherever he looked, he saw glorious battle. Scalussen was an island in an angry sea of steel and misplaced fervour. The smile he had been wearing faltered as he peered closer, saw past the sheer numbers. The proud war they waged was against farmboys and old women. There was barely a competent mage or archer or swordsman amongst them. These were not Scarred. These were not seasoned soldiers. No dragons had left Saker's side. Malvus was testing him. The true army waited beyond these lie-sold fools, throwing themselves against the gates in false hope. They might as well have brandished pitchforks, for all the threat they posed.

These Arka had realised it. More and more began to turn tail and run. Another cog in Malvus' display became apparent, as those who made it back to their lines first found Arka spears in their guts and throats.

'He's slaughtering his own kind to make a point,' Inwick snarled, looking almost gleeful. For a moment, Farden thought she might hurl herself from the parapet in pure bloodthirst.

Farden stared on in grim and private satisfaction, as hundreds, perhaps thousands realised they were trapped between two enemies. In desperation, those who retreated charged the fortress once more. The gates held fast, barely scratched by the onslaught. Soldiers died digging at the steel with broken sword blades and bare hands.

'Stow your weapons and spells!' Farden ordered. His generals and captains passed his words around the fortress until they came barking back at him.

'Farden! You can't be serious?' Inwick seethed.

'Let Malvus display his cruelty while we show this horde what real mercy looks like.'

The fortress slowly fell silent, letting the Arka flail uselessly at the walls until they realised the Scalussen were just staring from behind their shields.

'We'll show you mercy this one day!' Farden told them. Though mutters spread through Farden's forces, nobody disobeyed him. Not another arrow was loosed. One iron ball was accidentally dropped, crushing a skull with a shortened yelp, but otherwise a silence reigned.

The Arka took their chance to retreat. Dragging their wounded, they striped the ice red with scarlet streaks. Malvus, his point made, did not have the stomach to continue his slaughter. He let the first waves drag themselves back to their war camps, beaten and chided, but alive to fight again. His horde had witnessed the emperor's callousness, and whether that would work in his favour or drive them on like a cat of nine tails, only the days would tell.

Farden looked down upon his fortress as cheers began to rise into the air. Content and swollen with pride, the Scalussen made clearing the detritus of battle away look a joyous task. Some of the tribes began to chant. Farden wanted to curse them all to silence, but he did nothing except watch the Scalussen dead carried down the walls for the night's pyres. Two hundred, perhaps, but for Farden, it looked like a thousand. Such was the tortured, wrinkled pane of glass those in charge look through in times of war.

The celebration stalled slightly as the fallen were noticed. The cost of their win was witnessed. Some saw it a fraction of a price and continued to clap backs and growl for tomorrow. Others, like Farden, fell silent. Heads shook. Muttered prayers were offered.

If Mithrid had stared further daggers at the Outlaw King, she might have been accused of trying to assassinate him.

The battle had been nothing but hearsay to her. Ricocheted arrows and slingstones had scattered across the courtyards and come to die at her feet. Ice and snow dusted the polish of her armour. She had heard the cries of the soon to be dead, of magick against matter. She had seen the occasional spell bounce wayward from a shield.

That was the summary of her first victory. Sights and sounds. It might as well have been a fireside story, for all the involvement she felt in it. *And not to forget the smell.* That familiar and unavoidable stench of copper blood and voided bowels racing with the wind.

A woman was being carried past on a stretcher. A spear had run the poor soul through, with half still sticking up like a flagpole. A mage hovered over her, dragging at her hair. Mithrid lowered her eyes to keep from staring.

To the sound of hollering, Bull, Savask, and Aspala rounded the corner with a swathe of fellow soldiers. Recruits, they were no longer. They had whet their appetite on the Arka's blood and Mithrid was jealous of it. Bull, despite holding a longbow, wore a smear of blood across his mail, though whose it was seemed to be a concern for debate. Unlike many of the others, who still held suspicion for Mithrid, they failed to notice her until she blocked their path, arms folded.

'You seem pleased with yourselves.'

Aspala's oaken skin beaded with sweat. 'Vengeance is pleasing, girl.'

'Yeah, when you're allowed it,' Mithrid fell in with them. Savask gave her a wide berth. 'What's your problem?'

Savask pursed his lips. He was sweating so much he looked like he had taken a shortcut through the bathhouses.

'You don't still think I'm dangerous, do you?' Mithrid whispered over the marching clang of soldiers seeking berths, bowls, or booze.

'Well, I don't know, do I? You haven't told us a damn thing. Remina's still gone. All we hear are rumours of you knifing her or using your weird magick. That you're here to betray us all. Trenika doesn't like you one bit.'

'Fuck Trenika. That's why she blames me. It's ridiculous; I would never kill Remina. I was with you all night!' Mithrid looked up at her oldest friend. 'Bull? Surely not you as well?'

The big lad looked fidgety in his armour and mail. 'I—'

'You cretch! We grew up together, remember? Or are you so eager to believe absurd rumours that you've forgotten that?' she hissed, trying to keep this conversation from leaking to the passers-by. It was hopeless. Trenika and her brother Lurn had made a hobby out of following them around.

Trenika butted into their circle. 'What we're all wondering is what makes Mithrid Fenn so special. So secretive with the generals and King Farden.'

The crowd parted to leave Trenika and Mithrid facing off. 'Apparently nothing, otherwise I would have been on the walls with you.'

Trenika's eyes wandered down to the axe hanging from Mithrid's belt. 'None of us here were given a blade by the Forever King. Or train alone with Inwick or Modren. Why don't you sleep in the same quarters as we do? You barely eat with us, and yet you didn't even fight today. Maybe you are dangerous.'

Mithrid snorted. 'Careful, Trenika, you sound jealous.'

The Midgrir girl came close as she dared, wielding that accusing finger of hers. 'What did you do to Remina? You shook her hand that night.'

'I'd like to know the answer to that as much as anyone,' Mithrid said, barging past her. 'That way I could kill them.'

Mithrid walked through the crowds to where the mess lines had been set up in the training yards, at the roots of the Frostsoar. To her confusion, Bull and others had followed her. Perhaps they had not completely abandoned her yet.

The bowl of soup slopped hot lava on her sleeve. It took all her resolve not to throw it in the air. She daubed at her wrist as she stalked across the frozen flagstones and through the rings of inner walls to the outer. They still teemed with activity, but she squeezed in between a notch in the parapet so she could stare out across the Arka. Daring herself to look, vittles be damned, she peered over the stone to see the full carnage the Scalussen had wrought.

Black and white remained the land, but now with a thick and heavy streak of dirty crimson smeared across it. Mounds of dead had washed up against the walls like a nightmarish tide, mostly surrounding the gate. The wounded who mattered enough were still being dragged away across the ice. Many, many more were left to freeze or bleed to nothing.

The others followed still. Mithrid huffed. They were unwanted as wasps, and just as determined. Bull sat so close he practically barged Mithrid along the stone. Aspala remained standing and staring. Savask cursed his old bones as he bookended her.

'Don't let them prickle you, Mith,' Bull said.

He had not called her that since the *Winter's Revenge*. It jarred her sense of place. For a moment it was a slate-coloured sea of water she looked across, not an ocean of soldiers and armour. Mithrid looked back and caught sight of a red and gold speck crossing the fortress courtyard. 'There's more than them to be mad at,' she said.

'Did the king really give you that axe?' Bull asked, poking at the fine-etched swirls on the handle like ivy strangling a tree.

'He did. After I broke the handle in half in Efjar.'

'With the minotaurs.'

At least one rumour was true. 'Yes, with the minotaurs, Bull.'

Bull thought deeply on the situation, watching the mighty horned creatures heave on heavy catapults. 'I like them. Saw one fire a bow twice the size of mine. How can we not win this battle with beasts like that on their side?'

'A lot of ways, boy,' droned Aspala.

Savask slurped his soup down. Potatoes and some salted meat floated in it. 'I say we should march straight at Malvus and cut his head off. Put an end to him and call it a day. We can all go home.'

'Farden said that wouldn't work.'

'It would not. The emperor's lies have spread like rotgrass, growing across Emaneska, bearing fruit of his ideals.'

That was the longest Aspala had ever spoken for. 'Is it the same in Paraia?' Mithrid asked. 'So much world I haven't seen.'

Aspala spat a bone over the parapet, letting it lie with countless others. 'Malvus keeps vassals and mages there. They force my people to fight in arenas for the pleasure of northerners, or rich brethren who forget their blood and kind for coin. Magick is life for us. Gift of the gods. You cannot outlaw something like that.'

'Seriously,' Savask was muttering. 'Just charge straight in there. Slice off the head from the serpent. And that Grand Duke Wodehallow's while we're at it. Spineless dog 'e is.'

Aspala held her bowl in both furred hands, clearly enjoying the warmth. 'What of Albion? I hear it rains most days of the year.'

Savask weighed his head from side to side. 'Not *quite* every day. But it's the same as all of Emaneska. Wodehallow flaunts Malvus' power. Not a duke stands against him. Why would they, when he gets them fat on slave-gold and Arka trade? Conscription, too, and a bounty for every body they send to Krauslung. Funny thing is, I ran away so I wouldn't 'ave to fight. Now I'm here.'

'Did you kill any, today?' asked Mithrid.

'Three a piece.' Bull and Savask looked to Aspala. 'She got quite a few.'

'Twenty.' The woman did not look proud. She did not look pleased. She even patted the bow across her shoulders as if it had done the killing and not her. She looked more like a craftsman still looking for cracks in a masterpiece. 'It is the way fate demands it.'

'Is that what you believe?'

Aspala nodded. 'We believe in many gods, Mithrid. More than in your pantheon. And not all our gods are trapped in the stars. Some are the cold sea wind. Others a pattern of dust upon tiles. Fate is just one face of the gods. We all follow her threads. You Emaneska call her destiny.'

Mithrid pondered that. 'Are you saying we don't have a choice in our lives?' There was no comfort in knowing that. It did not feel like destiny, but doom. Her father had been cursed to die, and she was doomed to suffer.

'No, girl,' Aspala replied, beaming soup-stained teeth. 'She just knows us that well.'

'That was a fraction of his power, and the sooner we stop patting ourselves on the back, the better we will be for it!' Farden took aim at a wall and drove a gauntlet into it with a clang. The metal left an imprint in the stone. Shards crumbled to the floor.

Durnus blinked at him, tongue tracing the point of a fang. 'Did you come here to shout at me alone, or did you simply forget to invite the rest of the council members? And thank you for *that*.' He pointed at the gouge in his wall.

'It's Malvus. Prodding me when I wish he'd throw a punch. I can feel him toying with me.'

'More to the point, it seems to be working.'

'It is.' Farden seethed.

Durnus wove his fingers into a ribcage of white skin and bone. 'What is truly troubling you, Farden? I see worry in your face. Otherwise you would have gone to Modren and discussed ways of punishing Malvus. Something I would advise against, but that is me. Instead you came to me for the one thing I have always given you. Reassurance. And a—'

'A tongue-lashing?'

'Which you *deserved*. I have known you since before you were born, when I saw the same pervasive doubt in your uncle's eyes. Malvus, like those who have come before him, have always known how to prey on that. Loki knew that. Do not let them irritate you into rash action, Farden. That is what they want.'

Farden chose a chair to punish and almost broke it with his weight. He sprawled like a drunkard. He stared around at Durnus' shelves of books, and tables of books, stretching all the way into the limits of the mothlight. He poked at an old map of the Skap Islands. Durnus watched him closely.

'Today, on the walls. I have not seen your face like that since Kserak. Maybe not even since the Last War when the sky was falling on our heads. You are worried as well.'

'I prefer to call it educated concern. We would be stupid not to be. Overconfidence has been many a soul's downfall before, especially in war.' Farden sighed. 'So many driven to the death already, and far too many on our side.' He flinched as he drove his finger through the fragile paper. 'Gods.'

'Do you want to skip ahead and burn my haunt to ashes… ?' The vampyre tutted. Durnus was rarely speechless, and yet this was one of those times. Farden did not seem comforted.

'Any progress on a weapon?' he asked.

Durnus pinched his tired eyes. He had begun to hate that question long before now. 'I have been at this years, Farden. Another week has not made much difference. Aside from summoning something hideous from the other side that is altogether more dangerous, our only weapons are sitting right here in this fortress. You, and this girl, Mithrid. And myself, if you will let me.'

'Pardon the intrusion, gentlemen,' said Scholar Skertrict as he came bubbling through the door with an heap of aged books, 'but I believe I have found something that may help in your quest.'

While Farden looked angered by the invasion of the scholar – and his possible eavesdropping – Durnus waved Skertrict away dismissively. 'I have looked at all the elvish tomes before.'

'Not this one,' said the man, holding up a purple book clad in silk, badly aged and feasted upon by moths. 'At least not closely enough, if I may be so bold.'

'Explain yourself.'

'The Teh'Mani Spear. The Blade of Gunnir. This book points to it.'

'It is a metaphorical account, nothing more.'

'What's this spear?' Farden asked.

'A fable, and that is coming from a person who knows that within all myths lies a spark of truth,' Durnus lectured. He was glad to have an audience besides the scholar for once. Skertrict was enthusiastic to the point of irritating: the sort of chap that always answered a comment with a story of his own. Yet he was one of the finest researchers he had ever worked with. His memory for lore was almost as acute as Durnus' own. And, he wasn't afraid of long journeys hunting lost tomes.

Farden still looked clueless. Skertrict pounced on the opportunity. He opened the book to a page depicting a crude sketch of a spear.

'Teh'Mani translates to Skyrender, or the God-Corpser, depending on the text. Largely known as Gunnir, a spear made by the elven clan of Ivald. Actually, it's a lance, to be exact. It was so powerful it cut souls from bodies and the summits from mountains. Broke the sword of noble Sigrimur into nine pieces in the hands of the Allfather. It supposedly cut the very fabric of the air to carve doorways between the worlds of gods and men.'

Durnus shook his head. 'One world, actually. An arid plane, or so says the poem, where the elves were banished by the gods when the daemons were dragged into the sky. They used this spear to escape, and this book speaks of its final resting place, hidden by acolytes of the gods, thousands of years ago.'

'A fine tale. If I had a coin, I'd give you both one.' Farden's face broke into a broad smile.

'It's not a story.'

'You think I've got time to disappear and find this spear? Retrieving my Book from Albion was a close enough call,' he said, momentarily forgetting his company.

Skertrict was stuck smiling, his finger still prodding the open page and sketch.

'You have time to disappear every morning with Fleetstar,' Durnus couldn't help but mutter. He dug a claw into his desk. 'I will give it another look, Skertrict, fear not. Continue with your tasks. That Huskar commentary isn't going to decode itself.'

'At your service,' said the scholar, sketching a broad bow and grinning at Farden until he disappeared into a side chamber.

'Where did you find him again?' Farden asked.

'We practically dragged him from the ashes of Arfell when Malvus burned it, remember?'

'Don't remember him being so annoying. You trust him?'

'I do.' Durnus cracked a knuckle. 'Now, speaking of weapons…'

'If you dare start talking about necromancy,' Farden began, but Durnus slowly shook his head.

'Besides the fact I am a vampyre, Farden, and I know more of death and blood-curses and dark magick than even you suspect, you should trust me more. I meant another weapon. Somebody as old and as wise and as half-dead as I am.'

Farden caught the vampyre's sideways look. 'You've managed it?'

'I believe I have,' he said. Most of the luggage Durnus felt beneath eyes was due to late nights poring over the Grimsayer. 'You will not like it, but it will work. Hopefully Tyrfing can speak some sense into you.'

'As long as I don't have to die to talk to him,' Farden said, already halfway to the door.

'I do not think so…' Durnus trailed off, momentarily distracted by the page at which Skertrict had left the book open. It was upside-down, but recognisable as the spear against a strange blotch. He had seen it before, studied it at length. Now upturned, he saw it: the shape of a coastline he had seen before in misty dreams.

'Durnus.'

Farden's voice shook him away from the book, and with much biting of his lip, he followed.

The room was bare to the high winds. Windows without panes stared north, where fire raged as always. Farden tore his eyes away from Irminsul and assessed Durnus' contraption instead. it looked like a quickdoor fallen over, but instead of a pool of magick, there appeared to be just a pool of ice water. And by ice water, he meant the chunks of white ice floating in it. A crust had developed around the edge.

'Durnus…'

'Told you you would not like it,' Durnus sighed as Farden tested the water with his finger.

With the doors locked firmly behind them, he began to remove his sabatons and greaves.

'I suggest you keep that armour on. We're treading the line of death here. You will need all the life you have.'

Farden squinted at the vampyre's tired face. 'Have you done this before?'

'No.'

'I don't know whether to be glad or more anxious than I already am.'

With his helmet wrapping itself around his neck and face, he closed the visor and stood before the pool. The Grimsayer lay on a pedestal with all manner of copper wires running from it to the pool. Farden could hear its sibilant voice, muttering nothings to him.

'Shh,' he chided it.

'What?' Durnus raised an eye.

'The book. Don't you hear it?'

'I try to ignore it. Souls tend to talk too much if you start listening.'

'So that's what that is. Wonderful. The book is haunted.'

Durnus shrugged. 'A little.' He approached the book with spread hands. Crackles of energy pulsated across his paper skin. 'One more thing, I do not know how long I can hold this.'

Today was full of good news. 'Fair enough.'

'Show me Tyrfing,' Durnus whispered. The pages began to turn. As the lights emerged, Durnus let his magick flow into the huge tome. The Grimsayer quivered. The sparks spun out from the book and into the pool. Trails of amber light followed them. Within moments, the pool was aglow and spinning gently with the furious rotation of the lights.

The vampyre was straining already. 'Go.'

Hating the water even before its icy fingers stabbed beneath his armour, Farden sucked down a breath and jumped. The water did not merely puncture him with knives of cold, but tried to crush him. Through the bubbles and swirling current, the lights coiled and dazzled him. His breath poured from his lungs. Drowning seemed imminent. It was but a momentary struggle to die.

Farden opened his eyes to find himself windmilling his arms and one leg in the air. He froze, finding nought but a cave of darkness around him. He cleared his throat.

'You haven't aged a day,' said a figure behind him, etched in a ghost of orange light.

Even though his features stuttered, faded here and there, Farden knew him instantly. That sketch of a beard born from laziness and frozen in death. Those scars across his wrists and face. The hair, blowing in a wind that no mortal soul had ever tasted, and never wished to. Farden found a rare smile beaming across his face.

'Uncle.'

Tyrfing was squinting. *'I don't know how you're here, but I hope it has something to do with Durnus. You aren't dead, that's for sure.'*

'Thank fuck for that.' Farden put his chin to his chest. *'He toys with magick that verges on the dark.'*

'Let him, he's tasted enough of it to know its poison better than you,' his uncle replied. *'Remember what I told you of magick. There is no true dark or light, only shades and what we do with them, just as it is with human nature.'*

Tyrfing's time serving Hel in the underworld had not tempered his blunt fire. The same that ran through Farden's veins.

'I take it you didn't make your way all the way down here to complain about Durnus, did you, Nephew?'

Farden smiled. *'It's good to see you.'*

Tyrfing chuckled. *'And you, too, lad. Though I think we're now equal in age.'*

'Almost. How's the goddess of death treating you?'

His uncle cocked his head. Behind him, an obscured yet heavy presence shifted. Something ship-shaped and swollen. In the darkness a river burbled.

'It has its perks,' Tyfing smirked, but it was brief. *Where are you? I have heard the dead gossip of what Malvus is doing to Emaneska. Heard it in the whispering of the souls. Seen it in their wounds.'*

Farden's explanation was cut off by another amber ghost sprinting beyond him, muttering, *'please no, please no,'* in fearful gasps.

'In old Scalussen. With Malvus' horde on our doorsteps. You should see what we've built, Uncle.' Farden's voice faded without echo. *'Fifty thousand of us stand on our walls.'*

'You think you can beat him, Nephew?'

'He's got almost a million bodies under his banner. What's left of the daemons and Lost Clans.'

Tyrfing winced. *'I can't even count that high.'*

'And new mages. Scarred, he calls them, made from the stolen Books of dead Written.' Farden sighed. *'In short, I'm not sure.'*

'You don't fool me. I see something else gnawing at you. What is it?'

Farden couldn't hide from his uncle. The darkness shifted again. More souls drifted intermittently, as if walking between unseen trees.

'It feels like almost all of Emaneska would need to die for us to win.'

'Would you do it, to keep freedom alive?'

Farden nodded. 'Any decision I make could destroy us in trying to save us. And that outcome depends on so many things as to teeter on a cliff's edge above a gnashing sea. For now, that it is beyond my control. There is no retreat. No surrender. Just a waiting game. Now I see the horde that Malvus has gathered, I can't get it out of my head that I may have destroyed us already. With nothing but a single thought, Uncle. I cannot tell Durnus. I cannot tell Modren. I cannot tell anybody but trust to time and fate,' Farden gasped for breath, though what it was he breathed was highly questionable. 'I miss the fine old days of living on the outskirts of this world, when it was as simple as burning a sorcerer out of his fort or chasing trolls across moors.'

His uncle had begun to stroll back and forth. 'This isn't the first time you've had to make hard decisions for the survival of Emaneska, you know.'

Farden shook his head like testing his neck for pains. 'And yet this seems impossible. What should I do?'

'What are your weapons?'

'A girl who is the antithesis of magick.'

Tyrfing looked harrowed. 'What did you say?'

'She is the opposite of magick entirely. She can drain it from you like a drunkard empties a tankard, Uncle. She is as fiery as the colour of her hair. If I didn't know any better, I'd say she was a long lost sister or cousin of ours.'

'You can't be serious? That's unheard of.'

'Believe me, nobody is more shocked and disturbed by this power of hers than I am.' Farden sighed. He had dragged so much baggage into the underworld he should have brought a porter. 'And then there is my idea. Which even now—'

The ground quaked. Ghosts slewed between Tyrfing and Farden.

His uncle looked concerned. 'That's not from down here, Nephew. What is that?'

The mage glowered at a ceiling of pure imagination. He wasn't even sure if that was even up or down. 'I don't know, but I have a feeling it's Malvus' doing.'

Tyrfing stepped as close as Durnus' spell would allow.

'Choose the weapon Malvus least suspects,' he said, voice hollow as if the echo came before the words. 'You—'

Farden reached for his uncle's hand at the same moment as Durnus' spell collapsed. The dark water swirling around Farden's knees engulfed him. It caught him mid-shout. Primeval panic flowed with the water's icy touch as it forced its way down his throat. For a moment he hung in a place between worlds, where stars dared not to shine. A colossal void lingered below him. The silent surface a memory. For a brief moment, Farden felt a deep peace before a surge whisked him towards a light he had almost forgotten existed.

※

Farden slumped on the wet stone like an asthmatic seal. Painful fingers clawed at Durnus' arms. The vampyre hammered on his breastplate as if that would help.

'Cough it up!' Durnus urged. He slapped a hand to Farden's forehead and send a jolt running through him.

'Bleeding fuck, that stings,' spoke the mage through clenched teeth.

'Did you see him? Did it work?'

'I did.'

Another dull boom ran through the fortress. Farden looked around, bewildered. 'What is that noise?'

'An Arka bombardment, my good mage. Started not half an hour ago.'

Farden stared at the steaming pool. The lights spun lazily over the Grimsayer like flies circling a plate of rotten food.

'How long was I in there?'

'Two hours, perhaps,' Durnus said, feeling his throat dry.

'Two hours?!' Farden dragged the vampyre to a chair and told him to sit. 'Skertrict! We need your help!' he yelled.

Durnus half arose. 'Modren is seeing to—'

Farden was already striding to the door. 'You stay here and rest up. Skertrict!'

'What did he say? Tyrfing?' Durnus called

Farden hung onto the doorframe for a brief moment. 'He told me what I needed to do.'

'I—' But with a clang of steel, the mage was gone.

Durnus parried the wave of tiredness that tried to claim him with a swift push from his chair. Another impact sent faint shudders across the stone. He tottered to the window to witness the commotion.

Arcing smoke trails stretched like polluted rainbows from the Arka lines to Scalussen. Farden's mages dominated the walls, led by Modren and Eyrum, each fighting to roar louder as they coordinated defence and attack at the same time. Durnus watched as a flaming rock came falling like a star evicted from the sky. A dozen shields were already trained upon it. Bouncing from layer of magick to the next, the rock skidded harmlessly to the foot of Scalussen's walls.

The vampyre staggered back to his chair with gloom at the corner of his eyes. Skertrict came dashing through the door, lank hair flying and owlish eyes wide.

'General!' gasped the scholar, running to Durnus' side. He gazed around the room, trying to put the pieces together. 'What happened?'

'I am drained,' Durnus rasped, inaudible. 'Dungeons.'

'What?'

'Dungeons! You know what I mean.'

'Of course.' Skertrict swallowed. It was not the first time Durnus had pushed his mind and body too far. 'Of course,' he said, before slinging an arm under the vampyre and escorting him to the door.

By the time the lift had juddered deep enough into the Frostsoar, the scholar was supporting Durnus completely, hauling his old bones towards the bleak cold of Scalussen's dungeons. Not a soul lined the bare corridor. The spells upon the colossal iron doors did the work of guards, impenetrable to anyone without keys. Beneath the light of a moth lantern, Durnus pressed his hands to the first cell he came to. Light spread across runes in its surface as bolts slid back, one by one until the vampyre had counted a dozen. His vision had become a tunnel of shadow, but with the scholar's help, Durnus staggered into the dark of the featureless room. A shiver of primal hunger ran him through him.

'Stay outside,' he ordered Skertrict.

'Scalussen cunts!' came a weak cry from the back of the cell. Hands cast spiny shadows across a gaunt face to the chime of shackles. *The assassin.*

Durnus could sense the brittle thud of her heartbeat, the viscosity of the blood sloshing through her veins. *Smell the copper in her.* His lips drew back, revealing his fangs.

The woman stared up at Durnus in the shadow of the torchlight as if he was the very face of death himself. As Skertrict closed the door, she began to tremble.

'Kill me and be done with it.'

Durnus was more than happy to oblige her, half-pouncing, half-falling upon the woman. His fangs punctured flesh. Strength flowed with her sour blood. Durnus pinned her, claws sinking into her wrists while her cries withered. Ravenous, the vampyre drank until he drained her, yet still a hunger pulled at him. Durnus bit harder, tearing her skin. Only the crunch of cartilage stopped him, making him recoil and fall upon the stone. He pushed himself up, watching aghast as her faintly glowing soul bled back into her body.

Durnus shuddered, spitting blood, all the while wondering how he had let himself delve so deep.

CHAPTER 26
THE CRAFT OF KILLING

Before the wilderness of magick sparked power in even the most humble of lines, magickal aptitude was carried within blood. The families of the Arka were bred for their abilities for centuries, and those bloodlines have spread into the world through bastards and marriages like an oak's roots. Hereni of Dromfangar is an interesting case. Tracing her lineage, I discovered a distant ancestor who served in the council of Arkmages Beristo and Ferisson. Lineage that branched into none other than General Toskig's line.
FROM THE WRITINGS OF GENERAL DURNUS GLASSREN, YEAR 924

There was nothing like the constant crash and boom of a siege bombardment to spoil a good night's rest.

Malvus rained fire and rock on the fortress for three days and three nights. Even in the Underspire, where the sound of war would echo through the earth, not a wink was slept. The only comfort was hoping the Arka were just as wakeful.

By day, chunks of mountain stone and glacial ice met the walls and shield spells. At dark, rocks wrapped in flaming linens and tar. Most met the spells and either broke or bounced somewhere harmless. The menacing ones were those that arced high, landing within the inner walls, or the jars of flaming oil that burst and cast fire in clouds. Or the metal lumps painted with pitch; the ones the mages wouldn't see until the last moment, when they came crashing into the walls without mercy.

So it was that one eye out of every two was perpetually locked on the sky. Even the fire crews and water mages, as they ran around battling oil-fires or smouldering defences, constantly looked over their shoulder or posted a lookout.

Scalussen was not silent during the onslaught. Arrayed in the courtyards were dozens of ballistae, catapults, and trebuchets of curving design, etched with Siren swirls and blacksmiths' runes. Minotaurs and mages had worked on those war-machines without pause. For every missile that struck the fortress, a Scalussen siege engine retorted. They added their own stone and iron to the crowded skies.

Mithrid flinched as the gate rung with a resounding bang. 'Hurricane's balls,' she cursed, and went back to polishing the shining axe in her lap. Akitha had done her father's steel proud, forging a metal handle and battering the blade into more of a sweeping arc. Red steel ran through the ash-black metal.

Modren poked at the metal with his spear. 'A skipper, bouncing along the ice instead of striking the shields.'

'Well, it does wonders for my head.'

Hereni tutted, in the middle of massaging her own temples. 'Not a head in this fortress doesn't have an ache in it.'

'Except for him.'

Bull lay nearby, sleeping like a pine bear through winter. The big lump even had the audacity to snore softly. In recent days, he had followed Mithrid closely. Either Remina's death had transformed him, or the killing had. The carefree smile of a blissful naivety had been chiselled away to plain stone.

Mithrid took another one of those breaths Elessi had recommended, slow through the nose and out through the lips. All it brought her was the overwhelming smell of embers and burned flesh. She coughed and looked back to the brutish onager catapult that stood not far behind the gates.

Theirs was a rotary existence, not just within the confines of day and night, but within the span of minutes. Repetition was the rhythm of war, from the clanking of the cranks and handles, to the loading, to the pregnant pause as the shields were gapped. The enormous whoosh as pins were driven, and the entire machine bucked as its arm slung the projectile over the wall tops. By the catapult's side stood Inwick, face drawn and pale in the moon's light. Twirling her fingers, she lent magick to the missile, speeding it up with wind and emerald force spells.

Mithrid would always listen for the crash, but there were too many noises to know for sure.

'How long can this go on?' she asked.

'Days more, girl. Don't jinx it,' Modren replied.

A hoarse cry broke over the walls. 'Cover!'

Each one of them instinctively ducked. Mithrid even covered Bull with two insufficient arms, waking him. Though shields popped above them on the gatehouse, Modren cuffed the air. A shield spell crackled over them.

With ricocheting crashes, an iron lump came cannoning to the courtyard. It was not close to them, but close enough to a trebuchet crew several machines down. The missile scored a direct hit on the trebuchet, pulverising it to firewood and fenceposts. Mages and soldiers ran scattering.

Modren bellowed for some healers and smiths to get to work. His job done, he stood with his hands upon Elessi's shoulders. His wife was busy meditating, wincing one eye occasionally. Mithrid couldn't help but watch them. Everybody around her was supremely and irritatingly calm compared to the situation around them. Elessi and Modren most of all. The rain of fire seemed nothing more than an inconvenience.

'Still sense the daemons?' asked the undermage.

Elessi nodded. 'Like wakin' nightmares in my mind, husband. But they ain't any closer. They languish. They feel… bored.'

'I'll happily occupy the foul wretches,' Hereni swore.

Modren was not in agreement. 'You're just sore because one kicked your arse. And I mean literally kicked your arse. You're lucky it was only a small one.'

'Yes, thank you once again, oh, Undermage, for reminding me,' said Hereni, with mock pomp. Mithrid found herself snickering, only to be made the subject of Hereni's glare.

'When was this?' she asked.

Modren touched a scar across his head, pinker than the rest. 'Kserak, two years ago.'

Hereni's eyes were closed. 'The massacre. I'd been in Scalussen three years.'

Everybody present swallowed words, cleared their throat, watched yet another missile speed into the night. Elessi spoke for them.

'Farden and The Written took a chance in tryin' to save that city. Whether it was the wrong choice doesn't matter. Lines of 'em were pouring out the city when Malvus arrived. Instead of attackin' Farden, he treated the city like they'd all spat in his eye. Trapped them and burned 'em all alive with dragon and daemon fire. Six thousand died. Now there's barely a hundred Kserakan left in Scalussen. None of us have been the same since, 'specially Farden.'

Hereni had finished putting an edge to her sword. She motioned for Mithrid's axe. It took the girl a moment to give it up, and as she watched, Hereni used the whetstone like an artist daubing final touches on a portrait. 'That was the first time I saw Malvus' cruelty. Not that of his roaming mages, but *his*. It was his choice to burn them all. I've been looking forwards to a chance to show him the consequences,' she said.

'You'll get it,' whispered Elessi. 'We all will.'

'Then what?' Bull asked. 'Let's say we win. What happens to the empire and to us afterwards?'

Elessi chuckled wistfully. 'Peace, lad. Like Emaneska hasn't known before.'

Mithrid had known peace. Peace was not caring what lingered beyond a door or border. It had been weeks, barely, since Troughwake, and that concept seemed as foreign as Paraia. 'And what will you do with it?'

'Enjoy it,' said Elessi, staring at her constantly distracted husband while pulling her furs about her. 'We've never known a day of marriage without war to soil it. Modren has promised me a cottage, somewhere near a waterfall. Somewhere away from this bloody ice.'

'I wanted a castle at first, but she changed my mind,' added Modren.

Elessi smiled. 'Always served mages. Never owned a stone nor brick in my life. A cottage will do just fine. Just somewhere we can call a home without people wantin' to burn it down.'

'Wouldn't that be nice,' Modren clasped her hand. Mithrid watched their eyes glint as they held a gaze.

'I want a boat,' blurted Bull. 'Or a dragon. Somewhere I can go places in.'

When Hereni laughed without mockery, the boy looked put out. 'What's yours then?'

'Ale,' replied Hereni. 'Mother and father used to brew it. Best ale in Dromfangar, or so they said. If there's anything I've learnt about Emaneska, is that it's sodden in drink in both war and peace. I want my face on barrels.'

'Sure about that?' Mithrid quipped. Hereni shoved her in mock disgust, yet the captain's gaze lingered on her, roaming Mithrid's face

'And you?' she asked. 'What will Mithrid Fenn do with her powers if the world was hers to roam freely?'

Mithrid had not even begun to think of such a preposterous thing as a future. She was still getting to grips with the present and past. It seemed as fanciful as fable, especially when she knew nothing of what the world consisted of.

'Grow things,' she said. 'Mother did, and I'm good at it.'

Hereni was still staring. A smirk hovered on her lips. 'Is that why there's now a verglass sapling in your room?'

Mithrid's reply was overridden.

'Inwick! Change out!' Modren's holler cut through her thoughts. 'You've been at that for hours.'

The Written mage didn't respond, waiting with heaving shoulders for the minotaurs to reload. Her white hair was lank with sweat. Her rasping tone could be heard over the muted din. 'Come on, come on.'

'Inwick! Pay attention!'

It was as if somebody had poked her out of a trance. Inwick spat in the rubble around her feet and stalked like a bird over hot sand. 'I can keep going, Modren.'

'I don't want you to. It's time for Hereni's shift.'

Inwick didn't even look at the mage. She muttered something under her breath before constructing an audible reply. 'I need to.'

'You need water and to sit the fuck down, is what you need, Written! That's an order.'

The snarl she gave him was feral, but she obeyed with an ashamed, 'Yes, Undermage,' and disappeared into the shadow of the walls.

'What's wrong with her?' pondered Mithrid, watching the chunks of ice and rubble scatter before Inwick's boots.

'Mage problems,' Hereni muttered quietly, replacing the axe in Mithrid's hands as she went to work the onager.

Though power ran through her veins, Mithrid still nurtured some jealousy over the skills of magick. It did not matter that Mithrid could have rid the mage of her power, it mattered that it was all she could do. She watched Hereni setting a tar-painted rock alight with nothing more than a flick of the hand.

Durnus sighed dramatically, as if reminding everybody he was there. The withered old man sat upon a rock, devouring a small book by the light of the moon. He had stayed apart from them all evening, poring over whatever story or riddle the book held. Ever since Troughwake, Mithrid left books well enough alone, but her curiosity still soared.

'And what of you, General Durnus?' she asked him.

Modren snorted. 'Him? He's three thousand years old. He's seen and done it all.'

'Knowledge never ages, Undermage. I would not expect a spellwrangler like you to understand that,' Durnus hissed, occupied with his book. Mithrid could not keep from staring at his fangs as he spoke. The chap still looked ancient, but she swore some of the deeper wrinkles had been worn away. *Three thousand.*

The vampyre sighed as he shut the book and arose, cane tapping on the ice. 'I will not hope for a future until I know there is one to hope for,' he muttered.

Mithrid and the others regarded his slow totter with furrowed brows.

Elessi abruptly took a sharp intake of breath, reaching for the scar across her neck as if it were still an open wound. 'Husband! They're movin'.'

'What is it?'

'The daemons. They're gettin' ready to fight. I can feel it.'

Modren raced for the gatehouse, disappearing up the steps. Mithrid ran after him before anybody could say otherwise. Only Hereni shouted after her.

The hordes sprawled before her, a sea of fire in the night. Between their ranks and tents, dark bars of siege towers had risen from the ice. Tall and wedge-shaped like doorstops, reaching as high as Scalussen's mighty walls. They shone with torchlight as if aflame.

Horns blew, and the tremor shook the fortress as the Arka began to advance.

Modren waved his sword in the air, temporarily blinding Mithrid as light pulsed from its blade. It was so bright, it felt like an entire week of sun in one blink.

His voice boomed across the courtyard. 'To arms! Defend the walls! Dragons to the air! Siege engines, fire at will!'

As Mithrid took up a stance and looked for something to throw, Modren took her by the arm. 'You shouldn't be here.'

The girl wanted to spit in his face, the disappointment was so wrenching. 'I need to be. This is what I came for. You know that better than anyone here, even Farden.'

'Mithrid—'

'Please, Modren.' She kept her eyes trained on his, ignoring every whip of her scarlet hair.

The undermage glanced to the Frostsoar, where a pillar of flame burned atop its summit, a gryphon screeched with splayed wings behind it.

'Stay with that lump of a friend of yours and Hereni. Don't try anything. No heroism. Just fight.'

Mithrid couldn't reply, her lips were so busy straining not to grin.

'Go, girl!'

'Aye,' she blurted, as she sprinted down the steps. She hollered to the lad, even prodding him with a foot. 'Up, Bull! We've got a war to fight.'

Hereni was all too quickly beside her, catapult forgotten, eyes narrow and protective. She said nothing but followed them up the wall. Between armoured shoulders and the swollen arms of lycans and minotaurs, they found their space, overlooking the slowly shrinking gap of ice between them and battle.

'Any good with a bow?' asked the mage.

'I've shot once or twice.'

Elessi surprisingly barged in beside her. Modren guarded her side. 'Then pick one up. That shiny new axe won't be much use yet,' she suggested at Mithrid's confused look.

'What? Thought I was simply some wife? Some maid?' Elessi raised the black-lacquered bow and drew an arrow from the barrels set along the walls.

'I—'

'Just grab a bow, darlin'.'

Mithrid took the bow and tested its string. A barrel stuffed with arrows stood between them. Hereni stuck to her magick. Bull took up his longbow and stretched it to full. Some of the true archers around them nodded in respect.

'Shields!' Modren bellowed as the sky was engulfed by light. Countless flaming arrows rose up in a wave.

Towerdawn and his dragons had other ideas, swooping like dark jewels from the night and laying waste to the cloud of arrows with fire of their own. Those that got through clattered uselessly against the shields.

'Shields down and archers fire! Mages!'

Thanks to their height adding range, the Scalussen volley drove deep into the first five ranks. Fireballs and bolts of lightning carved furrows in the lines. The surge of screams and howls put some energy in the enemy's advance, and once more, the Arka charged the fortress.

With the dragons burning anything that rose more than a flagpole into the air to cinders, Scalussen was free to fire as they pleased.

A thunderclap made the walls jump, but it was Farden, emerging from thin, quivering air on the gatehouse. With their king wielding threatening fire in both hands, two dragons alongside him, everybody with a scrap of magick in their veins joined him with a will and a roar.

'No mercy 'til freedom!' Farden roared.

Mithrid was almost shaken to the ground by the blast of magick that was unleashed from the walls. Thousands of spells exploded at once against the Arka charge. Their shields, both magick and metal, kept some of them alive. The rest were subjected to the fierce will of Scalussen's might.

Mithrid stared, mouth agape and bow waiting on her string, as she saw soldiers ripped to their bones by lightning, burnt to a writhing crisp, or catapulted into the air to be snatched by dragons. Between the spells, arrows rained. She fired almost forgetfully, the twang of the string waking her from her reverie. She didn't even see where her arrow went.

'Keep firing!' yelled Hereni, spinning fire in her hands. A brave and stupid soul had broken free of the chaos and was running headlong for the walls.

Mithrid saw it wasn't a war cry that he screeched, but a yell of help. A cry of sanctuary.

Hereni's spell blasted his arm off, and he collapsed amongst the dirty, rubble-strewn ice to howl. Her second spell put him out of his misery.

Mithrid shook herself, affixing a scowl on her face instead. Arrow after arrow, she snatched, bettering her aim each time. By her ninth arrow, she had lamed two. Her tenth took a woman in the throat, and once again Mithrid felt the same thirst for more as she had in Efjar. She didn't care if it was a broken and foul feeling, it was like an armour in battle. A poison to her blade.

Three more sank to join the dead with her arrows in their guts. She was almost questioning her axe by the time the barrel of arrows was running empty. She snatched the last few out of Bull's reach and chased a beastly-looking wolf with her shots. It took several attempts, but she finally put an arrow in the back of its skull. The wolf came skidding to a halt at the gates.

Elessi clapped her on the back.

'Lucky shot,' muttered Bull.

'DOWN!'

The order sent ice coursing through Mithrid's heart.

Every Scalussen fighter threw themselves behind the mighty crenellations. A chunk of masonry exploded against the strong, dark mountain stone, more iron in places than granite. Modren shielded them from the shrapnel. More impacts sounded across the walls.

'Too close!'

Modren led a blast of shield magick, pushing a bubble of energy out from the walls for a moment that afforded them a quick breath. Not only Scalussen, but also the Arka, who quickly regrouped as the spells faded away. They could not keep the catapults at bay and repel the charge at the same time.

Farden came striding across the walls. Not a soul dared block his way. Towerdawn landed in the courtyard, the remains of a soldier dropping from his jaws. Nerilan's glaive was saturated in gore.

The mage raised his sword. 'Old Dragon! It's time we took those machines down. Force Malvus to use his towers. Bring your dragons in!'

'Why is it we alone are sent behind their lines?' hissed the queen

Towerdawn arched his back, rocking Nerilan and hushing her with a roar. 'It is because we can, and you know that.'

The Old Dragon raised his serpentine neck to the sky, uttering a barking call that put a ring as sharp as a needle in Farden's ears. Soldiers fell flat as the dragon took flight. He had an immense piece of rock clutched in his back claws, and as he hauled it high into the sky, a half dozen dragons did the same, sweeping high into a sky blotted with streaking fire and swarms of arrows. Lost Clan dragons rose up to chase them. Farden could see Saker wielding a scythe, standing atop his dragon Fellgrin instead of clamped into the saddle.

Modren cupped hands around his mouth. 'Every other mage fights! The other shields!'

'Aye!' trumpeted the walls.

Farden swept back to the gatehouse, standing upon the parapet and gleaming in the burning battlefield. 'Keep firing!'

A hail of spells, arrows, bolts, stones, and missiles began to pour from Scalussen. Mithrid was once again amongst them, firing at the Arka that were now pressing forward, step by grisly step across the dead. Their shields were locked in lines and shell-like barricades that bristled with spears.

For a moment, it looked to Mithrid as though Towerdawn's dragons were hideously outnumbered. The rocks they hauled slowed the Siren dragons down. Arrows clattered against their armour like black hail. Necks craned as Arka and Scalussen alike followed the golden dragon as he continued his vertical climb, mouths opened in awe.

'There!' Farden yelled. Towerdawn's call had been heard.

Gleaming colour barred the sky as the Siren fleet rose above the Tausenbar. Almost a hundred dragons, their armour shining as stars lost in daylight. The fleet plummeted down the face of the mountains in silence; gemstones falling down black canvas.

A cry went up from the walls. Not in cheer, but in shock. Bull went as far as wailing. The Old Dragon tumbled from the apex of his climb, twirling around Fellgrin in an eagle's duel. Steel glinted as scythe and glaive clashed briefly before Towerdawn and the other dragons plummeted to the earth. It was a wonderful distraction, falling in time to his dragons closing in on the horde's backside.

The Siren fleet struck moments before Towerdawn did, sowing panic as they laid waste to the Arka camp before they turned their fire on the rear ranks.

Towerdawn looked almost suicidal until the last possible instant, when he flared his wings and pulled up at a breakneck angle. His boulder of masonry shot from his claws, punching holes in a siege tower before scratching a bloody smear through the Arka lines. As his wings clipped lance-tips at dazzling speeds, he sowed an inferno in his wake. Dragonfire was ravenous, all-consuming, second only to the fires of Irminsul or the fiercest spells. Arka soldiers died shrieking as their armour melted into their bones. Others found their limbs turned to ash before death could ply its mercy.

Fire burst amongst the sky as rival dragons swooped in spirals upon Towerdawn's fleet. In their race back to the fortress, they tumbled and fought in mid-air with deafening roars, the like of which Mithrid had never heard. She watched two dragons intertwined, wings flapping though they were falling. A blue Siren serpent in silver armour was trying to escape the clutches of the other: an iron-plated dragon of ashen skin. Their jaws were sunk deep into each other's' necks, even up until the moment they crashed to the ice and rock. Bronze and blue blood stained the snow.

Farden's voice boomed across the fortress. 'Archers! Ballistae! Take those dragons down!'

The Lost Clan dragons that didn't chase Towerdawn's dragons descended on Scalussen in droves, spitting fire as they crashed into the shields. Several mages were thrown from the wall howling, landing upon Arka spears, or torn apart in the crush. Others were reduced to ribbons by airborne claws.

In the distraction, Arka forces had reached the walls. The gates began to pound incessantly, no matter how many spells were poured on the assailants. Crude battering rams were carried by teams under shields, but half fell before even reaching the stout gates. Soon enough, a fine hill of bodies had been built on the fortress' doorstep.

A rumble sounded along the walls. It took most fighters a moment to realise it was the siege towers, inching forwards under the power of wood and stone trolls. The beasts heaved and roared. Catapult missiles hit them square on, but wherever one was blasted apart, another filled its gap. The towers proceeded relentlessly.

A dragon managed to break through half the defences in one vicious dive, wings slicked back and aimed like a crossbow bolt. The lump of dragon flesh and iron armour pulverised a young mage bravely throwing everything she had into a shield spell. Both her spell and her skull were crushed in the pressure of the dragon's jaws.

In the confines of the courtyard, the dragon sowed carnage with its bladed tail and fire spewing from its bloodied jaws. The flagstones were scarred black.

It was Warbringer that put a stop to it. An inordinately violent and decisive stop. Mithrid didn't even see where she appeared from. The minotaur was all of a sudden arcing through the sky, warhammer raised so far behind her head, she could have itched her hooves.

With a bestial roar, the minotaur swung the hammer like a god forging mountains. A rending screech of metal sounded the impact. Scale and bone parted before steel. The ring of the hammer as it met the stone beneath was a death knell. The weapon whined as it drank the great soul of the dragon in wisps of blue vapour.

What was left of the serpent's head was not worth describing. Mithrid, though her heart ran fierce and her eyes unflinching, found her gorge rising at that. She made a mental note to never antagonise Warbringer as long as she managed to live.

Taking her eyes from the horde was a mistake sorely learned. A barrage of spells assailed the parapets, blasting fire past the nearest shield. An impeccably-timed catapult shot struck the wall feet from her.

'Mithrid!' Bull yelled, firing an arrow uselessly into the air as he whirled.

With a yell of something unpronounceable from Inwick, a net of green light captured most of the shrapnel, seizing it inches from Mithrid's face. It was too late; she was already falling.

Magick bit her as Hereni tried to catch her, but it took Eyrum's encompassing mitts to save her from injury. All that was bruised was pride.

'You might be able to kill magick dead, but blades and stones will stick break your bones,' he barked.

Mithrid panted her words. 'Please don't tell me that's some sort of Siren proverb.'

There, in the middle of battle, Arka and Scalussen roaring alike, the imposing general took a moment to ponder. 'No, but it should be.' And with a deafening, 'Yah!', Eyrum bounded up the stairs.

Mithrid followed him, joyed he had not told her to stay put behind the gates. Her approach to the wall was more cautious this time. Shields blazed all around her. She ducked as two dragons grazed the flags of the gatehouse, tumbling together before crashing into the Arka ranks. The Siren dragon landed on top. It gnashed again and again at the Lost Clan's neck until black blood washed across the ice. Lances stabbed the dragon from all sides, and no matter how many spells Farden and his mages hurled, the Siren dragon's wings did not taste the air again. With a saddening whine, the magenta beast toppled.

The cheer of the Arka stoked Mithrid to anger. Tears brimming her eyes, she pulled off her gloves and reached instinctively for the sea of enemies below her. Black smoke swirled around her hands. The feel of it only became more enticing. Mithrid clenched, trying to seize the cloud of magick she felt choking the air, assailing her skull. With a savage grin, she witnessed her power begin to work. The nearest mages stared cluelessly at their gauntlets. One man clutched at his neck as his fire spell seemed to rebound onto him, eyes turned to flame. Mithrid pushed and pushed, her shadow seeping through the marauders.

'Keep at it, Mithrid!' bellowed Modren.

A darting glance told her Farden was watching. While his face was encased in steel, the nod of approval spoke volumes. Weighty, inspiring volumes. The fireballs spinning in his hands screamed almost as loud as he did.

'Show them what you came to Scalussen for, Mithrid!'

Though Mithrid's body already ached from the effort, she let the shadow strangle her arms. She drove a wave of futility through a group of blue-clad mages. Farden's spells chased hers, exploding in tornados of fire. The screams were a symphony of chaos. Mithrid drank it in. She watched mage after mage stumble and fall or stare dumbly about them until a spell smashed into their faces.

Concentration stole her attention. Time slipped past like a thief. When Farden's orders forced her to turn, she was shocked to see the siege towers drawn so close. At that distance, she could see the glowing eyes of the strange beasts that hauled on the towers' huge chains. The trolls were never uniform, no two alike. The wood trolls were barely more than gnarled trees with faces. The stone trolls only differed in colour and how much glittering ore encrusted their faces and claws. The ice cracked and turned to slush beneath their feet and the colossal weight of the towers above, but their slog never paused for an instant. What whips Malvus used to motivate them, Mithrid had no idea. Surely they had no families to murder, no towns to burn.

'They respect might. Strength, wherever it rears its head,' said Farden, once again beside her.

Mithrid pointed at the thick tower rumbling towards the gatehouse. 'Why don't we show them some?'

'You're starting to get the hang of this,' Farden laughed, and in the same breath roared, 'Mages! Concentrate fire on the towers! Engineers! Let's clear these walls!' He punched the air, almost leaving a vacuum behind his shield. The acrid air caught in Mithrid's throat. Farden pointed down.

'You'll want to watch this.'

From the protrusion of Scalussen's gatehouse, Mithrid could look along the curvature of the walls and the churning masses below. Half of them sheltered beneath umbrellas of shields, cymbals for the rocks and arrows that rained on them. Others tried in vain to prop up ladders or returned fire whenever they got a moment between the spells that sowed the ground with dead. Thousands already lay broken and smeared across the ice, trampled by eager boots.

A fevered clanking made her think the gate was unlocking, until a covering on the outer ramparts fell open, proving itself fake stone. A metal rod was revealed, oar-thick and spanning a hundred yards of wall until it met a cog embedded in the stone.

'Now!' Farden bellowed, as Mithrid leaned over to see what the rod was attached to within the gatehouse.

With a sound like the pealing of a bell, a colossal blade swept from its hidden notch. It was the size and rough shape of a fishing boat, a foot thick and solid, honed steel. Scalussen steel for that matter.

Mithrid watched as the scythe cleaved through the Arka. Nothing slowed its pendulum arc, not armour, not bone, now sheer masses. A savage and uncompromising laceration was torn through hundreds. Heads and limbs and halved weapons fell in heaps. By the time the blade had swung to its apex, its steel was painted crimson.

The screams had barely dimmed by the time it began its return swing.

'And who says war can't be beautiful?' Inwick growled to apparently nobody but herself. Mithrid saw it as a strange definition, but the horrific sight certainly captivated her.

A twin blade wrought butchery on the other side of the gatehouse, too. Mages gathered in vain beneath shields, hammering the scythes with all manner of magick.

The siege towers stopped short of the walls, and for a moment, it appeared the onslaught had stalled them. Each one stood taller than the walls. They bore no windows, just armoured plates and fire-hardened wood. Thousands of soldiers must have been crammed into each one.

The Arka held by their towers, leaving only the whoosh of the scythes to fill the quiet of bated breath.

'Wh—why?' Wodehallow stammered. The man was a constant shade of pale. Malvus didn't blame him. After all, it was the grand duke's soldiers that Malvus had forced into battle first. Wodehallow's men and women, halved and quartered lying in pieces against the walls. He looked like a man on the uneasy brink of trying to decide whether he need to vomit or shit himself.

Malvus took the spyglass from his eyes. 'Spit it out, man.'

'Why do we pause?' Wodehallow squeaked.

'Because I say so.'

This did not appease Wodehallow at all.

'But the towers are so close. My men have been at the vanguard of every assault, and died in their—

Malvus whirled upon him, prodding Wodehallow in that pudgy, overlapping neck of his and making him choke. Though the Albion guards bristled, the imperial guard had already sprung like traps. An Arka blade hovered close to every Albion spine and throat. One of Wodehallow's captains was made an unfortunate example. He was dragged across the boards, his breastplate torn away, and a knife dragged from his groin to his ribs. Nearby, Gremorin grinned with appreciation.

At the sight of the dying man pawing at his spilled guts, Wodehallow finally decided upon a secretive third option: pissing himself profusely.

'*Your* men? All of this,' Malvus growled, 'all of this is *mine*. Mine to drive into any blade I wish. Mine to leave bloody on this confounded ice. Do you understand me?'

Wodehallow was too busy choking and hawking to answer, but his avid nod was good enough.

'Toskig!' Malvus yelled to the general, further down a level and busy scribbling paper orders for runners. He appeared to be sweating beneath his helm.

'Give these rebels a taste of Arka ingenuity.'

Toskig barely nodded, just grabbed a runner by the throat, scribbled a note on his forehead and practically threw him from the fort.

'Pay attention, Wodehallow. Unless you would like to know what it is to lead from the front?'

The piss-stained duke shook his head violently.

'Prince Gremorin,' Malvus called to the daemon. 'You may feast.'

Fire seethed through the daemon's veins before he disappeared in a roiling cloud of sparks and black smoke.

'Why are they falling short?' Modren yelled between lightning blasts.

Farden was standing with one foot on the parapet, fire swirling around his arms. Before him, the siege tower loomed: its iron, angular face staring right back. At the base, all the trolls had sheltered behind it save one, who wielded a thick hammer, the kind used for demolishing brick walls. It was aiming at part of the tower's structure. Farden watched the troll crack three of the scaffolding posts into pieces and take aim on the last one.

The mage's flames stuttered as realisation dawned upon him.

'They're not!' he yelled. 'SHIELDS!'

The air shook as Scalussen responded. The roar of battle was muted for a moment as the crackling wall of magick punched outwards. Even some of the corpse piles were pushed from the walls. Farden stretched his jaw as the pressure popped his ears. Nearby, Mithrid was wincing, blood trickling from her nose. Eyrum raised his own circular shield and raised his axe.

One by one, the siege towers began to topple like stumbling giants. Their metal edge became dastardly apparent as the first tower crashed through the shields and into the western curve of walls. A quake ran through the entire fortress. Soldiers and mages were sent flying. Those who escaped were shaken to their feet. Grey dust billowed. While the stone held, the fortifications were crushed. A giant gouge was cut into the parapet.

Before wind spells could clear the dust, the towers broke open. Hidden doors unfolded into ramps, crowded with howling Arka. They spewed onto Farden's walls like pus from a fetid wound: heavily armoured troops emblazoned with the hammer of the emperor. Fire spells rocketed back and forth as the Scalussen tried to repel them. The storm of battle cries were punctuated by another substantial boom as another tower hit the eastern walls.

'Modren!' he yelled, but his comrade was already sprinting towards the action, sword high and crackling with blue lightning.

Farden turned his attention to the tower standing before the gatehouse. With a terrible creaking, it teetered on its descent. The troll was still hammering at stubborn carpentry.

'Watch my back,' he growled to Eyrum.

The Siren peered over his shield, eyes full of worry. 'What are you doing?'

Farden slammed his visor shut. 'Something I haven't tried in some time.'

Planting his feet solidly, he locked eyes with the siege tower. He reached deep into the north's bones with one hand. He clawed at the sky with the other, searching for the rivers of magick that he knew surged there. His arms began to tremble. Farden's roar started as a growl, but before long he was howling with the effort. The magick tried to compress him into the stone, but he stood firm. His veins ran with the fire he sought.

The tower began to fall.

As though he lifted a mountain's edge, Farden raised his arms. Below the tower's wheels, the ice fractured and melted. Steam billowed for the briefest of moments before a pillar of raging crimson flame speared the tower's base. A spear through crowded ranks, it tore up through its levels one by one, growing as it gorged itself on bodies. The screams were drowned by the conflagration.

Within moments, the tower's roof exploded with fire. The spell looked set to spear the very sky, but as Farden stumbled backwards from the parapet, the pillar of fire withered like a tornado out of breath.

Eyrum put his hands to the mage's shoulders. Taking a knee and his helmet from his head, Farden felt the rush of wind as the smoke-marred sky was filled with dragons. Towerdawn led a charge against the other towers. With snarls, the dragons drove their weight against the wood and steel. Claws and tails hammered at the closest towers, and to the sound of creaking and the combined groaning of falling soldiers, the towers crashed to the incarnadined ice. Farden blew a private sigh of relief.

If Mithrid thought they deserved a moment to take a breath, she was sorely mistaken. That was made immediately clear by the arrival of the daemons.

Entrenched in disappointment, she watched a dozen of them burst into being along the walls. Spined, smoking, or burning with flame, the daemons entered the fray with a ravenous abandon. Their magick drove back the mages' shields, leaving room for their claws to gouge at bellies and rip heads from necks. She glimpsed one of the lycan guards ripped clean in two.

'Can you stand, Farden?' Mithrid hissed, trying in vain to help the man up. The mage weighed an anvil.

'I can,' he said, breathless.

'Good. Because I feel you're going to have to!'

Mithrid's words were chased by the arrival of another daemon, barely a spear's length from them. Farden pushed Mithrid back and in the same movement, drew his sword.

The daemon roared at them, its blast-furnace mouth spitting sparks and soot. The beast had an extra set of arms, and at the end of each were curled talons. Its orange bug-eyes were halfway popped from its charred head.

Farden stepped up to it, sword aimed straight for its flaring snout. It seemed afraid of Farden, and perhaps not because of his prowess or because of his sword, but because of his armour.

'Godblood!' it hissed, before trying its best to swipe at Farden.

The mage severed four of its claws before he pounced, his spell seizing the daemon by the throat and hauling its face towards the stone. Farden raced to greet it, hacking at its eyes until it flailed madly.

Its screeches brought another daemon to its brother's rescue. Mithrid saw it pounding its way across the walls, barging Scalussen left and right to reach Farden. Other daemons followed suit: one marching up the stairs to the gatehouse as Warbringer and Eyrum battered its iron shell.

Mithrid acted on instinct and the overwhelming desire to see pain wrought on these foul creatures. These incarnates of evil. She ploughed her hands into the thick air, letting shadow unravel towards the daemon. He cackled as he came at her, raising arms shaped like long glaives. It was then that he stumbled to a halt.

Mithrid felt the daemon's magick like another skin beneath his charred and pitted exterior. It was like seeing the ghost within a man and being able to throttle it. Closing her fingers, she did exactly that. The daemon grasped at his throat, somehow without cutting it with those malformed blades of his. She crushed her fist, relishing watching the daemon writhe.

Only when it crumpled to the floor did Mithrid realise she had caused a scene. The battle atop the walls and within the courtyard had wound to somewhat of a halt. The daemons were staring at her most avidly. The closest to them, a crown of fire on his head, uttered words in a hateful-sounding language. It was apparently an order, given that the other daemons started to fight their way to the gatehouse.

Mithrid paled, already weak in the stomach and knees from the effort her strange spell had exacted upon her. Farden stood between her and the daemon, sword aflame. Durnus was suddenly beside them.

'Not today, Gremorin!' he yelled.

'Foul traitor!' seethed the daemon prince, eyes narrowed at the vampyre.

Once again, it was the might of the dragons that intervened. Golden Towerdawn descended from the sky, striking Gremorin with a battering ram of talons. His rider Nerilan pierced the foul beast with her shining glaive, right through the shoulder. Gremorin battled the dragon halfway across the courtyard, smashing several siege engines in the process. Towerdawn blew fire, rearing onto hindlegs to use his claws like a sabrecat duelling. Nerilan swiped chunks from Gremorin's charcoal armour. The daemon did his best to keep the dragon at bay with his flaming sword, but when he found a wall at his back, he chose the coward's way and vanished into a crackling portal of lightning and smoke. Towerdawn roared, and Mithrid could hear the dragon's disappointment reverberating through her.

With their king gone, the other daemons followed suit, leaving only curses behind. The soldiers atop the walls finished off the last of the siege tower intruders with a mighty cheer, and Scalussen found itself looking over a dejected army that slunk back to the smoking camps of the Arka.

Modren clapped Farden on the shoulder with a clang. 'That took all we had, Farden, but we did it.'

'No,' he said, glancing at Mithrid with tired, smoke-smeared eyes. So glazed, in fact, she looked behind her to make sure he wasn't addressing somebody else. 'We've got more to give.'

Mithrid sagged onto one knee, exhausted yet filled with relief. Not merely because the battle was over – for now at least – but that she had tasted the revenge she had longed for so dearly. It ran through her like spiced wine. Churning her stomach but liberating at the same time.

Farden clanked his way down the steps to brush past her. 'Now everybody knows your secret,' he whispered. 'Careful what that brings you.'

CHAPTER 27
REAPING & SOWING

Ghosts do not glow nor shriek, nor rattle their chains in abandoned ruins. They are made of memory, haunting minds instead.
OLD PARAIAN PROVERB

In the wake of battle, the world was struck quieter. Where adrenaline was replaced by relief, exhaustion, hunger, tears, and all manner of other emotions, Scalussen began the slow business of clearing the dead.

Four thousand Scalussen had perished. The pyres were built in silence until a slow song began to emanate from the gathered. It began first with the snowmads, in their mellow voices, almost made for funeral dirges. The words were foreign, but where words failed, melody began to spread. By the time the fires seethed, all of Scalussen sang the dead to ash.

There was no feast that night. The mess lines were quiet with soft chatter over this kill and that lucky escape. It was human nature to try and make words out of feelings, especially the fog and clatter of war, and most failed.

The Outlaw King stood upon the walls, wrapped in the pyre-smoke. He did not stare at the dead, but out to the gathering dark, where the Arka licked their wounds. Farden did not see pyres amongst their camp. Piles of dead perhaps, but no cleansing flames to send the souls to Haven and Hel. Most of the fallen Arka lay below, in too boundless a mess to begin trying to clean. The unmistakeable scent of shit and the copper tang of blood was thick in his nostrils.

The scrape of a boot brought Inwick to his side. Her eyes had yet to recede back into her skull. She looked wild enough to still be in the throes of battle. 'I knew Malvus had little respect for the living, but abandoning his fallen to rot, unburned? Cheating them of an afterlife?' she rasped. 'He has no respect for the living or the dead.'

'And the more we keep that distinction between us, the more his forces will realise whose banner they stand beneath. What the emperor's lies has cost them.'

She spat on the muddied ice. 'Why do we play for time, Farden? We have the power, we have the vindication. Why not press outwards and bring the battle to Malvus?'

'We stay strong behind these walls. Open battle was never an option. You know that.'

Inwick muttered something so far beneath her breath Farden only made out the current of rage within her. She was staring at him with her fists clenching and unclenching.

'You look like you're waiting for something. Either that or you're afraid to do anything but hole up.'

Farden turned to her, lips pursed. 'Did you not have your fill of fighting today, that you have to pick one with me? The dead are barely burned yet.'

'You have never been the same since Kserak.'

'Nor should I be. That day scarred me. I witnessed Malvus' abject cruelty firsthand. It didn't make me a desperate fool. There is no open battle against a horde of that size. You know that.'

Farden saw a shine in Inwick's eyes he feared greatly. One he had first seen in his uncle's eyes, being dragged away bloody and raving for crimes against the Written rules. The last time he had seen it had been Gossfring, a mage who had fought alongside Farden for close on thirty years. Old Gossfring had been found trying to dig a hole in the ice, his fingers shredded past the bone. In the days of the magick council, a mad Written was given a gold coin and left to wander the wilderness to die. In Scalussen, Farden had ordained an end less barbaric, a warrior's end, with a blade to the back of the neck.

Inwick looked as if she were going to lay hands on him at any moment. Farden could feel her magick swirling around him.

Farden squared to her. 'Are you clear of mind, Inwick? Hearing voices? Struggling to sleep?'

Inwick twitched an eye. 'I am *fine*, Farden. How dare you question me?'

'With less than a dozen Written left in this world, I will question who I please to keep us alive. I am not your enemy, Inwick. They are out there.' Farden pointed to the Arka.

'And there they will stay,' Inwick hissed, striding away. She chose one direction, then another, came back to throw some more vitriol at Farden, thought better, and stormed along the walls, kicking at anything inanimate that wasn't bolted down.

'What wrong with the white haired one?' growled a heavy presence thumping along the walls. Warbringer had her axe resting against her swollen shoulder. A dozen cuts across her arms and torso streamed blood, but she didn't seem to notice, never mind care. The minotaur thumped her hoof, and nudged Farden, who was heavily distracted by Inwick. He looked up at Warbringer in surprise.

'She's consumed by this war, is all.' Farden prayed silently he was right.

'Bloodrage. We minotaurs call it blessing.'

'For us Written, it is a curse. A madness. For some, it is inevitable.'

Warbringer snuffled. 'That what you get for fooling with magick.'

Farden couldn't help but snort drily. 'You're probably right. There have been moments – dark, treasonous moments – when I wonder whether this world would be better off without magick.'

Turning back to the darkening ice fields and the wash of bodies waiting like a tide to drown them, Farden saw teams working away at the Arka trebuchets and onagers. Driving a spell into his eyes, he saw them up close. Several looked primed to fire. The mage's heart fell even further, expecting a night of bombardment once more.

He was partially right.

Just as Farden was drawing breath to rally the wall guards and mages to action, he heard several of the engines boom as they fired. What was strange was that a pitiful scream floated through the air. Most missiles fired in war didn't wail.

A speck of black silhouette rose up against the orange sky. It flailed as it flew, somewhat like a fledgeling bird, still screaming as if its lungs were bottomless.

'Raise shields!' cried Farden. He punched the air in time for a wounded Arka soldier to fall upon the gatehouse. His arc was shorter than he'd have probably liked. He landed directly on the parapets, his skull splitting him into silence.

Farden wiped blood and brain matter from his cheek as he stared, aghast, as more detestable missiles rose into the air.

Not all them were alive. Only the very unfortunate ones. Most were corpses. Limbs, decapitated heads, and even a lone foot still in a boot, rained down on the fortress. The screams of wounded men falling to their death stirred horror in Scalussen. The soldiers watched with pale, stony faces as the Arka dead splattered all across the fortress. They all knew the depths of Malvus' evil, but this was a tactic most vile.

Farden felt Inwick's brand of rage as he stormed from the walls. All manner of human detritus rebounded from his shield spell, but he tried his best to ignore it.

War was not as glorious as time had made its concept.

'What do we do, King?' yelled a young soldier. Despite the officer's bars on his arms, the horror had reduced him to a wreck.

'Stay strong,' he growled, almost as if was trying to chide himself into believing it. 'All of you! We are better than this!'

Farden met the gazes of his men and women, mages and soldiers. He forced a grim smile, and saw it reflected in but a few of them. Gullets bobbed. Hands trembled, but they were with him.

'Add them to the pyres,' he ordered.

'Let that be a lesson against today's failure!' Malvus screeched to the hundreds gathered around him. Their faces were full of fear or brimming with anger, but Malvus didn't care much for either. Snapping his fingers, his Scarred guards formed a wall around him and cut him a path from the ranks of siege engines to his makeshift fort.

'Leave us!' Malvus ordered them. All but one of the Scarred left. Corcoran remained, her face a tortured smile as always. She stood beside Toskig, making the general take several steps away. The Scarred stank of rot on most good days, like a bandage in sore need of changing. Whispers had it their wounds never quite fully healed.

In the glorified council room the engineers had built, encased in a chrysalis of pillows and blankets, was Wodehallow. He hunkered down at the emperor's entrance, so his head looked like a swaddled egg. His gaze switched between Malvus, Saker, and Gremorin, as if he didn't know of whom to be more afraid.

Malvus swaggered to his throne: a smaller version of the Blazing Throne in Krauslung, complete with flames that traced its smaller edges. An indulgence, perhaps, but in this freezing world, it was the warmest seat in the room. Except, perhaps, for Gremorin's lap, but that was out of the question.

'A fine day of battle, wouldn't you agree?' Malvus announced, watching the faces of his generals, testing their emotions.

Gremorin and Saker both rumbled, unconvinced.

'As I thought,' spat the emperor. His armoured fist rang the throne like a bell. In his other, he held his spyglass, metal already creaking under his grip. 'I want an explanation, gods curse it! What and who is this mage who can strangle a daemon with her bare hands?'

Silence ruled the tent.

'Speak!' Malvus crushed the spyglass, momentarily surprising himself at his strength. 'I saw her with my own eyes. At Farden's side no less.'

Toskig attempted to answer. 'She is the Hâlorn mage our spies told us of. They say she's unusual, favoured by the Outlaw—'

'And little else! I have read the messages, General, same as you! I do not want rumours and hearsay, I want answers!' Malvus shook the shards of the spyglass from his fingers.

None seemed to be coming any time soon. Malvus snarled at the gathering of morons before him. 'How many dead?'

'Four of mine,' answered the daemon.

'Nine dragons.'

'Eight thous—' Wodehallow ventured.

'Not our losses, you fools. *Their* losses. Have our spies reported?'

'Yet to, your Majesty,' said Toskig. The general's eyes looked glazed, as if his mind was somewhere else. 'But I would wager that fortress has merely days left in it.'

Another rumble from Saker. His needle teeth were bared more than usual. Stained with wine.

'A problem, Lord of the Wind?' the emperor demanded.

'None that you would heed, Malvus.'

The emperor leaned forwards in his throne. 'Your tone, Saker. I like it not. Two battles, and you are already eager to surrender?'

The challenge to the rider's honour was enough to convince him. Malvus wanted to laugh. These beings were far too easy to manipulate. Even the daemon, the throneless prince driven by hunger and not much else.

'No, Emperor,' Saker admitted.

'Much better.'

One of the Scarred entered, holding a small scroll. Toskig snatched it from the mage before Corcoran could. He cleared his throat. 'Four thousand dead.'

Malvus stared at the general. 'Is that all?'

'It appears so.'

Malvus felt like a grave robber opening an empty crypt. *Cheated*.

'Is there an error?'

'I don't believe so.'

'At that rate, this battle won't last days, but months,' Wodehallow said, with a whimper.

Malvus raised from his throne. 'Your lack of faith is pitiful, Duke. You should count yourself fortunate – all of you – that I am here to win this battle for you.'

He caught Saker and Gremorin trading glances and spoke louder.

'Anything of the girl?'

'They call her a leech, and that is all.'

Malvus wanted to burn the message with Toskig still holding it. 'Corcoran! I want a dozen of your best mages ready by the time the sun sets on this disgusting land.'

Corcoran didn't respond, she only grinned.

'What's in your mind, your Majesty?' Toskig asked.

'Just as I am the caulk and tar that holds this army together, Farden and his captains are theirs. We should remove their motivation.'

'You speak as if it were that simple?' Saker ventured.

'Farden always runs instead of fighting. Now he has no choice but to stay put. Farden has always been a powerful mage. Now we have our own mages.'

Corcoran beamed, still silent as a breeze.

'Send word to our spies, General. Tell them to be ready.'

Malvus stood with his hands on his hips, wondering why none of them moved.

'Now, General!'

'As you wish, Emperor.'

Saker left with Toskig. Wodehallow looked far too comfortable to move, but Malvus' glare made his feet move.

Gremorin hesitated, as if reading Malvus' mind. The emperor had always wondered if daemons had the same power as some dragons, but it was past the point of asking. Questions were the sign of weakness.

Gremorin sniffed at the emperor. 'I know my kind's blood when I smell it.'

Malvus smirked. 'Loki's suggestion. One of his best, if I'm not mistaken.'

'Be careful, Malvus. Such blood comes at a price, more than you may be willing to pay.'

'For how I feel, for the youth I sense in my muscles and veins again, I would pay any price.'

'And that, Emperor,' Gremorin said as he, for once, used a fucking door, 'will always be the downfall of your race.'

Malvus turned to Corcoran, who still stood nearby, teeth between her lips and eyes unblinking. Her gaunt and twisted face was a mask of fervour, like a hound obeying her master's orders yet straining to gobble the buffet before her.

'As much as it pains me not to have the glory, you may kill Farden. And the Hâlorn girl. I will not have some barely-weaned wretch interfere.'

Corcoran nodded painfully slowly and grinned as she left the emperor in peace and quiet.

Malvus itched at his short beard, finding tangles and scratching them free. When he brought his hand away, it trembled ever so slightly. He clenched his fist once, twice, and still a quiver.

Malvus felt the breath of a breeze on his cheek and stiffened. The smell of spices, of salt air, and foreign forests wafted past him. His breath curled before him as smoke. Whether it was the daemonblood lingering in his gut and veins, or simply a sense of always being watched, Malvus knew he was not alone.

'Where the fuck have you been? I thought you were my advisor,' he cursed the god.

Loki spoke soft as dying breath. 'Between the stars and back again. Beneath the ice and atop the clouds. Here and there and all around.'

'Enough riddles, Loki! I should have you strung up for disobeying me and for abandoning your emperor!' Malvus whirled on the god but found him gone. A candle snuffed by his side, and in its shadow, he met the amber eyes of the god staring back at him.

'You could try.' Loki shrugged. 'My, how well you're looking since we last spoke. A new remedy?'

'Tell me you have been making use of yourself,' Malvus threatened.

'Depends who's asking.'

Malvus sneered. He saw the human edge to the god, that ragged, chipped edge of mortality. 'I see you behind that visage, Loki. You have spent too much time in the company of men. God, you may be, but you think like flesh and bone.' Malvus stepped closer, relishing the smirk on Loki's face. 'You want to matter, just as we all do. Tell me, Loki. Matter.'

The god's smile was stubborn, like a stain that refused to die. 'I have been watching Farden, just as you have. Perhaps from a little closer than you.'

Malvus forced patience. 'And what can you tell me?'

'That you don't want to kill her.'

'Who? The Hâlorn girl? She stands with Farden. Why should she be allowed to live?'

'Because, my good Malvus, not all problems are be solved by killing them. The same sword can be wielded by both sides. She would be a powerful ally, even a strong insurance against the daemons.'

Malvus reached for the god's throat. Loki did not move. Instead, he let the emperor seize him. Just for a moment, until the pain started creeping along the emperor's fingers. A prickling stab he had not felt the like of in life.

The candles extinguished out as the god vanished into thin air. Malvus fingers were left sore and tingling at the touch of the god's skin.

'That would be the daemonblood. Loki's voice remained, ghostly and bodiless. 'Cheating time will always have a price, Malvus Barkhart.'

The emperor seethed for a moment, before yelling for Toskig.

The general burst in, a knife in his hands. Malvus couldn't tell whether he was disappointed or relieved to find the emperor sitting upright and glaring, swilling his wine thoughtfully.

'Catch Corcoran,' he ordered. 'Tell her to keep the child alive. Bring her to me, if possible.'

'Aye, Majesty.' Toskig disappeared as quickly as he had appeared.

In the quiet left in Toskig's wake, the emperor fished Loki's vial from his inner pocket, and silently contemplated the dark liquid within before emptying it into his wine.

CHAPTER 28
ABOMINATION

Malvus Barkhart's theft of power was a black ship docking in the dead of night, floating on false promises and coin. With Arkmage Durnus and Tyrfing preoccupied with the north and Krauslung distracted by the rise of religious cults, Malvus seized the thrones. It was fortunate he turned the army to his whims and brought Captain Toskig into his fold. Krauslung's streets might once again have washed with blood.
FROM 'THE MERCIES OF MALVUS BARKHART', BY COUNCIL JOHAN (SINCE DISGRACED)

A sun had to die before Farden let himself rest. The weariness had seeped into his bones like rot into a barrel. Farden denied it for as long as he could, walking the crowded walls until his feet felt like numb hooves and his hips crunched.

When at last, watching darkness creep across the ice and hordes beyond Scalussen's doorstep, Farden felt sleep trying to drown him, he found himself stalking the halls of the Frostsoar. Every spiral around the tower brought him the same view. Torch and campfire, burning in all directions save for the impassable north, where a more ancient fire brewed.

Moonless, the night reigned, black as pitch and devoid of stars. The day's breezes had brought a mist in from the south. Clouds followed. On the frozen and faraway sea, lightning flickered as if the gods played with flint and steel.

'What I wouldn't give for a storm giant right now,' he whispered to himself, remembering the first time he had seen them, duelling with thunderbolts above the Bern Sea.

A shadow caught his gaze and Farden whirled. A white cat, some pet of a captain or lord, sprinted past him on the stairs. Farden was cursing the muscle in his ribs that had decided to twang like a ljot string.

Sleep called him forever upwards, coiling around the steps until he trod vast hallways of black rock. Every guard nodded. Every lantern lent him a shadow.

The firelight from Durnus' room burned brightly. Farden forced himself to walk past, denying his curiosity, throttling his impatience. These were matters to sleep upon. Matters for tomorrow's morn. Though he told himself many times in that short moment, foot hovering in mid-air, he disobeyed his own orders.

Farden rewound his steps until he was leaning against the vampyre's doorframe. Durnus faced away from him, seated amidst a precarious mountain range of piled scrolls.

'You should be in bed, King. You have not rested in days.'

'That I should, but the same could be said of you.'

Durnus poked at some illegible scrawl. 'You should know by now that vampyres hardly sleep.'

'Still searching for your spear, old friend?'

The vampyre tutted irritably. 'It is not *my* spear, Farden.'

'You search for it like it is. I told you, it is no use to us now.'

Durnus strangled the scroll he was reading and threw it into the fire. Whatever its ink held, the flames shone green. 'You mages! You will be the death of me. Not that horde out there, but rather your incessant doubts, like a thousand needles in my skin.'

Farden held his tongue until Durnus had taken a breath and combed his threadbare silver hair back into place. The vampyre had grown irascible in recent days. 'I would wager it is not me that's angered you,' said the mage.

Durnus grumbled without words.

'Why don't you tell me?'

'Inwick,' Durnus replied, causing Farden to blow a pained sigh.

'What has she done?'

'This morning, she waded in here as if these were her own quarters, demanding books on Written. Skertrict was almost stabbed for trying to take a scroll from her. How it troubles me to say this, but she is losing control of herself, Farden. Her Book. The lines between friend and enemy are becoming blurred.'

'And what can I do about it? Perhaps you should be working on the cure for a Book's madness instead of searching for a godsdamned spear!'

The vampyre stared with murder in his eyes. In all their years, Farden had never seen that look directed at him

'I'm sorry, old fr—'

Durnus yelled at the top of his voice. 'Skertrict!'

Not a sound answered. Durnus strangled another scroll. 'Where is that blasted scholar now? He is forever getting lost!'

High above the ice, at the very boundary between sky and stars, where the air gave no life, yet the winds of the gods still blew, black dragons flew. Three of them, smoked and painted obsidian to blend with the night, heavily laden by equally dark bodies white-knuckled and hunched. Their hoods were strapped tightly over pale, masked faces, their armour extensive but light and fire blackened.

One stared bravely past their dragon's flanks, down to where the fortress was a dark hole on a summer field of light. Only when it was directly beneath them did she raise her fist and stand up in her saddle.

'Like we trained,' Corcoran hissed, barely audible over the shrieking winds. Where her voice failed, her actions spoke. As if she hovered no more than a dozen feet from the dirt, she swung herself free of the saddle, and jumped.

A second joined her fall without comment nor question. And a third, and so on, until nine bodies plummeted towards the ice and stone of Scalussen.

The rushing cold sought to freeze them before they struck the ground, which raced to embrace them. The wind hammered them relentlessly, its roar an almighty din. Half fell blind as the wind stole their tears.

The mages cast spells as they fell, wrapping themselves in their own tempests of wind. Faint green light traced them like smoke from a spat log.

The earth still dragged at them, as if they had dared to cheat its grasp and it was furious. The spells seemed to be failing. Harder and harder, they pushed, faces roaring silently behind masks as they fought to arrest their momentum.

Like trebuchet stones, they plunged towards the Frostsoar's peak. No beast occupied its stone, only two guards. Spell whining in strain, Corcoran landed upon the masonry between them with a heavy clang, sending them scattering. She bent her knee, almost shattering her leg with the force, and seized them both by the breastplate. Dark flame burnt their throats away before they could scream.

Seven more mages met the stone in varying degrees of grace. The last fell with an effusive stream of curses until the stone shut him up permanently.

Wiping blood spatter from their faces, the Scarred crouched low, hoods up and eyes fixed on the door ahead of them. The snowflakes blew around them as they paused.

※

'Skertrict, damn it!'

At last, there came a sound of falling literature. Skertrict emerged from an antechamber with arms full of loose parchments. 'Apologies, my lords. I was somewhat preoccupied.'

'Tell Farden what you've told me.'

The scholar coughed into his hands and twitched his eyes behind their spectacles. 'In my, erm. humble opinion, sire, the Spear of Gunnir could be the weapon to end all wars, not just this battle.'

Farden raised a brow. ' "Battle?" '

'Er... Siege, I mean, sire. *War*,' said the man, fidgeting with his robes.

'From what we have found, I am inclined to agree.'

'I care even less for the opinion of a scholar than I do for yours, Durnus!' Farden yelled.

The vampyre's eye were pinched narrow. His reply was a strangled hiss. He arose from his chair, closing books to create a pile. 'It is good to know my wisdom and expertise counts for so much.'

Farden held his hands as though summoning fire, but he sought patience instead. 'Where is this fucking spear, then?'

Durnus took a moment to reply. 'East, from what we can tell.'

'How far east?'

Skertrict was babbling. 'To our, er, best knowledge, which is, to say, erm… a guess. If you take into account—'

'Shut it, scholar. How far, Durnus?' Farden barked.

'Leagues. Countries. Swathes of land we don't have maps for! Content?'

'Hardly!' The mage threw his hands to the rafters as if trying to catch his evaporated patience. 'Why are we even having this discussion? We have neither the time nor the resources. Thousands of Scalussen are dying daily on the Arka's swords.'

'*You* chose to stand fast, Farden. You chose a siege. This is the price,' the vampyre said, voice hushed and dangerous.

Farden opened his mouth but no words came forth. Not now. *Not here*. Not with this scholar staring as if watching a swarm of bees slowly surround him. He held his tongue and its secrets.

In the silence, a muted thudding ran through the tower, likely a random catapult impact. Malvus had kept up occasional volleys to keep the fortress awake. It was like a door closing on the argument. Farden swept from the chamber at the same time as Durnus, simply in opposite directions.

Skertrict blinked owlishly at the swiftly emptying room, mouth agape.

'General?'

'Tonight's study is over, scholar. See to your quarters. Get some sleep, if you can. This fortress needs it.'

'I was—'

Durnus punctuated his order with a slam of his door.

'—going to do some further study on the spear…' Skertrict swept up his parchments, adjusted his glasses with a spare hand, and left the room with a smile.

'Do dragons dream?'

Mithrid sniffed and immediately regretted it. She thought she had grown used to the stink of the eyries by now, but the longer the days stretched, the more their musty scent filled the Frostsoar.

'I don't know, Bull, but that one over there looks like it is.'

A mighty blue beast lay curled like a cat in its nearby nest. Though its nose was tucked into its belly with its tail, and its wings wrapped around its hide like a blanket, its claws would occasionally flex, its muscles would twitch, or smoke would rise from its coils.

Bull readjusted his chainmail. 'Kevun says the more time you spend around dragons, the more you start to look like them.'

'Who in Hel is Kevun?'

'A Siren cook. He says that's why they've all got the scales.'

Mithrid hummed vague interest.

'Reckon we'll get them?' Bull itched his beginnings of a beard: patchy stubble that only sprouted on his chin.

'I hope not. I don't want scales.'

'You might not get a choice if we keep hanging out here,' Bull smirked, teasing her.

'It's quiet.' Mithrid's gaze returned to its default position: keeping an eye on the Arka horde as if she were Scalussen's only watchman.

Another question. 'You ever wonder what would have happened if Modren hadn't saved us?'

'No,' she replied honestly.

'I reckon we'd be out there, shouting Malvus' name instead of Farden's,' Bull opined.

Mithrid liked to think herself better than that, too suspicious, but Bull had her wondering. She wondered how many other Hâlorn cliff-dwellers were out there, sharpening blades and huddled around fires, on the wrong side of the future. That was nothing to crow about. Rather, she felt a pang of sadness, and a hollowness to her revenge.

A soldier bustled along the corridor, not far beyond the narrow column of nests. The noise made them both turn but the chap was already gone. The dragon's hollows spiralled around the exterior of the Frostsoar, never more than four or six nests tall, making the inner corridors always close at hand for riders. Their protruding balconies had shallow parapets; somewhere to dangle legs over prodigious heights and not worry about them being shot at.

The snow was coming stronger now, wind-driven and full of ocean fury. Mithrid watched the edges of the Arka's vast camp fade in brightness, but bloom with orange glow.

To the east, where the darkness of the ice fields still lurked, she caught a glimpse of another light. This was no torch, perhaps a string of moth lanterns, but they seemed to be drifting.

'Do you see that?' Mithrid pointed. Bull looked down her arm and squinted.

'Lights.'

A rustling sounded another passer-by, but this one hesitated at the doorway. Mithrid did not want to turn away from the lights, in case they should fade, but the scuffing of cloth shoes was curious.

It was Durnus' scholar. Sker-something. He held a bundle of old papers in his hands and was blinking at them through fogged spectacles. He stepped between the nests, staring up at their three levels. He seemed very cautious of the slumbering dragons occupying them.

'What are you doing?' he whispered. 'You're the Hâlorn girl everybody's been talking about, right?'

'And you're a scholar, right? A fellow of books?' she shot back at the nosy man. Not that she wasn't warmed by his comment.

He bobbed his head. 'Scholar Skertrict of Venheath, formerly of Arfell. Actually, we've met b—'

'Good. Then can you tell us what those are? It looks like a reflection of the Wake.'

The scholar came to look at what she pointed to. It took a lot of peering and cleaning of spectacles, but he had the answer. Apparently, it was something to grin about.

'It is not the Wake, miss, but souls.'

'Souls?' Superstitious Bull was immediately rattled.

'Of the dead. The deceased in battle.'

'I didn't think souls had to travel anywhere.'

'To ghostgates, miss. To places that lead to Hel, where daemons used to roam,' Skertrict pointed downwards, and then to the blinded stars. 'Or Haven, where the gods still dwell. The dead should be careful. Daemons subsist on them.'

'I thought they ate meat. Ate... us?' Bull asked.

'They do, but to get at the souls within. That is why they enslaved our kind, so many thousands of years ago. Gods' children were slaves for elves and daemons.'

Mithrid watched the man, beaming over his recollection and knowledge despite the dire subject. Men of history were peculiar like that. 'Where are the ghostgates?'

'Across Emaneska. Perhaps beyond if other lands treat their dead as we do.'

Mithrid kept digging. 'And who decides between Haven and Hel?'

'Not that there is much difference between the two, or so the scholars presume, but the gods do. With Evernia's golden scales.'

'But who made them right? Why do they get to decide?'

Skertrict grinned again. 'Precisely.'

The wind gnashed at the high reaches of the tower. Farden had forsaken his quarters for the cold air of the Wolf's Hall.

The council chamber was bare and empty. Not a cushion remained on the stone chairs. No lanterns were lit, though the ranks of poles still stood between the stalagmite statues. The Arka horde kindly lent the cave its glow.

Farden scuffed at snow sneaking in through the open windows and dragon door. His cape was tugged around his legs by the rushing air. His tired eyes half-closed to listen to the storm. No rain to ease his mind, but at least the hissing patter of the snow would do.

A distant cough of a guard echoed through the Hall. Farden raised his hands, poised for a light spell, and thought better of it. It was his tired mind playing tricks.

Something akin to a lantern falling caused him to turn. Nothing stirred that he could see, except a flicker from a door ajar that he swore he had closed behind him.

Farden sniffed, tasting nothing but snow in the air. And, perhaps a faint whiff of dragon. His tired mind populated the shadows with all manner of blades and dour faces. Try as he might to ignore them, his gut tended to agree.

The mage took a deep breath, stretched out his hands, and began to concentrate.

⁂

Corcoran resisted the urge to strike the Scarred mage across the face. 'I'll cut off your ballsack and use it as belt leather if you make another mistake, moron. Quiet!' she rasped.

With the help of another mage, they picked up the dead guard and propped him in an alcove. Bloody bootprints followed their scuttle through the dark corridors. Their blades already dripped crimson.

'Here,' Corcoran hissed, pointing towards a wide door that looked grander than the rest. It was ajar. 'Two of you, fetch that girl. Raise Hel once you hear us.'

A pair of Scarred disappeared without so much as a nod.

Inwards, the black-clad mages crept: knees bent, blades low and ready. A dark and vacuous room awaited them. Corcoran could have sworn she had wandered into a cave instead of a lofty chamber.

The wind rushed past them, peppered with snowflakes, as they trod softly between the statues and pillars. The carved stone faces were of so-called heroes and warriors of old the Scarred loathed. They met their marble eyes with scowls.

Corcoran hissed. A figure slumped over a grand, stretching table shaped like a map. Her mages spread like a blood pool, encircling the table from the shadows. With crackling light spells, they sprang their trap, rushing inwards from all angles to confront nothing more than a spare cloak, left hanging over a stone chair. The Scarred looked around their circle.

'Where the fuck is he?' Corcoran growled as she peered at her mages, and where the air rippled between them.

'You should look closer, abomination,' she heard a voice whisper, before a spell struck her hard and sharp in the gut.

※

The Scarred crept into the hall like wolves, but Farden knew the lambs that hid beneath their black armour. Lambs for the slaughter.

The magick he wielded was difficult enough to work on one mind, not to mention six. Farden tensed every muscle as he poured his magick into the mages' minds. A subtle, dangerous magick once banned by the old Arka Council, deemed reckless and draining. In the grip of such a spell, Farden knew why. It was not invisibility, but the idea of. He simply made the mages *forget* he was there the very instant they saw him.

Through narrowed eyes and with gritted teeth, Farden watched them take the bait of his cloak. They encircled him, one woman even striding within three feet of him. As he stared at her pallid, sweating skin, smelled the rot of her, Farden held himself strong and motionless with all his might.

'Where is he?' hissed the Scarred mage.

Farden smirked. 'You should look a little closer, abomination.'

He switched spells to drive a fist swirling with green light into the Scarred's armoured gut, just to the left of where he had been struck in Albion. The Scarred skidded across the stone, leaving Farden to unleash a spiralling wave of fire. The other mages scattered or were knocked flat.

Through the flames, Farden came swinging, slicing the throat from one mage before clashing with his shield spell. He tried to blast it aside but these Scarred were surprisingly strong. Another rushed him. With his spare hand, Farden deflected a stab of lightning and caught a blade inches from his head. The steel grated against his Scalussen gauntlet. A rare stalemate, until Farden bounced his spell from the shield right into the second mage's face. He went down, choking on sparks and his charred mask.

Pain wracked Farden as four force spells struck him simultaneously. He cartwheeled against the table, snapping a chair in half and leaving a Farden-shaped dent in the stone.

The mage sucked the blood from his split lip and spat it on the floor. 'How dare you wield dead men's Books so brazenly.'

The Scarred woman was upright. 'They are dead for a reason. A new guard is rising.'

Farden threw up his hands to block their fiery onslaught. He laughed behind his crackling shield. Fire was his magick, not theirs. He felt the heat of his Book blazing on his back as he seized their spells, twisting them around and back on themselves. One Scarred was thrown in front of the others. He collapsed to the ground, shrieking as his armour melted into his flesh. He fell face first with a perturbing clang.

The three remaining Scarred fanned out, each weaving spells between their hands, or winding their swords up to strike. Farden stood still between them, fingers crackling with magick and busy waiting for them to pounce. He did not have to wait long.

The scrawny one jumped at him, sword high and aimed for cleaving. Farden brought a narrow shield up under his guard and snapped his head back like the cork of an ale. The mage shifted slightly to let the man crash by his feet. He did not get up again.

The next rained lightning. Farden caught the blast on another shield, but the spell was fierce, wild. Pain shot up his leg, burning his flesh so that he took an impromptu knee. The mages charged him like sabrecats upon a lame goat. Farden snarled, raising rubble from the rock and clobbering them with stone while he fought upright.

With clawing fingers, he seized the nearest Scarred with his magick. Farden made a fist, and the man's armour crumpled inwards. His ribs cracked with loud pops. Hunchbacked and gasping for breath, he stumbled in front of the dragon door just in time for Farden's fireball to strike him. He was blasted from the hall and sailed into the black night.

Only one Scarred remained. Her ice bolts clattered against Farden's shield, driving him back inches with every impact. The mage could feel a weakness in his arms. He measured it grimly against the Scarred's assault. She had all the ferocity of madness and desperation, and Farden was morose to admit she was almost a match. Some of the ice shards punctured the edges of his shield, they were driven so hard. The woman had skill, that was for sure, but no restraint.

Farden pivoted, letting the ice storm sail past him to explode against the table. With a stamp of his foot, a ripple spread to the last Scarred. He had hoped to shake her from her feet, to rush in for a quick kill, but the woman stamped the spell dead. Instead, she snatched the shards of table towards him, assaulting Farden from both sides. The mage staggered as something sliced open his scalp.

With a clap of his hands, a shockwave cleared his path of ice and stone. He strode at the Scarred, sword weaving a barrier before him. The Scarred met it with her own blade. There, heaving against each other's strength, swords fighting to slash throats, Farden stared into the red-rimmed eyes of his enemy, and studied her. They reminded him far too much of Inwick's.

'Do you have a name, abomination?' he asked.

'Corcoran. And yours is Outlaw.'

'I will be the only one who remembers your name, Corcoran. You should have more respect,' Farden growled.

'Your kind are extinct without knowing it,' the Scarred spat. 'A wasted old man, cooped up in a tower. You don't feel the magick we do, coursing through our veins.'

Farden laughed heartily in the woman's face. 'Please,' he said, before bringing his knee up into Corcoran's thigh, knocking her off balance and detonating a force spell directly in her face. The woman somersaulted like a straw-doll, skull smacking against the stone.

Lightning sprang from the Scarred's hands; an admirably swift reaction, but Farden deflected it with a swipe of his sword, letting a statue take the brunt of the spell. In the ensuing shower of marble, Farden's sword ignited with flame. He drove it close behind Corcoran's shield and punctured her breastplate inches from the Scarred's heart. The spell withered, leaving only the burning sword. Flesh melted before its blade. When he met stone, Farden kept pushing, until the hilt pinned Corcoran against the floor. Armour sizzled as the fire began to spread through the woman's veins.

'There…' Corcoran rasped, 'there is only one abomination…'

Farden seized her by the chin, forcing her to look up to him. 'And that is?'

'That girl of yours, elsewhere in this tower.'

With a shudder, the woman died before she could speak again. Farden did not need to hear more. The mention of Mithrid was enough to send him sprinting.

🍎

Their first clue to something being amiss in the tower was the wretched man sailing through the night's sky. He wailed as he tumbled barely two spear's length from them.

'What in fuck's name was that?' Mithrid was up on her feet in moments.

Bull immediately drew his sword, even stepping in front of Mithrid like a tree with legs. 'Bad news, I'd wager,' he grumbled.

Skertrict's voice was a timid whisper. 'Assassins.'

At first, Mithrid thought he was merely speculating, but the two hooded and masked shadows that stood in the doorway, eyeing the dragons, were as concrete as evidence got.

Mithrid snuck around Bull and walked towards them, arms open as if surrendering. She felt the ice stir in her veins; reaching around her skull like the press of cold fingers.

'Have a go,' she snapped.

Spells blossomed between their fingers; swirling orbs of fire and surging water. Mithrid smiled as they approached and took aim. Though the spells rushed towards her, and Bull raced to seize her, Mithrid reached for their magick searing the air and seized it. Fire and water sputtered as cinder and steam against Mithrid's apparent shield.

The mages grasped at the air, but nothing happened. One even ripped his mask away to show her the grunt of effort he put into his magick. Mithrid throttled their power, smirking snidely.

'Bull, would you wake up the dragons?'

The boy had always had a knack for conjuring the most piercing of whistles between his fingers, and he did it now, waking dragon and rider alike. The sharp beasts were quick to taste the scent of Arka in their eyrie.

One mage was seized by two dragons at once. His body was sheared in two by their razor teeth. The survivor had only two options. Two directions, in truth. Run for the door or fulfil his orders and charge at Mithrid. To her delight, he chose her, bellowing at the top of his lungs as he aimed a sword at her.

The dragons snapped at his cloak but failed to catch him. Mithrid had her axe drawn and ready to swing, but it was Bull who stepped in, sweeping his blade over her head and into the mage's chest. The Arka blocked it awkwardly in his panic.

It was then that Skertrict appeared, brandishing some sort of writing implement like a dagger. With ferocity that belied his bookish and dusty appearance, he drove it deep into the Arka's neck until the man sputtered blood. Bull dispatched him with a sword between the ribs, and the dragons gnawed at the rest. A few trumpeted for the minuscule victory, raising the hairs on Mithrid's neck.

Farden sprinted past the eyrie before sprinting back. His gaze traced the splatter of blood to the body, and to Mithrid and Bull. And finally to Skertrict, who looked horrified at the blood on his hands, figuratively and physically.

'Thank the fucking gods,' gasped the mage.

Mithrid counted the scrapes and scorch marks on his armour. 'You look awful.'

Farden scowled. 'You don't look too picturesque yourself, girl.'

Mithrid tried to wipe the blood from her shoulder but ended up smearing it instead.

'How does it feel having the emperor himself wanting you dead?' said Farden.

'Makes me want him dead all the more.'

The mage nodded. 'Get in line, girl. It also means you are in danger. After what happened to Remina, from now on you won't be going anywhere alone. You'll stay in the training yards or the Underspire. I'll have one of the lycans watch you. Bull, is it? I'm trusting you to guard her, too.'

Bull nodded solemnly as though he had just been knighted.

'Farden!' Mithrid tried to interject, but the mage said no more. His decree uttered, he disappeared between the dragons.

'Farden!'

CHAPTER 29
WHAT RISES, FALLS

With dragons living spans far longer than any human, their minds become too crowded. Via their tears and magick tomes, they can store memories in paper and script. Tearbooks, they are called, and other than their eggs, they are the most coveted of dragon treasures. We riders envied them. The ability to store away the shrapnel of the past, pile it on a shelf to be forgotten? What a sublime gift.
TAKEN FROM LETTERS SENT BY THE EXILED RIDER DOORNA

Three bodies lay in rictus on the slab of rock, wretched, bloodied, and burned half to Hel. One Scarred still had half a sword melted into him.

To Durnus, it was as if they bore witness to a macabre piece of theatre. The dead were the most wooden of actors, gurning and glaring, holding their death poses. He looked across the audience. Farden, Modren, Durnus, Inwick, Eyrum, and Towerdawn all holding silent court with their thoughts. If they were anything like the vampyre's, they pondered deep depths, daring to question the how as well as the what could have been, more torturous than present facts.

Durnus cleared his throat, making half of them blink as if coming to. 'This was too close, Farden.'

The Outlaw King said nothing. He had no words for Durnus that morning.

'Must have come from above. Bodies start at the roof,' offered Modren.

'Bodies all down the Frostsoar,' Farden muttered, still quietly simmering. 'Good guards and mages all.'

Durnus, standing closest, could feel the raw heat coming from his armour and bare forearms. The sleep that Farden had bade him take had been forgotten. Scalussen had to search high and low for other Scarred first, of course. That pensive audience all looked exhausted. Deep hollows hung beneath their eyes like saddle bags. Durnus no doubt looked the same.

Three bodies. Face up and scarred Book on their backs hidden. Farden had obliterated the others to charred lumps. The one mage who had tried to fly had to be scraped up by shovels.

Towerdawn spoke. 'Dragons, most likely. Flying high and daring as we did in Krauslung. In the snowstorm we did not see them.'

It was no apology, but Farden shook his head as if he rejected it.

'We found one body of theirs smeared across the roof,' Inwick replied. She, too, looked incensed. Durnus peered at her, watching for signs to match his concern.

'Good,' spat Farden.

An applause of murmurs and grunts came from their little half circle.

Eyrum, hands folded leisurely over his axe head, sighed. 'They may try this again.'

Farden snarled. His orders reverberated around the statues as he left. 'I want a shield spell atop the Frostsoar day and night, and soldiers. Double the dragon patrols. And don't you dare burn these abominations. Throw them from the walls and let them rot.'

They watched him leave, knowing better than to chase him.

'What is in his mind, Durnus? Modren? You know him better than all of us,' rumbled Towerdawn. 'Should we be concerned?'

'No,' Modren replied staunchly. 'I don't know, truly, but I'd wager he's outraged.'

'I confess I do not know either, Old Dragon,' Durnus told them in a hushed voice, trying to keep his own confessions from spilling. The dead girl in the dungeons still haunted him. 'But he reminds me of the Farden of old, the Farden of Albion. The reckless kind. Some great weight occupies him.'

A chair flew across the hall as Inwick stormed off in her own direction.

Modren and Durnus shared a glance as the harsh echoes softened. 'Farden's told you about his fears? That her Book is beginning to rule her?' asked the vampyre.

The undermage pinched the bridge of his nose. 'I can see it with my own eyes,' Modren said, already following her path. 'I'll look after her.'

Eyrum sighed once again as he climbed atop Towerdawn's spine. 'Problems, problems. Ever since that mage washed up on Nelska shores, it's been one problem after another.'

Towerdawn winked at Durnus. 'Such is the downside of rule,' he said, before tumbling from the dragon door with a piercing screech.

'That it is,' Durnus muttered.

Skertrict was nearby, holding a fur cloak for the now shivering Durnus. 'Farden doesn't care about the spear, does he?'

'No, my good man. No, he does not.'

The scholar looked around before shrugging. 'Can we not make him?' he whispered.

'Make him?' Durnus gave the scholar an admonishing look. 'There is no making Farden do anything. And mind your tongue. He is your king as much as mine.'

Skertrict bowed his head. 'He's a troubled one, isn't he?'

'Putting it lightly, but yes. So would you be if you had the mantle of hero shoved on you at a young age and forced to wear it all your life.'

'I would have no doubt crumbled before adulthood.' Skertrict nodded, contemplating. 'But there is one aspect that I do question. Where does he go with his gryphon?'

Durnus looked up from the tome, following the scholar's pointing finger, and saw Ilios flash past the walls.

The games had exhausted themselves. The snowflakes fell fat and fluffy, and yet no matter how fast Mithrid swung the axe, she consistently failed to cut one in two.

The snow shook from the scarred wooden post once more.

Mithrid wrenched her axe free, levelling a threatening glare at the rudimentary snowman Bull had built. It was almost as tall as he was.

'Don't you bloody dare,' he warned, wiping snow from his gloves.

'Are you done training?' Aspala waggled her hand quickly before withdrawing it back into her fur sleeve. She spoke around a mouthful of Paraian chewing leaf. 'All feeling is gone in my toes.'

'It's been almost a month. How are you not used to this?' Mithrid snorted.

Aspala looked horrified by a snowflake landing on her nose. She blew it back into the air and sliced it with her sword.

Mithrid grumbled to herself.

The creaking of boots in fresh snow brought three bent and swaddled figures across the yards. As they emerged from the haze, one, Mithrid was glad to see. The other two, she could have done without.

'Fine weather you've picked for some training, Mithrid,' Savask greeted her. He came to stand by her side, leaving Trenika and Lurn outnumbered.

'They've come in peace, Mith,' Savask whispered, a faint hand on her chainmail shoulder. 'Do me a favour and let them speak.'

'Think it's time we put our minds together, instead of against,' Trenika said.

'What's brought this change?' Mithrid asked, on the cusp of mocking their joke. 'Got bored of being shunned, have you?' Since the incident with the daemon, the more unenthusiastic rumours of Mithrid had died away, and made pariahs of their pedlars. Suspicion had pointed backwards. The twins had stuck to themselves, eating on the walls or patrolling alone. She had seen Savask with them, too, and wondered who had convinced who of what was about to be said. Mithrid sheathed her axe but kept a hand on its steel.

'Got bored of this death and fighting and shitting on ice, more like,' grumbled Lurn. He was missing a tooth and had bandages around one leg. Trenika nudged her brother into silence with an elbow.

'Krommish caught an arrow to the eye this morning,' she explained.

Mithrid winced. 'Sorry to—'

Lurn cracked his neck from side to side, shedding snow from his hood. 'That makes ten now from our barracks. Who's next?'

'There's got to be a better way to win this war rather than hiding behind these walls. Savask and I've been talking, and his ideas are…' she paused to chew the words. 'Interesting.'

'Hurts you to say, doesn't it?' Mithrid replied. 'But for just a moment, let's get one thing straight. We're talking about the same idea you've been babbling on about for days, right? That somebody should sneak out there and kill Malvus themselves. Head from serpent and all that.'

'Right you are,' Savask answered, proudly bobbing his head so much that his spectacles were almost dislodged. 'And now that we've seen your magick, we thought who best to do it than you?'

Mithrid let the question hang while she attempted to gauge whether Savask was joking. She looked between them all, from the earnest siblings to Bull's furrowed brow. In the end, she found herself laughing. 'You can't be serious.'

'Why not?'

'Because Farden would never go for it. He says it won't work—'

'Farden doesn't have to know, Mithrid.' Savask cast an eye around the yards. 'We get the job done ourselves.'

'That sounds suspiciously like treachery to me,' Mithrid accused. 'Rebellion.'

'Aren't we all rebelling here?' proposed Lurn. 'This ain't about the king. It's about you.'

Trenika approached, fingers clasped and pleading. 'I saw you halt a daemon with your own hands, Mithrid. Only the Written can do such a thing. Now Bull tells us you took on two Scarred last night? I don't know how you do it, but if there's anyone that can strike at Malvus and cut right to the heart of the Arka, it's you. Newblood or not.' Her smile was pathetic, still halfway mocking through habit, but Mithrid saw the effort. 'The Outlaw King clearly doesn't see it. We do.'

Savask interjected. 'Save a lot of souls doin' it.'

Mithrid looked to Bull and Aspala, remaining silent and shivering in the cold. 'You two agree with this madness?'

Aspala spat her brown chewing leaf on the snow. The dark smear drew everybody's eyes, like a seer casting her stones. 'Though I hate to give Savask's yammering any credit, I've seen a lot of magick in my time, but none like yours, girl,' she whispered.

'And you, Bull?'

The lump's gaze was faraway but firm. 'I said it before, Mithrid. What if it was us out there? I think about it every time an arrow leaves my bowstring. I see now Malvus is the root of everything. He sent those men to Troughwake that night. Maybe they've got a point.'

Mithrid was distracted by Lurn staring at her in a way that made her skin prickle.

'This won't work without you,' he muttered.

She didn't answer. Not because their plan was preposterous, but because another white-wrapped figure was hobbling towards them, cane in hand and face bare to the snow.

Despite his cripple's amble, General Durnus seemed in a rush. Savask and the others bowed. Mithrid waited to hear what the vampyre wanted.

'Mithrid, training as always, I see!' he rasped. 'Would you accompany an old man on a simple mission?'

'What mission is that?'

Durnus looked at the small gang that stood around her. His eyes lingered on Savask's ample belly. 'I will inform you on the way. Time is wasting.'

Mithrid balanced going with Durnus to the preposterousness of the Trenika and Savask's ideas, and found the latter wanting. She moved to Durnus' side and extended an arm. She eyed the others until the snow obscured them.

Weaving through the doors and corridors of the Underspire and Frostsoar, with half its souls either asleep or on the walls, Mithrid spoke up. 'Where are we going, General? What's this mission?'

'Though we have not spoken much, Miss Fenn, you have been amongst us long enough for you to call me Durnus, please,' he said. He sounded tired, and in the lantern light, Durnus looked it, too. More paper than skin. The idea that he had not eaten in some time crossed her mind, and Mithrid, for a moment, wondered what his intentions where.

'And I need you to help me follow Farden.'

That morning seemed to be a breeding ground for ridiculous ideas.

'Because?'

'Because I want to know where our king is sneaking off to in the mornings. It is always the same. First, he inspects the forges, then he takes Ilios north again. This must be the dozenth time.'

'However kind it is telling me this, and clearly trusting me, Durnus, I can only wonder why you're telling me this. I can't leave Scalussen. He doesn't want me more than a hundred yards from the Frostsoar. Surely Modren or Elessi—'

'I have chosen you to accompany me, Mithrid, because I fear what is in our king's mind. I fear he is planning something with dire implications. Alone and without counsel. He is stubborn and bound to reject my wisdom, but I believe he might listen to you, Mithrid. You two seem to share the same mind.' Durnus cleared his throat. 'Besides, should Farden be engaged in something particularly foolish, I fear you might be the only one who can stop him. Much to my shame.'

Mithrid's feet scuffed to a halt. 'Did you say *stop* him? Why would I —'

'Our king has made some *questionable* decisions in the past. Taken some paths I would have urged him to stray from. I am certain he walks one now.'

Mithrid blinked hard. 'I…'

Durnus was already tapping his cane on the lift door.

'First, we need a Mad Dragon.'

'I'll say it again: go away, I'm sleeping,' said Fleetstar, puffing a cloud of smoke at them. Mithrid couldn't help but cough. 'I've been patrolling all night, carrying Siren knights hither and fucking thither.'

The vampyre affixed a curt smile. 'You can sleep afterwards. This will take but an hour at the most.'

'You're not my Old Dragon.'

Durnus leaned conspiratorially close to Fleetstar's snout. 'No, because the Old Dragon is precisely who I do not want you to tell. You cannot speak a word of a single detail of what you see. Not yet.'

One of Fleetstar's eyelids popped open, switching between Mithrid and the vampyre. 'Why so secretive?'

'You will see.'

Mithrid watched the dragon take Durnus' bait of mystery wrapped in intrigue. Durnus reeled it home with a challenge. The old coot certainly had some tricks in his vacuous sleeves.

'Besides, you will prove who is faster, you or Ilios.'

Fleetstar scattered straw as she got to her tree-trunk-like feet and extended a wing that nearly knocked Mithrid over.

'That little gryphon can't beat me,' snarled the dragon. A candle flame escaped her nostrils. 'Get on.'

Mithrid grabbed the saddle with eagerness and strapped herself tightly to it. Durnus was barely in his seat before Fleetstar dove from the eyrie and into the swirling, amber world of snowflakes and razor-sharp air. Mithrid knew no up nor down. With no horizon dividing land or sky, they could have sped upside down through a dream for all she knew. All that mattered was holding on and keeping her eyeballs from freezing.

How Fleetstar saw through the murk that drummed against her numb cheeks, Mithrid had no idea. It must have been some dragonsight that she immediately and sorely envied. Fleetstar swooped and weaved as if avoiding unknown obstacles. Once, Mithrid turned to find a wall of black and ragged rock barely a yard from Fleetstar's wingtip. She had to swallow her heart back into her chest.

Beyond the glow of the Arka hordes beneath them, the world turned a charcoal grey before blossoming a deep red. The snowflakes in places became flakes of ash that left her fingers dirty. A low and constant rumble accompanied the rush of the air.

Where the northern air grew too hot and soot-choked for snowstorms, the murk peeled back to reveal a landscape of fire and smoking rock. A mountain bigger than imagination's limits soared before Mithrid. Its jagged peak held the bright glow of fire. Molten rock dribbled from craters. Flaming stones hurled themselves down the mountain's charred slopes.

Farden and Ilios were nowhere to be seen at first. Then, between the crags, a flash of white, speeding through alleys of black rock. Fleetstar pivoted on her wingtip, tumbling from the sky like a bird struck by an arrow. Mithrid had to swallow her tongue to keep the vomit back. Somehow, Durnus turned even paler than usual.

Fleetstar chased the king and gryphon through the smoking canyons. Mithrid's eyes couldn't trace the threats fast enough. Just as she thought they would plough into one edifice, Fleetstar had snuck around it and was hurtling towards another. When they weren't choked by sulphurous vapours, or shielding their eyes from waterfalls of molten, vermillion lava, the gryphon's tail was always disappearing behind a wall of rock.

The Mad Dragon didn't play by Ilios' rules but rose above the canyon's black jaws. Mithrid could hear the rock whipping past them above the volcanic thunder.

Fleetstar aimed for an archway of stone, tucking her wings to thread the needle's eye of rock. Beyond it, the slopes of Irminsul rose violently upwards. Mithrid's neck crunched as she tried to take it all in.

At the base of the volcano stretched a halo of golden sand, and upon that sanctuary, huts stood on stone pillars, like sailors clinging to masts of sinking ships. They spread up a zigzagging mountain path. Canals of orange rock flowed past the settlement on either side.

'Who are these people?' Mithrid shouted.

She felt the vibration of the dragon's voice as much as heard it 'The Kharander. Lost snowmad types who think the volcano is a god.'

'And is it?'

'It is not merely a mountain, that much is true.' Durnus answered her. 'I cannot see Farden.'

No sooner had Fleetstar landed in a cloud of fine, choking dust, did the Kharander approach.

Bald men and women in ochre robes and burns decoratively scarring their face swept forwards in a small crowd. They beamed wide smiles as most snowmads did in greeting, except their teeth were dyed black with soot. On their feet were iron shoes with teeth that bit into the uneven ground.

Mithrid was more fascinated by their beasts nattering away behind the Kharander's procession. She had never heard of nor seen the like. They were sleek, weasel-like creatures, twice the length of a cow but half the height. Their skins were the colour of coal, and along their tails and legs orange fire simmered away. They seemed most intrigued by the dragon. Two snuck forwards to come sniff at Fleetstar.

The vampyre bowed deeply. 'We're here for a mage. Farden.'

'Farden!' Mithrid repeated in a louder voice, drawing a dry look from Durnus.

One of the Kharander stepped forwards to speak. '*Ker'a henu. Ratal sereni.*'

Durnus wrinkled his nose. 'That is one odd dialect. Erm... Tall man. Armour. Riding a gryphon.' He tapped his chest, mimicking clanging noises.

'*Fah haraden!*'

'That sounds close enough.' Durnus nodded, grinning back.

To a person, they all pointed to the volcano and its winding path. There, they saw the speck of the gryphon, perched like an eagle keeping watch over a field. With his hunched wings and swishing tail, Ilios looked somewhat threatening, no matter what Durnus and Farden had assured her.

Before they knew it, the Kharander were guiding them towards the peculiar fire weasels. Tutting at the fiery spots on the beasts and cooing over the furred sections and woven saddles on their spines, they guided Durnus and Mithrid each onto their own mount.

'*Pikalo*,' the Kharander kept repeating.

Mithrid wasn't sure if that the name of the beast or an instruction, but she decided on the former. She patted her pikalo and listened to it chatter, like a clamshell skittering across boards. Mithrid smiled. Whatever this journey was for, she was glad she had come.

Durnus clicked his tongue as if he were riding a cow. Riding a dragon should have taught him better; he almost tumbled along the beast's fiery tail before getting a grip. Mithrid cackled as she sped past him, leaving Fleetstar to take flight and hover above them. The Kharander bowed in the dragon's shadow, chanting something in a voice low like Irminsul's grumbling.

The pikalos scurried through the crags as though their minds moved twice as fast as their feet. The bursting vents of sulphur and steam didn't seem to bother them; they only spurred them faster with each blast. Mithrid would have found it exhilarating had she not been concentrating so hard on holding on.

It was the mage who ground them to a halt, stepping out from behind a rock and startling them into rearing. Seizing their reins in both hands, he dragged the pikalos back to the black earth and let them snuffle and lick at his armour with forked, red tongues. They seemed to know him.

Farden crossed his arms. His stubble-worn face was flush with anger for the vampyre. 'You shouldn't have come here. You especially shouldn't have brought Mithrid.'

'I was worried you might do something reckless.'

'Go back to the Frostsoar. You may take that as an order.'

'No, old friend,' countered Durnus, sliding from his mount while simultaneously singeing himself on the pikalo's leg. 'We have come for answers, and we shall not leave until we have them.'

Farden looked adamant, avoiding their eyes. 'No, Durnus. It's not time yet! This is my burden, not yours.'

Mithrid held herself back, watching them step closer together.

'Time for what?' asked Durnus, waving his stick as if fencing. 'What keeps drawing you here when you have the whole Arka horde on your doorstep?'

Farden scowled.

'What?' Durnus shouted. 'Does your trust in me finally fail after these long years, old friend? Or do you still think Mithrid is a spy?'

'No!'

'Then if we are not traitors, you must fear what we will say,' Durnus surmised. 'What have you done, Farden?'

Mithrid watched the mage wrestle with that for a moment. She jumped from her pikalo. Her scraping boots made Farden turn. The face that regarded her had an expression of pain, not merely anger. 'Follow me,' he growled.

They wound along the curves of the path, softening the sheer slopes, yet still precarious with frequent tremors and tumbling rocks. Mithrid could feel the heat emanating from the ground as if she waded chest-deep in summer waters.

Farden spoke as he walked, grinding out his excuses. 'With spies everywhere, I couldn't trust anyone with this knowledge. Not even the council. Even tongues waggling innocently could betray us. And you, Durnus, you would simply force me to do the right thing.'

'Are you saying you are doing the wrong thing, mage?'

Farden called over his shoulder. 'Only if it fails.'

Durnus stumbled, forcing Mithrid to catch him. 'What have you done, Farden? Tell me!'

The mage paused at the top of the path, where a great rift in the mountain breathed smoke. Scratched runes decorated very available surface. 'It's not what I've done, old friend. It's what I will do. This mountain is older than Emaneska itself. Here it sits, full of fire and hate, pent up over centuries, millennia even, or so the Kharander say. They pray to appease its anger, yet know one truth: that one day, this mountain will erupt in fire and lightning, and consume the north in flame.'

'We knew this when we built Scalussen and ran that risk willingly, knowing it could take decades. Centuries.'

'Yes, we did,' Farden raised his chin, swallowing as if his throat was choked by the ash. 'And Malvus' arrival has changed that. All the magick gathered here has only fuelled Irminsul. You've felt the tremors, surely. Seen the sky burn brighter at night?'

The mage stepped deeper into the rift, where heat and smoke billowed. Sparks scattered like corpse flies fleeing a body thought dead. Farden put his hand on the black, puckered rock. 'There is something within this mountain, Durnus. No dragon, no daemon, but a force older than both. Irminsul will erupt. It will explode, and when it does, I will wield its fire against Malvus and his hordes like the Book on my spine. I will wipe them from existence with Irminsul's rage.'

If Mithrid thought she had heard her quota of madcap plans that day, she was proved sorely incorrect. She tried desperately to hear Farden's words in any other way. Durnus was beside himself, pale eyes a raging blue. He looked every bit the fearsome beast the tales painted his kind.

'And what of Scalussen!' Durnus challenged, once he had finally summoned the wherewithal to speak. 'You would murder us all?'

Farden refused to meet their gaze. 'I ordered the digging of three tunnels the day before Malvus arrived, each of them deep and far-reaching. Dug in absolute secrecy. You told me not to worry about the small duties, Durnus. This one I did worry about. You will escape south, under the ice to the Tausenbar and Chaos Sound, where the Rogue's Armada will be waiting. I will let Malvus take Scalussen, I will let him think he's won, and then I shall reduce him and his army to cinders when Irminsul erupts. It is merely a matter of timing.'

'M—*merely* a matter, he says! Of course, just as simple as opening a quickdoor! How do you presume to control a volcano? What of all we have built? Our home is upon this ice, Farden.'

The mage shook his head. 'This was always a battleground, Durnus! You knew that. Towerdawn knew that. The High Crone and Ko-Tergo. Even Warbringer knew when she brought her clans here. Everything is temporary until we win our freedom and can build a new Scalussen. A new Frostsoar, right on top of the Arkathedral.'

'That is but pure fancy, Farden! Even you cannot control this power,' hissed the vampyre. 'And you say I toy with dangerous magicks! You will die attempting this, you fool!'

'A price Emaneska should have paid a long time ago,' Farden muttered, so low Mithrid strained to hear him. 'This mountain will erupt, as carelessly as a minotaur swats a fly. It could blow tonight, and end Scalussen and Arka both without hesitation. It hasn't yet, and I call that fate, if you will. This is the weapon Malvus does not, and will never, expect. We will wait, poised until Irminsul wreaks its fury, and then I will bend it to my will.'

Durnus looked as though he would snap his cane one moment and tugged at his ears as if they were broken the next.

Farden walked deeper into the mountain where the heat was fierce. His armour shone with firelight. Mithrid followed. She felt as if her skin might peel at any second. A fear began to build in her gut.

Beyond the rift, a balcony of raw and pitted stone thrust into a cavern afire with red and amber glow. The further Mithrid walked, the more of it she could see: the raging pool of molten rock, surging as fluidly as rapids. The acrid stench fought to shut her eyes and throat but she forced herself to stare deep into the shining crater, and see an immense shape churning beneath the fiery rock. The stone beneath her feet shook as if hating her gaze.

Durnus only saw the insanity of the Outlaw King's plan. 'This is madness, Farden! Utter madness! Never before have you suggested something so preposterous as this,' he hollered.

The mage whirled on him. 'And what else would you have me do, old friend? I have thought of this and nothing else for days upon days, watching every pyre after every Arka attack, knowing this could save us all! You knew that morning, when we saw the horde upon the ice. You knew we were doomed. I will not have those we've fought to save die slowly, rotting away as the weeks and months drag on until Malvus overwhelms us. I will not have people like Mithrid know what it is to have the whole world's hopes pinned on you, all for nothing and no end but choking on mud and blood. Nothing else than this can break such a horde. Not me! Not Mithrid! Not Scalussen!' Farden looked to her, hair wild in the scorching winds of the crater. 'This is the way of it. This is the weapon I've chosen! That is my order, and Emaneska will thank me for it when Malvus has been scorched from this earth! I will save us. I alone carry that duty. I always have.'

The painful pause was filled with roaring, and a momentary jet of molten stone that splashed against the cavern walls. Mithrid stood firm, watching the fiery globules spit and sputter. She could hardly tear her eyes away from the fire.

'How long until the tunnels are done?' Durnus asked.

'Two weeks, perhaps,' growled Farden.

'And should this blow before the tunnels are finished? Or Malvus breaks our walls before this volcano decides to speak?'

'Then we'll all die.'

The vampyre threw down his cane. 'You've risked us all without thought nor query, Farden! How dare you be so callous!'

Mithrid frowned. She had a voice in all of this lunacy. *And a say, for that matter.* She had earned that. 'What I want to know is if you would kill them all? Every last person, even if it they counted as innocent?' she interrupted. The others looked at her as though they had forgotten her.

Farden looked insulted. '*Innocent*? Have you had your fill of vengeance so quickly? What did you think would happen here? You are too young in this war to know, Mithrid, but Malvus is too adept a liar, too controlling. They all worship him, even if simply through fear. I will save the people who matter. His lies have to be burned out lest they spread. Trust me. No mercy until freedom.'

Mithrid advanced on him. 'What if it were me out there in the horde? What if Modren hadn't found me?'

The mage turned away, gnawing on her words. She chased his gaze until he snapped.

'If I'm the king of anything, Mithrid, it's what-ifs and what-could-have-beens! Nobody tortures themselves with past choices as I do! The world is how it is,' he yelled. 'The Arka chose their side. Sealed their own fates.'

Mithrid stared at the mage as if he were a stranger in Farden's armour. She backed away, not thinking of the direction until Farden raised a hand to stop her. Scarlet hair scattered across her face. Smoke curled around its threads. Disappointment ran through her as the mountain began to shake her bones.

'Don't. Fucking. Move,' Farden whispered, all argument faded, eyes wide.

Durnus spread his hands to the earth, concern etched into his wrinkled features. 'Calm yourself, Mithrid. Now.'

She barely heard the words. The increased rumble of the mountain was wonderfully distracting. As were the fountains of rock pluming in reach of their precarious balcony, and the blinding ferocity of the fire below. She realised the smoke was not the volcano, but her shadow.

Mithrid sank to a knee as she was shaken from standing. Ignoring the hot shards of rock beneath her palms, she scrambled for the grey light of day until she could run without toppling. She hawked and coughed at the air. Farden and Durnus rushed behind her, the mage's arm around the old skeleton. Smoke billowed around them. Sparks rose into the acrid air like a barrage of flaming arrows. The tremble in the rock seemed to quiet as they scrambled down the path. Ilios flapped around them, casting up clouds of ash.

'What was that?' Mithrid stared between Farden and the vampyre.

'You,' coughed Durnus.

'It would appear whatever magick is in this mountain doesn't like you,' said Farden. The accusatory atmosphere quickly returned to fill their vacuum of confusion. 'You continue to impress, Mithrid Fenn.'

A cold fist sat in her gut. 'What are you talking about, Farden?' Mithrid challenged.

Whistling sharply, Farden brought the gryphon to the earth and quickly climbed to his back. 'Ever fired a crossbow, girl?'

She had not.

Durnus had already guessed. 'No, Farden—'

'It would appear you are Irminsul's trigger, Mithrid'

Mithrid stood unblinking even when Fleetstar whipped up grit and ash into her face. Farden wanted to burn the world, and he wanted Mithrid to spark the tinder.

When Fleetstar skidded through the mush and ice, Mithrid did not wait for him to come to a halt. She jumped, landing hard but walking away without a word.

'Mithrid!' Farden shouted after her. 'Mithrid!'

All she did was hoist up her hood and walk a little faster through the snow.

'You hold your tongue, girl!' he hissed threateningly.

Mithrid whirled, gaze narrow and hot with disappointment. *Saviour, they called him.* 'I will. Don't you worry about that,' she muttered. 'As if anybody would believe me.'

Farden was left staring after her, dark hair masking his eyes.

Much to the guards' displeasure and mumbled insults, Mithrid kicked open the doors to the Underspire. The blurring stairs clattered past her boots, snow flying in clumps, until she reached the barracks' very depths. The day was half spent. Some shifts of soldiers slept, others slumped in quiet retrospection or chatted in hushed tones. The rest of the beds were vacant, whether through death or duty.

'Savask!' Mithrid hissed.

A head poked out from the bunks, swiftly followed by four others.

Beckoning them back up the stairs, the gang trod quietly and quickly until they made it to Mithrid's quarters. The piebald lycan was poking at the ice tree when they found him.

'We'll need some privacy, Roglurg.'

The piebald lycan licked a fang, eyeing Trenika and Lurn. He waited so long it verged on uncomfortable. He clearly did not enjoy being ordered by a group of recruits a fraction of his age.

'Please,' Mithrid repeated.

The lycan stalked from the room. He did not stop at the door but wandered the corridor with his feet thudding heavily on the stone.

'Changed your mind, Mithrid?' Savask breathed a sigh of relief that Roglurg was gone. His apparent fear of lycans had only intensified.

Mithrid chewed the inside of her lip, not trusting herself to speak.

'How come?' asked Trenika.

Mithrid held onto Farden's secret. The thread of respect she had left for him demanded that much. 'Call it perspective. All you need to know is that somehow you don't sound as mad as you did earlier. I'm in. When do we execute this little plan of yours, Savask?'

'I've been watching the guard patrols and the Arka lines. After the next battle, we'll go at night, on the second bell.'

Mithrid nodded. It felt as though she tumbled with an avalanche and did nothing to save herself. 'Tell me every detail.'

CHAPTER 30
THE DEATH OF MERCY

What strange creatures they must be, to spring from eggs fully formed, as though it were a chicken, or a monstrous goose! Be wary, in your travels, of stumbling across a dragon breeding ground. Closely guarded are they, and hold vicious retribution for the unwary trespasser! Be wary also of the eggs themselves, as rumour has it that they burn with a mystical and cursed fire. If ever you are unfortunate to come across an unprotected egg, leave it be, for the infant dragon may sprout at any time, and emerge hungry and snapping for its first meal!
EXCERPT FROM 'DRAGONS AND THEIR FEATURES: LESSONS IN IDENTIFYING THE SIREN BEAST', BY MASTER WIRD

The sound of breathing filled Modren's helmet. Slush sprayed as he pivoted on his boot. The notched sword dragged across the attacker's exposed neck, opening his throat to the spine. Blood fountained, stinging Modren's eyes before he could push the clinging soldier free of him.

A nimble duck saw an axe blade grind sparks against the parapet stone behind his head. A stab to the axe's owner pierced cheap Dromfangar tin to the guts. Modren ripped the sword through the woman as he charged onwards. She retched, clutching at her tumbling innards all the way to the baying masses below.

Modren was too late to rescue a young recruit skewered on an Arka lance, but he dealt revenge on his murderer. The undermage broke both his legs with a fierce shot of lightning and used his boot to make him pay the rest of the price. And more. By the time he moved on to the next fool climbing a ladder or grapple, the man barely had a skull to speak of, never mind a face.

Arka after Arka met the scarlet, half-melted snow before him. Through magick or steel, the walls were washed red.

A wolfish man covered in hair pounced upon his back. With a spell, Modren went from face-down in the muck to upright in a move so violent it threw the wolfman from his back. Eyrum was there to cleave his arm from his socket. The creature fell to the true lycans waiting below and truly rested in pieces.

A horn blasted across the walls. Modren punched the air with fire. Once more, the Arka onslaught tucked tail and retreated.

Light struck Modren's right cheek, rare warmth in the biting cold. It was as if the north itself smiled at the victory. Shafts of dawn were breaking through the ragged coattails of the storm. Its vanguard wind was sharp, smelling of salt to mix with the copper blood.

'Keep firing!' Inwick yelled. Dozens of mages followed her command until Modren countered it.

'They're retreating, Inwick!'

Inwick practically spat in his face she came so close and spoke so vehemently. 'Less for tomorrow. And the next day. It's been a week of this, Modren. A week spent exhausting nothing but ourselves day and night. We've lost two thousand more, and their horde has barely shrunk.'

Modren took a slow and deliberate step back. 'Lower your voice, General. There will be rank and order in Scalussen until the Frostsoar is rubble, understand me?'

Farden stood nearby, a dozen burned corpses at his feet, and fire still trailing on his shoulders. His visor was shut, but his gaze south, refusing to witness Inwick and Modren, said it all.

'We waste our chances. Again, and again,' Inwick hissed. She shouldered past the undermage and stormed through the ranks.

'Clear the dead. Collect the injured. See to any repairs. You know what to do,' Farden shouted to them.

The cries of, 'Aye!' were more muted than they had been at the start of the week. Malvus was attacking them with more than just ladders, towers, arms, and arrows. He assailed them with drudgery. A blunt weapon, sure, but enough to see even the proudest spirit pummelled into the earth with enough time.

Modren stood close to Farden. Even without touching the mage, Modren felt the tattoos on his arm glowing hot beneath his armour. Magick still poured from Farden. 'Eight attacks in five days is enough to drive anyone mad,' he said.

'It's her Book, Modren. You know that as well as I do.'

Modren had hoped for some easy conversation, but he guessed not. Every word spoken between the council members seemed too heavy of late, traded between them like blows. It was easy to blame the pressure of war, but it felt too much like sentience; a worm gnawing at all their hearts at once. *So be it*, he thought. 'Aye, but I haven't given up on her as easily as you seem to.'

'I have not given up on her!' Farden whirled on him. 'I haven't given up on a soul within these walls. But you know there is no cure for what awaits us in old age. Time and time again I've asked him to find a cure. But no.' The mage sighed. 'He is too obsessed with his mythical spear.'

Modren nodded. 'He's told me of it.'

'Even you two are at each other's throats like rutting boars.'

'A questionable comparison.'

'We're all swords half drawn. I saw Eyrum put a fist through a keg yesterday because some of his soldiers smuggled a drink. A single mug of wine, after the fourth attack in two days. Where's the camaraderie gone? The righteous unity of our cause? Gone, Farden, and it pains me to see it. No, it terrifies me, because without the Arka's numbers, the only way we win this is together. Even you, this last week, have seemed absent. Distracted. Always looking over your shoulder.'

Farden hung his head, saying nothing. Modren waited, and waited some more, until at last the mage seemed ready to speak.

Modren was wrong.

Farden walked away, leaving nothing but the words, 'We keep fighting,' for Modren's comfort. The undermage seized a discarded helmet and crushed it with a force spell. Half of him wanted to hurl it after the mage, just to get a reaction.

Modren caught a perfume on the wind. Turning, he saw Elessi on the steps. Her face was furrowed as a farmer's field and her arms crossed over her breastplate. She, too, watched Farden storm away to the inner walls, ignoring every hail and bow he was given.

'I haven't seen him like this in some time,' Modren sighed, as she came to clutch his arm. She daubed at the stranger's blood on his face.

'Neither have I, but it doesn't mean I don't recognise him.'

'What do you mean?'

'This is the Farden that has made a decision, and yet knows we will hate what he's decided.'

Modren shook his head at his wife. 'How did you get so wise?'

'Get? Was born wise, husband,' Elessi snorted. 'And I've known Farden almost as long as Durnus. I'm tellin' you: that mage has got something rollin' around his head. We better be prepared for it.'

'How?'

'By praying, is all. See if those gods aren't as useless as Farden says.'

'Tonight.'

The word was barely a breath from Savask. He brushed past her and proceeded along the crowded mess queue as if they were strangers. His conspiratorial leanings had only been exacerbated by the days of planning, plotting, and waiting. The first two had only cost a day at most. It had taken almost a week for the Arka to attack again.

So it was that Mithrid had stewed in a pot of discontent for days, made worse by being cooped up and kept away from battle. Her key to Farden's volcano lunacy had made her even more important to Farden than before. However, in Scalussen, importance apparently meant incarceration. Every chime of the hours had only fortified her decision to betray his trust.

With a single word from Savask in her ear, all the impatience faded. Mithrid's stomach began to churn in a dark form of anticipation. She did not dare call it fear. She was too determined and aggrieved for worry. It reminded her of the thrill of deciding to defy her father; of sneaking along the ladders of Troughwake, satisfying her will and only that.

Mithrid practically inhaled her stew. As did Aspala and Bull, whose ears Savask had also whispered in. They traded glances across their lonely bench but kept their mouths full instead of talking.

Mithrid almost threw her spoon across the yards in fright when Hereni clomped down next to them.

'There you are,' said the captain, smiling broadly at Mithrid. 'The king is still insisting you stay out of harm's way, I see? I—we missed you this morning.'

Though Hereni's eyes pierced her, Mithrid did not trust herself with small talk. She found the mage entirely too disarming, and though Mithrid longed to involve her, or at least have her blessing, she knew Hereni would do neither. 'It would appear that way,' was all Mithrid muttered.

'It's a wise choice. Those Scarred came after you as well as Farden. Shows how dangerous you are. Who knew, eh, cliff-girl?' Hereni smirked. 'How wrong was I?'

Mithrid could feel her kindness, but from the stares of Bull and Aspala, her wariness turned to rudeness. 'I'm flattered the emperor thinks so highly of me,' Mithrid spoke around a dumpling. 'So dangerous am I, that I should apparently stay indoors and not fight back.'

Hereni ripped her loaf in two. 'Farden's keeping you safe is all. Probably for something clever, knowing him.'

Mithrid snorted. *Clever.*

'If it were me, I'd let you wreak the havoc I can tell you were born for,' Hereni added.

The honesty struck Mithrid. 'Truly?'

'Truly. This is our world we're forging in fire and blood. Why shouldn't you help build it? But…' Hereni sighed. 'The king grows warier with every Scalussen body that hits the ice. Too troubled. He piles them on those red-gold shoulders of his and buries himself. Now he fears losing his friends so intensely, he's forgotten how to trust them with harm's way.'

'That's pretty bloody astute,' Bull whispered.

Hereni nodded. 'I've grown up around these people and grown up fast. Malvus might not be getting through our walls, but he's getting to us. All that fucker has to do is wait out our stores and patience.'

Waiting. Mithrid loathed it. She gazed north, past the busy, steaming cauldrons of the cooks to the bruised sky above the Emberteeth. Time was the true enemy of a siege, with its seconds counted in deaths.

'We have to go,' Mithrid said, standing abruptly. Bull and Aspala followed her.

Hereni looked disappointed, staring at the now empty table. 'Well... if you must.'

'It's time somebody reminded Farden what he's forgotten,' Mithrid said, in a quiet voice. 'That he doesn't get to make decisions for everyone.'

Hereni gave her a strange look, and for a moment, Mithrid lost herself in her eyes. Bull nudged her, and she hurried away across the dirty snow, back to the Underspire.

Savask was waiting with Trenika and Lurn. In their hands hung sacks of certain items appropriated from the expansive Scalussen armoury.

'What did the captain want?' Trenika hissed, eyes narrowed over Mithrid's shoulder.

'Nothing of importance,' Mithrid replied dismissively. 'Did you get it all?'

'That we did. Took it off the dead before they're burned. Did you doubt us, Hâlorn?' Trenika simpered. A week ago, Mithrid would have slapped it from her face, but she smirked instead.

'If all stays quiet when night falls, we'll go,' Savask whispered, constantly looking up and down the corridors.

Mithrid prodded him in the arm. 'You better be right, Savask.'

The Albion man chuckled, belly wobbling. He tapped his nose. 'I've got a feeling.'

Mithrid hoped he was right. She was done with waiting. Farden wasn't the only one in this fortress on whom the Scalussen fallen weighed heavily.

❦

Hereni had paced the outer walls twice, even completed a circuit of the Frostsoar, and in the end, once night had cloaked the lands, she still found herself in the training yards, staring at the door to the Underspire. Exhaustion pawed at her, bent her shoulders and put an ache in her temples, but she rejected sleep. Mithrid occupied her mind.

Hereni looked to the stars. The trapped gods and daemons had not shown their faces in a while, and the moon had yet to rise. There was a fog to them from the shields Farden had ordered held all night and day.

It was not so much Mithrid, but her words. They had echoed about Hereni's mind all afternoon until she had decided they seemed too purposeful. Weighted with intent.

It was an excuse, perhaps, to see Mithrid once more, but it was a worry that drove her to the door and sent Hereni striding towards her quarters.

Roglurg, the lycan guard, was asleep by Mithrid's door. That was something that lycans rarely did, especially in view of anyone else. They were private amongst their packs.

Hereni politely nudged him with her boot, letting him come awake with a snarl and slurred growl. They shared a look before both springing to the door. Roglurg barged it open, finding nothing but an empty room, save for a plant and some spare pieces of armour, spread about the room. Too many for one person.

'What happened, lycan?'

'I not know. She was here. Alone. She left me some of evening meal. I—'

'Fell asleep.'

'I do not remember,' the lycan snapped, angry at himself more than Hereni.

The mage looked up to him, feeling the warmth drain from her face. 'Find Farden. Find him now. I don't know why, but I fear Mithrid has made a very poor decision.'

The piebald beast whined for a moment before Hereni shoved him down the corridor.

'Go! Now!'

'Now!' Trenika whispered, face barely visible in the shadow of the ice.

Mithrid dashed through the shutters of light cast by the wall guards. It was twenty feet, no more, but she ran with her heart in her throat. Behind them, the echoing toll of the night's second bell chased them.

Bull skidded in the snow, almost tumbling. He wore a sheepish face once more.

Mithrid put her hand on Bull's wrist, reassuring him as much as she did herself. 'I've got your back.'

Lurn tutted loudly. 'You better have all our backs. Us surviving this whole plan rests on you. I ain't dying tonight.'

Savask prodded him. 'Shut your fucking mouths!' he hissed.

Trenika was last to sprint through the light. No shout was raised.

'Where now?' Aspala asked. Black cloth swathed her face and horns. She had blackened the shine of her sword.

Savask ambled along the edge of the ice, where it curled in on itself and left a thin, cold alleyway between the rock and the wall. 'To a door forgotten,' he whispered. 'The Outlaw King had most of the doors bricked up, but not this one. Not after it got claimed by the ice.'

The man's fingers traced a rough outline of a square door, armoured in an inch of ice. He brandished a key Mithrid had never seen until now, and before she could ask, Lurn barged past her. She could feel the lad's magick billowing behind him like a cloak.

'Ready?' Savask asked.

Lurn shrugged, pressing his hands to the frozen door. 'Stupid question.'

Fingers glowing and fire spitting against the cold, the ice was no match for fire. Meltwater ran in rivers around their feet, and every moment was spent staring at the dark parapet above, hoping nobody leaned far enough out to see them or the drifting steam that Trenika tried desperately to disperse. Mithrid was glad the moon hadn't shown her face.

With a crunch, a sheet of ice cleared the handle and keyhole, allowing Savask to rattle his key. The group shrank in on itself as some great cog clanked. Together, they inched the door inwards. More ice blocked their passage, and Lurn set to it.

'I got it,' said the mage, squeezing through the small hole he had melted. It was a tight fit, but it broke into a short passage through the wall.

The key went to work again, and again, Lurn had to melt the cold from around their escape. Trenika lent her magick to the effort. Bull lingered in the background, constantly looking behind him.

Mithrid sidled up to him. 'Are you ready for this?' she asked.

'For Troughwake,' was all he said, avoiding Mithrid's eyes.

'For Troughwake, indeed.'

A waft of air announced the twins' success. They disappeared into the dark hole burrowed into the layer of encroaching ice. Bull had some trouble, but Mithrid brought up the rear, ramming a shoulder into his buttocks to squeeze him through.

Something made her look behind, as if Modren or Farden or Hereni would come barging out of the passage at any moment. She dallied as long as she dared, but nobody came to stop her.

'Mithrid!' Bull hissed.

Beyond the shield of ice, there was nothing between them and the Arka horde but the wall of stakes that marked their camp.

'Cloaks,' Mithrid said.

They hoisted up their fur cloaks smeared with chalk and ash, blending almost perfectly with the ice on a moonless night. Beneath them, they wore traitorous attire: Arka mail and tabards stolen from the dead of recent battles and scrubbed of blood and char.

First came the dash, something they did in a sweeping curve from the walls, along the ripple of ice that gave them brisk cover, and then directly for the Arka lines, hoping neither watchmen saw their departure nor approach.

It was a mad and hair-raising scuttle across the brittle landscape, but they made it to a hollow a slingshot from the Arka lines, where torchlight and bonfires blazed. Sneaking glances, Mithrid counted a watchman every fifty yards along the stakes.

'I didn't realise how fucking stupid this plan was until right this moment,' Mithrid hissed, prodding Savask in the arm. 'Don't worry about their guards, you said. Their walls are full of them, all watching outwards!'

'What are we supposed to do?' Bull whined.

Savask prodded her back, unfortunately choosing her steel shoulder and bending one of his long nails. 'We wait for the change, is what I said.

I've watched these Arka shits for days. Half of the guards are Albion conscripts, already beaten and tired. Wait for the third bell from the fortress, then we dash right there.' He pointed towards a gap where a spur of rock pointed through the ice like a pen through parchment.

Trenika shoved them both. 'Both of you, shut up,' she whispered. 'If we have to wait, then we wait, and do it bloody quietly.'

'You'd better be right about this, Savask' added Aspala. From that dangerous woman, it sounded like a death threat; one that made the Albion man curl up on himself and grumble into his furs.

A cold and punishing period passed. Mithrid's eyes were drooping when Savask began agitatedly prodding them all.

'They're moving,' he hissed.

'Now?' Mithrid asked, lips numb from the northern air. It was colder beyond the fortress walls.

Ice sprayed as Savask scrambled out of the hollow. 'Now!'

Mithrid could have vomited, her insides were so strangled by panic. She dashed madly behind Savask and heard the panting of Trenika close at her heels.

Though almost impaling herself on a blackened stake, Mithrid reached the lines without hearing a single shout. They panted and heaved, fat Savask especially. Discarding their cloaks, they began to tread the slush-filled paths between the stakes with the casual lope of any other Arka guard, each quietly and desperately praying their gold and green colours camouflaged them.

Their invocations were heard. The first enemy soldier they crossed paths with belched, chuckled, and wished them a, 'fucking wink of sleep if you're lucky.'

Savask took initiative and garbled something back at the man in thick Albion accent. A laugh was shared and onwards they crept, weaving between tents, lean-tos, and anything else that could separate the soldiers and mages from the persistently bitter cold. It shocked Mithrid to see frozen corpses resting between the Arka tents: poor souls who had bedded down foolishly on the ice or been left without a scrap of shelter. None of the Arka seemed to pay them any attention besides giving them a wide and callous berth.

Deeper and deeper, they wound into the enemy camp. To Mithrid, every step felt like half a victory, half a step towards a noose with her name inscribed on its knot. Though they tried to keep their heads straight, their eyes wandered, eyeing the strange makeshift markets that had set up between soldiers, or the faint traces of battered siege engines, repurposed for firewood. Amongst the quiet chatter around braziers and bonfires, the injured and dying howled from healers' tents.

Besides the golden and green colours, Mithrid saw the same expressions on these men and women as she did in Farden's fortress. There were people of Paraia amongst the horde, such that Aspala stared longingly at their fires. People of the far reaches of the empire, too, and soldiers that looked cliff-born like Mithrid was. She saw one man weeping privately in the open door of his tent at some circumstance of his. Another two figures huddled close, foreheads touching and conversing too quietly for Mithrid to hear. Another, nose black with frostbite, absently scraped the ice from his axe.

All Mithrid saw during that agitated walk through that camp made her hate the emperor more. She fixed her eyes instead on his ship-keel fort, and let her power run cold through her arms.

Deeper still, and the intruders stumbled upon the edges of a daemon enclave. The reek of sulphur seized their throats immediately, and before they could retreat and find another way around, a nearby daemon took notice of them. It was a withered thing, sat stooped over a fire and grilling what looked to be a collection of amputated limbs on its coals. Its wings were hunched like damask umbrellas. It did not lunge after them, as Mithrid expected, but leered at them instead, like a hateful neighbour on his porch. The helbeast curled at its hooves seemed asleep.

'Scurry on, insects. Lest you wish to taste the flames,' the daemon said, stoking its fire.

Mithrid couldn't help but flex her powers in case the monster chose to come closer. It had the opposite desired effect, and she immediately cursed herself. The daemon twitched as if catching a foul scent of his own. The helbeast stirred with a cough of smoke, and Mithrid found memories of her first test stabbing her.

'Agh, your magick stings, insect. Begone with you,' it cursed, making the intruders scarper into a copse of tents as fast as possible. Much to Mithrid's worry, the daemon arose, and began to stalk after them. Curious, or hungry for fresh meat, she couldn't tell.

Between the haze of cooking fires and tobacco smoke, they lost sight of the creature, but their fear did not subside. They were drawing looks, for some reason, as if their armour or markings did not belong in that section of the camp. A few shouts in a dialect only Trenika and Lurn seemed to recognise assailed them. They yelled back something that seemed only mildly convincing. Mithrid didn't need to know the language to know what a challenge sounded like. Her first clue was the twins beginning to run.

'What's happening?' Mithrid breathed.

Trenika jabbing the crest of entwined eels on her breastplate. 'They don't like whatever shit-smeared Albion family we stole these off.'

'Fuck's sake!'

The winding makeshift roads of the camp and crowded tents saved them once more. The emperor's fort loomed now, still vaguely resembling the ships it was hewn from. Pennants hung limply on its flagpoles.

To Mithrid's dismay, two daemons stood before it, doubled in number by Scarred mages, who languished against pillars and ropes as if interminably bored. Or drunk. Some were both. Mithrid hoped they were attempting to drown the sorrows of their dead friends, if these half rotten bastards still knew sorrow. Atop the fort, mages held shields, necks craned to the sky.

'This is it,' Savask whispered, while they pretended to warm themselves on an unoccupied brazier.

'This feels too easy, Savask,' Mithrid said.

'Doesn't it just?' Trenika looked around, wide-eyed and wary.

Savask shook his head as if they had just suggested the sky was yellow. 'Easy because they don't expect it, like I said. Malvus is too confident.'

'Or they don't think anybody would be this stupid to try such a thing,' Aspala muttered.

'You ready, Mithrid?' Lurn asked, still looking as doubtful of her as ever. 'Because I told you, I want to walk away from this.'

Mithrid took out her axe, ignoring the looks they received from the men at the next brazier. In her other hand, she let the night curl around her fingers, sweeping all traces of magick from around her, feeling the living heartbeat of the daemons as the thudding of an axe against a tree. She eyed the others and nodded.

'Let's fucking do this,' snarled Lurn while unsheathing his sword.

Sweeping forwards in an arrowhead with Mithrid at its point, they charged the fort. The daemons barked orders for them to halt, but there was no retreat now.

Mithrid met the first daemon head-on, crippling it by dragging the magick and soul from its legs. She was glad these were small specimens; the effort dizzied her. Trenika and Savask hacked at its blistered hide as they dashed past. The other daemon spat fire but it faded a dozen feet from Mithrid, sweeping around her as black smoke and nothing more. It retched as Mithrid found its power and throttled it. The beast's wings cut through a tent and sent two braziers scattering before Bull put an arrow in its face. No sooner had it collided with the ice than Aspala was by its side, stabbing until her sword smoked with its blood.

As shouts rose up into the air, the Scarred advanced, gauntlet hands stretching to Mithrid. Spells sputtered, but she was now burning with her dark magick, ringed in shadow. She ripped their power from them, and smirked as they looked dumbfounded at their hands before Lurn cut them down without mercy. Mithrid swung her axe, taking a hand from one of them before Savask ran him through with his sword.

'For trying to kill me,' she hissed, spitting on his corpse before racing towards the fort's entrance behind Aspala. More mages sprang at them. The Paraian woman was a tornado of steel, slicing gizzards and nicking arteries in a dozen different directions before Mithrid could even be of use. Blood-spattered and bewildered, all she could do was press on, driving a wave of power before her.

At the mouth of the tent, magick lanterns withered before her. Shadow blasted through the tent. Mages clutched at themselves before succumbing to the advancing Scalussen blades. The four of them whirled in a tight circle around Mithrid, blades outwards and ruthless.

After cutting their way through several curtain walls and corridors, they found it: the throne room of the emperor. Malvus' grand throne – a polished stone seat with fire burning on its arched back – sat empty. Only a leather and fur-wrapped man waited for them, lounging on the ground before it. Not the emperor Mithrid had seen on coins, nor in the spyglasses atop the walls. This man bore a thin slick of obsidian hair and a wicked look in his eyes. When he grinned, he brandished needle-thin teeth crammed side by side, more dragon than human.

The intruders formed ranks, daring him to challenge them. He stayed put, waving a ringed hand in salute.

'You've done well, girl, to come this far. I wonder how well you would have done had we not known you were coming.'

As if hearing an order Mithrid was deaf to, Savask, Trenika, and Lurn all turned their weapons on their nearest comrade. Lurn pinned Bull to the nearest pillar with his wicked knife. Aspala froze as Savask's sword poked her gut. And Trenika, of all people, outmanoeuvred Mithrid by grabbing her axe and holding a dagger under her chin. She had never seen such finesse on the frozen yards.

'You utter cunt,' Mithrid hissed, trying to hide the weakness that surged through her. Legs trembling, she fought to stay above the dagger's blade. She wanted to vomit.

The cruelty in Trenika's laugh burned her.

'A cunt that still outfoxed you though, eh?' she said.

Mithrid shoved her axe, scraping the bitch's armour but drawing no blood. She ached to drain Trenika of every drop. It was not her cunning. Not the betrayal itself, but how Mithrid had walked into her trap as succinctly as a blind pig into a snare.

'What in Hel is happening?' Aspala screamed, eyes burning yellow in the gloom.

Caring not for the knife poking his belly, Bull roared, shoving Lurn with all his might. The lad tumbled across the floor. He came to a rest against the dragon lord's kneecap, sprawling with his eyes spinning in all directions. Maddened, he forced himself up, immediately succumbed to dizziness and plummeted onto his chin.

Bull had the crimson fog in him. The same intent glare her father had without the bottle of firewine in his hand.

'Careful, boy,' grinned the dragon lord, uttering a sharp whistle in the same breath.

Guards wearing the gold and green of imperial steel flooded into the tent. It took two of them to restrain Bull. It required four to handle Aspala, who strained to get her hands around Savask's neck. Even though Mithrid was pinned, her power leaked from her, cooped rage battling to be free. Shadow trailed from her arms. Trenika hissed as if stung by it.

'Stop her!' boomed an authoritative voice.

A swift punch from Trenika saw Mithrid reel.

In a waterfall of gold and white silks, Emperor Malvus appeared, fingers heavy with rings and two knives crossed at his stomach. A circlet of gold rested upon his brow. Behind him, a hulking daemon, nearly too large for the tent to accommodate. A fiery crown slowly rotated above his spiny head.

'Come now!' the emperor chided Trenika. His kindly, charming tone was at odds with the carnage Mithrid had seen him wreak on his very people. 'Restrain her, but do not harm her. I will not have her injured.'

Mithrid and the emperor met each other's gazes: one a hailstorm trapped behind glass; the other mildly intrigued, hiding a world of smugness.

Malvus Barkhart was not a foul man wrapped in drapery to hide a hideous shell. He wore his finery as if born wearing it. He had no pus-filled boils, no scars gruesome enough to mention. He did not leer. He did not lick pointed fangs like the dragon lord, and he did not itch to carve a name in Mithrid's belly like Trenika so clearly did. Malvus looked nothing like the grand villains that fairytales had sold her as a lie. In truth, she could see an attractive man behind his years, and even they did not show their crinkles and spots like his age suggested. Malvus was kingly, by all rights. Somehow, that made him more dangerous.

Before the emperor was done studying her in return, Mithrid sucked her teeth and tasted blood. 'You look at me like some sort of prize. A head for a plaque on the wall.'

'Halfway correct,' Malvus replied, sweeping across the floor in measured paces. 'You are a prize, are you not? Though I hardly had to battle to win you. You walked in here so confidently. It was almost no challenge at all. Noble causes can be manipulated so effortlessly.'

'No nobler than turning you into a headless corpse,' Mithrid muttered.

The emperor displayed teeth so white they looked porcelain. 'Such a tongue! Farden's taught you much, I see.'

Mithrid sneered. 'I taught myself.'

Malvus approached her slowly. 'Does that extend to your magick? Hmm? Leech magick, so they say, a breed never before seen in old or new blood.'

'I'm even better with an axe,' she snarled.

'Emperor,' a barrel-chested man who looked like a descaled version of Eyrum spoke up. 'Be careful.'

The cad laughed brazenly. 'She would not cross me. Not if she wants her friends to live a while longer.'

The blindness of Mithrid's anger parted like the curtain of a suspicious fishwife. She remembered Aspala and Bull on either side of her. The big lad struggled on half-heartedly. Blood dribbled from his lip and nose, courtesy of the soldiers' fists. Aspala was oddly still, letting the Arka guards bind her wrists.

Malvus stood mere feet from Mithrid. She hated herself for already being on one knee as if pledging allegiance. She tried to rise, but Trenika shoved her to the floor.

The emperor said nothing. Mithrid longed to rip the eyes from him, never mind the latent magick she could feel under his skin. Something in it tasted sour; the same stench as the daemon lurking nearby.

Malvus reached for her neck with a hand, whether to lift her or throttle her was worryingly unclear. All Mithrid saw were those ringed fingers of his, and how they began to shrivel the closer they came. How the nails yellowed, and how the age ravaged that hand all in three heartbeats and as many steps.

The emperor withdrew his hand as quickly as his stately posture would allow. Grasping it with his robes, he affected a false smile and ignored the stares of his generals.

'That is no leech magick,' rumbled the fire-eyed daemon building shadow in the corner.

'Chain her and the others together behind the fort. Fetch a fenrir cage. Put them out of sight. Guarded. No one touches the girl.' Malvus looked last to the dragon lord, whose eyes had not left Mithrid.

Trenika and Savask received a downpour of congratulatory pats on the back as they led their prisoners through the tunnel of guards. Even Lurn, who staggered behind the throng, grinned bloodily. Though they manhandled Bull and Aspala roughly, none dared to touch Mithrid, poking her towards their cage with staves and spears instead.

'Happy with yourself?' Mithrid snarled at their betrayers.

Savask beamed. 'Months we've had to endure not only your incessant moaning, but the repetitive blathering of that moronic mage you call king. I almost killed you myself.'

'Twice, in fact,' Trenika laughed. 'We had to settle for Remina instead, didn't we?'

Mithrid sprang at her but was swiftly whacked on the chin by Savask brandishing a blackjack club. The man was faster, sprier, and devoid of the bumbling nature that had defined him previously.

Bull and Aspala waited while Mithrid was poked in first and clapped in irons through the cage bars. Bull was next. The poor lad seemed to have been broken by the whole sordid affair. Aspala remained standing before the cage.

'I will not be caged,' she said. 'I am free and will remain it. I would rather die.'

Lurn levelled a short spear at her. Mithrid heaved against her chains.

'That's a service I can provide,' he said.

Trenika was an unexpected ally. 'Brother. Not without the emperor's orders.'

'Didn't say we couldn't wound her. Teach her a lesson!' cried Lurn. The crowd of guards grumbled in support. 'You don't even belong here anyway, so far from home.'

'This is all of Emaneska's war. Not that a child such as you would know it.'

Lurn stabbed at her thigh but hit nothing but air. Before he could look up, the Paraian woman had already spun him around, and looped her chains around the lad's neck. Aspala wrenched so savagely everybody present could hear the crunch of windpipe over the commotion. Lurn spat gore in Trenika's face as he fell to his knees. He clawed at his crushed throat, dragging nothing but blood into his lungs.

To Trenika's howls, the clubs descended on Aspala as though she were a war drum. By the time she was hauled into the cage, she was beaten bloody, and her horns broken and halved.

'Let that be a lesson to you.' Savask jabbed at Mithrid for reaching out to her.

She spat all she had in her dry mouth at the man. 'Your lesson is coming, snake.'

The crowds dispersed, leaving a ring of soldiers drifting around the cage. Whispers and harsh cackles filled the cold night. Mithrid shivered against the ice underneath the bare straw bedding. She met the eyes around the campfires one by one, all staring at her.

They soon got bored when a gentle trembling shook the ice, accompanied by thunder in the northern skyline. The clouds beyond the dark bar of the Frostsoar blushed red. Mithrid put her hands to the ice and felt it quiver. It was brief, but it put a quiet in the Arka camp, like chided dogs.

No prayer fell from her lips. No whimper. She stared at the fiery glow to the north and hoped it wouldn't explode with her in that cage.

CHAPTER 31
EXTANT

Time and pressure, I say they and they alone are what truly shapes the world.
FROM SCHOLAR AND SELF-PROCLAIMED 'CHILD OF JÖTUN', JORTHISH MENSK

'She is dangerous, I tell you.'

Malvus turned on the daemon prince, wearing his most mocking look even though his heart still beat at breath-snatching rates. 'Gremorin, you shock me. You would not happen to be scared of this mere peasant girl, now would you?'

The daemon flushed with fire, skin cracking and flame bursting through his pores. 'You insult me, mortal. I see the cold hand on your tiny heart. The shake in your hand. You fear her also. She is an atrocity of flesh.'

Gremorin's eyes wandered down Malvus' front to where he clutched his fingers tightly.

'Then the more bountiful for us, Gremorin, for she is all the more important to Farden. Important enough to make him fight for her, perhaps. We will find out her true value tomorrow. If she refuses us, you may eat her companions.'

Gremorin grunted as if offered scraps from the emperor's table. His dramatic departure left a ringing in Malvus' ears and a tang of char in his nose. He swiped his way through the lingering smoke and trod the stairs to his lavish room of silks pillows, tapestries, and sweeping chairs. The captains had not been happy with him pilfering their staterooms, but a swift beating of their most vocal complainer had soon changed their minds. Malvus had taken a man's hand for getting blood on his favourite cloak.

The lanterns glowed weakly, pulling the shadows close around him. The Albion whores Wodehallow had brought had been banished from his room. Malvus found himself momentarily wishing Jeasin was there to lash with his tongue. She never failed to return the favour. Had it not been so cathartic, and had she not her other uses, Malvus would have turned her skull into a goblet two decades ago.

'Gah,' he snarled, reaching out with his aged hand before remembering why he had hurried there in the first place. 'Curse that girl.'

Unlocking a chest, he snatched the remaining daemonblood into the light. Barely a mouthful remained in the vial. Before he could put it to his lips, a burst of light startled him. The vial tumbled to the floorboards and smashed into silvers.

'By Evernia's tits!' Malvus yelled, half blind and slashing at the air with one of his knives. 'Will you stop that?'

The god was lounging in one of the emperor's chairs. Where he had found some grapes that weren't black with frost by now, Malvus had no idea.

'You know, they say that all the way from the arsehole of Bethmuir to East Jorp and the Hammer Hills, as if she were the goddess of voluptuous bosoms instead of magick, and yet nobody has actually seen the goddess' tits except on a statue.' He spoke around a grape, smoothing his lapels down his chest. 'And let me tell you, the sculptors have been very generous.'

The daemonblood smoked and hissed quietly on the floor. 'You idiot!' Malvus plucked at the shards. I needed that.'

The god reached into his coat and pulled forth another vial of the vibrant blood. 'Here,' he sighed, placing it on the table. Malvus snatched it up and poured down his gullet. His frequent use of it had dimmed the foul taste and its complimentary burn. As it sank its teeth into his guts and trembled his legs, Malvus seized a flask of wine to quash the fire. It was a meagre solution. He stared at his hand, willing it to shed its years once again.

'Tell me how you do that. Is it the coat?' Malvus uttered.

'As I said, I know where to find lost things. Truly lost things. Not hidden. Not at the end of a treasure map's dotted line. But all that is lost. Trinkets. Baubles. Even faces.'

Malvus fought the urge to retch. He stared avidly at his hand. It took some squinting, but he saw the liver spots and strangled veins fade once more. The relief was a rush that dizzied him into a slump on a couch. 'Poison,' he breathed.

Loki looked suspiciously at his grapes. 'What of it?'

'It is high time you were some use to me, Loki. You have told me nothing of use. You have an ability my spies would slit throats for and that somehow isn't hindered by the shields and runes as the daemons are. You somehow come and go as you please, watching it all from afar.' It took some effort but Malvus propped himself up on an elbow. 'Do you have any poison in those pockets of yours?'

'Poison? A coward's weapon, some say.'

The emperor jabbed a knife on the nearby table. 'Are you calling me a coward?'

'Not currently.' Loki chewed slowly. 'There are many kinds of poison. Some are imbibed. Some are eaten or taken through the skin. Others float on the air into your ears, to find their way to your soul. What kind do you need?'

'The kind that kills men dead in moments,' Malvus bared his teeth. 'And plenty of them.'

Loki squinted knowingly. 'The sort that turns the tides of sieges, I would also wager?'

Malvus felt heat in his cheeks. 'Have you ever hanged somebody, god?'

'Not personally. Seen quite the few though. Perhaps one day I might try it for myself. They say—'

'I've seen prisoners hold their tongues for a year in the Arkathedral dungeons. They will remain silent all the way through the jeering clouds. All the way to the stage. But as soon as that noose wraps about their neck, that is when all prison cells and torturer's needles count for nought. That is when they realise they are set for the grave.'

'Fascinating.' Grape juice sprayed as he produced another fruit from his pocket.

'You're not the only one with a plan, Loki. The more desperate Farden gets, the closer to surrender he gets.'

Loki pulled a face. 'Are you sure of that, Emperor? Not to doubt your most dagger-like of wits, but every time I've seen Farden grow more desperate in the past, something normally explodes.'

Malvus laughed, reaching for a goblet of wine. It normally held a tang of sour berries, but all he tasted was ash in the wake of daemonblood.

'You have been gone some time, Loki,' he said. 'Farden has more to lose than he ever had.'

Loki spat a grape seed onto the carpet and smiled.

Farden stared at the waxen scowl he had carved into the candle. Its half-burnt hair resembled a tuft of hair on its crater skull. Farden could have admitted there was some of Malvus in that scowl.

Putting his knife down, he clasped the candle in his fist. Though snowmads and witches believed in curses crossing leagues, Farden had yet to see any proof. Be that as it may, as fire curled around his fist, he thought of Malvus' face, somewhere safe amongst his horde.

All he felt was a rumble instead, faint through the thick stone of the Frostsoar, enough to make his discarded gauntlets chime on the seat's arms. It was brief, but enough to send him stumbling from his inner chamber, staring at Irminsul from his windows, the glass speckled with dragon blood and cracked from arrow strikes.

'Not now, you bastard. Please not now,' Farden muttered to himself.

As if the mountain granted him that one favour, the trembling stopped. The sky in the north remained an angry scarlet, but the ice fields fell still.

With a hunched back and eyes half-open, Farden tottered for his bed, seeking a world of pillows and eider down instead of a landscape of hordes and daemons and walls painted with blood. He shed pieces of armour as he walked, all save for his vambraces.

His head had barely struck the pillow before there came a clamouring at his door.

A familiar voice was yelling insistently. 'I don't care what he said about not being disturbed, he will want to hear this!'

'Let the fuckers in!' Farden bellowed through his pillow, before punching his mattress several times. He heard tramping feet and panting and dug himself free of comfort to stare at them. Modren, Elessi, and Hereni, all dour and wringing hands.

Farden stared at them from a hole in his tangle of sheets. 'What? What could you possibly want from me now?'

'It's Mithrid,' Elessi spoke.

No good news had ever begun with such few words. Farden's bare feet hit the floor without hesitation. 'What of her? Is she safe?'

Hereni looked white with worry. 'She's left the fortress. Gone over the wall and into Malvus' camp with five other fools.'

'They're in the Arka camp, Farden. Dead or alive, we don't know,' said Modren.

'She's…' Realisation struck him as he stared between them, silently begging them to splutter with laughter and for Mithrid to come sauntering around the corner. Cruel jesting, maybe, but infinitely preferable. None of the three eased their furrowed brows. 'No demands. Messages?' he asked, feeling as though the Frostsoar swayed. 'A fucking horn blow?'

'Nothing.'

Hereni was muttering. 'I knew she was up to something—'

Farden began to pick up his armour, sliding piece after piece over his cold skin. 'No, you didn't. Otherwise you would have known enough to stop it. There are enough sharp edges to that girl without finding another to cut yourself on.' Farden regarded the sea of lights burning in the south. He had trusted Mithrid with everything, and she had charged full tilt at Malvus. Farden grit his teeth. 'All we can give her are fresh minds at first light. Frayed wits and foolish dreams led to this. I won't risk the same trying to save her now, unprepared, without even knowing if she is alive. Those are my orders.'

Elessi and Hereni marched from the room but Modren took his time. He stood by the door, arms barring his chest. 'You and I had our Rituals a week apart. You remember? Spent six years in the school together. Been in this game a long time, we have, and I've followed you through mountains of shit and not once have I questioned you,' he said.

Farden frowned. 'I assume that's now changed?'

'This fucked up world gave you a gift and you kept it in your back pocket to stifle it. You called her a weapon and then kept it sheathed, for what reason I can't understand. Now she's out there, perhaps already flayed alive, and I can't help but think you drove her to it. And even now, you're coldly indifferent. This is not the Farden I followed here.'

The honesty was a cold blade, puncturing a lung. 'This war has hardened us all, Modren, but all those years you mentioned spent at my side count for fuck all if you think I don't care about Mithrid, or anybody else in this fortress. It is because I care so deeply, as if each soul taking breath in Scalussen is a limb of my very own. Mithrid most of all. I would save her from all of this if I could. I would spare her the curse of duty and power that we've suffered all these years, and been bent and broken for it. But I cannot. She is more a weapon than you know.'

'What aren't you telling me, Farden?'

Farden turned away to the Arka lanterns, spread like cinders across black sand. 'What I told Mithrid,' he muttered. 'What drove her out there.'

Modren seized the door and left without another word.

To the sound of a door almost slammed off its hinges, the undermage stormed past the chamber guards, and stamped his way down the corridor.

As the echoes of footfalls faded, the guards relaxed, spears tilting as they stretched sore muscles. 'He didn't seem happy,' one mumbled to her fellow guardsman.

The chap twitched his moustache. 'No, he did not. Wonder what's afoot now?'

A booming crash came from inside Farden's chambers. The moustachioed guard made to seize the handles, but the woman waved a gauntlet.

'Better not,' she whispered.

The tirade continued with destructive abandon. At one point, something smashed into the door, rattling its construction. Smoke snuck from under the door.

After sharing a wide-eyed look, the two guards sidled away from the door as quietly and surreptitiously as possible.

Mithrid awoke to a morning full of smoke and drifting ash. A nearby smith was punishing a glowing spear, caring nothing for the hour. Every ring of his hammer shot through Mithrid's skull. Cows tramped past through slush dragging wagons full of wounded or weapons. Their lowing was another clamour that pained her, never mind the slap of wet ice on her neck.

Mithrid groaned, trying to right herself without digging the rough iron manacles deeper into her wrists. The ice had frozen her bones. One leg was completely asleep. Her spine clicked in a dozen places before she sat straight.

A hand rested on her shoulder. Mithrid recoiled so violently she almost tugged her arm from her socket. Blood oozed around the manacles.

'It's all right, Mith,' Bull said. His eyes were half-shut with bruises. One tooth was missing at the corner of his mouth. His other hand was on Aspala's neck, who could only be said to be alive from the faint steam emanating from her blood-encrusted lips. Mithrid tried to lift Aspala's head off the ice, much to the woman's groans, and pack straw beneath her.

'You got a funny definition of all right, Bull,' Mithrid croaked. Now she understood the bodies left in their tents: the ice preyed on all warmth. She rubbed her hands, rattling irons, and tried to knead some life into her leg. She didn't dare take off her boot; it felt as if her toes had simply vanished, replaced with numb pain instead. She knocked the snow from her limbs, and pain shot up her leg. She seethed but did not complain. The pain was a fine punishment for the mess she had got them into.

'They tricked us,' Bull whispered. He was no longer the raging beast of the night previous. He looked sullen, back bent and face dejected like a hound with too much cheek. He looked like Mithrid felt.

It took her some time to admit how deftly she had been duped. 'That they did. Lied and cheated us into this situation. Lied and cheated Scalussen, too.'

'Trenika and Lurn. I never liked them, but Savask…'

Mithrid looked longingly at the braziers the Arka guards gathered around. A few torches sat on snapped lances, spitting dust in the snow.

'Can we get some heat?' she rasped at the nearest soldier, an oar's length away. Between the mask and frosted helmet, all she could see of his expression were his eyes and they looked mirthful.

'Shut your mouth, gutter worm,' he retorted.

'You want to be responsible for the emperor's prisoners freezing to death? Suits me fine,' she challenged.

The guard snorted but Mithrid could see the hesitation in his flitting stare. Within moments, he was stamping his foot at some of the "camp skivs", as he called them. Junior soldiers by the look of them, tending to menial chores, one of which included prying any dead from the ice and lumping them onto a cart. Several eagerly put down their shovels and scurried over.

'Move that brazier closer to the cage. You two skivs, find another fire. Quick now, or I'll whip you with my sword.'

Two of them seized the brazier with bare hands. Mithrid heard the hiss of skin on hot metal before they yelped.

'Spears, you fucking idiots! In those metal loops there. Lift, don't drag. Fuck me, where'd they find you headless twats?'

Mithrid pressed herself to the bars so she could feel the heat sooner. The brazier seemed weighty, judging by the strained looks on their faces. They looked halfway through a difficult shit. Two lads smaller than Mithrid bent double under the spears, while a portly girl brought up the rear, sweating profusely despite the bitter cold. Another sapling of a girl traipsed behind them, chainmail hood up and eyes down.

Mithrid watched her. She seemed too out of place amongst a place of war. Filth decorated her trews and tabard. Shit encrusted her ill-fitting boots. A cheap steel dirk hung on her belt, looking like swordsmith's scrap.

As the girl came closer, she began to mechanically stoke the flames with her blade. Something shone at her neck, peeking just beyond her armour. A sun-coloured stone on a muddy twine. The last time Mithrid had seen such a thing, it had been on a beach in Hâlorn, clasped by a girl called —

'Littlest!' Mithrid breathed. 'By Hurricane and all the gods, she's alive! Bull!' She frantically tapped the big lad on his arm. 'Bull, she's alive. She didn't die in the battle!'

The lad opened his eyes, winced, and then tried again. 'Fuck me,' Bull said. 'It is.'

A spear butt rapped their fingers, sending them both reeling from the bars. The guard lifted his mask and sneered at them. The frost had bitten his cheeks black. 'Shut your fuckin' mouths! You skivs. Bring another brazier, then back to shovelling those dead bastards. Before they start to reek. Daemons don't like 'em reekin'!'

Mithrid waited until the guard had shuffled farther away before she tried to call to the girl. 'Littlest!'

There was no response, as if she had been struck deaf since Hâlorn.

'Littlest!' she said louder, before trying her true name. 'Larina Hag!'

The girl looked up at the cage as if noticing it for the first time. Her eyes fluttered, confused. Bull and Mithrid pressed their faces to the frigid bars, caring little for the cold. The girl pulled at her chainmail hood, loosing long, lemon-yellow hair hacked short as a boy's. Her nose looked crooked. Sores hid at the corners of her mouth.

Mithrid's heart couldn't decide whether to soar or sink. 'We thought you were dead!' she whispered. 'Is Crisk alive, too?'

'Crisk. Crisk.' Littlest's eyes roved to the sky. 'Dead. Burnt to ash.'

Mithrid tried to reach for her, to take her hand, but Littlest didn't move. 'Do you remember me?'

Littlest cocked her head like a bird examining a seed. 'Mithrid,' she breathed, creeping closer. her eyes, once so full of fiendish energy, had no sheen to them. As if it had been beaten out of her. 'But you're dead, too.'

'We were taken by a mage. Brought here on a ship,' said Bull.

'I…' It seemed the memory was already distant. 'The survivors took me to Krauslung, but they got their throats cut in the night by Arka. They took me the rest of the way, till I was shown before his imperial majesty. Then they chose me for the army.'

'Hag, you're going to get us flogged!' whispered another skiv. His skin was as pale as a snowmad's, eyes red and bloodied.

Bull bowed his head. Mithrid swallowed the tough knot in her throat. 'We… We didn't know. We were told you were dead.'

Littlest picked at a tooth with her tongue. 'You left me.'

'What? No! We... Littlest!' Mithrid yelled after her, but she was already seeing to the corpses.

The guard jabbed the blunt end of his spear through the cage bars and winded Mithrid before whacking Bull in the side of the head.

'Shut. Your fucking. Faces! In fact, I won't tell you again, I'll carve it into your legs instead.'

Mithrid hunkered down, silent yet eyes avid, like an owl peering out of a burrow. She watched Littlest until she disappeared in the throngs.

'Another four hundred dead from the cold in the night. A Lost Clan food wagon was raided by some Albion miscreants. Lord Saker has seen to dispensing his own justice, namely disembowelment, which Grand Duke Wodehallow is far from pleased about. Some mediation might be a good idea, Your Imperial Majesty. Also, a trebuchet collapsed from the weight of ice, killing another five. Thirty deserters were caught by helbeast patrols in the night. And finally, there is still no word of the fled Scalussen bookships.'

Malvus was looking at General Toskig with a horrified expression, as if he had delivered his reports without trews. 'By the gods, I have never been more bored in my entire life,' he snapped.

'I...' Toskig began to explain but thought better of it. His eyes returned to the heavy lidded, imagined spot an inch above the emperor's head and remained there. 'Shall I refrain from the morning reports, Your Majesty?'

'Morons who are foolish enough to steal from the Lost Clans or who forget to bring a blanket to the north are far from what concerns me.'

Toskig bit into the old and far too familiar wounds at the edges of his tongue. Blood seeped. 'Yes, Majesty.'

Malvus was surveying his camp, particularly his new prisoners. Their cage could be seen over the fort's parapet. Some soldier recruits were manhandling braziers closer to it. 'Who is that?' he demanded.

'Camp workers and latrine daggers, by the looks of it.'

The emperor pointed. 'Not them. *Her.* That waif of a scrotum in the chainmail that doesn't fit her. Yellow hair!'

Toskig peered. 'I have no idea, Your Majesty.'

'Bring her to me.'

Toskig accidentally let out a groan. The battle to be the brunt of the emperor's moods, requests, and ceaseless blood spilling was a greater siege than Scalussen. After all these decades, Toskig was noticing his walls failing. His honour being sapped like dwindling supplies, day by day.

'A complaint, General?' Malvus snapped.

Toskig ground his teeth. 'None, Emperor. Confusion is all. What could you want with a small child?'

'You look at me as if I had the bedchamber tastes of our Lord Saker. No. I want her to do a favour for me, if she is willing. Send a hawk to the fortress. Farden will be most pleased to hear we have his prized pet,' Malvus instructed, raising his hands to the sky like some street preacher in the Bowels. 'And bring those deserters to me in chains. I will have them fed to Gremorin's ilk while I watch.'

'Aye, Emperor.'

Toskig set foot on the steps, tasting nothing but his own blood in his mouth. Though even he branded such thoughts traitorous, the old days were a glimmering, unattainable lighthouse in his mind. He longed for them, for the rule of the last arkmages; when war was nothing more complicated than sticking somebody before they stuck him, not slicing throats in alleys with poisoned knives.

As he had learned to do years before, the general inhaled long and deep through his nose. That day was not a good day for such practices: Toskig hawked on the stench of rotting meat and shit.

CHAPTER 32
FOUL HANDS

How in Emaneska a spellsmith wrought the quickdoor spell into such small an object as a Weight has antagonised every scholar and blacksmith who's lived since, and will likely fox them forever more. Gifts from the gods, they once were, and now only one remains.
FROM THE WRITINGS OF ARKMAGE TYRFING

Farden had given up counting. The Siren wizards, surer with their mathematics than most in Emaneska bar the Rolia numeralists, had counted at least a hundred thousand Arka dead. Farden couldn't see a difference in the horde. The Arka still dominated the ice fields like a forest of tent-spikes and spears. The stink of latrines and sweat and blood and charcoal swept across the wastes on a northerly gust. More towers and battering rams had sprung up with the dawn light.

Twenty thousand lay dead on the Scalussen side, ash on the pyres, never to see freedom or justice. *Twenty thousand.*

Farden looked to his generals, solemn and steady upon the wall by his side. The horde captivated them also. At the sound of a piercing screech, the mage held out his arm.

The hawk gripped his gauntlet with its spindly claws. Flapping its chestnut wings, it fought the wind while Modren untied the scroll, wrapped in green Arka silk.

Farden hefted the hawk into the sky. It did not fly south back to its cage but east, to whatever freedom its golden eyes had spotted. Farden envied him. 'Our enemy speaks at last,' he said. Within him, if felt as though his innards had been twisted into a bowstring and were aiming an arrow at his heart. The scroll threatened to loose it.

Modren read aloud. ' "Your presence is requested by order of the Emperor Malvus Barkhart, Lord of…" blah blah. "Should you wish to see the safe and whole return of Mithrid Fenn." '

Farden exhaled. 'She's alive, then. For now.'

'And hopefully you can keep 'er that way,' added Elessi. 'Right?'

'Mithrid is bait,' Durnus muttered.

Inwick scraped her nails across the parapet. 'Malvus seeks to murder us outside the walls in a trap.'

Farden's laugh was the sound of pebbles striking. 'Of course it's a trap. That's why we'll be ready to fight our way out of if we must. Mithrid might be bloody fool but she is important.' Farden caught Modren's sidelong stare. 'What the emperor doesn't know is her true potential. We'll hear the emperor's demands, and perhaps we'll get to finish what Mithrid started.'

Inwick snarled, veritably trembling with anticipation. 'Finally,' she said.

Farden hid his cringe, wishing he had any hope of ordering her to stay behind. 'I can see the bloodlust in you, Inwick. If you want to fight, I told you I need you clear of mind.'

'Hmph,' was all the reply Farden got, reassuring him not one bit.

'Gather Towerdawn, tell him I need another favour. Accompany her, please, Modren.'

Modren and Inwick departed without a word, leaving Hereni to step out from behind the vampyre.

'I want to help.'

Farden recognised the sharp line of her jaw and mouth, the fists white as snow at her side. The very same as when they had found her, fighting tooth and bone to be free of her Arka captors. 'Get your full armour on. We'll need it.'

Hereni drummed a frantic path down the stairs, outstripping Modren and Inwick before they had even reached the ground.

'She thinks much of Mithrid, that one,' Elessi hummed contemplatively.

In the days since Irminsul, scant conversation had passed between Durnus and Farden. Now they traded confused looks.

'What do you mean?' Farden rubbed a tired eye.

Elessi harrumphed. 'You men. You're half blind to anythin' you can't kill, fuck, or eat.'

Durnus looked particularly insulted. 'I am a scholar, madam, and—'

'You both look famished. Now, Durnus, I know your kind don't eat stew, but you do, Farden, last time I checked. You aren't fightin' on an empty stomach, so come on. To the training yards and mess lines with you. You can eat with your soldiers for once,' ordered Elessi.

Farden put up no fight. If there was a war he could never win, it was against Elessi. Durnus let her go ahead, assuring her they would follow.

'We should send her out there to chide Malvus to death,' the vampyre whispered.

'She'd be empress within the hour, and then we'd all be truly doomed.'

'Speaking of doomed...'

'Thron's balls. Don't start,' tutted the mage.

'I have said my piece and you know my heart, Farden. I will say nothing further on your mad plan.' Durnus swung his hand over the inner walls, where Hereni could be seen bolting through crowds. 'But at some point in this siege, you *will* have to tell the council, preferably before Scalussen is razed to the ground. When, is your choice. Yours and yours alone. That is a king's prerogative.'

Farden eyed blood frozen into the snow. 'I am no king. No grand royal or fable.'

'No matter what I think and what you want to believe, you are a king to them,' Durnus muttered as a contingent of snowmads came to attention until Farden had passed. Beyond their fur-swaddled ranks, a Paraian with spiralled horns raised his hands in salute.

'See? Those who did not believe before have now seen you fight. Seen you stand for them. They now stand for you as king. And more so, a saviour.'

'Enough! Leave the lyrics for the skalds and bards. Let them believe the myth.'

'All myths were made of flesh and bone once,' whispered Durnus.

Elessi had noticed their lagging behind and shooed them. 'Go on, damn it!'

Ahead of them, the snaking lines of soldiers and mages were taking shape upon the yards. Tables took the place of targets. Wagons for detritus and crockery waited in spread ranks. A great bank of vats and cauldrons steamed in the northern air. Their clouds billowed from under the slate roofs of the kitchens as if they were ablaze. A cohort of apron-clad soldiers toiled away on final touches, readying mountains of boards and bowls.

Farden was content to let the lines proceed ahead of him, but everywhere he stood, the crowds parted for him. Farden wished he hadn't left his visor in his chambers, but he affected a grim smile and nodded to all those who moved aside with shouts of, 'After you, sire!'

The stamping of feet began to spread, line by line, hammering a slow yet increasing rhythm.

'A cheer for the Forever King!' somebody shouted. It was enough to spark the crowds into a deafening holler. 'And a cheer for Scalussen!'

With the ice shaking under his feet, Farden found himself standing at the front of the lines, Durnus and Elessi at his back. He could not deny the grip around his throat, the imagined hand seizing his chest. Farden raised his chin. *Twenty thousand dead, and still they cheered.*

'Stew, milord?' said a grinning cook. Farden took two bowls, offered his thanks, and headed for a table across the yards. The steam clouding his face was hot, fragrant of cloves and salt pork. Hunger twisted his stomach within moments. He had not realised how long he had gone without breaking his fast.

The snow had turned brittle, but Farden scraped it away with his sword before sitting. Elessi, lending Durnus her arm, sat opposite Farden.

'It is quite literally boiling,' said the vampyre, poking at Elessi's bowl.

'I'd rather hot food than cold.'

Farden folded his arms and waited, much to the complaint of his stomach. 'Durnus prefers his still beating.'

The vampyre tutted. 'I am glad we are joking once more, mage. Shame it is in poor taste. Vampyric eating habits are not suitable conversation for dinner.'

'Why wouldn't you two be jokin'?' Elessi asked.

As she hoisted a spoonful of pork into the air to let it cool, Durnus wrinkled his nose at the steam in his face. 'What is that smell? It is unfamiliar.'

A strangled cry came racing across the ice from a nearby table. Farden's head turned so fast his neck clicked. A bearded barbarian of a man was clutching at his throat. He looked to be choking, all save for the violet shade of his teeth and lips.

Farden whirled, swinging a flat palm. Though he heard the crunch of bones in Elessi's hand, he regretted nothing. The spoonful of stew sprayed across the snow before it had touched her lips.

'It's poisoned!' Farden gasped, bounding onto the table. 'POISON!' he roared. 'Not a soul is to touch a single morsel! Captains! Sergeants! Round up every one of those cooks!'

In the scramble that followed, more screams and wretched coughing filled the air from the poor souls for whom Farden's warning came too late. From the atop the table, Farden stood aghast as he watched scores of men and women collapse across the yards. Not a soul stood by to help, as if their skin or furs were contagious. Horror froze the crowds faster than any northern gale.

'Elessi, bring Peryn and Wyved to me as fast as their legs or finches can carry them!' he bellowed.

'Right you are!' She wasted no time in sprinting across the yards.

'Healers!' Farden yelled, seeing only a handful raise their hands. 'We need healers! All others to your barracks or posts!'

Stomachs empty yet devoid of hunger, the Scalussen forces dispersed with shocked whispering and gaping eyes. They left a field of contorted corpses behind them. The poison still wrought its curse on the unlucky few. They writhed and screeched. Some tore at their insides. One man, before Farden could reach him, saw fit to gouge open his belly with his knife, as if he could cut the poison out of him.

When at last the yards had grown still, Farden spent the next hour treading the ice between the corpses and scattered steaming bowls. Finches flittered through the air. One was determined to perch on his pauldron and twitter in his ear.

Wyved and a dragon named Glassthorn were still making their way along the lines of cooks and scullery souls, interrogating each one's mind and soul. It wasn't utterly accurate, but a dreadlocked witch and a huge dragon with fangs spilling from its mouth staring at a person will usually make them crack enough for further questioning.

The impatience grew too much for continued silence. 'Anything, Wyved?'

The witch shook her head.

'Durnus!' Farden bellowed.

At last, the vampyre reappeared from the kitchens. Peryn was in tow, and her face was unusually grave.

'We searched a quarter of the stores so far. But everything we have found has some whiff of poison about it,' Durnus said.

'Gutshade. Amaranth. Devil's Spool,' recited Peryn, face gaunt.

Farden wiped sweat from his brow, now cold in the northern air. '*Three* poisons?'

Peryn shook her head. She held up the blue stem and the broken bulb of some tortured rose-like plant. 'All and the same, King. It has many names. Shaped small, but when it blooms, its spores spread on faintest breath. They are like grains of sand. I wager you dig in pockets, you still find sand from Albion waste, correct?'

Farden didn't have to test her.

'Sand gets everywhere you don't want it. Lingers. As does amaranth. One grain can make a cauldron the death of fifty men.'

Farden's tongue rasped against his dry palate. 'How much food is spoiled?'

Peryn shrugged as she let a finch land on her fingers. 'Almost all.'

'How long does that give us?'

Durnus' voice was but a cold breeze. 'Days, only,' he said. 'Why does this stink of Loki to me, Farden?'

'Because you're not wrong,' Farden admitted, scanning the yards, half-expecting to see the golden-haired bastard smirking from behind a barrel. 'Count and make sure, witch.'

Peryn swept away, leaving the mage and the vampyre staring at each other. Durnus held his tongue, letting Farden stew until he could keep silent no longer.

'Call the council,' he ordered. 'Looks like you'll get your wish, Durnus.'

The vampyre looked no happier than Farden felt.

🌑

The Wolf's Hall had the feel of a fireplace left to burn out: the cold charcoal seemed to suck in warmth, rather than give it.

Farden looked around the small gathering. They could have been a pack of archers for how skewered he felt beneath their accusing gazes. Peryn, Wyved, the High Crone, and Ko-Tergo sat close and conspiratorial. Nerilan had yet to dismount Towerdawn. Warbringer and Inwick hunched over opposite ends of the table, brooding.

'Excuse me?' Ko-Tergo growled, as if his translation of the Commontongue had failed him. 'Say that again. You wish to—?'

Farden sucked at his teeth loudly. 'Burn Scalussen to the ground using a volcano, taking Malvus and his horde with it in the process? Yes.'

Durnus quietly cleared his throat while the silence deepened like a yawning sinkhole.

'You knew about this?' Modren glared at the vampyre.

'For a short time, yes. I have already said my piece.'

'This is our home, Farden.'

Warbringer thumped her warhammer on the floor, eliciting a distant wail. 'One home already burned. Now we must find another?'

'Has the pressure of command utterly dissolved your mind, mage?' Nerilan stared at him as though he were fit for a sleeveless coat and the dungeons, rather than standing at the head of the scorched table, still with chunks of Scarred armour melted into the table's coastlines.

'Only the pyres I see almost daily, with hundreds of our men, women, and beasts burning upon them. What is the point of this war, if there are none of us left to build on its ruins?' Farden urged. 'I only aim to save us. We underestimated Malvus' numbers and his willingness to slaughter thousands to climb these walls. I realised the first day of battle that this would be our only chance at victory.' His gaze turned to hold Modren's narrow scowl. 'I kept it to myself to ensure Malvus would never know. I trust you all implicitly, I merely did not trust myself.'

Towerdawn shook the table with his growl. 'How close are your escape tunnels to being finished, Farden?'

'A week. Quicker, if I have my way.'

The dragon continued. 'And your only true control over Irminsul, which could erupt at any moment or not for the next month, is Mithrid Fenn?'

Farden nodded slowly. 'It would appear so.'

'Who is now in the hands of Emperor Malvus,' interjected Elessi.

'Somewhat, yes,' replied the mage.

The groans spread around the table as Farden held up his hands. 'There's more,' he said, already wincing at piling dire news atop bad news. 'Without Mithrid, our option was to hold out and wait for Irminsul. Months, perhaps, as we originally planned. As of this morning, that will not be possible.'

Nerilan's scales were flushed dark amber. 'Why is that?'

'Poison,' Farden uttered.

Chairs squeaked as the council looked between its members, as if the poisoner was within the hall.

'Malvus has managed to poison our food stores. How he did it changes nothing of the facts. What remains is that we only have days of food left, rather than months.'

Eyrum was far from impressed. 'How would you all like to die? Starving, burning, or on Arka swords?' he snarled. Warbringer was already on her hooves. The mutters grew to fever pitch.

'The solution, my friends, is simple!' Farden yelled over them.

'And what is that, pray!' barked Nerilan.

'We rescue Mithrid Fenn.'

The Wolf's Hall fell still.

Nerilan pointed her claw of a finger. 'You'd risk us all for that girl?'

'I would risk everything for any of you,' replied Farden, looking around the table. 'And who knows, we might come back with an emperor's head, and we can put Irminsul far behind us.'

Ko-Tergo and Inwick gave him the slightest smirk, wolfish and eager. It took several long, jaw-clenching and uncomfortable moments for anybody to speak.

'And how do you propose to do such a thing?' Eyrum grunted.

Farden, relief swelling in his heart, slumped into his chair with a clang. 'I'm glad you asked, Eyrum,' he said. 'Because I was hoping you might want to show off your steel dragon.'

The big siren's normally stoic face creased into an unusually broad grin.

CHAPTER 33
A WRETCH IN SILK

Yon elixir of discontent is brewed from the fruits of inattention.
A LINE FROM THE BANNED THEATRE PRODUCTION 'REGAL FOLLY'

Sleep had come easily to Bull and Aspala. Mithrid told herself it was their injuries that kept them slumbering. Sleep was healing, they said. Too much sleep was what they called death. Every time the guards came past on their circular patrol, she poked them to make sure they were still alive.

Rewarded by two different groans, Mithrid went back to her staring. If she stretched high enough, she could watch the gold echelons of the Arka wander in boredom about the walkways of the fort. The dragon lord Saker – or Lord of the Winds as the guards called him, a haughty title for one so repugnant – was a frequent taker of the cold air. He spent almost an hour staring across the horde and swilling wine. Whenever Mithrid happened to stare in his direction, she always caught his gaze. Those amber eyes never failed to put a shiver in her.

The sight of Littlest dragging her boots towards the cage and unhindered by the guards, was a surprise that caught her like a fishhook in the cheek. She looked away at first, only to be snapped back around.

Mithrid met her at the bars. Littlest avoided her stare. It was likely hopeful thinking, but there seemed a brighter light behind the windows of her eyes that day.

'I'm so sorry, Littlest,' Mithrid began. 'Bull would be, too, if he were awake. We asked after you, wanted to go back, but we were told you had perished. You, Crisk, and Hassamer. We thought you were all dead. We added you to the pile in our heads and kept on moving where we were told.'

Mithrid found herself babbling and put a stop to it. She told herself she talked to fill the awkwardness, but it was to chip away at Littlest's blame. Such was human nature: to be terrified of being wrong.

Littlest scuffed at the ice and mud.

'What happened to you?' Mithrid asking, giving her the floor instead.

'Why would you care?'

'Why wouldn't I? We're all that's left of Troughwake. We're family.'

Littlest looked around, swinging her hands over the tent tops and armoured figures. 'I have a family now. An army and an emperor to serve.'

Mithrid swallowed that lump again. How close had Mithrid come to standing on her end of the bars? She could see now the paths of fate and consequence did not run beside each other but diverged violently with each inconsequential choice. How close a path they had begun, and now she and Littlest stood on opposite sides of a chasm that crumbled wider every day.

'What happened, Littlest?' she asked again.

Gaze turned inwards in memory, Littlest told her. 'Don't remember the village much, but I remember the dragon coming. I got buried under a dead man. It was the foulest stench I ever did smell, but it kept me from the dragonfire. Mostly.' She poked absently at the scars on her hands. 'The handful that survived took me and three others east through scratching forest and rivers I've never seen the like of. I saw mountains for the first time, Mith. Made our cliffs look like steps. Every morning, every sunset, they beat us before staking us out in the cold. Starved us. They took an old one – a woman – into a tent and she never came out. Never made another sound. Two ran south, deserted, after.

'The night our saviours came, they were playing games with knives. Drunk like your father used to get, Mith. They came all gold and green, shining in the campfires. They made no noise, just dealt their justice. Showed us a wagon and straw to lie on. Rattled our way south this time until we came to a valley stuck between two mountains. I saw it. A city so big it should only be able to fit in dreams. White stones piled so high they hurt my neck to look at.'

'Krauslung.'

'I never saw it properly. Just from a distance in Manesmark. They kept us other survivors together in barracks. Gave us beds. Water. Told us what we already knew. We were safe, rescued, and in the care of the emperor.'

Mithrid scraped at the ice with her fingernails.

'He taught us how lucky we were to be out of the clutches of the rebels. And that we had a glory—glorious duty. I got all angry, Mith. Angry with you and angry with Mam. Angry with everyone who wasn't there, doing what was right. They told me I could be a soldier. Fight for the emperor himself to avenge my family.'

Same story, told by two skalds. 'Didn't they hurt you? Your bruises. Scars. They can't all be—'

'The emperor's hand is firm but just. Hard trials make hard hearts,' she interrupted in a drone, looking past Mithrid's shoulder as if reading lines. 'And now we are here, fighting for justice and peace.'

'You shovel shit and corpses.' Mithrid couldn't believe the words spilling out of the girl's mouth. A girl who had only cared for trinkets and her mother's hotpots. A girl so innocent she thought the dead ships on the shore were gifts from the sea. They had beaten or lied all the innocence out of her.

Again came that drone of a voice. 'All in service to the emperor. A war is fought by many hands,' she said.

Mithrid leaned closer, seizing part of the girl's tabard. 'Littlest – Larina – you're in danger here.'

'The emperor will protect me. He protects us all.'

'Tell that to the dead men you were picking up this morning.'

Littlest was unconvinced, blind to the evidence that littered her surroundings. Watching her, Mithrid heard her father's words: *a man will do almost anything if it suits him,* he had said. Convenience and necessity were the two most important threads in the tapestry of any person's life. Bathed in blood and fire, fed nothing but lies, Littlest had settled on an easy existence. The monster under the bed was preferable to the one outside the door. Mithrid tried to change it.

'You've been lied to, Littlest. Those were not rebels. They were Arka. The dragon that burned the camp? That dragon is in the Frostsoar as we speak. Her name is Kinsprite. Along with a mage, she tried to save us all. Those men that dragged you south and were murdered by your saviours were one and the same. It is a great ruse, Littlest, all to convince you of one thing: that the emperor is right and the Outlaw King is wrong. Bull would tell you the same thing. Malvus breathes lies.'

Littlest backed away. Mithrid's weak fingers peeled from her tabard one by one.

'No,' said the girl. 'You're the traitor, of course you'd lie. The Outlaw King's pet, they call you.'

Mithrid had hoped for something along the lines of "daemon killer". She was stunned. 'I am no pet! Farden might be... Farden, but he is no liar. Not constantly clawing for power. He is not—'

'Falsehoods.'

'Littlest—'

'My name is Larina,' spat the girl, retreating through the slush.

'Larina!' Mithrid shouted, but it was no use. She settled back against the cage bars. A sob of doubt and dejection took her, unexpected, unwanted. She fought its successor back but could not stop the tears that gathered at her eyes. She stared at Malvus' fort with abject hatred until it stung to keep looking. She closed her eyes, wedged her head against the bars, and sought a darkness without any thoughts.

All she could see behind her eyelids was a shadow. A colossal shape writhing in fire. A face, laughing at her.

Rough hands awoke her from the sleep of boredom that had kidnapped her. A leash choked her neck. She felt the manacles come free and ice scrape beneath her. She tried to curse them, but the words were strangled in her throat.

No respect nor care was paid to her, nor Bull and Aspala, who were dragged behind in equal thuggish fashion. The sun was now high on the southern mountains. It blinded her every time she tried to open her eyes.

The journey to the fort was swift. The heinous waft of the camp was replaced by candle smoke and sweet incense, barely welcome. It stung Mithrid's throat.

Malvus Barkhart sat upon his Blazing Throne. His bear of a general loomed behind the throne's flaming ridge. An obese Albion duke stood by his side, with a cumbersome gold chain across his chest. The dragon lord, Saker, too, yet no daemon prince. Another fellow she didn't recognise stood nearest to the emperor. Short of stature and golden haired, he wore no armour, nor nothing of gold nor silk, only a simple dusty, weather-beaten coat and a confident smile. There was a shine in his eyes that Mithrid recognised.

Surrounded by hooded Scarred, they all waited in silence for Mithrid and the others to stop struggling against the shackles that hooked them to the floorboards. Mithrid loathed looking up at the men, but she had little choice. Between the guards and mages, she spotted the haughty leers of Savask and Trenika, now dressed in their Arka finest and new ranks on their shoulders.

'Let me guess,' Mithrid began. 'I've heard a few eddas in my short years. Is this the part where you crow about your grand plan in an effort to impress me?'

Malvus stared at her for a long moment before sputtering with laughter. 'My, my, girl. It has been some time since any of my wards dared to speak to me with such bluntness. It is almost refreshing.' He snapped his fingers. 'I have changed my mind. Leave us.'

The duke yelped like a kicked dog. 'But...'

At Malvus' burning glance, Wodehallow immediately shuffled from the throne room.

'And you, Saker. Take your filthy proclivities elsewhere. I want Mithrid to feel comfortable.'

The rider snarled but did as he was told, taking his lecherous stare with him. He bit at a long fingernail and spat it upon Bull. Even the Scarred shuffled out, each one of them staring at Mithrid as Lurn had in the training yards, each silently betting they could take her. Mithrid let them believe it.

Soon enough, it was the emperor, the general, and the quiet man left.

'Privacy is best, I believe, for our conversation.' The emperor's tone was oleaginous.

Mithrid snorted. 'Ah, I was wrong. This is where you convince me that Farden is actually the villain, and you've been suing for peace all along.'

Malvus shrugged nonchalantly. 'Basically, yes.'

'It won't work.'

'First, however, I wish to know your secret. Your power, miss. What exactly is it that makes the daemons and mages alike fear you?'

Malvus' eyes roved over her, and Mithrid felt an itching spread across her skin. 'Nothing of note.'

'With my own eyes, I saw you kill a daemon atop the walls. It takes a strong Written to do that, and you, miss, are not Written.'

'Leech magick, they say,' commented the shorter man. Mithrid wracked her brains why she recognised his eyes.

Malvus mused through templed fingers. 'Was it you who killed my mage Corcoran, or was it Farden?'

'I won't tell you a thing,' she replied.

'Don't you dare,' Bull affirmed.

Malvus chuckled. 'General Toskig?'

The impassive lump thudded his way from the dais. He looked the soldier type, but the fire sparking in his palm said different. He seized Aspala with his spare hand and lifted her beyond her tiptoes.

Malvus inspected his rings as if bored. 'Burn her.'

'No!' Aspala croaked. Bull thrashed against his chains.

Mithrid went rigid, seeking to manhandle her anger into a cohesive force. Toskig's hands came closer, poised at the side of Aspala's head. Ice stabbed Mithrid's arms as shadow crept from her shackled fingers, twirling towards the general. His flames began to crackle like a torch in a gale. Within seconds, the spell had sputtered out and Aspala was dropped.

Mithrid saw Toskig's worry, his confusion. She mentally tore at him, forcing him to stagger backwards and clutch at his steel chest as if Mithrid had physically cut the magick from him.

'That feels... inhuman,' he gasped.

Malvus was on his feet and clapping. His golden rings chimed. 'Well, well. Not in almost thirty years have I seen the general so indisposed. Especially by one so young. So untested. What are you, indeed?'

Mithrid simmered quietly. Malvus came as close as he dared. Mithrid strained as far as her chains would allow to close the distance, but he was cautious, and she could not grasp the scant amount of sour magick that washed through his veins.

'You are something else, are you not? Something new,' Malvus breathed. 'War is an ugly, terrible thing, is it not? So barbaric. So cheap. And yet, some view it as their only option. Do you know how this war came to be?'

Aspala answered before Mithrid could. 'Because of you. You denied us our freedom. Our way of magick.'

'Denied your freedom? Oh, dear me, madam. All in the Arka empire are free. No. Your precious Farden started this war.' Malvus waited for his lies to blossom in laughter or outrage, but Mithrid and the others were barren soil. They merely waited for the preposterousness to unfold.

'All I did was notice an opportunity for peace and seize it,' he boasted. 'Trace every edda and account back to times before you were born and it has always been magick at the root of the problem. The old arkmages thought they were helping this world by allowing magick to flow. They checked it here and there, damming it and corralling it as farmers would a river. But they singularly underestimated it, and in their underestimations, evil flourished. Take the daemons, for example, who should still be locked in the sky. But here they are, and here to stay, all because of magick. I wished to save Emaneska by cutting free the poison that had plagued it for so long. It was a bold edict to ban magick, I understand that. Unheard of even! And yet, a united Emaneska was unheard of before I broke the Twin Thrones, and built my own,' Malvus waxed.

Still, the captors held their tongues.

'If Farden had relented his endless crusade to be called a hero, had he seen past his own ego, had he seen the slimmest iota of sense, we could have created the finest empire Emaneska has ever seen. A time of peace the histories have never written about. But.' Malvus waggled his finger. 'Farden did not relent. He instead came here to this frozen wasteland and built himself a monument that stood against everything I longed to build. He insisted on freedom when I gave it willingly. He fought his own war on the fringes, torching villages and kidnapping people exactly like you, Mithrid, to his cause.'

The girl smiled as sweetly as she could pretend. 'And what of the mages who came to my village one night, posing as Farden's rebels? Who sent them?'

Malvus played the sorrowful one. 'That mage has forced my hand in many ways.'

'Just like Kserak?' rasped Mithrid. 'You massacred every man, woman, child, and beast.'

Malvus had the gall to look proud. 'Yes, I did. In fact, Toskig here did that on my orders. Farden signed their death warrants the day he showed his face in Kserak.'

Facing away from his emperor, Mithrid could tell Toskig still remembered that day very well. A little too well, from the paleness of his face.

'You foul bastard,' Aspala rasped.

'Cut the shit. What do you want, Malvus? What am I to you?' Mithrid demanded. Something about her vehemence made the quiet, coated man chuckle.

'My dear,' Malvus beamed, 'you are fascinating. A freak of nature and magick, perhaps. But you are the embodiment of what Emaneska shall become: free of corrupting magick and therefore free of strife, of greed, and of war. The Arka shall reign for a thousand years, and our peace will last a thousand more. How fitting, you should emerge into the world as I fight to keep it. You and I have a fate entwined, Mithrid, a common purpose that Farden cannot begin to understand.'

Mithrid glowered. 'You slaughtered my family. Murdered a part of me. My purpose is to kill you.'

'A common career choice, these days,' Malvus let his words hang. 'Cupbearer!'

A small figure shuffled into the room carrying a carafe of wine and a jewelled goblet. To Mithrid's dread, it was Littlest, dressed in a smock of linen in the emperor's colours. Though her clothing had changed, her dull eyes had not gained any gleam besides what the candles and lanterns lent her.

Mithrid watched her with captured breath.

'I understand you know my latest servant, Larina?' enquired the emperor, sweeping to his throne and snatching wine from Littlest's hands.

'You lay a finger on her—!'

'I shall do no such thing, Mithrid, but would Farden? All he sees is the Arka colours. He would split her little skull open just to see her bleed.' Malvus clutched Littlest's head with his hand. 'What do you see?'

'A girl who should be let free. To live in peace, as any child should.'

Malvus cut the air with his hand. 'That is what I want.'

'Cowshit,' hissed Mithrid.

'She can walk out of this camp this very evening,'

'Do not believe it, Mith!' Bull whispered. Toskig struck him across his battered jaw.

'Even these... *friends* of yours can go with her,' offered Malvus.

Mithrid wanted to laugh but she lacked the spit. 'And why would a cutthroat like you do that?'

Malvus sprawled in his throne. 'Because you're going to tell the good Outlaw King to surrender.'

The three captors all croaked and coughed in amusement. 'He'd never do it,' said Mithrid.

'Oh,' Malvus replied with a grin, 'I think he might. What with his prized daemon slayer in mortal danger.'

'Then *I* won't.'

The emperor sighed. 'I can be persuasive, Mithrid.'

With another click of his fingers, Toskig began to beat Bull and Aspala. His steel fists elicited enough cries and moans for Mithrid. She blasted him with her shadow, but it seized nothing. Toskig needed no magick.

'Stop it!' she cried.

Malvus let the beating last another moment before clapping his hands. 'Do as she says.'

The fists halted mid-strike. Toskig receded. Bull and Aspala were left on the carpet, bleeding and wheezing. They both stared at her through their slits of eyes, and Mithrid caught the gentle shake of their heads; the silent pleading not to give in.

'Well?' Malvus asked. 'Unless you want your friends and Larina here to die, and the many like her who have only come here to serve their good emperor.'

Mithrid dug her wrists into the manacles, as if the pain was what she deserved for... she couldn't even bring herself to think it. *For agreeing with such a man as the emperor.* Malvus was a wretch in silk, refined evil sporting gold rings, but he was right. The fires of Irminsul raged within her mind. She imagined them washing across the waste, incinerating all. Even the innocent and the deceived, conned by a cause dressed up in whatever false promises.

Mithrid stared at Littlest as she spoke, fragile and barely audible. She hated every word that spilled from her mouth, but there was no choice in the matter. Mithrid knew that plain as she knew the sky was up. She was not formidable enough to watch friends flayed before her. Not for any cause. 'Send for Farden, then. I will talk to him, as you ask.'

The coated man spoke up. 'A hawk has already been sent.'

Mithrid glowered at both of the men. 'But whatever he decides, you will free them. Understand? Even a liar such as you can agree to that much.'

'While you are in no position to be making bargains, I shall abide,' Malvus said, with a grand twirl of his hands.

'You should bow in gratitude for the emperor's mercy,' grunted Toskig, but the emperor laughed.

'No need, General. They will thank me, in time, when this horde has gone home to its hearths and wives and hounds. Fetch them water. Stitch their wounds. Clean clothes, too. Guards!'

It could have been the whirlwind of guards swarming the room, or the conversation of knots and loops, but Mithrid's head spun. What made it worse was that every time she shut her eyes, the dark face of shadow was there to grin at her.

It was Toskig who shook her from her loathing stupor. 'Just do as he says,' the general whispered in her ear, nearly drowned out by clanking armour and the squelch of feet. 'There's no escaping him. You'll live a lot longer if you just do what he says.'

It was so unexpected, Mithrid almost stumbled. But he had said his piece and spoke no more.

Loki pulled a flagon of something dark and syrupy from one pocket, and a slim cup of crystal from another. The taste was sharp, burning sugar. 'I told you she would impress.'

The emperor seemed distracted, staring towards the door. 'She is a razor in the hands of a child, but she is most intriguing.'

'Powerful, Malvus. I think that's the word you're looking for. Her existence is still a surprise even to me. An anomaly, they call it in the east.'

'She will have many uses,' Malvus mused. 'Nevermar in human form. Who could have imagined such a blessing? With her by my side… Alas, I get ahead of myself. Tell me it is done, Loki?'

Loki raised his glass in toast. 'It is. Nothing like Devil's Spool to ruin a party.'

'How long can the fortress' stores last?'

'Days, at most.'

'You do have your uses, I see! Fine work.'

The god chuckled. 'You still believe Farden will surrender?'

Malvus snatched the glass from the god's hand and took a sip for himself. He did not hand it back. Loki merely produced another, much to Malvus' apparent displeasure.

The emperor talked between frequent sips of the liquor. 'I heard a story once of the Huskar steppe riders. Each Highfrost they embark upon a traditional hunt, seeking a fearsome krasilisk for their cooking fires. Now, with six legs, the krasilisk is a rapid beast, known to charge in an instant.' Malvus snapped his fingers. 'Their trick, refined over years, is to lasso it. A long noose, thrown from the back of their cows. One lasso is not enough. Even an impressive snare around the neck will not do. The beast is strong and violent; it can rip the rider straight from his mount and into the krasilisk's mandibles. It takes many lassoes, one around its stag horns, perhaps. Another around its legs. And another. You get the idea.'

'It's a lovely story.'

'The point is that Farden is that krasilisk. One rope will not stop him. The capture of Mithrid is one such rope. The poison of his stores is another. My ultimatum delivered from the mouth of his favoured pet, a third.'

Loki tutted. 'What of your promise—'

'And then I will crush him from all sides, and let his brave soldiers watch as I hang him from a siege tower for all to watch. Mayhaps I'll leave him in his armour. Maybe it will prolong the suffering, let him watch as I raze his fortress to the ground, dismantle it brick by brick, and throw each one in the Lonely Ocean, never to be seen again.' Malvus got to his feet. 'There will be no trace of Scalussen's existence. No trace of his name. The Forever King will be nothing but a curse.'

The god swilled his sweet wine, examining the rafters while pondering. His silence seemed to irk the emperor.

'Have you nothing to say to that?' Malvus challenged.

Loki shook himself as if cold. 'To your continued health,' he smirked, and with that, he raised his glass, and let it smash upon the arm of the Blazing Throne before he vanished with a crackle of scorched air.

'So this is a steel dragon,' remarked Towerdawn, growling at the monstrosity he saw before him.

For almost two years, Eyrum had been slaving away in Farden's forges, refining a tactic that seemed made for that very day, and that very situation that vexed them.

The steel dragon, like the Old Dragon's armour and skin beneath it, was no machine nor construction, but a formation made of broad scales. Shields, to be exact, complex and interlocking to form a long arrowhead in the rough shape of a dragon's head. Where the polished scales joined, steel spears bristled from vents designed to spew fire from mages, or even two dragons side by side.

The humans and Sirens the general had gathered to wield such a heavy formation all looked as though they had gathered for a competition of who looked most like Eyrum. To a person they were brawny, swollen with muscle, battle-scarred, and raring to split skulls.

'You've built a moving fortress, Eyrum.'

Though Towerdawn thought the Siren could not get any bigger, he swelled with pride.

'I am gratified, Old Dragon.'

'This will do nicely,' said Farden, touring the stack of shields, expertly crafted to resemble the ebb and flow of dragon scales. 'Tyrfing would have been proud.'

'No better weapon to have in a trap.'

'Shivertread. Are you ready?'

The lithe dragon switched his scales to the bright steel of the shields. 'Ready as ever, Old Dragon.'

Farden placed his helmet under his arm and strapped his scabbard on tightly. 'Then let's go see what Malvus Barkhart wants of us.'

CHAPTER 34
REPERCUSSIONS

Of all the schools of magick, fire is the most common. Call it the embodiment of anger, the casualty of a tortured soul, only the most aggrieved will burn the brightest.
FROM THE WRITINGS OF SIREN WIZARD KORZ

At the front edge of the horde, standing before the blood-painted walls of Scalussen, the wind rushed across the wastes with little care for what cheeks or knuckles it froze.

The Outlaw King was keeping them waiting.

Behind Mithrid, the Arka was a sea of steel and iron, fidgeting in their impatience. Clouds of breath hovered over the ranks. Not a soul gave voice. The banners crackled loud enough. The silence had grown heavy and cloying.

Mithrid stood atop the expansive imperial chariot. It was more of a glorified platform with wheels, pulled by a score of the largest and ugliest birds she had ever seen. They were featherless but coated in fingernail scales that refused to stay one colour.

Closest to her was Littlest, standing at her side and giving her a constant deadpan stare that clutched Mithrid's insides with sharp nails. Bull and Aspala were shackled and in the care of General Toskig. The healers had patched them up and bundled them in furs.

Emperor Malvus stood behind them, in all manner of golden armour and regalia. The two Arka spies stood at his heel, gleaming in polished armour. The bastard Savask had taken Mithrid's axe for himself, and it now rested against his pudgy belly. Trenika glared daggers at Aspala.

The man with golden hair stood apart from the rest of the crowd. Mithrid had heard the emperor call the man Loki. The name had put a shiver in her. She swore she had heard that name in a recital of gods. It was preposterous, gods walking the ice like men. She simply ignored him. It was easier to face what she understood and think nothing of it. Her mind was already hurtling like a drunkard towards a precipice.

'Come on, come on,' she muttered. The waiting was a sharper blade than her impending task. She eyed the crowded walls of Scalussen, trying again to recognise the shades of armour and visored faces.

At that moment, a long horn blast came from Scalussen. The walls began to thunder. Spears, swords, shields, and boots all hammered rhythmically. With heavy clanking of cogs and chains, the great gates opened for the first time since the Arka had arrived.

A sliver of bright steel caught the meek sunlight. Mithrid blinked in its mirror glare. To the beat, still shaking ice from the walls, a square wall of polished shields emerged from the shadow of the gates. Mithrid had never seen such shields in the fortress before. They were almost as tall as the brawny soldiers that bore them: curved rectangles covered in ridges and spikes. Interlocked side by side, with long lances rested on their edges, the formation was fearsome. A wide wagon populated with archers sat at the centre of their ranks. A mound of what looked to be rags and spare shields was piled at its centre.

Heads held high, their formation smart enough to make an architect glow with pride, the Scalussen formation approached. Once halfway between the walls and the horde, they came to a rest with a jarring clang. There, they stood quietly until a muffled order could be heard. With the sound of hammers striking bells, the frontmost shield bearers collapsed inwards. Three figures strode forth: Farden, covered in red and gold; Modren in ashen armour with a streak of copper; and Durnus, for once wearing a suit of mail and scale-plate such as the dragon-riders wore.

Mithrid could feel Malvus stirring behind her: a rasp of boots, a caught breath, a lick of wind-bitten lips. Her tangled mind and heart that kept skipping its rhythm envied the simplicity of his hatred.

'Come, Mithrid. Your king awaits you!' the emperor announced. The surrounding soldiers and smattering of remaining Scarred leapt to obey his order. The birds were whipped until they began to pull. The chariot juddered beneath them, creeping across the ice to close the gap.

The tension was beyond palpable, almost sickening in the way it squeezed Arka and Scalussen alike. Every jaw clenched. Every arsehole tightened. Mithrid could smell the sweat and nervous piss on the wind.

With fifty yards left between them, the emperor's glorified wagon halted. Standing before the curving lines of Arka, with barely a hundred soldiers at his back, Farden resembled a sandcastle defying an ocean storm. And yet, somehow, he still put a chill in every soul present.

Farden removed his helmet. His face was the picture of exhaustion, no matter how he tried to hide it with a smug smile. His black hair tried to untangle itself in the wind.

Malvus cleared his throat. Two imperial guards sprang to place wooden, velvet-clad steps before them. Mithrid was pushed down them unceremoniously, much to the delight of her injuries. Her boots crunched on the ice as if it were broken glass. With the emperor at her side, surrounded by Scarred, they walked towards Farden.

'One move. One slip of the tongue. One betrayal, and your friends will be gutted before you can blink,' the emperor whispered to her. Mithrid believed him. A quick glance showed her Bull, Aspala, and Littlest still standing by the chariot. Trenika's sword was unsheathed and ready.

Farden met them halfway, leaving at least twenty yards between them. He paid the emperor no heed for now. He stared at Mithrid, eyeing the cuts and bruises on her face.

'Have they hurt you, Mithrid?' Farden called out.

She shook her head. 'Nothing that won't heal.'

Malvus tutted loudly. 'You are not the only one to see her potential, Farden.'

Mithrid could hear Farden's growl even at that distance, but he kept his face smug. *Uncaring.*

'My, my. You look as if this war has taken a toll on you, my good mage,' Malvus spoke. 'Tell me: when was the last time you sought a bed? Or a hot meal, perhaps?'

From the slight fall in Farden's face, Mithrid could see the sting in Malvus' words, but she did not understand why.

'What do you want, Malvus? Speak your piece. Tell me what you want in return for Mithrid. I grow bored of waiting.'

Malvus shook his head. 'It is not I who has summoned you, Farden. It was Mithrid, here. She has seen this war from the other side of your walls and has learned a great deal. Go on, Mithrid. Tell Farden what you told me.'

Mithrid could taste blood in her mouth she bit her lip so hard. Taking a deep breath and a step ahead, she looked Farden straight in the eyes.

'Surrender,' she said.

'I don't think he heard you,' Malvus chided mockingly.

Farden had. As had the others: the anger, confusion, and disappointment were a wave breaking across their faces.

Mithrid spoke louder. 'You should surrender, Farden. End this war with words and save thousands of lives that don't deserve to bleed and die here on this ice.' She kept her stare, unblinking. 'You know as well as I do, they're all doomed if we keep fighting.'

Farden took a moment to answer. Modren spoke instead, his voice quiet and strained. 'Never thought I'd hear those words in your mouth, girl.'

Malvus beckoned a finger. Littlest was summoned to stand before them. 'Tell him, Mithrid,' the emperor called out. 'Tell him about little Larina here.'

Mithrid loathed every moment that crawled past like a dying man, slower than time should go, as if torturing her on purpose. 'She's from Troughwake, Farden.' Her voice cracked as she put a hand on Littlest's shoulder. 'Where Modren found us. Remina's sister. She is innocent in all of this. She's barely seen a dozen winters. All she wants is to go home, like the rest of us.'

Littlest made no sound, but she nodded vacantly. She looked to Bull and Aspala, but their bruised eyes were nothing but condemning.

Farden's face was now as impassive as a cliff face. He barely looked at Mithrid or Malvus, but through them. 'It matters not,' he said, with all emotion dead in his voice.

Mithrid let her mouth hang open as her act crumbled. 'How can it not matter?'

'You would slaughter this child to win your war? And these?' Malvus gestured to Bull and Aspala. 'How many souls bound for Haven and Hel, until you have had enough?'

'I will kill as many as I have to until I cut you from Emaneska in all forms, Malvus. Until I burn every one of your lies from the eddas and histories. Until every mind knows the truth of how you betrayed this land. I would drown Emaneska in blood to destroy you, Malvus. Because even after all of that, it would still be preferable to the future you have planned. It is you, who condemn these thousands to death.' Farden swept a hand across the endless Arka lines. 'I am simply the hand that swings the sword.'

The words fell on Mithrid, but they landed like hail and stinging rain. Even Modren and Durnus were staring at Farden in disbelief. Inwick stared murder at him.

Malvus clapped, and when that wasn't mocking enough, he laughed loud and brashly. 'The true villain at last revealed for all! Witness the enemy of Emaneska, brave soldiers, mages! Here he stands, poised to strike you down without thought or mercy.'

Booing and peals of laughter burned through the crowded ranks like a brushfire. Farden endured it all without reaction, even though Mithrid could see the waves of heat rising from his shoulders. His magick emanated from him like dawn light creeping across the ice, clashing quietly with the Scarred.

'However,' Farden interjected, looking troubled now. He held up a hand. 'Mithrid Fenn is one of mine. One who has seen the truth. I won't let her or any of mine be harmed.'

'Then save her, Farden. Save thousands like her,' Malvus urged. Mithrid could hear the quiver in his breath. The emperor was excited, damn him. 'Like young Mithrid here, I have seen the need for mercy. To save us all from bloodshed. I swear that you and yours will be treated with fairness.'

'Lies!' Modren yelled.

Malvus looked injured. 'I have plenty of witnesses to my oath. What would the Arka think of its emperor then?'

Farden hesitated, and Mithrid cursed him for it. She felt an abandoned object, thrown about in an angry sea.

'Give her back to me and we'll discuss this peace. Or fight me for her, and we will decide this war in combat. Send me your best champion. Or better yet, face me yourself,' he said.

In the corner of her vision, Mithrid saw Malvus put a hand on a knife hilt. He cackled.

'You're the Hero of Efjar. A slayer of minotaurs, a dragon killer, clad in the armour of the lost Knights of the Nine, with sixty years of slitting throats under your belt. You take me for a fool?'

'Allow me, Your Majesty,' Toskig called, stepping from the chariot. The thing practically breathed a sigh of relief to lose the weight of the big general. He was encased in full plate, a shield and a sword the height of Mithrid in his grip. 'I will face him.'

Malvus tutted. 'I fear even you, General Toskig, would fail to live up to the challenge.'

Toskig stared at Farden like a bull at crimson.

'No,' Malvus decided. He whipped his knife free of its scabbard and held it an inch from Mithrid's throat. She hissed between bared teeth. The idea that she might not be valuable enough to either Farden or the emperor to live through this slunk into her mind. Despite the frigid air, her skin beaded with sweat.

'Magick might not touch this one, but steel will. Hand me your sword, swear peace, and open your fortress to me, Farden, Outlaw King. Then you can have your Mithrid.'

Modren whispered something unheard to Farden, but the mage shook his head. He stepped ahead, but Durnus tried to hold him back. Inwick stared murder at him. Farden wrenched himself free, placed his helmet in the vampyre's hands, and drew his sword.

Behind Mithrid, the Scarred bristled, creeping forwards with fingers crackling with lightning and green energy.

Farden stopped a spear's length short of the emperor's entourage. He did not look at Mithrid. If he had, he would have seen a face wracked with panic and guilt. She had betrayed an entire fortress for a handful of lives, and yet Farden thought her worth the trade. She knew the emperor was lying about their safety. Farden could not have fallen for it either. It did not make sense, even when he turned his sword around hilt first, and offered it to Malvus. The emperor was wide-eyed and ecstatic. He likely could not believe his luck, and yet still he pushed it.

'Kneel,' Malvus ordered.

Farden sneered. 'You have your surrender.'

Malvus' knife drew a line of blood across Mithrid's throat. She didn't dare swallow lest it cut deeper.

'Kneel.'

Farden looked to the sky as he shook his head, chewing words beneath his breath. It took an eon of waiting, but with little alacrity, the Outlaw King slowly but surely bent a knee to the ice.

Mithrid could feel the shock washing over the Arka ranks. She could hear the muted cries of distress coming from the fortress walls. Even she reeled against the emperor's grip.

'How long I have waited for this moment,' Malvus breathed. Mithrid forgotten, he took a step, caught himself, and pointed with his knife. 'Bring me that sword, General Toskig.'

Mithrid stared in disbelief. At any moment, she expected Farden to spring up, slicing Toskig in half before burning Malvus to charcoal. But Farden did not. Although keeping his head high, he handed the general his blade, flat on the palms of his hands.

'You've fallen far for somebody who has climbed so high, Toskig,' Mithrid heard Farden mutter. Still not a smile dared show itself on his face. A sick feeling, awash with guilt, almost bent Mithrid double.

Farden stayed kneeling as the sword was carried to Malvus. Sheathing his knife, he seized the sword by the handle and held it flat as the horizon before him, his eyes switching between the blade and Farden, particularly his unarmoured neck.

Malvus began to laugh. He gave the sword an experimental swing. Ice crunched beneath his boots. *One, two, three steps.* His Scarred followed, shield spells ready in their hands. The emperor stopped short with the sword levelled at Farden, three feet from his face.

'I always knew you would fall.'

A broad smile spread across Farden's face, feeling almost foreign it had been so long. 'And that is why you took the bait. Overconfidence is a bitch.'

Ducking Malvus' lunging, rabid swing, Farden pressed his fists to the ice, blasting a shockwave under the Scarred's shields. Their footing cracking and splintering beneath them. Mage and emperor alike stumbled and fell.

Barely moments after the spell had abated, Eyrum's roaring voice could be heard. The archers fled the wagon in the centre of the Scalussen formation. To Mithrid's shock, the pile of shining steel and cloth exploded into the air in the shape of a dragon. With three mighty heaves of his wings, Shivertread rose into the air, dragging the wagon in his claws. With a roar and a violent, somersaulting manoeuvre, Shivertread tossed the wagon high into the air. Flames enveloped it, and within the space of a gasping breath, a blazing mass of wood was sailing towards the emperor's entourage.

'Flee!' yelled Toskig, shortly before barrelling the emperor aside with no dignity at all. Mithrid threw herself and Littlest in the other direction, leaving the Scarred in the wagon's path. She dragged her hair out of the way to see Farden now standing, arms ablaze, and winking at her.

'Any time you like, Mithrid!' he yelled.

Pent-up shadow surged from her, ripping the magick from the Scarred just before the wagon crashed to the earth. Their screams were silenced by the rending crash and cloud of flaming debris.

Mithrid was now standing. A roar climbed in her throat, spilling out as a shriek. She poured her all into her dark and wicked spell, detonating a wall of shadow that tore through the Arka ranks. Mages reeled left and right. Even the soldiers seemed stunned.

Farden himself stumbled across the ice in his charge, and yet in his stagger, he seized his discarded sword and began to cleave his way through the remaining, utterly bewildered, Scarred.

Through the smoke, Bull and Aspala could be seen struggling with the traitors. Aspala was free but weak as an hour-old calf. Bull was taking hit after hit from Trenika, gradually sinking to the ice.

'Littlest! We have to—'

A searing pain in her shoulder knocked Mithrid to her knees. Colours exploded in her eyes. She turned to find Littlest with bloody murder written across her face and a stained dirk in her hands.

'What the fuck? What are you—gah!' Mithrid recoiled as Littlest swiped at her again, slicing a crimson line across the back of her hand.

'You are a traitor, just as he told me you were,' she said, in that hideous drone of blinkered eyes. 'The emperor is a god amongst men. Our saviour!'

Again, she came at her. Mithrid dragged herself across the ice, trying to push herself up with her good arm.

'Stop it! It's me! You know me!'

Littlest ran at her, dirk slashing in wild, vicious arcs. Mithrid kicked one of Littlest's legs from beneath her, snapping a knee, but Littlest crawled instead, narrowly missing Mithrid's thigh with a fierce stab. She drove her fist into Littlest's chin. The girl reeled backwards, and for the briefest and most wrenching of moments, she looked just like the little girl on a stormy beach, confused and tearful when asked to give up her trinkets.

It lasted no longer than a hiccup. Littlest gnashed at her like a mad hound and raised her bloody blade once more.

A knife appeared before the golden-haired man did. A curved and savage thing, dropping heavy onto Mithrid's heaving chest. She looked up to see a brown coat, and a pale faced man with a fiendish smirk standing over her.

Loki held a finger to his lips before promptly folding into a burst of light and lingering smoke. Through it came charging Littlest, eyes wild as a sabrecat's and mouth slavering.

Mithrid fumbled to raise the knife in time, acting on instinct. She felt the blade grate against bone as Littlest collided with her. She looked down, across Littlest's writhing shoulder, and saw the knife tip poking from the girl's back, making a tent of her tabard. Biting back tears, Mithrid pinned the twitching Littlest to her, and though she felt the warmth spreading across her chest, she drove the knife in once again to end the nightmare.

Retching, she clambered free of the dead girl. It took her precious moments to drag her horrified eyes away from Littlest, face down in bloodied snow. Mithrid staggered away from the growing pool of blood.

The world was a deafening cocoon of smoke and fire. Farden and his captains were holding back the Scarred, wielding what magick Mithrid had left them, and carving through plenty more with their blades. She saw Farden battering Toskig's shield while the emperor cowered behind a wall of mages.

'Bull! Aspala!' she cried out. She could hear the thunder of a charging army and the roar of a dragon. Fear controlled her until, between a gust of smoke, she saw them.

Aspala had Trenika in a headlock just as Inwick ran her through. It gave her no pleasure: Bull was down, slumped against the wagon and clutching a bloody stomach. Mithrid started to run, but skidded to see Savask sprinting at her, her own axe high above his head.

'Yaah!' came his reckless cry.

Mithrid raised her knife, shuddering with panic. Then she saw his grip: not an axeman's grip, but far too narrow. She leaned to the side throwing him into a wild swing she could dodge. As the axe bit into the ice, up came her knife, disappearing into the flabby meat under Savask's chin. This death, she enjoyed.

Mithrid brought him close as he gurgled and spat, tongue impaled by the knife. 'A treacherous worm like you deserves every moment of this,' she hissed.

Savask landed hard, boggle-eyed and intensely disappointed. On any other battlefield, on any other day, she would have watched him until the end, but that was not to be. Farden came from nowhere, sweeping her away from the spy and towards the fortress. Modren and Durnus were dragging Inwick away. She still had somebody's scalp in her hands. Aspala and Bull were there, too, helped by Warbringer and Ko-Tergo.

Their feet pelted the ice, and Mithrid soon found out why: beyond the smoke, the Arka were swarming to the rescue of their emperor. Like a snare, they were beginning to close around Eyrum's formations.

'Good to have you back,' Farden said between snatching breaths.

'Was this always your plan?'

'More or less?'

'Then you'd better have something saved for this lot,' Mithrid yelled. The Arka had begun their charge.

Farden laughed. 'Eyrum! Now!'

Mithrid watched as a dragon came to life upon the ice and snow. Not one of fire and scale, but of steel. The formation of soldiers collapsed inwards again, raising their shields as they did so. One by one and in rapid succession, they interlocked to form a seamless shell of steel that looked suspiciously like a dragon's head.

The shields opened for them, and Mithrid rushed into the darkness beneath the steel. Before the trap closed behind Farden, he yelled to the swooping dragon. 'Shivertread! Back to the fortress!'

Flashing sky blue to red, Shivertread pirouetted across the lines, spraying fire to break the Arka's charge. When the flame retreated, the dragon was already swooping for the walls.

In the heavily panting half-gloom, with the thunder of an army in their ears, Farden clapped his gauntlets. 'That went better than expected.'

'I can't believe you kneeled,' Mithrid gasped for breath.

Modren tutted. 'Me neither.'

Farden looked momentarily sick to his stomach. 'Necessary for the ruse.' He pointed at Mithrid. 'Looks like we were both playing actors for a moment there. Were we not?'

Even with Littlest's blood still warm on her clothes, she met his pained stare. 'You were right,' she muttered. 'There's no saving them. Burn them all, I say.'

Farden seemed satisfied, if not a little awkward. He hovered between clapping her on the shoulder and checking her injured hand. He did neither.

'Thank you,' she said, 'for coming for me. I didn't think you would. I don't know what I thought.'

'We can talk about apologies later,' grunted the mage.

Warbringer looked mightily uncomfortable beneath the confines of the steel dragon. She snorted and snuffled while she attempted to keep her horns from poking the shields. 'Can we get the fuck out of here?'

'Right you are,' grunted the general. He was holding one of the foremost and largest shields and somehow looked barely inconvenienced. He barked something in the Siren tongue and the steel dragon began to move. Even though the soldiers jogged, their carapace stayed locked together.

'Brace!' Eyrum yelled. The shields dropped into the frozen ground.

A battering ram of bodies and armour struck them. Boots skidded through ice but did not falter. Spears were threaded back and forth through the holes in the shields. Mages, their spells returned, put their hands to steel gates and rained fire on anything that moved beyond their metal shell. Farden joined them. The screams of the Arka deafened them.

'Onwards!'

The steel dragon began to move, lifting and heaving, almost caterpillar-like in their march to the fortress gates. All those who didn't hold a shield manned a spear, wrought spells, or sent finches swirling around enemy legs. In moments where the Arka reeled, the shields unlocked. Spears and blades shot outwards, cutting down anything that still moved.

Foot by foot, death by death, the steel dragon approached the gates. Arrows and spells began to rain, beating the Arka back.

Spells began to hammer the shields. Heavy and hard, even when glancing from the metal. The Arka had regrouped under the emperor's screeching orders and were seeking restitution. The Scalussen soldiers spread along the gates as they creeped open, all too slowly. The inside of the steel dragon steamed as fire rained upon them. Arka blades began to pry under the shields, slashing feet and legs.

Part of the carapace stumbled. Daylight spilled. Raging faces could be seen. Fingers and hands reached over to pry the shields apart. Farden and Modren severed them with lightning.

'Escape!' Warbringer bellowed, frightening Mithrid half to death.

Light shone from the back of the dragon. She pushed Aspala and Bull ahead towards the courtyard. Next came Modren and Durnus. Last, as the shields began to fall apart under the sheer onslaught, Farden and Eyrum. They dragged soldiers as they rushed for the gate, spells and blades clattering around their heads.

'Close it!' Farden yelled, firing spell after spell through the slim gap in the thick steel and stone. 'Close it now!'

Lances, spears, and pikes shoved their way through. Lightning ricocheted inwards, igniting fires within the courtyard. But the gates of Scalussen were powered not by hands and muscles, but by inexorable cogs and machinery.

Inwick held the last stand, pushing Farden out of the way and spouting a steady stream of fire at any soldier that dared to darken the fortress' doorway.

'Inwick!' Farden shouted.

Mithrid, even though her head whirled, and the exhaustion was doing its best to drag her to the earth, heard the panic in that shout. It sounded wounded.

In the last moment before the gate become a crushing vice, Inwick stepped into the fray beyond the walls. Fierce white flame burnt through the gap before it slammed with thunder.

Farden was yelling so loudly it sounded as though he would do himself injury. 'Get her back! Get ropes! Shivertread, bring her back here!' The dragon flapped and danced along the walls, trying to dodge spears, spells, and arrows.

Breathless, they raced up the gatehouse and threw their heads over the parapet. Inwick had charged from the gate, deep into the horde.

'INWICK!'

Farden's shield stole the air from Mithrid's lungs as it sought to envelop the mage. It was no use. From that height, and with so many spells raging, reaching Inwick seemed impossible. Even with Mithrid's shadow snaking out to choke their magick, the Arka were too many, and Inwick was moving too fast, sealing her fate each new yard she charged.

'Come back, Inwick!' Modren bellowed as Farden and the other mages threw rope and grapple out into the horde. They, too, fell short, and maddeningly, the Arka began to climb them. Knives and axes soon saw to that.

Aghast and powerless, the walls cried out to the Written mage. Inwick did not hear or did not care. She was wrapped in crimson rage, a blur of steel and fire that wrought havoc in all directions. Every step she took she filled with three corpses. The emperor could be heard baying from somewhere behind Toskig's shield. Both had retreated deep into the masses. 'Kill her!'

Dozens shrivelled like chaff against fire before Inwick's reign of blood began to slow. Where her fire spells melted the ice, she sloshed through water. Steam billowed alongside smoke. The bodies tangled her feet.

'She can't keep it up.' Durnus spoke all their thoughts aloud in a low and trembling tone. The finality in his voice sank Mithrid's heart. She hunkered down between the parapets to watch between the stone.

Even when Inwick's spells failed her, the corpses kept mounting. She claimed the limbs or life of any Arka that got close enough. She was a raging beast with a sword-master's arm. Even when her blades were notched like saws, one even broken to a dagger, she hacked and hacked at the half dead around her, unstoppable.

Silence fell upon the walls as the first arrow broke through her armour, chased by the second, both deep under the arm. Inwick screeched, almost inhuman. But it was not pain in that echo, it was madness.

Even from on her knees, Inwick was lethal. Swords discarded, nails and teeth became her weapons. The last man to try and stab her up close was dragged to the filth, his neck ripped clean away.

Not a single eye on the fortress walls stayed dry as the Arka cowards rushed Inwick with long spears. It took a dozen to stop her thrashing, and half that again to bleed the rage from her. Cries of pain and vows of vengeance rose up from Scalussen. Farden said nothing. The stone beneath his gauntlets creaked. Mithrid could not tear her eyes away. A hand rested on her shoulder, and she found Hereni behind her, a fine cut across her brow and cheek. The tears cut channels through the blood.

In the end, Inwick died with her back to Scalussen, but her head to the sky. It was impossible to see, but as Mithrid choked, she imagined Inwick wore, at last, a face of peace.

Not a word was spoken, nor order given. The Arka withdrew in tense silence. The dead they left in their wake must have numbered a thousand.

Only Toskig and Malvus remained, standing before the wreath of carnage around Inwick. The emperor was striding towards the fallen mage with a sword in his hand.

Farden and Modren bristled. Mithrid had to shield herself from the heat coming off their armour. 'You fucking dare…' the king could be heard whispering.

He dared. And boldly so. The emperor had longed for a head all day. He had been denied Farden's and Mithrid's. He would have his prize.

The sword flashed in the winter light as it severed Inwick's head. Farden did not wait for the emperor to raise it up as hideous trophy, or for Toskig to begin dragging her body to the Arka lines. He stormed from the roaring Scalussen walls and barged a path towards the Frostsoar.

Without a word, Mithrid sprinted after Farden. Trading glances of tearful and smoke-red eyes, Hereni, Durnus, and Modren were given no time to grieve and no choice but to follow. Like Mithrid, they knew calamitous things usually happened when Farden was pushed to the edge.

'Where are you going, Farden?' she called after him.

Hereni was surprisingly fast. She would have done well in Troughwake's races.

'What the fuck did they do to you, Mithrid? You're hurt.' she said, worry thick in her voice as she noticed the hole in the girl's shoulder and the cuts across the legs.

Mithrid shook her head. 'We're all hurt.'

Down, into the Frostsoar's foundations, they marched, taking the winding stairs as Farden had. Stone clattered beneath their feet. Still the mage said nothing. His face was a portrait of madness. Those who paid attention got out of the way swiftly. Smiths and exhausted workers scattered before the king. A few cheers rang out, but it was far from the right time.

'Where is he going?'

'The new tunnels, I wager,' said Hereni.

'You know about those?'

'And Irminsul. Farden called a council when the food stores were poisoned.'

'What?' Mithrid tripped on a piece of coal. 'I've been gone two days.'

'And we have three days left before we all start starving. The fortress won't last too long with weakened soldiers behind it.'

'But the tunnels?'

'Far from finished,' Durnus snarled at them, at last catching up on flatter ground.

At the edge of the forges, three yawning holes each as wide as a dragon burrowed into the ice and rock. Lines of diggers passed along rocks and lumps of ice. A handful of mages sat nearby, wiping their foreheads with rags. They sprang up as Farden stormed past them with flame already streaming from his fists.

More workers escaped the tunnel, looking behind them in worry. The others pushed forwards where others wouldn't, following Farden into the dark, water-strewn tunnel. Moth light lanterns were wedged into the ice at intervals, but it was too cold to eke much light from them. Water ran past them in hewn gutters.

Farden did not care. He was a torch in his own right.

When they came to the end of the tunnel, where mages burnt away at the ice in bursts and workers manhandled wooden supports, Farden barely let them escape before unleashing his spell at the wall of ice and captured boulders. The blast forced the others to cover their eyes and retreat slightly. Water poured out of the gutters and washed around feet.

With grim nods and hearts of stone, they left the mage there to burn through the earth. Modren and Hereni cracked their fingers and began to nurse tongues of flame in their hands. In silence, they climbed into the companion tunnels, leaving Mithrid and Durnus standing in the growing torrent.

A cloak of exhaustion wrapped around her. Mithrid sagged against the old vampyre, who caught her with his bony, iron hands before she could stumble.

'Time,' Durnus whispered. 'Time is our enemy now.'

CHAPTER 35
MASKS

No empire was ever built upon roses, perfume, and soft words. Empires are built of blood, fire, and betrayal.
OLD SAYING, SOURCE UNKNOWN

The fleeting shadow was spied too late. Admiral Lerel dodged to the side, evading the barrage, but she was not fast enough. The splatter was tell-tale. Pale shit decorated the admiral's trews and one boot with unnerving accuracy. The gull flapped away, crowing victoriously.

Lerel reached for the crossbow hanging from the woodwork but left it on its hooks. The bird was already lost in the mists that perpetually clung to the black coasts of Nelska.

The bookships strained against their colossal anchors. Only iron chain and the efforts of the wind mages keeping them from sweeping into the bristling spears of volcanic rock that gnashed with every valley-sized swell of the steel ocean.

At least the dragons seemed to enjoy it. Towerdawn's kin littered the bookship decks, shining bright even in the dour day and steaming gently. Barely a dozen had remained to tend the coveted eggs of the Siren dragons. Their riders preferred the braziers and hammocks of below decks, and Lerel did not blame them one bit.

Wrenching the wheel a notch to port, she swung the *Autumn's Vanguard* around a roguish wave, bouncing off the sharp edges of the inlet they had sheltered in.

A wall of spray burst over the bow, reaching her on the aftcastle. Even over the water's constant voice, she could faintly hear Roiks upon the *Revenge*, cursing every drop of seawater under the skies. Beyond him, the *Summer's Fury* was barely a haze. The half-score other ships in the Rogue's

Armada, including her old ship, the *Waveblade*, all scattered across the wild bay, enduring. Waiting.

'Watch it, Admiral,' warned her first mate, pointing to another dark shape against the murky sky.

Lerel seized her crossbow, took aim, and then tutted loudly. 'Fuck's sake, Hasterkin. You're going blind in your old age. That's a hawk.'

The bird fluttered to a chaotic land on the bookship's wheel. The winds kept its wings aloft, its claws locked on its perch. Lerel took the scroll from its wet leg and gave the bird a cursory pat. 'Get it some worms or a mouse or something. It's come a long way.'

'Scalussen?'

Lerel was already distracted by the message. Scrunching it in her fist, she seized wiry Hasterkin by the shoulder and shook him lightly. 'Looks like we'll be in the battle after all. Signal the armada!'

It felt as though the world had taken a breath and strained to hold it. Broken sleep and growling stomachs were all the next trio of days brought Scalussen. Sombre moods dominated. Conversation was dimmed. The buoyancy of rebellion and victory had sunk, leaving only trepidation and red-rimmed eyes behind. The gap between the fortress and the bristling Arka lines seemed to shrink every unctuous hour.

The walls and courtyards between the fortifications were still. The remaining soldiers were milling and drifting from menial chore to the next, but only a few knew the toil that raged in the forges. The only sign above was the demolition of a handful of buildings at the edge of the main courtyards. War was the only reason given.

Below the ice and steaming rock, the purpose was plain. Scaffolded steps now reached to the ceiling of the cavern beneath Scalussen, a far easier escape than winching lifts up and down a score at a time. A third of the fortress had already been stowed beneath the surface, happy to be warm and safe, unaware they were to fill the tunnels at Farden's order. Scalussen's lean chance at salvation was still held in high secrecy, lest Malvus spoil it.

Even though the hammers had now ceased, they still reverberated between Mithrid's ears. She had taken up camp in the forges, partly for the warmth, partly on Farden's orders, and partly to be with Hereni, who had been charged with the digging once Farden was hauled away half-conscious. Few had seen him since Inwick had passed. The loss had scorched every soul between the walls.

Another rumble shook the cavern, causing Mithrid to drop her whetstone.

Bull reared up from his cot, clutched his stomach with a wince, and lay back down. 'What is that?'

Mithrid watched frost and dust tumbling from the distant ceiling. The tremors had become more frequent in recent days. Everyone caught their breath like sprinting throat first into a taut rope. The forges powered by the fire of the Emberteeth belched sulphurous smoke. Heat washed over the cavern like a tide.

'The end,' Mithrid muttered, patting the big lad's arm. Trenika had gouged Bull well, leaving three knife wounds in his belly. Even half dead he had refused to leave Mithrid's side. Aspala had made the same promise. It seemed as though she had sharpened her new sword for three days straight, as if scraping her soul into it. Mithrid had imitated her in boredom.

'Fenn!' hollered a familiar voice. Akitha came trundling between the makeshift walls hiding the tunnels, dragging a handcart. 'There you fuckin' are.'

With a grimace, the Siren dragged her small cart around the wooden gutters hewn to keep the meltwater from drowning the forges. A lone mage wielding water spells saw to the task. Everyone else was deep in the tunnels, hewing at rock and ice with magick and steel.

Akitha bobbed her head to the tunnel. 'Any closer?'

'A day more, says Hereni.'

'I'll have shrivelled to a ballsack by then, I'll be so hungry.'

Mithrid knew the feeling well. The penultimate meal had been doled out that morning. It was now victory or starvation.

'What's that?'

Akitha hauled the cart in front of her. 'Something to keep you alive, at least a little longer.'

Casting aside a blanket, she revealed smartly overlapping black steel waiting beneath. Mithrid took a moment to realise it was armour. Gold and crimson trim decorated its edges.

'Not a rune or spell in sight. Makes it more pervious to magick, but from what I hear, you won't have trouble with that. Not exactly Scalussen red and gold, but it matches the manner of your spells, too, and it pisses on what you've worn until now. This is Nelska, not Scalussen.'

Piece by piece, Mithrid let Akitha strap it onto her. The bruises and cuts of the escape from Malvus complained, but with the weight of each section, the more temporary they felt.

'Helmet,' Akitha said, once she was fully clad.

A simple knight's helmet with an angled visor completed the ensemble, and through its grates she stared down at Bull and Aspala.

'Don't suppose you made us some?' murmured the woman, momentarily – and gingerly – checking her broken horns.

Akitha cackled. 'Wish I had the time. You three went for the emperor's throat, and that's got to be admired, if not envied. You did us proud.'

Mithrid only murmured her thanks; Littlest was still wedged firmly in her mind like a bloody splinter.

'You got the same look on you that you had on the ship, when you came to sharpen your axe. Angry. Nervous.'

'Sounds about right. Back to where I started, even though the world looks different now. I thought knowing more would make it easier to handle.'

'It's a wide world, Mithrid. Wider even than Emaneska, they say. That's the trouble with knowing how much of a speck you are in the void of history and miles, yet feeling so sure you matter. Well, say the rest of us. For you, it might just be true.' Akitha put her hand on the girl's shoulders, a touch stiff and a poor excuse for a smile on her face, but it seemed the equivalent of a bear-hug from the Siren.

Before Mithrid could thank the blacksmith, a flood of water sloshed through the gutters of the first tunnel. Hereni appeared, pale as the ice cladding the walls, and half bent with exhaustion. Workers bearing buckets of gravel streamed behind her. Mithrid rushed to the captain's side, slower and heavier than she would have liked.

'Are the tunnels done?'

'Almost,' panted the mage, eyes rolling and fighting to focus. She was roasting hot. Even through Akitha's steel, Mithrid could feel a weak magick resonating within her, like the slumbering embers of a fire still hot by morning. 'We're close to the mole tunnels. We have to be.'

Another tremor rattled the earth. Mithrid braced herself and the breathless Hereni.

'It's getting worse,' she told her.

But the mage arose with shaking legs, staring up at the thin shafts of daylight peaking through the cavern roof. Dust fell in curtains.

'That wasn't Irminsul,' she hissed. 'It's begun.'

Mithrid seized her axe, making the metal of her new gauntlets screech.

*

The growl was audible.

'Gods, do I hate fighting on an empty stomach,' muttered the undermage, standing like a pillar while Elessi circled him, checking every strap and plate.

'I told you, it's fine.' Elessi patted Modren's belly, rings clanging on his armour. 'And at least you've got some paddin' beneath that metal to keep you warm.'

The mage looked appalled. 'Now listen here, wife, it's stress weight. You can blame Farden if you don't like it!'

Elessi tutted. 'What I don't like is how close we're cuttin' it. Another day and we'll all be too weak to fight properly. What if Malvus doesn't attack today?'

'Then we'll make him,' Modren replied.' As much as I hate to admit it, that tattooed bastard was right. He had the foresight to see Malvus' dirty tricks and sheer numbers. Without his tunnels, the poison would have finished us all. We have hope, thin as thread, but hope.'

Elessi stretched to brush her lips against his stubbled cheek and scars. 'And that's why I married you. Ever the optimist.'

'Tough work, but somebody has to do it,' he said. For possibly the tenth time, Modren checked the buckles of his cloak, strapped to his pauldrons. Elessi's hands calmed his.

'That they do, Undermage,' she replied. 'At least for one more day, and then you and I will talk about this castle idea of yours.'

A polite knock sounded upon their chambers. Eyrum thumped into the room, encased in Siren scale plate and only a circle of his face showing. An axe hung on each hip.

'Farden wants you at the peak.'

Elessi's affection turned sharp as she prodded her husband, straight at the red and balanced scales etched into his dun-metal breastplate. Her brown eyes brimmed with an emotion Modren found inescapable, even with the Siren waiting.

'Don't fight battles you can't win,' she whispered. We already have two heroes; we don't need more. You meet me by those ships, understand?'

'I understand.' Modren bowed his head as Elessi turned to Eyrum, skewering him with a look.

'And you, you big troll, you keep him safe, you hear me?'

Eyrum bowed in a royal gesture. 'Yes, madam.'

Modren swept past Elessi, grinning to shrug the heaviness from the moment. 'And you, woman, don't you take any chances either. Get those people to safety and nothing more.'

Elessi patted her own armour, light and simple just as she preferred it.

'Go on. Get,' she shooed them out the door, lingering to watch before they disappeared down the corridor.

'At least you aren't starving, Durnus,' said Skertrict cheerily, patting his stomach. The smile was a fleeting thing, dying from being so plainly out of place.

The vampyre shook his head as he packed another tome into his seal-leather satchel. With the bulk of his tomes aboard the bookships already, he could choose but precious few to escape with. He stared over the spread of poems and scrolls and kneaded his eyes with a knuckle. 'Not the time, scholar, for frivolity.'

'Apologies, General. I feel drowned by the mood, is all. It lies heavy and dark like fog over this fortress,' Skertrict sighed as he looked out the window.

'Such is the shadow of death's wings,' Durnus replied. 'And they will fall on all of us by the end of this day if we do not make haste.'

The scholar smiled again, and this time it held as Skertrict watched the vampyre from across the table, framed by the pallid daylight.

'Skertrict!' snapped Durnus.

'Yes, sorry. Of course,' the scholar scrambled to the vampyre's bidding, making space in his already straining pack.

The vampyre poked his tongue with a fang. 'These two, the discourse of southern Paraia and Moxel's tributaries. And that will have to suffice.' Leaving the rest to be burned was heresy of the highest order, but choice was lacking in Scalussen these days.

'What of this?' The scholar pushed an open tome across the table, shoving books aside. The faded diagram of a spear faced Durnus, and he traced it with a claw.

'Leave it. Go gather in the courtyards with the others,' he instructed, waving the scholar away. 'It's time.'

'You still haven't explained—'

'And neither shall I. You're a fine scholar, Skertrict. You always have been. But curb that inquisitive mind of yours for a moment and do as I say.'

'As you wish, General.' It was with a stony face and hidden sneer that Skertrict left the vampyre's lair. Durnus shook his head. *A dark fog indeed.*

With a sigh, he looked around at his ransacked bookshelves. What had once been a home now looked like a body on the pyre, shining with oil and waiting for the torch. It had set Durnus adrift, uprooted him and left him floating on uncertainty. For all his centuries, for all his wisdom, for all his great power, he felt inescapably fragile. Perhaps, he thought, this was how Farden felt most often.

A fist sounded at the door. 'Skertrict, I swear to Ever—'

A balding head poked through. 'It's me,' said Modren. 'Farden wants us.'

'I am ready.' Durnus nodded, hauling his rucksack over his shoulders, wearing fur and chainmail. He turned from the desk, hesitated. His gaze crept back to the tome still open on the desk.

'Durnus?'

'Yes!' With a hiss, the vampyre snatched the tome from the table and stuffed it into the satchel.

The slam of the door chased them down the hallway. Bustling beside Modren, pale eyes ahead and mind abuzz, Durnus didn't see the wiry, bespectacled man hovering at a distant corner, one lens creeping beyond the wall. Watching.

The silence of his footsteps would have put a cat to shame.

The gryphon's trill was damning.

Farden sighed patiently. 'I don't care, Ilios. You're going to the ships and Lerel. Fleetstar will take Durnus and Mithrid to Irminsul.'

Ilios whistled so piercingly it put a ring in Farden's ear.

'No, you fool, it's because you matter most to me. I promised Tyrfing I would take care of you, and I will.'

A clack of the gryphon's beak was the only reply. In a sour mood, the gryphon retreated to the edge of the Frostsoar and hunched his wings, staring east.

Farden rolled his eyes, finding his gaze resting on the horde below him. Though the sky was clear, a faint snow of ash drifted on the breathless breezes and dirtied the ice fields. Plumes of smoke arose from the Arka as forges raged. He stared at the wooden fort deep behind the enemy lines. Even without spells, Farden could tell Malvus stood watching also. A god by his side. Both poised to die. *All it took was wrangling a volcano.* The mage relaxed his stern jaw and took a shuddering breath.

Hinges creaked behind him. Guards emerged and moved aside to let Modren and Durnus through. Both of them grimaced at the cold slapping them in the face. The guards shut the doors behind them.

'Fine day for it,' muttered Modren, flicking ash from his armour.

Farden met them at the centre of the tower. 'Isn't it just?'

The undermage pointed at Ilios, who promptly spread his pinions and took flight. 'What's wrong with him?'

'He's sulking.'

'Ah.'

Farden held open his hands. 'Are we ready?'

'Eyrum's at the gatehouse. Hereni's closing in on the Tausenbar tunnels. We're as ready as we'll ever be for the cataclysm you have planned.'

Without a word, the three turned north to the anvil-cloud of smoke that hid Irminsul. Its fire still lit the clouds. 'Think Mithrid can do what you need her to?' Modren whispered.

Farden nodded. 'She'll have to. No time for doubt now.'

'And you, Farden,' interjected Durnus, 'do you truly believe you can do this?'

The mage looked between them. 'Is there anyone else who can?'

Durnus shook his head.

'Then who else, besides the Forever King?' Farden told him, swelling more with bravado than belief, but he did not dare admit it. For the first time, the name did not turn his stomach, and he saw the glint in his friends' eyes. There were no smiles. No quips of speeches and kings now. Durnus put a hand on the mage's armoured shoulder and bowed his head as if offering a prayer. Something clanked and cried out far below, breaking the moment's meaning. Merely a trebuchet being manhandled, most likely.

'Come, old friend,' said Farden, clasping the vampyre's bony knuckles. They felt stronger than before. 'I have one more favour to ask of you.

'I am still in the middle of the last dozen you have asked of me.'

Farden moved to a trunk perched on the stone and produced a leather-wrapped bundle. 'These will be better in your care. In case…'

'What?' Modren pounced.

Farden ignored him and unveiled the Grimsayer. 'Take this, Durnus.'

The vampyre visibly tensed under the weight of the tome as he manhandled it into his satchel.

Farden took another sheaf of battered parchment from the leather and let the wind take the empty wrapping. The parchment wavered with faint heat against the cold air as he clutched it to him. 'You know what this is.'

Though he handled the parchment gingerly, Durnus gave Farden a solemn nod. 'Your Book.'

Modren recoiled slightly. 'I thought you went to Albion to destroy it.'

'I didn't. Couldn't,' Farden confessed. 'Nobody should have to bear this curse but me, and yet it is a piece of me I can't let die, not now there are only two of us left, Modren. I trust nobody with it but my oldest friends. Keep it, bury it, destroy it if you have to, but it cannot be lost.'

The sound of door hinges sounded once more. Modren turned, but Farden was fixed by Durnus' keen gaze, cutting to his core. The vampyre placed one hand on the parchment and left it there outstretched.

'This sounds remarkably like a goodbye, Farden,' Durnus accused.

'I was just about to say the same thing,' announced a voice. It was the scholar, wiping blood from his hands with a kerchief. He was wearing a brown leather travelling coat, dusty and sunburnt at the edges.

Durnus was outraged. 'Skertrict! I ordered you to the courtyards.'

'Away with you, scholar,' Farden ordered.

As though he had misplaced something, Skertrict reached into the pocket of his coat and withdrew an orb of blue glass. 'Ah,' he said, relieved, shortly before hurling it between their feet.

Violet smoke erupted, engulfing them in a choking cloud. Concussions pounded Farden's ribs as spells exploded about him. Something steel struck him hard in the cheekbone. As pain wracked him, he staggered backwards, and cried out as he felt the parchment ripped from his hands. Magick burst from him, blasting aside the thick veil.

By the door, the scholar stood, parchment under his arm and spectacles smashed by his feet. He was shaking a hand limply.

'Gods, did that feel satisfying after so many years,' he crowed. 'Now we're even, Farden.'

'Spy!' Durnus screeched, outraged. Force magick unfolded from his claws.

'Please,' Skertrict tutted. With the sound of boulders splitting, he folded into himself to reappear on the other side of the Frostsoar. They whirled to find him peeling at the corner of his face. Skin scraped away in one great slough. As horrifying as it seemed, no blood came. Skertrict's face buckled like rotten leather as it was stripped away, proved nothing but a grotesque mask of skin and scalp, long cut from its owner. Beneath the stain of muddy hair and boyish cheeks, golden hair emerged, and a weathered face occupied with a familiar broad and victorious grin. Farden's breath caught in his craw as he felt the stab of realisation in his gut.

'Finally!' Loki stretched his face as if it were frozen. 'You don't know how dull it was to play your scholar these past weeks, Durnus. But at last, Farden! You bring your precious Book into the open for me. I must confess my gratitude that you didn't burn it or bury it under that mountain. It would have made my ruse somewhat singular. Fortunately for me, I took the chance and trusted in your sentimental side, the one I glimpsed in that Albion hovel decades ago. It will make a fine addition to the Hides of Hysteria, I think.'

There were no words yet invented for the insidious depravity of this creature standing before Farden, and he sought to wipe it from the world. Withering lightning forked from his fingers, but it struck nothing but stone and thin air. Loki cackled from behind them.

'It's been fun, I must admit, watching you all scurry around like toads aflame,' he gloated. '

'You've been here all along?' growled Farden, cursing his own stupidity as much as Loki's prowess at trickery. 'Right under my nose.'

'I found your scholar wandering about Kroppe three months ago. I knew his face would suit me well here amongst you. He did not want to give it up, but you know how convincing I can be. I arrived before you shut the quickdoors.' Loki pouted. 'You've grown serious with the years, Farden. I dare say the king's life suits you not. And yet, you're still as easy to push and prod as I remembered. Predictable.'

'You poisoned our stores.' It was no question. Farden already knew the answer.

'At Malvus' request, yes. You were dallying too much for his liking. Rich, coming from him. I was content to wait you out. Sit back and enjoy the performance.'

'With me!' Farden roared.

All three of them levelled their spells against him. Fire, lightning, and choking threads of red magick shredded the stone. Loki was too quick, vanishing but a dozen paces to the left.

'You should thank me, Farden! Without me, you might still be waiting for Malvus to arrive, watching everyone grow old around you.' Loki grinned. 'I wish you well in the coming battle. I trust you'll survive it somehow. Your work is not done yet, Forever King.'

The name took a foul turn in Loki's mouth. Farden reached for him with his spells once more, and this time Loki met them head on, skidding across the stone but holding a shield before him. The dismay was acute, stabbing. The reminder that he was a true god was a jarring one.

Modren and Durnus summoned their magick to the fray. Combined, their raging spells turned to pure fire and light. A whining built to fever pitch. Farden found his own boots scraping against the black rock. Beside him, Modren and Durnus strained.

'I'll see you again soon!' Loki yelled over the screeching. He clenched a fist, repelling their onslaught in a crescendo of light. Farden stumbled to his knees, and, to his horror, found nothing but blank air beneath his hands. His weight was already too far gone, and he felt the gut-wrenching sensation of falling.

Curses streaming from his mouth, he tried desperately to fall face first. Green light trailed from his hands. It was all in vain.

Ilios swept up beneath him, and Farden almost bit his tongue clean off with the jolt. Seizing Ilios' feathers a mite too hard judging from the gryphon's trill, Farden poised on the saddle, ready to pounce.

With a piercing cry, Ilios rose above the Frostsoar's rooftop. For all his airs of cunning and masterfulness, Farden would have sworn the god would have shit were he human. Loki stumbled, eyes wide at the splayed talons reaching for him, and the beak crammed with rows of teeth seeking god-flesh.

Ilios snapped at nothing but shaking, crackling air. He whined in disappointment, scraping gouges in the stone.

'That fucking god!' Farden bellowed. Bounding from the gryphon's back, he ripped open the doors to find the guards slumped and bleeding, dead to a man. 'He's played me for a fool! He didn't steer me to Albion to clash with Malvus, but to find and reclaim my Book! And now he has it! He has… *me!*'

As fire crackled on the mage's shoulders, below them, horns began to wail. Through the lingering trails of purple smoke, as if they had taken as it some manner of signal, they saw the Arka missiles loose from their siege engines.

'It's begun,' Modren murmured.

As trembling with outrage as the vampyre was, Durnus stowed his emotions momentarily to take Farden's Weight from his belt, press it against the mage's chest, and speak with the calm of wisdom. 'As much as I wish to skin that detestable star-born cunt with my own báre hands, there is nothing we can do now save for chasing him with Irminsul's fire. Wield the volcano, like you say you can, old friend,' he said. The runes in the Weight began to glow under his touch. 'Keep to the path you chose.'

Every part of him tensed like iron struts, Farden had to physically force himself to nod. The Weight's spell rattled against Farden's breastplate. He felt the heat in the tattoo of his wrist as Modren seized his vambrace.

'I'm not fucking walking this time.'

The world folded into black and blaring white as the spell seized them.

'What by Hurricane's arse is that?' Mithrid yelled, pointing to the sky.

Hereni spared a moment from heaving with breath to stare up to the fortress' heights. Purple smoke drifted from the summit of the Frostsoar.

'Trouble, I'd wager,' whispered Aspala. Her sword quivered as she cast around, searching the skies. Mithrid's eyes were still aching in the transition from smoky light to bright day. Ash fell in faint specks. The north was black with smoke and cloud.

The horns jolted her. Her head snapped south to see dark streaks polluting the skies. Eyrum's orders echoed across the walls, creating a waterfall of activity. The air grew thick and hot with magick as shields spread over the fortress, thousands of mages pouring out their all. Dragons took flight from the Frostsoar like birds fleeing a falling tree. The bland white sky became a riot of colour and noise. Only one pirouetted to the ground. *Fleetstar.*

Breaking from the guarded hole in the Scalussen ice, Hereni and Mithrid battled their way through the siege engines and waiting soldiers to catch the dragon. The first bombardment struck just as they reached her, colliding uselessly with shields and stone.

Mithrid could barely speak a word to Fleetstar before the Outlaw King emerged from thin air with a deafening strike of lightning. Durnus and Modren stood behind him, looking perturbed yet determined.

'Fucking hell,' Mithrid muttered, clutching her chest.

'Tunnels?' Farden asked of Hereni.

'Hundred yards from the Tausenbar mole tunnels, can't be any more,' Hereni surmised. 'I'll need an hour or two.'

Modren winced. 'This will be close.'

'I'll get back to it. No rest for the doomed,' Hereni said, affecting a mocking roll of the eyes. Before she turned, she caught Mithrid's hand. The touch was slight, but lingering.

'Remember when I said you weren't special?' Hereni snorted. 'How wrong was I? Do me a favour and don't die.'

The touch broke. 'I bet I beat you to the bookships,' she said, and the captain flashed a smile.

Mithrid watched her hurry crookedly across the ice, wondering how in Hel the girl had come to matter so much to her. Behind her, Farden and Durnus were waiting silently.

'What?'

'You ready?' Farden asked.

Mithrid snorted. 'Are you?'

'I'll be fine,' replied the mage, avoiding Mithrid's gaze. All she heard was Durnus grumbling as he saw him clambering up Fleetstar.

Farden crossed his arms. 'I've never been one for believing in a god of fate. Never heard of one, yet I'm starting to believe something brought you here for this. I don't dare question it, but I hope it's our fate to win this, not to fail. No god could be that cruel, and I know my share. They call me a saviour, but it looks like it might be you,' he said. 'What I'm saying is I never doubted you, you merely scared the shit out of me for a while.'

Watching those grey-green eyes flit about, Mithrid couldn't deny her grim smile. To matter, large or small and beside the circumstances, was a gift worth the hardship. She nodded. 'I'm sorry I doubted you. Hard to trust anything after finding your existence is a lie.'

Farden smirked wryly. 'I've been there, Mithrid Fenn,' he said. Another volley hammered the shields, and Farden's face hardened into stone-carved duty. 'Watch for my signal. Then unleash everything within you at that mountain and run for the ships. No heroism, Durnus.' Farden levelled a finger at the vampyre.

'Same to you, Farden. Our future needs no more martyrs for its foundations,' warned Durnus. Inwick's name was not spoken but heard all the same.

'Are we going, or shall I take a quick fucking nap?' growled Fleetstar, irascible as ever.

Mithrid clambered onto the dragon, her heart beating faster the closer she got to the saddle. She buckled her straps quickly, remembering last time.

'Fast as you can fly, Fleetstar,' Farden bade the dragon, who wasted no time in rearing onto her hindlegs and lurching into the sky. Ducking the shields, she sped around the perimeter of the walls before racing east, so fast the wind sought to drag Mithrid from her saddle. As the dragon sped into the smoke and soot of Irminsul's wrath, she focused her entire being upon holding on.

CHAPTER 36
HOPE'S EMBERS

Grave's god and magick's root.
Mountain high, sulphur, soot.
Cleansing fire and furnace mercy.
Righteous anger burn thee, scorch thee.
KHARANDER PRAYER

Farden ascended to the gatehouse to the deafening roar of the enemy. To a horn cry, the entire Arka horde advanced as one, its charge rippling across vast ranks as its shout reverberated through the fortress. Again, and again. A step, a shout, a step, until they grew faster, baying like starved hounds.

As the fire ignited in Farden's palms, Scalussen roared in return, clashing hilts and fists on shields and stone until the fortress thrummed.

'This is different, Farden,' Modren muttered by his side. 'Not just Albion spell fodder and recruit mages.'

Farden weaved his spells together. 'We buy as much time as Hereni and Elessi need.'

No sooner had Modren spoken than did daemons appear at the vanguard of the ranks. Helbeasts snarled. In their midst, Gremorin could be seen, with two fenrir leashed on chains, one held in each gnarled hand. They howled and spat at the smell of rotting meat at Scalussen's door. Nothing of Malvus could be seen besides his fort, a boulder in a sea of armour, spears, and banners.

Again, a volley struck the fortress. Farden watched the boulders and flaming wood crumble before his mages' power. Spells fluttered here and there with strain and weakness.

With a cry, Farden let fly his spell, watching the fireball streak across the churned battleground and cast ice and embers on the front ranks. A daemon beside Gremorin was singed, yet all the prince offered was a cackle.

'Archers! Mages! Ready yourselves!' Modren hollered.

Farden donned his helmet, shuddering at the cold rush as the metal slithered around his neck. 'Siege crews, fire!'

Smoke washed the walls as Scalussen fired its own barrage. These reached the advancing, roaring lines with ease. Each cut great swathes through the ranks. Screams replaced battle cries, and to the blast of horns and rabid pounding of drums, the Arka began their charge.

'Scythes!'

Once more, machinery began to clank within the walls. The blades reared their vicious heads, making mincemeat of those fleet of foot and eager to meet their deaths. Blood sprayed the walls as the scythes completed their arc. Scalussen cheered.

'Loose!' Modren yelled.

Along the walls, shields lifted to let fire and lightning cascade from the walls. Arrows chased the spells. The charging Arka stumbled over their dead.

The thunder of troll feet and colossal wheels filled the air as Malvus' siege engines advanced. Farden spied a battering ram under which four daemons laboured. Soldiers surrounded it, heaving thick shields and longswords. As the Arka crashed against the fortress like winter waves, the battering ram aimed straight for gate, caring not who it trampled. Farden glimpsed the face of the ram, iron carved like a snarling helbeast. Despite the volleys of archers and mages, the giant contraption collided with the gate with a burst of fire and a tremor that shook the Scalussen stone.

Farden sighed. 'Shall we?'

'Let's.' Modren placed two fingers in his mouth and blew sharply. Below them, Eyrum and Warbringer loitered ahead of their formations of minotaurs and heavily armed Sirens.

'I think it's high time we put out the welcome mat.'

Warbringer looked clueless, while Eyrum grinned. With a barking order, engineers sprinted to attention with javelins of solid steel two inches thick, one end sharp and the other blunt. Farden loosed a shield spell as he hovered over the crenellations. He knew just how well those javelins fit the drilled holes in the gate, opened by the very clanking he could hear over the first juddering hammer of the ram. Just long enough to poke from the gates, ready to be hammered by spell or strength.

'Now!' Modren yelled to Warbringer and Eyrum. Farden heard the clang as war hammer and axe met the ends of the loaded javelins. The battering ram immediately slumped. One daemon fell limp beyond its iron-clad roof, a steel javelin embedded in its throat.

'Swing all you like!' Farden yelled.

Javelin after javelin shot from the gate, until they could barely be shot through the mound of dead that had accumulated. Farden watched the last shot pierce three soldiers before sticking them upright in the ice like some Paraian delicacy.

The mage's shield buckled as a daemon spewed fire against the walls. Looking up, he saw the siege towers making faster progress than their precursors. Though Towerdawn's dragons harried and scorched them as much as possible, their iron skins kept them rolling, all converging along a single stretch of the wall.

Two ladders slammed along the parapets to the right. Modren was already hacking at them. Arrows began to clatter against the shields like hail, one in every dozen sneaking through. Farden saw two of his mages fall with fletching poking from their eyes and mouth.

The Arka refused to cease their chanting. Even though the front ranks perished pressed up against the walls and sweeping blades, the horde kept marching.

Between the crowded masses, Farden saw iron ladders being passed over heads and spears. For every soldier or mage that died carrying them, more filled their space.

As one came crashing onto the walls, Farden mounted the gatehouse parapet, a shield in one hand and lightning surging in the other. He poured his rage into every glowing thread of that spell, driving it into the nearest ladder. The score or so of impetuous Arka convulsed as the energy shot through them, turning muscle to cooked meat and bone to ash.

'Take them down!' Farden roared between spells.

No axe or hammer could dislodge the ladders. Not even the scythes could reach that far. With the collision of the other two ladders, they formed broad ramps for scores of Arka to ascend at a time. Under Modren's orders Scalussen shields rallied and spears gathered to stab at anything that reared its head above the walls.

Farden laid a barrage of fire and lightning upon anything that moved. Modren lent his fire to the fray, and as archers and mages kept the rungs peppered, they managed to melt two of the ladders enough for them to crumble. Those at its peak fell into the path of the scythe, sliced in two before they could scramble free.

For a blessed moment, the barrage seemed halted, but from the smoke and blur of chaos, Gremorin's fenrir scaled the ladders and bounded into the fortress. One fenrir wasted no time in turning the minotaur ranks into a bloodbath. One minotaur was seized in its jaws, and chewed nearly in half by the time the clan had sank its blades and horns into the fenrir's pelt. The other fenrir had torn a line through the Scalussen mages. Burnt from fire spells and coated with arrows, the beast rent ranks into bloody strips. It took Eyrum removing its back legs for the giant wolf to fall, howling. The Siren's axes fell once more, turning its yelps to silence.

Fire bloomed as Towerdawn led a scorching assault across the Arka ranks. Dragon after dragon fell from the sky, burning furrows of flame through the chanting crowds. Screams filled the air as thousands found their limbs burning before their melting eyes.

Farden turned to eye the hollow buildings where escape waited for the masses below. All of Scalussen stood between the walls and the Frostsoar. He squeezed his eyes shut.

'Come on, Hereni!'

Steam choked her. Dripping ice drenched her. The hammering of the brace builders was a constant thunder drilling into her soul. The heat singed her fingers, and yet Hereni's fire spells remained unabated. Too much counted on her and the other mages burning their way through the underworld of cold ice and volcanic rock.

Behind her, a dark tunnel tracing miles stretched into shadow. Only the light of engineers and the mages flanking her lit their efforts. Even at that distance, they could feel and hear the clamour of battle.

Hereni took a breath, winding back her magick only to focus all her frustration and panic into one stream of fire; one glowing spot of sputtering, boiling water. She was convinced she would be half blind after this, but with narrowed eyes, she pressed on.

'Come on, you bastards!' she yelled.

The mage to her right responded by promptly passing out, landing in the slush before the engineers dragged her away. 'Fetch me another mage!'

'That's all there are!'

'Gods damn it!' Heat scorched the tunnel as Hereni delved into depths the undermage and Farden had always warned against, those deeper levels that verged on abandon, the kind that scorched mages to the bone. Grinding teeth, she surrendered herself, letting fire stream from her entire body.

Hereni collapsed into the meltwater in surprise as the wall of ice collapsed, revealing a black spell-hewn tunnel beyond. 'Kill your spells,' Hereni gasped, half choking on the torrent of water that flooded past her. 'Pass the word along quick as you can. We're through! You, come with me.'

Hereni half jumped, half collapsed into the mole tunnel. The other mage slid down the ice wall. After tracing the sled tracks with her shaking fingers, Hereni began to run, thanking the gods their tunnel bored mercifully close to the southern end.

She spread her hands over the ice door, glowing white with sunlight, and let the magick spread alongside the other mage's. After digging out the tunnel, this was easy work, and within minutes, they collapsed upon fresh snow, blinking in sunlight and gasping at mountain air.

Beyond them lay the swathe of black gravel and snow leading to a bay of indigo water, filled with Arka ships at anchor. A score of golden sails bearing the hammer of the Arka stretched between them and the walls of ice between the Tausenbar and the sea.

All fervour and energy fled Hereni's body. Try as she might, she couldn't rise past her knees. 'Where the fuck is the armada?' she panted.

Her question was answered gloriously quickly, and not by the mage at her side, but by the eruption of fire that engulfed the furthest Arka ship. Black sails emerged from the doorway of ice beyond the bay, and within moments, Chaos Sound was earning its name. Hereni would have cheered if she had had the breath for it. Instead, she feebly pushed the mage back into the tunnel, where she could see light breaking through the ice as the other two tunnels connected.

'Go! Get everybody moving!' she yelled.

꽃

The news came in the form of a screaming engineer, wailing all the way from the forges to the courtyard. Even Farden heard him, only needing Elessi's frantic waving to confirm his hopes: the tunnels were finished.

He seized the undermage by his side, pulling him close. 'Get this fortress to safety, Modren,' he ordered, keeping his voice low. 'I'll hold the gatehouse. Eyrum! Help the undermage.'

Once more, the heat burned through his forearms as he held Modren close. 'Go, you ugly bastard.'

'Ha!' Modren cackled as he bounded down the stairs. With the Siren in tow, they raced through the crowded soldiers. With the help of the engineers, the walls to the hollow buildings were collapsed, and with voices honed by years of conducting recruit drills, they began to shepherd the rear ranks and inner courtyards to the scaffolding leading down into the forges. Elessi was amongst them, pushing bewildered bodies past her with reckless shoves.

The river of bodies was not moving as fast as Farden would have liked, but it was moving nevertheless. His heart beat a vicious rhythm, stealing his wind for a moment as he balanced every passing moment with every life it spent. With a bloodcurdling cry, Farden raised blistering fire in his hands, and rained havoc upon the crowded ranks churning below him.

'No rest 'til freedom!' he cried. 'No mercy!'

With renewed fervour, Scalussen sowed slaughter amongst the crowded Arka. Barely did the mages and archers have to aim. The ice had been replaced with bodies, both dead and overwhelmingly alive.

The gatehouse trembled beneath Farden's feet. Another battering ram had broken past the wreckage of the last, driven by crowds of heavily armoured Arka soldiers. Its hammer tested the gates repeatedly. Beneath the gate, stone and earth trolls roared as the siege towers filled the skyline, taller than the Tausenbar. Dragons filled the sky with fire. Behind him, Scalussen began to teem with fire as spells and burning wreckage escaped the shields. And still the crowds evacuated at a trickling pace.

Time slid past Farden one death at a time, his eyes racing from one to the next, watching bodies fall from the walls, scorched by lightning and plagued by fire. The steady thunk of arrows in flesh counted the seconds, underpinned by the deafening thud of the battering ram.

Farden bared teeth and crushed his hands together until they glowed white hot. Slowly, he lifted them, trusting in the shields around him for cover while he stretched his arms up, until the fire spell crackled loudly in his face, caged between his fingers. With a lurch and a yell, he threw it to the heavens. The spell tore vertically through the chaos of the skies, streaking between twirling dragons and the smoky trails of missiles. Farden watched it as long as he dared, until it had exceeded the Frostsoar's height and remained a pinprick of light amongst the ash.

It was Mithrid's turn now.

'I cannot see a damn thing!' Durnus raised his cloak over his head to block the incessant gusts of steam and smoke, half resembling a bat in the process. Ash decorated his pale face in smears like a charcoal sketch.

Mithrid did the same. The helmet and visor had been useless in the heavy, acrid air. Sweat had blinded her. Irminsul had already been fuming when they arrived; now it raged. A constant stream of ash spewed from the mountain's crooked mouth. Lightning crackled amongst the billowing stack. Fresh new rivers of molten rock spewed down its sides. It was almost impossible to hear the vampyre's voice without having him yell in her ear. Together, they stared up into the blackened sky and strained to spy the dragon through the ash. They could barely see the neighbouring mountain, never mind spy Scalussen amongst the muck.

The girl flinched as she caught voices on the turbulent air, floating up from below, where the moronic Kharander were kneeling in clumps across the trembling red rock and raising chants to Irminsul.

Mithrid took another step towards the rift at the end of the path. Her outstretched hands shook under the sheer draught rushing past her, the breath of the mountain's forge. The heat was intense. More so than before, and for that, she was glad she was encased in steel. In the threads of smoke and waves of heat, Mithrid could feel the magick of Irminsul swatting against her. She did not dare loose her power yet. Not without Farden's signal and the dragon close by.

'You have faith in him, then? Last time we stood here you told him it was impossible.'

'I have more hope than faith. Blind, desperate hope that scholars are not used to trusting in. Farden is a force that there is often no arguing with. He is as stubborn as a mountain. As determined as fire. If there was anyone who could bend Irminsul to a weapon without dying in the act, it is Farden.'

Mithrid raised her chin. 'I hope he survives it.'

'Farden might act foolish, but that man does not know how to die,' Durnus yelled. 'Gods damn it! If we cannot see, how will we know when Farden signals.'

Durnus squeezed his eyes shut. Mithrid thought he might be blinded by the grit, but she also had seen how the riders could whisper to their dragons, without words, using minds only. Durnus was deep in conversation.

'Either the blasted serpent can't hear me, or she's gone, and ruined us all. I should have taken Ilios—'

'And you would have found yourself a roasted vampyre!' boomed Fleetstar, as the dragon emerged from the swirling haze. The wind of her wings threatened to tear their cloaks away. Gravel chimed against armour as they shielded their faces. 'Farden's given the signal! Fire, rising above the Frostsoar.'

'Bless your dragon eyes!' Durnus cried. 'Miss Fenn. I believe it is over to you.'

Blowing a deep sigh, Mithrid advanced, step by step towards the rift. 'No pressure. Just light the tinder that sparks the world aflame,' she muttered. Behind her, Fleetstar was poised to flee, already half-turned south but looking back in earnest. Durnus walked behind Mithrid, hands spread like talons and face grimacing against the heat. The shiver of a shield covered his extremities, and Mithrid found herself jealous.

The balcony beyond the rift was charred black. Half of it was missing, the rest looked like the night's canvas spread with molten stars. A sun's fury churned beyond: that tempest of liquid rock. Glowing fountains cascaded down the walls.

Mithrid heard the tense call of Durnus. 'Use your emotion, girl! As you did before.'

Dredging up every memory she had ever quashed – of her father lying dead, of the callousness of the mages, of the blood dripping from Troughwake's rafters – she poured it into one point of concentration. Above her metal palm, a shadow coalesced. An orb of darkness, spinning and raging as the magick tugged at it. Mithrid felt the volcano tremble.

Shadow wrapped her hands, spun around her wrists. Mithrid did not seek out the magick this time. Magick flowed about her. She merely pushed it, like a canopy against a storm.

Harder, Mithrid strained, finding her very bones shaking. She felt her face form into a mask of effort, lips drawn back, and her jaw iron. She felt herself screaming but heard nothing but the roar of fire and magick.

Mithrid took a step, and another, forcing the winds to wither before her. She stared down into that roiling stone. Its light was blinding, and yet in the threads of her own harried shadow, she saw the dark face waiting beneath, a yawning skull of flame and darkness. Mithrid thought of Littlest's foaming mouth, of Malvus' sneer, and added anger to her sorrow. The mountain screeched in unison with her. A column of fire sprang forth from the crater, spewing up into Irminsul's reaches. Great claws of molten rock raked at the charred walls. Despite the danger, Mithrid advanced. She stood in the doorway of the rift, shadow streaming from her like daemon wings. Durnus shrank back, both the heat and Mithrid's power scorching him.

'Keep going!' came his muffled shout.

Mithrid speared the column of fire with her shadow. Irminsul shook with outright rage. The molten claws reached higher, tearing the balcony until Mithrid stood on the precipice of the volcano. Jaws of flowing, white-hot stone emerged from the glowing maelstrom, and Mithrid sought to choke it.

Irminsul inhaled. The wind would have swept her from her feet had it not been for the vampyre's clutches. Weak as he seemed, his grip was steel, dragging her back against the influx of air and ash.

'I think you've done enough!' Durnus bellowed.

Bones still rattling from the effort, muscles convulsing, Mithrid ran in lurching stumbles. Irminsul's breath clawed at her all the way to the dragon's scales, where rough ridges gave her purchase enough to scramble into the saddle. Durnus was a whisker behind.

Fleetstar needed no bidding. With a neck-cracking lunge, she tore along the ragged slopes of Irminsul, skimming the Kharander, who stared in misplaced awe. The wind fought them with every blast of Fleetstar's wings, so much so that at the crescendo of the volcano's roar, the dragon was being swept backwards across the smoking landscape.

With a rending boom, Irminsul let out its breath in fire and molten rock. Flame burst from a thousand pores along the volcano's slopes. Its throat gushed fire and black smoke in a cascade of primordial fury.

'Fly, Fleetstar!' Durnus cried, as the initial wave of scorching heat swept over them. The dragon rode it, wings quaking as she battled to ride the onslaught. Mithrid dared a glance over the vampyre's shoulder, and what she saw ran her blood colder than her dark power ever had.

A wall of sulphur, fire, and vengeful magma chased them, mountain-high and all consuming. The Kharander's settlement had already been engulfed. The pikalos squealed as they scampered into rifts beneath the scarred and shaking earth.

Fleetstar howled as the conflagration charred her forked tail. Mithrid felt the strain of the dragon's muscles beneath her. The volcano's wrath sought to engulf them with every wingbeat, but Fleetstar's determination outpaced it. Towers of rock exploded into shards behind them as the dragon raced through the canyons of the Emberteeth. Mithrid swallowed vomit on every other violent turn.

Bursting through a veil of ash, Scalussen was sighted, shining with light and fire in the Arka barrage. The black stone had never looked so welcoming, yet so painfully small in distance. Fleetstar blazed a path towards it, spurting fire from her jaws, part in signal and part in panting breath.

'We're not going west to the ships?' Mithrid cried. The gale stole her voice, but Durnus heard her.

Durnus gave her but a look and hammered his hand on Fleetstar's scales. Mithrid's stomach crowded her throat as the dragon dropped like a stone to skim the ice.

❦

Death ruled the Scalussen walls, sweeping her scythe without mercy. More iron ladders had fallen upon the battlements. Two siege towers had smashed their way into the stone, leaking Arka across the parapets. Battles were fought in pockets along the fortifications.

Feeling the tremor pounding through the gatehouse, Farden reigned in his spells. It was no fist of a battering ram, but something deeper. North, he looked, and saw fire painting the sky orange.

Though a cold dread burned through him, the mage reached for his Weight, but before he let the spell seize him, the sight of his generals stalled him.

The High Crone had appeared beside Warbringer, bristling with finches. Ko-Tergo, too, swollen to his full yetin form, almost stretching to the minotaur's height.

'This is no time for last stands!' Farden called to them. 'Get your people to safety. Forge the Emaneska we dream of!'

All except Warbringer followed his directions. Farden glared, but she shouldered her mighty hammer and flared her nostrils. 'I fight to the end, Forever King!' she bellowed.

'As do I,' he growled, not caring if she heard him. He was preoccupied with the wash of magick and heat he felt crash against the fortress walls. Farden peered into the sky, trying to spy a dragon racing west beyond the roiling clouds, but there was not a sign of Durnus and Mithrid.

Whispering words of the oldest magicks Farden knew, he raised the Weight and let its magick flow through him.

Even without Toskig's reports, the spyglasses told Malvus all he longed to know. His cheeks ached his grin was that expansive.

'Two siege towers have reached the wall, Your Majesty. One stretch is being held. It appears we have breached the fortress.'

'Keep pushing, Malvus ordered. 'I wish to take my supper in Farden's halls this evening, while the mage kneels at my feet, and this time, means it. And remember, the mage's head is mine and mine alone. My knives thirst for his blood.'

'Your will be done, Your Majesty.' Toskig bowed.

Malvus looked to Wodehallow, whose face was a sicklier colour and even slicker with sweat than was usual. A flux of the cold had taken him in recent days. Truth be told, the man looked dreadful.

'Cheer up, Grand Duke. Your days here are numbered.' At the sight of Wodehallow's immediate abject fear, Malvus elaborated. 'You may return to your swamp of a city soon enough.'

The man sagged like a punctured bellows, utterly relieved.

'Though,' Malvus added. 'I regret to inform you that you shall do it on foot or by carriage. Since Arfell I have taken a liking to that sky-ship of yours. I believe I shall take it as a spoil of war,' Malvus boasted as he eyed the contraption anchored behind the fort.

'But I'm not the enemy! I—'

'Remain that way,' Malvus warned with a stern glare.

'Lord Saker returns, Majesty!' Toskig yelled.

While all eyes were fixed on the silhouette of a dragon as it spiralled down to the fort, a whiplash of air sent the guards scurrying. Loki appeared. Blades formed a circle around the god before Malvus bade them calm.

'Where have you been?' the emperor tutted.

'Burning bridges,' Loki replied, forcing others from his path as he came to stand at Malvus's side.

'Farden…' he began, but Fellgrin's roar silenced him. As the dragon hovered above the fort, Saker raised a bloody lance of black steel. Spots of crimson covered his furrowed face.

'Ships are burning in the bay beyond the mountains! Something's happening within the fortress.'

Malvus glared at Loki.

'Escape,' explained the god, playing at calm, but Malvus saw the indecision in his gaze, flirting back and forth between the walls and the emperor. 'Farden is planning an escape.'

'What good is your insight now, Loki?' Malvus snarled.

The god snorted mockingly, 'Use your eyes, Emperor. You have Farden cornered. He will not leave his sinking ship. He—' Loki's voice trailed away with his gaze as its fled north. Malvus had heard it, too. The deep crack of a tree snapping. The ice shook worryingly. Beyond Scalussen, above the black mountains of the world's crest, the sky bloomed like a sunset, its only sun a broadening wall of fire and hot ash spreading like dragons' wings. A black mushroom-shaped cloud was rising above the tallest peak. Purple lightning traced its ever-expanding bulk. A wave of acrid air raced across the battlefields. Pennants and banners reversed, crackling in the hot winds.

Though Malvus stared accusingly at the god, Loki was enraptured.

'Well played, Farden,' he could be heard saying to himself. 'Well played.'

Malvus clutched his stomach as a rush of nausea flooded his gut.

'You don't recognise it, do you?' uttered Wodehallow, as if in a daze, eyes wide and mirroring the horizon's fire. 'That feeling in your gut? It's called failure, Malvus.'

'Gah!' Malvus cried, sweeping his knife from its scabbard and drawing an ugly line across the duke's throat. Wodehallow sank to his knees, his front a mess of dark blood. He sputtered only the once, spurting ichor from his wound before toppling. Malvus stepped over him before Wodehallow could stop twitching.

'Give them everything we have!'

Toskig blustered between the confines of his helmet, 'But Majesty! Malvus!'

'EVERYTHING!' the emperor screeched.

Modren clanged his sword blade against the scaffolding strut. 'Hurry yourselves, damn it! Enough of that gawping. Move!'

Elessi helped a wounded lad into the arms of Aspala, whose face had yet to leave the direction of the sky. 'How many left?'

The undermage stretched desperately over the churning crowds all pouring eagerly into the forges. He had cursed the gods for many things over the years, but his lack of height was a fond favourite. The walls were a teeming blur. Smoke hung heavy, veined with lightning and fire. Eyrum was half pushing and half dragging dozens across the courtyards, while Warbringer's minotaurs and the Siren knights blocked the stairs with thick muscle, ensuring not a single Arka boot touched fortress soil. Not alive, in any case. Corpses had begun to pile inside the walls.

'Thousands still!' Modren yelled.

Sulphurous yellow smoke gushed from the chimneys of Scalussen as the ice began to quiver underfoot. The scaffolding rattled so violently that faces turned to the blushing sky. Fingers and swords pointed north. Daylight halved as the horizon was choked with ash. Though bitter air swept the crowds, the blood of Scalussen ran cold in dread. Those who saw the meaning of the stairs and the bolthole of the forges began to flood in earnest.

Modren felt it acutely: they were pinned, and nothing could erode training, faith, and camaraderie faster than panic. But the undermage preferred panic to indecision. 'Get moving if you want to live, damn you!' he stoked their hurry.

Thunder crackled over the gatehouse as Farden disappeared. Modren craned to see light swirling above the Frostsoar. 'Come on, you bastard. Do us proud once more,' he murmured privately, before wading through the churning crowds. 'Eyrum! Form a line! Mages, with me!'

'Modren!' Elessi's cry halted him only momentarily.

'Go, Elessi! Get everybody to safety. That is all that matters!' Modren held her eyes as long as he could before she was stolen from view by a lumbering minotaur.

Ash swirled around Farden's boots in the wake of the spell. The battle was an ocean's drumming against a shore far below, and though he dared not count the burning siege engines nor the scars upon the fortress walls. Even the dragons swirling in a constant storm of fire and flashing armour far beyond the Frostsoar's walls were no longer of interest. It was the north that commanded his attention, the hammering of his heart, and every needle of fear worming its way into his insides.

Magick. Born to wield it, they had said of him in the Manesmark School, an age before this one. The Hero of Efjar, they had branded him. The chosen weapon of greed and evil, he had been, the sire of Emaneska's foiled doom. Forever King, they called him now, and Farden tried to hold it all in the brink of his mind as he looked out upon the advancing blast of Irminsul's anger. It was a cliff face of bubbling ash and rock. Veins of fire and crimson lightning ran through it, belying the fury chasing the choking, eviscerating vanguard. It was preceded only by shooting stars of molten rock that bombarded the ice like the engines of another horde.

Farden held his hands low. He seized the great roots of power buried beneath the ice, sweeping up from the Emberteeth. He even clawed at the battlefield, and the storm of magick that roiled around the tower. Magick rose through his knees, his ribs, and put a stutter in his heart. By the time it had met the power of his own Book streaming from the base of his skull, Farden's arms convulsed. The wind railed at him as he fought to control the heat burning across his back. Farden felt the pressure in his legs as he heaved. The sky sought to crush him.

Beyond the fortress, drifts and wind-cut sculptures of ice began to shake themselves apart. Their shards arose into the sky, unbothered by the sweeping gales of heat. Black, became the skies, as ash swept ever forwards and to greater heights. Steam exploded to join the advance as Irminsul's inferno swept over the Dragonfields' spires and onto the ice. Farden tensed, betraying a garbled prayer – not to any god, but to all those who believed in him. *Praying that they were right.*

With a defiant casting of his hands, the mage unshackled the pressure he had built. A ship's length from the walls, Farden's spells clashed with Irminsul's fire. Fists of empty air and spitting shield magick drove a wedge in its onslaught. His shields grew blinding as they fought to keep the melting heat, ash, and raw magick at bay. Vast columns of smoke billowed upwards as the conflagration was divided in two seething rivers before a bow of Farden's pure will.

Sparks ground from his sabatons as he ground against the rock, sliding backwards. Again, the Frostsoar's precipice called to him. With seething, rapid breaths, Farden fought the pressure that sought to sweep him aside. He reclaimed his step, laughing not with glee but utter surprise. *He was doing it.* Though the fiery storm continued to rise over the fortress, bringing gnashing night to an already brutal day, its force swept around Scalussen's walls in two engulfing thrusts.

With a roar, Farden pivoted, turning his back to the edifice of black sky and lightning, holding his fists out straight as if enduring a lashing. He stared down the aim of his shaking arms, watching the ash and fire claim the ice like a tidal wave.

Beyond the reach of their captain's cries, where the encroaching calamity was hidden by the walls and barrage of spells, thousands of Arka battled on unabated. As the walls began to shake beneath their ladders and rams, the realisation rippled through the ranks as the first molten rocks began to fall on the flanks. Chants died mid-gasp. Even swords paused in mid-air.

Farden barely heard the screams over the deafening bellow of the volcano's fire meeting the crowded horde. He imagined them short-lived all the same. As he watched, the chaos continued without pause. He saw trebuchets blown to splinters. Siege towers were sent cartwheeling as if they were mere staves. Even some of the slower and heavier dragons couldn't outrun the fire. Farden saw one Lost Clan beast swatted from the sky by a blinding streak of rock, and spiral to the Arka with only one wing. Through the smoke he could see regiments beginning to turn tail as the two walls of fire sought to join. Despite the muscle-shredding strain, he found a moment to roar in gratified defiance as he watched his enemy laid waste before him.

Farden was forced onto one knee as Irminsul seemed to redouble its efforts. Another shockwave of force slammed into his spells. To Farden's horror, his spells crumbled momentarily; enough to bring the fire to Scalussen's walls. Despite the pain wracking his bones, Farden hit the volcano back, pushing it back for all of a moment before it swallowed a length of wall and blasted its stone to bricks. The brave few who were not crushed fled.

Again, Farden's feet slid across the stone. As molten rock began to rain around him, he felt the primal hunger in Irminsul's chaos. It held no complex grudge. It was pure, consuming hunger, and it was now levelled at Farden for having the gall to interrupt it.

Farden watched the stone's edge come closer, letting the force reveal the gatehouse, now swarming with battle. The Arka were in the courtyard, clashing with Modren's makeshift defences while the remainder of the fortress fought to escape. Far too many remained, at least several hundred, corralled by thin stairs. Though it almost shattered his arm, Farden held the spells with one hand while he snatched for his Weight.

It was but the space of a blink, but in that short journey, the fires tore at Scalussen. He found himself staring up in open-mouthed awe. Flames now lashed the Frostsoar's northern sides. The sky had been completely consumed with ash. Farden's spell slammed into the fire, holding it back beyond the inner walls with an unearthly screech that was beyond any magick clashing. Though he gave it his entire effort, the chaos engulfed the fortress yard by shrinking yard.

Through the slits of his visor, Farden caught sight of Modren wielding fire and blade against the Arka who spilled over the walls in desperation. Scalussen soldiers and mages fell like culled herds. No longer kept back by shields, daemons exploded onto the parapets. Helbeasts swarmed.

And despite it all, Farden could do nothing but concentrate. Even when a carapace-clad daemon began to pound its way across the battlements towards him, a fiery whip raised high. Farden cursed at the top of his lungs.

The dragon fell moments before the whip did. Talons hooked the daemon's face and crushed its skull against the wall top. Fleetstar had gouged its throat out with her fangs and spat in disgust.

'Protect the king!' bellowed Durnus, as he dropped from the dragon's flank, Mithrid alongside him. Warbringer mounted the steps with Aspala, now drenched in blood. She held a notched golden sword in both hands like a walking stick. Flame burnt in Fleetstar's mouth.

Farden had not the voice nor time to argue. It was all he could do to keep Irminsul's fire from consuming them. The thin bubble of Farden's magick was becoming brittle. Over his shoulder, he saw the Arka in the shadow of the walls, still daunting in their tens of thousands.

A wedge was shortly driven between Modren's shrinking enclave of shields and darting spears. A snatching glance showed the undermage and Eyrum surrounded by circles of corpses. Yet still the Arka pressed them, clambering rabidly for the same safety the Scalussen fought to claim. It was blood-drenched madness.

'Durnus!' Farden roared. Every word trembled his spell, but he had to try. 'Do what I forbade you to do!'

The vampyre took the briefest of moments to look shocked before his lips drew back in snarl. He, too, sought magick, though a darker kind than Farden had ever tasted. By the time his hands were clawing at the sky, tentacles of cyan light were seeping from amongst the churning masses. Farden saw it himself: the shiver that spread through the mounds of dead. They arose to the stuttering weave of Durnus' fingers. A different kind of scream began to fill the courtyard and the crimson ice beyond the walls. Not of pain nor rage nor fear, but the utter horror that comes from one when forced to question the order and permanence of death.

Durnus eyes and mouth were now aglow with light. Under his power, half the dead had risen and now ravaged the Arka with tooth and claw.

The dead yelled as one through slashed and crooked throats, even as they fell twice to Arka swords.

'Leave, Modren!'

'Remind me to talk about this to Durnus when we see him next!' Modren shouted to Eyrum. The Siren was too busy cleaving a man from neck to hip to respond. He snatched a breath as Modren redoubled his shield, casting a line of struggling mages to the ground.

Though the vampyre's dark magick had slowed the Arka assault, it had not halted it. Blood sprayed as a dead man sank a knife into an Arka mage's skull, one who had been dangerously close to pouncing on Modren.

'Do as he says!' the undermage ordered Eyrum, eyes focused on the right flank, where the evacuees were being overrun. 'And break the steps once you see me coming down!'

'Don't you dare risk yourself, Modren—'

Two daemons cut their way through the crowds, their fire-drenched swords sweeping through all: foe, ally, dead or alive. It did not matter to them.

Lightning was already pouring down Modren's arms. 'Do it! This is not a fight you can win!'

Eyrum had little choice. A quake spell ripped from the undermage, flattening the daemons and forcing half the survivors towards the forges whether they liked it or not. Eyrum alone guarded the last dregs limping to safety. Half of them tumbled down the scaffolding before he, too, put foot to the stairs, yet he still refused to leave.

But Modren saw Scarred barging their way into view. With a cackle, he bathed the ranks in lightning, watching with grim satisfaction as his spells reverberated through the slush of the churned ice. Armour and flesh melted before his onslaught. Step after step, the undermage closed the gap between the stairs, one eye on Farden all the time, a burning pyre of magick against the black sky.

'Now, Modren!' he could hear Eyrum urging him. Feeling the hot rush of air from the forges on his back, Modren threw out another blast of a quake spell before turning to flee.

A thunderclap drove the wind from his lungs as the prince of daemons appeared barely inches before him. Gremorin's fist struck Modren like a boulder, driving him into the ice. Even within his helmet, Modren felt the impact crack his skull. He fought desperately to rise, even glimpsing Eyrum's axe spinning past him during his struggle. It dug deep into the daemon's shoulder, but nothing could keep Gremorin from his prey. He swatted the Siren into the scaffolding and down the spiral of stairs.

The daemon's claws ripped aside Modren's shield spell and stabbed the seams of his armour. Once, twice, thrice they stabbed, driving deeper every time until Modren felt the metal puncture.

Even as his lungs collapsed, as the blood filled his throat, as Gremorin sneered unbearably close to his face, Modren reached for the scaffolding, and for the woman he knew waited beyond it.

What Gremorin gleefully mistook as death-throes and desperate pleas to his gods was his undoing. Modren let the magick pour from him, to burn through his veins as Written were taught to shy from at any cost. *What better moment for recklessness was there than his last breath.*

Lacking the breath for curses and cries, Modren just sneered as the daemon. 'No rest 'til freedom,' he rasped, shortly before the magick exploded from him.

'NO!'

The cry ripped from Farden's throat as he watched lightning consume the courtyard, savage and wordless, chorused by Mithrid and Durnus. Though his knees sought to crumble, Farden's magick kept him aloft. Once more, the force pushed him backwards, until his heels scraped the battlements. It was no decision, but a reaction of rage.

Farden raised his hands, letting the flames billow around the Frostsoar, letting the ash cloud consume half the courtyards before he dragged the fire from it. With a combined roar of effort and sorrow, the mage swept the conflagration across the walls, scorching every Arka and animated corpse from his sight. He turned one last time to the Arka with his hands rigid, bones threatening to snap at any moment, and his searing gaze fixed on Malvus' fort. He clawed the volcano's fire inwards.

Malvus' avid grin was at last proved an imposter. It had endured the obliteration of half his horde from the ice. It had endured the sight of Farden glowing like a god atop his gatehouse. But now, as he saw the volcano's fury surge inwards, rearing up like a great fist poised to smite him, no longer could he maintain it. His horrified gaze flitted before the searing edge of the destruction rushing towards him, watching men turned to char before his very eyes.

The emperor began to edge backwards and quickly found the railing behind him. He sought the stairs instead, but at the creak of wood, he found Toskig turned around, glaring murder at him. The general's sword was drawn, his face streaked with ash and what looked like tears.

'You,' he breathed. Not a single one of the imperial guards moved to stop him. Half of them were already sprinting for other escapes. 'You've killed us all,' Toskig accused.

'Now you listen here!' Malvus was already clattering down stairs, halfway to the ice. Toskig clomped after him with all the purpose of a storm cloud. The emperor drew one of his knives and spun it around his fingers.

'Back away, you oaf! You think this is the end, General? Mark my words. We'll chase them to the ends of Emaneska if we—'

'Emaneska will be better off without you.'

Toskig raised his sword, poised for a lunge. Malvus shrank under his shadow, framed by the encroaching fire. The ice was jarringly cold against his hand, as he stumbled to his knees. It was then the old seer's words rushed back to him. *Coughing blood on white snow.* Terror gripped him.

'Toskig! I'm warning you.'

Blood spattered his face, making Malvus cough and wipe his eyes. He slashed menacingly with a knife, but Toskig's sword had already fallen from his grip. Toskig reached not for the emperor, but for his face, where a lance protruded from his mouth. The general lived long enough to stare cross-eyed at the bloody blade before collapsing. Behind him stood Loki, brushing his hands of splinters and frost.

'Never trusted him,' he surmised. Loki strode to the emperor's side and seized his hands despite the disgust he showed.

'You've got more work to do, Malvus Barkhart,' he told him, and together they folded into nothing. The air was still wobbling when the fire reached the fort and reduced it to a hail of splinters.

Mithrid pried herself from her knees and from what remained of the scaffolding. Modren's spell still crackled. She saw the daemon prince trace a wound across his face before the he disappeared into the fire. She watched the dead consumed, watched yards of fallen and bloodied ice swallowed by the looming jaws of flame. She shielded herself with a hand as flame swooped close, blocked only by Durnus' magick. A mighty hand threw her down by the gate, and she reeled to find Warbringer standing over her.

'Farden!' Durnus bellowed. Mithrid only made out the words from the shape of his mouth.

The mage did not respond. Above them, Farden now burned with his own white fire. She did not have to see his eyes to know they were pits of fire. As she had stared, part in horror, part in awe, the winds lifted Farden from his feet as if drawn on ropes lashed to his clawed hands. He had left nothing of the sky besides ash.

The fire washed interminably close. The sulphur smoke gagged her and left her eyes burning. As she tried desperately to see, she found the vampyre clutching at her.

'Your role is not over yet, Mithrid!' He had to scream to be heard. 'Farden has given into the emotion and given in too far! It will not solely be us who perish. The very earth is splitting. He will consume himself and the whole north in the process!' Durnus slapped the dragon's scales. 'Fly, Fleetstar! We will meet you!'

Without a word, Fleetstar took her chance to escape. Mithrid stared longingly after the dragon until Durnus seized the collar of her breastplate and shook her. 'You remember what I told you?'

Mithrid shook her head. Warbringer and Aspala were staring at her.

'You may be the only one to stop him!'

She tore her eyes from the vampyre's gaze as a geyser of steam exploded barely a stone's cast from the gatehouse. She pressed herself to the iron gate. It juddered like the ice beneath her boots. Once again, the fire edged closer as Farden's shield shrank.

'Now, Mithrid! Your tale does not end here.'

That it did not. She had not come here to die. Blind desperation drove her onwards, step by exhausting step. Shadow swirled about her like a ragged cloak. She held an orb of power in each palm.

'Farden!' she yelled, still in hope he might relent. His magick bombarded her, driving needles into her skull. Mithrid almost tottered, but Aspala was close behind, using her somewhat as a shield. Durnus and Warbringer brought up the rear. The vampyre's shield was possibly the only barrier remaining between them and death. The fire now revolved about the gatehouse in a maelstrom. The neighbouring walls were staring to crumble, even melt in places.

Mithrid tried one final time. 'You have to stop!'

Farden chose that moment to fix her with a glare, white hot eyes burning through his visor. The armour glowed in places. Mithrid felt her fingertips burning, smelled her hair singed. Irminsul was a sandcastle to the wall of steel that was Farden's power. Flinging her hands, her shadow strangled his limbs. Mithrid reeled in pain yet refused to give in. Behind her, she could hear Durnus straining, fire now a mere yard from his claws.

'The Weight! Get the Weight and hold onto him!'

Mithrid poured all her remaining strength into her dark spell, pushing the heat and choking the bright fire aside long enough to place her hands on the Weight at Farden's belt. Fire scorched her arm, hot enough to burn through Akitha's armour.

With desperate hands, the Weight was passed to Durnus, while Mithrid strained to grasp Farden. Barely an inch remained between her and Farden, yet it felt like seizing coals. The cold grip of her power lent her no relief.

'Mithrid!' the vampyre howled. Above their head, the Frostsoar thundered as the tower split. She had seen enough trees fall in her time to know they had moments only.

Mithrid threw herself at the mage, clamping her numb hand onto his Scalussen armour. The skin peeled from Mithrid's fingers as the magick railed against her. In her anguish, behind her clamped eyes, she saw the eyes of Irminsul fixed upon her. Blinding. Vengeful. Her defiant scream was snatched away as the world was crushed into a cloud of blistering ash.

The bitter battle of Chaos Sound ended with the *Autumn's Vanguard* splicing an Arka warship in two before biting into the ice. Ko-Tergo and Hereni were already by the black shore. The mage levelled every fire spell she had left in her at any Arka that made it ashore. The witches filled the sky with finches, all a-twitter at the smoke breaking over the Tausenbar.

Elessi stood by the tunnel's entrance. The sky, streaked orange and black, held no interest for her. Even the increasingly bloodied bodies that poured from the tunnel on foot or by sled were mere numbers, every face a disappointment in being the wrong face.

A vicious tremor shook her to the glassy wall, and Elessi steadied herself. The evacuees dwindled to a desperate trickle. Elessi ducked and weaved to examine the dark figures deeper within. Hands wringing, Elessi rushed to the three tunnels. Smoke was belching from them. Only one shadow could be seen against the lantern light. Steel armour shone.

Elessi was already backing away, tears brimming as Eyrum tumbled onto the ice. He sought to grab her.

'We have to run,' he gasped.

'Modren!' she cried, trying to get past the Siren and into the tunnels.

'Elessi! We have to leave!'

Her fists pounded against his breastplate. 'You promised me!'

As if she was no more than a sack of grain, Eyrum hauled her from her feet and dragged her towards the tunnel's light. Ignoring every pummel and scream, the Siren ran doggedly for the waiting ships and crowds, all staring north and past the mountains. Elessi's sobs were cut short by a shower of ice and charcoal spewing from the tunnels. She watched, nauseated, as the ash continued to claim the horizon.

Elessi spoke nothing when Eyrum sat her down, his face a mask of sorrow. Her heart soared momentarily when the Siren dragons burst through Tausenbar's crags, but they bore only their riders. Their news was solemn: they had seen Frostsoar fall; they had seen the fortress incinerated, they had seen Malvus' enclave destroyed.

Even the news of a scattered, fleeing horde, scorched to a mere shade of the numbers that had arrived on the ice, fell on deaf ears and numb heart. Elessi walked herself aboard the *Autumn's Vanguard*, as if Eyrum had swept her body from the ice but left her soul in the tunnels.

An hour, the ships waited, until no more dragons came. Though Elessi shared the bookship's rail with other sorrowed hearts, their victory over the Arka was mute, and sorely-bought.

While the survivors of Scalussen were crowded across the armada's ships, glad to be alive, no songs were sung. No cheers risen. Not yet. The Forever King was still missing. Scalussen remained a smouldering husk. The ice fields were blackened, awash with grim floodwaters of countless charred corpses.

Elessi spent the hour with the others, staring at the scarred sky until Irminsul seemed to be spent, and its fury was dragged west and out to sea.

It was Lerel who came to her at last, once the armada had nosed through the battle scarred remnants of Arka ships. She was dressed in even more furs than Elessi, her face just as stony.

'Ilios and the dragons have been roaming far and wide,' she said. 'Scalussen still burns, and there is no sign yet of Durnus, Mithrid, or Fleetstar. The gryphon refuses to come down.'

A quiet grumble came from Bull, hunched over a railing like a discarded mattress.

'The minotaur Warbringer and a woman named Aspala are missing, too. Thought you would want to know, as you are the ranking member left. *General* Elessi.' Lerel's smile was a furtive, awkward thing.

Elessi nodded, closing her eyes to the salt air striking her face as the ship turned. 'How many saved?' she whispered.

Lerel rapped the railing with her fist. 'Twenty thousand saved, so my officers say. A better count will be taken tomorrow. Far more would have died today had it not been for Farden. Even if our worst fears are true, he won.'

'At what price?' Elessi murmured.

Lerel turned her back to the sea, watching her crew run about their duties, readying the ship for the ocean. 'What now, Elessi? What becomes of the rest of Scalussen?'

'South.' Elessi's tone was flat, hoarse. 'We sail to Krauslung. That was always the plan, wasn't it?'

It took time for Lerel to draw her eyes from the sky. The quarry of words seemed barren for all.

'Nothing has changed, and yet everything feels different.'

'We still have hope,' Elessi muttered as she set a course for the peace and companionless vacancy of her cabin. Her footfalls were loud, drawing stares. 'At least that didn't burn with Scalussen.'

EPILOGUE

Birds.

She couldn't remember the last time she'd heard the chirruping song of birds. And what peculiar specimens, too. No mew of a gull nor squeak of the flitting finches, but a music rare summers scraping knees had been filled with. She wondered what birds there were beyond the veil of death,

Mithrid clenched her fists in sudden fright. Grass. She plucked a handful of verdant grass from the black soil. Though her hands were scorched to blisters and still aflame, Scalussen's pyre had disappeared. The only heat was a sun upon her back, a contrast to the cold knife of wind that found the gaps in her armour.

Rolling onto her back showed her trees. Not pines. Not verglass trees, but those of twisting trunks and broad, flat leaves of red and amber.

A snuffle sounded nearby. Mithrid froze, only her eyes shifting.

Warbringer came awake with a bellow and a flurry of turf. In her panic, Mithrid must have seemed an enemy, for her warhammer came swinging before the girl could ever raise a hand.

Opening an eye, she briefly examined the pitted surface of the warhammer, blearily tracing its skull shape before it was hoisted clear.

'We're alive,' breathed Mithrid as if reality were a spell she could shatter at any instant. 'We're fucking alive. Unless either Hel or Haven is a forest, we escaped.'

The minotaur snorted. The noises of the forest pulled her snout in every direction. 'Hel is where we escaped from, girl.'

Fronds of blue flowers rustled as something else stirred. Aspala was dragged free, draped half over Durnus. Whether protecting him or using him as padding for her fall was unclear, but the vampyre was unconscious. Burns scorched his face. Not a shade of colour infused his skin. His fingers were still clutched around a blackened Weight.

'Girl,' rumbled Warbringer. She was staring over a patch of black soil, or what she'd thought was black soil. It was char.

Farden lay sprawled on his face. The grass around him was still smoking. Ash fell from the treetops like lost and travel-weary snow. A vague hole had been torn in the canopy where they had presumably fallen.

'Is he alive?'

Caring not for possible injuries, Warbringer hoisted Farden to face the light. The minotaur snarled as her fingers hissed against his armour. The Scalussen metal was forge-hot, scorched black in places, and deeply scored. Half of his cuirass scales warped outward.

Aspala tottered to stare down at the mage. 'Is he…? He can't be.'

With a rising yell, Mithrid endured the heat long enough to wrench Farden's visor opened. His eyes were shut, face marred with soot, but faint mist appeared on Aspala's shattered sword.

Mithrid sprawled on her arse by his side, consciousness fragile. The woods wavered before her eyes. She could see no end to the cathedral of autumn leaves.

'Where's the ice? The cold?' Mithrid muttered. Even the sky looked too unnaturally blue. Far too peaceful for her liking. 'Where's the fire and ash?'

Aspala uttered the true question she was trying to avoid. 'Where are the others?'

Durnus groaned between the foliage. It took the minotaur to haul Mithrid to her feet, and she fell upon the vampyre instead. Durnus' breath rattled in his throat, and with the others' help, they propped him against the nearest knuckle of a root. Still, the Weight refused to fall from his skeleton's fingers. They looked fused to the gold.

'Where are we, Durnus?' Mithrid spoke louder with every word. 'Where did you take us?'

The vampyre's eyes refused to open, but a fang snuck beyond his lips.

'Where, old man?' pressed Mithrid, going as far as to pull at his armour, even as Aspala dragged her away.

'East,' came the vampyre's whisper, causing them all to fall statue still.

Mithrid was yelling now. 'How far?'

But the vampyre's brief sentience had passed. Mithrid looked up, eyes darting between Aspala and Warbringer.

'How far east can Emaneska go?' whispered the girl.

Farden & Mithrid will return in

SCALUSSEN CHRONICLES BOOK TWO

Join Ben's Guild to stay notified, get sneak
peeks, and see behind the scenes:
WWW.BENGALLEY.COM/GET-INVOLVED

More Books

If you need some more epic fantasy in your life, try Ben's other complete series:

THE CHASING GRAVES TRILOGY

In this Egyptian-infused fantasy, ghosts are bound for eternity as slaves for the rich, and whomever controls the most souls rules the cut-throat empire. Master thief Caltro must fight for his freedom from beyond the grave.

THE SCARLET STAR TRILOGY

High-born orphan Merion finds himself struggling to survive after his father's will sends him to the frontier of the known world. His only ally? A foul-mouthed faerie, exiled by his own kind. Weird western fantasy meets alternate history in this action-packed mashup.

All books by Ben Galley

THE EMANESKA SERIES
The Written
Pale Kings
Dead Stars - Part One
Dead Stars - Part Two
The Written Graphic Novel

THE CHASING GRAVES TRILOGY
Chasing Graves
Grim Solace
Breaking Chaos

THE SCARLET STAR TRILOGY
Bloodrush
Bloodmoon
Bloodfeud

STANDALONES
The Heart of Stone

SHORT STORIES
Shards
No Fairytale

ANTHOLOGIES FEATURED IN
Lost Lore
Heroes Wanted
Lone Wolf
Inferno! 5
The Art of War

DID YOU ENJOY THE FOREVER KING?

If you enjoyed this new epic tale in the world of Emaneska, then feel free to tell a friend, spread the word on social media, or leave a review on Amazon and Goodreads. Your support keeps an indie author like me writing.

Follow me on social to stay up to date with new books, competitions, funny fantasy stuff, and news. Come chat to me on Facebook and Instagram:
@BENGALLEYAUTHOR

Or find me on Twitter and vlogging author life on YouTube:
@BENGALLEY

You can also visit my website for all the details on my fantasy books and series:
WWW.BENGALLEY.COM

Or join **The Guild** for a monthly newsletter of behind the scenes content and a copy of the exclusive Emaneska short story The Iron Keys:
WWW.BENGALLEY.COM/GET-INVOLVED

THANK YOU FOR READING!
— BEN

Lightning Source UK Ltd.
Milton Keynes UK
UKHW010107021220
374457UK00001B/65